Reader's
Digest
CONDENSED BOOKS

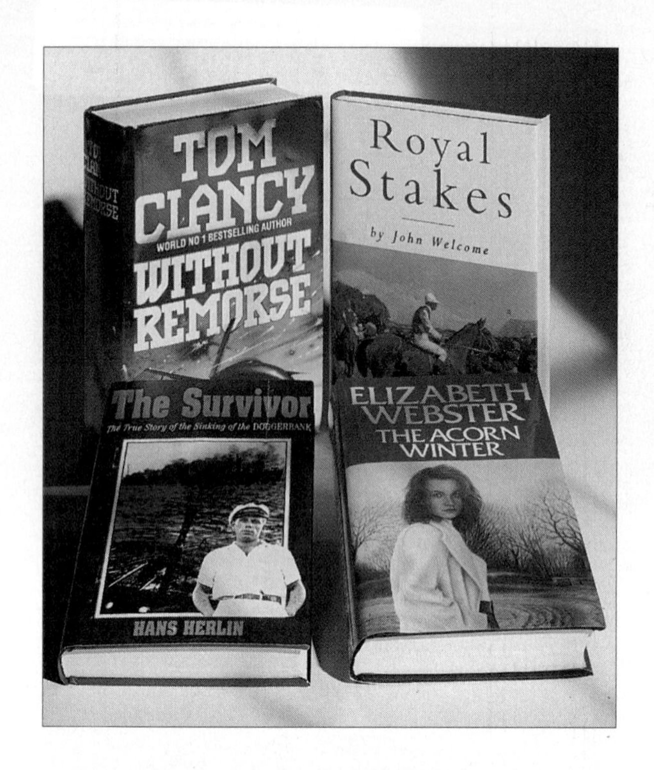

THE READER'S DIGEST ASSOCIATION LIMITED
Berkeley Square House, London W1X 6AB

THE READER'S DIGEST ASSOCIATION
SOUTH AFRICA (PTY) LTD
Reader's Digest House, 130 Strand Street, Cape Town

Page make-up by MS Filmsetting, Frome, Somerset
Separations by Magnacraft, London
Printed by BPC Magazines (East Kilbride) Ltd,
A MEMBER OF THE BRITISH PRINTING
COMPANY LTD
Bound by BPC Hazell Books Ltd, Aylesbury

WITHOUT REMORSE

Tom Clancy

PUBLISHED BY HARPERCOLLINS

THE ACORN WINTER

Elizabeth Webster

PUBLISHED BY SEVERN HOUSE

THE SURVIVOR

Hans Herlin

PUBLISHED BY LEO COOPER

ROYAL STAKES

John Welcome

PUBLISHED BY SINCLAIR-STEVENSON

CONTENTS

In Vietnam John Kelly served behind the lines as a navy SEAL, a member of that elite band of US commandos. Now, in 1970, he's back home, with a steady job, a woman he loves and a bright future ahead of him. John Kelly is sure his fighting days are over. But he's wrong. For suddenly a new enemy confronts him: a network of evil, operating virtually on his own doorstep. And it will take all Kelly's courage—and his military skill—to win on this new battlefield.

The latest blockbuster from the author of *The Hunt for Red October* and *Patriot Games*.

The pain of losing first her husband and then her little son has driven Beth Halliday to the edge of despair. What is there left for her to live for if those she loves most are no longer there? But then she meets Stephanie Edmondson, her husband Finn and daughter Chloë, and is drawn into their circle of warm friendship. Slowly she begins to feel that she might just have a future after all, if only she has the courage to let others into her heart again. Then tragedy strikes the Edmondsons and this time it is Beth who must find the strength to help the people she loves to heal their wounds.

THE SURVIVOR

Hans Herlin

It was March 3, 1943. The *Doggerbank*, a British auxiliary cruiser captured and converted into a blockade-runner by the Germans, was sailing towards Bordeaux. On board were 365 seamen and a precious cargo of indispensable materials for the Nazi war effort. Suddenly she was hit by three torpedoes and sank. Only one man survived and that man, Fritz Kuert, suspected that the submarine that had sunk them was German.

Here is Fritz Kuert's story, as told to Hans Herlin. A gripping investigation into how the accident happened and how Fritz Kuert survived.

page 321

ROYAL STAKES

John Welcome

It was one of the great scandals of the twenties when racing trainer Lieutenant-Colonel Richard de Lacey was warned off the Turf by the Jockey Club for the alleged doping of a horse in his care. However, de Lacey's son, Danny, was determined to clear his father's name. In so doing he began to unravel a plot that threatened the Prince of Wales, racing's most glittering personality and the man destined to become Britain's future King Edward VIII.

This is a colourful and compelling novel written by a distinguished author and close follower of the Turf.

page 405

WITHOUT REMORSE

Tom Clancy

ILLUSTRATED BY MICHAEL HERRING

Who is John Kelly?

The navy SEAL whose valour in Vietnam made him an almost legendary hero?

The newly recruited agent just beginning to find his way around CIA headquarters?

The unforgiving vigilante seeking justice on the crime-infested streets of Baltimore?

The anwer is, he is all of them.

And he is about to go to war.

Prologue *MEETING PLACES*

NOVEMBER

Camille had either been the world's most powerful hurricane or the largest tornado in history. Certainly it had done the job to this oil rig, Kelly thought, donning his tanks for his last dive into the Gulf of Mexico. The superstructure was wrecked and all four of the massive legs weakened—twisted like the ruined toy of a gigantic child. Everything that could safely be removed had been torched off and lowered by crane onto the dive barge. What remained was a skeletal platform, which would soon make a fine home for local game fish, he thought, entering the launch that would take him alongside. Two other experienced divers would be working with him, but Kelly was in charge. They went over procedures on the way over, while a safety boat circled nervously to keep the local fishermen away. Events like this attracted the curious. And it would be quite a show, Kelly thought with a grin as he rolled backwards off the dive boat.

It was eerie underneath. The sunlight wavered under the rippled surface, making variable curtains of light that trained across the legs of the platform. The C4 charges were already in place, wired tight against the steel and fused to blow inwards. Kelly took his time, checking each one carefully. The men behind him ran the prima-cord, wrapping it tight round the steel blocks. Kelly checked their work, and they checked his, for caution and thoroughness was the mark of such men. When you dealt with explosives, you didn't rush and you didn't take chances.

COLONEL ROBIN ZACHARIAS concentrated on the task at hand. There was a North Vietnamese SA-2 site just over the next ridge. Already it had volleyed off three missiles, searching for the fighter-bombers he was here to protect. In the back seat of his F-105G Thunderchief was Jack Tait, his weapons-systems operator, or 'bear', a lieutenant-colonel and an expert in the field of defence suppression. The two men had helped invent the doctrine that they were now implementing. He drove the Wild Weasel fighter, showing himself, trying to draw a shot, then ducking under it, closing in on the rocket site. It was a deadly, vicious game, not of hunter and prey, but of hunter and hunter—one small, swift and delicate, and the other massive, fixed and fortified. This site had given fits to the men of his wing. The commander was just too good, whoever the little bastard was. He was probably Russian-trained. He'd killed two Weasels under Robin's command in the previous week, and so the colonel had drawn this mission for himself. It was his speciality: diagnosing, penetrating and destroying air defences—a vast, rapid, three-dimensional game in which the prize of winning was survival.

Zacharias was roaring low, never higher than five hundred feet, while his eyes watched the hilltops and his ears listened to the talk from the back seat.

'Launch—two, two valid launches,' Tait warned. 'Time to do some pilot magic, Rob.'

Zacharias rolled left and ducked back behind a ridge, pulling out at a dangerous low altitude. The SA-2 Guideline missiles went wild four thousand feet over his head.

'I think it's time,' Tait said.

'I think you're right.' Zacharias turned hard left, arming his cluster munitions. The F-105 skimmed over the ridge, dropping back down again while his eyes checked the next ridge.

'His radar is still up,' Tait reported. 'He knows we're coming. Some light flak at ten o'clock.'

Maybe they could see him, maybe not. The F-105 moved faster at low level than anything ever made, and the camouflage on the upper surfaces was effective. They were probably looking up. There was a wall of jamming there now, part of the plan he'd laid out for the other Weasel bird, and normal American tactics were for a medium-altitude approach and steep dive. But they'd done that twice and failed, and so Zacharias decided to change the technique. Low level, he'd Rockeye the place; then the other Weasel would finish things off. His job was killing the command van and the commander within. He jinked the F-105 left and right, up and down, to deny a good shooting track to anybody on the ground. You still had to worry about guns, too.

Robin centred the command van on his bombsight pipper. 'Selecting Rockeye,' he said. 'Looking good. Release . . . now!'

Four of the decidedly unaerodynamic canisters fell free of the fighter's ejector racks, splitting open in midair, scattering thousands of bomblets over the area. The strike force could come in now, and that surface-to-air missile battery was out of business. OK. He selected a notch in the ridge, racing for it, straight and level now that the threat was behind him. Home for Christmas.

The red tracers that erupted from the small pass startled him. That wasn't supposed to be there. He jinked up, but the body of the aircraft passed right through the stream of fire. It shook violently, and in the passage of a second, good changed to evil.

'Robin!' a voice gasped over the intercom, but the main noise was from wailing alarms, and Zacharias knew in a fatal instant that his aircraft was doomed. It got worse almost before he could react. The engine died in flames, and then the F-105 started a roll-yaw that told him the controls were gone. His reaction was automatic—a shout for ejection—but another gasp from the back made him turn just as he yanked the handles. His last sight of Jack Tait was blood that hung below the seat like a vapour trail, but by then his own back was wrenched with more pain than he'd ever known.

'FIRE IN THE HOLE,' Kelly said. He twisted the handle on the detonator. The results were gratifying. The water round the rig's legs turned to foam as the legs were chopped off bottom and top. The fall was surprisingly slow. The entire structure slid off in one direction. There was an immense splash as the platform hit. Then the see-through collection of light girders sank below sight, to rest right on the bottom, and another job was done.

Kelly disconnected the wires from the generator and tossed them over the side.

'Two weeks early. I guess you really wanted that bonus,' the executive said. A former US navy fighter pilot, he admired a job well and quickly done. 'Dutch Maxwell was right about you.'

'The admiral is a good guy. He's done a lot for Tish and me.'

'Well, we flew together for two years. Good to know those nice things he said were true.' The executive liked working with people who'd had experiences like his own. 'What's with that? I've been meaning to ask.' He pointed to the tattoo on Kelly's arm—a red seal, sitting up on his hind flippers and grinning impudently.

'Something we all did in my unit,' Kelly explained offhandedly.
'What unit was that?'
'Can't say.' Kelly added a grin to mute the refusal.
'I bet it's something to do with how little Dutch got out—but OK.' A former naval officer had to respect the rules. 'I'll radio in so your wife can pick you up, Mr Kelly.'

TISH KELLY WAS GLOWING her me-too look at the women in the Stork Shop. Not even three months yet, she could wear anything she wanted—well, almost. She thanked the clerk, deciding that she'd bring John here in the evening and help him pick something out for her, because he liked doing that. Now it was time to pick him up. The Plymouth station wagon they'd driven down from Baltimore, Maryland, was parked outside. She brought the station wagon onto the street, heading south for the oil company's huge support yard. Even the traffic lights were in her favour. One changed to green in such a timely fashion that her foot didn't have to touch the brakes.
The truck driver frowned as the light changed to amber. He was late and running a little too fast, but the end of his 600-mile run from Oklahoma was in sight. He stepped on the clutch and brake pedals with a gasp of surprise as both pedals went all the way to the floor. The road ahead was clear and he kept downshifting to cut speed, frantically blowing his diesel horn.
She never saw it coming. Her head never turned. The station wagon just jumped right through the intersection, and the driver's lingering memory would be of the young woman's profile disappearing under the bonnet of his diesel tractor and then the awful lurch.

HELEN WAS HER FRIEND. Helen was dying, and Pam knew she should feel something, but she couldn't. The body was gagged, but that didn't stop all the sounds as Billy and Rick did what they were doing. The sounds were those of a woman soon to leave her life behind, but the trip had a price that had to be paid first, and Rick and Billy and Burt and Henry were doing the collecting. Helen was bad. Helen had tried to run away, and they couldn't have that. It had been explained to them all more than once, and was now being explained again in a way, Henry said, that they would be sure to remember. Pam felt where her ribs had once been broken, remembering her lesson. She knew that there was nothing she could do as Helen's eyes fixed on her face. Presently Helen stopped making noise, and it was over, for now. Now Pam could close her eyes and wonder when it would be her turn.

THE CREW THOUGHT it was pretty funny. They had the American pilot tied up right outside their sandbagged emplacement so he could see the guns that had shot him down. They had the other body, too, and they set it right next to him. The intelligence officer from Hanoi was here now, checking the man's name against a list he'd brought along. It must have been something special, the gunners all thought, from the way he reacted to it and the urgent phone call he'd made. After the prisoner passed out from his pain, the intelligence officer had swabbed some blood from the dead body and covered the live one's face with it. Then he'd snapped a few photos. That puzzled the gun crew. It was almost as though he wanted the live one to look dead. How very odd.

KELLY WALKED OUT of the emergency room. A police officer explained that it hadn't been the driver's fault. The brakes had failed. Mechanical defect. Just one of those things. All the things he'd said on other such occasions, trying to explain to some innocent person why the main part of his world had just ended. This Mr Kelly was a tough one, the officer saw, and all the more vulnerable because of it. His wife and unborn child were dead by an accident. Nobody to blame. There was nothing to be done for a man who would have accepted hell rather than this—because he'd seen hell. But there was more than one hell, and he hadn't seen them all quite yet.

1 *ENFANT PERDU*

MAY

He'd never know why he stopped. Kelly pulled his Scout over to the shoulder without a conscious thought. She hadn't had her hand out soliciting a ride. She was just standing at the side of the road, but her posture was that of a hitchhiker, one knee locked, the other bent. Her clothes were clearly well used, and a backpack was slung over one shoulder. Her tawny, shoulder-length hair moved about in the rush of air from the traffic. Her face showed nothing, but Kelly didn't see that until he was already pressing his right foot on the brake pedal. In a few seconds she was at the passenger window.

'Where you goin'?' she asked.

Kelly hesitated for a second or two. Twenty-one, perhaps, but old for her years. She wore a man's cotton shirt that hadn't been ironed in months. But what surprised him most of all were her eyes. Fetchingly grey-green, they stared past Kelly into . . . what? He'd seen the look before often enough, but only on weary men.

'Back to my boat,' he answered finally.

'You have a boat?' she asked. Her eyes lit up like a child's. A smile started there and radiated down the remainder of her face.

'Forty-footer—she's a diesel cruiser. You want to come along?'

'Sure!' She yanked open the door and tossed her backpack on the floor in front of the passenger seat. Kelly pulled back into the traffic.

You want to come along? he'd asked, and she'd said, *Sure*, his mind reported to him. What the hell? Kelly frowned in frustration at the traffic because he didn't know the answer, but then there were a lot of questions to which he hadn't known the answers in the last six months. He told his mind to be quiet and watched the Memorial Day weekend traffic.

His guest was staring forward, her face serene. It was a pretty face in profile. She was thin—perhaps willowy was the right word—her hair halfway between blonde and brown.

Kelly ran a hand across his jaw, feeling the sandpaper texture. The hand itself was dirty. Letting yourself go, Kelly.

He remembered what he'd once been. He remembered all the things that he had survived, amazed that he had done so. And perhaps the worst torment of all was that he didn't understand what had gone wrong, leaving what had once been a tough, smart, decisive man to blunder about in confusion and despair. He was on autopilot. He knew that, but not where fate was taking him.

She didn't try to talk, and Kelly sensed there was something he ought to know. He'd always trusted his instincts, the warning chill on his neck and forearms, and he found himself checking the mirror for no good reason.

The boatyard was a swarm of activity. The three-day weekend, of course. Kelly manoeuvred to *Springer*'s transom and backed up to the slip he'd left six hours before. It was a relief to crank up the windows and lock the car. His adventure on the highways was over, and the safety of the trackless water beckoned.

Springer was a diesel-powered motor yacht, forty-one feet long. She was not especially pretty, but she had two sizable cabins, and the midships saloon could be converted easily into a third. Kelly had a high-quality marine radar, every sort of communications gear that he could legally use, and navigation aids normally reserved for offshore fishermen. The Fibreglass hull was immaculate, and there was not a speck of rust on the chromed rails, though he had deliberately done without the topside varnish that most yacht owners cherished because it wasn't worth the maintenance time. *Springer* was a workboat, or was supposed to be.

Kelly and his guest alighted from the car. He opened the cargo door and started carrying cartons of groceries aboard.

'What do I do?' the girl asked. Kelly had the impression that she was trembling a little and trying to hide it.

'Just take a seat,' Kelly said, pointing to the flying bridge.

'OK.' She beamed a smile at him guaranteed to melt ice.

Kelly secured the last of the groceries in the saloon. Common decency told him to wash his face and hands. Two minutes later he went topside.

'I, uh, forgot to ask you something—' he began.

'Pam,' she said, extending her hand. 'What's yours?'

'Kelly,' he replied.

'Where we going, Mr Kelly?'

'Just Kelly,' he corrected her. Pam nodded and smiled again.

'OK, Kelly, where to?'

'I own a little island about thirty—'

'You own an *island*?' Her eyes went wide.

'That's right.' Actually, he just leased it.

'Let's go!' she said with enthusiasm, looking back at the shore.

He flipped on the bilge blowers. He didn't really have to worry about fumes building up, but Kelly was a seaman and he followed a strict routine, observing all the safety rules that had been written in the blood of less careful men. After the prescribed two minutes, he punched the button to start the port-side, then the starboard-side diesel. Both engines caught at once.

He left the flying bridge to slip his mooring lines, then came back and eased the throttles forward to take his boat out of the slip, checking tide and wind—there was not much of either at the moment—and looking for other boats. Pam was looking round at the boats, too, mainly aft, and her eyes fixed on the parking lot for a long couple of seconds before she looked forward again, her body relaxing.

'You know anything about boats?' Kelly asked.

'Not much,' she admitted, and for the first time he noticed her accent.

'Where you from?'

'Texas. How about you?'

'Indianapolis, originally, but it's been a while.'

'What's this?' she asked. She reached out to touch the tattoo on his forearm.

'It's from one of the places I've been. Not a very nice place.'

'Oh, over there.' She understood. 'What did you do there?'
'Nothing to talk to a lady about,' Kelly replied.
'What makes you think I'm a lady?' she asked.
It caught him short, and for the first time he answered her smile with one of his own.
'Well, it wouldn't be very nice of me if I assumed that you weren't.'
'I wondered how long it would be before you smiled.' You have a very nice smile, her tone told him.
How's six months grab you? he almost said. Instead he laughed, mainly at himself. That was something else he needed to do.
'I'm sorry. Guess I haven't been very good company.' He turned to look at her again and saw understanding in her eyes. Just a quiet look, very human and feminine, but it shook Kelly. Her hand reached out again, ostensibly to stroke the tattoo, but that wasn't what it was all about. It was amazing how warm her touch was, even under a hot afternoon sun. Perhaps it was a measure of just how cold his life had become.
But he had a boat to navigate. They were out of the yacht basin now, and there was a freighter about a thousand yards ahead. Kelly was at full cruising power, and the ride was smooth until they got into the merchant ship's wake. Then *Springer* started pitching up and down three or four feet at the bow. Kelly manoeuvred left to get round the worst of it.
Pam went below. She reappeared in a few minutes wearing short shorts and a halter and no shoes. She had dancer's legs, Kelly noticed, slim and very feminine. She grasped his upper arm and sat on the vinyl bench, leaning against him.
Kelly settled down to a steady cruising speed of eighteen knots as he worked his way out of Baltimore harbour. He kept to the main shipping channel all the way out into the Chesapeake Bay.
'What's that?' Pam asked. Kelly turned and winced. He'd been so content with the girl on his arm that he'd neglected to pay attention to the weather. 'That' was a thunderstorm.
'Looks like we're going to get some rain,' Kelly replied, switching on his marine radio. He caught a weather forecast at once, one that ended with the usual warning.
'Is this a small craft?' Pam asked.
'Technically it is, but you can relax. I used to be a chief bosun's mate in the navy. Besides, this is a pretty big boat. If you're worried, there are life jackets under the seat you're on.'
'Are you worried?' Pam asked. Kelly smiled and shook his head.
'OK.' She resumed her previous position, her head on his shoulder,

a dreamy expression in her eyes, as though anticipating something that was to be, storm or no storm.

Kelly wasn't worried—at least not about the storm—but he wasn't casual about things either. Passing Bodkin Point, he continued east across the shipping channel. He didn't turn south until he was in water he knew to be too shallow for anything large enough to run him down. Every few minutes he turned to keep an eye on the storm, which was charging right in at twenty knots or so. It had already blotted out the sun.

'Won't be long now,' Pam observed, just a trace of unease in her voice as she held onto him.

Kelly throttled back some. There was no reason to hurry. With the throttles eased back, there was no need for two hands on the controls either. He wrapped his arm round the girl, and despite the approaching storm everything was suddenly right with the world.

The rain arrived quickly, the first warning sprinkles followed by solid sheets that marched across the surface of the Chesapeake Bay. Within a minute the sky was as dark as late twilight. The waves started kicking up in earnest, driven by what felt like thirty knots of wind. Kelly knew that he was in a good anchoring place now and wouldn't be in another for five hours. He brought *Springer* into the wind and eased the throttles until the propellers were providing just enough thrust to overcome the driving force of the wind.

'Take the wheel,' he told Pam. 'Just hold her steady and steer the way I tell you to. I have to go forward to set the anchors. OK?'

'You be careful,' she shouted over the gusting wind. The waves were about five feet now, and the bow of the boat was leaping up and down. Kelly gave her shoulder a squeeze and went forward.

Pam looked nervous until the moment Kelly returned to the flying bridge and sat back down on the bench. Everything was covered with water now, and their clothes were soaked through. Kelly eased the throttles to idle and switched off the diesels.

'I could fight the storm, but I'd prefer not to,' he explained. 'You can go down to your cabin and—'

'You want me to go away?'

'No. I mean, if you don't like it here—'

'I like it here.' Her hand came up to his face.

Kelly asked himself why it had taken so long. All the signals had been there. There was nothing to be afraid of, just a person as lonely as he. Loneliness didn't tell you what you had lost, only that something was missing. It took something like this to define that emptiness. Her skin was soft, dripping with rain, but warm.

Pam pressed her face against his, her hands pulling him forward, taking charge in a very feminine way. Somehow her passion wasn't animalistic. Something made it different. Kelly didn't know what it was, but didn't search for the reason—not now. Both stood for the next embrace, weaving as the boat pitched and rocked beneath them. Then Pam took his hand and they went below.

Long minutes later Kelly's arms were wrapped round her thin form, and so they stayed until the storm passed. Kelly was afraid to let go. He tried to smile at her, but the hurt was back, all the more powerful from the joy of the previous hour, and he wept. She held him tightly until he was done.

'I'm sorry,' he said after a while.

'You don't have to explain. But I'd like to help,' she said, knowing that she already had. She'd seen it from almost the first moment in the car: a strong man, badly hurt.

'It's been nearly seven months. Down in Mississippi on a job. She was pregnant and . . . It was a truck, a big tractor-trailer rig. The linkage broke.' He couldn't make himself say more.

'What was her name?'

'Tish—Patricia.'

'How long were you . . .'

'Year and a half. Then she was just . . . gone. I never expected it. I mean, I never thought—' His voice cracked again.

'You never let it out, did you?'

'No,' he whispered.

'Thank you.'

Kelly looked up in surprise. 'I don't understand.'

'Yes, you do,' Pam replied. 'And Tish understands, too. You let me take her place. Or maybe she did. She loved you. And she still does. Thank you for letting me help.'

He started crying again, and Pam cradled him like a small child. Later he fell asleep at her side, and she kissed his unshaven cheek. That was when her own tears began, at the wonder of what the day had brought after the terror with which it had begun.

2 ENCOUNTERS

Kelly awoke at his accustomed time, thirty minutes before sunrise, to the mewing of gulls, and saw the first dull glow on the eastern horizon. At first he was confused to find a slender arm across his chest, but other feelings and memories explained things in a few seconds. He extricated himself from her side and moved the blanket to cover her from the morning chill. Time for ship's business.

Kelly got the coffee machine going; then he headed topside. The sky had cleared; the water was a flat, oily calm and the breeze gentle. It seemed as fine a morning as he could remember.

His head turned at the low, muted rumble of marine diesels. A few minutes later the familiar shape of a coastguard 41-foot patrol boat eased alongside *Springer*.

Quartermaster First Class Manuel Oreza stepped from one gunwale to the other with practised ease. 'Morning, Kelly.'

His outstretched hand held a Styrofoam cup filled with coffee. Kelly took it and laughed. Oreza was famous for his coffee.

'Long night,' the coastguardsman said wearily.

'Trouble?' Kelly asked.

Oreza nodded. 'Kinda. Some fool in a little day sailer turned up missing after that little rainstorm we had last night, and we've been looking all over for him. You see anything unusual?'

'No. Came outa Baltimore. Two and a half hours to get here. Anchored right after the storm hit. Visibility was pretty bad. Didn't see much of anything before we went below.'

'We,' Oreza observed. The look on his face was neutral, but there was interest behind the eyes. He hoped his friend had found someone. Life hadn't been especially fair to the man. 'Anyway, you see a little day sailer with an orange and white candy-striped sail, you want to give me a call?'

'No problem.'

Oreza jumped back aboard the cutter. A moment later its engines rumbled anew and the boat moved northwest.

'Good mornin'.' It was Pam. 'What was that?'

Kelly turned. Her hair was a Medusa-like mass of tangles.

'Coastguard. They're looking for a missing boat. How'd you sleep?'

'Just fine.' She came over to him. Her eyes had a soft, dreamlike quality that seemed strange so early in the morning but could not have been more attractive to the wide-awake sailor.

'I DON'T LIKE THIS.'

'You don't have to like it,' the taller man said. He unfolded his pocketknife and slit the heavy paper to reveal a plastic container of white powder. 'A few hours' work, and we turn three hundred thousand.'

'And this is just the start,' the third man said.

'What do we do with the boat?' asked the man with the scruples.

The tall one looked up. 'You get rid of that sail?'

'Yeah.'

'Well, we can scuttle the boat. Yeah, that's what we'll do.'

'And Angelo?' All three looked over to where the man was lying—unconscious still, and bleeding.

'I guess we scuttle him, too,' the tall one observed without much in the way of emotion. 'Right here ought to be fine.'

'Maybe two weeks, there won't be nothin' left. Lots of critters out there.' The third one waved outside at the tidal wetlands.

'See how easy it is, Eddie? No boat, no Angelo, no risk, and three hundred thousand bucks.'

'His friends still ain't gonna like it.'

'What friends?' Tony asked without looking. 'He ratted, didn't he? How many friends does a rat have?'

Eddie bent to the logic of the situation and walked over to Angelo's unconscious form. He pulled a small .22 automatic from his pocket, placed it to the back of Angelo's skull, and fired once. Eddie set his gun aside and dragged the body outside, leaving Henry and Tony to do the important stuff. They'd brought some fish netting, which he wrapped round the body before dumping it in the water behind their small motorboat. A cautious man, Eddie looked around, but there wasn't much danger of intruders here. He motored off a few hundred yards, then stopped and drifted while he lifted a few concrete blocks from the boat and tied them to the netting. Six were enough to sink Angelo about eight feet to the bottom. The water was pretty clear here, and that worried Eddie a little until he saw all the crabs. Angelo would be gone in less than two weeks. Disposing of the little sailboat would be harder. He'd have to find a deeper spot, but he had all day to think about it.

KELLY ALTERED COURSE to starboard to avoid a gaggle of sports craft. The island was visible now, about five miles ahead. Not much to look at—just a low bump on the horizon, not even a tree—but it was his, and it was as private as a man could wish.

Battery Island had a long and undistinguished history. Its current name had come in the War of 1812, when some enterprising militiaman decided to place a small gun battery there to guard a narrow spot in the Chesapeake Bay against the British, who were sailing towards Washington DC. One British squadron commander took note of a few harmless puffs of smoke on the island, brought one ship within gun range and let loose a few salvos. The citizen soldiers manning the battery hadn't needed much encouragement to make a run for their rowboats and hustle to the mainland.

The Second World War had brought the sleepy island back to life. A nearby naval air station needed a rescue station from which a crash boat might respond to an aircraft accident. That had required building a concrete quay and boathouse and two bunkers on the island. Then the advent of helicopters made crash boats unnecessary, and the island had been declared surplus. It remained on a register of unwanted federal property until Kelly managed to acquire a lease.

Pam leaned back on a blanket as they approached, basting in the warm sun beneath a thick coating of suntan lotion. She wasn't wearing any more now than when he'd put the blanket on her.

Kelly eased the wheel to the right to pass well clear of a large fishing yacht.

The sound startled both of them—rapid short blasts on the fishing boat's diesel horns. The boat lay two hundred yards to port. On the flying bridge a man was waving. Kelly brought *Springer* to a halt twenty feet away.

'What's the problem?' Kelly called over the loudhailer.

'Lost our props,' a swarthy man hollered back.

Kelly brought his boat closer in to survey the situation. It was a medium-sized fishing cruiser, a fairly recent Hatteras. The man on the bridge was about five eight, fiftyish, and bare-chested. A black-haired woman was also visible, also rather downcast.

'I think we hit a sandbar,' the man explained. 'About half a mile that way.' He pointed to a place Kelly kept clear of.

'Sure enough, there's one that way. I can give you a tow if you want. You have good enough line for it?'

'Yes,' the man replied. He went forward to his rope locker.

Kelly manoeuvred his stern in close, then went aft to his well deck to take the towing line, which he secured to the big cleat on the transom. He hustled back to the flying bridge and coaxed his throttle a crack.

'Get on your radio,' he told the Hatteras owner. 'Leave your rudder amidships till I tell you different. OK?'

'Got it.'

'What happened to him?' Pam asked.

'People forget there's a bottom under this water. You hit it hard enough and you break things.' He paused. 'You might want to put some more clothes on.'

Pam giggled and went below. Kelly increased speed carefully to about four knots before turning south towards Battery Island.

Kelly brought *Springer* alongside the quay very slowly, mindful of the boat he was towing. He scurried off the bridge to drop his rubber fenders, then jumped ashore to tie off a pair of lines before heading towards the Hatteras. The owner already had his mooring lines set up, and tossed them to Kelly on the quay. It only took five minutes to get the boat snugged in; then Kelly did the same with *Springer*.

'This is yours?'

'Sure enough,' Kelly replied. 'Welcome to my sandbar.'

'Sam Rosen,' the man said, holding his hand out. While he had a strong grip, Kelly noted that his hands were so soft as to be dainty.

'John Kelly.'

'My wife, Sarah.'

Kelly laughed. 'You must be the navigator.'

Sarah was short, overweight, and her brown eyes wavered between amusement and embarrassment. 'Somebody needs to thank you for your help,' she observed in a New York accent.

'A law of the sea, ma'am. What went wrong?'

'The chart shows six feet where we struck. This boat only takes four. And low tide was five hours ago!'

'Sandbar. It's been building there since last winter's storms, but my charts show less than that. Besides, it's a soft bottom.'

Pam came up just then, wearing clothing that was nearly respectable, and Kelly realised he didn't know her last name.

'Hi, I'm Pam.'

'Y'all want to freshen up?' Kelly asked his guests. 'We have all day to look at the problem.' There was general agreement on that point, and Kelly led them off to his home.

'What is that?' Sam Rosen asked. It was one of the bunkers built in 1943, two thousand square feet, with a roof fully three foot thick. The entire structure was reinforced concrete and was almost as sturdy as it looked. A second, smaller bunker lay beside it.

'This place used to belong to the navy,' Kelly explained.

'Nice dock they built for you,' Rosen noted.

'Not bad at all,' Kelly agreed. 'Mind if I ask what you do?'

'Surgeon,' Rosen replied.

'Oh, yeah?' That explained the hands.

'Professor of surgery,' Sarah corrected. 'But he can't drive a boat worth a damn!'

'The charts were off,' the professor grumbled as Kelly led them inside. 'Didn't you hear?'

'People, that's history now, and lunch and a beer will allow us to consider it in comfort.' Just then Kelly's ears caught a sharp crack coming across the water from somewhere to the south.

'What was that?' Sam Rosen had sharp ears, too.

'Probably a kid taking a muskrat with his twenty-two,' Kelly said.

'You hunt?' Rosen asked.

'Not any more,' Kelly replied.

Rosen looked at him with understanding. 'How long?'

'Long enough. How'd you know?'

'Right after I finished residency, I made it to Iwo and Okinawa. Hospital ship. What were you on?'

'Usually my belly,' Kelly answered with a grin.

'Underwater demolition? You look like a frogman,' Rosen said. 'I had to fix a few of those.'

'Pretty much the same thing but dumber.' Kelly dialled the combination lock and pulled the heavy steel door open.

The inside of the bunker surprised the visitors. It looked almost like a house, with painted concrete and rugs. The furniture showed the influence of Patricia, but the current state of affairs was evidence that only a man lived here now. Everything was neatly arranged, but not as a woman would do things.

'How do you get a place like this?' Sam asked.

'A friend got me the lease. Surplus government property.'

'He must be some friend,' Sarah said.

'Yes, he is.'

VICE-ADMIRAL WINSLOW HOLLAND MAXWELL, USN, had his office on the E-Ring of the Pentagon. It was an outside office, allowing him a fine view of Washington—and the demonstrators, he noted angrily to himself. *BABY KILLERS!* one placard read. There was even a North Vietnamese flag. The chanting, this Saturday morning, was distorted by the thick window glass. He could hear the cadence but not the words, and the former fighter pilot couldn't decide which was more enraging.

'The freedom to do that is one of the things we defend, Dutch,' Rear-Admiral Casimir Podulski pointed out, not quite making that leap of faith despite his words. It was just a little too much. His son had died over Haiphong in an A-4 strike-fighter.

'So why are you in such a great mood, Cas?' Maxwell grumbled.

'This one goes in the wall safe, Dutch.' Podulski handed over a heavy folder. It bore the codename Boxwood Green.

'They're going to let us play with it?' *That* was a surprise.

'Just a few of us. We have authorisation for a complete feasibility study.' Admiral Podulski settled into a deep leather chair and lit up a cigarette. His face was thinner since the death of his son, but the crystal-blue eyes burned as bright as ever. 'They want us to keep it off the books.'

'Jim Greer, too?' Dutch Maxwell asked.

'Best intel guy I know, unless you're hiding one somewhere.'

'He just started at CIA, I heard last week,' Maxwell warned.

'Good. We need a good spy.'

'HOW LONG HAVE you had the boat?' Kelly asked about halfway through his second beer.

'We bought it last October, but we've only been running it two months,' the doctor admitted.

'You a doc, too, ma'am?' Kelly asked Sarah.

'Pharmacologist. I also teach at Johns Hopkins University.'

'How long have you and your wife lived here?' Sam asked.

'Oh, we just met,' Pam told them artlessly. The Rosens merely accepted the news as a matter of course.

'Let's take a look at that propeller.' Kelly stood up. 'Come on.'

Rosen followed him out of the door. The secondary bunker on the island housed Kelly's workshop. He selected a couple of wrenches and wheeled a portable air compressor towards the door.

Two minutes later he had it sitting next to the doctor's Hatteras. He buckled a pair of weight belts round his waist, stripped off his shirt and headed for the ladder. Rosen spotted three separate scars that a really good surgeon might have been skilful enough to conceal, but a combat surgeon didn't always have time for cosmetic work.

Four minutes later Kelly was climbing back up the ladder.

'Found your problem.' He set the remains of both props on the concrete dock.

'What did we hit?'

Kelly sat down for a moment to strip off the weights. It was all he could do not to laugh. 'Water, Doc, just water. What destroyed your props was electrolysis. Galvanic reaction. It's caused by having more than one kind of metal in salt water. Corrodes the metal. All the sandbar did was to scuff them off. They were already wrecked. You'll have to replace the zinc anodes on the strut. What they do is to absorb the galvanic energy. You replace them every couple of years, and that protects the screws and rudder. Your rudder needs replacement, too, but it's not an emergency. Sure as hell, you need two new screws.'

'So what do I do now?'

'I make a phone call and order you a couple of props. I'll call a guy I know over in Solomons, and he'll have somebody run them down here, probably tomorrow.' Kelly gestured. 'It's not that big a deal, OK? I want to see your charts, too.'

Sure enough, when he checked their dates, they were five years old. 'You need new ones every year, Doc.'

The doctor smiled. 'Sarah'll never let me forget it.'

'Blame the charts,' Kelly suggested.

'Will you back me up?'

Kelly grinned. 'Men have to stick together at times like this.'

'I think I'm going to like you, Mr Kelly.'

3 *CAPTIVITY*

After returning all the diving gear to the machine shop, Kelly took a two-wheel hand truck out onto the quay and started wheeling the groceries towards the bunker. Rosen insisted on helping.

'So,' Kelly said, 'you teach surgery?'

'Eight years now, yeah. Speaking of surgeons'—Rosen pointed at Kelly's chest—'some good ones worked on you. That one looks like it was nasty.'

'Yeah, I got real careless that time. Not as bad as it looks, though, just grazed the lung.' Kelly moved the boxes into the pantry.

'How long were you over there?'

'Total? Maybe eighteen months. Depends on if you count the hospital time.'

'That's a Navy Cross hanging on the wall. Is that what it's for?'

Kelly shook his head. 'That was something else. I had to go up north to retrieve somebody—an A-6 pilot. I didn't get hurt, but I got sicker 'n hell. I had some scratches—you know, from thorns and stuff. They got infected from the river water. Three weeks in the hospital from that. It was worse 'n being shot.'

'Not a very nice place, is it?' Rosen asked as they came back for the last load.

'No, I didn't like it there much. But that was the job, and I got that pilot out, and the admiral made me a chief and got me a medal. Come on, I'll show you my baby.' Kelly waved Rosen aboard. The tour took five minutes. The amenities were there, but not glitzed up. This guy, the doctor saw, was all business.

'Let me get Pam's stuff.' Kelly headed aft and picked up her backpack. Rosen was already on the quay, and Kelly tossed the backpack across. Rosen looked too late, and the pack landed on the concrete. Some contents spilled out, and Kelly saw what was wrong even before the doctor's head turned to look at him.

There was a brown plastic prescription bottle without a label. The top had been loose and a couple of capsules had fallen out.

Some things are instantly clear. Kelly stepped slowly off the boat to the quay. Rosen picked up the container and placed the spilt capsules back in it before snapping down the white plastic top.

'I know they're not yours, John.'

'What are they, Sam?'

'The trade name is Quaalude. It's a barbiturate, a sedative. We use it to get people off into dreamland. Pretty powerful. A little too powerful, in fact. No label. It's not a prescription.'

Kelly suddenly felt tired and old. And betrayed somehow. 'Yeah.'

'You didn't know?'

'Sam, we just met. I don't know anything about her.'

Rosen looked round the horizon for a moment. 'Now I'm going to be a doctor, OK? Have you ever done drugs?'

'No! I *hate* the stuff. People die because of it.' Kelly's anger was immediate and vicious, but it wasn't aimed at Sam Rosen.

The professor took the outburst calmly. 'OK, your lady friend may have a problem. But she seems like a nice girl. So do we try and solve the problem or not?'

'I guess that's up to her,' Kelly observed, bitterness creeping into his voice. He'd started giving his heart away again, and it might all have been a waste of time.

Rosen became a little stern. 'That's right, it is up to her, but it might be up to you, too, a little. She's not a bad girl, John. But something's bothering her. She's nervous about something. Come on, we have work to do.' Rosen took the hand truck in his large, soft hands and wheeled it towards the bunker.

The cool air inside was a harsh blast of reality. Pam was trying to entertain Sarah but not succeeding. Doctors' minds are always at work, and Sarah was starting to apply a professional eye to the person in front of her. When Sam entered the living room, Sarah gave him a look that Kelly was able to understand.

'And so, well, I left home when I was sixteen,' Pam was saying. Her eyes focused on the backpack Kelly held in his hands. 'Oh, great. I need some of that stuff.' She came over and took the pack from his hands, then headed towards the master bedroom. Kelly and Rosen watched her leave, then Sam handed his wife the plastic container. She needed only one look.

'I didn't know,' Kelly said, realising what Pam's dreamy eyes had really been after all.

Pam came back into the room a few seconds later, telling Kelly that she'd left something on the boat. Her hands weren't trembling, but only because she was holding them together to keep them still. She was trying to control herself and almost succeeding.

'Is this it?' Kelly asked. He held the bottle in his hands.

Pam's eyes fixed on the brown plastic container with a hungry expression, as though her thoughts were already reaching for the bottle. Then the shame hit her—the realisation that whatever image she had tried to convey to the others was rapidly diminishing. Her eyes swept over Sam and Sarah, then settled on Kelly. At first hunger vied with shame, but shame won. And then the sobs began.

'I'm s-s-s-orry, Kel-el-y. I di-didn't tel-el . . .' she tried to say, her body collapsing into itself. Pam turned away, sobbing, unable to face the man she'd begun to love.

It was decision time for John Terrence Kelly. He could feel betrayed, or he could show the same compassion to her that she had shown to him less than twenty hours before.

Kelly's eyes filled with tears as well. He went to her and wrapped his arms round her, pulling her head against his chest, because it was now his time to be strong for her.

'I've been trying,' she said, 'I really have—but I was so scared.'

'It's OK,' Kelly told her. He was concentrating so hard on the girl in his arms that he didn't notice Sarah at his side.

'Pam, how about we take a little walk?' Pam nodded agreement, and Sarah Rosen led her outside.

Kelly looked at the bottle still in his hand and then at Sam. 'So what do we do now?'

'We wait a little while.'

Sarah and Pam came back twenty minutes later, holding hands like mother and daughter.

'We got a winner here, folks,' Sarah told them. 'She's been trying for a month all by herself.'

'She says it isn't hard,' Pam said.

'We can make it a lot easier,' Sarah assured her. She handed a list to her husband. 'John, how close is the nearest town with a pharmacy?'

'Solomons, I guess.'

'OK, get your boat moving. Now.'

'What happens?' Kelly asked Sam Rosen thirty minutes and five miles later. Solomons was already a tan-green line on the horizon.

'The treatment regime is pretty simple, really. We support her with barbiturates and ease her off.'

'You give her drugs to get her off drugs?'

'Yep.' Rosen nodded. 'That's how it's done. It takes time for the body to flush out all the residual material in her tissues. The body becomes dependent on the stuff, and if you try to wean them off too rapidly, you can get some adverse effects—convulsions, that sort of thing. Look, you know how to drive a boat, right?'

'Yep,' Kelly said, turning, knowing what came next.

'Let us do our job. OK?'

THE LOCKHEED DC-130E Hercules cruised well above the low cloud deck, riding smoothly and solidly. Everything had the appearance of a pleasant flying day. In the front office, the flight crew of four watched the various instruments, as their duties required. All in all, the atmosphere was one of total normality. But anyone seeing the exterior of the aircraft could tell different. This aircraft belonged to the 99th Strategic Reconnaissance Squadron.

Beyond the outer engines on each wing of the Hercules hung additional aircraft. They were Model-147SC drones, and they bore the informal name Buffalo Hunter. In the rear cargo area of the DC-130E was a second crew, which was now powering up both of the miniature aircraft, having already programmed them for a mission sufficiently secret that none of them actually knew what it was all about. The chief technician, a 30-year-old sergeant, was working a bird codenamed Cody-193.

Cody-193's engine was turning at full power now. The sergeant gave it a final look out of a small porthole before turning back to his instruments.

'Be careful, baby,' the sergeant breathed as the drone dropped free of the mother aircraft. Cody-193 was on its own.

SARAH HAD A LIGHT dinner cooking. Kelly smelt it even before opening the door. He came inside to see Rosen sitting in the living room. 'Where's Pam?'

'We gave her some medication,' Sam answered. 'She ought to be sleeping now.'

'She is,' Sarah confirmed, passing through the room on the way to the kitchen. 'I just checked. Poor thing, she's exhausted. She's been doing without sleep for some time. It's catching up with her.' She paused. 'There's something else. She's been abused, John. I didn't ask about it, but somebody's given her a rough time.'

'What do you mean?' Kelly asked in a low voice.

'I mean she's been sexually assaulted. She's almost certainly been raped. Probably more than once. There is also evidence of physical abuse.'

'You mean that somebody's been working her over, and maybe got her on drugs?' Kelly said. 'But why?'

'Kelly, please don't take this wrong . . . but she might have been a prostitute. Pimps control girls that way. She's young, pretty, a runaway from a dysfunctional family. The physical abuse, the undernourishment—it all fits the pattern.'

Kelly sat on the sofa, looking down at the floor. 'But she's not like that. I don't understand.'

'She's fighting back, John.' Sarah sat across from Kelly. 'She's been on the road for over four years. She's got guts. But she can't do it alone. She needs you. Now I have a question.' Sarah looked hard at him. 'Will you be there to help her?'

Kelly looked up, his blue eyes the colour of ice. 'You guys are really worked up about this, aren't you?'

Sarah spoke with focused passion. 'Do you have any idea how bad it's getting? Ten years ago drug abuse was so rare that I hardly had to bother with it. Now I spend nearly all of my time in clinical work, trying to keep children alive who have their systems full of chemicals that never should have made it outside a laboratory!'

'And it's going to get worse,' Sam noted gloomily.

Sarah nodded. 'Oh, yeah. The next big one is cocaine. She needs you, John,' Sarah said again, leaning forward. 'You be there for her! She's *fighting*. There's a *person* in there.'

'Yes, ma'am,' Kelly said humbly. 'What do I do first?'

'More than anything else, she needs rest, good food and time to flush the barbiturates out of her system. Her physical problem is not so much addiction as exhaustion and undernourishment.' Sarah looked over towards the open bedroom door. 'She'll probably be out for the rest of the night. Tomorrow we start feeding her. For now,' she announced, 'we can feed ourselves.'

ONLY THIRTEEN FOOT LONG, the Buffalo Hunter angled towards the ground as it accelerated to an initial cruising speed of over five hundred knots. Already its navigational computer was monitoring time and altitude. The drone was programmed to follow a specific flight path and altitude, all painstakingly predetermined. Cody-193, a sporty-looking beast, had a profile remarkably like that of a blue shark, with a protruding nose and underslung air intake for a mouth. It was also stealthy. Blankets of RAM—radar-absorbing material—were integral with the wing surfaces.

Cody-193 crossed the border between Laos and North Vietnam at 11.41.38 local time. It levelled out at five hundred feet and turned northeast. The low altitude and small size of the speeding drone made it a difficult target, but by no means an impossible one, and outlying gun positions of the dense and sophisticated North Vietnamese air-defence network spotted it. The drone flew towards a recently sited 37mm twin-gun mount, whose alert crew loosed twenty quick rounds, three of which passed within feet of the diminutive shape but missed. Cody-193 took no note of this and continued along its flight path.

The drone turned north, dropping down to three hundred feet as it found the right valley, following a small tributary river. It had burned a third of its fuel by now and was consuming the remaining amount very rapidly at low level, flying below the crests of hills to the left and right. The programmers had done their best, but there was one chillingly close call when a puff of wind forced it to the right before the autopilot could correct, and Cody-193 missed an unusually tall tree by a scant seventy feet. The drone flew blindly on.

COLONEL ROBIN ZACHARIAS, USAF, was walking across the dirt of what might in other times and circumstances be called a parade ground, but there were no parades here. A prisoner for over six months, he'd been shot down on his eighty-ninth mission, within sight of rotation home—a completely successful mission brought to a bloody end by pure bad luck. Worse, his 'bear' was dead. And he was probably the lucky one, the colonel thought as he was led across the compound by two small, unfriendly men with rifles. His arms were tied behind him, and his ankles were hobbled because they were afraid of him despite their guns.

Zacharias didn't feel very dangerous. His back was still injured from the ejection. He'd hit the ground severely crippled, falling right into the arms of the gun crew that had shredded his aircraft.

The abuse had begun there. Paraded through three villages, stoned and spat upon, he'd finally ended up here. Wherever here was. In the preceding months he had been subjected to all sorts of physical abuse, but it had strangely slackened off in the past few weeks. There were other prisoners here, but his cell had no windows, and his attempts at communicating with them had all failed. This was not what he had been briefed to expect. It wasn't the Hanoi Hilton, where all the POWs were supposed to have been congregated. Beyond that he knew virtually nothing.

'Good morning, Colonel Zacharias,' a voice called across the compound. He looked up to see a man taller than himself, Caucasian, and wearing a uniform very different from that of the guards. He strode towards the prisoner with a smile.

That was when Zacharias heard a noise, a thin screeching whine, approaching from the southwest. It appeared in an instant, before the guards had a chance to react.

Buffalo Hunter, Zacharias thought, standing erect, staring at it, holding his head up, seeing the black rectangle of the camera window, whispering a prayer that the device was operating. When the guards realised what he was doing, a gun butt in the kidneys dropped the colonel to the ground.

'Do not get excited,' the other man said. 'It's heading to Haiphong to count the ships. Now, my friend, we need to become acquainted.'

CODY-193 CONTINUED northeast, holding a nearly constant speed and altitude as it entered the dense air-defence belt surrounding Haiphong, North Vietnam's only major port. Its cameras snapped away, recording the images on 2¼-inch film.

The drone went into its final climb as it reached its preprogrammed point thirty miles offshore. Circling at five thousand feet, Cody-193 finally ran out of fuel and became a glider. When the air speed fell to the right number, explosive bolts blew a hatch cover off the top, deploying a parachute. A navy helicopter was already on station, and the white chute made for a fine target. The chute was snagged on their first attempt, and the helicopter turned at once, heading for the carrier USS *Constellation*, where the drone was carefully lowered into a cradle, ending its mission. Processing the drone's film required a brief six minutes in the ship's elaborate photo lab. The still damp film was wiped clean and handed over to an intelligence officer. It was better than good. The film was run from one spool to another over a flat glass plate, under which was a pair of fluorescent lights.

'Well, Lieutenant?' a captain asked tensely.

'We have two, three frames! Good ones.'

'Let me see.' The captain nearly shoved the junior officer out of the way. There was a man there, an American, with two guards and a fourth man—but it was the American he wanted to see. 'He's one of ours!'

'Sure as hell, sir—and this guy isn't. Let's take these back to the lab for positive prints and blowups.'

Fully two months of work had gone into the flight of Cody-193, and the captain lusted for the information he knew to be on those three 2¼-inch frames.

An hour later he had it. An hour after that he boarded a flight to

Da Nang. From there he flew to the Philippines and took a KC-135 directly to California. Despite the rigours of the next twenty hours of flying, the captain slept, having solved a mystery whose answer just might change the policy of his government.

4 COMMITMENTS

Kelly slept nearly eight hours, again rising at the sound of the gulls to find that Pam wasn't there. He went outside and saw her standing on the quay, looking out over the water. The bay had its usual morning calm, the glassy surface punctuated by the circular ripples of bluefish chasing after insects. It was the sort of time that allowed you to be alone with nature, but he knew that Pam merely felt alone. Kelly walked out to her as quietly as he could and touched her waist with both his hands.

'Good morning.' He stood still, holding her lightly, just enough that she could feel his touch.

'So now you know,' she said, unable to turn and face him.

'Yes,' Kelly answered quietly.

'What do you think?' Her voice was a painful whisper.

'I think you're beautiful. I think I'm real glad we met.'

'I do drugs.'

'The docs say you're trying to quit. That's good enough for me.'

'It's worse than that. I've done things—'

Kelly cut her off. 'The things you did before we met don't matter. You're not alone, Pam. I'm here to help if you want me to.' He pulled her tighter. 'I love you, Pam.'

'How can you say that?' she asked. Kelly gently turned her round and smiled.

'Maybe it's your tangled hair—or your runny nose. No, I think it's your heart. No matter what's behind you, your heart is just fine.'

'You mean that, don't you?' she asked. There was a long moment, then Pam smiled up at him. The orange-yellow glow of the rising sun lit up her face and highlighted her fair hair.

Kelly wiped the tears from her face, and the wet feel of her cheeks eliminated whatever doubts he might have had.

'THAT TOOK LONG ENOUGH,' Tony observed, sipping coffee from a paper cup.

'Where's mine?' Eddie demanded, irritable from lack of sleep.

Tony was tired as well. 'The coffeepot's outside.'

Eddie Morello grumbled and went outside. Henry Tucker, the third man, was bagging the product. It had actually worked out a little better than he'd planned. There was at least three hundred thousand dollars' worth of finished drugs now being weighed and sealed in plastic bags for sale to dealers. The expected 'few hours' of work had lingered into an all-night marathon as the three had discovered that what they paid others to do wasn't quite as easy as it looked. Still, over three hundred thousand dollars of profit from sixteen hours of work wasn't all that bad. And this was just the beginning. Tucker was just giving them a taste.

Eddie was still worried about the repercussions of Angelo's demise. He grimaced as he looked out of a porthole of what had once been a ship. Was he safe, linked up with these men? They—he—had just killed Angelo Vorano not twenty-four hours earlier. But Angelo wasn't part of the outfit, and Tony Piaggi was. Tony was their legitimacy, their pipeline to the street, and that made him safe—for a while. As long as Eddie stayed smart and alert.

Henry Tucker stood, stretching, wondering why it was that he had to do all the hard work. The answer came easily enough. Tony was a 'made' man. Eddie wanted to become one. He would never be, and neither would Angelo, Henry reflected—glad for it. He'd never trusted Angelo and now he was no longer a problem. One thing about these people, they seemed to keep their word—and they would continue to as long as he was their connection to the raw material and not one minute longer. Tucker had no illusions about that. It had been good of Angelo to make his connection with Tony and Eddie, and Angelo's death had had exactly the effect on Henry that his own death would have on the other two: none.

With luck that would be the last killing for a while. Tucker disliked complications that often came from killing. A good business ran smoothly, without fuss, and made money for everyone. For that reason he'd selected his associates for their experience, connections and security. His processing site had also been selected with an eye to security. They had a good five miles of visibility and a fast boat with which to make their escape. Yeah, there was danger, but all life was danger, and you measured risk against reward. Henry Tucker's reward for a single day's work was one hundred thousand dollars in untaxed cash, and he was willing to risk a lot for that.

THE BOAT FROM SOLOMONS arrived with the propellers, and Kelly attached them to the Rosens' Hatteras.

'What do I owe you?' Sam asked.

'For what?' Kelly said as he took off his diving gear.

'I always pay a man for his work,' the surgeon said somewhat self-righteously.

Kelly had to laugh. 'Tell you what—if I ever need a back operation, you can make it a freebie. Now, let me get the gear stowed and we'll see how well you can really drive this thing.'

'I bet I'm a better fisherman than you are,' Rosen proclaimed.

Fifteen minutes later they were drifting lazily on the tide, fishing lines out under a warm holiday sun. Kelly had little interest in fishing, and instead assigned himself lookout duty on the flying bridge while Sam taught Pam how to bait her line. Her enthusiasm surprised all of them. Sarah made sure that she was liberally covered with Coppertone to protect her pale skin, and Kelly wondered if a little tan would highlight her scars. Alone with his thoughts, Kelly asked himself what sort of man would abuse a woman.

'LET'S GET OUTA HERE,' Tony Piaggi said, settling into his seat. Tucker took the engine of their eighteen-footer out of idle.

Tony looked at the cooler. Under the fifteen or so cans of National Bohemian was a layer of ice, under which were twenty sealed bags of good Asian heroin. In the unlikely event that anyone stopped them, it was unlikely that they'd look further than the beer. Tucker drove the boat north, and Tony and Eddie laid out their fishing rods as though they were trying to find a good place to harvest a few rockfish from the Chesapeake.

MEMORIAL DAY, Dutch Maxwell thought, alighting from his official car at Arlington National Cemetery. To many just the traditional start of the summer beach season. But not to him, and not to his fellows. This was their day, a time to remember fallen comrades. Admiral Podulski got out with him, and the two walked slowly. Casimir's son, Lieutenant (junior grade) Stanislas Podulski, was not here. His A-4 had been blotted from the sky by a surface-to-air missile. The small attack bomber had dissolved into a greasy cloud of black and yellow, leaving little behind. And so the son of a brave man had been denied his resting place with comrades.

Rear-Admiral James Greer was at his place, as he'd been for the previous two years, about fifty yards from the paved driveway, setting flowers next to the flag at the headstone of his son.

'James?' Maxwell said. The younger man turned and saluted. All three wore their navy-blue uniforms. Their gold-braided sleeves glistened in the sun. Without a spoken word, all three men lined up to face the headstone of Robert White Greer, First Lieutenant, United States Marine Corps. They saluted smartly, each remembering a young man whose luck had proved insufficient to the moment, fifty miles southwest of Da Nang. As each man standing there had taken his chances, so had Bobby Greer and Stas Podulski. It was just that luck had not smiled on two of the three sons.

Greer and Podulski told themselves at this moment that it *had* mattered—that freedom had a price, that some men must pay that price else there would be no flag, no Constitution.

The three men turned and left the grave, heading slowly back to the driveway.

'Have you been briefed in on Boxwood Green, James?' Dutch Maxwell asked.

'No.' Greer turned. 'Do I want to be?'

'We'll probably need your help.'

'Under the table?'

'You know what happened with Kingpin,' Casimir Podulski noted.

'They were lucky to get out,' Greer agreed. 'Keeping this one tight?'

'You bet we are.'

'Let me know what you need. You'll get everything I can find,' Greer said. 'How's little Dutch doing?'

'Flying for Delta now,' Maxwell said. 'Copilot. He'll make captain in due course.'

'Really? Congratulations, my friend.'

'I don't blame him for getting out. I used to, but not now.'

'What's the name of the SEAL who went in to get him?' SEALS, for Sea Air Land, were special-operations commandos.

'Kelly. He's out, too,' Maxwell said.

'You should have gotten the medal for him, Dutch,' Cas Podulski said. 'I read the citation. That was as hairy as they come.'

'I made him a chief. I couldn't get the Medal of Honor for him.' Maxwell shook his head. 'Not for rescuing the son of an admiral, Cas. You know the politics.'

'Yeah,' Podulski said. 'Yeah, I know about politics.'

TUCKER EASED THE BOAT into the slip. He cut the engine and grabbed the mooring lines, which he tied off quickly. Tony and Eddie lifted the beer cooler out while Tucker collected the loose gear before joining his companions at the parking lot.

'Well, that was pretty easy,' Tony noted. The cooler was already in the back of his Ford Country Squire station wagon.

'You know where to find me,' Tucker said.

'You'll get your money,' Eddie Morello said. 'End of the week, the usual place.' He paused. 'What if demand goes up?'
'I can handle it,' Tucker assured him. 'I can get all you want.'
'What kind of pipeline do you have?' Eddie asked.
'Gentlemen, if I told you that, you wouldn't need me.'
Tony Piaggi smiled. 'Don't trust us?'
'Sure.' Henry Tucker smiled. 'I trust you to sell the stuff and share the money with me.'

SARAH CHECKED PAM one last time while Sam packed up their gear. On the whole she liked what she saw. 'I want you to gain five pounds before I see you again. John's going to bring you in to see us in two weeks so that we can get you a complete physical.'
'You have to leave?'
Sarah nodded. 'We really should have left last night.'
Kelly and Pam walked her out to the dock, where Sam's boat was already rumbling with life. She and Pam hugged. Kelly had to submit to a kiss. Sam jumped down to shake their hands.
'New charts!' Kelly told the surgeon.
'Aye, Cap'n.'
Rosen backed out, turning his Hatteras and heading directly for water he knew to be deep. Pam just stood there, holding Kelly's hand, until the boat was a white speck on the horizon.
'We need to talk,' Pam said finally. 'It's time.'
'Wait here.' Kelly went back into the workshop and returned with a pair of folding lounge chairs. He gestured her into one. 'Now tell me how terrible you are.'
Pamela Starr Madden was three weeks shy of her twenty-first birthday, Kelly learned. Born to a lower-working-class family in the Texas Panhandle, she'd grown up under the firm hand of a father who was strict because he didn't know how to love, who drank from frustration with life. When his children misbehaved, he beat them, usually with a belt or a switch of wood. The final straw for Pam had come on the day after her sixteenth birthday, when she'd stayed late at a church function and ended up going on what was almost a date with friends. Arriving home at ten twenty on a Friday evening, Pam came into a house whose lights blazed with anger, there to face an enraged father and a thoroughly cowed mother.
After sustaining the worst beating of her sixteen years, Pam had slipped out of her ground-floor bedroom window and walked the four miles to the centre of the bleak, dusty town. She'd caught a Greyhound bus for Houston before dawn. So far as she could

determine, her parents had never even reported her as missing. A series of menial jobs and even worse housing in Houston had merely given emphasis to her misery. With what little money she'd saved, she'd caught yet another bus and stopped in New Orleans. Scared, thin and young, Pam was spotted almost at once by a well-dressed and smooth-talking 25-year-old named Pierre Lamarck. She'd taken his offer of shelter and sympathy, and three days later he had become her first lover. A week after that, a firm slap across the face had coerced the young runaway into her second sexual adventure, this one with a salesman from Springfield, Illinois.

By nineteen Pam had escaped Lamarck and three more pimps, always finding herself caught with another. One in Chicago had started Pam on heroin. Unable to go home—she'd called once and had the phone slammed down by her mother even before she could beg for help—and not trusting the social services, which might have helped her along a different path, she finally found herself in Washington DC, an experienced street prostitute with a drug habit that helped her to hide from what she thought of herself.

The final chapter had begun in Baltimore with someone named Henry Tucker. Wanting to broaden his drug business, he'd set up a stable of girls to run drugs from his operation to his distributors. He had bought the girls from established pimps in straight cash transactions, which the girls found ominous. Pam tried to run almost at once, but she'd been caught and beaten severely. Henry had used the opportunity to cram barbiturates into her, which both attenuated the pain and increased her dependence. He'd augmented the treatment by making her available to any of his associates who wanted her. Henry finally cowed her spirit.

Over a period of five months, the combination of beatings, sexual abuse and drugs had depressed her to a nearly catatonic state until she'd been jarred back to reality only four weeks earlier by tripping over the body of a twelve-year-old boy in a doorway, a needle still in his arm. Remaining outwardly docile, Pam had struggled to cut her drug use. She'd waited for a time when Henry was away, because his associates got looser when he wasn't around. Only five days earlier she'd packed what little she had and bolted. Penniless, she'd hitched her way out of town.

'Tell me about Henry,' Kelly said softly when she'd finished.

'Thirty, black, about your height.'

'Did any other girls get away?'

Pam's voice went cold as ice. 'I only know of one who tried. Her name was Helen. It was around November. He . . . killed her. He made us all watch.' She looked up. 'It was terrible.'

Kelly said quietly, 'Do you have any idea how brave you've been to tell me all this? You're one very courageous lady, honey.'

'If they ever find me . . .' Emotion was coming back now. Fear. 'Every time we go back to the city, they might see me. I'll never be safe. Never.'

'Yeah, well, there's two ways to handle that. You can just keep running and hiding. Or you can help put them away. I've a friend in the police . . .'

She shook her head emphatically. 'The girl they killed. They knew she was going to the cops. I can't trust the police. Besides, you don't know how scary these people are.'

'We'll be careful,' Kelly said.

THE NEXT FEW DAYS settled into a surprisingly easy routine. Whatever her other qualities, Pam was a horrible cook. But she learned quickly, and by Saturday she'd figured out how to make hamburger into something tastier than a piece of charcoal. Through it all Kelly was there, encouraging her. A quiet word, a gentle touch and a smile were his tools. She spent her afternoons in the sun and acquired the beginnings of a tan. Her smiles gained confidence, and twice Kelly caught her looking into the mirror with something other than pain in her eyes.

She was changing. Her ribs were less pronounced. She'd gained weight on a regular, healthy diet. But it was the person inside who had changed the most. Kelly wondered what miracle had taken place, afraid to believe that he was part of it but knowing that it was so. Pam had begun to look at the future as more than a dark place where she could hide and forget. It was now a place of hope.

5 *AMBUSH*

By the end of her second week with Kelly, Pam had started to run. Her leg muscles were toning up; what had been slack was now taut, as it ought to be on a girl her age. She still had her demons. Twice Kelly woke to find her trembling. Both times his touch calmed her.

Mainly he loved her. He found himself slightly anxious if he failed to see her every few minutes, as though she might somehow disappear. But she was always there, smiling back playfully.

Ten days after Sam and Sarah had left, they had a little ceremony. They took *Springer* out, tied the bottle of barbiturates to a large rock and dumped it over the side. The splash it made seemed a fitting and final end to one of her problems. Kelly stood behind her, his strong arms about her waist.

'You were right,' she said, stroking his forearms.

'That happens sometimes,' Kelly replied with a distant smile, only to be stunned by her next statement.

'There are others, John, other women Henry has . . . like Helen, the one he killed.'

'What do you mean?'

'I have to go back. I have to help them before Henry . . . before he kills more of them.'

'There's danger involved, Pammy,' Kelly said slowly.

'I know . . . but what about them?' It was a symptom of her recovery, Kelly knew. She had become a normal person again, and normal people worried about others. 'I can't hide for ever, can I?'

'No, you can't. That's the problem. It's too hard to hide.'

'Are you sure you can trust your friend on the police?' she asked.

'Yes. He knows me. He's a lieutenant I did a job for a year ago. A gun got tossed, and I helped find it. So he owes me one.' Kelly paused. 'You don't have to do it, Pam. If you just want to walk away from it, that's OK with me. I don't *have* to go back to Baltimore ever.'

'If I don't do something, then it'll never really be gone, will it?'

Kelly thought about that. You simply could not run away from some things. He knew. He'd tried. 'Let me make a phone call.'

'LIEUTENANT ALLEN,' the man said into his phone.

'Frank? John Kelly,' the detective heard, bringing a smile.

'How's life in the middle of the bay, fella?'

'Quiet and lazy. How about you?' the voice asked.

'I wish,' Allen answered, leaning back in his swivel chair. A large man, and like most cops of his generation, a Second World War veteran, Allen had risen from foot patrol to homicide. 'What can I do for you?'

'I, uh, met somebody who might need to talk with you.'

'How so?' the cop asked.

'It's business, Frank. Information regarding a killing.'

The cop's eyes narrowed a bit. 'When and where?'

'I don't know yet, and I don't like doing this over a phone line. It's drug people.'

Allen's mind went *click*. Kelly had said his informant was 'somebody', not a 'man'. That made the person a female, Allen figured. He had heard reports of a drug ring using women for something or other.

Nothing more than that. But it wasn't his case. It was being handled by Emmet Ryan and Tom Douglas downtown.

'My friend doesn't want much involvement, Frank. If it goes further, we can re-evaluate then. We're talking some scary people if this story is true. My rules: it's for information purposes only, and it's a quiet meet. OK?'

Allen considered that. He'd never dwelt upon Kelly's background, but he knew he was a trained diver, a bosun's mate who'd fought in the brown-water navy in the Mekong Delta, supporting the 9th Infantry. He'd done a nice job retraining the force's divers. And he did know Kelly to be a serious man. If nothing else, it sure sounded interesting.

'You know, anybody else, I'd probably say come right in here and that would be it, but I'll play along with you for now.'

'Thanks. What's your schedule like?'

'Working late shift this week,' Allen explained. 'I get off around midnight, one o'clock.'

'Tomorrow night. I'll pick you up at the front door. Thanks, Frank. Bye.' The line clicked off.

'ARE YOU SCARED?' he asked.

'A little,' she admitted.

He smiled. 'That's normal. But you heard what I said. He doesn't know anything about you. I'll be carrying a gun. It's just a talk. You can always back out. And I'll be with you all the time.'

She smiled and relaxed. 'I have to fix dinner,' she said, heading off to the kitchen.

Kelly went outside. He walked into the equipment bunker and took his .45 Colt automatic down from the rack. He took two loaded magazines from a drawer, along with a single loose round. He now had a total of fifteen rounds with which to face danger. Not nearly enough for a walk in the jungles of Vietnam, but he figured it was plenty for the dark environs of a city. He'd never once rattled under fire, and he'd killed men before. Whatever the dangers might be, Kelly was ready for them. Besides, he wasn't going after the Vietcong. He was going in at night, and the night was his friend.

'WE NEED TO GET YOU some new clothes,' he said, watching her face, the new confidence. He had her on the wheel, steering past Sharp's Island Light, well east of the busy shipping channel.

'Good idea,' she agreed. 'Where will we stay tonight?'

'On board,' Kelly answered. 'We'll be secure here.'

'I'm sure you're right,' Pam said, turning to smile at him. The confidence in her face warmed his blood.

They made port three hours later. They walked straight from the boat to the Scout, and Kelly drove off the property at once. It was still early in the day, and they drove immediately out of the city, finding a suburban shopping centre in Timonium, where Pam selected three nice outfits, for which he paid cash. She dressed in the one he liked best, an understated skirt and blouse.

Dinner was eaten in the same area, an upscale restaurant with a dark corner booth. 'You look pretty good—relaxed, I mean,' he said, sipping his after-dinner coffee.

'I never thought I'd feel this way. I mean, it's only been . . . not even three weeks?'

Kelly set his coffee down. 'In a couple of months everything will be different, Pam.' He took her left hand, hoping that it would some day bear a gold ring on the third finger.

'I believe that now. I really do.'

'Good.'

'What do we do now?' she asked. Dinner was over and there were hours until the clandestine meeting with Lieutenant Allen.

'Just drive around some?' Kelly left cash on the table and led her out to the car.

It was dark, and rain was starting to fall. Kelly headed south towards the city, feeling confident and ready for the night's travail. On getting in the car, he'd put his .45 Colt automatic in its accustomed place, a holster just under the front seat that he could reach faster than one in his belt.

'Pam?' he asked. 'How much do you trust me?'

'I do trust you, John.'

'Where did you . . . work, I mean?'

'What do you mean?'

'I mean, it's dark and rainy, and I'd like to see what it's like down there.' Without looking, he could feel her body tense. 'Look, I'll be careful. If you see anything that worries you, I'll make tracks like you won't believe.'

'You promise you'll be careful?'

'Believe it, Pam,' he assured her.

'OK, then.'

It was amazing, Kelly thought, fifty minutes later. The things that are there but which you never see. For years his survival had depended on his noting everything—every bent branch, every footprint in the dirt. But he'd driven through this area a hundred times and never noticed what was happening, because it was a different sort of jungle filled with very different game.

The environment was ideal. Dark, under a cloudy, moonless sky. The only illumination came from sparse streetlights that created lonely globes of light along trash-laden sidewalks. Showers came and went—enough to keep heads down and limit visibility.

The dealers were a diverse group, Kelly saw as he cruised past their sales area. Their posture told him of their confidence. They owned the streets at this hour. The customers were diverse, too. Some were local, you could tell from their colour and shabby clothing. Then there were the others, the ones with medium-expensive cars, who had come from the suburbs.

Kelly looked over at Pam. She seemed all right, though a little tense. These people were dangerous, but not to the two of them. He'd been careful to remain invisible, to drive like everyone else, meandering round the few blocks of the 'business' area in an irregular pattern. If anyone had eyeballed him and his vehicle, he would have noticed. And besides, he had his Colt .45.

Fifty yards away was a dealer dressed in a silk shirt. Probably real silk, Kelly was willing to bet. There was a flashiness to these vermin. They had to let people know how bold they were.

'They're so stupid.' Kelly waved at the dealer near the corner. 'I mean, he's holding a lot of money, right? So what if somebody tries to rob him?'

'It happens,' Pam replied. 'But he's carrying a gun, too, and if anyone tries—'

'Oh! The guy in the doorway?'

'He's the real dealer, Kelly. The guy in the shirt is his lieutenant. He's the guy who does the actual transaction.'

Kelly had failed to spot something, allowing his pride to overcome his caution. Not a good habit, he told himself.

'I get it,' Kelly said. 'The lieutenant holds the drugs and makes the exchange, but he gives the money to his boss. The boss holds the earnings, but he also has a gun to make sure nothing goes wrong. They're not as dumb as I thought they were.'

'They're smart enough.'

Kelly smiled, ignoring the warnings that the combat-experienced part of his brain was beginning to generate.

Hmm. He hadn't seen that car before. It was a muscle car, a red Plymouth Runner, half a block away. There was something odd about the way it—

'Kelly . . .' Pam suddenly tensed in her seat.

'What is it?' His hand found the .45.

'I know that car. It's—'

Kelly's voice was calm. 'OK, I'll get us out of here. It's time to leave.' He increased speed, manoeuvring left to get past the Road-runner. He thought to tell Pam to get down, but that really wasn't necessary. In less than a minute he'd be gone, and—damn!

It was one of the gentry customers, someone in a black Karmann-Ghia convertible who'd just made his transaction and, eager to have this area behind him, shot left from beyond the Roadrunner only to stop suddenly for yet another car doing much the same thing. Kelly stood on his brakes to avoid a collision. But the timing worked out badly, and he stopped almost right next to the Roadrunner, whose driver picked that moment to get out. Instead of going forward, he opted to walk around the back of the car, and, in turning, his eyes ended up not three feet from Pam's cringing face. Kelly saw the look in the man's eyes. He recognised Pam.

'OK, I see it,' Kelly's voice announced with an eerie calm, his combat voice. He stepped on the gas, reaching the corner a few seconds later. After the briefest pause to check traffic, he executed a hard left turn to evacuate the area.

'He saw me!' Her voice hovered on the edge of a scream.

'It's OK, Pam,' Kelly replied, watching the road and his mirror. 'We are leaving the area. You're with me and you're safe.'

Bright, low-slung headlights made the same turn Kelly'd executed twenty seconds earlier. The car was accelerating hard and fishtailing on the wet asphalt. It wasn't the Karmann-Ghia.

You are now in danger, Kelly's instincts told him calmly.

He put both hands on the wheel. He started evaluating the situation, and not much of it was good. His Scout was not made for this sort of thing. It wasn't a sports car, wasn't a muscle car. He had four puny cylinders. The Plymouth Roadrunner had eight.

'Pam,' Kelly said as quietly as he could manage, 'you want to get down on the floor, honey?'

'Are they—?' She started to turn, the fear still manifest in her voice, but Kelly's right hand pushed her down towards the floor.

'Looks like they're following us, yes. Let me handle this, OK?'

Kelly turned hard right. He couldn't corner as well as the Roadrunner, but these streets were wide and being in front gave him the choice of path and timing. Losing them would be hard, but he knew where the police station was. It was just a matter of leading them there. They'd break contact at that point.

They might be armed, but they sure as hell weren't trained. How many? Two? Maybe three? He ought to have checked, Kelly told himself, remembering that there hadn't been time.

Kelly looked in the mirror. The headlights of another, uninvolved car a block away shone straight through the Roadrunner. Three of them. He wondered what they might be armed with.

The Roadrunner was ten yards behind now. Its driver made a move to the right. Kelly snapped the wheel to the right to block. He heard tyres squeal as the Roadrunner braked to avoid a collision. He immediately learned that the other driver didn't have the stomach to hurt his car. Then the Roadrunner snapped left, but Kelly covered that move also. It was like sailboats in a tacking duel.

'That's Billy's car. He loves to race,' Pam said, her voice cracking on every word.

'Billy, eh? Well, Billy likes his car a little too much.'

Kelly turned hard left, taking a street through a wide strip of vacant lots that the night's rain had changed to mud. He turned to look at the Roadrunner. Uh-oh. The right-side passenger window was coming down. That meant a gun. Cutting this a little close, Kelly. He stood on the brakes and turned hard right. The Scout bounded over the kerb, obviously a manoeuvre of panic. Pam screamed with the sudden jolt.

The Roadrunner mimicked his turn, also bouncing over the kerb, following the Scout right into the trap Kelly had sprung.

Kelly had already downshifted. The mud was a good eight inches deep and he felt his car slow, felt the tyres sink a few inches into the gooey surface, but then the big, coarsely treaded tyres bit and started pulling again. Only then did he turn round.

The headlights told the story. The Roadrunner yawed wildly to the left as its tyres spun on the gelatinous surface, and when the vehicle slowed, their spinning merely dug wet holes. The headlights sank as the car's powerful engine excavated its own grave.

The race was over.

Three men got out of the car and just stood there, uncomfortable to have mud on their shiny punk shoes, looking at the way their once clean car sat in the mud like a weary sow hog. Nice to know I haven't lost it yet, Kelly thought.

Then they looked up to where he was, thirty yards away.

'You dummies!' he called through the light rain. 'See ya 'round!' He started moving again, careful, of course, to keep his eyes on them. That's what had won him the race, Kelly told himself. Caution, brains, experience. Guts, too. He nursed the Scout back onto a strip of pavement, upshifted and drove off.

'You can get up now, Pam. We won't be seeing them again.'

Pam did that, smiling for him, showing bravery she didn't feel at the moment. Kelly checked his watch. Another hour or so until shift change at the police station. The smart move was to find a quiet place to wait. He drove for a little while, then, finding an area with no major street activity, he parked.

'How are you feeling?' he asked.

'That was scary,' she replied, looking down and shaking badly.

'Look, we can go right back to the boat and—'

'No! Billy raped me . . . and killed Helen. If I don't stop him, he'll just keep doing it to people I know.'

'How many other girls?' he asked.

'Doris, Xantha, Paula, Maria and Roberta.'

'Well, with a little luck you can help them, honey.' He put his arm round her, and after a time the shaking stopped.

'I'm thirsty,' she said.

'There's a cooler on the back seat.'

Pam smiled. 'That's right.' She turned in the seat to reach for a Coke—and her body went rigid. She gasped, and Kelly's skin got that all-too-familiar unwelcome feeling. The danger feeling.

'Kelly!' Pam screamed. She was looking towards the car's left rear. Kelly was already reaching for his gun, turning as he did so, but it was too late and part of him knew he'd erred badly, but he didn't know how. Before he could reach his gun, there was a flash of light and an impact on his head, followed by darkness.

6 *RECOVERY*

It was a routine police patrol that spotted the Scout. Officer Chuck Monroe, sixteen months on the force, noted that it was an unusual vehicle for this area. He decided to check it out, record its tag number, and then came the heart-stopping realisation that the car's left side had taken at least two shotgun blasts.

Officer Monroe called for back-up and for an ambulance, and then he notified his district desk of the licence number of the subject automobile. Only then did he step out of the radio car, his police baton in his left hand, his right at the grip of his revolver. He approached the Scout. What he saw froze him in his tracks.

The head rested on the steering wheel. Blood had sprayed all over the inside. The man was still breathing, which surprised the officer. Clearly a shotgun blast, it had hit the victim's head, neck and upper back. Who was he? Monroe reached for the wallet pocket. Unsurprisingly, it was empty.

Just then Monroe heard the banshee wail of a fire-department ambulance approaching. The large, boxy, red and white vehicle turned the corner a few seconds later. It halted just past the radio car, and its two occupants came at once to the officer.

'What d'we got?' The senior fireman-paramedic hardly needed to ask. In this part of town at this time of night, it would be 'penetrating trauma', in the dry lexicon of his profession.

The other paramedic was already moving back to the ambulance for supplies when another police car arrived on the scene.

'What gives?' the watch supervisor asked.

'Shotgun, close range. The guy's still alive!' Monroe said.

'ID?' the police sergeant asked.

'No wallet. I haven't had a chance to look around yet.'

The sergeant played his flashlight on the inside of the car to help the firemen. A lot of blood, otherwise empty. Both officers stood back to give the paramedics room to work.

'Where you taking him?' the sergeant asked.

'Hopkins,' the junior paramedic advised.

PROFESSOR SAM ROSEN was not in a good mood, as the resident saw at once. It had been a twenty-hour day for him already. The patient lay face down on an ER—emergency room—treatment table.

'Tell me what we have,' Sam Rosen ordered curtly.

'Shotgun wound, several pellets very close to the cord, sir.'

'OK.' Rosen bent down. 'What's with the glass?'

'He was in a car.'

'We need to get rid of that, need to shave the head, too,' Rosen said, surveying the damage. 'We're going to be busy.' He paused. 'Overall condition of the patient looks good; good muscle tone. Let's get the neck cleaned off, Margaret. I need to take a look.'

Margaret Wilson, the senior ER nurse, selected a pair of forceps, grabbed a large cottonwool ball, which she dipped in distilled water, then wiped across the patient's neck, clearing away the blood and exposing the actual wounds. While she swabbed the patient off, Rosen looked for and got sterile garb. By the time he got back to the bedside, Margaret had a sterile kit in place and uncovered.

Rosen picked a small, round hole on the patient's shoulder, well away from anything really vital. With a delicacy that his large hands made almost comical, he probed for and retrieved a single lead ball, which he held up to the light. 'Number seven shot, I believe.

Somebody mistook this guy for a pigeon. That's good news.'

'What's this, I wonder?' Margaret said after a moment.

'Hmph?' Rosen walked round to her side of the table while the rest of the ER team did its work.

'A tattoo on his arm,' she reported. Nurse Wilson was surprised by the reaction it drew from Professor Rosen.

'THE SHOULDER WOUND was extensive but superficial,' Rosen told the neurosurgical resident.

'Bloody enough. Four units,' she noted.

'Shotgun wounds are like that. There was only one real threat to the spine. Took me a little while to figure how to remove it without endangering anything.'

'Two hundred and thirty-seven pellets, but'—she held the X-ray up to the light—'looks like you got them all. This fellow just got a nice collection of freckles, though.'

'Took long enough,' Sam said tiredly.

'He's coming out, but it'll be a while,' Sandy O'Toole said, arriving from the recovery room. She handed over the chart, which showed his current vitals. 'You know this one, don't you, Doctor?'

Professor Rosen nodded. 'Yeah. He's a friend of mine. Would you mind terribly if I asked you to take—'

'A special interest?'

'You're our best, Sandy.'

'Anything I need to know?' she asked.

'He's a good man, Sandy. Sarah likes him, too.'

'Then he must be all right.' She headed back into recovery, wondering if the professor was playing matchmaker again.

'NICE TAN,' Billy observed with a smirk. 'I wonder where she got it.' There was general amusement. 'What do we do with her?'

'Find a spot,' Henry said after a moment's consideration. 'If she's found, it doesn't matter much.' Then he looked round the room, cataloguing the expressions he saw. The lesson had been learned. Nobody else would try this again, not anytime soon.

'What about the guy?' he asked Billy.

Billy smirked again. It was his favourite expression. 'Blew him away. Both barrels, ten feet. We won't be seeing him no more.'

'OK.' Henry left. There was work to be done and money to collect.

The body remained in place on the floor. Doris and the others sat in the same room, unable to look away from what had once been a friend, learning their lesson, as Henry wished.

KELLY OPENED HIS EYES and saw a woman. His age, perhaps a year or two younger, with brown hair stuffed under a green cap, and light eyes that sparkled in a friendly way.

'Hello,' she said. 'I'm your nurse, Sandy O'Toole.' She gave him her beaming feminine smile.

'Where am I?' Kelly asked in a raspy voice.

'Johns Hopkins Hospital. Somebody shot you.' She reached out to touch his hand.

The softness of her hand ignited something in his drug-suppressed consciousness. For a minute or so Kelly couldn't figure out what it was. Then the missing pieces began to come together, and he understood it was horror that awaited him.

'Oh, God . . . Pam.' The look on his ruggedly handsome face was one of black despair.

JUNE 20 WAS A HOT DAY and a dull one. Bob Preis, a photographer for the *Baltimore Sun*, had a new camera, a Nikon, and the new camera, like a new love, had all sorts of new features to enjoy. Preis was sitting in his car on Druid Lake Drive listening to his police radio, hoping for something interesting to happen, but nothing was. And so he was playing with his new camera, changing from one lens to another, scanning the area.

It was the crows that caught his attention. Located off-centre in the irregularly shaped lake was a fountain. It was a plain concrete cylinder sticking six or eight feet up from the water's surface, and in it were a few jets that shot water more or less straight up. Crows were circling the water, trying to get in. What were they interested in? His hands searched the camera case for the 200mm lens, which he attached to the camera, bringing it up to his eyes.

'Oh, God, no . . .' Preis instantly shot ten rapid frames. Only then did he get on his car radio, telling his base office to notify the police at once. There was a body in the fountain—a young woman.

'JOHN, THEY FOUND HER,' Rosen said.

'Dead?' Kelly couldn't look up. The tone of Sam's voice had already told him the real news.

Sam nodded. 'Yeah.'

'How?'

'I don't know yet. The police called me a few minutes ago.'

'Thanks, pal.' Kelly's voice sounded dead.

Rosen grasped Kelly's hand. 'I'm sorry, John. I . . . you know how I felt about her. Is there anything I can do?'

'Not right now, Sam. Thanks.'

'The police want to talk to you. I told them tomorrow morning.'

'OK.'

The surgeon wanted to say more, but couldn't find the right words. He left without any others.

'I HEARD,' Sandy O'Toole told him. It bothered her that his grief wasn't right. He was a tough man—perhaps one of those who did his weeping alone, but she was sure he hadn't done it yet. The nurse sat beside his bed. 'I'm a widow,' she told him.

'Vietnam?'

'Yes. Tim was a captain in the First Cavalry.'

'I'm sorry,' Kelly said.

'It's hard. I know.'

'Last November I lost Tish, and now—'

'Sarah told me. Mr Kelly—'

'John,' he said softly.

'Thank you, John. My name is Sandy. Bad luck does not make a bad person,' she told him in a voice that meant what it said.

'It wasn't luck. She told me it was a dangerous place, and I took her there anyway because I wanted to see for myself. I was careless and stupid, and I killed her.'

'Other people killed her, and other people tried to kill you. You're a victim.'

'Not a victim. Just a fool.'

'You gave her love, didn't you, John?'

'Yes. Yes, I did love her.'

'Let it out,' the nurse told him. 'You have to.'

First he closed his eyes. Then he shook his head. 'I can't.'

'THAT WAS really stupid.'

'That's one way of looking at it,' Tucker agreed. 'But I can't have my girls leaving without permission, can I?'

'You ever hear of burying them?'

'Anybody can do that.' Henry Tucker smiled in the darkness, watching the movie. They were in the back row of a downtown cinema. It was a good place for a covert meeting with a confidential informant, which was how this meeting would go on the officer's time sheet.

'Sloppy not killing the guy, too,' said Lieutenant Mark Charon of the Narcotics Division, Baltimore City Police Department.

'Will he be a problem?' Tucker asked.

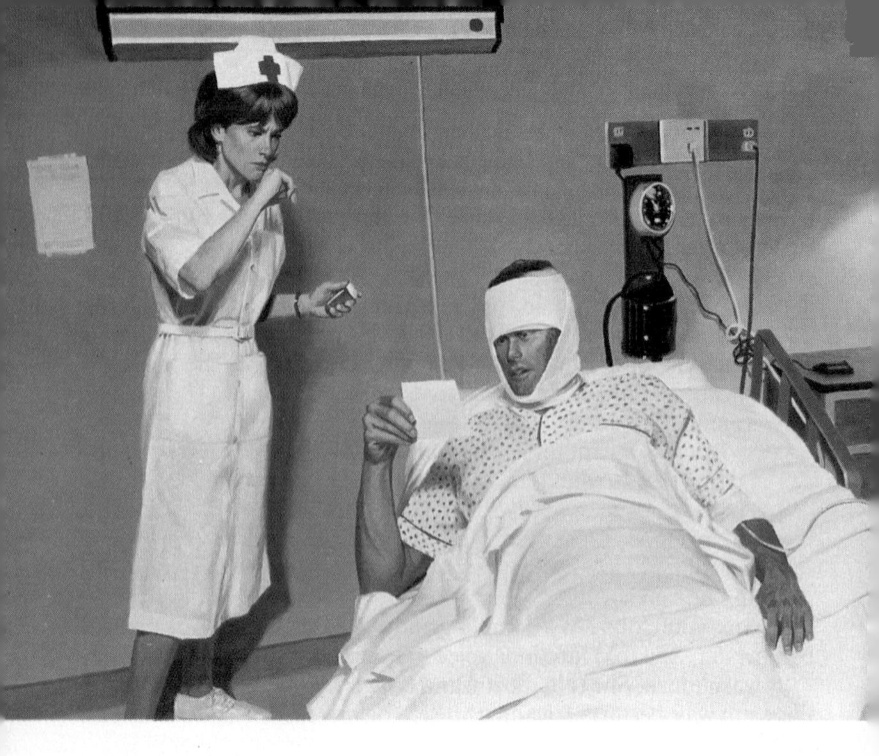

'No. He didn't see anything, did he?'

'You tell me, man.'

'I can't get that close to the case, remember?' The man paused for a handful of popcorn and munched away his irritation. 'He's known to the department. Ex-navy guy, skin diver, lives over on the Eastern Shore somewhere, sort of a rich beach bum from what I gather. Ryan and Douglas are going to be working the case, but it doesn't look like they have much of anything.'

'You want me to get him in the hospital?' Tucker asked lightly.

'No! You damned fool, this is going on the books as a robbery. If anything else happens, it just gets bigger. We don't want that. Leave him be. He doesn't know anything.'

'So he's not a problem,' Tucker wanted to be clear on that.

'No. No problem.' He ate another handful of popcorn. 'What do you have for me?'

Tucker smiled in the darkness. 'Mr Piaggi is starting to like doing business with me.'

A grunt in the darkness. 'I wouldn't trust him.'

'It does get complicated, doesn't it?' Tucker paused. 'But I need his connections. We're about to hit the big time.'

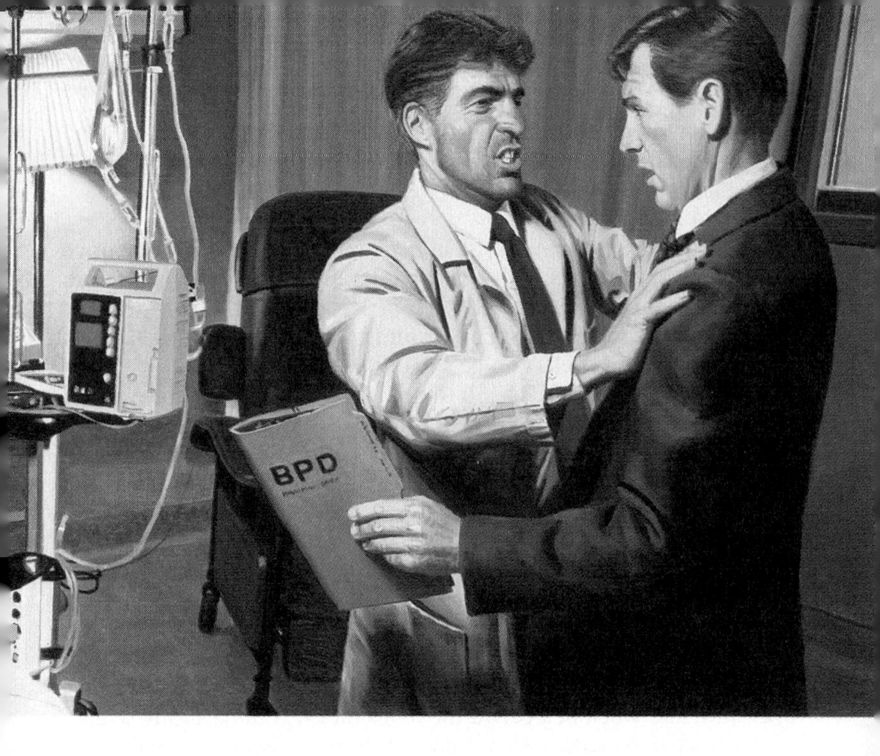

'TAKE IT EASY ON HIM,' Rosen said, opening the door of the private room. 'He's recovering from a major injury.'

'I have my job, too, Doctor,' said Detective Sergeant Tom Douglas. He was about forty and looked every bit as angry as Kelly, Rosen thought, as he followed the detective into the room.

'Mr Kelly, we're sorry,' the detective said after introducing himself. Douglas opened his notebook. 'Two nights ago you were in the company of a young lady named Pamela Madden?'

'Yes.' Kelly's eyes were closed when Nurse O'Toole came in with his morning antibiotic dose. She was surprised to see the two other men there.

'Mr Kelly, yesterday afternoon we discovered the body of a young woman who fits the physical description of Miss Madden.' Douglas reached into his coat pocket. 'Is this she?' Douglas asked, holding the photo before Kelly's face.

'No!' Rosen said, pushing the cop against the wall. In the process the photo dropped on the patient's chest.

Kelly's eyes went wide in horror, his skin pasty white. Everyone turned away but the nurse, whose eyes were locked on her patient.

'Look, Doc, I—' Douglas tried to say.

'Get out of my hospital!' Rosen fairly screamed. 'You can *kill* somebody with that kind of shock. Why didn't you tell me?'

'He has to identify—'

'*I* could have done that!'

The antibiotic medication still in her hand, O'Toole tried to remove the photograph from Kelly's view, but her own eyes were first drawn to the image and then repelled by it as Kelly's hand seized the print and held it a scant twelve inches from his own wide-open eyes. Then his face composed itself, and he spoke.

'It's OK, Sam. He has his job to do, too.' Kelly looked down at the photo one last time. Then he held it up for the nurse to take.

And things settled down for everyone except Nurse O'Toole. She watched Kelly swallow the oversized pill and left the room for the calm of the corridor.

Sandra O'Toole walked back to the nurses' station, remembering what she alone had seen—Kelly's face turning so pale that her first reaction to it was that he must be in shock. However, the pallor of his face was not that of shock, but of rage. His hands balled briefly into fists of quivering stone. And then his face had changed again. There had been comprehension to replace the blind, killing rage. Kelly's eyes shut, and when he opened them, his face was unnaturally serene. The complete sequence had not taken four seconds, she realised, all of it while Rosen and Douglas had been scuffling. He'd passed from horror to rage to understanding, then to concealment—but what had come in between comprehension and disguise was the most frightening thing of all.

What had she seen in the face of this man? It took her a moment to answer the question. Death was what she'd seen. Controlled. Planned. Disciplined.

But it was still Death, living in the mind of a man.

'I'M SORRY, MR KELLY. I really am,' Douglas said with genuine sincerity, 'but there's no easy way to do this. Whatever happened, it's our job to try and identify the people who did it. We need your help to do that. Did you see the people who—'

Kelly shook his head. 'No. I was looking the wrong way.'

'What were you doing at the time?'

'Observing. Look, you talked to Lieutenant Allen, right?'

'That's correct.' Douglas nodded.

'Pam witnessed a murder. I was bringing her in to talk to Allen about it. She was linked up with people who deal drugs. She saw them kill a girl. I told her she had to do something about it.'

'Names?'

'None that I remember,' Kelly answered.

'Come on,' Douglas said, leaning forward. 'She must have told you something.'

'No. Like I said, she was linked up with this bunch, and I—dumb as it sounds—didn't ask much.' *I'll be finding out, though.*

ALONE IN HIS BED, alone with his mind, Kelly's eyes calmly surveyed the ceiling, scanning the white surface like a movie screen.

What had happened fitted what Pam had told him. It was something they had done before. He had allowed himself to be spotted—twice. His guilt was still quite real, but that was history now and he couldn't change it. Whoever had done this to Pam, they were still out there, and if they had done this twice already, they would do it again.

OK, he thought. But they've never met anyone like me before.

I need to get back into shape.

The injuries were severe, but he'd survive them. Recovery would be painful, but he'd do what they told him. Then the really hard part would start. The running, the swimming, the weights. The weapons training. The mental preparation . . .

'DOES KELLY KNOW anything?' asked Lieutenant Emmet Ryan.

'Nothing we can use,' Douglas replied. 'He didn't see any faces.'

Ryan looked up from a large collection of photos, half taken at the scene, half at the coroner's office. What he saw there sickened him despite all his years of police work. 'Maybe Narcotics will shake something loose.'

'Sure,' Douglas replied. As so often happened in police work, you played for breaks, for mistakes the other side made. These people didn't make many, but sooner or later they all did, both officers told themselves. It was just that they never seemed to come soon enough.

'GOOD TO SEE you're eating.'

Kelly looked up from a mostly empty plate. 'I have to get better, Sam.'

'What are you going to do?' asked Rosen, sitting down on the bed.

'I don't know.'

'You think you can fool me? John, you have to stay aloof, you can't get too involved. You understand me?'

'Yes, sir, I do.'

'What are you going to do?'

'You don't want to know, Sam.'

'I want to help. I really do,' Rosen said, genuine wonder in his voice. 'I liked her, too, John. So what can I do?'

'Get me better.'

7 LABOUR

It was almost grim to watch, Sandy thought. The strange thing was that he was being a good patient. He didn't whine. He did just what the physical therapist told him to do. When the therapist asked for more, more was delivered, and on and on until the therapist began to worry. 'You can ease off now,' he advised.

Kelly slowed his pace on the stationary bike to a reluctant stop.

'I've come to take him back,' O'Toole announced.

Kelly got off. 'To what do I owe this honour, ma'am?'

'I'm supposed to keep an eye on you,' Sandy replied. 'Trying to show us how tough you are?'

Kelly had been a touch light-hearted but turned serious. 'Mrs O'Toole, I'm supposed to get my mind off my troubles, right? Exercise does that for me. OK?'

'OK.' She pointed to the door. Out in the bustling anonymity of the corridor, she said, 'I worry about my patients.'

'Well, you don't have to worry about me. I know my limits.'

'Where are the limits?'

'A long way off,' Kelly said with the beginnings of a smile, which he quickly extinguished. 'How am I doing?'

'Very well. But why the big show?'

'I don't know. It's the way I am, Sandy.'

Who is this guy? Sandy asked herself. His furious effort in rehab. His outward toughness. How to reconcile that with his gentleness and good manners?

Whatever else she might say about the patient, he was rapidly getting himself back in shape. She wondered what the urgency was.

'SO WHAT HAVE you found out for us?' Dutch Maxwell asked.

'Good news and bad news,' James Greer replied. 'The good news is that the opposition has very little in the way of regular ground forces within response distance of the objective.'

'And the bad news?' Admiral Podulski asked.

'Do I have to tell you? Enough triple-A along the coast to turn the sky black. It's dangerous there for fast movers, Cas. For helicopters?

One or two rescue birds, sure, it's doable, but a large lift will be real dicey. We went over all this before. Kingpin failed, remember?'

'That wasn't our fault!' Podulski objected.

All three men hovered over the reconnaissance photos. It was a good collection. The camp was two hundred metres square, with a guard tower at each corner. Inside the wire were three large buildings and two small ones. Inside one of the large buildings were, they believed, twenty American officers, lieutenant-colonel/commander rank or higher, for this was a special camp.

It was the Buffalo Hunter photos that had first come to Greer's attention. One was good enough to have identified a face, Colonel Robin Zacharias, USAF. His F-105G Wild Weasel had been shot down eight months earlier; he and his weapons-systems operator had been reported killed by the North Vietnamese. Even a picture of his body had been published. This camp, whose codename, Sender Green, was known to fewer than fifty people, was located in the most unlikely of places, not acknowledged in any way. However the war would turn out, America wanted her pilots back. Here was a place whose very existence suggested that some would never be returned. A statistical study of losses had shown an ominous irregularity: flight officers of relatively high rank were reported killed at a higher rate than those of lower rank. It was known that the enemy had dossiers on senior American officers—who they were, what they knew. It was possible that those officers were being held in a special place, that their knowledge in areas of special strategic interest was being used by North Vietnam as a bargaining chip for dealing with their Russian sponsors.

'We've got to find a way,' Casimir Podulski said. 'If we don't, we'll never see these men again.'

'I concur in the nature of the camp,' Greer said. 'Zacharias is someone they'd be interested in.' Zacharias had been part of the joint-targeting staff that selected the destinations for strategic weapons, and his knowledge of America's most secret war plans was encyclopaedic. 'If you want, I can try to sell the idea, but I'm not very hopeful.'

'If we don't, we're breaking faith with our people!' Podulski slammed his fist on the desk. But Cas had an agenda, too. Discovery of this camp, rescue of its prisoners, would make it clear that North Vietnam had publicly lied. That might poison the peace talks enough to force Nixon to adopt yet another plan being drawn up by a Pentagon working group: the invasion of the north. That plan, whose cover name changed on a monthly basis—currently it was Certain

Cornet—was the holy grail of vengeance for all the professionals who had for six years watched their country blunder about in indecision and the profligate waste of America's children.

'Don't you think I know that?' Greer said. 'I'm on your side, remember?'

Unlike Cas and Dutch, Greer knew that Certain Cornet would never be more than a staff study. But Sender Green was still there, and this mission, Operation Boxwood Green, was possible—just.

Greer shifted his gaze to the relief map. He pointed to a red line that ran from a coastal town nearly to the camp's main gate. On the overhead photos it looked like a good blacktopped road. 'Twenty minutes in a helicopter, but the road follows the river most of the way up.'

'You know,' Maxwell said, 'this is right where my son was shot down. That SEAL went in and recovered him right about here,' the admiral said, tapping the map.

'Somebody who knows the area from ground level?' Greer asked. 'That's a help. Where is he?'

SAM BROUGHT THE SCOUT up to the hospital entrance himself. The bodywork was all fixed and there was a new window on the driver's side. Kelly got out of his wheelchair and gave the Scout a long look. The doorframe and adjacent pillar had broken up the stream of incoming shot and saved his life. Bad aim on someone's part, really, after a careful and effective stalk—helped by the fact that he hadn't troubled himself to check his mirrors. But that was history. And history could not be changed.

'Back to your island, John?' Rosen asked.

Kelly nodded. 'Yeah. I have to get myself back into shape.'

He thanked Sandy O'Toole for her care and was rewarded with a smile. She'd almost become a friend in the preceding eighteen days. Almost? Perhaps she already was, if only he would allow himself to think in such terms. Kelly got into his car and fixed the seat belt in place. He smiled at them and drove off.

Next to him, on the passenger seat, was a manila envelope marked 'Patient Records/Bills' in Sam Rosen's coarse handwriting.

Springer was in her accustomed place, twenty minutes later. Kelly assembled his things and went aboard. Ten minutes after that, the diesels were chugging away and he was ready to cast off. Kelly's left shoulder was distressingly stiff despite his having been able to use it, after a fashion, for almost a week, and his line handling was awkward. Finally the lines were slipped, and *Springer* headed out.

Only after clearing the shipping channel an hour later did Kelly look away from the water. He leaned back in the captain's chair and opened the envelope Sam had left him, while the autopilot drove the boat south.

Only the photos had been left out. He'd seen one of them, and that one had been enough. A handwritten cover note—every page in the envelope was a photocopy—showed that a professor of pathology had got the copies from his friend, the state medical examiner, and could Sam be careful how he handled this.

The 'wrongful death' and 'homicide' blocks on the cover sheet were both checked. The cause of death, the report said, was manual strangulation. Beyond that, the victim had been raped and subjected to violent and extensive traumatic insult prior to death, all of which was catalogued at length in dry medical prose.

'This was deliberate torture, from some really sick folks,' the handwritten page said. 'One thing the report leaves out. Her hair was combed or brushed out, almost certainly post-mortem. I gather you knew the girl. I'm sorry, my friend.' Kelly slid the package back into the envelope.

'Never again, Johnnie-boy,' he said aloud in a conversational tone. 'We're not going to make any more mistakes. Not ever.'

THE C-141 LANDED at Pope Air Force Base, adjacent to Fort Bragg, North Carolina, soon after lunch, ending a routine flight that had originated over eight thousand miles away.

In most previous wars Americans had lain close to where they fell. Not so for Vietnam. It was as though people understood that no American wanted to remain there, living or dead, and every recovered body came home, and having passed through one processing facility outside Saigon, each body would now be processed again prior to transshipment to whatever home town had sent the mainly young men off to die in a distant place.

Awaiting the bodies in the receiving centre were civilian morticians. But a uniformed officer was always present to verify identification, to make sure that the right body went off to the right family, even though the caskets that left this place were in almost all cases sealed. The physical insult of combat death, plus the ravages of often late recovery in a tropical climate, were not things families wanted or needed to see on the bodies of their loved ones. As a result, positive identification of remains wasn't really something that anyone could check, and for that very reason it was something the military took as seriously as it could.

It was a large room, where many bodies could be processed at once. One body, that of Specialist Fourth Class Duane Kendall, bore numerous wounds to the torso. Of more interest to the mortician was a white tag located between the right arm and the chest, which confirmed an apparently random mark on the card on the outside of the container in which the body had arrived.

'Good ID,' the mortician said to the captain who was making his rounds with a clipboard. The officer checked the required data against his records and moved on, leaving the mortician to his work.

There was the usual number of tasks to be performed, and the mortician went about them, lifting his head to make sure the captain was at the other end of the room. Then he pulled a thread from the stitches made by another mortician at the other end of the pipeline. The stitches came undone almost instantly, allowing him to reach into the body cavity and remove four plastic envelopes of white powder. It was his third and last such recovery of the day. After spending half an hour on one more body, it was the end of his working day. The mortician walked to his car and drove off duty. He stopped at a supermarket to pick up a loaf of bread, and on the way out dropped some coins into a public phone.

'YEAH?' HENRY TUCKER SAID, picking it up on the first ring.

'Eight.' The phone clicked off.

'Good,' Tucker said, really to himself, putting the receiver down. Eight kilos from this one. Seven from his other man. The arithmetic was simple enough. Each kilo was one thousand grams. Each kilo would be diluted with nontoxic agents like lactose. Then after careful mixing to ensure uniformity throughout the entire batch, others would divide the bulk powder into smaller hits of the drugs that could be sold in smaller batches.

Tucker had started his operation small. But his supply of pure refined heroin was far more extensive than his partners knew. They were, for now, happy that its quality was so high, and he would gradually reveal to them the magnitude of his supply, while never giving them a hint of his method of shipment, for which he regularly congratulated himself.

The sheer elegance of his operation was striking. The distant end required only six people: two who procured the drugs from local sources and four on-site morticians. All six were very well paid and had been selected for their businesslike stability. The United States Air Force handled transportation. The two at the receiving station were also careful men. From there it was merely a matter of transport by automobile to a convenient place, and that was handled by a trusted and well-paid man who never exceeded a speed limit. Doing things on the bay, Tucker thought, sipping his beer and watching a baseball game, was his masterstroke. In addition to all the other advantages that the location gave him, he'd given his new partners reason to believe that the drugs were dropped off ships heading up the Chesapeake Bay to the port of Baltimore. Angelo Vorano had proved that, by buying his dumb little sailboat and offering to make a pick-up. Convincing Eddie and Tony that he'd betrayed them to the police had been so easy.

With a little luck Tucker could take over the entire east-coast heroin market for as long as Americans continued to die in Vietnam. In the meantime he needed to think about finding a way to expand his distribution network. But one thing at a time.

8 *FABRICATION*

Five miles can be a long walk. It is always a long swim, particularly alone and for the first time in weeks. That fact became clear to Kelly before the halfway point, but even though the water east of his island was shallow enough that he could stand in many places, he didn't stop. He gutted it out until he touched the mud that marked the eastern side of Battery Island. Instantly his muscles began to tighten up, and Kelly had to force himself to stand and walk. It was then that he saw the helicopter. He'd heard one during his swim but made no note of it. He had long experience with helicopters, but having one land on his sandbar was not all that common, and he walked over towards it until a voice called him back towards the bunkers.

'Over here, Chief!'

Kelly turned. The voice was familiar, and on rubbing his eyes, he saw the undress whites of a very senior naval officer.

'Admiral Maxwell!' Kelly was glad for the company, especially this man, but his lower legs were covered in mud from the walk out of the water. 'I wish you'd called ahead, sir.'

'I tried, Kelly.' Maxwell took his hand. 'We've been calling here for a couple of days. Where were you? Out on a job?' The admiral was surprised at the instant change in the boy's face.

'Not exactly.'

'Why don't you go get washed? I'll look for a soda.' It was then that Maxwell saw the recent scars on Kelly's back and neck.

Their first meeting had been aboard USS *Kitty Hawk*, three years earlier—he as AirPac, Kelly as a very sick bosun's mate first class. Kelly had gone in to rescue the flight crew of Nova One One, whose pilot had been Winslow Holland Maxwell III, USN. Two days of crawling about in an area that was just too hot for a rescue helicopter to go trolling, and he'd come out with Dutch 3rd, injured but alive. And how, Maxwell still asked himself, how did you thank a man for saving your only son? Maxwell had done what he could for Kelly, making him chief bosun's mate.

Dutch Maxwell had stayed on *Kitty Hawk* for three more days, ostensibly to conduct a personal inspection of flight operations, but really to keep an eye on his wounded son and his rescuer, who'd caught a vicious infection from the putrid water. He'd been with Kelly for the telegram announcing the death of his father. And now, he realised, he'd arrived just after something else.

Kelly returned from his shower in a T-shirt and shorts, dragging a little physically but with something tough and strong in his eyes.

Maxwell handed over a Coca-Cola for his host. 'What happened to you?' he asked. 'That mess on your shoulder is new.'

Kelly told his story briefly, and for the second time Dutch Maxwell sat and listened like the surrogate father he had become.

'That's a hard hit, John,' the admiral observed quietly.

'Yes, sir.' Kelly looked down for a moment. 'So what brings you out here, sir?'

'I want to go over something with you.' Maxwell opened his portfolio and unfolded a map on Kelly's coffee table.

The younger man grunted. 'Oh, yeah, I remember this place.'

'Chief, what we're going to talk about is very sensitive.'

'Why me, sir?'

'You're the only person in the country who's seen this area from ground level. How far did you go up the river, John?'

'About to here.' Kelly's hand wandered across the map.

'The objective is here.' Maxwell tapped a spot marked in red.

'That's a long way to swim, sir. What is it?'

'Chief, when you retired, you ticked the box for being in the fleet reserve,' Maxwell said benignly.

'Hold on, sir!'

'Relax, son, I'm not recalling you.' *Yet*, Maxwell thought. 'You had a top-secret clearance, John. This stuff is higher than TS.' And Maxwell explained why, pulling additional items from his portfolio.

Kelly looked up from a reconnaissance photo. 'You want to go in and get them out, like Song Tay?'

'What do you know about that?'

'Just what was in the open,' Kelly explained. 'It sounded like a pretty slick job.'

'Yeah, *but* there was nobody home. This guy'—Maxwell tapped a photo—'is positively ID'd as an air-force colonel. Kelly, you can never repeat this.'

'I understand that, sir. How do you plan to do it?'

'We're not sure yet. We want your information to help look at alternatives. Tell me about the river valley.'

Fifty hours, Kelly remembered—picked up from Da Nang by helo, deposited aboard the submarine USS *Skate*, which then had moved Kelly right into the surprisingly deep estuary of that damned stinking river. Fighting his way up against the current behind an electrically powered sea scooter, staying underwater until his air tanks gave out, and he remembered how frightening it was not to be able to hide under the rippled surface. And now this flag officer was asking him how to risk the lives of other men in the same place, trusting him, much as Pam had, to know what to do. That sudden thought chilled the retired chief bosun's mate. Fifty hours, Kelly remembered—no rest, no sleep, just fear and the mission.

'You say these guys will never come back unless we get them?'

'No other reason for them to set this place up in the way they did,' Maxwell replied. He collected the photographs and the maps. He handed Kelly a fresh set of the latter.

'Will this be a SEAL job?'

'We're not sure yet. Kelly, I can give you two weeks while we work on other aspects of the mission.'

'How do I get in touch, sir?'

Maxwell dropped a Pentagon pass on the table. 'No phones, no mail, it's all face-to-face contact.'

Kelly stood and walked him out to the helicopter. He grabbed the admiral's arm as the rotor started turning.

'Was the Song Tay job betrayed?'

That stopped Maxwell in his tracks. 'Why do you ask?'

Kelly nodded. 'You just answered my question, Admiral.'

Maxwell ducked his head under the rotor and got into the back. The helicopter lifted off, turned, and headed northeast.

KELLY WATCHED THE HELO disappear into the forenoon haze. Then he went into his machine shop. The admiral had given him two weeks. That was about the time he'd given to himself for his physical preparation. Now it was time for another sort.

Kelly took down the .45 automatic from its place on the wall, unloaded and disassembled it before giving the slide and barrel a very careful look inside and out. He then reassembled the pistol, attaching a silencer he had made. Then he grabbed a cold Coke and headed outside with a box of .22 Long Rifle ammunition.

Kelly had never been intimidated by the large, heavy Colt automatic, but the cost of .45 ACP was far higher than that of .22 rimfire cartridges, and so the previous year he'd purchased a conversion kit allowing the lighter rounds to be fired through the pistol. He finished the Coke and tossed the can about fifteen feet before loading three rounds in the magazine. He didn't bother with ear protection. He stood as he always did, relaxed, hands at his sides, then brought the gun up fast, dropping into a crouching two-hand stance. Kelly stopped cold, realising that the silencer he had screwed onto the barrel blanked out his sights. That would be a problem. The gun went back down, then came up again, and Kelly squeezed off the first round without actually seeing the target. With the predictable results—when he looked, the can was untouched. That was the bad news. The good news was that the sound suppressor had functioned well. The noise of the firing was muted to a whisper.

All of which was fine, Kelly thought, but missing a soda can at fifteen feet did not speak well of his marksmanship. He relaxed and tried again, bringing the gun up from his side in a smooth and quick arc. This time he started pulling the trigger just as the silencer began to hide the target. It worked, after a fashion. The can went down with a .22-inch hole an inch from the bottom. Kelly's timing wasn't quite right. His next shot was roughly in the centre of the can, however, evoking a smile.

'Still have the old touch, Johnnie-boy,' Kelly said to himself.

'LOOK, COLONEL, I was just an aide, OK? How many times do I have to tell you that? I did the same thing your generals' aides do.'

It was sad, Colonel Nikolay Yevgeniyevich Grishanov thought, that a man had to go through this, but Colonel Zacharias wasn't a man. He was an enemy, the Russian reminded himself with some reluctance, and he wanted to get the man talking again.

It was their sixth session. Grishanov was the only Soviet officer allowed to interview these Americans, the Vietnamese were playing their cards so carefully. Twenty of them—all the same, all different. Zacharias was as much an intelligence officer as fighter pilot, his dossier said. He'd spent his twenty-odd-year career studying air-defence systems. A master's degree from the University of California, Berkeley, in electrical engineering. The dossier even included a recently acquired copy of his master's thesis. It was a very clever examination of what happened to low-frequency search-radar energy—and how, incidentally, an aircraft could use mountains and hills to mask itself from it. Three years after that, following a tour of duty in a fighter squadron, he'd been assigned to Offutt Air Force Base, just outside Omaha, Nebraska. Part of the Strategic Air Command's war-plans staff, he'd worked on flight profiles that might allow American B-52 bombers to penetrate Soviet air defences.

Grishanov could not bring himself to hate this man. A fighter pilot himself, the Russian colonel was in a curious way Zacharias's counterpart. His job, in the event of war, was to stop those bombers from ravaging his country, and in peace, to plan methods of making their penetration of Soviet airspace as difficult as possible.

Grishanov laid the most recently arrived document on the table. 'I read your thesis last night, Colonel. It's excellent work.'

The Russian's eyes never left Colonel Zacharias. The American's face proclaimed what he was thinking: How could they know so much about me?

'How is it that this was never classified?' Grishanov asked.

'It's just theoretical physics,' Zacharias said, shrugging his thin shoulders, recovering enough that he tried to conceal his despair.

Grishanov tapped the thesis with his finger. 'Brilliant! Tell me, what sort of place is Berkeley?'

'Just a school, California style,' Zacharias replied before catching himself. He was talking. He wasn't supposed to talk. He was trained to evade and disguise.

'You come from Utah. What sort of place is it?'

'Zacharias, Robin G., Colonel—'

Grishanov raised his hands. 'Please, Colonel. I know all that. I also know your place of birth, in addition to the date. But I know nothing of Utah. There is a large lake there. It's called Salt Lake, yes?' He didn't give the American time to reply. 'There are mountains there, too, yes?'

'Wasatch Mountains,' Zacharias confirmed somewhat drunkenly.

One clever thing about the Vietnamese, Grishanov thought, the way they fed their prisoners—food a hog would eat only from necessity. Resistance, physical and mental, required energy, and you could watch these men lose their strength during the hours of interrogation, watch their courage wane as their physical needs drew more and more upon their supply of psychological resolve.

'The skiing, is it good, Colonel?'

Zacharias's eyes blinked. 'Yeah, it is.'

'I like cross-country skiing. I had wooden skis, but in my last regiment my maintenance officer made me steel skis from a wing panel on our new interceptor, project E-266.'

'What's that?' Zacharias knew nothing of the new MiG-25.

'Your people now call it Foxbat. Very fast, designed to catch one of your B-70 bombers.'

'But we stopped that project,' Zacharias objected.

'Yes, I know that. But your project got me a wonderfully fast fighter to fly. When I return home, I will command the first regiment of them.'

'Fighter planes made of steel? Why?'

'It resists aerodynamic heating much better than aluminium,' Grishanov explained. 'So how well do you think we would do with my steel fighters and your aluminium bombers?'

'I guess that depends on—' Zacharias started to say, then stopped himself cold. His eyes looked across the table, first with confusion at what he'd almost said, then with resolve.

Too soon, Grishanov told himself with disappointment. He'd pushed too soon. This one had courage. But Grishanov had time.

9 OUTFITTERS

Nineteen sixty-three VW, low mlge, rad, htr . . .

Kelly dropped a dime in the pay phone and called the number. 'Hello? I'm calling about the ad for the car . . . That's right . . . Right now if you want . . . OK, say about fifteen minutes? . . . Fine, thank you, ma'am. I'll be right there. Bye.' He hung up.

It was a blazing hot Saturday. *Springer* was tied up in a guest slip at one of the marinas on the Potomac. He hailed an empty cab that was driving past the marina's entrance.

'The forty-five-hundred block, Essex Avenue, Bethesda,' he told the driver.

It was an upscale residential neighbourhood, and the house was easy to spot. There it was—a VW Beetle, an awful peanut-butter colour, speckled with a little body rust. It could not have been much better. Kelly knocked on the door of the house.

'Hello?' It was a face to match the voice. She had to be eighty or so.

'Mrs Boyd? I'm Bill Murphy. I called a little while ago about the car.' Kelly smiled benignly.

Gloria Boyd handed him the keys. 'Here. Take a look.'

Kelly unlocked the car door. The seats were well worn, and one had a long slash in it. He turned the key in the ignition and the engine started immediately. There was even a full tank. He asked for and got permission to take it round the block. The car was mechanically sound, he decided, bringing it back to the waiting owner.

'How much do you want for it, ma'am?'

'My grandson says it's worth one thousand five hundred dollars.'

Your grandson must be a lawyer to be that greedy, Kelly thought. 'How about twelve hundred? I can pay cash.'

'Cash? Then you can have the car.'

The paperwork took thirty minutes. Kelly promised to take care of the title transfer for her, and the number plates, too, of course.

'What are you going to use it for?' Mrs Boyd asked.

'Business.' Kelly smiled and left.

AT QUARTER TO NINE that night two cars pulled into a half-full parking lot north of Maryland House, a rest stop on the John F. Kennedy Highway. The first was a Dodge Dart, the one behind it a red Plymouth Roadrunner. The Dart stopped three spaces from a white Oldsmobile with Pennsylvania plates and a brown vinyl top. The Roadrunner parked in the next row. A woman got out and walked towards the restaurant, a path that took her past the Olds.

'Hey, baby,' a man said. The woman stopped and took a few steps towards the vinyl-topped automobile. The man was Caucasian, with black hair and an open-necked white shirt.

'Henry sent me,' she said.

'I know. Get the stuff.'

Doris walked back to her car, as though she'd forgotten something. She returned with a large bag. As she walked past the Olds, the man's hand reached out and took it. Doris proceeded into the building, returning a minute later holding a can of soda, her eyes on the Roadrunner, hoping that she'd done everything right.

'That was easy enough,' Henry Tucker said, fifty yards away at the outdoor eating area.

'Good stuff?' another man asked Tony Piaggi. The three of them sat at the same table.

'The best,' Piaggi assured him.

'And if the carrier gets caught?' the man from Philadelphia asked.

'She won't talk,' Tucker assured him. 'They've all seen what happens to bad girls.'

'The money?' Piaggi asked.

'I need a cup of coffee.' The other man got up and walked inside, leaving his briefcase, which Piaggi took in his hand. He and Tucker walked off to his car, which was a blue Cadillac.

'Not going to count it?' Tucker asked.

'If he stiffs us, he knows what happens. This is business, Henry.'

'BILL MURPHY,' KELLY SAID. 'I understand you have some vacant apartments.' He held up the Sunday paper.

'What are you looking for?'

'A one-bedroom,' Kelly told the man. 'I travel a lot.'

It was an old garden-apartment complex, composed exclusively of three-storey brick structures. Kelly looked round approvingly as the manager took him to a ground-floor furnished unit.

'This is fine, just what I need,' Kelly announced. The furniture was obviously used, but in decent shape.

Twenty minutes later Kelly was in a cab heading downtown. He caught the next train to DC, where another taxi delivered him to his boat. By nightfall *Springer* was headed down the Potomac. Six hours later, just before midnight, Kelly arrived at his home.

Despite a weekend of almost nonstop motion, there was no time to dawdle. Kelly packed clothing, most of it purchased in the suburbs of Washington. Linen and food he would buy in Baltimore. His .45 automatic, plus the .22–.45 conversion kit, was packed in with old clothing, along with two boxes of ammunition. By three thirty in the morning he was back aboard *Springer*, headed north, looking forward to a few hours' sleep once he got past Annapolis.

It was a lonely night, with scattered clouds, and his mind churned over variables. The less-than-satisfactory thought was that he still knew little. Billy with his red Plymouth muscle car. A black guy named Henry. He knew their area of operation. And that was all.

THE PILLS HELPED shut out reality, but not all the way. Doris was too dependent on the barbiturates now. Sleep came hard to her, and in the emptiness of the room she was unable to avoid herself. She would have taken more pills if she could, but all they allowed was a brief oblivion, a short-term liberation from her fear. Twice now she'd watched friends die, sitting there, drugged but unable to sleep and blot it out, the horror so vast that it became numbing, watching their eyes, seeing and feeling the pain, knowing that she could do nothing. Doris had prayed that Pam had gotten away, only to see her dragged in and to watch her die. Doris's only act of resistance, thankfully unnoticed by the men, had been to brush out her friend's hair, crying all the while, hoping somehow that Pam would know there was someone who cared, even in death.

'I'M IMPRESSED, JOHN,' Rosen said, staring at his patient. Kelly sat on the examining table, his shirt off. 'What have you been doing?'

'Five-mile swim for the shoulders. Better than weights, but a little of that, too, in the evening. A little running.'

'How are you otherwise?'

The reply was a neutral expression that told Rosen all he needed to know. One more try. 'There's an old saying: Before setting out on revenge, dig two graves.'

'Only two?' Kelly asked lightly.

Rosen nodded. 'I read the post-mortem report, too. I can't talk you out of it?'

Just then Sandy O'Toole came in. 'You're looking healthy for a guy who got shot a few weeks ago,' she said.

'Clean living, ma'am. Only one beer in thirty-some days.' Kelly put his shirt on. 'Where do you get lunch around here?' he asked.

'I'd show you myself,' said Rosen, 'but I have a conference in about ten minutes. Sandy?'

She checked her watch. 'About time for mine. You want to risk hospital food or something outside?'

'You're the tour guide, ma'am.'

She guided him to the cafeteria, where the food was hospital-bland. Kelly selected something filling to compensate.

'Been keeping busy?' he asked after they selected a table.

'Always,' Sandy assured him.

'Where do you live?'

'Off Loch Raven Boulevard. It's an old bungalow. Half an acre. That reminds me,' she added. 'I have to cut the grass this weekend.' Then she remembered that Tim had liked cutting grass, had decided to leave the army after his second Vietnam tour and get his law degree and live a normal kind of life—all of that taken away from her by people in a distant place.

Kelly didn't know what she was thinking, exactly, but he didn't have to. The change in her expression, the way her voice trailed off, said it all. How to cheer her up?

'You were very kind to me while I was upstairs. Thanks.'

'We try to take care of our patients,' she said with a friendly and unaccustomed expression.

'A face as pretty as yours should do that more,' Kelly told her.

'Do what?'

'Smile.'

'It's hard,' she said, serious again.

'I know. It's Tim, isn't it?' he asked, jolting her.

She stared into Kelly's eyes. 'I just don't understand. I'll never understand why Tim had to die. It still doesn't make sense.'

'Maybe the *thing* doesn't make sense, but the *people* do,' Kelly suggested. 'Maybe we're all trying to save the world, Sandy, one little bit at a time.'

They finished their lunch, then Kelly insisted on walking her back to the unit. There was something he wanted to say.

'You know, I'd like to have dinner with you. Not now, but—'

'I'll think about it,' she allowed, knowing as Kelly did that it was too soon for both of them.

10 AGENDAS

It was his first-ever visit to the Pentagon. Kelly felt ill at ease, wondering if he should have worn his khaki chief's uniform, but his time for wearing that had passed. He wore a blue lightweight suit, with a miniature of the Navy Cross ribbon on the lapel.

'How are you feeling, John?' Dutch Maxwell asked first of all.

'Fine, sir, thank you.' Civilian now or not, Kelly could not help feeling uneasy in the presence of a flag officer. A door opened to admit two more men, one in civilian clothes, the other a rear-admiral. Maxwell did the introductions.

'I've heard a lot about you,' Podulski said, shaking Kelly's hand.

'Thank you, sir.'

The other man was Greer. In addition to wearing soft clothes, this admiral had the map case. He took one out. Then came the photographs, and Kelly got another look at Colonel Zacharias.

'I was within three miles of the place,' Kelly noted.

'It wasn't there then. This place is new,' Greer explained. 'Tell me how you got little Dutch back. Every step of the way.'

Kelly needed fifteen minutes for that. It was an easy story to tell.

'That was some job,' Greer said when he finished. 'So this area is densely populated?'

'Yes and no, sir. Some farms and stuff. I heard and saw traffic on this road. Only a few trucks, but lots of bicycles, oxcarts, that sort of thing. How are you planning to get in?'

'There's nothing easy, John. We've looked at a helicopter insertion, maybe even an amphibious assault and racing up this road.'

Kelly shook his head. 'It ain't much of a road, sir. I've been there. Drop a few trees and it's closed. Has to be choppers.'

He could see the news was not welcome, and it wasn't hard to understand why. This part of the country was dotted with antiaircraft batteries. Getting a strike force in wasn't going to be easy.

'Dutch, we have a meeting in five minutes,' Podulski said reluctantly. This meeting had not been a successful one, he thought. Greer and Maxwell weren't so sure of that. They had learned a few things. That counted for something.

'Can I ask why you're keeping this so tight?' Kelly asked.

'You guessed it before,' said Maxwell. 'The Song Tay job was compromised. We don't know how, but we found out later that they expected Operation Kingpin.'

'Dear God,' Kelly breathed. 'Somebody over here deliberately betrayed them?'

'Welcome to the real world of intelligence operations,' Greer said with a grim smile. 'Mr Kelly, where's your car parked?'

'In the city, sir. I took the bus over here.'

'Come with me. There's a shuttle bus you can take back later.'

They walked out of the building in silence. Greer's car was parked in a visitors' lot by the river entrance. He waved for Kelly to get in and headed towards the George Washington Parkway.

'Dutch pulled your dossier. I got to read it. I'm impressed, son. Every commander you had sang your praises.'

'I worked for some good ones, sir.'

The highway sign didn't say anything about CIA. Kelly didn't tumble to it until he saw the oversized guardhouse.

Greer found his parking place and popped his door open. 'Come with me, Chief.' The out-of-uniform admiral led Kelly in the front door and got him a special visitor's pass.

For his part, Kelly felt like a tourist in a strange land. Though an ordinary and rather new government office building, CIA headquarters had a sinister aura. It wasn't like the real world, somehow. Greer caught the look and chuckled, leading Kelly to an elevator, then to his sixth-floor office. Only when they were behind the closed wooden door did he speak.

'How's your schedule?'

'Flexible. I don't have anything tying me down,' Kelly answered cautiously.

James Greer nodded soberly. 'Dutch told me about that, too. I'm very sorry, Chief, but my job right now concerns twenty good men who probably won't see their families again unless we do something.'

'Sir, I'm real confused right now.'

'Well, we can do it hard or easy. The hard way is that Dutch makes a phone call and you get recalled to active duty,' Greer said sternly.

'The easy way is, you come to work for me as a civilian consultant.'

'Doing what?'

'You fly down to Eglin Air Force Base, where the Kingpin people trained, via New Orleans and Avis, I suppose. I want you to go over their operations plan as a model for what we want to do. From the outside you're just a junior consultant gathering information for a low-level report.'

'Are you really serious about this?'

'Colonel Zacharias is officially dead,' Greer said sternly. 'The other side even published a photo of a body. Our side will not screw up the peace talks over something like this. If the lives of twenty more men are necessary to end the war, then that's what it takes.'

It was almost too much for Kelly to believe. How many people did America write off every year? And not all were in uniform, were they? Some were right at home, in American cities.

'It's really that bad?'

The fatigue on Greer's face was unmistakable. 'You know why I took this job? I was ready to retire. I've served my time, commanded my ships. Chief, too many people come to places like this, and reality to them is a memo. They focus in on process and forget that there's a human being at the far end of the paper chain. That's why I re-upped. Somebody has to try and put reality back into the process. We're handling this as a black project. That means it doesn't exist. It's crazy. It shouldn't be that way, but it is. Are you on the team or not?'

New Orleans . . . Kelly's eyes narrowed for a moment. 'If you think I can help, sir, then I will.'

Greer managed a smile and tossed a folder into Kelly's lap. 'Your ID is in the name of John Clark. I want to see you next Friday. My card and private line are in there.'

'Aye, aye, sir.'

IT WAS AN UNEVENTFUL flight, and when Kelly arrived in New Orleans the Avis counter had a car waiting, along with a map.

Kelly tossed his suitcase into the boot and headed east. It was rather like driving his boat, though somewhat more hectic—dead time, in which he could let his mind work, examining possibilities and procedures, his eyes sweeping the traffic while his mind saw something else entirely.

FOUR HOURS AFTER LANDING, he stopped his car at the main gate of Eglin Air Force Base. A fitting place for the Kingpin troopers to have trained, the heat and humidity were an exact match with North

Vietnam. Kelly waited outside the guard post for a blue air-force car to meet him. When it did, a young officer got out.

'Mr Clark?'

'Yes.' He handed over his ID folder. The officer saluted him. Clearly someone was impressed with CIA.

'If you'll follow me, please, sir.' The officer, Captain Griffin, led him to a ground-floor room at the Bachelor Officers' Quarters, which was like a medium-quality motel. After helping Kelly get unpacked, Griffin walked him to the Officers' Club where, he said, Kelly had visitor's privileges.

'I can't knock the hospitality, Captain.' Kelly felt obligated to buy the first beer. 'You know why I'm here?'

'I work intelligence.'

'Kingpin?'

As though in a movie, the officer looked around before replying. 'Yes, sir. We have all the documents ready for you. I hear you worked special ops over there, too.'

'Correct,' said Kelly, between sips. 'When do I start?'

'Supposed to be tomorrow morning, Mr Clark, but the documents are all in my office.'

'I need a quiet room, a pot of coffee, maybe some sandwiches.'

'I think we can handle that, sir.'

'Then let me get started.'

Ten minutes later, Kelly got his wish. Captain Griffin had supplied him with a yellow legal pad and a battery of pencils. Kelly started off with the reconnaissance photographs. The configuration of Song Tay was not terribly different from the camp that he was interested in now, he saw, making notes. One document was a memo indicating that the Song Tay mission would open all sorts of special-ops possibilities. It concluded with a note that political factors made this aspect extremely sensitive. Some would see it as a widening of the war.

Kelly spent three hours going through reams of paper between Eglin and CIA, concerns of deskbound bean-counters distracting the men in green suits, 'helpful' suggestions all of which required answers . . . and so Kingpin had grown from a relatively minor insertion mission to a Cecil B. DeMille epic which had become known to the President's National Security Council staff.

And that's where Kelly stopped, at two thirty in the morning, defeated by the next pile of paper. He left notice for a seven o'clock alarm call and bounced from the bed when the phone rang.

The days continued. The paperwork was surprisingly stimulating.

He had never tried to figure things out in quite this way, and was surprised to find he had a talent for it. The planning had all taken so long, the soldiers practising while the higher-ups had dithered, pondering the intelligence information so long that the prisoners had been moved. If the operation had been betrayed, the leaker was probably one of the last people to discover what was afoot.

The operation itself had been meticulously planned, everything done just right. Crashing a huge Sikorsky helicopter right in the camp for the strike team to get at the objective. Using miniguns to take down the guard towers. No finesse, no pussyfooting, just brutally direct force. But the soldiers had assaulted and liberated an empty camp. It wasn't hard to imagine how quiet the choppers must have been for the ride back to Thailand, the bleak emptiness of failure after having done everything better than right.

There was, nonetheless, much to learn here. Whatever else it had been, Kingpin was a supremely valuable lesson. So much had gone right, he saw, and all that could be shamelessly copied. All that had gone wrong, really, was the time factor. The quest for perfection hadn't been demanded at the operational level, but higher, from men who had grown older and lost contact with the enthusiasm and intelligence of youth. If the real hazard to the operation was oversight, then why not eliminate the oversight?

'CAPTAIN, YOU'VE BEEN very helpful,' Kelly said.

'Find what you wanted, Mr Clark?' Griffin asked.

'Yes, Mr Griffin,' he said, dropping back into naval terminology for the young officer. 'The analysis you did was first-rate.' Kelly handed over his notes. Under his eyes they were sealed in an envelope with red wax. 'Courier the package to this address.'

'Yes, sir. Did you get any sleep at all?' Captain Griffin asked.

'Well, I think I'll depressurise in New Orleans before I fly back.'

'Not a bad place for it, sir.' Griffin walked Kelly to his car.

One other bit of intelligence had been stunningly easy, Kelly thought, driving out. His room had contained a New Orleans telephone directory in which had been the name he'd decided to look up while sitting in James Greer's office in CIA.

PIERRE LAMARCK'S PROFESSION demanded a certain flash, a personal flair. He accentuated his uniqueness with a white linen suit complete with waistcoat, white shirt and a red, solid-colour tie, which fitted his own image as a respectable if ostentatious New Orleans businessman. That went along well with his personal automobile, an eggshell-white Cadillac. He eschewed the ornamental excesses that some other pimps placed on their automobiles.

Lamarck opened the door of the Cadillac for his newest acquisition, fifteen years old and possessed of an innocent look that made her a noteworthy and enticing member of his eight-girl stable. The luxury car started on the first turn of the key, and at seven thirty Lamarck set off on another night's work, for the nightlife in this city started early and lasted late.

It had to be him, Kelly thought, half a block away, behind the wheel of his rented car. Who else would wear a three-piece suit and be accompanied by a young girl in a tight mini? Certainly not an insurance agent. Kelly slipped the car into gear, following. The Cadillac moved on a few more blocks, finding a parking place by a seedy, flashy bar. Kelly found himself a place to park three blocks away. There was a dual purpose in parking so far from his objective. The walk in along Decatur Street gave him both a feel for the territory and a look at likely places for his action.

He walked into Chats Sauvages at eight seventeen. A small but enthusiastic rock band played at the far end. There was a dance floor, where young people moved with the music; and there was Pierre Lamarck, sitting at a table in the corner with a few acquaintances. The nearest path to the white Caddy led past the bar, and that told Kelly where his perch had to be. He ordered a beer and turned conveniently to watch the band.

At nine ten, two young women came to Lamarck. One sat on his lap while the other nibbled at his ear. The other two men at the table watched with neutral interest while both women handed cash over to him, and the pimp ostentatiously wrapped the bills round a roll removed from his pocket. Flash money, Kelly had troubled himself to learn—an important part of a pimp's public image. The first two women left, and Lamarck was soon joined by another, in what became an intermittent stream that didn't stop.

Just after midnight Kelly made a trip to the men's room. In the toilet stall he took the automatic he'd hidden inside his slacks and moved it to the waistband.

His timing was good. Washing his hands for the fifth time, Kelly saw the door open in the mirror. Only the back of the man's head, but under the dark hair was a white suit. The man turned, and their eyes met in the mirror.

Kelly stepped away from the basin, still drying his hands with a paper towel. 'I like the ladies,' he said quietly. 'The ones that come up to you. They, uh, work for you?'

'You might say that, my man.' Pierre Lamarck took out a black plastic comb to readjust his coiffure. 'Why do you ask?'

'I might need a few,' Kelly said with embarrassment. 'Some friends in town with me. One's having a birthday, and—'

'A party,' the pimp observed pleasantly. 'How many ladies do you require, sir?'

'Three, maybe four. Talk about it outside? I could use some air.'

The street was quiet. Busy city though New Orleans might be, it was still the middle of the week.

'It's nothing to be embarrassed about,' Lamarck said. 'We all like to have fun, especially when we're away from home, right?'

'I'll pay top dollar,' Kelly promised with an uneasy smile.

Lamarck grinned. 'Anything else you might need?'

Kelly coughed and took a few steps, willing Lamarck to follow, which he did. 'Maybe some . . . well, something to help us party?'

'I can handle that, too,' Lamarck said as they approached an alley.

'I think I met you before, couple years back. I remember the girl, really. Her name was . . . Pam? Yeah, Pam. Thin, tawny hair.'

'Oh, yeah, she was fun. She's not with me any more,' Lamarck said lightly. 'But I have lots more, young and fresh.'

'I'm sure you do,' Kelly said, reaching behind his back. 'They're all on . . . I mean they all use things that make it . . .'

'Happy stuff, man. So they're always in the mood to party.' Lamarck stopped at the entrance to the alley, looking outwards. Behind him, he had not troubled to see, was a dark corridor of blank brick walls, open at the far end. 'Let's see. Four girls, shall we say, and something to help get the party started—'

'Both hands in the open,' Kelly said, the Colt automatic levelled twelve inches from the man's chest.

Lamarck's first response was a disbelieving bluster: 'My man, that is a very foolish—'

Kelly's voice was all business. 'Turn, walk down the alley.'

'You must need money real bad to try something this dumb,' the pimp said, trying an implied threat.

'Your roll worth dying for?' Kelly asked reasonably. Lamarck measured the odds and turned, moving into the shadows.

'Stop,' Kelly told him after fifty yards. He grabbed the man's neck and pushed him against the wall. 'Hand me your gun—real careful.'

'OK, OK,' Lamarck said. 'Let's be real cool. It's only money.'

'That's smart,' Kelly said approvingly. A small automatic appeared. Kelly put his index finger into the trigger guard. There was no sense in taking chances at this point and putting fingerprints on the weapon. The pistol fitted nicely into his coat pocket.

'Let's see the roll next.'

'Right here, man.' Lamarck was starting to lose it.

'Thank you, Mr Lamarck,' Kelly said, to calm the man.

Just then he wavered. 'Wait a minute—you said you knew Pam.'

'I did,' Kelly said. 'And you're one of the guys who ruined her life.'

Outrage: 'Hey, man, she came to *me*!'

'And you got her on pills so she could party real good.'

'That was *business*.'

'She's dead,' Kelly told him, reaching in his pocket. 'Somebody killed her.'

'So? I didn't do it!'

'I know that,' Kelly said, screwing the silencer onto the pistol.

'Then what are you doing this for?' the man said.

Kelly thought about that for a second or two. He could have said many things, but it was only fair, he decided, to tell the man the truth as the gun came up quickly and finally.

'Practice.'

11 *LESSONS APPLIED*

The early flight back from New Orleans to Washington National was too short for a movie, and Kelly had already eaten breakfast. He settled on a glass of juice at his window seat and, as after every combat action of his life, he went over every detail.

Lamarck's wounds had been immediately and definitively fatal. Two screws that Kelly had drilled in the top of his pistol held a small cloth bag which had caught the two ejected cartridge cases, leaving the police who'd investigate the scene without that valuable bit of evidence. His stalk had been effectively carried out and his hastily selected site for the elimination had also worked well enough.

The ending of a human life was vaguely sad, but Lamarck had long since forfeited his right to life. In any just universe, a person who exploited helpless girls simply did not deserve the privilege of breathing the same air used by other human beings.

And what did Kelly feel about it? He pondered that question for a while. A quiet voice—perhaps conscience—told him that he ought to feel *something*, and he searched for a genuine emotion but could find none. There was no loss, no grief, no remorse.

In ending the life of Pierre Lamarck, he had removed something harmful from the surface of the planet. It had not avenged Pam's life.

It had not changed very much. It had been like stepping on an offensive insect—you did it and moved on. Now Kelly's mind could focus on the mission before him. Having killed many men better than Pierre Lamarck, he could now think with confidence about killing men worse than the New Orleans pimp.

PODULSKI AND MAXWELL sat in Greer's office at the CIA.

'Dutch, you were right about this kid,' Greer said. 'I spent a whole night last week going through his dossier. This guy's a self-starter. I've gone over our in-house assessment of Kingpin. Kelly's assessment tracks on every major point.'

'Who did the CIA assessment?' Maxwell asked.

'Robert Ritter,' Greer said. 'Good man, a little terse, knows how to work the field, though. If Boxwood Green goes, we need an operations guy from this house. Are we agreed on that?' Greer looked round the table, seeing the reluctant nods.

Podulski said what they all thought. 'Can we trust him?'

'He's not the one who betrayed Kingpin. Cas, I'm new here. Ritter knows the bureaucracy here better than I do. He's an operator; I'm just an analyst type. And his heart's in the right place.'

Podulski looked up the table. 'Sounds like our kind of guy.'

'What about Kelly?' Maxwell asked.

'His CIA identity is Clark now,' Greer told them. 'If we want him in, we can utilise him better as a civilian.'

'Make it so,' Maxwell said. It was convenient, he thought, to have a naval officer seconded to CIA, wearing civilian clothes but still subject to military discipline.

'Aye, aye, sir. If we get to training, where will it be done?'

'Quantico Marine Base,' Maxwell replied. 'General Young is a pal from the old days. He understands.'

'You know, if we bring this off,' Podulski said, 'we have to get Kelly his medal.'

AIRPORTS WERE USEFUL places, with their bustling anonymity and telephones. Kelly placed his call as he waited for his baggage.

'Greer,' the voice said.

'Clark,' Kelly replied. 'Do you still want me this afternoon?'

'No. I'm tied up.' Greer flipped through his daybook. 'Make it Tuesday . . . three thirty. See you Tuesday.' The line clicked off.

Kelly hung up, surprised to have been bumped. Twenty minutes later he had his bags and was walking off to his car. About an hour after that he was in his Baltimore apartment. It was lunchtime and he fixed a couple of sandwiches, chasing both down with Coca-Cola. He hadn't shaved today and his heavy beard made a shadow on his face, he saw in the mirror. He'd leave it. Kelly headed into the bedroom for a nap.

'SO WHAT'S NEW?' Peter Henderson asked. They were dining just off the Hill, two acquaintances from New England, one a Harvard graduate, the other from Brown, one a junior aide to a senator, the other a junior member of the White House staff.

'It never changes, Peter,' Wally Hicks said resignedly. 'The peace talks are going nowhere. We keep killing their people. They keep killing ours.'

Both had been seniors at Andover Academy in 1962, close friends and room-mates. After graduation, though each went his separate way, their friendship and their mission in life continued and grew. Both majored in political science. Both got master's degrees and, most important of all, both were noticed by people who mattered. Their parents helped there, and in finding a form of government service that did not expose them to uniformed servitude.

In screening information for their bosses and deciding what appeared on the master's desk, both young men had a real effect on the decision process; they also had access to data that was wide, diverse and sensitive. As a result, in many ways both knew more than their bosses did. And that, Hicks and Henderson thought, was fitting, because they often *understood* the important things better than their bosses did. War was a *bad thing* and had to be avoided entirely or else ended as rapidly as possible.

There was only one difference between the two, really. As a White House staffer, Wally Hicks worked inside the system. But he shared everything with Peter Henderson, which was OK because both had special-access security clearances.

Hicks didn't know that Henderson had taken one step beyond him. If he couldn't change government policy from the inside, Henderson had decided to get help from the outside—some outside agency that could assist him in blocking government actions that endangered the world. The first contact had come at Harvard, a friend in the peace movement. Now he communicated with someone else.

KELLY ROSE after 5pm, feeling rested and alert. He selected his clothing. Dark, baggy and shabby. Old white gym socks and sneakers were more serviceable than their appearance suggested. A wig completed the picture. It was made of coarse black Asian hair, not *too* long, and he brushed it out in a deliberately sloppy way. He'd have to find a way to make it smell, too, Kelly thought.

Nature provided some additional cover. Evening storms were rolling in, bringing wind and rain. He purchased a bottle of cheap yellow wine and a paper bag to semi-conceal it. He poured about half of it into a gutter. Then it was time to go.

It all looked different now, Kelly thought. It was no longer an area he could pass through, seeing the dangers or not. Now it was a place of sought danger. He drove the Volkswagen past the spot where he'd led Billy and his Roadrunner. He shook his head. That was in the past, and it was the future that occupied his thoughts.

In Vietnam there always seemed to be the tree line, a spot where you passed from the openness of a field into the jungle—an imaginary boundary where safety ended and danger began. In looking around this area, he saw the same thing. Only this time he was driving through the barrier. He accelerated and, just like that, Kelly was in the jungle and again at war.

He found a parking place, got out and headed into an alley dotted with trash and several discarded appliances. He took a mouthful of the cheap wine and sloshed it around before letting it dribble out onto his face, neck and clothing. Bending down, he got a handful of dirt, which he rubbed onto his hands and forearms and face, and by the time Kelly had passed through the city-block-length of the alley, he was just one more street bum. He adjusted his gait, becoming deliberately sloppy in his movements while his eyes searched for a good perch. He settled for a vacant corner house with upstairs bay windows.

Kelly entered from the back, made his way upstairs and found the corner bedroom with the bay windows. He crouched there, took out a small pair of binoculars and began his reconnaissance.

His first task was to learn the environment. The rain showers passed, leaving the air still warm. It was Friday night, the start of the weekend, and people were making their purchases. Kelly identified one probable dealer a block and a half away. Twenty minutes' observation gave him a good physical picture of both the dealer and his lieutenant. Both were in their early twenties, and they had a thriving trade. The two were of roughly the same height and build and he assigned them the names Archie and Jughead.

During his reconnaissance Kelly identified and classified two other operations within his field of view. He thought of the dealers as Charlie Brown and Dagwood. Archie and Jughead seemed to be doing the most business. They were the last to call it quits for the night. Kelly checked his watch: three twenty. He was stiff when he rose. He descended the stairs as quietly as he could and walked away from the house. Ten minutes later his car was in sight. He got in quickly, started the engine, and pulled away, leaving the not-so-imaginary jungle and heading north towards his apartment.

THE FACE IN THE BATHROOM mirror was becoming foreign, and that was good. His grime and odour were part of his disguise. His looks and smell had to make people look away from him, to avoid coming too close. He couldn't be a person now. He had to be a street creature, shunned. Invisible.

Kelly fortified himself with a good meal. Then came the push-ups. At long last his left shoulder was fully recovered, and the aches in his muscles were perfectly bilateral. Finally came the hand-to-hand exercises, which he practised for general quickness in addition to the obvious utilitarian applications.

He'd left his apartment in daylight the day before, taking the risk of being seen in his disreputable state, in order to visit a Goodwill store, where he'd found a bush jacket to go over his other clothing. It was so oversized and threadbare that they hadn't charged for it. Kelly realised that disguising his size and physical conditioning was difficult, but that loose, shabby clothing did the trick.

He'd spent the previous night continuing his reconnaissance. No one had given him as much as a second look as he'd moved along the streets—just one more dirty, smelly drunk, not even worth mugging. He'd also acquired a Ka-Bar marine combat knife in a surplus store. The knife, along with his pistol, went into his waistband in the small of his back, well hidden by the loose bulk of a dark shirt and the bush jacket. Into one of the jacket pockets went a whisky flask filled with tap water. In his trouser pocket was a pair of rubber gloves. He already had a pair of cotton work gloves in the car, which he wore when driving. After buying the car, he'd cleaned it inside and out, wiping every glass, metal and plastic surface, hoping that he'd removed every trace of fingerprints.

Kelly switched on the TV and watched the news to get a weather forecast—cloudy, chance of showers, low around seventy-five. He made and drank two cups of instant coffee for the caffeine, waiting for night to fall, which it presently did.

Leaving his apartment, he walked directly to the Volkswagen, which he unlocked and entered. At once he put on the work gloves, and only then did he close the door and drive south into the city.

Part of him was surprised at how tense it was, driving in. He'd scouted the parking place the night before, two blocks from the objective. As before, he left the car quickly, ducking into an alley for the cover of darkness and the assumption of his physical disguise. Within twenty yards he was just one more shambling drunk. He went up the same rickety stairs, finding his accustomed place in the southeast corner, sat down and looked out.

Archie and Jughead were also in their accustomed place, a block away. It was ten twelve at night. Now it was just a matter of waiting.

Traffic slowed perceptibly just after two.

OK.

Kelly made his way down the stairs and out of the back door. He crossed the street, still walking in a shambling but now exceedingly quiet gait. Then he reached into his waistband for his silenced pistol and moved in.

Archie was leaning back against a wall, smoking a cigarette. Jughead was also smoking, sitting on someone's car bumper, and every ten seconds the flaring of their cigarettes degraded their vision.

'Don't move,' Kelly whispered. Archie's head turned, more in annoyance than alarm, until he saw the pistol with the large cylinder screwed onto the end. Jughead froze without being bidden.

'Business good tonight?' Kelly asked.

'Fair 'nuf,' Archie responded quietly. 'What you want?'

'You a cop?' Jughead asked.

'No. I'm not here to arrest anybody. Actually, I need your help.'

'What with?' Archie asked.

'Looking for a guy, name of Billy, drives a red Roadrunner.'

'What?' Archie asked in rather a disgusted voice.

'Answer the question, please,' Kelly said reasonably.

'You get outa here,' Archie suggested spitefully.

Kelly turned the gun slightly and fired two rounds into Jug's head. Archie's eyes opened wide in horror and surprise, like little lights in the darkness. He had not expected that.

'I said please, didn't I?'

'Hell, man!' the voice rasped, knowing that to make any more noise would be death.

'Billy. Red Plymouth Roadrunner, loves to show it off. He's a distributor. I want to know where he hangs out,' Kelly said quietly. 'Sorry about your friend, but I had to show you that I'm serious. Do you understand what I just said?'

Archie did, or thought he did, and he talked freely until the time came for him to rejoin Jughead.

A quick search of Archie's pockets turned up a nice wad of cash and a collection of small drug envelopes, which also found their way into Kelly's jacket pockets. He stepped carefully over both bodies before renewing his drunken gait and taking a roundabout path back to his car. Thank God, he thought, driving north again, he'd be able to shower and shave tonight. But what would he do with the drugs? That was a question that fate would answer.

12 EXERCISES

The door to his cell opened. Armed Vietnamese wearing khaki uniforms took him to a larger room. But even before he passed through the doorway, the muzzle of a rifle stabbed hard into his back, right at the spot that still hurt, fully nine months after his painful ejection, and he gasped in pain. The Vietnamese didn't ask questions. There wasn't a plan to their abuse that he could recognise, just the physical attacks of five men operating all at once, and Zacharias knew that resistance was death.

It didn't matter. In a brief span of seconds his ability to do anything at all was taken away, and he merely collapsed on the rough concrete floor, his muscles paralysed by agony as the blows and kicks and pain went on and on and on—

A screaming voice blasted its way past his catatonia, and then he saw their boots draw back. His peripheral vision saw their faces cringe, all looking towards the door at the source of the noise. Strong hands lifted him, sitting him up against the wall, and the face came into view. It was Grishanov.

'My God,' the Russian said, his pale cheeks glowing red with anger. He turned and screamed something else in oddly accented Vietnamese. Instantly a chair appeared. Then he screamed something else and Zacharias heard the door close.

The Russian helped him up into the chair. He was in obvious pain.

'I have only one thing for pain, Robin,' Grishanov said apologetically, holding out a flask.

The American colonel shook his head. 'I can't.'

Grishanov spoke with the frustration of a man trying to reason with a friend. 'Robin, pain serves no one—not you, not me. Let me help you a little. Please?'

Zacharias was a Mormon and had never touched alcohol in his life. Can't do it, he told himself. To do so was to break his covenant. His body was a temple. But the temple was broken. Would his body be able to heal itself? Easing the pain might make it easier to heal, and easier to stick to his duty. So what was the right thing? His eyes

looked at the metal container. There was relief there. Not much, but some, and some relief was what he needed.

Grishanov handed the flask over. 'Here.'

Just this once, Zacharias thought. Just for the pain. He took a swallow. He felt the warmth in his belly as it spread out and allowed his body to relax.

EMMET RYAN and Tom Douglas stood back, letting the forensics people do their jobs. The discovery had happened just after five in the morning. On his routine patrol pattern, Officer Chuck Monroe had come down the street and spotted the two bodies.

'Time of death?' Ryan asked the representative from the coroner's office.

'Not too long ago,' the man said. 'Probably after two.'

'Monroe?' Ryan called. The young officer came over. 'What do you know about these two?'

'Both pushers. Older one on the right there is Maceo Donald, street name is Ju-Ju. The one on the left I don't know, but he worked with Donald.'

Douglas and Ryan took their time examining the crime scene.

'Nothing at all, Em,' Douglas said, finishing his third sweep. Both men approached the bodies and squatted down close to them for the first time.

'Not bad shooting.' Douglas had his pencil out, pointing to the holes in the forehead of the unidentified victim. They were scarcely half an inch apart, just above the bridge of the nose. The pencil moved to Maceo Donald. The two holes in his forehead were even closer together. 'Our shooter has a real steady hand, Em.'

Ryan shrugged and began his search of the bodies. He found no weapon on either man, and though both had wallets and ID—from which they identified the unknown as Charles Barker, aged twenty—the amount of cash discovered wasn't nearly what men in their business would customarily have on their persons. Nor were there any drugs.

'Monroe?' Douglas said.

'Yes, sir?'

'Our friends Barker and Donald—experienced pushers?'

'Ju-Ju's been around since I've been in the district, sir.'

'Somebody got Ju-Ju!' It was Lieutenant Mark Charon from Narcotics, who had just arrived. 'I had a case running on him.'

'Well, tell me about him,' Ryan ordered.

'Major street pusher, big clientele. Drives a very nice red Caddy.

Pretty smart one, too. Drug rip-off?' Charon asked.

Douglas answered. 'Looks that way, Mark. Whoever did it knew their business. Looks real professional. Any noise on the street about a turf war?'

'No, not really, nothing organised.'

'You might want to ask around,' Lieutenant Ryan suggested.

'No problem, Em. I'll have my people check that out.'

Ryan headed off to his car, accompanied by Tom Douglas. Junior detectives would have the rest of the routine work.

'Somebody that knows how to shoot—better than me, even,' Douglas said as they drove back downtown.

'Well, lots of people with that skill are around now, Tom. We'll let Mark do some of the work on the intelligence side.'

'That makes me feel warm all over.' Douglas snorted.

KELLY ROSE AT TEN THIRTY, feeling clean for the first time in several days. Before breakfast—brunch—he drove to a local park and ran for thirty minutes, then drove back home, where there was work to do. All the clothing from the previous evening was in a brown paper grocery bag—slacks, shirt, underwear, socks and shoes. It seemed a shame to part with the bush jacket, whose size and pockets had proved to be so useful. He'd have to get another, but this was not the time to take any chances. Leftover food and coffee grounds went on top of the clothing and found their way into the apartment complex's Dumpster. Disposing of the four empty .22 cases was easy. He'd dumped them down a sewer while jogging.

'WHAT CAN I DO FOR YOU?' Sam Rosen asked from behind his office desk.

'Gloves,' Kelly said, holding his hand up. 'The kind you use, thin rubber. Do they cost much?'

Rosen almost asked what the gloves were for but decided he didn't need to know. The surgeon pulled open a drawer in his desk and tossed over ten of the paper and plastic bags. 'You look awfully respectable.' And so Kelly did, dressed in a button-down white shirt and his blue CIA suit, as he'd taken to calling it. It was the first time Rosen had seen him in a tie.

Kelly smiled. 'I have a new job, consulting. I can't say about what, but it requires me to dress properly.'

'Feeling OK?'

'Yes, sir, just fine. How are things with you?'

'The usual. More paperwork than surgery.' The small talk was making Sam uneasy. It seemed that his friend was wearing a disguise, and though he knew Kelly was up to something, in *not* knowing exactly what it was, he managed to keep his conscience under control. 'Can you do me a favour?'

'Sure, Doc.'

'Sandy's car broke down. I was going to run her home, but I've got a meeting that'll run till four. She gets off shift at three.'

'If it's OK with her, it's OK with me.'

It was only a twenty-minute wait, which Kelly disposed of by going to the cafeteria for a light snack. Sandy O'Toole found him there.

'I hear your car's broke,' he said.

She nodded. Sandy looked tired, with puffy dark patches under both eyes. 'Something with the starter . . . wiring. It's in the shop.'

Kelly stood. 'Well, my lady's carriage awaits.' His remark elicited a smile, but it was one of politeness rather than amusement.

'I've never seen you so dressed up,' she said on the way to the parking garage.

'Well, don't get too worked up about it. I can still roll in the mud with the best of 'em.' And his jesting failed again.

'I didn't mean—'

'Relax, ma'am. Your driver has a crummy sense of humour.'

Nurse O'Toole stopped and turned. 'It's not your fault. Bad week. We had a child—auto accident. She faded out on my shift, day before yesterday. Sometimes I hate this work,' Sandy concluded.

'I understand,' Kelly said, holding the door open for her. 'We all try to fix the broken parts as best we can, Sandy. You fight your dragons. I fight mine.'

'And how many dragons have you slain?'

'One or two,' Kelly said distantly, trying to control his words.

Her eyes examined him in a professional sort of way. Something's changed in you. I wonder what it is, Sandy thought. Something had resolved itself. The sadness she'd seen, which had almost matched her own undying grief, was gone now, replaced with something she couldn't quite fathom.

When they reached her house, he walked her to the door.

'I don't know why I like talking to you,' she said.

'I wasn't sure that you did. You do?'

'I think so,' O'Toole replied with an almost smile. The smile died after a second. 'John, it's too soon for me.'

'Sandy, it's too soon for me, too. Is it too soon to be friends?'

She thought about that. 'No, not too soon for that.'

'Dinner some time? I asked once, remember?'

'How often are you in town?'

'More now. I have a job—something in Washington.'

'Doing what?'

'Nothing important.' And Sandy caught the scent of a lie.

'Next week, maybe?'

'I'll give you a call. Get some rest.' Kelly didn't attempt to kiss her, or even take her hand. Just a friendly, caring smile before he walked away. Sandy watched him drive off, still wondering what there was about the man that was different.

'WHAT'S THE STORY on Ju-Ju?' Henry Tucker asked.

'Looks like a rip-off. One of yours, eh?' Lieutenant Mark Charon said.

'Yeah. He moved a lot for us. Who did it?' They were in a library, hidden between some rows.

'No telling, Henry. Ryan and Douglas were there, and it didn't look to me like they had much. Douglas was talking mob hit.'

Tucker turned his head. 'Oh?'

Charon spoke calmly, his back to the man. 'Tony isn't going to do anything like that, is he?'

'Probably not.' But Eddie might.

'I need something,' Charon said next.

'What?'

'A dealer.'

'Too many of 'em are mine now, remember?' It had been all right—better than that, really—to use Charon to eliminate the major competition, but as Tucker had consolidated his control on the local trade, he was able to target fewer and fewer independent operators for judicial elimination.

'If you want me to be able to protect you, Henry, then I have to be able to control investigations. For me to control the investigations, I have to land some big fish from time to time.'

'I'll get back to you.' Tucker replaced his book and walked away. The police lieutenant spent another few minutes searching for the right book. He found it, along with the envelope.

GREER HANDLED the introductions.

'Mr Clark, this is General Martin Young . . . and Robert Ritter.'

Kelly shook hands with both. The marine was an aviator. He hadn't a clue who Ritter was, but he was the one who spoke first.

'Nice analysis. You hit all the high points.'

'Sir, it's not really all that hard to figure out. The ground assault ought to be fairly easy. Figure two guys in each tower.' Kelly moved his hands round the diagram. 'Here's the barracks, only two doors, and I bet there's not forty guys in there. The trick's getting the initial strike team in close. Two gunships, just regular rockets and miniguns to hose these two buildings. Land the evac choppers here. It's all over in under five minutes from when the shooting starts. If you want to do another Song Tay, you can duplicate the whole plan, crash the chopper in the compound—but I hear you want it done small.'

'There's no way we can sell this as a major operation,' Ritter said.

'Fewer assets, sir, and you have to use different tactics. The good news is that it's a small objective, not all that many people to get out, not many bad guys to get in the way.'

'We need an additional safety factor,' Young said, looking at the large-scale map, figuring how the helicopters would get in.

'Yes, sir. Somebody has to go in early and eyeball things.' Hell, Kelly thought, why not one more crusade? 'I guess that's me.'

13 *INTERFERENCE*

Billy's bright red Roadrunner was easy to spot.

Kelly had sighted the car just after seven in the evening, close to the bar Archie had identified. Kelly, driving the Beetle, trailed Billy, never closer than half a block.

After forty minutes the pattern became clear. The Roadrunner came to a stop at the end of a block. Kelly kept going, slowly. As he approached, he saw a girl get out, carrying a bag. She walked up to a supplier. The two walked into a building and remained hidden for a minute or two until the girl came out.

In his rearview mirror Kelly saw the Roadrunner cross the street. The girl headed the same way, disappearing from his view as the light changed. Kelly turned right and right again, spotting the Plymouth as it proceeded south with three people inside. He hadn't noticed the man crouching in the back before.

Darkness was falling. Kelly continued to follow the Roadrunner, seeing it stop at a brownstone corner house where all three occupants got out, having made their deliveries for the night to four pushers. He parked his car a few blocks away and came back on foot to observe, again disguised as a street drunk. The local architecture made it easier. All of the houses had marble front steps. Picking the right set of steps, not too close to a working streetlight, gave him a nice shadow in which to conceal himself. Kelly adopted a drunken huddle, occasionally lifting his bag-covered bottle for a simulated sip while he watched the corner brownstone for several hours.

Four hours, finally, had passed when the three came out again, the men in the lead. Kelly risked lifting his head to watch. He needed to get a look at Billy, whom he assumed to be the driver. Not a very impressive figure, really, perhaps five nine, slim; he moved with brisk economy—and arrogance. The other was taller, more substantial, but a subordinate, Kelly thought. The girl followed, her head down, her movements slow and uneven, probably from drugs.

The car started as he watched, and Billy's manner with the car matched the name to the driver. The car jerked a few feet to the corner, then turned left, accelerating with the squeal of tyres across the intersection and out of Kelly's sight. *Billy, five nine, slim, arrogant.* The positive identification was set in Kelly's brain, along with the face and the hair. He wouldn't forget it. The other male form was recorded as well, the one without a name—just a destiny far more immediate than its owner knew.

'NURSES' STATION, O'Toole.'

'Sandy? It's John. Still getting out at three?'

'You do have good timing,' she said, allowing herself a private smile. 'The car is broke again.' And taxicabs cost too much.

'Want me to look at it?' Kelly asked.

'I wish somebody could fix it.'

'I make no promises,' she heard him say. 'But I come cheap.'

'How cheap?' Sandy asked, knowing what the reply would be.

'Permit me to buy you dinner? You can pick the place, even.'

She was weary of being alone and alone and alone. 'Three fifteen,' she told him, 'at the main entrance.'

'IIERE'S THE STORY,' a marinc coloncl said at Camp Lcjcunc, North Carolina, while another was doing much the same thing at exactly the same time at Camp Pendleton, California. 'We have a special job. We need fifteen people. It's dangerous. It's important. It's something you'll be proud of doing. The job will last two to three months. That's all I can say.'

At Lejeune there were perhaps seventy-five men—all combat veterans, all members of the corps's most exclusive unit. Recon marines, they'd all volunteered to become marines first—there were no draftees here—then done so again to join the elite within the elite. These men specialised in going out in small groups, to look and learn, or to kill with a very high degree of selectivity.

But they were also men. More than half had wives and/or children. Now their job was to train their juniors, passing along the lessons that had enabled them to return home when others almost as good as they were had not.

After a few moments the men rose and filed out. Perhaps twenty-five or thirty stayed behind to register their names. Their personnel records would be collected quickly and evaluated, and fifteen of their number would be selected. By the end of the day the men who were going were assembled and briefed on departure times and nothing more. A bus would be taking them, they noted. They couldn't be going very far. At least not yet.

'OK, I KNOW what's wrong with your car,' Kelly said. He leaned over Sandy O'Toole's Plymouth Satellite, jacket and tie off, sleeves rolled up. 'It's the solenoid switch, a loose wire.'

Sandy stood next to Kelly, looking at the engine.

'I'm going to be too dirty to take you to dinner,' Kelly said, as he disappeared under the car. A minute later he was back out. 'Try it now.'

Sandy got in and turned the key. The engine caught at once.

Kelly looked at his clothes and grimaced. 'Could I wash up?'

Sandy led him into the house. Kelly got the grime off his hands before rejoining her in the living room.

'Where'd you learn to fix cars?' she asked, handing him a glass of wine.

'My dad was a small-time mechanic. I learned from him. Thanks.' Kelly toasted her with the glass.

'Was?'

'He died while I was in Vietnam, heart attack. Mom's gone, too. Liver cancer, when I was in grade school.'

Sandy was beginning to understand him a little better now. Losing his mother at a young age and in a particularly cruel and lingering way. He'd probably always been a big kid, tough and proud, but helpless to change things. Every woman in his life had been taken from him—his mother, his wife and his lover. How much rage he must face. It explained so much. As big and tough as he was, there was nothing to fear from this man. It seemed an odd observation with which to begin a relationship, if that was the thing happening.

KELLY SETTLED into a spot on the marble steps across the street from the corner brownstone and waited for the Roadrunner to arrive. Every few minutes he'd lift the wine bottle, while his eyes continuously swept left and right.

It was a quarter past two when the Roadrunner finally appeared. He turned his head to give the man a good look. Billy and his sidekick. Laughing about something. The other one stumbled on the steps, and when he fell there was a flutter of light little twirling rectangles that had to be banknotes.

That's where they count their money? Kelly wondered. Both men bent down to recover the cash before entering the house.

Kelly rose, tiredly, crossing the street and heading to the brownstone with his accustomed drunken gait. The door, he confirmed, wasn't locked. He took a single long look while he passed by. As he moved, he began planning his mission for the following night. He heard Billy's voice filtering through the upstairs windows. A voice he already loathed and for which he had special plans. For the first time he was close to one of the men who had murdered Pam. Probably two of them. He'd do this one right.

Be seeing you, guys, he promised in the silence of his thoughts. This was the next really big step forward, and he couldn't risk blowing it.

Kelly headed up the block, his eyes fixed on the dealers he called the two Bobs, a quarter-mile away up the wide city street.

This was another test—he had to be sure of himself.

At one block's distance Kelly stopped, lifting the bag-wrapped bottle to his lips before moving on. Big Bob, the dealer, was six three. Little Bob, the lieutenant, was fully six five, muscular. Both were formidable enough. Better to pass by and leave them be?

No.

But he did pass by first. Little Bob was looking across the street. Big Bob was leaning back against the building. Kelly drew an imaginary line between the two and counted three steps before turning left slowly so as not to alert them. He moved his right hand under his new-old bush jacket as he did so. As the right came out, the left covered it, wrapping round the handle of the Colt automatic in a two-hand grip. His arms extended full-length without locking the elbows, and the physical manoeuvre brought the gun in alignment with the first target. Big Bob saw the move. His street-smart instincts made the correct analysis and screamed for action. Too late.

Kelly's fingertip depressed the trigger twice. Without shifting his feet he swivelled right, a mechanical turn that took the gun towards Little Bob, who had reacted already, seeing his boss starting to fall and reaching for his own weapon at his hip. Moving, but not fast enough. Kelly's shot was a good one. Little Bob fell on his face. Kelly lingered only long enough to be sure that both were dead, then turned and moved on.

HER NAME WAS VIRGINIA CHARLES, and her night wasn't going well. A nurse's aide at St Agnes Hospital, she'd had her shift extended by the late arrival of her relief worker. Having just missed one bus, she'd had to wait what seemed to be for ever for the next.

She was tired when she got off the bus, and she walked quickly and alertly. How the neighbourhood had changed. She could remember a lively and *safe* street life with friendly neighbours. But now she watched the streets for danger.

'Hey, mama, spare a dollar?' a voice said, already behind her. She kept moving, lowering her head.

A hand was on her shoulder.

'Give me money,' the voice said next.

'Ain't got enough to interest you, boy,' Virginia Charles said, still not looking back. Then she heard a click.

'I'll cut you,' the voice said, explaining the hard facts of life.

She stopped, whispering a quiet prayer, and opened her small bag. She turned slowly. He was just a boy, seventeen or eighteen, and his eyes had the lifeless amplification of some sort of drug. She reached into the bag and extracted a five-dollar bill.

'Five whole dollars?' The youth smirked. 'More, or you bleed.'

Kelly turned the corner. He hadn't heard anything, but as he made the turn he saw two people not twenty feet from his Volkswagen. A flare of reflected light told him that one was holding a knife.

He stopped cold, looking. He didn't have much time to make a decision. The boy had the woman by the arm, brandishing a knife, with his back to him. Kelly started to move that way. That's when things changed. The boy cut the woman's upper arm.

Virginia Charles gasped when the knife sliced her arm, and she yanked away, dropping the five-dollar bill. The boy's other hand grabbed her throat, and she could see he was deciding the next place for the knife to go. Then she saw movement, a man perhaps fifteen feet away, and in her pain and panic she called for help.

The youth turned to see a street wino ten feet away.

'Maybe you got some money, too, Pop?' he asked, intoxicated with power. On a whim he took a step towards the man, extending his knife hand. There was no time now to bring the gun out. Kelly stopped, backing off a half step and coming up to an erect stance.

The mugger's first lunge with the knife was clumsy, and he was surprised at how easily the wino batted it aside, then stepped inside its arc. A stiff, straight right to the solar plexus deflated the mugger's lungs, winding but not stopping him. The knife hand came back wildly as he started folding up. Kelly grabbed his arm, twisting it

hard, then stepped over the body already headed to the pavement.

'Why don't you go home, ma'am?' he told Virginia Charles quietly, turning his face away and hoping she hadn't seen it very well.

The nurse's aide stooped down to recover the five-dollar bill from the sidewalk and left without a word. Kelly was grateful that she didn't need any help. He really ought to have helped her deal with her wound, but the risks were piling up. The mugger was moaning now. And this one had definitely seen his face, close up.

Well, he'd attempted to hurt a woman, and he'd attacked Kelly with a knife—both of them, arguably, failed attempts at murder. Mistakes like that had a price. Kelly took the knife from his limp hand and shoved it hard into the base of his skull, leaving it there. Within a minute his Volkswagen was half a block away.

14 *QUANTITY OF MERCY*

It was becoming routine, Lieutenant Ryan told himself. Two pushers down, both with a pair of .22s in the head, but not robbed this time. Then had come the call from only a few blocks away, and he and Douglas had rolled to that one. The call had identified the new crime scene as interesting.

'Whoa,' Douglas said, getting out first. One did not often see a knife sticking in the back of a head. 'They weren't kidding.'

'The victim's shoulder appears to be dislocated. Make that wrecked,' the medical examiner said.

'Karate move?' Douglas asked.

'Something like that. That sure slowed him down some. You can see the cause of death.'

'Lieutenant, over here,' a uniformed sergeant called. 'This is Virginia Charles, she lives a block over. She reported the crime.'

'Are you OK, Miss Charles?' Ryan asked. A fireman-paramedic was checking the bandage she'd placed on her own arm, and within four minutes Ryan had a goodly quantity of information.

'A bum, you say?'

'Wino. That's the bottle he dropped.' She pointed. Douglas picked it up with the greatest care.

'Can you describe him?' Lieutenant Ryan asked.

THE ROUTINE WAS so exactingly normal that they might have been at any marine base. The daily-dozen exercises followed by a run, everyone in step. But turning back off the main road, into the woods towards their training site, they were surprised to see a general officer waiting for them.

'Welcome to Quantico, Marines,' General Martin Young told them after they'd had a chance to cool down. Off to the side they saw two naval officers and a pair of civilians, watching and listening. Eyes narrowed collectively, and the mission was suddenly very interesting indeed.

During Young's lecture Cas Podulski looked round the training site. 'Just like the photos,' he observed quietly.

'The dimensions are accurate to within three inches,' Bob Ritter said. 'We have the Soviet manual for building places like this. Your General Young did a nice job.'

The marines looked around after having learned a little of the mission. The site had been carefully selected for its similarity with another place—the marines hadn't needed to be told that; it had to be so. After the welcoming speech, the men divided into predetermined units to draw their weapons. They'd start training in daylight for feel and proficiency, but almost immediately they'd switch exclusively to night work. This sort of job, they knew, only happened at night.

'THE KNIFE SEVERED the spinal cord just where it enters the medulla,' the medical examiner observed to Emmet Ryan. 'Death was instantaneous.'

Ryan looked at his notes. 'White, forty or older, long black hair, short, dirty.'

Douglas came over to his lieutenant. 'Our victim was still alive when Mrs Charles walked away. Em, in the past week we've seen five very expert murders.'

'Different MOs, Tom. Four were pushers. But this guy's just a street hood. Have we ID'd him yet?'

The uniformed sergeant answered. 'Junkie. He's got a rap sheet, six arrests for robbery.'

'It doesn't fit,' Ryan said. 'It doesn't fit anything, and if you're talking about a clever guy, why let somebody see him, why let her leave, why talk to her? Whoever this guy was, he sure wasn't real careful.'

'A wino with a sense of justice, Em?' Douglas prodded.

LOOKING BACK, reliving the incident, Kelly realised that he faced a difficult situation. On coming home he'd looked in the mirror, wig and all. Whatever that woman had seen, it had not been John Kelly, not with a face shadowed by his heavy beard, smeared with dirt, under a long and filthy wig. His hunched-over posture made him appear several inches shorter than he was. But he'd somehow left his wine bottle behind. He remembered dropping it to parry the knife thrust, and then in the heat of the moment he'd not recovered it. Dumb! Kelly raged at himself.

What would the police know? The physical description would not be a good one. He'd worn a pair of surgical gloves and he had never touched the wine bottle with ungloved hands. The police would know a street bum had killed that punk, but there were lots of street bums, and he only needed one more night. It meant that he'd have to alter his operational pattern even so, and that tonight's mission was more dangerous than it ought to be, but his information on Billy was too good to pass up. It was time to set his thoughts aside. There were other responsibilities as well. Kelly lifted his phone and dialled.

'Greer.'

'Clark,' Kelly responded.

'We're going to need you soon,' Greer said. 'It's started.'

That's fast, Kelly thought. 'OK, sir.'

'Ever been to Quantico?' James Greer asked.

'No, Admiral.'

'Bring your boat. There's a marina there, and it'll give us a place to chat. Sunday morning. Ten sharp. We'll be waiting, Mr Clark.'

'Aye, aye.' Kelly heard the phone click off.

Sunday morning. He hadn't expected that. It was going too fast, and it made his other mission all the more urgent.

'HOW DOES THIS GRAB YOU?' Douglas asked, setting it on Ryan's desk. The wine bottle was in a clear plastic bag, and the smooth, clear surface was uniformly coated with a fine yellow dust.

'No prints?' Emmet looked it over in considerable surprise.

'Not even a smudge, Em. Zilch.' The knife came down next. It was a simple switchblade, also dusted and bagged. 'One partial thumbprint, matched with the victim. Either he stabbed himself in the back of the neck or our suspect was wearing gloves.'

It was awfully warm this time of the year to wear gloves. Emmet Ryan leaned back, staring at the evidence items on his desk, then at Tom Douglas, sitting beside them. 'OK, Tom, go on.'

'The two pushers were a couple blocks away, time of death almost identical. Our friend does them, walks over this way, turns a corner, and sees Mrs Charles being hassled.'

Lieutenant Ryan shook his head. 'Why get involved? A killer with morals?' Ryan asked. That was where the theory broke down. 'And if the same guy is wasting pushers, what's the motive? If we're dealing with a robber, then it doesn't connect with Mrs Charles and her friend. Tom, it's just speculation.'

'No physical evidence, a street wino wearing gloves!'

'Not enough, Tom.'

'I'm going to have western district start shaking them down.'

Ryan nodded. That was fair enough.

IT WAS MIDNIGHT when he left his apartment. Kelly drove out quietly, passing darkened office buildings downtown in his continuing routine. But tonight there was a difference. Tonight would be his first major payoff.

The Roadrunner was right there, a block away from the corner brownstone. Kelly parked as close to it as he dared, then got out and walked away from the target house, heading back to the next block before dropping into his disguise.

It was after one in the morning now, and activity on the street was diminishing. Kelly turned yet again, heading for the objectives. One of those who had hurt Pam was now within a hundred yards. Probably two of them. Kelly allowed his mind to see her face again, to hear her voice. Then he took five deep breaths, slowing his pace and watching the corner house, now only thirty yards away.

The sentry, if that's what he was, betrayed himself. The streetlights revealed puffs of cigarette smoke coming out of the door, telling Kelly exactly where the first target was. Approaching the wide steps, he slumped against them, coughing. Then he walked up towards the door, which he saw was ajar, and fell against it. He tumbled to the floor, finding himself at the feet of the man whom he'd seen accompany Billy. Along the way, the wine bottle broke, and Kelly ignored the man, whimpering over the broken glass and the spreading stain of cheap California red.

'Come on, Pop.' Strong hands reached down. Both hands, lifting him. Kelly allowed his own arms to dangle, one going behind as the man started to turn him towards the door. He staggered, and now the sentry was supporting him almost fully. Weeks of training and careful reconnaissance came together in a single instant.

Kelly's left hand slapped against the sentry's face. The right drove the Ka-Bar through his ribs. The eyes were wide and shocked, the knees already buckling. Kelly let him down slowly.

'Remember Pam?' he whispered to the dying body in his hands. Kelly withdrew the knife, which he wiped off on the victim's shirt.

Everything was going according to plan. He'd gotten the right target, the subordinate. The principal objective was upstairs.

The stairs were creaky. Kelly attenuated that by keeping close to the wall, moving slowly. He'd replaced the knife in its scabbard, and his .45/.22 was in his right hand now, suppressor screwed on.

Halfway up, he started hearing sounds: a slap, a whimper, a whine, followed by a cruel chuckle.

'Please . . .' A despairing whisper that caused Kelly's knuckles to turn white round the pistol grip. There was light coming from one room, and he could see shadows on one wall.

'What's the matter, Dor?' a male voice asked as Kelly reached the doorframe.

There was a mattress in the room, and on the mattress a woman, kneeling. The face staring down at her was smiling when Kelly took a step into the room.

Kelly's voice was light, relaxed, almost comical. 'This looks like fun.'

Billy turned and saw an extended arm with a big automatic. He was naked, and his left hand held a pair of pliers, but not a knife or a gun. Those tools were elsewhere, in a holdall ten feet away, and his eyes could not bring them closer.

'On your face, Billy, spread-eagle. Down! Now!'

Billy did what he was told. Kelly pushed the girl back on the mattress and reached in his belt for the length of electrical wire which he had previously wrapped round his waist. In a few seconds Billy's hands were securely wrapped and knotted.

The girl was staring at Kelly's face, eyes wide, breath heavy, but her movements were slow. She was drugged to some extent.

'Get dressed,' Kelly told her. 'Do it now.'

'Who are you?' Billy asked, giving Kelly an outlet for his rage.

'You even breathe loud, and your brains go on this floor, got it?'

Billy's head nodded by way of an answer.

Kelly checked the wire on Billy's wrists and decided to do another loop at the elbows. He then lifted Billy by the arms to a standing position, which evoked a scream.

'Hurt a little, does it?' Kelly asked. Then he applied a gag and turned him to the door. 'Walk.' To the girl: 'You, too.'

Kelly conducted them down the steps and was surprised by the girl's reaction to the body at the bottom.

'Rick!' she gasped.

It had a name, Kelly thought.

Looking out of the door, he could see his car, and there was no activity in his view. There was danger in what came next, but danger had again become his companion. Kelly led them out.

He unlocked the car, forcing Billy in, then the girl into the front seat. Before starting the car, he leaned over the seat and wired up Billy's ankles and knees.

'Who are you?' the girl asked as the car started moving.

'A friend,' Kelly said calmly.

ONE DOES NOT EXPECT to hear doorbells at a quarter to three in the morning. Sandy first thought she had dreamed it. Even so, she rose, slipped on a robe and went downstairs, too disorientated to be frightened. She turned on the lights as she opened the door.

'Turn that light off!' The rasping voice was familiar. The command caused her to flip the switch without so much as a thought.

'What are you doing here?' There was a girl at his side, looking thoroughly horrible.

'Call in sick. You're not going to work today. You're going to take care of her,' Kelly said. 'Her name is Doris.'

'Wait a minute!' Sandy stood erect, and her mind started racing. Kelly was unshaven, had on awful clothes, but his eyes were burning with something. Rage was part of it, a fury at something.

'Remember about Pam?' he asked urgently. 'This girl's in the same spot. I can't help her. Not now. I have to do something else.'

'What are you doing, John?' Sandy asked. And then, somehow, it was very clear. The TV news reports she'd been watching, the look she'd seen in his eyes in the hospital; the look she saw now, the desperate compassion and the trust it demanded of her.

'She needs help, Sandy.'

'John,' she whispered. 'You're putting your life in my hands.'

Kelly actually laughed, after a fashion. 'Yeah, well, you did OK the first time, didn't you?' He pushed Doris in the door and walked away, off to a car, without looking back.

15 *DEPRESSURISATION*

It was after four when Kelly pulled into the marina, and he was tired. He backed up to his boat, got out and opened the rear door.

'Hop,' he told Billy, and that he did. Kelly pushed him aboard, then directed him into the main saloon. Once there, Kelly fastened Billy's wrists to a deck fitting. Ten minutes more and he had cast off, heading out to the bay. Kelly was tired. With the boat on autopilot he settled into the control chair, drinking some strong black coffee and stretching by way of reward to his body for its efforts.

'Who are you?' Billy asked, relieved of his gag.

Kelly sipped his coffee, ignoring the voice behind him.

'Look, I want to know who you are! I don't know what the problem is, but we can talk, OK?'

This time Kelly turned, looking down at the naked man chained to the deck. There was a remarkable long silence, punctuated by a deep intake of breath.

'You're . . .'

'That's right.'

'I killed you,' Billy objected. He'd never gotten the word.

'Think so?' Kelly asked, looking forward again.

'So that's what it's about . . . she told us all about you before we snuffed her.'

Just past the Bay Bridge, Kelly disengaged the autopilot and turned ten degrees to port. There was almost no morning traffic.

'Did Pam tell you about the passion marks?' Billy sneered. He didn't see Kelly's hands tighten on the wheel.

'The marks about the breasts appear to have been made with an ordinary set of pliers,' the pathology report had said. Kelly had it all memorised, every single word of the dry medical phraseology.

'I don't know what the big deal is. I mean, she's just a dead whore. I can make it up to you. Let's make a deal, OK?'

'TOM, I THINK you may be right after all,' Ryan said.

According to his driver's licence, Richard Oliver Farmer was twenty-four. He had expired from a single knife thrust into the chest. Whoever had killed him had wiped the knife on the shirt. Three wipes, it appeared, and one of them had left a permanent impression of the knife, marked in the blood of the victim. Douglas pointed to one of the stains with his pencil.

'You know what it is?' Douglas asked. 'It's a Ka-Bar, standard-issue marine combat knife. I own one myself.'

'Nice edge on it, too,' the ME told them. 'Very clean cut. He must have sliced the heart just about in half. A very accurate thrust, gentlemen. Our friend knew exactly what he was doing.'

'One more, Em. Our friend got in close and did him so fast—'

'Yeah, Tom, I believe you now.' Ryan nodded and went upstairs to join the other detective team. In the front bedroom was a cloth satchel with a ton of cash in it, a gun and a knife. Also a lady's bag. So much evidence for the younger men to catalogue.

'You know Farber, that psychiatrist over at Hopkins?'

'Yeah, Em. I set up a date for you. He's real smart.'
'I owe you a beer, Tom. You figured this one faster than I did.'
'Well, thanks. Maybe I can be a lieutenant, too, some day.'

AFTER TYING UP to the quay, Kelly helped Billy down from the boat and walked him towards the machinery bunker. He dialled the combination lock, turned on the lights and pushed Billy inside.

It looked like—was, in fact—a steel cylinder, seventeen inches in diameter, sitting on its own legs with large castor wheels at the bottom. The steel cover on the end was not in place, hanging down on its hinge.

'You're going to get in that,' Kelly told Billy, forcing his head and shoulders into the opening. 'Inside!' A push helped, and when his feet were inside the rim, Kelly lifted the hatch and bolted it into place. Then he walked out, flipping the lights off. He needed something to eat and a nap. Billy could wait.

'HELLO?' HER VOICE sounded very worried.
'Hi, Sandy, it's John.'
'John! What's going on?'
'How is she?'
'Doris, you mean? She's sleeping now,' Sandy told him.
'Sandy, I want you to listen to me very carefully. This is important. Number one, don't tell anybody that she's there.'
'John, she's badly injured, she's hooked on pills, she probably has severe medical problems on top of that. I have to—'
'Sam and Sarah, then. Nobody else. Sandy . . .' Kelly hesitated. He had to make it clear. 'Sandy, I have placed you in danger. The people who worked Doris over are the same ones—'
'I know, John. I kinda figured that one out. John, she told me that you—killed somebody.'
'Yes, Sandy, I did.'
Sandra O'Toole wasn't surprised. But hearing it from him—it was the way he'd just said it. Calm, matter-of-fact. *Yes, Sandy, I did.*
'Sandy, these are some very dangerous people. I could have left Doris behind—but I couldn't, could I?'
'I'll have to get her proper medical attention. I'll call Dr Rosen. We'll take care of her.' She paused. 'John?'
'Yes, Sandy?'
'What you're doing . . . it's *wrong*.'
'I know,' Kelly told her.
'But I don't care about that, not any more. I understand, John.'

'Thank you,' Kelly whispered. 'I'll be back as soon as I can. Sandy?'

'What, John?'

'Thanks.' The line clicked off.

You're welcome, she thought, hanging up. What a strange man. He was killing people, ending lives with an utter ruthlessness. But he'd endangered himself to rescue Doris.

DR SIDNEY FARBER looked exactly as Emmet Ryan expected: forty or so, small, bearded, pipe smoker. Ryan had messengered extracts from the case files to the psychiatrist, and clearly the doctor had read them. All of them were laid open on the desk.

'How sick is this one?' Lieutenant Ryan asked.

Farber looked up. 'He's as healthy as we are—rather healthier, physically speaking. But that's not the important part. What you just said—"this one". You're assuming one murderer for all these incidents. Tell me why.'

'I didn't think so at first. Tom saw it before I did. It's the craftsmanship.'

'Correct.'

'Are we dealing with a psychopath?'

Farber shook his head. 'No. The true psychopath is a person unable to deal with life. He sees reality in a very individual way. This fellow is all business. He's killing people for a reason that is probably rational, at least to him.'

'Why, then?'

'Obviously it's not robbery. It's something else. I've met people like this before—in World War Two.'

'I was in Europe myself,' the detective said. 'I jumped into Normandy and Eindhoven. Airborne. One-Oh-One.'

'Well, that's what you're up against, Lieutenant Ryan. Here's the key to it.' Farber held up the transcribed interview with Mrs Charles. 'The disguise. Has to be a disguise. It takes a strong arm to slam a knife into the back of the skull. That wasn't any wino.'

'But that one doesn't fit the pattern at all,' Ryan objected.

'I think it does, but it's not obvious. Turn the clock back. You're in the army, you're an elite member of an elite unit. You take the time to recon your objective, right?'

'Always,' the detective confirmed.

'Apply that to a city. How do you do that? You camouflage yourself. So our friend decides to disguise himself as a wino. How many of those on the street? Dirty, smelly, invisible. But how does he get in and out? You think he takes a bus—a taxi?'

'Car.'

Farber held up the photo of the Charles murder scene. 'He makes his double kill two blocks away, he clears the area and comes here. Why, do you suppose?' And there it was, right on the photo, a gap between two parked cars.

Ryan felt humiliated. 'What else did I miss, Dr Farber?'

'Not much else. This individual is very clever, changing his methods, and this is the only case where he displayed his anger. That's it, do you see? He was angry, but *why* was he angry? He wouldn't have planned something with Mrs Charles there. For some reason he had to do something that he hadn't expected to do, and that made him angry. Also, he let Mrs Charles go—*knowing* that she saw him.'

'You still haven't told me—'

'He's a combat veteran. He's very very fit. That means he's younger than we are and highly trained. Ranger, Green Beret. He's watching his victims. He's picking the same time of day, when they're tired. He's not robbing them. He may take the money, but that's not the same thing.'

'But he's not crazy, you say.'

'No, I doubt he's disturbed in a clinical sense at all, but sure as hell he's motivated by something and highly disciplined. Discipline shows in how he operates—but his anger also shows in *why* he operates. Something made this man start to do this.'

'He's not killing for fun.'

'Correct.' Farber nodded. 'Everything has a purpose, and he has a lot of specialised training that he can apply to this mission. It is a *mission*. You have one really dangerous cat prowling the street.'

'He's after drug people. That's pretty clear,' Ryan said.

'One other thing. If you have police looking for this guy, remember that he's better with weapons than almost anybody. He'll avoid a confrontation. He doesn't want to kill the wrong people, or he would have killed Mrs Charles.'

'But if we corner him—'

'You don't want to do that.'

'ALL COMFY?' Kelly asked.

The recompression chamber, made of high-quality steel, was designed to reproduce the pressure that came along with scuba diving. At one end was a triple-paned four-inch-square Plexiglas window. Under the chamber itself was a powerful, gasoline-powered air compressor, which could be controlled from a fold-down seat, adjacent to which were two pressure gauges. One was labelled in 'bars', or multiples of normal atmospheric pressure. The other gauge showed equivalent water depth. Each thirty-three feet of simulated depth raised the atmospheric pressure by one bar.

'Look, whatever you want to know, OK?' Kelly heard over the intercom.

'I thought you'd see things my way.' Kelly started the compressor. He made sure that the spigot valve was tightly shut. Then he opened the pressurisation valve, venting air from the compressor to the chamber, and watched the needles rotate slowly clockwise.

'Ever do any skin-diving?' Kelly asked.

'No, no, I haven't,' replied a very confused drug distributor.

'OK, well, you're going to learn what it's like. You should yawn and work your ears to get used to the pressure,' Kelly told him.

Kelly steadied the depth gauge at one hundred feet. While Billy adjusted to the pressure, Kelly spent an hour tidying up the machine shop, cultivating his memories and his rage before coming back to his fold-down seat.

'Ready to answer some questions?'

'Anything, OK? Just let me outa here!'

'OK, good.' Kelly lifted a clipboard. 'Have you ever been arrested, Billy?'

'No.' A little pride in that one, Kelly noted. Good.

'Been in the service?'

'No.' Such a stupid question.

'Never been in jail, never been fingerprinted, nothing like that?'

'Never.' The head shook inside the window.

'How do I know you're telling the truth?'

'I am, man. I am!'

'Yeah, you probably are but I have to make sure, OK?' Kelly twisted the spigot valve and air hissed loudly out of the chamber.

In the preceding hour, Billy had been surrounded by four times the normal amount of air for the space he was in. His body had adapted to that. Various gas bubbles, mainly nitrogen, were dissolved into his bloodstream, and when Kelly bled the air out of the chamber, those bubbles started to expand. The pain came in waves, evolving into the most intense and unpleasant sensation Billy had ever experienced. Kelly listened to the scream. The air pressure was only that of sixty feet. He shut the valve and restored the pressure.

'That's the penalty for a lie. I thought you should know. Now let's talk about Henry and his organisation.'

'LEFT THE MONEY?' Tucker asked.

'More than fifty thousand. They were still counting when I left,' Mark Charon said. They were back in the cinema, the only two people in the balcony. But this time Henry wasn't eating popcorn, the detective saw. It wasn't often that he saw Tucker agitated.

'I need to know what's going on. Tell me what you know.'

'We've had a few pushers whacked in the past week or ten days—'

'Yeah, I know that. You think they're connected?'

'It's all we got, Henry. Was it Billy who disappeared?'

'Yeah. Rick's dead. Knife?'

'Somebody cut his damn heart out,' Charon exaggerated. 'One of your girls there, too?'

'Doris,' Henry confirmed. 'Left the money . . . Why?'

'Maybe what happened last night was . . . well, something else.'

'Like what?'

'Like maybe a direct attack on your organisation, Henry,' Charon answered patiently. 'Who would want to do that? Somebody's sending you a message, Henry. Not taking the money is a sign of contempt. Who do you know who doesn't need money?'

THE SCREAMS WERE getting louder. Billy had just taken another excursion, staying at sixty feet for a couple of minutes. Kelly saw him claw at his ears.

'Billy,' he said, after restoring the pressure and eliminating most of the pain, 'I'm not sure I believe that one. If I think you're lying, it hurts. You want me to hurt you some more?'

'No, please!'

'Now let's get back to business, OK? Tell me more about Henry. Where does he live?'

'I don't know,' he gasped.

'Wrong answer!' Kelly snarled.

'I don't know. We meet at a place off Route 40—'

'Billy, I don't have much reason to be nice to you,' Kelly reminded him. 'You killed Pam, remember? You tortured her to death. You used pliers on her. You say you've worked for this guy for almost two years and you don't even know where he lives? I have trouble believing that,' Kelly said, reaching for the valve.

'I just know the phone number,' Billy said.

'Give it to me,' Kelly ordered. Billy did as he was told, and Kelly wrote it down. He had two full pages of pencilled notes now. Names, addresses, a few phone numbers. Seemingly very little, but far more than he'd had only twenty-four hours before.

'How do the drugs come in?'

Billy's head turned away from the window. 'Don't know . . .'

'We have to do better than that.' *Hisssssssssssss* . . .

Again Billy screamed, and this time Kelly let the depth-gauge needle rotate to seventy-five feet. Billy started gagging. The pain was beyond anything he had ever felt.

'Please . . . please . . .' The whisper carried over the speaker next to Kelly. He brought the pressure back up slowly, stopping this time at one hundred and ten feet.

'The last question was about how the drugs come in.'

'I don't know,' Billy whined.

Kelly spoke quietly into the microphone. 'Billy, there's something you have to understand. Up until now what's happened to you—well, it hurts pretty bad, but I haven't really hurt you yet. So it's a good idea not to lie to me, OK? Now . . . how do the drugs come in? Tell me what you know, Billy, or it just gets worse. Talk fast.'

Billy broke. He started talking in a choked and uneven voice, but one that, finally, was completely truthful. The information was somewhat remarkable, but it had to be true. No person like this had the imagination to make it up. The final part of the interrogation lasted for three hours. Kelly revisited questions to see if the answers changed, but they didn't. In fact the renewed question developed yet more information that connected some bits of data to others, formulating a clear, overall picture, and by midnight Kelly was sure that he'd emptied Billy's mind of all the useful data that it contained.

Kelly was almost captured by humanity when he set his pencils down. If Billy had shown Pam any mercy at all, perhaps he might have acted differently. But Billy had tortured a young woman whom Kelly had loved, and for that reason Billy was not a *man* at all and did not merit Kelly's solicitude.

It didn't matter in any case. The damage had been done, and it progressed at its own speed as tissues torn loose by the barometric trauma wandered about blood vessels, closing them off one at a time. Though the final depressurisation was a slow and gentle one, what came out of the chamber was not a man—but then, it never had been.

Kelly loosed the retaining bolts on the hatch, pulling Billy out and laying him on the concrete floor. He wondered if he had to chain him to something, but the body at his feet was useless to its owner now, the central nervous system good only to transmit pain. But Billy was still breathing, and that was just fine, Kelly thought, heading off to bed, glad it was over. With luck and good medical care, Billy would live for several weeks. If you could call it that.

16 POSSIBILITIES

It would be a trip of several hours, more than half in darkness. Heading south for Point Lookout, Kelly took the time to scan the collection of derelict 'ships' near Bloodsworth Island. Built for the First World War, they were an exceedingly motley collection. Some made of timber, others of concrete—which seemed very odd indeed—all of them had survived the world's first organised submarine campaign, but had not been commercially viable even in the 1920s. Kelly went to the flying bridge, and while the autopilot handled his southerly course, he examined them through binoculars, because one of them was probably the clever hiding place for the activity in which Billy had so recently played a part. Kelly altered his course to the west. This matter would have to wait. He made a conscious effort to change his thinking. He would soon be a team player, associated again with men like himself. A welcome change, he thought, during which he would have time to consider his tactics for the next phase of his operation.

'OK—I FOUND something out,' Charon said. His car sat in the parking lot outside a supermarket, next to a Cadillac.

'What's that?' Tucker asked.

'They're looking for a guy disguised as a bum. White, not too tall, strong, moves real good when he has to. This guy is a pro.'

'Tony and Eddie,' Tucker said quietly.

'That's my best guess, Henry, but it's only a guess.' The detective pulled out of his parking place.

But none of it made any real sense, Tucker told himself, driving out. Why would Tony and Eddie try to do . . . what? What was going on? They didn't know much about his operation, merely that it existed, and that he wanted it and his territory left alone while he evolved into their principal supplier. For them to harm his business without first learning his method of importing the product was not logical. Why would they cross him now, just when things were blooming?

Perhaps Eddie was making his move, betraying Tony and Henry at the same time.

Perhaps a lot of things. Whatever was happening, Henry still controlled the import pipeline. More to the point, he had to defend what he had—his own territory and his connections. Things were just starting to pay off big. He had to stand and fight.

A plan began to form. He'd talk to Tony and sound him out on the chance that Eddie was playing a game of some sort, that he was connected with rivals. That was his starting point to gather information. Then he would act on it.

THERE'S A LIKELY SPOT, Kelly told himself. *Springer* was just crawling along quietly. The trick was to find a place that was populated but not alert. He'd risk it here, round a bend in the river.

Kelly idled his motors and went forward to drop a small anchor. He moved quickly, lowering his small dinghy into the water. He put a life jacket on Billy before tossing him over the side. He tied the jacket off to the stern, then rowed to the shore. It only took three or four minutes before the dinghy's bow touched the muddy banks. There was a school, Kelly saw. It probably had a summer programme, and almost certainly had a maintenance staff that would show up in the morning. He stepped out of the dinghy and hauled Billy onto the bank before removing the life jacket.

'You stay here, now.'

'. . . stay . . .'

'That's right.' Kelly pushed the dinghy back into the river and began rowing back. He'd left Billy naked. No identification. No distinguishing marks. Billy had said that he'd never been fingerprinted. If true, then there was no way for police to identify him easily, probably not at all. And he couldn't live too long the way he was. Soon Kelly had *Springer* moving back up the Potomac.

Two more hours and Kelly saw the marina at Quantico Marine Base. Tired, he made a careful approach, selecting a guest berth at the end of one of the piers.

'SO WHAT'S SO DAMNED important?' Tony Piaggi asked.

'I think somebody's making a move on me. I want to know who. Somebody's been taking pushers down,' Tucker said.

'I read the papers,' Piaggi assured him. He poured some Chianti into his guest's glass. 'Why is that important, Henry?'

'The same guy took down two of my people. Rick and Billy. One of my girls is missing, too.' He lifted his glass and sipped, watching Piaggi's eyes. 'The police say it looks like a pro doing this.'

'It isn't one of mine, Henry,' Tony said after a moment.

'I don't think you're doing it. I think you're too smart.'

'Glad to hear that.' Tony smiled.

'What about Eddie?'

'No,' Piaggi said. 'Nobody thinks Eddie's got what it takes.'

'Who, then?' Tucker asked. 'Who else knows enough? Who else would do a bunch of killings to cover up a move like this? Who else would make it look like a pro job?'

'Henry, taking Eddie out would cause major problems.' He paused. 'But I'll check around.'

'Thank you.' Tucker stood and left Tony alone with his wine.

GRISHANOV WAS in the embassy. Hanoi was a strange city, a mixture of French architecture, little yellow people and bomb craters. Travelling about a country at war was dangerous, but it had been worth the trip to be here in his country's embassy, where he could speak his native tongue for a precious few hours.

'So? What are you learning, Comrade Colonel?' the general asked.

'Colonel Zacharias is everything that we were told, and more.' Grishanov leaned forward. 'In another two months, perhaps six weeks, I will be able to think as the Americans think. I will know not only what their current plans are, but I will also be able to duplicate their thinking into the future. Zacharias is giving me a graduate course in American doctrine and philosophy. I've *seen* the intelligence estimates we get from KGB and GRU. At least half of it is wrong. That's only one man. Another one has told me about their carrier doctrine. Another about NATO war plans. It goes on, Comrade General.'

'How do you do this?' the general asked.

Grishanov leaned back in his chair. 'Kindness and sympathy.'

The general nodded. 'So why are you here?'

'I need more people! I can't interrogate all of these prisoners myself, especially now that they are beginning to talk. I take more and more time with each. There are not enough hours in the day.'

The general sighed. 'I've tried. They offer you their best—'

Grishanov almost snarled in frustration. 'Their best *what*? Best barbarians? That would destroy my work. I need Russians. Pilots, experienced officers. And one more thing,' he added, inwardly trembling at his boldness. 'Hope, Comrade General. I need hope.'

'Explain.'

'We can't let them die,' Grishanov said. 'Not all of them. Some we must have. Some will serve us, but I must have something to offer to them.'

'Bring them back?'

'After the hell they've lived here—'

'They're *enemies*, Colonel. They all trained to kill *us*! Save your sympathy for your own countrymen.'

Grishanov stood his ground. 'They have knowledge that is useful, Comrade General. Is it too much to ask that we treat them with kindness, that we give something in return for learning how to save our country from possible destruction? We could torture them, as our "fraternal socialist allies" have done, and get nothing! Does that serve our country?'

General-Lieutenant Rokossovskiy pulled a bottle of expensive vodka from his desk. He poured two small glasses. 'I can't get you more men, Kolya. But, yes, I will try to get you some hope.'

'YOUR LAD SEEMS to know his business—till now, anyway,' General Young observed.

'It's a lot to ask him to do something like this the first night, Marty,' Dutch Maxwell countered.

'Well, hell, Dutch, if he wants to play with my marines . . .' That's how Young was. They were all 'his' marines.

They stood on a hilltop overlooking the site Young had erected. Fifteen marines were on the slopes, and their job was to detect and eliminate Clark as he climbed to his notional perch.

'What do you think of Clark, Irvin?' asked Young.

'Seems like he knows a thing or two,' replied the master gunnery sergeant. 'Pretty decent shape for a civilian—and I like his eyes.'

'Oh?'

'You notice, sir? He's got cold eyes. He's been around the block.'

They were speaking in low murmurs. Kelly was supposed to get here, but they didn't want to make it easy for him. They settled into silence, waiting for three o'clock, the operation's agreed stop-time. That took an hour. Finally it was 0255. Marty Young stood and stretched, fishing in his pocket for a cigarette.

'Anybody got a smoke?' a voice murmured.

'Here you go, Marine,' Young said. He held one out to the shadow and flicked his trusty Zippo. Then he jumped back a step. 'How long have you been there?'

'I "killed" you around one thirty, sir,' Kelly said. He stood there, a rubber knife in his hand, his face painted with green and black shadows. The young face split into a grin as he pocketed his 'knife'.

Irvin stood up from his place of repose and walked up to the civilian. 'Mr Clark, sir, I think you'll do.'

DORIS BROWN CLOSED her eyes and lapsed into sleep.

'Sarah, I'm worried,' said Sandy O'Toole.

'So am I. I'm worried about her physical and psychological

condition. I'm worried about her "friends"—'

'I'm worried about John,' Sandy said discordantly. Doris was under control. She could see that. Sarah Rosen was a gifted clinician, but something of a worrier, as many good doctors were.

They headed out of the room and downstairs. There was coffee there. Sarah could smell it. 'Yes, that, too,' she said. 'I know what I think. Tell me what you think.'

'I think he's killing people.'

'I think you're right.' Sarah Rosen sat down. 'You never met Pam. Prettier than Doris—willowy. We had her saved, Sandy, and then something happened, and something changed in John.'

'Part of me says he's a good man, but there's something very scary about him . . .' Sandy's voice trailed off.

'Sandy, if he were a bad person, why did he bring Doris up here? He could have just walked away from her. Maybe he's just the sort of person who thinks he has to fix everything himself. But now we have to help.'

'What are we going to do with her?' Sandy asked.

'We're going to get her well,' Sarah said, watching Sandy's face change, returning to her real dilemma.

'But what about John?'

'DO YOU KNOW how many Ka-Bar knives there are?'

From the tone of Douglas's question, Lieutenant Ryan knew the news had to be bad. 'No, but I suppose I'm about to find out.'

'Sunny's Surplus just took delivery of a thousand of the damn things a month ago. I didn't know how many were out there.'

What neither man wanted to admit openly was that they were stymied again, despite what had appeared to be a wealth of physical evidence in the brownstone. Ryan looked down at the open file and about twenty forensic photographs. The murder victim—probably a hood himself, but still officially a victim—had been identified immediately from the cards in his wallet, but the address on his driver's licence had turned out to be a vacant building. A full set of fingerprints from Richard Farmer merely generated a new card. The FBI register did not have a match.

The bedroom had provided three complete sets of Farmer's prints. There was also a selection of partial prints, one of a girl (supposition, from their size), and one of a man (also supposition). Worst of all, by the time the latent-prints team checked out the Roadrunner parked outside, the August sun had heated the car up so much that what might have been something to match prints with the registered owner of the car, one William Grayson, had merely been a collection of blobs. Finally, Mark Charon's narcotics team had nothing on the names Farmer or Grayson.

'We just need the one thing,' Douglas said quietly.

'The one thing,' Ryan repeated. It was a private bit of shorthand. *The one thing* to break a case could be a name, an address, a person who knew something—the crucial piece in the jigsaw puzzle that made the picture clear. And it was out there. Ryan was sure of it.

'TWO WEEKS,' MAXWELL SAID. 'Two weeks' more training, one week of travel and set-up.'

James Greer leaned forward. 'Dutch, that's really fast.'

Maxwell nodded. 'Cas flies out tomorrow to *Constellation*.'

'I have a lot of briefing to do. What does your man Clark say?' Podulski asked.

'He tells me he's comfortable with how things are going at Quantico,' Greer said. 'Mr Ritter will want to see a rehearsal.'

'That's fair,' Maxwell said. 'We have a full-up live-fire rehearsal tomorrow night.'

'We'll be there, Dutch,' Greer promised.

THE TEAM WAS in an old barracks designed for at least sixty men, and there was plenty of room for everyone. They were enjoying their first night off since arriving at Quantico, and some kind soul had arranged for three cases of beer.

'Mr Clark,' one of the grenadiers asked, 'what's this all about?'

It wasn't fair, Kelly thought, to make them train without letting them know. But it wasn't unusual either.

'I can't tell you, Corp. All I can say is, it's something you'll be mighty proud of. You have my word on that, marine.'

'Mr Clark?' Master Gunnery Sergeant Paul Irvin gestured to the door. It was just as sticky hot out as it was inside, with a gentle breeze coming through the long-needled pines.

'What is it?' Kelly asked, taking a long pull of his beer.

'That's my question, Mr Clark, sir,' Irvin said lightly. Then his voice changed. 'It's Song Tay, isn't it?'

'Something close to that, yes. They should be telling you soon.'

'You have to tell me, Mr Clark. I have marines to worry about.'

'Hey, I'm going in, too, remember?'

'Keep talking,' Irvin ordered gently.

'I helped plan the insertion. With the right people we can do it.'

'You sure it's worth it?'

'I can't tell you this, but I will anyway. The place we're hitting—it's a prison camp, like you think, OK?'
Irvin nodded. 'More to it. There has to be.'
'It's not a regular camp. We think our guys, they'll never come home unless we go get 'em. There's Russians in the camp, probably interrogating our people—grilling them real hard for what they know. If we don't do anything . . . what's that make us?'
'Thank you, Mr Clark,' Sergeant Irvin said. 'That's a mission. So you're first in and last out?'
'I've worked alone before.'

17 *HELLOS*

'Where am I?' Doris Brown asked in a barely understandable voice.
'You're in my house,' Sandy answered. She sat in the corner of the guest room. 'A friend brought you here. I'm a nurse. The doctor is downstairs fixing breakfast. How are you feeling?'
'Terrible.' Her eyes closed. 'How long?'
'Almost a week.' Sandy took a sponge and wiped her face.
'Thank you.' Doris turned her head and opened her eyes. 'Why are you doing this for me?'
That answer was an easy one: 'I'm a nurse, Miss Brown. It's my job to take care of sick people.' Sandy got her sitting up.
'That's a step forward,' Sarah Rosen observed from the door. 'You're looking much better today, Doris.'
'I feel awful.'
Doris closed her eyes. Sandy took a brush and started working on her patient's hair. It was filthy and needed washing, but just getting it straightened out would help, she thought. She was surprised by Doris's shudder a minute or so after she started.
'Am I alive?' The alarm in the question was startling.
'Very much so,' Sarah answered.
'Pam . . .' It took Doris a moment to go on. 'Hair . . . when she was dead . . . brushed her hair.'
Dear God, Sarah thought. Sam had related that one part of the post-mortem report to her. Dr Rosen came over and touched her patient's face as gently as she could.
'Doris, who killed Pam?' she asked.
'Rick and Billy and Burt and Henry killed her. Watching . . .' The girl started crying.
'They made you watch?'

'Yes . . .' Doris's voice was like one from the grave.

'Let's not think about that now.' Sarah stroked the girl's cheek.

'Tired.' Doris faded off into sleep almost at once.

'LET'S ALL STAY back here,' Marine General Marty Young said. 'They're shooting all live stuff.'

'Makes sense to me,' Dutch said. 'I'm used to having things go off a couple hundred yards behind me.'

'Flying at four hundred knots,' Greer added for him.

'A lot safer that way, James,' Maxwell pointed out.

They stood behind an earthen berm, the official military term for a pile of earth, two hundred yards from the camp.

'How long have they been moving in?'

'About an hour. Any time now,' Young breathed.

'I can't hear a thing,' Admiral Maxwell whispered.

It was hard enough to see the site in the darkness. The buildings were visible only because of their straight lines. All they heard was the wind whispering through the treetops. There was a surreal element to being in the woods like this.

Kelly ran over the Boxwood Green assault plan in his mind. The insertion would put the recon marines on the ground one ridge away from Sender Green. Thirty minutes for the marines to approach the camp. M-79 grenades to eliminate the guard towers. Two Huey Cobra gunships—known with lethal elegance as 'snakes' to the troops—would hose the barracks and provide heavy fire support; but the grenadiers on the team, he was sure, could take out the towers in a matter of five seconds, then pour white-phosphorus into the barracks and burn the guard force alive with deadly fountains of flame, doing without the snakes entirely if they had to.

The radio sitting on the berm had been transmitting only the noise of static. That changed now, with four long dashes. They were answered at intervals by one, then two, then three, then four dots.

'Teams in place,' Kelly whispered. 'Hold your ears. The senior grenadier shoots when he's ready, and that's the kickoff.'

The first thing they heard was a distant mutter of twin-bladed helicopter rotors. Designed to make heads turn, and even though every man at the berm knew the plan in intimate detail, it still worked, which pleased Kelly no end. He'd drawn up much of the plan, after all. All heads turned but his.

Kelly saw the muted flash of a single launch, and not a second later the blinding white-red-black flash of a fragmentation grenade against the floor of one of the towers. The tower, where men and guns would have been, disintegrated. The echo had not yet dispersed when the other three towers were similarly destroyed. Seconds later the gunships came skimming in over the treetops, not fifty feet separating their rotors as miniguns ripped into the barracks building—two long neon fingers reaching in. The grenadiers were already pumping white-phosphorus rounds into the windows.

The fire element of the marine assault force continued to pour fire into the barracks and admin buildings while the snatch team raced to the prison block. Now the rescue choppers came in, behind the Huey Cobras, landing noisily close to the main gate. One of the gunships began circling like an anxious sheepdog on the prowl for wolves.

The first marines appeared, dragging dummies that simulated prisoners. Kelly could see Master Gunnery Sergeant Irvin checking and doing a count at the gate. There were shouts now, men calling off numbers and names, and the roar of the big Sikorsky choppers almost covered it all. The last marines in were the fire-support teams, and then the rescue choppers lifted off into the darkness.

'That was fast,' Ritter breathed as the sound faded.

'That was fifteen seconds under nominal,' Kelly said, holding up his watch.

'What if something goes wrong, Mr Clark?' Ritter asked.

Kelly's face lit up in a wicked grin. 'Some things did, sir. Four of the team were "killed" coming in—maybe a broken leg or two.'

'Wait a minute, you mean there's a chance—'

'Let me explain, sir?' Kelly said. 'I eliminated four people at random. Call all of them broken legs. They had to be carried into the objective and carried out. Back-ups on everything. Sir, I *expect* a clean mission, but I messed it up some tonight just to check.'

Ritter nodded, impressed. 'I expected everything to be run by the book for this rehearsal.'

'In combat, things go wrong, sir. I allowed for that. Every man is cross-trained for at least one alternative job.' Kelly rubbed his nose. He'd been nervous, too. 'What you just saw was a successful simulated mission. This one's going to work, sir.'

Ritter turned to Greer. 'When do you want me to brief the White House?'

'I'll let you know, Bob.'

'SO? WHAT'S THE BEEF?'

'Look, Eddie,' Tony Piaggi said patiently. 'Our friend's got a problem. Somebody took down two of his people.'

'Who?' Eddie Morello asked.

'We don't know. His contacts, my contacts—we got nothin'. What we want to know is, who's taking his people down? You catch anything about somebody from out of town?' Tony's eyes bored in across the table at Eddie.

'I haven't heard anything about that.'

'Put feelers out,' Tony ordered. 'Check around.'

'Sure,' Eddie snorted.

SHE MADE IT all the way down the stairs, holding onto the banisters, following the sound of conversation.

Sandy's face broke into a smile. 'Well, good morning!'

'Hi,' Doris said, still pale and weak, but she smiled back as she walked through the doorway. 'I'm real hungry.'

'I hope you like eggs.' Sandy helped her to a chair.

'I'll eat the shells,' Doris replied.

'You can start with these, and don't worry about the shells,' Sarah Rosen told her, shovelling the beginnings of a normal breakfast from the frying pan onto a plate.

Doris had turned the corner. Her movements were painfully slow, but the improvement from only twenty-four hours before was miraculous. She was turning back into a person.

But they still didn't know anything about her except her name—Doris Brown. Sandy got a cup of coffee for herself and sat down at the table. 'Where are you from?' she asked.

'Pittsburgh. There's just my father. Mom died in sixty-five, breast cancer,' Doris said slowly.

'Nobody else?' the nurse asked evenly.

'My brother . . . Vietnam.'

'I'm sorry, Doris,' Sarah said. 'Tell us about your father.'

'I ran away,' Doris replied. 'Right after David . . . after the telegram. Daddy had some trouble, and he blamed me.'

RAYMOND BROWN was a foreman at the Jones and Laughlin Steel Company. He worked the night shift because his house was especially empty at night. Nevermore to hear the sounds of his wife, nevermore to take his son to Little League, nevermore to worry about his daughter's dates at weekends.

It had just been too much. His wife discovering a lump, still a pretty young woman in her thirty-seventh year, his best and closest friend. He'd supported her as best he could after the surgery, but then came the downhill slide and always having to be strong for her until the end. It would have been a crushing burden for any man, and then followed by another. His only son, David, drafted, sent to Vietnam, and killed two weeks later. He'd crawled inside a bottle, desperately trying to cling to what he had left, but too tightly. Doris had borne her own grief, something Raymond hadn't fully understood, and when she'd come home late, her clothing not quite right, the cruel and hateful things he'd said. He could remember every word, the hollow sound as the front door had slammed.

Only a day later he'd come to his senses, driving with tears in his eyes to the police station, desperate again to get his little girl back, to beg from her the forgiveness that he could never give himself. But Doris had vanished. The police had done what they could, and that wasn't much. And so for two years he'd lived inside a bottle, until two fellow workers had taken him aside and talked as friends do once they have gathered the courage to invade the privacy of another man's life. His minister was a regular guest in the lonely house now. Raymond Brown was drying out. Man that he was, he had to face his loneliness, had to deal with it as best he could. Prayer also helped some, and in the repeated words he often found sleep. He was tossing and turning in his bed when the phone rang.

'Hello?'

'Hello, is this Raymond Brown?'

'Yeah, who's this?' he asked with closed eyes.

'My name is Sarah Rosen. I'm a doctor in Baltimore. I have somebody here who wants to talk to you, Mr Brown.'

'Daddy?' The voice was a whisper.

From hundreds of miles away, the whispered word came through as clearly as a church bell. 'Dor?'

'Yes . . . Daddy, I'm sorry.'

'Are you OK, baby?'

'Yes, Daddy, I'm fine.'

BOB RITTER ENTERED the Executive Office Building and searched for the right room. He found it on the second floor, the room of Roger MacKenzie, special assistant to the President for national security affairs.

'Hi, Bob. How are things at Langley?' MacKenzie asked.

'The usual.' Ritter smiled back. He gestured with his head towards MacKenzie's private office. His host nodded.

'Wally, we need someone to take notes.'

'Coming, sir.' His executive assistant rose from his desk in the secretarial area and brought a pad.

'Bob Ritter, this is Wally Hicks. I don't think you've met.'

'How do you do, sir.' Hicks extended his hand. Ritter took it, seeing yet one more eager White House aide. New England accent, bright-looking, polite. A minute later they were sitting in Roger MacKenzie's office, the doors closed.

'So what brings you in, Bob?' MacKenzie asked. Hicks flipped open his notepad to take down every word.

'Roger, a rather unique opportunity has presented itself over in Vietnam. We've identified a special prison camp southwest of Haiphong.' Ritter quickly outlined what they knew and what they suspected. He then took a photo folder from his briefcase, set it on the desk and opened it.

'We know who this guy is. Colonel Robin Zacharias. Air force. He spent quite some time at Offutt Air Force Base, SAC war plans. He knows everything, Roger.'

MacKenzie looked up and whistled. 'And this guy?'

'He's a colonel in the Soviet air force. It isn't hard to figure what he's there for. But here's the real punch line.' Ritter handed over a copy of the wire-service report on Zacharias's death.

'Damn. This sort of thing could wreck the peace talks,' MacKenzie thought aloud.

Walter Hicks was not supposed to say anything. 'Wreck the peace talks,' he scribbled down, taking the time to underline it.

'Roger, the men we believe to be in this camp know enough to seriously compromise our national security. I mean *seriously*,' Ritter said calmly. 'Zacharias knows our nuclear war plans.'

'You have my attention, Bob.'

'Mr Hicks, right?' Ritter asked, turning his head.

'Yes, sir.'

'Could you please excuse us?'

'Yes, sir.' Hicks stood and walked out of the door, closing it quietly.

This could wreck the peace talks, he raged to himself, sitting back down at his desk. Even MacKenzie thought that.

All those kids from his generation dead. And now they might risk not ending the war because of fifteen or twenty professional *killers*, who probably liked what they did. Hicks lifted his phone and dialled a number.

'Senator Donaldson's office.'

'Hi. I was trying to get Peter Henderson.'

'I'm sorry. He and the senator are in Europe right now. They'll get back next week.'

'Oh, that's right. Thanks.' Hicks hung up. Damn.

SOME THINGS HAVE to be done very carefully. Peter Henderson didn't even know that his code name was Cassius. It had been assigned to him by a Soviet analyst who loved Shakespeare's plays.

His senator was in Europe on a fact-finding tour, mainly having to do with NATO, though they would stop in on the peace talks at Paris. In fact, the 'tour' was mainly a shopping trip, punctuated by a brief every other day. Henderson, enjoying his first such trip as the senator's expert on national security issues, had to be there for the briefs, but the rest of the time was his. At the moment he was touring the White Tower, centrepiece of the Tower of London.

'Warm day for London,' another tourist said.

'I wonder if they get thunderstorms here,' the American replied casually, examining Henry VIII's immense suit of armour.

'They do,' the man replied, 'but not as severe as Washington.'

Henderson headed towards an exit. A moment later he was strolling round Tower Green with his new companion.

'Your English is excellent.'

'Thank you, Peter. I am George.'

George was his real name—actually Georgiy, which was the Russian equivalent. He was a full colonel in the KGB. He smiled at the American. 'Your senator has access to many things.'

'Yes, he does.' Henderson didn't have to add, And so do I.

'Such information is useful to us. We need your help to control the unreasonable people on our side—leftovers from the Stalin era. What I am asking, Peter, is that you let us know from time to time certain things that you have learned about us. I won't even tell you what, exactly. I think you are intelligent enough to see for yourself. We will trust you on that. The time for war is behind us. The coming peace, if it does come, will depend on people like you and me.'

'Peace . . . That would be nice,' Henderson allowed.

'So can you help us?'

'I've been helping you, George.' Which was true. Henderson had been nibbling at the hook for nearly two years.

'Yes, Peter, I know that, but now we are asking for a little more, some very sensitive information. The decision is yours, my friend. It is easy to wage war. Waging peace can be far more dangerous.'

Henderson made his decision. 'Somebody has to help make the peace. I'll help you, George.'

'Peter, I thank you. You will be contacted when you get home. I must go now.'

'See you, George,' Henderson said. It caused George to turn and smile one last time.

'No, Peter, you will not.' George walked down the stone steps towards Traitor's Gate. It required considerable self-control not to laugh aloud at the mixture of what he had just accomplished and the irony of the portcullised stone arch before his eyes.

18 *DEPARTURES*

Kelly was working on his woodcraft, as he'd been doing for several weeks. He'd picked his weapons in the fervent hope that he would not need to fire a single shot. The primary weapon was a carbine version of the M-16 assault rifle. A silenced 9mm automatic went into a shoulder holster, but his real weapon was a radio, and he would be carrying two of those, just to be sure, plus food, water, a map—and extra batteries. It came to a 23-pound load, not counting his special gear for the insertion. The weight wasn't excessive, and he found that he could move through the trees and over the hills without noticing it. Kelly moved quickly for a man of his size, and silently. The latter was a matter of where he walked more than anything else—where he placed his feet, how he twisted and turned to pass between trees and bushes.

Overtraining, he told himself. Take it easier now. He headed down the hill and found the marines training in small groups, miming the use of their weapons. Kelly was just approaching the site's landing zone when a blue navy helo landed and Admiral Maxwell emerged. Kelly, by chance, was the first one there.

'We're going?'

'Tonight,' Maxwell confirmed with a nod.

Despite the expectation and enthusiasm, Kelly felt the usual chill. It wasn't practice any more. His life was on the line again. The lives of others would depend on him.

The admiral clapped Kelly on the shoulder. 'I guess you want that quick liberty you asked for. You be back here by midnight.'

'Aye, aye, sir.'

Fifteen minutes later Kelly was in a staff car en route to Baltimore. Since leaving *Springer* tied up at the guest slip, the world had stopped and he'd moved backwards in time. Now he was in forward motion for a brief period.

'SO WHAT'S THE STORY, Mr MacKenzie?' Wally Hicks asked.

What the hell, MacKenzie thought. Hicks had a clearance. In two minutes he covered the high points of Boxwood Green.

'Sir, that's an invasion,' Hicks pointed out as evenly as he could.

'I suppose they might think so, but I don't. Wally, we have *people* over there, and what they know is vital to our national security.'

'But—'

MacKenzie looked up. Didn't this kid get it? 'But *what*, Wally?'

'It's dangerous.'

'War is that way, in case nobody ever told you.'

'Yes, sir.' What else could he say? Damn, he really needed someone to talk to about this.

'JOHN!' HE WAS ALIVE.

'Hello, Sandy.' Kelly smiled, dressed decently in a tie and blue blazer. It was so different from the way she'd last seen him.

'Where have you been?' Sandy asked, waving him in.

'Off doing something. Nothing illegal, I promise.'

'You're sure?' An awkward moment developed out of thin air.

'I'm going somewhere, and I wanted to stop over before I left.'

'Where to?'

'I can't say.' The answer chilled the room.

'John,' Sandy said. 'I know.'

'OK.' Kelly nodded. 'I figured you would. How is she?'

'She's doing fine, thanks to you.' The nurse and her former patient drifted into the kitchen. 'John, we need to talk, OK? What exactly have you been doing?'

'You're better off not knowing, Sandy.'

'Billy and Rick?' she said, putting it on the table. 'John, you can't do things like that! The police—'

'Are infiltrated,' Kelly told her. 'The organisation has compromised somebody, probably someone very high up. Because of that I can't trust the police, and neither can you, Sandy.'

'How do you know that?'

'I asked Billy some questions.' Kelly paused. 'If you want to turn me in, well, I can't stop you. I won't hurt you—'

'I know that!' Sandy almost screamed. 'John, you can't do this,' she added more calmly.

'Why not?' Kelly asked. 'They kill people. They do horrible things, and nobody's doing anything about it. What about the victims, Sandy? Who speaks for them?'

'The law does.'

'And when the law doesn't work, then what? Do we just let them die? Remember the picture of Pam?'

'Yes,' Sandy replied.

'Sandy, your houseguest—they made her *watch.*'

'She told me. She's told us everything. After . . . after Pam died, she's the one who brushed Pam's hair out, John.'

The reaction surprised her. It was immediately clear that Kelly's pain was behind a door, and some words could bring it out in the open with a sudden speed that punished him badly. He turned away for a moment and paused before turning back.

'Sandy, it's like this: they killed Pam. They raped and tortured and killed her as an *example*, so they could use other girls the same way. I'm going to get every one of them, even if I die in the process.'

She took a deep breath. 'You said you're going away.'

'Yes. If things work out, I should be back in about two weeks.'

'Will it be dangerous?'

'Not if I do it right.' Kelly knew she would see through that one.

'Doing what?'

'A rescue mission, and please don't repeat that to anyone. I'm leaving tonight. I've been off training for it.'

'Vietnam?' Sandy asked after a few moments.

'That's right.' Kelly paused.

'Damn you, John! I've started to *care* about you.'

The pain returned to his face one more time. 'Don't, Sandy. People who get attached to me get hurt.'

Doris came into the kitchen just then. The girl was transformed. Sandy had trimmed her hair and found decent clothes for her. Her soft brown eyes fixed on Kelly.

'You're him,' she said quietly.

'I guess I am. How are you?'

She smiled. 'I'm going home soon—Daddy wants me back.'

'I'm sure he does, ma'am,' Kelly said. She was so different from the victim he'd seen only a few weeks before.

The same thought came into Sandy's mind just then. Doris was the innocent one, the real victim of forces that had descended on her, and but for Kelly she would be dead.

'SO MAYBE IT WAS EDDIE,' Tony Piaggi said. 'I told him to sniff around, and he says he doesn't have anything.'

'And nothing's happened since you talked to him. Everything's back to normal, like,' Henry replied. 'How much you want to bet that if Eddie takes a little trip, nothing else happens?'

'Anything happens to Eddie, there could be trouble.'

'Let me handle it. I have a way that'll work just fine.'

'Tell me,' Piaggi said. Two minutes later he nodded approval.

'WHY DID YOU COME here?' Sandy asked while she and Kelly cleaned up the dinner table. Doris had gone back upstairs for more rest.

'I wanted to see how she was doing.' But that was a lie, and not an especially good one.

'It's lonely, isn't it?'

Kelly took a long time to answer. 'Yeah.' She'd forced him to face something. Being alone was not the sort of life he wanted to have.

She touched his hand. 'What you're going off to, it's not—'

He smiled. 'No. It's a real job. Official stuff and everything.'

'How will I know, John? I mean . . .'

'About me?' Kelly pulled a pen from his coat and wrote down a phone number. 'An admiral named James Greer. He'll know.'

'Please be careful.' Her eyes were desperate now.

'I have to go now, Sandy.'

'Just make sure you come back.'

'I will. Promise.' But the words sounded empty, even to him. Kelly moved away from the table, feeling her hand still on his. 'See you in a couple weeks. Say goodbye to Doris for me, OK?'

'Yes.' She followed him towards the front door. 'John, when you get back, let it stop. Try to find another way.'

'I'll think about it.' Kelly opened the door. It was dark outside now, and he'd have to hustle to get back to Quantico on time.

'John?'

'Yes, Sandy?'

'Come back.'

'HOW WAS ENGLAND, Peter?'

'Pretty nice. It rained in Paris, though,' Henderson said.

Their apartments were only two blocks apart, solid, comfortable places in Georgetown built during the late thirties for the bureaucrats of a growing government. Wally Hicks had a two-bedroom unit, which compensated for the smallish living-dining room.

'So what's happening that you wanted to tell me about?' the Senate aide asked, still recovering from jet lag.

'We're invading the north again,' the White House aide answered.

'What? I was at the peace talks, OK? Things are moving along.'

'Well, you can kiss that goodbye for a while,' Hicks said morosely. On the coffee table was a plastic bag of marijuana, and he started putting a smoke together.

'You should lay off that garbage, Wally.'

'Doesn't give me a hangover like beer does. Hell, Peter, what's the difference?'

'The difference is your security clearance,' Henderson said pointedly.

'Like that matters.' Hicks lit up and took a long pull. 'There's supposedly this camp . . .' he began. He related what he knew. 'They *think* there's a bunch of people there, but it's just supposition. We only know about one. What if it's all for one guy?'

What a remarkable chance this was, Henderson thought.

THE CHARTERED BUS drove to Andrews Air Force Base. There was a new C-141 on the ramp, its strobe lights already rotating. The marines got out of the bus, finding Maxwell and Greer waiting.

'Good luck,' Greer said to each man.

'Good hunting,' was what Dutch Maxwell told them.

Built to hold more than double their number, the Lockheed Starlifter was outfitted for stretcher patients with a total of eighty beds. That gave every marine a place to lie down and sleep, plus room for all the prisoners they expected to rescue. The Starlifter started turning engines as soon as the cargo hatch was shut.

'I hope this works,' Maxwell said, watching the aircraft taxi into the darkness.

'You've trained them well, Admiral,' Bob Ritter observed. 'When do we go out?'

'Three days,' James Greer answered. 'Got your calendar clear?'

'For this? You bet.'

19 ***TRANSIT***

The problem was the first thing on his mind when his eyes opened. What do I do about this? Henderson asked himself. Now he had something the other side really needed. It was just that he didn't have anyone to tell it to. Did the Russians really know what they had there at that camp southwest of Haiphong? It was information that, if used properly, would make them feel far more comfortable about détente, would allow them to back off a little, in turn allowing America to back off a little. That was how it had to start.

Henderson rode the bus to work. He found a seat in the back. Two blocks later the bus came to a stop, and immediately thereafter a man sat down next to him.

'How was London?' the man asked in a conversational voice. Henderson looked over briefly. It wasn't someone he'd met before. 'I have a friend there. His name is George.'

'George said he had a friend in town,' Peter said cautiously.

The man smiled. 'My name is Marvin; you can call me that. What are you doing for dinner tonight?'

'Nothing much.'

'Do you know a place called Alberto's?'

'Wisconsin Avenue—yeah.'

'Seven thirty,' Marvin said. He rose and got off at the next stop.

ALBERTO'S WAS A SMALL Italian place where the veal was especially good. Henderson found a booth in the back and ordered a gin and tonic. Marvin arrived a few minutes later. He was of Henderson's age, totally nondescript, wearing glasses, his hair a neutral brown.

'The house red for me,' Marvin told the waiter when he arrived with Henderson's drink.

'How will it work?' Henderson asked when the waiter had brought the wine.

'First of all we need to set up a way of contacting me. Your apartment has curtains on the front windows. When they are all the way open or all the way closed, there is nothing to concern us. When there is, leave them halfway closed. Is that acceptable?'

'Yes, Marvin.'

'For starters, Peter, we'll use a simple transfer method. I will park my car on a street close to your home. It's a dark blue Plymouth Satellite with licence number HVR-309. Put your messages in this.' He passed something under the table. It was small and metallic. 'There's a powerful magnet in it. When you walk past my car, you can bend down to pick up a piece of litter or rest your foot on the bumper and tie your shoe. Just stick the container on the inside surface of the bumper. The magnet will hold it in place.'

It seemed very sophisticated to Henderson, though everything he'd just heard was kindergarten-level spycraft. The dinner menu arrived, and both men selected veal.

'I have something for you now,' Henderson told the KGB officer.

IT WAS A RELIEF when the C-141 thumped down at Da Nang in South Vietnam. They'd been in transit for a total of twenty-three noisy and mind-numbing hours, including refuelling stops in Alaska and Japan, and that was quite long enough, they all thought.

Two trucks were waiting, and they drove to a different part of the air base, where two aircraft waited. The marines selected seats for the next part of their journey, a one-hour hop to USS *Constellation*. Once there, they boarded a pair of helicopters for a transfer to USS *Ogden* where, disorientated and exhausted by travel, they were led to capacious and empty troop quarters—and bunks. Kelly watched them file off, wondering what came next for him.

'How was the trip?' He turned to see Admiral Podulski, dressed in wrinkled khakis.

'Aviators gotta be crazy,' Kelly complained.

'Does get kinda long. Follow me,' the admiral ordered, leading him into the superstructure of the ship. Kelly looked around first. *Constellation* was on the eastern horizon, with aircraft flying off one end while others circled to land on the other. Two cruisers were in close attendance and destroyers ringed the formation.

Inside the superstructure there was a comfortable sitting room, and the ship's captain was there.

'Welcome aboard!' Captain Ted Franks said. 'You're Clark?'

'Yes, sir.'

Franks waved Kelly to a chair next to a table in the centre of which was a bottle of Jack Daniel's whiskey.

'That ain't legal,' Kelly observed at once.

'I arranged it,' Casimir Podulski explained. 'Brought over from *Connie*. You need something to steady down.'

'Sir, I never argue with admirals.' Kelly dropped ice cubes into a tumbler and covered them with alcohol. 'So when do we start?'

'Four days. You need two to recover from the trip,' Podulski said. 'The submarine will be with us two days after that. The marines go in Friday morning, depending on weather.'

'Fair enough.' There was nothing else he could say.

SARAH'S BUICK WAS PARKED outside, and today would see them in Pittsburgh. Sandy had worked on Doris's hair a little more and made one more trip to get clothes that befitted the day—a beige silk blouse and a burgundy skirt that ended just above the knee.

'I don't know what to say,' Doris Brown told them.

'You just keep getting better,' Sarah Rosen replied. They went out to the car and Doris got in the back.

It was a quiet ride. In the silence of the car Sandy and Sarah could feel the tension build. It was something they'd talked about. Doris was returning to a home and a father she'd left for a life that had nearly become a death. For many months the principal component of her new life would be guilt, part earned, part not. But with her confidence and self-esteem restored she might in two or three years be able to continue her life on a normal course.

The hills were steep in Pittsburgh. Doris directed them along the

Monongahela River and up the right street. And there it was. Sarah pulled the Buick into a parking place, and everyone took a deep breath.

There was nothing remarkable about Raymond Brown, Sandy saw a moment later. He was nervous coming down the steps, holding the rail as he did so with a trembling hand. He opened the car door, helping Sandy out with awkward gallantry. Then he reached inside, and when his fingers touched Doris's, he burst into tears. Doris tripped coming out of the car, and her father kept her from falling, and clutched her to his chest.

'Oh, Daddy!'

'Let's get you inside, baby,' Ray Brown said, taking his little girl up the steps. Sandy O'Toole and Sarah Rosen followed.

In the security of the house, father clutched daughter again. That hug lasted over a minute, and then she drew back with a giggle.

'I have to go.'

'The bathroom's in the same place,' her father said.

Doris moved off, finding the stairs and going up. Raymond Brown turned his attention to his guests. 'I, uh, I don't know what I'm supposed to say.'

'That's OK.' Sarah smiled her benign doctor's smile. 'This is Sandy O'Toole. Sandy's a nurse, and she's more responsible for your daughter's recovery than I am.'

'Hi,' Sandy said, and handshakes were exchanged all round.

'Doris still needs a lot of help, Mr Brown,' Dr Rosen said. 'She's been through a really terrible time.'

'Doc,' he said softly, 'she's my little girl. She's all I have, and I'm not going to . . . foul up and lose her again. I'd rather die.'

'Mr Brown, that is exactly what we needed to hear.'

KELLY AWOKE AT ONE in the morning, local time, feeling unusually rested. The gentle rocking of the ship had soothed his body. He made his way to the shower, and in ten minutes he was dressed and presentable in striped fatigues. There was a name tag that said CLARK, but no badges of rank. In the eyes of the crew that made Mr Clark a civilian, and already they were whispering that he was CIA.

Kelly headed into the superstructure, wandering forward and upwards until he found the combat information centre. Warships never sleep and Captain Franks was there, sleepless, as many captains tended to be.

'You need to look at some charts?' the CO asked. 'I have the whole package under lock in my cabin.'

'Sounds like a good idea, Cap'n. Maybe some coffee, too?'

Franks's cabin was comfortable enough. A steward brought coffee and breakfast. Kelly unfolded the chart, again examining the river he'd be taking up to the camp.

'Nice and deep,' Franks observed.

'As far as I need it to be,' Kelly agreed, munching on some toast. 'The objective's right here.'

'Long swim, Mr Clark,' Franks observed.

'I'll have some help, and I don't have to swim back, do I?'

'I suppose not. Sure will be nice to get those guys out.'

'Yes, sir.'

PHASE ONE of Operation Boxwood Green began just before dawn. The carrier USS *Constellation* reversed her southerly course at the transmission of a single codeword. Two cruisers and six destroyers matched her turn to port. That left *Ogden* with two Adams-class missile-destroyer escorts.

At eight that morning a pair of AH-1 Huey Cobra helicopters from the marine air base at Da Nang landed on *Ogden*'s ample flight deck. Members of *Ogden*'s crew were still not briefed on the mission, but it was clear now that something most unusual indeed was under way. Cobra gunships meant action, and every man aboard knew they were a lot closer to North Vietnam than South. Speculation was running wild. In officers' country, the latest set of photos had come aboard. Kelly lifted the blow-ups.

'Still people in the towers. No changes I see,' Kelly told the others. 'Only one car. No trucks . . . nothing much in the immediate area. Gentlemen, it looks pretty normal to me.'

'*Connie* will hold position forty miles off seaward. The medics cross-deck today. The command team arrives tomorrow, and the next day—' Franks looked across the table.

'I go swimming,' Kelly said.

THE FILM CASSETTE SAT, undeveloped, in a safe in the office of a section chief of the KGB's Washington station, in turn part of the Soviet Embassy, just a few blocks from the White House. The volume of material generated by over a hundred trained field officers meant that not all the information that came in through the door was processed locally. The cassette finally went into a small manila envelope, which found its way into the canvas bag of a diplomatic courier who boarded a flight to Paris. At Orly, eight hours later, the courier walked to catch an Aeroflot jet to Moscow.

Upon arriving in Moscow and walking past customs control, the courier was taken by car to KGB headquarters. The cassette landed on the desk of a KGB major, who called a subordinate to convey it to the photo lab for development.

PERHAPS THE WORLD'S MOST sophisticated weather-prediction service supported air operations over Vietnam. The senior meteorologist had come across from *Constellation* with Greer, Maxwell and Ritter. Now he moved his hands across a chart of isobars and the latest satellite photo.

'The showers start tomorrow, and we can expect rain on and off for the next four days. Some heavy stuff,' he told them.

All of the officers were there. The four flight crews assigned to the mission evaluated this news soberly. 'Our main search radar is pretty good for weather surveillance. We can steer you round the worst of it,' Captain Franks offered. The pilots nodded.

'Mr Clark?' Admiral Greer asked.

'Rain sounds good to me. The only way they can spot me on the inbound leg is the bubbles I leave on the surface of the river. Rain'll break that up. It means I can move in daylight if I have to.' Kelly paused. '*Skate* ready for me?'

'Whenever we say so,' Maxwell answered.

'Then it's "go mission" on my end, sir.' Kelly could feel his skin go cold. But he'd said it anyway.

Eyes turned to Captain Albie, the young marine officer who would take the main force in. A vice-admiral, two rear-admirals, and an up-and-coming CIA field officer now depended on Albie to make the final decision. His was the ultimate operational responsibility. It seemed very strange indeed to the young captain that seven stars needed him to say 'go', but twenty-five marines and perhaps twenty others had their lives riding on his judgment. It was his mission to lead, and it had to be exactly right the first time. He looked over at Kelly and smiled.

'I think it's time for your swim, sir. This mission is go.'

There was no exultation. In fact, every man round the chart table looked down at the maps. Maxwell spoke first to one of the helicopter crews. 'I guess you'd better get your helo warmed up.' Maxwell turned. 'Captain Franks, would you signal *Skate*?' Two crisp aye, aye, sirs answered him.

Kelly put his fear aside as best he could. You can do it, man. You know how. He could feel the determination begin to take over as he walked out of the compartment to pack up his gear. All the decisions were made. He was committed to action now. Kelly's face took a hard set. Dangers were no longer things to be feared, but to be dealt with. To be overcome.

KELLY'S SEA SLED was wheeled out to the flight deck. The helicopter was up and running now, its five-bladed rotor turning in the predawn darkness as Kelly walked through the watertight door.

'Batteries are fully charged. Your gear's in the container. It's watertight, so no problems there, sir. The rifle is loaded and chambered in case you need it in a hurry, safety on. New batteries for all the radios, and two sets of spares,' the chief machinist's mate shouted over the sound of the helicopter engines.

'Sounds good to me,' Kelly shouted back. 'See you—and thanks!'

The big Sikorsky rescue chopper lifted off a few feet. A crewman attached the sled to the bottom, and the helo headed aft, flying off into the darkness without strobes and disappearing in seconds.

USS *SKATE* WAS an old-fashioned submarine, modified and developed from the first nuclear boat, USS *Nautilus*. Her hull was shaped almost like that of a real ship, rather than a whale, which made her relatively slow underwater, but her twin screws made for greater manoeuvrability, especially in shallow water. For years *Skate* had drawn the duty of inshore intelligence ship, creeping close to the Vietnamese coast to snoop on electronic emissions. She'd also put more than one swimmer on the beach. That included Kelly, several years before. He saw her on the surface, a black shape darker than the glistening water. The helicopter pilot first of all set the sled on *Skate*'s foredeck, where the sub's crew secured it in place. Then Kelly and his personal gear were lowered by hoist. A minute later he was in the sub's control room.

'Welcome aboard,' Commander Silvio Esteves said.

'Thank you, sir. How long to the beach?'

'Six hours. Coffee? Food?'

'How about a bed, sir?'

'Use the executive officer's cabin. We'll see you're not disturbed.'

Kelly headed forward to the last real rest he'd have for the next three days—if things went according to plan. He was asleep before the submarine dived back under the waters of the South China Sea.

'THIS IS INTERESTING,' the KGB major said. He dropped the translation on the desk of his immediate superior.

'So the Americans know about this at last,' the other man said.

'Keep reading,' the major suggested.
'Indeed! Who exactly is this Cassius fellow?'
'Glazov did the final recruitment only a short time ago.' The major explained on for a minute or so.
'Well, I'll take it to him, then. I'm surprised Georgiy Borissovich isn't running the case personally.'
'I think he will now.'

'PRETTY CLOSE.' Kelly needed only one look through the periscope to see that Esteves was a cowboy. *Skate* was scraping off barnacles. The periscope was barely above water, the water lapping at the lower half of the lens. 'I suppose that'll do.'
'Good rainstorm topside,' Esteves said.
'Good is right.' Kelly finished his coffee. 'I'm going to use it.'
'Then you better get ready.'
As warm as the waters were, Kelly still had to worry about the cold. Eight hours in water with only a small temperature differential could sap the energy from his body. Alone in the executive officer's stateroom, he worked his way into a green and black wet suit, adding double the normal amount of weight belts.
There was now no turning back, Kelly told himself, opening the door. But for him there rarely was.

20 *FIRST IN*

The sea sled was slightly longer than Kelly was tall. It was, in fact, a modified torpedo, with attachments allowing a man to steer it and control its speed. There was a depth gauge and an up/down-angle indicator, along with a battery-strength gauge and the vital magnetic compass. The electric motor and batteries had originally been designed to drive the shape through the water at high speed for over ten thousand yards. At lower speeds it had five-to-six-hour endurance at five knots.
The whirring of the twin props couldn't be heard any great distance, but Kelly was a mere six feet from them; the steady high-speed whine was already making him grimace inside his diving mask. Part of that was all the coffee he'd drunk. He had to stay nervously alert, and he had enough caffeine in him to enliven a corpse.
So many things to worry about. There were boats on the river. Running into one could be lethal. Visibility was almost nil, and so

Kelly had to assume that he'd have no more than two or three seconds to avoid something. He held to the middle of the channel as best he could. Every thirty minutes he'd slow down and ease his head above the surface for a position fix.

Time crept by, and Kelly concentrated on driving the sled.

PASTOR CHARLES MEYER had been a minister for thirty years, all of his adult life. He was not a stern man; his message of faith was that of mercy and love.

'Welcome back, Doris,' Meyer said as he entered Ray Brown's house. He took both her hands in his, smiling warmly. 'Our prayers are answered.'

For all his pleasant and supportive demeanour, this would be an awkward meeting. Doris had erred, probably rather badly, Meyer thought. Still, the really important thing was that the prodigal had returned. All of Christianity in a single story: no matter how grave one's misdeeds might be, there would always be a welcome for those with the courage to return.

Father and daughter sat together on the old blue sofa, with Meyer to their left in an armchair.

'I'm surprised how good you look, Doris.'

'Thank you, Pastor.'

'It's been hard, hasn't it?'

'Yes. I've seen . . . and done . . . such awful things.'

Meyer was a difficult man to shock. Clergymen were in the profession of listening to stories about the reality of hell. But what he heard now did shock him. Doris told the story in the manner of a motion picture, seemingly leaving nothing out. Prostitution, drugs, sexual abuse.

Pastor Meyer couldn't know what he hadn't been told, the things that Doris had deliberately left out. He knew that a Baltimore physician and nurse had restored his parishioner to physical health. He didn't know how Doris had come to that point, and Meyer assumed that she'd escaped, as the girl Pam had almost done. He also knew that there were other girls still in trouble. As he had dedicated his life to denying souls to Lucifer, so also he had a duty to deny their bodies to him. He had to be careful. A conversation like this one was privileged in the ultimate sense. He would counsel Doris to speak to the police, though he could never force her to do so. But as a man of God, he had to do *something* to help those other girls. Exactly what, he wasn't sure. He'd ask his son about that, a young sergeant with the Pittsburgh city police force.

THERE. KELLY'S HEAD was above the water only enough to expose his eyes. He reached up with his hands to pull the rubber hood off his head. To his north was darkness that his acclimatised eyes began to break into shapes. There was 'his' hilltop, a mile away past another, lower hill. He knew there was a road only a hundred yards away, and at the moment it was totally vacant. It was time.

Kelly steered the sled close to the bank. He selected a place with overhanging trees for the additional concealment, and stripped off the wet suit, stuffing it in the waterproof container on the now surfaced sled. Kelly quickly donned his camouflage fatigues. Next he did his camouflage make-up—dark green on forehead, cheekbones and jaw, with lighter colours under his eyes and in the hollow of his cheeks. Shouldering his gear, he flipped the power switch on the sled. It motored off towards the middle of the river, its flotation chambers vented now, sinking it to the bottom. Kelly turned to the land and climbed the bank, disappearing at once into the thick foliage, moving slowly and deliberately up the first hill.

Climbing the hill took half an hour. It was approaching three in the morning, local time. He stopped to look and listen, then moved on, going down the hill. At the bottom was a small stream that fed into the river. He took the opportunity to fill one of his canteens, dropping in a purification tablet as he did so. He looked up at 'his' hill, a grey mass under the cloudy sky. The rain was picking up as Kelly started his climb.

Halfway up, his eyes got their first look at the prison camp. It was an open space amid forest. He saw a flare of light from one of the guard towers—someone with a cigarette, no doubt.

It almost came as a surprise when he reached the top. He sat down for a moment, making himself still, looking and listening some more before he began his examination of the camp. He found a very good spot, perhaps twenty feet below the crest. This was his place on his hill. He reached into his jacket and pulled out one of his radios.

'Snake calling Cricket. Over.'

'Snake, this is Cricket, reading you five by five,' one of the communicators replied from the *Ogden*.

'In place, beginning surveillance. Over.'

Kelly took the binoculars from their case and began examining the camp. There were guards in all four towers, two of them smoking. There was a single automobile present, parked near the building that had to house the officers at this compound. There were no lights at all, and no sounds.

At quarter to four Kelly saw some flickering lights in the barracks.

Guard change? The two soldiers in the tower nearest him were stretching, chatting to each other. They were bored.

Good news, Kelly told himself. Stay bored, guys.

COLONEL GLAZOV DIDN'T LIKE working at weekends any more than his Western counterparts, even less so when it was because his administrative assistant had set this report on the wrong pile. 'Bloody hell,' he said in English as he examined the thing. The case officer had described the first-contact meeting in exquisite detail.

'Boxwood Green,' Glazov said. The question was whether or not to forward the data to the Vietnamese. The colonel lifted the phone and dialled his most immediate superior, who was also at home and instantly in a foul humour.

SUNRISE WAS GREY. Kelly checked his watch, making mental notes at every point. The guard force was forty-four men, plus four officers. There was one Russian officer, a tall colonel. All except the eight on tower duty formed up just after dawn for calisthenics, which lasted half an hour, until the soldiers headed off for morning chow. The tower guards spent most of their time leaning on their elbows.

Kelly made another check of his surroundings, catching the pattern of birdcalls, getting used to it so that a change would register at once. He had a green cloth across the muzzle of his weapon, a floppy hat to break up the outline of his head within the bush, and the facial camouflage paint, all of which conspired to make him invisible.

At eight the guard cycle changed again. Those relieved from the towers went in. Kelly watched the Russian colonel walk across the parade ground. A Vietnamese major went towards him and saluted. Two men took posts at the gate, bored before they got there, looking out at the road for traffic that would probably never come to this backwater camp.

SERGEANT PETER MEYER smoked. His father didn't approve, but accepted his son's weakness so long as he did it outside, as they were now, on the back porch of the parsonage after dinner.

'It's Doris Brown, right?' Peter asked. At twenty-six he was one of his department's youngest sergeants. 'I remember her. She had a reputation as a hot number a few years back.'

'Peter, you know I can't say. This is a pastoral matter. I will counsel the person to speak to you when the time is right, but—'

'Pop, you have to understand, we're talking two homicides here. Two dead people, plus the drug business. That's heavy stuff.'

'Even worse than that,' his father reported more quietly still. 'They don't just kill the girls. Torture, sexual abuse. It's horrible. I know I have to do something, but I can't—'

'Yeah, I know you can't. OK, I can call the people in Baltimore and fill them in. I'll call first thing tomorrow morning.'

'Will it put the person in danger?' Meyer asked.

'Shouldn't,' Peter judged.

THE KGB *REZIDENT* in Hanoi had general-major rank, and his job was mainly that of spying on his country's putative allies. The enciphered dispatch on his desk was interesting, all the more so since it did not give him direct guidance on what to do about it. How like the Moscow bureaucrats!

He knew about the camp, of course. Colonel Grishanov was using irregular methods, but he was reporting good results. Now the colonel had come up with the boldest idea of all. Instead of letting the Vietnamese kill the prisoners in due course, bring them home to Mother Russia. It was brilliant in its way, and the KGB general was trying to decide if he'd endorse the idea to Moscow. On the whole, he thought that the idea had real merit . . . and that decided matters.

As entertaining as it might be for the Americans to rescue their people with this Boxwood Green operation, it would also mean that the knowledge locked in those American minds would be lost to his country, and it was knowledge they must have.

How long could he wait? The Americans moved quickly, but not that quickly. Operation Kingpin had gone on for ever, else it would have succeeded. Only good luck had allowed them to warn Hanoi, and then almost too late—but now they had real forewarning.

The general lifted his phone.

21 *LAST OUT*

In their quarters aboard USS *Ogden*, the marines were assembled around a sand-table model of the objective. They'd already gone over the mission once and were doing so again.

'Captain Albie, sir?' A yeoman came into the compartment. He handed over a clipboard. 'Message from Mr Snake.'

'Thanks, sailor.' Albie read the dispatch. 'People, our friend is in place. He counts forty-four guards, four officers, one Russian. Normal duty routine, nothing unusual is happening there.' He looked up. 'That's it, marines. We're going in tonight.'

'HOMICIDE.'

'Hi, I'm trying to get Lieutenant Frank Allen.'

'You got him,' Allen replied. 'Who's this?'

'Sergeant Pete Meyer, Pittsburgh,' the voice replied.

'What can I do for you, Sarge?'

'Lieutenant, I have some information for you. Two homicides, both victims female, in their late teens, early twenties.'

'Back up, please. Who's your source?'

'I can't reveal that yet. It's privileged. I'm working on changing that, but it might take a while. Can I go on?'

'Very well. Names of victims?' Allen got a sheet of paper.

'The recent one was Pamela Madden—only a few weeks ago.'

Lieutenant Allen's eyes went wide. 'The fountain murder. And the other one?'

'Her name was Helen, some time last fall. Both murders were ugly, Lieutenant—torture and sexual abuse.'

Allen hunched forward with the phone very close to his ear. 'You telling me you have a witness to both killings?'

'That is correct, sir. I got two likely perps for you, too. Two white males, one named Billy and the other named Rick.'

'OK, they're not my cases. It's being handled downtown—Lieutenant Emmet Ryan and Sergeant Tom Douglas. These are high-profile cases, Sarge. How solid is your information?'

'I believe it to be very solid. I have one possible indicator for you. Pamela Madden—her hair was brushed out after she was killed.'

In every major criminal case, several important pieces of evidence are always left out of press accounts in order to screen out false confessions. This thing with the hair was sufficiently protected that even Lieutenant Allen didn't know about it.

'What else do you have?'

'The murders were drug-related. Both girls were carriers.'

'Bingo!' Allen exclaimed. 'Is your source in jail or what?'

'I'll level with you. My dad's a preacher. He's counselling the girl. Lieutenant, this is really off-the-record stuff, OK?'

'I understand. What do you want me to do?'

'Could you please forward the info to the investigating officers? They can contact me.' Sergeant Meyer gave over his number.

'Very well, Sergeant. I'll pass that along. Thanks a lot. You'll be hearing from Em and Tom.' Allen switched buttons on his phone.

'HEY, FRANK,' Lieutenant Ryan said as he picked up his pen. 'Keep talking. I'm writing this down.'

Sergeant Douglas came in with his usual coffee and Danish, to see his boss scribbling furiously.

'Brushed out the hair? He said that?' Ryan asked. Douglas leaned across the desk. 'OK, Frank, where is this guy? Thanks. Bye.'

'Break?'

'Call from a police sergeant in Pittsburgh—a possible witness in the murders of Pamela Madden and Helen Waters. This is the one who brushed her hair, Tom. And guess what other names came along?'

'Richard Farmer and William Grayson?'

'Rick and Billy. Close enough? Possible carrier for a drug ring. Wait.' Ryan leaned back. 'There was a girl there when Farmer was killed . . . we think there was,' he corrected himself. 'It's the connection, Tom. Pamela Madden, Helen Waters, Farmer, Grayson, they're all related, and that means—'

'The pushers, too. All connected somehow. What connects them, Em? We know they were probably all in the drug business.'

'Two different MOs, Tom. The girls were slaughtered like . . . no, you don't even do that to cattle. All the rest, though, all of them were taken down by the Invisible Man. Man on a mission! That's what Farber said—a man on a mission.'

'Revenge,' Douglas said, developing Ryan's analysis. 'If one of those girls was close to me . . . Em, who could blame him?'

There was only one person connected with either murder who'd been close with a victim, and he was known to the police department. Ryan grabbed his phone and called back to Allen.

'Frank, what was the name of your friend who was shot in the fountain murder case—the navy guy?'

'Kelly, John Kelly.'

'Tell me about him, Frank.'

'Hell of a nice guy. Quiet, kinda sad. Lost his wife—auto accident or something.'

'Veteran, right?'

'Special-operations group, a spin-off of underwater demolitions, but called SEALs now, for Sea Air Land.'

'Keep going.'

'Physically he's pretty tough, takes care of himself.' Allen paused. 'He's seen combat. I got his address and all if you want.'

'I have it in my case file, Frank. Thanks, buddy.' Ryan hung up. 'He's our guy. Kelly's the Invisible Man.'

NIGHTFALL. IT HAD BEEN a dreary day for everyone at Sender Green except for Kelly. The parade ground was mush, with fetid puddles.

Weather like this made the soldiers irritable and dull of mind, all the more so if their duty was also boring, as it was here.

Kelly took the opportunity of the darkness to move around, stiff from the inactivity. He sat up under his bush, eating some of his rations. He drained down a full canteen, then stretched. He could see the landing zone and had already selected his path to it. At 2100 he made his final radio transmission.

'LIGHT GREEN,' the technician wrote on his pad—Activity normal.

'That's it. That's the last thing we need.' Maxwell looked at the others. Everyone nodded.

'Operation commences at twenty-two hundred. Captain Franks, make signal to *Newport News*!'

'Aye, aye, sir.'

On *Ogden*, flight crews walked aft to preflight their aircraft. In the troop spaces the marines were donning their striped utilities. No smiles or joking now.

In the squadron ready room aboard USS *Constellation*, a young squadron commander led the briefing for the air attack.

'We're covering a special operation tonight. Our targets are SAM sites south of Haiphong,' he went on, not knowing what it was all about, hoping it was all as important as Admiral Podulski had said. Playing games with surface-to-air missile sites wasn't exactly fun.

USS *Newport News* was twenty-five miles off the coast, approaching a point that would put her exactly between *Ogden* and the beach. The captain was sitting in his bridge chair. He checked his watch and opened a sealed envelope, reading quickly through the gunnery targets in the action orders he'd had in his safe for two weeks.

IT WAS THE TIME for nerves now. What could go wrong? Kelly asked himself atop his hill. Lots of things. He'd seen missions go wrong for any number of dumb and unpredictable reasons. But not tonight; not with all this preparation. He'd made no mistakes for this mission. Nobody had. The former chief of SEALs checked the illuminated dial of his watch and commanded himself to take a deep breath and continue the mission. For him that meant laying the carbine across his lap and concentrating on his binoculars. His reconnaissance had to continue right to the moment the first M-79 grenades were fired at the guard towers. The marines were counting on him.

EDDIE MORELLO DROVE up Route 40 towards Aberdeen, Maryland, in his Cadillac convertible. The top was down. Eddie liked the sun and the wind. It was almost like being out on his fishing boat. It also gave him fine visibility. That it made him somewhat easier to spot and trail hadn't occurred to him. Next to him, on the floor, was a leather attaché case. Inside that were six kilos of pure stuff. Big cash deal. Two guys. Nothing to worry about. Make the transfer and drive back. Dinner with Tony.

Morello was right on time as he pulled into the half-empty parking lot of a diner—the old-fashioned kind, made from a railroad car.

The other car pulled in. It was a blue Oldsmobile, as he'd been led to expect. The two guys got out. One carried an attaché case and walked towards him, while the back-up man stayed at the car, watching, just to be on the safe side.

'Got the stuff?'

'Got the money?' Morello asked in return.

'You made a mistake, Eddie,' the man said without warning as he opened the briefcase.

'What do you mean?' Morello asked, suddenly alert.

'I mean, it's goodbye, Eddie,' he added quietly.

The look in the eyes said it all. Morello immediately went for his weapon, but it only helped the other man.

'Police, freeze!' the man shouted just before the first round burst through the opened top of the case.

Eddie got his gun out, just, and managed to fire one round into the floor of his car, but the cop was only three feet away and couldn't possibly miss. The back-up officer was already running in. As he watched, the attaché case fell aside and Lieutenant Charon extended his arm, nearly placing his service revolver on the man's chest and firing straight into his heart.

'Back-up!' Charon screamed over the dying man. He reached down to seize Eddie's revolver. Within a minute two state police cars screeched into the parking lot.

'Damned fool,' Charon told his partner five minutes later, shaking as he did so, as men do after killing. 'He just went for the gun—like I didn't have the drop on him.'

'I saw it all,' the junior detective said, thinking he had.

'Well, it's just what you said, sir,' the state police sergeant said. He opened the case from the floor of the Cadillac. It was filled with bags of heroin. 'Some bust.'

'Yeah,' Charon growled. Remarkable, he thought, succeeding in his struggle not to smile at the mad humour of the moment. He'd just committed the perfect murder, under the eyes of other police officers. Now Henry's organisation was safe.

ALMOST TIME NOW. The rain continued to fall. Good. Thc soldiers in the towers were huddling to stay dry. All the lights were out now. Kelly made a slow sweep with his binoculars. There was a human shape in the window of the officers' quarters, a man looking out at the weather—the Russian, wasn't it?

Now it was up to the air force, then the marines. His part was almost done, Kelly thought.

'COMMENCE FIRING,' the captain of *Newport News* ordered.

The first rounds off were from the port-side five-inch mount. The sharp bark of noise was very hard on the ears, but along with it came something oddly beautiful. With each shot, the guns generated a ring of yellow fire. Then after its few milliseconds of life it vanished. Six thousand yards downrange, the first pair of star shells ignited, and the wet, green landscape of North Vietnam turned orange under the light.

THE MARINES WERE lightly loaded as they filed aft. Albie and Irvin counted them off, directing them to their choppers.

The last sailors in line were Maxwell and Podulski. Both were wearing their oldest and most disreputable khakis—shirts and trousers they'd worn in command at sea, things associated with good memories and good luck. Even admirals were superstitious.

'All ready, Captain?' Maxwell asked.

'Yes, sir,' Albie replied. 'See you in about three hours.'

'Good hunting.' Maxwell saluted the younger man.

ONLY MINUTES NOW until the marines were on the ground. The rain remained steady though the wind had died down.

Kelly was in the open now. It was safe. He wasn't skylined. There was ample flora behind him. His clothing and skin were coloured to blend in. His eyes were sweeping everywhere, searching for danger, for something unusual, finding nothing. He was concentrating so much with his eyes that he almost neglected his ears.

It was hard to pick it out through the rain—a distant rumble, low and tenuous, but it didn't fade. It grew in intensity. Kelly lifted his head from the eyepieces, turning, trying to figure it out.

Motors. Truck motors. Well, OK, there was a road not too far away. A supply truck maybe. Delivering food and mail.

Kelly moved to the top of the hill, leaning against a tree, looking down to where a dirt road traced the north bank of the river. Movement. He put the glasses on it.

Truck . . . two . . . three . . . four. Oh, my God!

They had lights on—just slits, the headlights taped over. That meant military trucks. People in the back, lined on both sides.

Soldiers.

They turned round the base of his hill. A guard in one of the towers shouted something. Lights came on in the officers' quarters. Somebody came out, not dressed, shouting a question.

The first truck stopped at the gate. A man roared for somebody to open it. The other truck stopped behind it. Soldiers dismounted. Kelly counted: ten . . . twenty . . . thirty . . . more . . . But it wasn't the number, it was what they started to do.

Kelly reached for his radio and flipped it on.

'Cricket, this is Snake. Over.'

'WHAT GIVES?' Podulski asked.

Maxwell took the microphone. 'Snake, this is Cricket Actual. What is your message? Over.'

'Abort, abort, abort—acknowledge,' was what they all heard.

'Say again, Snake. Say again.'

'Abort the mission,' Kelly said, too loudly for his own safety. 'Abort, abort, abort. Acknowledge immediately.'

It took a few seconds. 'We copy your order to abort. Acknowledged. Mission aborted. Stand by.'

'WHAT IS IT?' Major Vinh, the camp commander, asked.

'We have information that the Americans may try to raid your camp,' the captain replied, looking back at his men. They were deploying skilfully, half heading for trees, the other half taking positions inside the perimeter. 'Comrade Major, you are ordered to take your Russian guest to Hanoi for safety.'

'DAMN IT, DUTCH! Now what—'

'The mission's aborted, Cas,' Maxwell said.

'But *why*?'

'Because Mr Clark said so,' Ritter answered. 'He's the eyes. He makes the call. You don't need anybody to tell you that, Admiral. We still have a man in there, gentlemen. Let's not forget that.'

'We have *twenty* men in there.'

'That's true, sir, but only one of them is coming out tonight.' *And then only if we're lucky*.

HE COULD HEAR THEM coming. Far off, moving without a great deal of skill, probably tired, but coming.

'Cricket, this is Snake. Over.'

'We read you, Snake.'

'I'm moving. There are people on my hill, coming my way. I will head west. Can you send a helo for me?'

'Affirmative. Be careful, son.' It was Maxwell's voice.

22 TRAVEL AGENTS

Had he had the time to reflect, Kelly might have considered how quickly things could go from good to bad. But he didn't. Survival was an all-encompassing game, and at the moment it was also the only game in town.

The only thing that made sense was to put as much distance as possible between himself and the North Vietnamese Army. They'd probably keep their firepower in close. It wasn't a time to panic, but he couldn't dally either. Failure to get out before dawn would materially degrade Kelly's chances of ever escaping this country. Move. Find a good spot. Call the helo. Get out of here. He had four hours until dawn. The helo was about thirty minutes away. Make it two or three hours to find a spot and make the call. Kelly took a few minutes to look around, orientating himself. Then he started moving.

Kelly got to the bottom of the hill, into thicker growth. There. Right across the road was an open space, a meadow or something. That would do just fine. He grabbed his radio.

'Snake to Cricket. Over.'

'This is Cricket. We read you, and we are standing by.'

'West of my hill, past the road, about two miles west of objective, open field. I'm close. Send the helo. I can mark with strobe.'

Albie looked at the map, then the aerial photos. 'Roger, copy. Rescue One is moving in now, two zero minutes away.'

'Copy that. I'll be ready. Out.'

MISERABLE ROADS, Grishanov thought, even worse than those in Russia. Remarkably enough, the car ran fairly well, or would have done so except for the driver. Major Vinh ought to have driven it himself. As an officer he probably knew how, but status-conscious fool that he was, he had to let his orderly do it, and this little lump of a peasant probably didn't know how to drive anything more complicated than an ox. The car was swerving in the mud. The driver was having trouble seeing in the rain, as well. Grishanov closed his eyes in the rear seat, clutching his backpack.

EUT-U 68

KELLY TOOK HIS TIME NOW, moving slowly and quietly towards the road. He waited, listening for the sound of a truck's engine, which was the greatest danger to him. Nothing. OK, about five minutes on the helo now. He started to cross the road.

The sound of the approaching car, swishing through the muddy surface of the road, was a little too close to the environmental noises, and by the time Kelly recognised the difference, it was too late. When the car came round the bend, he was right in the middle of the road, standing there like a deer in the headlights, and surely the driver must see him. What followed was automatic.

Kelly brought his carbine up and fired a short burst into the driver's area. The car didn't swerve for a moment, and he laid a second burst into the front passenger seat. The car changed direction then, slamming into a tree. The entire sequence could not have taken three seconds. He ran to the car. Who had he killed?

The driver had come through the windscreen, two rounds in his brain. Kelly wrenched open the passenger door. The person there was—the Vietnamese major! Also hit in the head. Kelly yanked him out of the vehicle and had knelt down to search him before he heard a groan from the inside. He lunged inside, finding another man—Russian!—on the floor in the rear. Kelly pulled him out, too. The man had a backpack clutched in his hands.

The routine came as automatically as the shot. Kelly clubbed the Russian unconscious with his buttstock, then quickly turned back to rifle the major's uniform for intelligence material. He stuffed all documents into his pockets.

'What the hell do I do with you?' Kelly asked, turning to the Russian. He knelt there, opening the backpack and finding whole sheaves of paper, which answered his question for him.

'I GOT THE STROBE!' the copilot said.

'Coming in hot.' The pilot was driving his Sikorsky as hard as the engines would allow. The rescue helicopter came to a steady hover two feet over the clearing.

'Did I see *two* people out there?' he asked over the intercom.

'Go, go, go!' another voice said. 'Pax aboard now, go!'

'Getting the hell outa Dodge City, now!' The pilot pulled for altitude, heading back to the river as the helicopter accelerated. Wasn't there just supposed to be one person? He set it aside. He had to fly now, and it was thirty twisty miles to the water and safety.

'Who is this?' Gunnery Sergeant Irvin asked Kelly.

'Hitchhiker,' Kelly answered above the noise of the engines.

Explanations would be lengthy and would have to wait. Irvin understood, offering him a canteen. Kelly drained it. The door gunners scanned the river valley while their aircraft screamed out, barely a hundred feet over the meandering surface. What had gone wrong? they all wanted to know. The answer was in the man they'd just picked up. But who was the other one, and wasn't that a Russian uniform? Two marines sat over him. One of them tied his hands up. A third secured the pack's flap in place with the straps.

LIEUTENANT MARK CHARON was surprisingly chipper for a man who'd been through a fatal shooting and the almost as rigorous interrogation that had followed it.

'Anything you might have done to spook him?' Frank Allen asked.

Charon shook his head. 'No. I didn't shout or anything until he went for his piece. I tried to calm him down, y'know. But he just jumped the wrong way. Eddie Morello died of the dumbs,' the narcotics-division lieutenant observed, impassively enjoying the fact that he was telling the exact truth.

'Well, I'm not gonna cry over the death of a doper. Good day all around, Mark.'

'How's that, Frank?' Charon sat down and stole a cigarette.

'Got a call from Pittsburgh today. Seems there may be a witness for the fountain murder that Em and Tom are handling.'

'That's good news. What do we have?'

'Somebody—probably a girl from how the guy was talking—who saw Madden and Waters get it. Sounds like she's talking to her minister about it and he's trying to coax her into opening up.'

'Great,' Charon observed, concealing his inward chill. One more thing to clean up. With luck that would be the end of it.

THE HELICOPTER FLARED and made a soft landing on USS *Ogden*. As soon as it was down, Irvin and another marine climbed out, holding a body. Kelly alighted next.

'Let's get this guy inside and isolated right now,' Ritter said.

'He's unconscious, sir.'

'Then get a medic, too,' Ritter ordered.

They picked one of *Ogden*'s many empty troop-berthing spaces for the debrief. Kelly was allowed to wash his face, but nothing else. A medical corpsman checked out the Russian, pronouncing him dazed but healthy. A pair of marines stood guard over him.

'Four trucks,' Kelly said. 'They just drove right in. A reinforced platoon—weapons platoon, probably—they showed up while the assault team was inbound, started digging in. About fifty of 'em.'

Greer and Ritter traded a look. No coincidence.

Kelly looked at Maxwell. 'I'm sorry, sir.' He paused. 'It would not have been possible to execute the mission. The chances of success were exactly zero.'

'You're sure?' Maxwell asked.

Kelly nodded. 'Yes, sir. Sure as hell.'

'What about our guest, Mr Clark?' Ritter asked.

Kelly explained how the car had got so close. 'I killed the driver and the camp commander—I think that's what he was. He had all this on him.' Kelly reached into his pockets and handed over the documents. 'Lots of papers on the Russian. I figured it wasn't smart to leave him there. I thought maybe he might be useful to us.'

'These papers are in Russian,' Irvin announced.

'Give me some,' Ritter ordered. 'My Russian's pretty good.'

'We need somebody who can read Vietnamese, too.'

'I have one of those,' Albie said.

'WHERE AM I?' Grishanov asked in Russian. He tried to reach for his blindfold, but his hands couldn't move.

'You're aboard USS *Ogden*, Colonel,' Ritter told him in English.

'I am a Soviet officer. You have no right—'

'We have as much right as you had to interrogate American prisoners of war and to conspire to kill them, Comrade Colonel.'

'ARE YOU KIDDING ME?'

'Mr Clark, the world can be a very complicated place. Anyway, this Grishanov guy was going to a considerable effort to keep our people alive.' Ritter held up another sheet. 'Here's a request for better food—for a *doctor*, even.'

'So what do we do with him?' Admiral Podulski asked.

'That, gentlemen, is our department,' Ritter said, looking at Greer, who nodded.

'And finally'—Ritter tapped a translation of the Vietnamese message—'we know that somebody betrayed the mission. We're going to track that bastard down.'

'WHERE'S JOHN?'

Sandy O'Toole looked up from her paperwork. It was close to the end of her shift, and Professor Rosen's question brought to the fore a worry that she'd managed to suppress.

'Out of the country. Why?'

'I got a call today from the police. They're looking for him.'
'Why?'
'He didn't say.' Rosen looked around. They were alone at the nurses' station. 'Sandy, I know he's been doing things . . . I mean, I think I know, but I haven't—'
'I haven't heard from him either. What should we do?'
Rosen grimaced and looked away before replying. 'As good citizens, we're supposed to cooperate with the police—but we're not doing that, are we? No idea where he is?'
'He told me, but I'm not supposed to . . . He's doing something with the government, over in . . .' She couldn't finish. 'He gave a number I can call. I haven't used it.'
'I would,' Sam told her, and left.

'PITTSBURGH?'
'That's what he said,' Henry Tucker confirmed.
'It's cute, by the way, having him as your man on the inside. Very professional,' Tony Piaggi said with respect.
'He said we need to take care of it quick. She hasn't said much yet. The family name is Brown. Her name is Doris. Her father's name is Raymond. You got connections. I need you to use 'em fast.'
Piaggi copied down the information. 'OK. Our Philly connections can handle it. It's not going to be cheap, Henry.'
'I didn't expect it would be.'

'SEVEN ONE THREE ONE,' the female voice said.
'Hello. I'm trying to get Admiral James Greer,' Sandy told the secretary. 'It's important.'
'Could you tell me who's calling, please?'
Sandy took a deep breath. 'A friend of mine gave me this number to call. He's with Admiral Greer. He said I could call here to find out if he's OK.'
'I don't understand.'
'Look, I *know* he went to Vietnam.'
'Miss, I cannot discuss where Admiral Greer is.' *Who violated security?* She'd have to make a report on this.
'It's not about him, it's about John!'
'John who?' the secretary asked.
Deep breath. Swallow. 'Please get a message to Admiral Greer. This is Sandy. It's about John. He will understand. OK? This is most important.' She gave her home and work numbers.
'Thank you. I will do what I can.' The line went dead.

USS *OGDEN* PULLED into Subic Bay Naval Station in the Philippines in the early afternoon. The marines filed off to a bus that would take them to Cubi Point, where their C-141 was waiting for the flight stateside. Mr Clark, they saw, wasn't with them.

'JOHN, IT SEEMS you have a lady friend who's worried about you,' Greer said, handing the message over.

It was the friendliest of the dispatches that had been brought up from Manila to Subic Bay. Kelly scanned it while three admirals reviewed the other, less welcome messages. Admirals Maxwell and Podulski were being summoned back to Washington soonest to report on the failure of Boxwood Green. Ritter and Greer had similar orders, though they also had an ace in the hole—a plane waiting at Clark Air Base.

Colonel Grishanov came into the sunlight along with the admirals. Ritter was talking to him quietly in Russian as all six men walked down to the waiting cars. Ten minutes later they climbed into an air-force Beechcraft to fly to Clark. Half an hour later that aircraft taxied right alongside a large Boeing jet, which got off less than an hour after they'd left *Ogden*. Kelly found himself a nice wide seat and was asleep before the transport started rolling. The next stop was Hickam in Hawaii.

23 *HOME IS THE HUNTER*

The flight wasn't as restful for Greer and Ritter and their Russian guest. Ritter handled most of the interrogation. His first task was to explain to Grishanov that they had no plans to kill him. Yes, they were CIA. Yes, Ritter was a field officer—a spy, if you like. But that was his job, as Kolya—do you mind if I call you Kolya?—had *his* job. Now, please, Colonel, can you give us the names of our men? (That was already listed in Grishanov's voluminous notes.) Yes, we are very grateful indeed for your efforts to keep them alive. Of *course* you'll go home to your family.

Damn, Greer thought, but Bob is good at this sort of thing. It wasn't about courage or patriotism. It was about humanity. Colonel Grishanov was a tough hombre, but he was fundamentally a man, and the quality of his character worked against him. He didn't want the American prisoners to die. That plus the stress of capture, plus the whiplash surprise of the cordial treatment, plus a lot of good brandy, all conspired to loosen the Russian's tongue.

A HARD LANDING at Hickam startled Kelly into wakefulness. The aircraft taxied to a remote part of the base for refuelling and servicing. Kelly took the time to get out and walk around. He found a phone in the distinguished-visitors' lounge and placed a call.

'Hello?' the groggy voice said, five thousand miles away.

'Hi, Sandy. It's John,' he said with a smile.

'John! Where are you?'

'Would you believe Hawaii?'

'You're OK?'

'A little tired, but, yes. No holes or anything,' he reported. Just the sound of her voice had brightened his day. But not for long.

'John, there's a problem.' As Kelly listened, the sergeant at the reception desk saw his face change.

'OK. It must be Doris,' Kelly said. 'I mean, only you and the docs know about me, and—'

'It wasn't us,' Sandy assured him.

'OK. Please call Doris and . . . be careful, but . . .'

'Warn her off?'

'Can you do that?'

'Yes!'

Kelly tried to relax a little. 'I'll be back in about . . . oh, nine or ten hours. Will you be at work?'

'I have the day off.'

'OK, Sandy. See you soon. Bye.'

'John!' she called urgently.

'What?'

'I want . . . I mean—' Her voice stopped.

Kelly smiled again. 'We can talk about that when I get there, honey.' Maybe he wasn't just going home. Maybe he was going home *to* something. Kelly made a quick inventory of everything he'd done. He'd left behind no evidence that he knew of. The police might be interested in talking to him, fine. He did *not* have to talk to them. That was one of the nice things about the Constitution, Kelly thought as he walked back to the aircraft and trotted up the stairs.

He sat with the CIA officers. The Russian, he saw, was snoring loudly and blissfully.

'So what's the story?' Kelly asked.

Ritter explained what he knew. The camp had indeed been established as a bargaining chip for use with the Russians, but it seemed that the Vietnamese had used that particular chip in a rather inefficient way and were now thinking about eliminating it, along with the prisoners.

'You mean because of the raid?'

'Correct. But settle down, Clark. We got us a Russian, and that's a bargaining chip too. Mr Clark,' Ritter said with a tight smile, 'I like your style.'

'What do you mean?'

'Bringing that Russian in, you showed commendable initiative. And the way you blew the mission off showed good judgment.'

'Look, I didn't . . . I mean, I couldn't . . .'

'You didn't screw up. Somebody else might have. You made a quick decision, and it was the right decision. Interested in serving your country?' Ritter asked.

REVEREND MEYER PARKED near the Brown house. He had to persuade Doris to speak to his son. Peter had assured him that they'd be extremely careful. Yes, Pop, we can protect her. Now all he had to do was to get that message across to a frightened young woman and her father.

Meyer climbed up the worn concrete steps and pushed the button. He could hear the doorbell's two-tone chime. Raymond's white Ford was parked right here. He knew they were home, but no one came to the door. He pushed the button again. He was slow to note that the door wasn't quite closed all the way. With a degree of uneasiness he pushed it open and stuck his head inside. The TV was on.

'Hello? Raymond? . . . Doris?' he called, loudly enough to be heard anywhere in the house. 'Hellooooo!'

This was odd. He stepped inside. There was a cigarette burning in an ashtray, almost down to the filter, and the vertical trail of smoke was a clear warning that something was amiss. Meyer walked through the living room, quiet now, listening. He found the kitchen empty too. The basement door was open as well, the light on. He couldn't stop now. He started down. He was halfway to the bottom when he saw their legs.

Father and daughter were face down on the bare concrete floor, and the blood from their head wounds had pooled together. Meyer's mouth dropped open with a sudden intake of breath as he looked down at them. They were holding hands. He recovered after a few seconds, continued down the stairs and knelt, touching the intertwined hands and entreating God to have mercy on their souls.

'HELLO.'

'Mr Brown?'

'No. Who's this?'

'This is Sandy. Is Mr Brown there?'

'How do you know the Brown family?'

'Who is this?' Sandy asked with alarm.

'This is Sergeant Peter Meyer, Pittsburgh Police Department. Now, who are you?'

'I'm the one who drove Doris back. What's the matter?'

'Your name, please?'

'Are they OK?'

'They appear to have been murdered,' Meyer replied in a harshly patient way. 'Now, I need to know your name and—'

Sandy O'Toole brought her finger down on the switch, cutting the circuit. To hear more might force her to answer questions. Her legs were shaking, but there was a chair close by. It wasn't possible, she told herself. How could anyone know where Doris was?

'Why?' She whispered the question aloud. She couldn't have hurt anyone . . . Yes she could, but how did they find out?

They have the police infiltrated. She remembered the words from John's mouth. He was right, wasn't he?

'Damn it, we saved her!' Sandy told the kitchen. That was her task in life, to make sick people well. She'd done that. She was proud of that. She started crying and had to go to the downstairs bathroom, grabbing tissue to wipe her eyes. Then she looked in the mirror, seeing eyes that she'd never beheld before. And seeing that, she truly understood. Disease was a dragon that she fought forty hours or more per week. But there was more than one kind of dragon, wasn't there? Some couldn't be killed with kindness and medications and skilled nursing care. She'd defeated one, but another had killed Doris anyway. *That* dragon needed the sword, in the hands of a warrior. Someone had to hold that sword. John wasn't a bad man at all, just realistic.

She fought her dragons. He fought his. *It was the same fight*. She'd been wrong to judge him. Now she understood, seeing in her eyes the same emotion that she'd beheld months earlier in his, as her rage passed, but not very far, and the determination set in.

'WELL, EVERYBODY lucked out,' Hicks said, handing over a beer.

'How so, Wally?' Peter Henderson asked.

'The mission was aborted. Everyone's flying home right now.'

'Good news, Wally!' Henderson said, meaning it. He just wanted the damned war to end, the same as Wally did. It was a shame about the men in that camp, but some things couldn't be helped. 'What happened exactly?'

'Nobody knows yet. You want me to find out?'

Peter nodded. 'But you have to be careful.'

'No problem.' Hicks lit up his first joint of the evening.

THE FOLLOWING WINDS had allowed the transport to make the hop from Hawaii to Washington without a refuelling stop, and the landing was a gentle one. It was five in the afternoon.

'Can I get a day or two off?' Kelly asked.

'We'll want you back to Quantico for an extended debrief,' Ritter told him, stiff and sore from the flight.

'Fine. Just so I'm not in custody or anything. I could use a lift up to Baltimore.'

'I'll see what I can do,' Greer said as the plane came to a halt.

Two security officers from the Agency were the first up the mobile stairs, even before the oversized cargo hatch swung up.

Ritter woke the Russian up. 'Welcome to Washington.'

Grishanov was groggy, rubbing his head. He went with the security officers, down the steps to their waiting car. It left at once for a safe house near Winchester, Virginia.

Maxwell and Podulski also had a car waiting. From the hatch, Kelly watched them enter it.

Greer led Kelly out and down the stairs. He, too, had a ride waiting. He directed his driver to head to the wing-headquarters building, where he arranged a car to take Kelly to Baltimore. 'Get some rest and call me when you're ready. Bob was serious about what he said. Think it over.'

'Yes, sir,' Kelly replied, heading to the blue air-force car.

It was amazing, Kelly thought. Everything about him—the highway exit signs, the rush hour—proclaimed the normality of life, when three days earlier everything had been alien and hostile. Most amazing of all, he'd adjusted to it. The driver didn't speak a word all the way to Kelly's apartment except to enquire about directions.

Five minutes after arriving there, Kelly was in the shower. Another five and he was dressed in slacks and a short-sleeved shirt and headed out of the door to his Scout. Another ten and he'd parked the car within sight of Sandy's bungalow. He'd come home to something, Kelly told himself. For the first time.

'John!' He hadn't expected the hug—less so, the tears.

'It's OK, Sandy. I'm fine.' He was slow to grasp the desperation of her hold on him, pleasant as it was. But then the face against his chest started sobbing, and he knew that this event was not for him at all. 'What's wrong?'

'They killed Doris.'

Time stopped. It seemed to split into many pieces. Kelly closed his eyes. 'What happened, Sandy?'

She still clung to him. 'We got her well, John. We took her home, and then I called today, like you told me to, and a policeman answered. Doris and her father—both murdered.' Her face came up. 'Doris said there were others, other girls, they still have.'

'Billy said the same thing. I'm going to try to get them out.'

'WELL, HENRY, that little job was taken care of this morning,' Tony Piaggi told him. 'Nice and clean.'

'They didn't leave—'

'Henry, they were two pros, OK? They didn't leave anything behind except two bodies.'

'Then that's that,' Tucker observed with satisfaction. He reached into his pocket and pulled out a fat envelope. He handed it to Piaggi, who had fronted the money himself. 'With Eddie out of the way and with that leak plugged, things ought to go back to normal.'

'Henry, the other girls?' Piaggi pointed out. 'You've got a real business now. People inside like them are dangerous. Take care of it.' He pocketed the envelope and left the table.

'JOHN, I UNDERSTAND,' Sandy told him quietly. Both were surprised at how strong her voice was, how determined. 'I didn't before, but I do now.' Sandy took his hand and smiled. 'You love too much, John,' she said. 'You're like me.'

Those words brought his head up.

'We lose patients all the time—and I hate it! I hate being there when life goes away. I hate knowing that we couldn't stop it from happening. And with Doris—we won that one, John, and somebody took her away anyway. Somebody meant to do it. She was one of *mine*, and somebody killed her and her father. So I do understand, OK? I really do.'

She really does, thought Kelly . . . better than me.

'Everybody connected with Pam and Doris—you're all in danger now.'

Sandy nodded. 'You're probably right. She told us things about Henry. I know what kind of person he is. I'll tell you everything she told us.'

'You do understand what I'll do with that information?'

'Yes, John, I do. Please be careful.' She paused and told him why he had to be. 'I want you back.'

24 *HOME IS THE PREY*

The one bit of usable information to come out of Pittsburgh was a name—Sandy. A female voice, young, she'd hung up before saying anything, though it hardly seemed likely that she'd had anything at all to do with the murders.

How did it fit in? Ryan leaned back in his chair, staring at the ceiling while his trained mind examined everything he knew.

Kelly had rescued Pamela Madden, but he'd had help getting her straightened out—Professor Sam Rosen and his wife, another doctor. So Kelly finds Doris Brown—who would he take her to? *That* was a starting place! Ryan lifted his phone.

'Hello.'

'Doc, it's Lieutenant Ryan.'

'What's up?' Farber asked.

'Do you know Sam Rosen?'

'Professor Rosen? Sure. Hell of a good cutter—world-class.'

'And his wife?' Ryan could hear the man sucking on his pipe.

'I know her quite well. Sarah. She's a pharmacologist, research fellow across the street, also works with our drug-abuse unit.'

'One more name. Sandy.'

'Sandy who?'

'That's all I have,' Lieutenant Ryan admitted.

'Let me make sure I understand things. Are you asking me to check up on two colleagues as part of a criminal investigation?'

'Yes, Doctor, I am,' the detective admitted after a pause. 'I have no reason to believe that either of them is implicated in any illegal act. But if my speculation is correct, they may be in some danger.'

'Give me a few minutes.' Farber broke the connection.

'Not bad, Em,' Douglas said.

It was scraping the bottom, Ryan thought, but he'd tried everything else. It seemed a long five minutes before the phone rang.

'Ryan.'

'Farber. No docs by that name. One nurse, though—Sandra O'Toole. I don't know her myself. Sam thinks highly of her. She was working something special for him recently.'

'When was that?' Ryan asked casually.

'Two or three weeks ago.'

'Thank you, Doctor. I'll be back to you.'

'Connection,' Douglas observed after the circuit was broken. 'How much you want to bet that she knows Kelly, too?'

SANDY DROVE HIM to Quantico. It was her first time on a marine base, but only briefly, as Kelly guided her to the marina. Sandy was not yet back on Interstate-95 when he pulled away from the dock, heading out for the middle of the river.

The lady had brains and a good memory to go with her guts, Kelly told himself, sipping his first beer in a very long time. Henry, it seemed, had been a talker, especially when he had a girl under his direct control. Kelly still didn't have an address to go along with the phone number, but he had a new name, Tony P-something—Peegee, something like that. Italian, drove a blue Cadillac, along with a decent physical description. Somebody else named Eddie—but Sandy had matched that name with a guy who had been killed by a police officer; it had made the front page of the local paper. Kelly took it one step further: what if that cop was the man Henry had inside? It struck him as odd that a senior officer like a lieutenant would be involved in a shooting. Speculation, he told himself, but worth checking out—he wasn't sure yet exactly how. He had all night for it, and a smooth body of water to reflect his thoughts as it did the stars.

THERE WAS A PROCEDURE for what Ritter had to do. You were supposed to have official sanction for it, but he didn't want to wait that long, not with lives at stake. He couldn't make the call from his office, nor from his home. He decided to drive into town, and picked the Smithsonian's Museum of Natural History. He walked past the elephant in the lobby and found the public telephones, into one of which he dropped a dime and called 347-1347. It was almost an institutional joke. That number connected him to a telephone that rang on the desk of the KGB *rezident*, the chief of station for Washington DC. They knew, and knew that people interested knew they knew. The espionage business could be so baroque, Ritter told himself.

'Yes?' a voice said.

'This is Charles. There is a matter of concern to you. I propose a brief meeting and discussion. I'll be at the National Zoo in an hour, at the enclosure for the white tigers.'

'How will I know you?' the voice asked.

'I'll be carrying a copy of *Newsweek* in my left hand.'

'One hour,' the voice grumbled.

THE WORRISOME PART was the time element, Kelly thought, finally rounding Point Lookout. There was a clock on this. The police were sniffing at him. While he thought there was nothing they could possibly have to use against him, he still couldn't feel good about it.

The other worry was the safety of those four young women. There was no such thing as a good *long* operation. Well, he'd have to be patient on one thing, and with luck, just the one.

RITTER HEADED OVER to the tiger cage. He rolled the *Newsweek* in his left hand, watching the large cats and waiting.

'Hello, Charles,' a voice said beside him.

'Hello, Sergey.'

'I do not know you,' the *rezident* observed.

'This conversation is unofficial,' Ritter explained.

'Aren't they all?' Sergey noted. He and Ritter started walking, with the *rezident*'s security guard in close attendance.

'I just returned from Vietnam,' the CIA officer said.

'Warmer there than here.'

'Not at sea. It's rather pleasant out there.'

'The purpose of your cruise?' the *rezident* asked.

'A visit, an unplanned one.'

'I believe it failed,' the Russian said, not tauntingly, just letting 'Charles' know that he knew what was going on.

'Not completely. We brought someone home with us.' Ritter handed over Grishanov's paybook. 'It would be an embarrassment to your government if it were to be revealed that a Soviet officer was interrogating American POWs. You see, the people he's been interrogating have been reported as being dead by your little friends.' Ritter explained for a few minutes.

'I did not know any of that,' Sergey said after hearing the facts of the matter.

'It's true, I assure you.'

'And where is our colonel?'

'In a safe place. He's enjoying better hospitality than our people are.'

'Colonel Grishanov hasn't dropped bombs on anyone,' the Russian pointed out.

'That is true, but he did take part in a process that will end with the death of American prisoners, and we have hard evidence that they are alive. As I said earlier, a potential embarrassment for your government.'

Sergey Voloshin could see where this discussion was headed. 'What do you propose?'

'It would be helpful if your government could persuade Hanoi to restore these men to life, as it were. That is, to take them to the same prison where the other prisoners are, and make the proper notifications so that their families will know they are alive after all. In return for that, Colonel Grishanov will be returned unharmed and uninterrogated.'

'I will forward that proposal to Moscow.' With a favourable endorsement, his tone said clearly.

'Please be quick,' Ritter warned.

'Your assurance that Colonel Grishanov is alive and well?'

'I can have you to him in about forty minutes if you wish.'

Voloshin thought about it. 'I will take you at your word, Mr . . .'

'Ritter, Bob Ritter. When can I call you?'

'I'll need two days . . . Shall I call you?'

'Forty-eight hours from now. I'll make the call.'

'Very well. Good day.' They shook hands like the professionals they were and headed for their respective cars.

'HOW WELL DO YOU KNOW Mrs O'Toole?' Ryan asked.

'Her husband's dead,' the neighbour said. 'He went to Vietnam right after they bought the house. She's not in any trouble, is she?'

The detective shook his head. 'No, not at all. I've only heard good things about her.'

'It's been awful busy over there,' the elderly lady went on.

'What do you mean?'

'I think she had a houseguest a while back. She sure was shopping a lot more than usual. And somebody else came almost every day, stayed overnight a lot, even.'

'Who was that?' Ryan asked, sipping his iced tea.

'A woman, short like me, but heavier, messy hair. She drove a big car, a red Buick, I think. I was out with my roses when the girl came out.'

'Girl?' Ryan asked innocently.

'Young, like nineteen or twenty, dark hair. Kinda pale, like she was sick. They drove away . . . When was that? Oh, I remember. The day my new roses came from the nursery. The eleventh. I waved at Sandy. She's such a nice girl. She's a nurse, you know. She works at Johns Hopkins, and . . .'

Ryan finished his tea without letting his satisfaction show. Doris Brown had returned home to Pittsburgh on the afternoon of the eleventh. Sarah Rosen drove a Buick. Sam Rosen, Sarah Rosen, Sandra O'Toole—they had treated Miss Brown. Two of them had also treated Miss Madden. They had also treated Mr Kelly. After months of frustration, Lieutenant Emmet Ryan had a case.

'There she is now,' the lady said. Ryan turned and looked to see an attractive young lady, on the tall side, carrying a bag of groceries.

'I wonder who that man was?'

'What man?'

'He was there last night. Maybe she has a boyfriend after all. Tall, like you, dark hair—big. He must be nice, though. I saw her hug him. That was just last night.'

THE ONE BAD THING about the demise of Eddie Morello was that it had required the loss of a large quantity of pure, uncut heroin to the police evidence locker. That had to be made up. Philadelphia was hungry for more. He'd do one last batch on the ship. Tony was setting up a secure lab that was easier to reach, but until that was ready, one more time the old way. He wouldn't make the trip himself.

'How soon?' Burt asked.

'Tonight,' Henry said.

'Fair enough, boss. Who goes with me?'

'Phil and Mike.' The two new ones were from Tony's organisation, young, bright, ambitious. Tony guaranteed their reliability. Henry accepted that. He'd also accept Tony's counsel now that he trusted him. He'd rebuild his distribution network, removing the need for his female couriers, and with the removal of the need for them so would end the reason for their lives. They were becoming dangerous.

But one thing at a time.

'How much?' Burt asked.

'Enough to keep you busy for a while.' Henry waved to the beer coolers. There wasn't room for much beer in them now, but that was as it should be. Perhaps Burt would become his principal lieutenant. He was loyal, respectful, tough when he had to be.

'Take Xantha with you.'

'Boss, we're going to be busy,' Burt objected.

'You can leave her there when you're done.' Perhaps one at a time was the best way to do it.

'TOUGH ONE, DAD?'

'Eleven months' worth, Jack,' Emmet admitted over dinner. He did his best to keep that part of his life out of the house. He decided to comment on a decision his son recently made. 'Marines, eh?'

'Well, Dad, it pays for the last two years of school, doesn't it?'

'My son, a jarhead,' Emmet grumbled good-naturedly.

'What falls out of the sky, Pop?' Jack asked with a college-boy grin, repeating something marines like to say.

What falls out of the sky? Trouble! the detective almost told his son, for his own 101st Airborne, too, were a proud group. But the thought stopped before it got to his lips.

Kelly. He'd vanished. He was back now, though, if the little old lady was right. The killings just plain stopped after the Farmer-Grayson-Brown incident. The marina had remembered seeing the boat about that time, but he'd left in the middle of the night—*that night*—and just vanished. Connection. *What falls out of the sky? Trouble.* That's exactly what had happened before. It just dropped out of the sky. Started and stopped.

He'd saved Doris Brown. He'd given her over to people he trusted. He'd seen one of them last night. He knows she's dead. He saved Pamela Madden, she died, and he was in the hospital, and after he got out, people started dying in a very expert way. Then the killings just stopped and Kelly was nowhere to be found.

What if he's just been away?

He's back now.

Something's going to happen.

'LOOKEE, LOOKEE,' Kelly breathed. It wasn't hard, really. Billy had told him all he needed to know. They had a laboratory in that morass of derelict ships. They came in the bay side, by boat, usually at night, and usually left the following morning. Turned in at the red lighted buoy. Hard as hell to find, almost impossible in the dark. Well, probably was if you didn't know the water. Kelly did. He lifted his binoculars. There was the boat. *Henry's Eighth* was the name. Check. He settled back, watching it move south, then turn east at the red buoy. Kelly marked his chart. He'd wait for sunset. While waiting, Kelly got out a can of spray paint and put green stripes on his dinghy. The inside he painted black.

25 *POISONED CHARM*

It usually took all night, Billy had told him. That gave Kelly time to eat, relax and prepare. He moved *Springer* in close to the cluttered ground he would be hunting tonight and set his anchors. The meal he prepared was only sandwiches but it was better than he'd had on 'his' hill less than a week ago.

His small dinghy, now camouflaged, went into the water after midnight. He'd attached a small electric trolling motor to the transom. With darkened face and hands he steered the dinghy into the tangled waters, moving at perhaps two knots, while his eyes and ears searched for something that didn't belong. The sky helped. There was no moon, and the starlight was just enough to show him the grass and reeds which had grown in this tidal wetland that had been created when the hulks had been left there.

The marsh grass grew to perhaps six or seven feet above the water. The 50-year-old hulks around him looked like ghosts of another age, as indeed they were, relics of a war that had been won.

A voice. Kelly stopped his motor, drifting for a few seconds, pivoting his head to get a fix on it. Carefully now, slowly, he came round the bend. There were three of the derelicts. The westernmost one listed to port. The profile was an old one, with a low superstructure whose tall steel funnel had long since rusted away. But there was a light where the bridge ought to be. Music, he thought—some contemporary rock from a radio station.

They'd been clever selecting this place. It was an unlikely spot, ignored even by local fishermen. Kelly crept up, sticking close to the side of the old ship until he got to their boat. He tied off to the nearest cleat. A rope ladder led up to the derelict's weather deck. Kelly took a deep breath and started climbing.

THE WORK WAS EVERY BIT as menial and boring as Burt had told them it would be, Phil thought. Mixing the lactose in with the pure heroin was the easy part, sifting it into large stainless-steel bowls, like flour for a cake. Then came the tedious job of doling out precisely measured portions into the little plastic envelopes, which had to be stapled shut and piled and counted and bagged. He shared an exasperated look with Mike. Burt probably felt the same way, but didn't let it show. They had a radio playing, and for breaks this Xantha girl, half blasted on pills. She was sleeping in the corner.

'Hello.'

There had been no warning at all. Suddenly there was someone at the door, holding a pistol. He was dressed in military clothes, striped fatigues, and his face was painted green and black.

Kelly had reconverted his Colt back to .45 calibre. He pointed with his left hand. 'That way. On the deck, face down, hands at the back of the neck, one at a time.'

Then Kelly saw the girl sleeping in the corner. He'd let that continue for the moment. His first task was to search them for weapons. Two had small handguns. One had a useless little knife.

'Hey, who are you? Maybe we can talk,' Burt suggested.

'We're going to do that. Tell me about the drugs,' Kelly said.

HE STOPPED OFF for fuel at the Cambridge town dock before heading back north. He had it all now—well, he had enough now, Kelly told himself. Full bunkers, and a mind full of useful data, and for the first time he'd hurt the bastards. Two weeks, maybe three weeks of their product. That would shake things loose. He might have collected it himself and perhaps used it as bait, but no, he wouldn't have it around him, especially now that he suspected he knew how it might come in. Somewhere on the east coast, was all that Burt actually knew. But it was Asian heroin, and the bags it arrived in smelt of death. How many things from Asia that smelt of death came to the eastern United States? Kelly could think of only one, and the fact that he'd known men whose bodies had been processed at Pope Air Force Base only fuelled his anger and his determination to see this one thing through. He brought *Springer* north, heading back into a city that held danger from more than one direction. One last time.

THERE WERE FEW PLACES in eastern America as sleepy as Somerset County, Maryland. An area of large and widely separated farms, it was also an area with a crime rate so low as to be nearly invisible. About the only problem was the way people drove, and for that they had the state police.

Trooper First Class Ben Freeland was on his regular patrol routine when he spotted a pedestrian on Postbox Road. She was walking unevenly and she wasn't dressed like a local. That was odd. You didn't get here except by car. The trooper eased the Ford over to the gravel, bringing it to a stop fifty feet from her, and got out, putting his uniform Stetson on and adjusting his pistol belt.

'Hello,' he said pleasantly. 'Where you heading, ma'am?'

She stopped after a moment, looking at him with eyes that belonged on another planet. 'Who're you?'

The trooper leaned in close. There was no alcohol on her breath. 'What's your name?' he asked in a more commanding tone.

'Xantha, with an *X*,' she answered, smiling.

'Where are you from, Xantha?'

' 'Lanta.'

'You're a long way from Atlanta, ma'am. Can I offer you a ride?'

'Sure. Tired a walkin'. Where we goin'?'

'Well, Xantha, I think you need a place to lie down and rest.'

'Burt and the other two restin', 'cept they ain't gonna wake up.'

'What's that, Xantha?'

'He killed them, *bang bang bang*.' She mimed with her hand.

'Who's that?'

'He a white boy. Di'n't get his name, di'n't see his face neither.'

'Where?'

'On the boat. An' you know the funny thing? He left all the drugs right there, too, the white boy did. 'Cept'n' he was *green*.'

Freeland didn't have much idea what this was all about, but he intended to find out. For starters he lit up his rotating lights, heading fast for State Police Barracks V in Westover.

'YACHT *SPRINGER*, take a look to your port quarter.'

Kelly lifted his mike. 'Anybody I know?'

'Where the H have you been, Kelly?' Manuel Oreza asked.

'Business trip. What do you care?'

'Hey, Kelly, one seaman to another, back down, OK?'

Kelly cut his throttles, allowing the cutter to pull alongside in a few minutes. Oreza hopped aboard.

'Hey, Chief,' the man said. 'I was down your sandbar twice looking to share a beer with you, but you weren't home.'

'I had to go out of the country. Business,' Kelly answered. It was clear that he'd go no further.

'Fair enough. Be around for a while?'

'I plan to be, yeah.'

'OK, maybe I'll stop by and give you a safety inspection.'

'I thought this was a friendly visit,' Kelly observed.

Suddenly it was clear that both men were uneasy. Oreza tried to cover it with a smile. 'OK, I'll go easy on you.' But that didn't work. 'Catch you next week, Chief.'

They shook hands, but something had changed. Oreza waved for the cutter to come back in and jumped aboard. The cutter pulled away without a further word.

Kelly advanced his throttles anyway.

'SO WHAT HAPPENED?'

'Roger, they knew we were coming,' Ritter answered with a steady look.

'How, Bob?' Roger MacKenzie asked. 'Leak?'

Ritter reached into his pocket and extracted a photocopy of a document and handed it across to the special assistant to the President. The original was written in Vietnamese. Under the text of the photocopy was the handwritten translation.

'We got lucky, Roger. Nobody got hurt. We put a guy on the ground in early. Navy SEAL, very good at what he does. Anyway, he was watching things when the NVA reinforcements came in. He's the guy who blew the mission off. Then he just walked off the hill. On the way out he bagged the Russian who was talking to our people, and the camp commander. We have them in Winchester. Alive,' Ritter added with a smile. 'That's the good news.'

'I'm not sure I want to hear the bad news.'

'We have an indicator that the other side might want to eliminate the camp and everyone in it.'

'Henry Kissinger is over in Paris right now,' MacKenzie said.

'Wrong approach. If he brings this up, they'll just deny.'

'True. What, then?'

'We're working through the Russians.'

'Let me know how it turns out?'

'You bet.'

'THANKS FOR LETTING me talk to you,' Lieutenant Ryan said.

'What's this all about?' Sam Rosen asked. They were in his office. Sarah and Sandy were there, too.

'It's about your former patient—John Kelly. I need to talk to him. But I don't know where he is.'

'About what?' Sarah asked.

'About a series of killings,' Ryan answered at once.

'Killing who?' This question came from the nurse.

'Doris Brown, for one, and several others.'

'John didn't hurt her—' Sandy said before Sarah Rosen was able to touch her hand.

'Then you know who Doris Brown is,' the detective observed. 'Someone named Sandy called the Brown house in Pittsburgh. It was you, wasn't it?'

'Officer,' Sarah said, 'I'm not sure I understand why you're asking all these questions.'

'I'm trying to develop some information, and I want you to tell your friend that he needs to talk with me.'

'Wait a minute,' Sam said. 'If you think John might have done something wrong, and you want us to find him for you, you're saying that you think we know where he is, right? Doesn't that make us possible accessories?'

'Did I say that? Look, your friend Kelly is a very tough guy, but he's not as smart as he thinks he is. If he comes in now, it's one thing. If he makes us catch him, it's something else. You tell him that. Kelly is out there killing people, and that's *wrong*. I don't like druggies either. Pamela Madden, the girl on the fountain, that's *my* case. I want those people in a cage; I want to watch them walk into the gas chamber. That's *my* job, to see that justice happens. Not his, mine. Do you understand?'

'Yes, I think we do,' Sam Rosen answered.

THE PROBLEM WAS making sense out of what Xantha said. A physician had been called in and had diagnosed her problem as barbiturate intoxication.

'Three dead people on a boat somewhere,' Trooper Ben Freeland repeated. 'Names and everything.'

'You believe it?'

'Her story hasn't changed for several hours.'

'Yeah.' The captain looked up. 'You like to fish out there, Ben. What's it sound like to you?'

'Like around Bloodsworth Island.'

'We'll hold her overnight on public drunkenness.'

'And then, sir?'

'Like helicopter rides?'

KELLY PICKED a different marina this time. He moved into one of the guest slips, paid in cash, and announced to the dockmaster that he'd be sleeping aboard this night.

He didn't say what would be happening the next day.

26 *STALKING*

'We missed something, Em,' Douglas announced.

'What was it this time?' Ryan asked. Missing something wasn't exactly a new happening in their business.

'How they knew she was in Pittsburgh. I called that Sergeant Meyer, had 'em check the long-distance charges on the house phone. None—not a single outgoing call for the last month.'

Ryan stubbed out his cigarette. 'The story is, Sergeant Meyer's dad is a preacher. He was counselling the girl and told his son a little of what he knew. OK. The sergeant goes up the chain to his captain. The captain knows Frank Allen, and the sarge calls him for advice on who's running the case. Frank refers him to us. Meyer didn't talk to anybody else. So how did the info get to our friends?' He lit up another cigarette.

'I suppose you could call this progress, Em. Now we're sure. There has to be a leak inside the department.'

'What other good news do we have?'

THE STATE POLICE HELICOPTER arrived on the Barracks V helicopter pad at a quarter to nine. Captain Ernest Joy and Trooper Ben Freeland were waiting. Mainly used for medevac missions, the aircraft had a pilot and a paramedic, both of whom were gun-toting state police officers in sporty flight suits. The ground-pounders strapped in and the helicopter spooled up.

'Where to?' the pilot asked over the intercom.

'Bloodsworth Island, the graveyard,' Captain Joy said.

'Roger that,' the pilot replied.

The Chesapeake Bay was a wide blue band below them. 'Sure looks different from up here,' Freeland said. 'I fish around there. From the surface it just looks like marshes.'

But it didn't now. From a thousand feet it looked like islands at first, connected by silt and grass. As they got closer, the islands took on regular shapes, lozenge-like at first and then with the fine lines of ships—grown over, surrounded by grass and reeds.

'What exactly are we looking for?' the pilot asked.

'Not sure, maybe a boat. We picked up a druggie yesterday,' Captain Joy explained. 'Said there was a drug lab in there, and three dead people.'

'Got a flash down this way.' The paramedic pointed the pilot over to the right. 'Off glass or something.'

'Let's check it out.' The pilot eased the chopper down to about two hundred feet. 'Yeah, I got a boat by those three derelicts.'

'Lower,' Captain Joy commanded. In a few seconds they were fifty feet over the deck of one of the derelicts. The boat beside it was empty. There was a beer cooler in the back, but nothing else.

'Whoever owns that boat sure isn't real interested in us,' the pilot said over the intercom. In the back, Freeland mimed three shots with his hand. Captain Joy nodded.

'I think you may be right, Ben.' To the pilot: 'Can you mark the exact position on a map?'

'Right.' The paramedic pulled out a chart and made the appropriate notations. 'Seen what you need?'

'Yeah. Head back.'

Twenty minutes later Captain Joy was on the phone.

'Coastguard, Thomas Point.'

'This is Captain Joy, state police. We need a little help.'

KELLY TOOK A CAB to pick up his Volkswagen. Then he drove the car back to the marina and started unloading the things he needed. Nobody paid much attention, and in fifteen minutes he was gone.

Kelly took the opportunity to drive through the area he'd be hunting. It was agreeably vacant, an industrial part of the city where nobody lived and few would want to. Many of the buildings in the district looked unused. More to the point, there was much open ground here, many buildings separated from one another by flat areas of bare earth. The place he was interested in was a single freestanding building with only three doors, and though they were on two different walls, all could be observed from a single point. To Kelly's rear was another vacant building, a tall structure with plenty of broken windows. His initial reconnaissance complete, Kelly headed north.

XANTHA WAS MORE or less sober, though weak. She was aware that she was under arrest now, and that her rap sheet had arrived on Teletype. She was also canny enough to have requested the presence of a lawyer.

'My client,' the attorney said, 'is willing to cooperate.' The agreement had taken all of ten minutes to strike.

'They was gonna kill me!' Xantha said.

'Who's "they"?' Captain Joy asked.

'They dead. He killed 'em—the white boy. Shot 'em dead.'

'Tell us about the white man,' Joy asked.

'Big dude, like him'—she pointed to Freeland—'but face all green like a leaf. He blindfold me after he took me down; then he put me on that pier an' tol' me to catch a bus or somethin'.'

'How do you know he was white?'

'Wrists was white. Hands was green,' she said. 'He wear green clothes with stripes on 'em, like a soldier, carry a big .45. I was asleep when he shoot. That wake me up, see? Take me away, drop me off, boat just go away.'

'What kind of boat?'

'Big white one, tall, like, big, like thirty feet long.'

'Xantha, how do you know they were going to kill you?'

'White boy say so. He show me the things in the little boat—fishnet, like, and cement blocks. He say they tell him they do it before.'

The lawyer decided it was his turn to speak. 'Gentlemen, my client has information about what may be a major criminal operation. She may require protection.'

'Counsellor,' Joy replied quietly, 'may I suggest that we keep your client in our lockup for the time being? For her own safety. All charges against her are dropped pending verification of her story. You'll get everything you want, in return for her cooperation.'

'My client agrees to your conditions and suggestions,' the lawyer said without consulting her. 'A pleasure doing business with you, Captain Joy,' he continued as the state police captain left for Freeland's car.

'Ben, you really fell into something. You handled her real nice. I won't forget. Now show me how fast this beast goes.'

'You got it, Cap'n.' Freeland engaged the lights before passing seventy. They made it to the dock just as the coastguard turned out of the main channel.

THE MAN CALLED HIMSELF a captain, and Quartermaster First Class Manuel Oreza saluted him as he came aboard. Both police officers were given life jackets to wear because coastguard regulations required them on small boats, and then Joy showed him the chart.

'What gives?' asked Oreza.

'A possible triple homicide, possible drug involvement. We overflew the area this morning. There's a fishing boat right here.'

Oreza nodded and took the wheel himself, pushing the throttles to the stops. It was a bare five miles to the graveyard—that was how Oreza thought of it—and he plotted his approach carefully.

'No closer?' Freeland asked.

'No. From here on we use our launch.'

Oreza's crewmen got the fourteen-foot launch deployed, and the three men motored in. The cops were fingering their revolvers, and Oreza asked himself, too late, why he hadn't brought one too.

'Looks like a Starcraft eighteen,' Oreza breathed.

Suddenly things got very tense. Oreza eased his launch right up to the Starcraft. The cops got aboard gingerly.

Freeland pointed to the back. Joy nodded. There were six cement blocks and a rolled-up section of nylon netting. There was also a rope ladder going up. Joy went first, his revolver in his right hand. Oreza just watched as Freeland followed. Once they got to the deck, the men headed for the superstructure. When Joy came back, his revolver wasn't visible.

'We have three bodies up here, and a large quantity of what looks like heroin. Call your boat, have them tell my barracks that we need crime lab.'

'OK,' said Oreza, making his radio call.

IT WAS A HOT DAY at the zoo. Better to have met in the panda enclosure. The place was air-conditioned and comfortable, but intelligence officers usually were uncomfortable in places like that, and so today Ritter was strolling by the remarkably large area that contained the Galapagos tortoises.

'Hello, Bob.'

'Hello, Sergey. What's the word from Moscow?'

'You forgot to tell me something.'

'What's that?'

'That you have a Vietnamese officer also.'

'Why should that concern you?' Ritter asked lightly, clearly concealing his annoyance that Voloshin knew this, as his interlocutor could see.

'It is a complication. Moscow doesn't know yet.'

'Then don't tell them,' Ritter suggested. 'It is, as you say, a complication. I assure you that your allies don't know.'

'How can that be?' the Russian demanded.

'Sergey, do you reveal methods?' Ritter replied.

A judicious man, Voloshin thought, which pleased him. 'OK, Bob. You assure me that our allies do not know their man is missing?'

'Positive. My offer for you to meet your man is still open,' he added.

'Without reciprocal rights?' Voloshin tried.

'For that I need permission from upstairs. I can try if you ask me to, but that also would be something of a complication.'

'I ask.' Voloshin wanted that made clear.

'Very well. I'll call you. And in return?'

'In return I will consider your request.' Voloshin walked off without another word.

Gotcha! Ritter thought, heading towards where his car was parked. He'd played a careful but inventive game. There were three possible leaks on Boxwood Green. He'd visited each of them. To one he'd said that they actually had got a prisoner out, who had died of wounds. To another, that the Russian was badly wounded and might not survive. But Ritter had saved his best piece of bait for the most likely leak. Now he knew. That narrowed it to four suspects—Roger MacKenzie, that prep-school aide Wally Hicks, and two secretaries.

IT WAS AN UNUSUAL way to gather information, something he'd never done before. Kelly sat at a corner booth in Mama Maria's, dressed in his suit, well groomed and sporting a new businesslike haircut. The excellence of the food explained the crowded room, and the crowding explained why it was a convenient place for Tony Piaggi and Henry Tucker to meet. Mama Maria's was, in fact, owned by Piaggi. The owner was a bon vivant, greeting favoured customers,

guiding them to their tables with Old World hospitality. Snappy dresser, too, Kelly saw, recording his face and build, gestures and mannerisms as he ate through his calamari. A black man came in, dressed in a nicely cut suit.

Piaggi looked up and headed to the front, stopping only briefly to shake hands with someone on the way. He did the same with the black man, then led him back past Kelly's table and up the back stairs to where the private rooms were. So that's Henry Tucker, Kelly thought. That's the one who killed Pam. He didn't look like a monster. Monsters rarely did. To Kelly he looked like a target, and his particulars went into Kelly's memory, alongside Tony Piaggi's. He was surprised when he looked down and saw that the fork in his hands was bent.

'WHAT'S THE PROBLEM?' Piaggi asked, upstairs. He poured each of them a glass of Chianti, good host that he was, but as soon as the door had closed, Henry's face started telling him something.

'Phil, Mike and Burt—they haven't come back.'

'OK, settle down. How much stuff did they have?'

'Twenty kilos of pure, man.'

'Lot of stuff, Henry. Maybe it just took a while,' Tony said, sipping his wine and trying to appear calm and reasonable. 'Why are you getting excited? They're probably on their way here now.'

'Something's wrong, man.'

'What?'

'I don't know.'

Piaggi thought he understood Tucker's anxiety. Now it was big-time. Twenty kilograms of pure translated into a huge quantity of street drugs. This was the really big score that Tucker had been working towards for several years. Just assembling all the cash to pay for it was a major undertaking. It was an understandable case of nerves.

Tucker's anxiety was partly what Tony thought it was, but something else, too. The things that had happened earlier in the summer, he had told himself, were Eddie Morello's doing. He'd managed to convince himself of that, but only because he had wanted to believe it. Somewhere else a little voice had told him otherwise, and now the voice was back, and it was telling him things that he didn't understand, couldn't reason out.

'Give 'em until tomorrow.'

'HEY, WALLY?'

The tape was disappointingly scratchy. That was due to the old phone lines, the technician explained.

'Yeah, what is it?' the somewhat uneven voice replied.

'The Vietnamese officer they got. You sure about that?'

'That's what Roger told me.' Bingo! Ritter thought.

'Where they have him?'

'I guess out at Winchester with the Russian.'

'I wanted to check up on that before—well, you know.'

'Sure thing, man.' With that the line went dead.

'Who is he?' Greer asked.

'Walter Hicks.' Ritter tightened his hand into a fist. 'You want to know why those people are still in Sender Green? That's it.'

'So what are you going to do about it?'

'I don't know.' But it won't be legal. The tape wasn't. The tap had been set up without a court order.

'Treason is still a capital crime, Bob.'

Ritter looked up. 'It's supposed to be.'

27 *RITE OF PASSAGE*

Mark Charon found himself in rather a difficult position. He'd just hung up the phone after a conversation with Quartermaster Oreza of the coastguard. The first order of business was that Henry would not be pleased to learn that his lab was gone and three of his people with it. Worse still, it sounded as though a vast quantity of drugs had been lost. Worst of all, the person or persons who had accomplished that feat were unknown, at large, and doing—what?

According to Oreza, the captain running the case was a guy named Joy in Somerset County. Charon lifted his phone.

'State police.'

'Trying to get Captain Joy. This is Lieutenant Charon, Baltimore City Police.'

'Please hold.' The next voice that came on was a tired one.

'Captain Joy.'

'Hello, this is Lieutenant Charon—Mark Charon—city police. I work narcotics. I hear you just took down something big.'

'You might say that.'

'Could you give me a quick sketch? I may have some information on this one myself.'

'Who told you about this anyway?'

'Coastguard sailor—Quartermaster Oreza. I've worked with him on a couple cases.'

'OK, Lieutenant. What do you need from me?'

'What can you tell me?' Charon took several minutes of notes. 'What are you doing with Xantha?'

'Holding her as a material witness. We want to take care of this girl. Looks like we're dealing with some pretty nasty folks here.'

'I believe it,' Charon replied. 'OK, let me see what I can shake loose for you at this end.'

'Thanks for the assist.'

Charon hung up. Burt and the two people Tony had evidently seconded to the operation—back of the head, .45s. The coldness of it gave Charon a chill. But it wasn't so much coldness as efficiency. Like the pushers. Like the case Tom and Em were working.

About the only good news was that he could call Henry in safety. Charon knew every drug-related wiretap in the area, and not one was targeted on Tucker's operation.

'Yeah?'

'Burt and his friends are dead,' Charon announced. 'The state police in Somerset have them bagged. The lab is gone, Henry. The drugs are gone, and they have Xantha in custody.'

'I'VE KNOWN HIS FATHER for thirty years,' Roger MacKenzie said, pale and suddenly nauseous. They were standing on the breakfast porch of his house in northwest Washington. Ritter had arrived unannounced at six fifteen, fully dressed and grim.

Ritter sipped his orange juice, though the acid in it didn't exactly do his stomach any good either. This was treason of the worst sort. Wally Hicks had *known* what he did would hurt fellow citizens.

'I can't fault you for taking him into your office, Roger, but the boy's guilty of espionage. That's a criminal offence.'

'I could pull his security clearance, kick him out—'

'Not good enough,' Ritter said coldly. 'The little bastard betrayed his country. People may die because of him. He is *not* going to walk away from it.'

'Your tap was illegal.'

'National-security investigation—slightly different rules. There's a war going on, remember? All that has to happen is to let him hear it, and he'll split open.'

'And run the risk of bringing down the President? Now? Do you think that'll do the country any good? What about our relations with the Russians? This is a *crucial* time, Bob.'

'Well, I'm coming to you for guidance,' Ritter said, and then he got it, after a fashion.

'We can't afford an investigation and a public trial. That is politically unacceptable.' MacKenzie hoped that would be enough.

Ritter nodded and stood. The drive back to his office at Langley was not all that comfortable. MacKenzie had said to handle it. Not in so many words, but that's what he meant. There was no sense in confusing the issue.

'MRS O'TOOLE?' Sandy was checking off some forms when the phone rang. 'This is James Greer. You've spoken to my secretary, I believe.'

'Yes, I have. Can I help you?'

'I hate to bother you, but we're trying to track John down.'

'I think he's in town, but I don't know where exactly.'

'If you hear from him, could you please ask him to call me?'

'I'll be glad to.' And what's that about? she wondered.

It was getting to her. The police were after John, and she'd told him, and he hadn't seemed to care. Now somebody else was trying to get hold of him. Why? Then she saw a copy of the morning paper sitting on the table in the lounge area. On the lower right side of the front page was the headline DRUG MURDER IN SOMERSET.

RYAN FLIPPED OPEN the thin manila folder that Frank Allen had sent over. It was part of John Terrence Kelly's service record, and it included a photograph. Kelly had joined the navy two weeks after his eighteenth birthday and stayed in six years, honourably discharged as a chief petty officer. The three rating sheets in the folder were all 4.0, the highest navy grade, and there was a flowery letter of recommendation from a three-star admiral.

Ryan set the file down and called Allen.

'Thanks for the info on Kelly, Frank. Now I got a tough one for you. When that Sergeant Meyer called in from Pittsburgh, anybody else you mention that to?'

'That was the day Mark Charon popped the dealer, wasn't it?' Allen thought back. 'I might have said something to him.'

'OK, thanks, Frank.' Ryan looked up the number of Barracks V of the state police.

'Captain Joy,' said a very weary voice.

'Lieutenant Ryan, city police, homicide.'

'You big-city boys sure are interested in us now,' Joy commented wryly. 'What do you want to know?'

'What do you mean?'

'I mean I was on my way to bed last night when another one of your people called, Lieutenant Chair—something like that.'

Charon. He keeps appearing, doesn't he?

'Could you fill me in? I'll take the short version.' It turned out that the short version was plenty. 'The woman is in custody?'

'You bet she is.'

'Captain, you keep her that way until I say different, OK?'

'She isn't going anywhere for a while,' Joy promised.

'Nothing more on the shooter?'

'Just what I said: male Caucasian, six foot or so, and he painted himself green, the girl said, like camouflage stuff. There is one more thing,' Joy added. 'He's a right good shot.'

Ryan flipped the folder back open. At the bottom of Kelly's list of awards: Distinguished Rifleman, Master Pistol.

'I'll be back to you, Captain,' Ryan said, hanging up.

'You're in early,' Douglas observed, arriving late. 'See the paper?'

'Our friend's back, and he got on the scoreboard again.' Ryan handed the photo across. 'Want to drive down to Somerset and interview the girl?'

'You think . . .'

'Yes, I think we have our witness. I think we have our leaker, too.' Ryan explained that one quietly.

HE HAD JUST CALLED to hear the sound of her voice. So close to his goal, he was allowing himself to look beyond it.

'John, where are you?'

'I have a place,' was all he was willing to say.

'I have a message for you. Call James Greer.'

'OK.' Kelly grimaced.

'Was that you in the paper?' she whispered. 'Three dead people on the Eastern Shore!'

'I'll get back to you,' he said almost as fast as the chill hit him.

Kelly didn't have the paper delivered to his apartment, for the obvious reason, but now he needed one. There was a dispenser at the corner, he remembered. He only needed one look.

What does the girl know about me?

It was too late for recrimination. He'd faced the same problem with her as with Doris. She'd been asleep when he'd done the job, and the pistol shots had woken her. He'd explained to her that Burt had planned to kill her, then he'd given her enough cash to catch a Greyhound to somewhere. But the cops had her already.

OK, so now what do you do?

For starters, he had to get rid of the .45. Even if he had left no evidence at all behind, it was a link. When this mission was over, it was *over*. But now he needed help, and where else to get it but from the people for whom he had killed?

'Admiral Greer, please. This is Mr Clark.'

'Hold, please,' Kelly heard, then: 'You were supposed to call in.'

'I can be there in two hours, sir.'

'I'll be waiting.'

'HELLO, JOHN,' Admiral Greer said. Greer pointed him to a seat, and the door was closed.

'Glad to be back home, Mr Clark?' Ritter asked. There was a copy of the *Washington Post* on his desk.

'Yes, sir, I guess you can say that.' Both of the older men caught the ambivalence. 'Why did you want me to come in?'

'I told you on the airplane. It may turn out that your action bringing that Russian out might save our people yet. We need people who can think on their feet. You can.' Ritter pulled a thick folder from his desk. 'I had this brought in from St Louis.' Kelly recognised the forms. It was his complete navy personnel-records package. 'I'm offering you a job in my part of the house.'

'Doing what?'

'Whatever we tell you to do,' Ritter answered. He already had something in mind.

Kelly's instinct battled against his reason. Then he decided that he had to tell the truth to somebody. 'There's a problem.'

'What's that?' Ritter asked.

Kelly reached across the desk and tapped the article on the front page of the paper. 'You might want to read that.'

'I did. So? Somebody did the world a favour,' the field officer said lightly. Then he caught the look in Kelly's eyes, and his voice became instantly wary. 'Keep talking, Mr Clark.'

'That's me, sir.'

'THE FILE'S OUT, SIR,' the records clerk said over the phone.

'What do you mean?' Ryan objected. 'I have some copies from it right here.' He'd called the military's central records-storage facility, located in St Louis. Every piece of paper relating to every man or woman who had ever served in uniform was there, in a secure and carefully guarded complex. 'I'm Lieutenant Emmet Ryan, Baltimore City Police. I need information from that file.'

'Sir, the file's not here. My clerk just showed me the notes. It's been taken out and will be returned, but I do not know when.'

'Who has it?'

'I'm not allowed to say, sir.'

Out. Why? For whom? What the hell's so different about this case? Ryan knew that it had many differences. He wondered if he'd ever have them all figured out. 'Thank you, I'll get back,' Ryan said.

'THAT'S WHAT THEY DID to her,' Kelly told them. It was the first time he'd actually said it all out loud and, in recounting the details of the pathology report, it was as though he were listening to the voice of another person. 'I got two more girls out. One they killed. The other one, well . . .' He waved at the newspaper.

'The article says twenty kilograms of the stuff,' Ritter observed. 'Is that true?'

'Probably.' Kelly shrugged. 'I didn't weigh it. There's one other thing. I think I know how the drugs come in. The bags smell like . . . embalming fluid. It's Asian heroin.'

'Yes?' Ritter asked.

'Don't you see? Asian stuff. Comes in somewhere on the east coast. They're using the bodies of our killed-in-actions to bring the stuff in.'

THE AMERICAN PRISONERS were brought out in the darkness. The only illumination came from flashlights and a few torches. Every prisoner had his feet hobbled; in each case the hands and elbows were bound behind their backs. Every man had in close attendance a conscript to chivvy him along, right to the centre of the compound.

Robin Zacharias stumbled. His posture made it hard to look up, and he didn't see the truck until he was only a few feet away. It was a beat-up Russian vehicle with fence wire over the top. They were going somewhere. Robin had no real idea where he was and could hardly speculate on where he might go. Nothing could be worse than this place had been—and yet he'd survived it somehow, Robin told himself as the truck rumbled away. The camp faded into the darkness, and with it the worst trial of his life.

28 DANGEROUS DRUGS

Kelly's hands squeezed the wheel as he drove south on the Baltimore-Washington Parkway. He'd never done anything like this before at the behest of others, except for Vietnam, which was a different set of circumstances altogether. He hoped Ritter understood why he was doing what he had been asked to do. He simply could not turn away. Not from Pam. Not from the men of Boxwood Green. He shook his head. But he wished they'd asked someone else.

IT WAS ALL COMING TOGETHER. Blowing the whistle on that raid was the best thing he had ever done, Hicks thought, lighting up his third joint of the night. He heard the phone ring.

'How's it going?' It was Peter Henderson. 'Got a few minutes? I want to go over something with you.'

'Half an hour?' Wally said.

'See you then.'

Not a minute later, there was a knock on the door. Hicks stubbed out his smoke and went to answer it. Too soon for Peter.

'You're Walter Hicks?'

'Yeah. Who are you?'

'John Clark. I need to talk to you for a few minutes.'

'What about?'

'Operation Boxwood Green. There's some things you need to know,' Clark told him. He was working for the Agency now, so Clark was his name. It made it easier, somehow.

'Come on in. I only have a few minutes, though.' Hicks waved him to a chair. 'Can I get you anything?'

'No, thanks, I'm fine,' Clark answered. 'I was there.'

'What do you mean?'

'I was at Sender Green, just last week.'

'You were on the team?' Hicks asked, intensely curious and not seeing the danger that had walked into his apartment.

'That's right. I'm the guy who brought the Russian out. One of the documents I took off his body was an order to make preparations to kill all of our POWs.'

'That's too bad,' Hicks said with a perfunctory shake of the head. *Oh—your dog died? That's too bad.*

'Doesn't that mean anything to you?' Clark asked.

'Yes, it does, but people take chances. Wait a minute . . .' Hicks's eyes went blank for a moment. 'I thought we had the camp commander, too, didn't we?'

'No. I killed him myself. That bit of information was given to your boss so that we could identify the name of the guy who leaked the mission.' Clark leaned forward. 'That was you, Mr Hicks. I was there. We had it wired. Those prisoners ought to be with their families right now—all twenty of them.'

Hicks brushed it aside. 'I didn't *want* them to die. Look, like I said, people take chances. That was a black operation. You can't reveal it. The White House will never let you do that.'

'That's correct. I'm here to kill you.'

'What?' Hicks almost laughed.

'You betrayed your country. You betrayed twenty men.'

'Look, that was a matter of conscience.'

'So's this, Mr Hicks.' Clark reached into his pocket and pulled out a plastic bag. In it were drugs he'd taken off the body of his old friend Archie, and a spoon and a glass hypodermic needle. He tossed the bag into Wally's lap.

'I won't do it.'

'Fair enough.' From behind his back came his Ka-Bar knife. 'I've done people this way, too. There are twenty men over there who ought to be home. Your choice, Mr Hicks.'

IT WAS A WEEKDAY NIGHT, and Washington went to bed early. It made for empty sidewalks in Georgetown. Peter Henderson saw two elderly folk walking their dog, but only one other on Wally's block—a man getting into a Beetle. A few seconds later he knocked on Wally's door. It wasn't fully closed. Wally was sloppy about some things. Henderson pushed the door open, ready to reprove his friend, until he saw him there, sitting in the chair.

Hicks had his left sleeve rolled up. His right hand had caught on his collar, as though to help himself breathe, but the real reason was on the inside of his left elbow. Peter knew he had to get out.

He removed a handkerchief and wiped the doorknob, closed the door and walked away. Damn you, Wally! Henderson raged. I needed you. And to die like this—from a drug overdose.

But there remained his beliefs, Henderson thought.

KELLY WAS RELIEVED it was over. There was no satisfaction in the death of Walter Hicks. He'd been a traitor and a coward, but there ought to have been a better way. He was glad that Hicks had decided to take his own life, for he wasn't at all sure that he could have killed him with a knife—or any other way.

Kelly packed his clothing into the suitcase and carried it out to the car, and with that his residence in the Baltimore apartment ended. It was after midnight when he drove south again, into the centre of the danger zone, ready to act one last time.

OFFICER CHUCK MONROE drove his radio car in his regular patrol pattern, looking for things out of the ordinary. Maybe the narcs from downtown could start making a few things happen out here. Someone had, however briefly. A street bum. That made Monroe smile in the darkness. The informal name applied to the case seemed so appropriate. The Invisible Man.

He reached the western border of his area, a north–south street, and was about to turn onto it when he saw a bum. Tired of sitting in his car, he pulled over.

'Yo, hold up there, sport.' The figure kept moving, slowly, unevenly. Monroe walked quickly to catch up. His hand came down on the bum's shoulder. 'I said hold up, now.'

Physical contact changed everything. This shoulder was firm and strong—and tense.

Almost immediately, Monroe saw the world rotate wildly from low right to high left, his view interrupted by a pistol.

'Who—'

'Quiet!' The pistol against his forehead ensured that, almost. It was the surgical gloves that forced the officer to speak.

'You're him.'

'Yes, I am. Roll over—now!' The policeman did so. Kelly pulled the cuffs off his belt and secured them to both wrists. 'Relax. I'm not going to kill any cops.' Kelly stood him up and started walking him back to the patrol car. 'Where do you keep your keys?'

'Right side pocket.'

'Thank you.' Kelly took them as he put the officer in the back seat of the car. There was a screen there to keep arrested passengers from annoying the driver. He quickly started the car and parked it in an alley. 'Your hands OK—not too tight on the cuffs?'

'Yeah, I'm just damned fine back here.' The cop was shaking now—mainly rage, Kelly figured. That was understandable.

'I don't want you to get hurt. I'll lock the car.'

Kelly walked away quickly, heading west again, keeping to the shadows and alleys as much as possible.

It was an out-of-business store, just as Billy had told him and Burt had confirmed, with vacant houses to the left and right. Kelly looked at it from across the street. Despite the vacant ground level, there was a light on upstairs. The front door was padlocked.

He crossed the street briskly. First he did his best to check out the street level for people. Finding none, Kelly took the Ka-Bar from his sheath and started attacking the caulking round the full-length glass pane in the old wooden door. It took six endless minutes before he was able to lower the glass. Then he stepped sideways through the opening and headed for the back of the building, where there were

stairs. Kelly could hear noise, and he went up, his .45 leading the way.
'It's been a nice party, honey, but it's over now,' a male voice said. 'Sorry, honey, but that's just the way things are.'

Kelly eased down the corridor. The wooden floor creaked—

'What's that?'

There was neither time nor a place to hide, and Kelly darted the last fifteen feet, then dived in low and rolled to unmask his pistol.

There were two men, both in their twenties. One was reaching for a gun and coming round when two rounds entered his chest.

'OK! OK!' A small revolver dropped to the floor. There was a scream from the front of the building, which Kelly ignored as he got back to his feet, his automatic locked on the second man.

'They're gonna kill us.' It was a surprisingly mousy voice, frightened but slow from whatever she was using.

'How many?' Kelly snapped at her.

'Just these two. They're going to—'

'I don't think so,' Kelly told her. 'Which one are you?'

'Paula.' He was covering his target.

'Where are Maria and Roberta?'

'They're in the front room,' Paula told him.

'Who are you?' Kelly asked the man.

'Frank Molinari.'

'Where from, Frank?' Kelly kept the gun level.

'Philly. Hey, man, we can talk, OK?'

Why was somebody from Philadelphia doing Henry's dirty work? Kelly's mind raced. 'Ever been to Pittsburgh, Frank?' Somehow the question just popped out. 'Killed Doris and her father, right?'

'It was a job, man. Ever do a job?'

Kelly gave him the only possible answer, and there was another scream from the front as he brought the gun back in close to his chest. Time to think. Kelly walked over and yanked Paula to her feet.

'Come on, let's get your friends.'

Kelly got Paula, Maria and Roberta together and forced them down the stairs, then outside, making them move fast. The police car was still where he'd left it. Kelly unlocked the front and told the women to get in. He handed the keys to Paula, who seemed the best able to drive.

'Officer Monroe, these ladies will be driving you to your station. I have instructions for you. You ready to listen?'

'I got a choice? Go ahead.'

'Sergeant Tom Douglas is the man you want to talk to—nobody else, just him. These ladies can help you break some major cases.'

Monroe caught the message and nodded his head. 'Yeah.'

'Paula, you drive. Don't stop for anything. Get moving!'

She really was too intoxicated to drive. The police car crept away, scraping a telephone pole halfway down the alley. Then it turned the corner and was gone. Kelly took a deep breath. He hadn't saved Pam. He hadn't saved Doris. But he had saved these three, and Xantha, at a peril to his life. It was almost enough.

But not quite.

THE TWO-TRUCK CONVOY didn't arrive at the destination until after noon. It was Hoa Lo Prison, the Hanoi Hilton, and its reputation was well known to the Americans.

When the trucks had pulled into the courtyard and the gates were secure, the men were let down. Again each man was given an individual guard, who took him inside.

Robin Zacharias found a nice piece of floor and sat down, resting his head against the wall. Then he closed his eyes and gave thanks to his God.

'THIS BETTER BE GOOD,' Tom Douglas growled into the phone.

'Sergeant, this is Chuck Monroe, western district. I have three witnesses to the fountain murder.' He paused. 'I think I have two more bodies for the Invisible Man, too.'

It was nine months now since the death of Helen Waters. Then Pamela Madden. Then Doris Brown. He was going to get the bastards now, Douglas told himself, incorrectly.

IT WAS TRICKY and dangerous. There were four automobiles parked out front, and he couldn't afford to make any noise. He was standing on the marginal space provided by the sill of a bricked-up window, reaching for the telephone cable. Kelly hoped nobody was using the phone as he clipped into the wires, quickly attaching leads of his own. With that done, he dropped down and started walking along the back of the building, trailing out his own supply of wire, just letting it lie on the ground. Another hundred yards and he entered the deserted building and climbed to his perch.

The rifle wasn't properly sighted in. Mad as it seemed, the most sensible course of action was to use the building as his target. Kelly shouldered the weapon, searched the wall for a likely brick and squeezed gently.

The bullet created a puff of dust. He adjusted the scope and fired again. Perfect. Kelly then fed three rounds into the magazine.

'DID YOU HEAR something?' Piaggi asked tiredly.

'What's that?' Tucker looked up from his task. More than twelve hours now and not even half done, despite the two 'soldiers' who were with them, down from Philadelphia.

'Like something falling,' Tony said, shaking his head and getting back to it. He slit open another bag and dumped the fine white powder into the bowl. Next he dumped in the milk sugar. 'Forget it.' He concentrated on his task.

'WHAT CAN I DO for you, Lieutenant?' said the sergeant who ran the central evidence-storage room.

'I need to check the numbers on the drugs I brought in last week,' Charon told him. 'I know where to go.' Official policy was that nobody wandered around in this room without an official escort, but Charon was a lieutenant.

The ten kilos he had taken from Eddie Morello's car were in a labelled cardboard box on the third shelf. He took down the box of ten one-kilo bags. Charon reached into his shirt and trousers, pulling out plastic bags of icing sugar, which was of the same colour and consistency as the heroin.

Only his office would ever touch this evidence, and he could control that. Since the case on it was closed, he'd dump it down the drain with several other people watching, and the plastic bags would be burned and nobody would ever know. It certainly seemed simple enough. Within three minutes he was walking away from the evidence racks.

'Numbers check out?'

'Yeah, Harry, thanks,' Charon said, waving on the way out. They'd pay him big-time for this, he thought.

'SOMEBODY GET the phone,' Piaggi growled.

Tucker walked over.

'Hi, Henry,' Kelly said. He'd wired a field phone into the building's telephone line, cutting it off from the outside world.

'Who's this?'

'The name's Kelly, John Kelly,' he told him. 'Four of you killed Pam. You're the only one left, Henry. I got the rest. Now it's your turn. I got Rick and I got Billy and I got Burt, and now I'm going to get you.' The line went dead.

'It's him,' Henry said quietly. 'It's *him.*'

'Well, who is *him,* Henry?' Piaggi lifted the phone.

Kelly heard the buzz and lifted his handset. 'Yeah, what is it?'

'Who are you?'

'It's Tony, right? Why did you have to kill Doris, Tony? Now I have to do you, too.'

Piaggi slammed the phone down. 'How could he know . . . ?' Piaggi said, his voice trailing off.

There was only one window with clear glass. It had a crank, allowing the panes to open upwards at an angle. Piaggi cranked the window open.

Kelly saw it move and wondered if he should announce his presence in a more direct way. Better not to. Better to be patient. Waiting grows hard on those who don't know what's happening.

It was ten in the morning now, a clean, sunny late-summer day.

Piaggi squatted to look out of the window. 'There's nobody around.'

'Let me look,' Henry Tucker said. 'Nothin',' he agreed.

Piaggi snarled. 'You two!'

'Yeah?' It was Bobby, the taller of the two Philly guys.

'Take a walk around the building—'

'No!' Henry said, thinking. 'What if he's right outside? You want to risk that? We gotta out-think him, OK?'

'What do you mean?' Piaggi asked, looking over to his partner. Henry was looking up. The acoustical panels had been removed from the drop ceiling. Right there, in the flat roof, was an access door with a simple latch. It would open easily to the tar and gravel roof, and a guy could get up there, walk to the edge, look down and whack whoever was waiting there.

'Bobby, Fred, come here,' Piaggi ordered. He filled them in on the tactical situation. Both had handguns. Both were clever. The two of them slid a desk under the access door.

Fred stood on the desk, which allowed him to open the trapdoor and look out on the roof. He then lifted himself up on the roof and moved very slowly towards the front of the building.

Fred was very concentrated now. He approached the parapeted edge. Then quickly he leaned forward, gun aimed downwards at—nothing. Fred turned and called, 'There's nobody here.'

'What?' Bobby's head came up in the opening to look.

As soon as Kelly's peripheral vision caught movement at the opening, he brought the gun left. A face—white, twenties, dark eyes—a pistol in his right hand. Take him first. Kelly squeezed gently.

Smack. Fred's head turned when he heard a sound that was both wet and hard. There was nothing there. But now there was also a clatter, as though Bobby had slipped and fallen. Nothing else, but for no apparent reason the skin at the back of his neck turned to ice. He backed away from the edge of the roof, looking all round. Nothing. He started moving back to the opening.

Kelly couldn't allow that. He squeezed again. *Pinggggggg*.

Two for the price of one.

29 *TRIAL BY ORDEAL*

'You're looking much better than the last time, Colonel,' Ritter said pleasantly in Russian. Ritter was carrying an attaché case, which he set on the coffee table and opened.

'When can I go home?' Grishanov said warily.

'This evening, probably. We're waiting for confirmation that our people are in Hoa Lo Prison.'

The attaché case was quite full with papers, Grishanov saw. Ritter took out two large cards and an ink pad. 'Could I have your hands, please?'

Ritter took the Russian's left hand and inked the fingertips, rolling them one at a time in the appropriate boxes on one card, then the other. The procedure was duplicated with the right hand. Ritter slid one of the cards into a file, substituting it for one he removed. The other just went on top. He then carried the old card to the fireplace, where he ignited it with his cigarette lighter.

'I don't understand,' said Grishanov.

'You just helped me out on something, that's all. What say we have lunch? If your side sticks to the bargain, you'll be on your way home in about eight hours. Fair enough?'

MARK CHARON PULLED his unmarked Ford to the front of the building, got out and walked to the front door. It was locked. He had to knock. Tony Piaggi yanked it open, a gun in his hand.

'What the hell is going on?' Charon demanded. Then he saw the body on the floor.

'It's him! He's out there,' Tucker said. 'The one who got Billy and Rick and Burt—'

'Kelly!' Charon exclaimed. He unloaded the bag of heroin from his clothing onto the table.

'You know his name?' Tucker asked.

'Ryan and Douglas want him for a string of killings.'

'We have to think this one through, OK?' Tony rubbed the heavy stubble on his face, collecting himself. 'He's got a rifle, and he's in that big white building.'

'You wanna walk over and get him, Tony?' Tucker asked.

'Ever hear of nightfall, Henry? We can wait for night and make our move. He can't get us all. If we move fast he might not get any.'

'AND HOW ARE YOU, Colonel?' Voloshin asked.

'It has been an interesting trip.' Ritter and Grishanov were sitting on the steps of the Lincoln Memorial, just two tourists, tired after a hot day, joined by a third friend, under the watchful eyes of a security guard.

'And your Vietnamese friend?'

'What?' Grishanov asked in some surprise. 'What friend?'

Ritter grinned. 'That was just a little ploy on my part. We had to identify the leak, you see.'

'I thought that was your doing,' Voloshin observed sourly. It was such an obvious trap, and he'd fallen right into it. Almost. You moved too fast, my young American friend. You managed to kill this Hicks boy, but not Cassius. Impetuous, my young friend. You miscalculated, and you really don't know it, do you?

'What about our people?'

'As agreed, they are with the others, Mr Ritter.'

'Very well, there's a Pan Am flight from Dulles to Paris tonight at eight fifteen. I'll deliver him there if you wish to see him off. You can have him met at Orly.'

'Agreed.' Voloshin walked away.

FIVE THIRTY. KELLY HAD long since decided what to do. It was going to be dangerous, and there was again a clock running. But he knew that he could delay no longer.

Kelly checked his Colt automatic and headed down the stairs, pulling out the keys to the VW. He let the engine warm up while watching traffic on the north–south street in front of him. He darted across, fitting neatly into the rush-hour traffic.

'SEE ANYTHING?' Charon asked.

'Just traffic on the other side,' Henry said.

'Don't get too close to the window, man,' Tony told him.

Charon was the most uncomfortable of the three. Could there be a way out of this? He had a gun. He watched them there, left and right of the window. They were the criminals. He could come out of this a hero, couldn't he? Got a tip, walked right into it. Crazy shoot-out. He could even help Kelly. All he had to do was to get on the phone and *reason* with the man. Except for one little thing.

KELLY TURNED LEFT, proceeded west one block, then left again, heading south towards O'Donnell Street. His hands were sweating now. There were three of them, and he'd have to be very, very good. He stopped the car a block away, getting out, locking it, and walking the rest of the way to the building.

He stood right there at the corner of the building, looking in all directions. Better from the other side . . . He walked to the corner with the phone and electrical service, using the same half-windowsill he'd used before, reaching for the parapet.

OK, now you just have to walk across the roof without making any noise. On tar and gravel?

There was one alternative. Kelly stood on the parapet. It was at least eight inches wide. It was also quiet as he walked the flat brick tightrope towards the opening in the roof.

CHARON HAD TO MAKE his move soon. He stood, looking at the others. His coat was off, his tie loose, and his gun was at his right hip. Just shoot the bastards and then talk to this Kelly character on the phone. Why not? Why should he die for what they did?

'What are you doing, Mark?' Henry asked.

'Tired of sittin'.'

Piaggi just didn't like the look in Charon's eyes. 'Why not just sit back down and relax, OK? It's going to get busy soon.'

'Back off, Tony, OK?' Charon said. He didn't know that his eyes had given him away. His hand had barely touched the revolver when Tony aimed and fired one shot into his chest.

'Real smart guy, huh?' Tony said to the dying man. Then he noticed that the oblong rectangle of light from the roof trapdoor had a shadow in it.

THE SHOT STARTLED Kelly—thinking it had been aimed at him—but he was committed, and jumped into the square hole.

He hit hard, rolled at once, straightening his arm. The nearest one was Piaggi. Kelly brought the gun up, levelling the sights with his chest and firing twice.

Kelly rolled again. There he was. Time stopped in that moment. Henry had his own gun out and aimed, and their eyes met, and for what seemed the longest time they simply looked, hunter and prey. Then Kelly's finger depressed the trigger, delivering a finely aimed shot into Tucker's chest, dropping him to the floor.

Mission accomplished, Kelly told himself. He walked to Henry Tucker. He wanted to say something to the face that was still alive, but Kelly was out of words. If the dead still lived on the surface of this earth, then it was in the minds of those who remembered them, and for that memory he'd killed Henry Tucker and all the others. Perhaps Pam would not rest any more easily. But he would. Kelly saw that Tucker had departed this life while he'd been thinking, examining his thoughts and his conscience. No, there was no remorse for this man, none for the others. Kelly safed his pistol and looked round the room. Four dead men, and the best thing that could be said was that he wasn't one of them. He walked to the door and out of it. His car was a block away, and he still had an appointment to keep, and one more life to end.

THE BOAT WAS where he'd left it. Kelly parked his car, took out the suitcase, then locked the car with the keys inside, for it was something he'd never need again. He hefted the suitcase, walked to *Springer* and hopped aboard. Kelly slid open the door to the main saloon and stopped dead when he first smelt smoke, then heard a voice.

'John Kelly, right? Emmet Ryan. My partner, Tom Douglas.'

'What can I do for you?' Kelly set his suitcase down.

'You can tell me why you've killed so many people,' Ryan suggested.

'If you think I've done it, then you know why.'

'True. I'm looking for Henry Tucker at the moment. Maybe you could help me, then?'

'Corner of O'Donnell and Mermen might be a good place to look. He's not going anywhere,' Kelly told the detectives.

'Just what do you think you accomplished?' Ryan asked. 'This drug problem isn't going away.'

'Henry Tucker won't kill any more girls. I accomplished that. I took that drug operation down.' Kelly paused. There was more this detective needed to know. 'There's a cop at that building. I think he was dirty. Tucker and Piaggi shot him. Maybe he can come out of this a hero. There's a load of stuff there. It won't look too bad for your department that way. I'll give you one more. I know how Tucker was getting his stuff in.' Kelly elaborated briefly.

'I have to take you in. For murder, Mr Kelly.'

'It's only murder when innocent people die.'

'The law doesn't say that. I can't just let you go,' the detective said, though part of him wished it were otherwise.

'Can you give me one hour? It'll make things better for everybody.'

The request caught Ryan by surprise. It was against everything he stood for—but then, so were the monsters the man had killed. *We owe him something* . . . and besides, where could he go?

Ryan rose. 'Your hour starts now.'

Kelly didn't watch him leave. He hit his engine controls, warming up the diesels. One hour should just about do it.

As soon as he was out of the yacht basin, he brought *Springer* to her top speed of twenty-two knots. He had to. He knew who they'd send after him.

'COASTGUARD, Thomas Point.'

'This is the Baltimore City Police . . .'

Forty-one Bravo was warmed up and ready. Seconds later it rumbled away from the dock.

THE MAN SURE DIDN'T GIVE me any slack, Kelly thought, seeing the cutter closing from starboard. Well, he'd asked for an hour, and an hour he'd received. It was a race now, but with a complication—a large French freighter standing out to sea right where Kelly needed to be. He would soon be caught between her and the coastguard.

'WELL, HERE WE ARE,' Ritter said, dismissing the security guard who'd followed them like a shadow all afternoon. He pulled a ticket from his pocket. 'First class. The booze is free, Colonel.'

'Thank you for your hospitality.'

'Your behaviour to our prisoners was as correct as circumstances allowed,' Ritter said formally. 'Thank you for that.'

'It is my wish that they get home safely. They are not bad men.'

'Neither are you.' Ritter led him to the gate.

THEY WERE TOO CLOSELY matched. *Springer* had a slight advantage since she was in the lead, while the cutter needed her half-knot speed advantage to draw closer.

Manuel Oreza watched the other man slide his boat across the wake of the freighter, sliding her onto the front of the ship-generated wave and riding it to port, gaining perhaps half a knot's momentary advantage. Oreza had to admire it.

Oreza started his slide to port now, riding through the freighter's wake, using the energy generated by the ship to gain speed. Interesting. This is how a dolphin does it. That got me a whole knot's worth, and my hull's better at this than his is . . . Contrary to everything he should have felt, Manuel Oreza smiled. He'd just learned something new about boat-handling, courtesy of a friend he was trying to arrest for murder.

IT WAS DEVILISHLY CLOSE. Oreza was just too good at driving his boat, and that made it all the harder to risk what he'd planned, Kelly thought. The control for the pyrotechnics charge was next to him. Five seconds after he hit that, the fuel tanks would blow, but that wasn't worth a damn with a coastguard cutter two hundred yards back.

Now what?

The quickest and simplest solution was to pull the cutter up behind him on the starboard side of the freighter, then duck across the bow, and *then* blow the boat up. But there was another way, a better way.

He was amidships on the freighter now and Oreza had swallowed the bait—as he had to, Kelly thought. That guy was good. Another mile and he'd be alongside, reducing Kelly's options to precisely zero, but he did have his plan now, seeing the freighter's bulbous bow, partly exposed. Kelly looked back for the first time in this race, measuring distance, and it was damnably close.

Oreza was barely half a ship's length back now.

It was then that Kelly did something unexpected. He eased his rudder right to catch the bow wave, his eyes watching the foaming forefoot of the freighter. When the moment was right, he put the rudder over.

Springer lurched to starboard from the force of the radical turn, then even more from the small hill of water raised by the freighter's bow. Kelly held onto the wheel with his left hand and reached with his right for the air tank, round which he'd strung six weight belts.

OREZA WATCHED from only a hundred yards away, but the distance might as well have been a thousand miles for all the good it did, and his mind saw it before reality caught up: already heeling hard to the right from the turn, *Springer* rode up high on the curling bow wave of the freighter and, crosswise to it, rolled completely over, her hull instantly disappearing in the foaming forefoot of the cargo ship.

It was no way for a seaman to die.

FORTY-ONE BRAVO backed down hard, rocking violently with the passage of the ship's wake as she came to a stop. The freighter stopped, too, but it took fully two miles, and by that time Oreza and his cutter were poking through the wreckage. Searchlights came on in the gathering darkness.

'Coastguard Forty-one, Coastguard Forty-one, this is US Navy sailboat on your port beam. Can we render assistance? Over.'

'We could use some extra eyes, Navy. Who's aboard?'

'Couple of admirals. The one talking's an aviator, if that helps.'
'Join in, sir.'

HE WAS STILL ALIVE. It was as much a surprise to Kelly as it would have been to Oreza. He and the air tank had plummeted seventy feet to the bottom. He fought to strap the tank to his chest in the violent turbulence of the passing ship overhead. Then he fought to swim clear of the descending engines and heavy gear from what had seconds earlier been an expensive cruiser. Looking up, Kelly could see the coastguard hull over to the east . . . and to the west the deeper shape of a sailboat—pray God the right one. Kelly disengaged four of the weight belts from the tank and swam towards it. His head broke the surface on the west side of the sailboat.
'Is that you?' Maxwell called.
'I think so.' His hand reached up.
Maxwell reached over the side, hauled the bruised and sore body aboard and directed him below.

'FORTY-ONE, THIS IS NAVY. This doesn't look real good.'
'I'm afraid you're right, Navy. You can break off if you want. I think we'll stay a while,' Oreza said. It had been good of them to quarter the surface for three hours. Oreza and Forty-one Bravo would continue their search all night, finding only wreckage.

IT MADE THE PAPERS in a big way. Detective Lieutenant Mark Charon, following up a lead on his own time, had stumbled into a drug lab and in the ensuing gun battle had lost his life in the line of duty while ending those of two major traffickers. The coincidental escape of three young women resulted in the identification of one of the deceased traffickers as a particularly brutal murderer, which perhaps explained Charon's heroic zeal. On page six was a story about a boating accident.
Three days later a filing clerk from St Louis called Lieutenant Ryan to say that the Kelly file was back, but she couldn't say from where. Ryan thanked her for her effort. He'd closed the case, and didn't even try the FBI records centre for Kelly's card, and thus made unnecessary Bob Ritter's substitution of the prints of someone unlikely ever to visit America again.
Five months later Sandra O'Toole resigned her position at Johns Hopkins and moved to the Virginia tidewater, where she took over a whole floor of the area's teaching hospital on the strength of a glowing recommendation from Professor Samuel Rosen.

Epilogue *FEBRUARY 12, 1973*

'We are honoured to have the opportunity to serve our country under difficult circumstances,' Captain Jeremiah Denton said, ending a statement that rang across the ramp at Clark Air Base with 'God bless America'.

'How about that?' the commentator said. 'Right behind Captain Denton is Colonel Robin Zacharias of the air force. He's one of the prisoners about whom we had no information until very recently . . .'

John Clark didn't listen to the rest. He looked at the TV, at the face of a man to whom he'd been so close in body, closer still in spirit not so long before. He saw the man embrace his wife after five years of separation. He saw a woman who'd grown old with worry but now was young with love for the husband she'd thought dead. Kelly wept with them, seeing the joy that really could replace pain, no matter how vast. He squeezed Sandy's hand. She rested his on her belly to feel the movement of their soon-to-be first-born. It was then that the phone rang.

'I hope you're proud of yourself, John,' Dutch Maxwell said. 'We're getting all twenty back. I wanted to make sure you knew that. It wouldn't have happened without you.'

'Thank you, sir.' Clark hung up. There was nothing else to be said.

'Who was that?' Sandy asked, holding his hand in place.

'A friend,' Clark said, wiping his eyes as he turned to kiss his wife. 'From another life.'

TOM CLANCY

Since the phenomenal success of his first novel, *The Hunt for Red October*, Tom Clancy has become one of the world's fastest-selling authors. The book grew out of a long-term ambition to write a novel and a fascination with military technology. 'More than anything else I'm a technology freak,' he admits. 'And the best stuff is military.' His interest in military detail combined with painstaking research has made him just as popular with military personnel as with the general book-buying public. His subsequent six books, including *Without Remorse*, have all built on his first novel's success and enhanced his worldwide popularity.

It comes as no surprise that Hollywood has already snapped up three of Clancy's action-packed books to make into films. *The Hunt for Red October*, starring Sean Connery, was the first, followed by *Patriot Games*, which starred Harrison Ford. Tom Clancy is currently working as co-executive producer on the forthcoming film of *Without Remorse*.

Although the success of his novels has led to increased demands on his time, Clancy disdains the social circuit. Instead, he prefers to be at home in Calvert County, Maryland, in the United States, overlooking the waters of Chesapeake Bay, writing his next novel, helping around the house and enjoying the company of his wife and their four children.

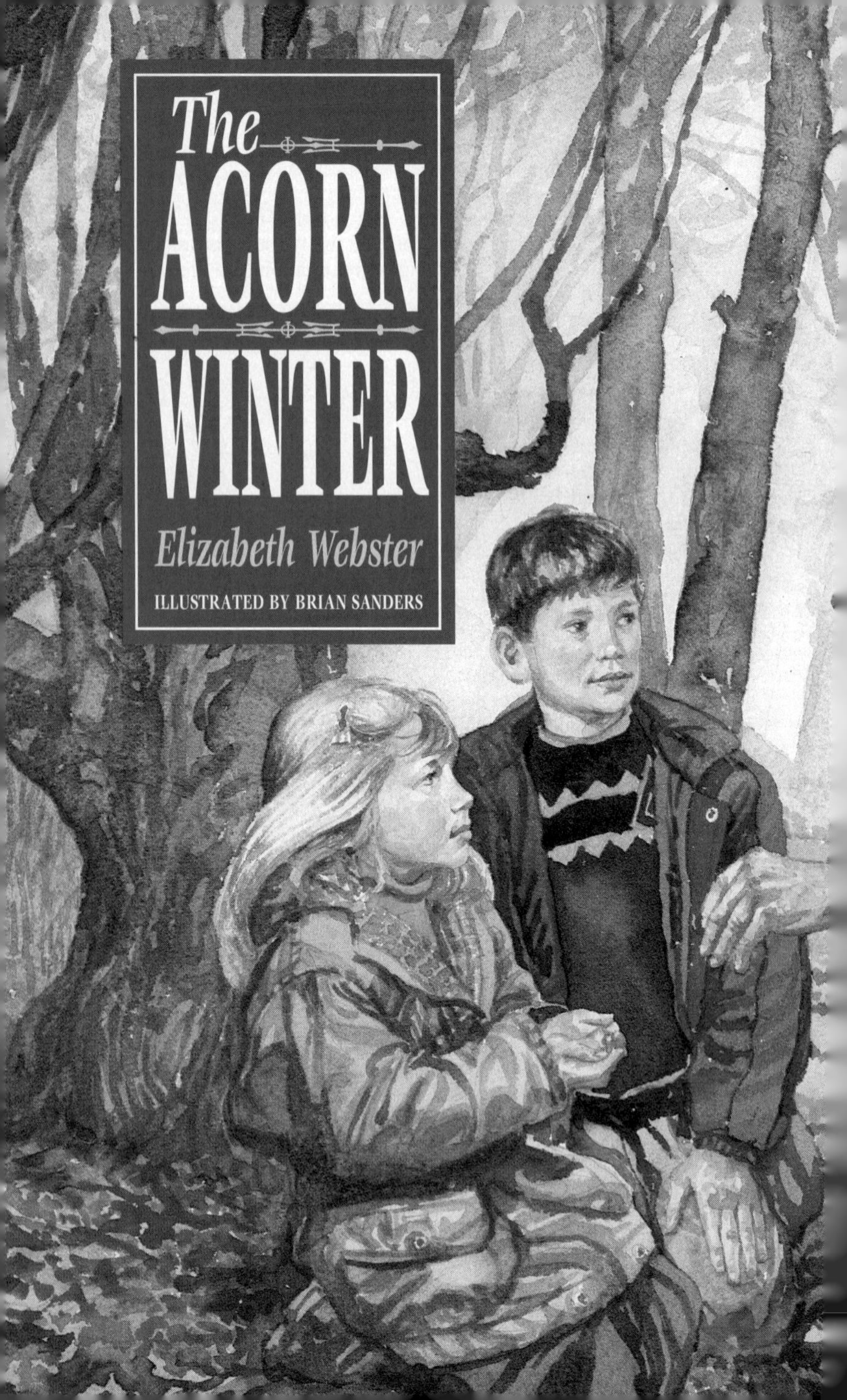
The
ACORN
WINTER
Elizabeth Webster
ILLUSTRATED BY BRIAN SANDERS

When her husband returns from his triumphant, single-handed sailing trip, Stephanie Edmondson and her daughter Chloë are overjoyed to see him. But, even in the midst of all her family's happiness, Stephanie is aware of the distress of the young woman who day after day stands on the shore staring out to sea. Something about the lonely figure touches Stephanie's heart and she seeks her out, discovering that her name is Beth Halliday and that she has been devastated by the deaths of her husband and son. Little by little Stephanie pieces together Beth's story and sets her on the road to recovery. Then tragedy strikes again.

PART I
The Empty Sea

She stood at the edge of the sea, staring out at the horizon. A small, slim girl—graceful too, probably, only now she was standing too straight and taut, staring out, straining to see something beyond her reach, beyond the horizon, beyond the sky, too far, too far away to reach.

The look on her face was one of bewilderment rather than loss—a puzzled disbelief that what she searched for was unreachable, was gone for ever, would never come back.

Never come back.

If I wait long enough, she told herself, he might come back. They both might. I think they are just out there, just round the point, searching for crabs, like they used to. They'll come back hand in hand—tall Robert, smiling and handsome, and little Mo, trying to keep up on his four-year-old legs, and smiling, too, at the father he adored . . .

She stood a little straighter and gazed out even harder at the cold grey sea, trying to pierce the veils of distance and see what could not be seen. Curls of white foam were breaking round her feet now, and spray rose up in rainbow plumes. She looked drenched and cold, and somehow beyond recall.

But a sudden explosion of sound startled her, a burst of cheering way down the beach near the jetty, and a cacophony of whistles and sirens from the small boats in the bay, a clapping of many hands and a chorus of excited shouts of encouragement.

The girl turned her head and looked down the beach to where a crowd of cheerful people jostled one another on the little harbour wall, all peering out to sea. Someone, or something, was clearly coming. But who? Or what?

The cheering broke out again as a small battered yacht slipped round the harbour entrance and came gently to rest at the end of the concrete pier.

The cheering grew louder and the solitary figure of the yachtsman, poised on deck, raised a cheerful hand in salute and then leaped ashore, mooring rope in hand.

So it was that Beth Halliday, cold and bereft and bewildered, first saw Finn Edmondson coming home in triumph from his lonely single-handed voyage aboard *Dancing Lady*. And the brilliance of his coming seemed to spark in her a kind of desperate anger, it was so beautiful and so full of certainty.

He leaped ashore and sunlight glinted on his golden beard, laid sparks of light on his tangled sea-wet hair and lit his eyes with sudden fire. He strode up the jetty like a Viking marauder, a hero of ancient legend—and the light of victory was in his face as he walked through the cheering crowd.

And then the friendly press of people parted, leaving a pathway down the middle of the jetty, and at the end of the open space stood Finn's wife and small daughter, waiting to greet him. The pretty young wife stood still, smiling and calm, but the little girl could not wait any longer and ran towards him, white-gold hair flying, calling out to him over the voices of the crowd as she ran, 'Daddy-Finn, Daddy-Finn! You're home!'

He swept her up in his arms and his stride scarcely lessened as he went on, straight into his wife's open embrace. Something about this joyous, sun-gilded encounter seemed to pierce Beth to the core and she turned away with tears in her eyes.

It was all very well for him. At the harbour end of the beach the sea was blue and spangled with sunlight, and the little scene she had just witnessed seemed bathed in an almost mythical, golden light. But here, where she stood, the sea was cold and grey and empty—terribly empty—and no one was coming home to her, no one at all.

No one at all. Not ever again. No tall, wind-browned Robert, no sturdy little Mo. They would not come round the corner, hand in hand. It was all a dream—a futile, self-deluding, cruel dream—and she was a fool to let herself believe it. Time to come to terms with reality, to leave the far horizons where hope laid a false brightness on the shadowed sea.

Stumbling a little, and shaking her head as if to rid it of visions and mirages, she began to walk furiously away along the shore, and tears of rage and grief blinded her as she went.

'WHO IS SHE, I WONDER?' said Stephanie Edmondson, holding her breakfast coffee cup suspended in midair and staring out of the hotel dining-room window at the slight, lonely figure on the shore.

Finn's gaze followed hers for a moment, but soon returned to his wife's expressive face with smiling affection. 'How should I know? I just got here, remember?'

'She's been standing there since early morning, and I think she was there most of yesterday, too, only I was too excited to pay much attention.' There was concern in the clear grey eyes. 'I can't help thinking . . .'

'You and your lame ducks,' growled Finn. But he was too happy just now to protest very much, even when Stephanie left the breakfast table and went across to the reception desk in the foyer to ask discreetly if anyone knew who the solitary sea-gazer was.

'No,' said the man at the reception desk, who, like Finn, was unable to stop smiling at Stephanie and her palpable happiness. 'She's not staying here. But I think I've seen her coming out of the Harbour View.'

'Thank you,' said Stephanie. 'Maybe I'll enquire there.'

She returned to find Finn busy explaining the intricacies of a sea chart to his small daughter. 'You see, Chloë, that big dot is an island. But the little dots are reefs.'

'Reefs?' It was incomprehensible to six-year-old Chloë, but she didn't mind. Anything her splendid hero of a father said was worth listening to, even if she didn't understand a word of it.

'What are you doing today?' asked Stephanie, looking at the two of them with loving indulgence.

'Seeing to the repairs.' Finn stretched in lazy contentment and got to his feet. 'Coming, Sprat?'

'Yes, *please*!' Chloë put her hand firmly in his.

Finn twitched an enquiring eyebrow in Stephanie's direction, but she hesitated and then said in an offhand voice, 'I'll follow you down later. I want to make a call on the way.'

Finn nodded amiably. He was used to Stephanie's determined independence. It was one of the things he liked best about her and a blessing when he was so often away on his endless pursuit of new projects and adventures. 'We'll be at the boatyard,' he said, and strode off with Chloë's warm brown hand in his.

Stephanie watched them go, then turned and went out into the street. She walked briskly down the road and up the white steps into the sunny glassed-in porch of the Harbour View Hotel.

It was an old-fashioned place with an air of tranquillity about it that Stephanie liked immediately. The woman behind the reception desk was middle-aged and, like her surroundings, pleasant and homely. Stephanie approached her directly, somehow certain that she would not be rebuffed.

The proprietress, Mrs Foster, clearly recognised her. Finlay Edmondson was a very famous man these days, always in the news, and (rumour had it) extremely rich. His wife was undoubtedly someone to be reckoned with too, but her warmth and friendliness were totally disarming.

'Oh, you mean Mrs Halliday—Beth Halliday.' Mrs Foster looked up at Stephanie with genuine concern in her eyes. 'Yes, I'm afraid she is very much alone now, poor young lady. The three of them used to come down here quite a lot in the old days—her husband and the little boy. Such a lovely child. He and his father used to go out together, looking for crabs.' She glanced at Stephanie, a faint smile softening the tired lines of her face.

Stephanie was staring at her hard. 'They *used* to come?'

The woman nodded. 'Yes, quite often. He got a lot of short leaves, you see. He was an airline pilot. There was some kind of accident, I believe, at some foreign airport. She was widowed very young, poor girl.' She paused as if not quite sure how much to say. 'But even after that, she came back with the little boy. I think, maybe, she felt better in the place where they had been happy.'

Stephanie nodded silently. That made sense.

'And now . . . this,' added the proprietress, as if driven by a kind of angry outrage she could not express.

'Now *what*?'

'The little boy. He died of meningitis.'

'When?'

'Oh, only a short while ago, I think. She didn't say exactly, just rang to explain why she was coming down alone. The poor young thing, she just stands there on the beach all day.' Mrs Foster shook her head sadly, then seemed to recollect that she was stepping outside her role of discreet guesthouse proprietress and sighed. 'I shouldn't be gossiping about my guests, really.'

'It's not gossiping,' Stephanie told her roundly. 'She needs help. She needs company. I'll see what I can do.'

And, with that, Stephanie left the hotel and strode off along the beach.

'AREN'T YOU COLD?' she said, standing close to the lonely figure at the edge of the water.

'Cold?' The girl turned her head. The dark blue eyes, unfocused and overbright, stared blankly at the stranger beside her.

Cold? She was always cold now. There seemed to be no warmth left in the world, none at all.

'Yes, I'm cold.' Her voice was cold, too—brittle and strange.

'Why not come and have a coffee?' suggested Stephanie, looking back into the brilliant, unseeing gaze with compassion.

Beth shook her head. 'I have to wait,' she explained reasonably to the kind face opposite. And then, since the face did not look convinced, she added earnestly, 'If I wait long enough, you see, they will come back.'

'Do you think so?' The gentle voice was not sceptical, merely calm and quiet.

'They went round the point, you know,' Beth told her. 'They only went round the point.'

'To look for crabs?' The voice was even gentler now.

Beth smiled, and the pinched, bewildered face was suddenly flooded with light. 'Yes, that's it. How did you know?'

'My daughter, Chloë, likes looking for crabs, too.' Stephanie was watching her carefully. 'Sometimes she goes on her own when the tide is low . . . I can see her from the hotel window.'

'Can you?' The girl stood looking at her uncertainly.

'Shall we go and see?'

Once more the girl's eyes turned to look at the sea, but it was still empty and cold. There was no one there. No one coming back. 'Well, all right,' she said, and then, more fiercely, 'but I have to watch.'

'Of course.' Stephanie put a warm, comforting arm round her shoulders and led her away towards the warmth of Stephanie's hotel.

In the quiet lounge, they sat by the big picture windows that looked out on the bay so that Beth could still watch the swirl of water round the point. 'Drink your coffee,' prompted Stephanie, and carefully wrapped Beth's cold fingers round the warm china cup.

Obediently, Beth sipped at the hot liquid and felt some of the icy numbness begin to thaw a little. She knew this friendly stranger was being extraordinarily kind and she tried vainly to focus on the concerned face opposite, but somehow she couldn't seem to reach it. She couldn't seem to reach the world around her at all. There was this awful silence, this veil between her and reality, like an invisible pall.

Like a pall.

A pall . . . He lay in a pall, consigned to the cold, dark earth. His small body laid out neatly, stiff and cold as death . . . Death? How could he cope with death all on his own? He was only four. I ought to be with him, helping him through. Through to where?

In her mind she saw a sudden, very clear picture of an enormous staircase, huge and dazzling white and empty—save for one tiny figure bravely struggling to master those massive, steep steps.

'He was always brave,' she said suddenly and, as she spoke those words, the whole distorted fantasy of her hopeless vigil by the sea collapsed, and she was through the veil and back in the real world again, and the tears were running down her cheeks.

'I know,' said Stephanie, watching both sanity and pain return to the girl's face. 'They are much braver than we are.' And then, seeing how much that weight of sorrow needed to come out, she put a hand on Beth's arm and suggested, 'Shall we go upstairs? It's quieter there.'

Beth nodded, not able to speak just now, and allowed herself to be led away to Stephanie's sunny room overlooking the bay.

'You can still look out,' Stephanie said, standing near the window so that Beth could see the beach below.

'No,' whispered Beth, her voice choked with tears. 'They won't come back . . . not now.' And her shoulders began to shake.

'Oh, my dear girl,' said Stephanie, and folded her in her arms.

When the storm of tears was over, Stephanie sent for more coffee and some brandy, and they began to talk. It seemed to her very important that Beth should tell someone, anyone, about what had happened. It didn't matter how long it took. She had all day to spare.

'I ought not to . . .' Beth began, already ashamed of her collapse.

'Yes, you *ought*,' said Stephanie firmly. 'You need to talk. And I want to hear it.'

'Why?'

Stephanie looked at her with curious intensity. 'Because I need to know.' She spoke obscurely, and when Beth did not go on she prompted her gently. 'Tell me about your husband first.'

'Robert?' She sighed. 'He was an airline pilot, older than me, and he was away a lot. So . . . so every leave was somehow exciting and special, like an extra honeymoon.'

'Yes.' Stephanie nodded comprehension. 'Like Finn and me.'

Beth glanced at her with sudden awareness. 'Of course . . . on the beach yesterday. I saw him arrive.' A faint smile touched her for a moment. 'He looked like a Viking.' But the smile faltered then. 'I thought it looked such a . . . such a *joyous* meeting.' The tears almost threatened to spill out again at the memory of that reunion, and she hurried on. 'It reminded me so much of how it was every time Robert

came home. But then, of course, one day he didn't.'

Stephanie sighed. It could so easily happen to Finn.

'It was such a senseless accident!' Beth exploded into sudden anger. 'After all those flying hours, all those journeys all over the world, and never a mishap, never any trouble . . .'

'And?'

'He was just walking back to the airport for his next flight, and some car came round the corner too fast. It simply mowed him down, never saw him at all.'

Stephanie looked shocked. 'How dreadful.'

'Yes.' Her tone was dry. 'There was a court case of some sort out there. And the company did their best to be helpful.' She pushed the hair out of her eyes in a childish, distracted manner. 'I don't know why I'm telling you all this.'

'Because I asked you to,' said Stephanie. 'Besides, it's sometimes easier to talk to a stranger.'

Beth looked at her then in an odd, searching way and almost said, But you're not a stranger, are you? But it was too difficult to say, so she merely shook her head wordlessly and gave a shaky smile.

But Stephanie was not to be deflected. 'How long ago was this?'

'Oh . . . two and a half years. Mo was just two when it happened.'

'It must have been terribly hard for you.'

'Yes, I suppose it was.' Beth paused, and then went on in a cool, light voice. 'Though in a way it was easier to cope with because I had got used to managing on my own most of the time. Of course I missed Robert terribly, and so did Mo . . .' She took a deep breath. 'It's the little things . . . Not being able to say, "Look, Robert!" when you see something beautiful, or having someone around who knows your thoughts without being told.' She shook her head, angry at her own weakness. 'Anyway, I thought I was coming to terms with it. Life was a bit bleak but we managed, Mo and I. I suppose I concentrated everything on little Mo. He became the . . . the *focus* of my life.' She was silent then, unable to continue.

Stephanie's comment was gentle. 'That's only natural.'

'Is it?' Beth swallowed hard. 'He was such a . . . such a happy child. I never thought anything else could happen to us.' She shook her head in helpless disbelief. 'It didn't seem possible.'

Stephanie waited for her to go on and, when she failed to say anything more, gave her another quiet prod. 'Then what went wrong?'

Beth glanced at her rather wildly and shivered. 'I can't . . .'

'Yes, you can. Please?' Her voice was still soft, but Beth could feel the steel behind it. Stephanie was difficult to resist when she was determined to have her own way.

'He seemed so well . . .' Beth said slowly, 'so full of life that day . . .'

He had been running round the garden with her, laughing in the sun, looking for tadpoles in the little pond, chasing a dragonfly across the grass and laughing, always laughing in the sunshine. *'Look at me, I'm high—high as a dragonfly!'*

There had been nothing to indicate disaster, no shadow on that bright spring day. And then nothing more than a headache, a tossing restlessness, a faint glaze in the blue, trusting eyes . . . And the fever rising and rising . . .

'You'll feel better soon,' she had said, laying a cool hand on his small hot head. And his answering voice, vague and drowsy, had faded on a sigh: *'Better . . . soon . . .'*

But he hadn't been better. He had been worse. And the nightmare had begun. The doctor—grave and concerned, the fever rising and rising, and sudden, frightening convulsions and then the deep, dreadful unconsciousness. The rush to the hospital, and the shocked, terrible wrench in her arms, in her heart, as they took him away from her. It felt like the stroke of death, even then.

'He just . . . got ill so suddenly,' she said. 'Meningitis is like that. I called the doctor as soon as . . . as soon as the fever rose . . . He did everything he could. So did the hospital. But it was too late. He just never came round.'

I never held him again, she thought. Never. And my arms will always feel empty. Always. As long as I live.

And now my life is utterly changed, and the worst thing is not knowing where he is, whether he can cope. Is Robert with him? Or is he alone? Terribly alone? What is heaven, anyway? Is it there at all? How can I tell?

'Where do they go?' she said suddenly, turning a beseeching gaze on Stephanie 'Where are they now?'

Stephanie looked at her sadly. 'I don't know. I wish I did.' She paused and then added, almost shyly, 'Are you religious?'

'I don't know what I am.' Beth shook her head. 'I don't know what I believe, though I was brought up a Christian, I suppose, but . . .' The tears threatened again and made her voice shake. 'I only know I'd like to think they went on . . . and that Mo was safe.' She took another wavering breath and continued, in a faintly puzzled tone, 'I thought I might feel close to Robert, you know, after the accident, that I might feel him nearby or something . . . but I never did. I got quite angry with him, at times, for *not* coming back. But as for little

Mo'—again her voice shook a little—'he was too small to cope with eternity.'

'I don't know,' repeated Stephanie, but in a different, altogether more certain tone. 'I think a child might understand eternity better than we could. Everything would seem possible to him.'

Beth stared at her. 'Do you think so?'

Stephanie smiled. 'Yes. He'll be all right, he and your Robert. It's you we have to think about now.'

At that point the door opened suddenly and Finn and Chloë burst into the room.

'You never came!' reproached Chloë, and Finn added, smiling, 'We missed you!' Then, seeing Beth, he stopped short.

Stephanie looked up at him undismayed, and said calmly, 'This is Beth. She is coming to lunch with us downstairs.'

'Oh, but—' began Beth.

'No buts.' Stephanie got briskly to her feet. 'Chloë can choose her favourite pudding. Shall we go?'

Finn shrugged broad shoulders and grinned with the greatest good humour. 'Why not?' he said.

OVER LUNCH, FINN WAS his usual brilliant self, and described in much hilarious detail the hazards of his single-handed voyage. He was not a stupid man, and he knew without being told that Stephanie required him to keep things light and cheerful and cover for this distressed young woman's silence.

Chloë played up, too, plying her father with questions, chattering with excitement, spreading her wide-eyed admiration of Finn's exploits like a cloak of many colours round their enchanted table. But even little Chloë somehow knew she ought to do something about that bewildered silence, and she turned to Beth suddenly with the utmost sweetness. 'Would you like to come and see Daddy's boat? I'm sure he'd let you.'

'I . . .' Beth tried to focus her flying thoughts on the bright, eager little face beside her. You can't quench that brightness with your own sorrow, she thought. It's not her fault. 'Yes,' she said at last, summoning a smile, 'I'd be honoured.'

Beside her, Stephanie nodded quiet approval. It was a start. Trust Chloë to break the ice.

A waiter approached, looking concerned at Beth's untouched food. 'Try to eat something,' murmured Stephanie.

'I . . . I can't,' Beth said. I can't. How can I eat when he is dead? How can I go on living and doing ordinary things? The world and its noise and clutter simply choke me. What's the point of it all?

'Never mind.' Stephanie spoke softly. 'It will come.'

Beth glanced at her new friend in mute protest and suddenly realised that she had never really looked at her closely before.

Stephanie's face had a clear-cut bone structure, a rather determined chin and the same luminous grey eyes as her six-year-old daughter. Beth was rather afraid of those eyes. They probed too deep. The mouth, though occasionally stern, was full of the same quiet compassion as those disturbing eyes, but the set of her head was somehow alert and watchful despite its frame of fair flyaway hair. It was a face she could trust, Beth told herself. And I have this extraordinary feeling that we knew each other before, she thought suddenly. She didn't approach me like a stranger, and somehow I think our lives are already linked.

'Let's go, then,' Stephanie suggested.

'But I haven't had my pudding!' cried Chloë, outraged, and Finn began to laugh.

'Oh, you must have that. What is it to be?'

And they all watched in fascination as the small girl's face puckered in concentration over the dessert trolley.

When she had successfully demolished a mound of chocolate gâteau they went to inspect the boat, which was propped up on wedges high up on the slipway at the edge of the little boatyard.

'How long will it take?' asked Stephanie, eyeing the shabby paint with some respect. It had seen a lot of storms, she thought, that sturdy little boat. And it had brought Finn safely home.

'About a week,' said Finn.

Stephanie looked at Beth and smiled. 'We can potter about together then, can't we?'

Beth scarcely knew how to answer. She could not understand why this amazingly kind woman was taking so much trouble. 'What will you do next?' she asked Finn, wondering if he would be off on some new adventure immediately.

'Oh, it's the family's turn,' he said, smiling. 'We're going to sail her down to the Greek islands. There's a development project I'm involved with out there that wants looking at.' He winked at Stephanie and sunlight sparked in his golden buccaneer's beard.

'When isn't there?' laughed Stephanie. But there was a plan forming in her head, only it was too soon yet to put into words.

'A family holiday,' pronounced Finn, and hoisted Chloë up onto his shoulder. 'How does that grab you, Sprat?'

'Magic!' said Chloë, and grabbed at her father's golden hair.

ALL THAT WEEK Stephanie kept it up, filling Beth's day with cheerful, unimportant excursions. She did not let her walk on the beach alone any more, but took her up onto the green hills beyond the town and along the deep leafy lanes of the Devon valleys. Mostly she left Chloë with Finn, who was still haunting the boatyard, determined to supervise his repairs personally. It was good for the two of them to be together—Chloë saw little enough of her famous father as it was.

Then one morning, Stephanie said suddenly to Beth: 'Would having Chloë along with us bother you?'

Beth looked at her in amazement. '*Bother me?* She's enchanting.'

'Yes, but—'

'No,' said Beth firmly. 'She doesn't remind me of Mo—not really. Except her zest for life. But then most children have that, don't they?' She looked at Stephanie, half smiling. 'After all, I used to be a teacher. I can't banish all children from my life, can I?'

'No,' agreed Stephanie slowly. 'You can't.'

Beth was still looking at her and wondering if she dared to ask a leading question. Things were unexpectedly easy between them now, especially since Beth herself was not quite so shocked and disorientated.

'Can I ask you something?'

Stephanie lifted expressive eyebrows and smiled. 'I should think so.'

'Then, *why*? Why take all this trouble?'

Stephanie regarded her calmly. 'I suppose . . . because I'm an interfering woman, and you remind me of myself when I was young.'

'But you're still young.'

'Not as young as you.' The smile still lurked behind her eyes but there was now a curious, reflective sadness in her gentle voice. 'I married very young—like you. And I knew from the start that Finn would always be off on new ventures—like your Robert.'

'Didn't you mind?'

Stephanie sighed. 'Oh yes, I minded. But that's the way it is with men like Finn. He can't stay in one place for long. There has to be a challenge.'

Beth nodded. 'Yes, I know.'

'Well, like you, I learned to manage on my own.' She grinned with sudden mischief. 'And I've been managing ever since!'

Beth actually laughed.

But Stephanie was suddenly grave. 'Of course, it's hard on Chloë. And she—' Stephanie broke off and then added in a softened tone: ' *"The focus of your life"* you said, about your little Mo. You're not the only one.'

Beth understood her very well. But she did not speak.

'I sometimes wish . . .' went on Stephanie, and then paused, as if uncertain of her own thoughts. 'I wish Chloë would get attached to someone besides me. She relies on me too much. It's dangerous.'

Beth looked at her then. 'Oh, yes. It's dangerous.'

Stephanie took a strange, long breath. 'But I wouldn't have it otherwise. Every moment, every small happening, they are all extra special—extra precious, really.' Her voice had taken on a soft, reflective resonance, filled with unexpressed thoughts. Then she turned to Beth with sudden insistence. 'Weren't they for you?'

'Of course.' Beth bent her head to hide the sudden tears.

'Don't you see?' persisted Stephanie. 'You still have them—all those special moments. You only have to remember.'

This time, Beth did not answer at all.

'There,' said Stephanie, laying an apologetic hand on Beth's arm. 'I've said too much, as usual!' She was smiling again and Beth could not help responding. 'But do you see now why you matter to me?' She tilted her head sideways in an interrogative way. 'It could so easily have been me . . . But I have been much too lucky.'

At this, Beth looked up and smiled with sudden generosity. 'Well, thank God one of us has,' she said.

AFTER THIS, STEPHANIE often brought Chloë along too, and Beth found herself curiously drawn to the outspoken, fair-haired child with eyes so like her mother's.

It was while they were sitting on the springy turf of a nearby clifftop, finishing a picnic lunch, that Stephanie dared to talk of the future. 'What will you do now?' she asked.

'Do?' Beth looked panic-stricken for a moment, and then seemed visibly to pull herself together. 'I don't know. Go back to work, I suppose.'

Stephanie prompted her gently. 'You said you were a teacher?'

'Yes. I went on working after I got married, till Mo was born.'

Stephanie nodded.

'And after Rob was killed I went back part-time, to . . . to have something to do. I took Mo with me, then. The school had its own nursery.'

'What subjects?'

'Subjects? Oh, general—junior-school stuff. And music.'

'Music?' Stephanie sat up straight and looked at her with sudden attention. 'What kind of music?'

Beth looked surprised. 'Any kind. Class music—singing—piano

and all that. And the recorder, of course—a must in junior-school life.' There was almost a glimmer of a smile on her pale face. 'And percussion. For all the duds who liked banging things.'

Chloë, following the conversation in spite of the egg sandwich half-in and half-out of her mouth, said suddenly, 'Tubular bells.'

'What?' Stephanie was mystified.

'Tunes,' explained Chloë, swallowing more sandwich. 'Not only bangs. Like xylophones.'

Beth smiled. 'You're right. Not only bangs.'

'We're not all duds,' stated Chloë, looking at Beth with challenge.

'Of course not.' Beth was ashamed of her stupid generalisation. She knew very well that percussion could be both subtle and immensely skilled.

'Do you know anything about music therapy?' asked Stephanie, sounding oddly offhand and casual all of a sudden.

Beth considered for a moment. 'No, I don't.' Then she went on more slowly, 'Though I suppose all music is a kind of therapy.' She turned to look at Stephanie and caught a strange, speculative gleam in her eye. 'Why?'

'Oh, it's just something I'm interested in.' She spoke carelessly. 'I'll tell you about it later.'

But at that point they saw Finn climbing up the cliff path to meet them, and Chloë leaped to her feet and went running to meet him.

'Daddy-Finn!' she shouted, a mixture of joy and reproach in her voice. 'You're late and we've eaten all the sandwiches.'

'Never mind,' he said, hoisting her up in the air and swinging her round. 'I've brought a pork pie.'

Stephanie looked at Beth's still face and knew she was seeing another summer's day and another joyful meeting, and desperately trying to stave off hurt. But it would not do. That way she would never mend.

Gently, she broke into Beth's dark dream. 'Don't shut them out,' she said.

'WHY?' ASKED FINN as he and Stephanie sat late in their room to discuss the day.

'Oh, Finn, *think*! She's lost everything in the world she loved. There's nothing left. How would you feel if you lost Chloë? Or me, for that matter?'

Finn went pale. The thought was unendurable. 'I wanted you to myself,' he grumbled.

'You can still have me to yourself,' said Stephanie, laughing.

'There's room on the boat for four. We won't get in each other's way.'

'That's what you think!'

'And, anyway, she can help to look after Chloë if we should want to go out on our own.' She looked into Finn's face with sudden appeal. 'Please, Finn. It's important.'

'Is it? Why?'

She looked at him strangely and said, in an oddly shaken voice, 'Because we're so happy.'

Finn was silent for a while, but he knew very well what Stephanie meant. Wasn't his whole life lived as a hostage to fortune?

Sighing, he acquiesced and laid his golden head close to his wife's in perfect accord. 'Have it your own way,' he said.

BUT STEPHANIE DIDN'T have it her own way. When she made her offer, Beth flatly refused.

'No.' She sounded unexpectedly firm and decisive, but then she smiled at Stephanie with sudden warmth to mitigate her refusal. 'It's wonderful of you to suggest it, especially when I know your time with Finn is so precious! But I can't.'

'Why not?' Stephanie was surprised and not a little impressed by Beth's new air of decision.

'I have to get what's left of my life together. There are decisions to take about the house . . . and I've got to find a job for the autumn term. That means applying now.' She paused, and then added, 'I must be out of my tiny mind to refuse a yacht trip to the Greek islands! But no, Stephanie, though I can't thank you enough for asking.'

Stephanie knew when she was defeated. So, being a practical woman, she promptly discarded Plan A and prepared to put forward Plan B. But, being skilled in negotiation, she went about it in a roundabout way. There were things she needed to know first.

'What about your parents, Beth? Are they still alive?'

Beth sighed. 'My father is. My mother died a few years ago. She split up with my father when I was ten, and he married again. We've never really kept in touch. I believe he lives in the north of England somewhere.'

Stephanie nodded quietly. She had got the picture now. 'What about the house? Will you keep it?'

'No.' She sounded even more definite than before. How could she go on living in that house, with the ghost of little Mo in every corner? 'No,' she repeated, and shivered. 'I must start again. Somewhere else.'

'Then maybe what I've got to say might interest you,' said

Stephanie, and she waited for Beth's haunted gaze to come back into focus.

'Yes?' Beth asked at last.

'We live in Gloucestershire,' began Stephanie carefully. 'And there's a very nice school in the village that Chloë goes to. It has an ordinary curriculum, but it also has extra remedial classes for children with problems of one kind and another. Music therapy is one of their special interests.'

'I see.' Beth was beginning to get the drift.

'Don't freeze up,' said Stephanie hastily. 'I think you might like it and I know they have been looking for someone to take it on since the last music teacher got married and moved up north. Not many general teachers today seem to include music in their skills.'

'That's true,' admitted Beth. 'And there are no funds for specialist teachers.'

'Exactly. Well, I know the headmistress, Margaret Collier, quite well. I'm on the board of governors.'

'Oh, *honestly*, Stephanie!'

'No, it's only because of Finn being famous, damn him! I get asked to do all sorts of things.' She paused, and then added, with intent, 'But I care about this one.'

Beth was silent. The idea was beginning to interest her. And what had she got to lose? It didn't matter where she went or what she did.

'A few of the children are quite badly disturbed,' Stephanie warned her. 'They need a lot of care and patience, and a certain toughness, too. It would be a challenge.'

Beth did not reply to this. She was still thinking it out.

Stephanie watched the thoughts chasing themselves across Beth's expressive young face, and went on quietly. 'I know it sounds unlikely, Beth, after what you've been through, but I have a strange feeling you'd be just what they are looking for. And getting those mixed-up kids to fit into this sorry world would be something worth doing.' She gave Beth another shrewd, half-humorous glance. 'Is that too corny?'

'Yes,' said Beth, smiling. 'Much too corny. But it does sound interesting.'

Stephanie heaved an exaggerated sigh of relief. She was rather terrified of trying to order someone else's life. 'I'll give you the address—and ring Margaret about it, if you like. You could go over to Gloucestershire and have a look for yourself. No obligation!'

Beth laughed. 'You're a conniving woman, d'you know that?'

'Yes,' agreed Stephanie smugly. 'Isn't it fun?'

BETH STAYED ON until Finn's boat was ready for the trip to Greece—partly because she was dreading the decisions ahead of her at home, and partly because she found herself very reluctant to leave Stephanie and cheerful little Chloë. They had become important to her and she was ashamed to find how much she had come to rely on their company and their unfailing kindness.

All too soon, however, the day of departure came. *Dancing Lady* was loaded with stores and luggage, and it was time to go.

A small group of well-wishers came down to the jetty to see them off and Beth stood alone, just in front of them, looking up at the gleaming new-painted hull of the sturdy boat.

'Good luck,' said Finn, smiling down at her. 'I hope things work out for you,' and he gave her a swift, comforting hug.

'Goodbye,' said Chloë, and then added obscurely, 'Remember the tubular bells.'

Both she and Finn leaped on board the yacht and stood waving at her.

And then it was Stephanie's turn. She simply put her arms round Beth who, not knowing how to express all she felt about the extraordinary kindness she had been given, could only stumble into incoherent thanks. 'I can't tell you . . . what it's meant to me . . .'

'Hush,' murmured Stephanie. 'You'll be all right. I know you will.' She gave her an extra hug of reassurance and then climbed rather swiftly on board to stand beside Finn.

They cast off, and the sails filled with the gentle west wind. Gently, quietly, the graceful boat nosed her way out of the harbour towards the open sea. The little crowd cheered and waved her off, and the three figures on board waved back.

Beth lifted her hand to them once, and then stood to watch them go. It seemed to her that the only bit of light and warmth in her grey, centreless days was going from her with those three bright figures in their charmed circle of family happiness. Her world seemed very bleak and empty without them, and she knew it was going to be hard to fill it with other things.

For a long time she stood there, watching the little boat get smaller and smaller, and then at last she turned away from the sunlit sea. Time to go. Time to face facts. Time to put her own life in order. Somehow she had got to make some sense out of it.

I'll go to Gloucestershire today, she told herself. No point delaying. I'll go there now, before I have time for second thoughts. I'll ring Margaret Collier. Taking a long breath of resolve, she began to walk back towards the town.

PART II
The Beehive

Beth arrived in Gloucestershire on a golden summer day which seemed to smile and pose no threat. Her first impression was one of space—high hills and open skies, and wide fields of wheat that moved in a continuous green-and-gold dance like silken water under the gentle wind. She had been dreading this journey and the difficult decisions ahead, but somehow she was already disarmed by the timeless beauty of her surroundings.

The village of Ashcombe stood on the curving southwest slope of a hill, the grey spire of its church reaching for the sky above a close-knit jumble of mossy stone-tiled roofs. Grey stone dominated the houses, too; at least, Beth thought it was grey, but in this bright wash of sunlight it was a grey laced with many soft shades of weathered gold.

She came to the school before she knew she was there. It was a long, neat building made of the same gold-grey stone, with tall windows under pointed Victorian eaves and a narrow porch with an inscription carved into the lintel above the door. There were other buildings scattered round the tidy green lawns, a couple of modern Portacabin annexes and what looked like a converted stone barn.

The grounds looked cared-for and there were flowers all round the main schoolhouse in neatly tended beds. Clearly, someone took a pride in its appearance and this comforted Beth a little. Someone loved this place, whoever it was.

As she drew up in the drive near the front of the school, the door opened and a woman stood there, smiling a welcome. Margaret Collier was about forty-five, squarish and sturdy, with a hawk nose, a wide smile and telltale flecks of grey at the edges of the thick dark hair on her strong, fighting head.

She looked at Beth with frank, assessing eyes and held out her hand. 'Welcome to Ashcombe School. You must be tired after that long drive. There's coffee brewing.'

Beth found herself being led into a sunny staff room where she was firmly guided into a comfortably shabby armchair. While Margaret got busy with the coffee she said, with her back to Beth, 'If it makes things easier, Stephanie Edmondson has told me all about your circumstances so you needn't go in for a lot of background explanation unless you want to. I should just like to say how sorry I am—how truly sorry—and I hope maybe we can come to some arrangement that will help us both.' Having said all this, she turned round, smiling, and came towards Beth with two steaming mugs of coffee in her hands.

'Thank you,' said Beth, meaning more than just the coffee. It was a relief not to have to say anything—just to sit and wait for this curious interview to take its course.

'I must tell you a bit about the school,' began Margaret, giving Beth time. 'It is a local-authority primary school, of course, but it also has an old Victorian trust fund which was set up long ago by the school's founder, Josiah Madley. This enables us to add a few extras to the school curriculum, and music is one of them. I think Stephanie has told you of our special programme of music therapy?'

'Yes. But she didn't enlarge on it.'

'Well, inevitably there are some difficult children in any school. But we have built up a reputation for being able to deal with them, so we get extra problem cases sent to us as well as our normal intake.'

Beth looked into the tough, committed face before her with sudden sympathy. 'It's quite a responsibility.'

'Oh, yes,' agreed Margaret at once. 'It is—but it's worth while.'

'I can see that.' Beth met the shrewd, kind eyes with an unexpected sense of camaraderie. 'Tell me what you do.'

Margaret leaned back in her chair and looked at the ceiling. 'Well, mostly we just let them make a frightful noise!'

Beth smiled. 'That sounds easy!'

She's really quite pretty when she smiles, thought Margaret, watching the tension ease a little in the pale, haunted face before her. She grinned. 'On the surface, yes.' Margaret hesitated for a moment and then continued with her explanation. 'We realised, from bitter experience, that the worst scenes and tantrums usually occurred at the beginning of the day and, worst of all, at the beginning of the week. Some of them hated coming to school, some of them hated being told what to do and where to go, some of them just hated everyone and everything.'

Beth nodded. She had met some of that before.

'So we decided to have the special music class first, before the serious work of the day began.' She glanced at Beth again, half apologetically. 'Not that we feel music isn't a serious subject—please don't think that. Anyway, you would be plunged in head first, as it were, if you took it on. I can't pretend it would be easy. But you could try any kind of music-making you like—let them work out their frustrations in whatever way they can. Let them sing, let them dance, let them shout . . .'

'Let them bang?'

Margaret laughed. 'Exactly. We're not afraid of noise.' Then she grew serious again. 'You would have to take on some of the ordinary subjects as well. What other subject would you be willing to offer?'

Beth pushed the hair out of her eyes nervously. 'Oh, English? History? Not maths, unless I have to!' She paused, and then added in a tentative voice, 'I used to teach art sometimes.'

'That might come in very handy. Do you paint, yourself?'

'No,' said Beth. 'Not seriously. I used to daub some wishy-washy landscapes.' She stopped suddenly. Those were the days when Robert was away and she needed to fill her time—and little Mo would climb on her knee and dab at her sketchpad with a wobbly brushful of improbable colour.

'Look, Mummy, a cloud. That's a cloud.'

'Purple?'

'Yes. A purple cloud.'

'I . . . I wasn't very good,' she said, trying to steady her voice, 'but at least it made me look at the countryside.' She took a shaky breath, grasping at normality. 'It's very beautiful round here.'

'Yes, it is.' Margaret noted that silent struggle for composure. 'You could take small sketching parties out sometimes, if you liked. They love any excuse to get out of doors!'

Beth saw the pattern of her days beginning to emerge. They would be full enough, but still the world felt empty. It was like a dreadful unassuageable ache. It would never go, she knew, but maybe she would learn to live with it, somehow. Fill her days with ceaseless activity—that was the only way.

'Let's go and look round the school,' suggested Margaret, with surprising gentleness. 'I'm sorry the children aren't here, but some of their work is still on the walls.'

They walked round the classrooms, stopping to admire a lot of weird and colourful drawings, and inspected the gym and the school hall with its small working stage. As they strolled round the playground Beth commented on the flower-filled borders round the house.

'Yes, we're rather proud of those. The children do a lot of it themselves, but Beech keeps the place in order. He's a born gardener. I don't think there is anything that wouldn't grow if Beech told it to!'

'Who is Beech?' asked Beth.

Margaret Collier smiled. 'Who is Beech? How can I answer you? He's as much part of this place as the hills—or the ancient beech trees themselves. He used to be head gardener on a big estate round here. Now he lives in a cottage up at the edge of the beech woods, along with a menagerie of stray animals that come to him for shelter.' She stopped suddenly in her tracks and banged a hand against her forehead, exclaiming, 'What a fool I am! I forgot to tell you about the Beehive.'

'The Beehive?'

'It's a small house that goes with the job, if required.' She looked into Beth's mystified face and went on to explain, 'It belongs to the old Madley Trust, and they allow it to be rented out to any of our staff who need accommodation.' She saw the glimmer of interest in Beth's shadowed eyes, and said quickly, 'It's empty now. Let's go and look at it, shall we?'

Silently, Beth followed Margaret past the clump of pines and up a narrow, overgrown path at the far end of the school grounds. The little cottage stood alone in a patch of sunlight between two tall beech trees, and looked away from the path over the sloping valley below. It had a curious, oval-shaped dome for a roof—the old stone tiles cut into small overlapping layers that formed subtle downward curves—hence the name the Beehive.

'Oh,' breathed Beth, 'isn't it lovely!'

I would feel safe here, she thought. I could dream dreams and they would not hurt me. Mo would have loved it. And so would Robert. All that space to look out at, but somewhere small and safe to be in when you needed comfort. Yes, they'd have loved it.

'Mornin', missus,' said a deep, slow voice behind her. 'Dozy old day, ent it?'

Beth turned sharply as Margaret answered the voice with a warm one of her own. 'What are you doing here, Beech?'

'Thought I'd keep an eye,' he said, laying down the sickle with which he had been attacking the nettles at the edge of the overgrown little lawn. 'We can't let her go to rack and ruin, can we?' He straightened up and turned his faded blue eyes in gentle enquiry on Beth's startled face.

'This is Beth Halliday,' said Margaret. 'She might be needing the cottage, so we've come to look it over.'

'Ar,' said Beech, nodding a wise head. 'Dusty, I dessay. But she'll stand till doomsday, she will.'

He turned back then to the nettles and picked up his sickle, deliberately, with instinctive courtesy, leaving the inspection of the cottage to Beth and Margaret.

Margaret put the key in the lock and led her inside. Sunlight poured through the windows in dusty shafts and laid gold fingers on the bare oak floor. The room itself was smallish and almost circular under the beehive dome of the roof, with an extra bulge at one side for the little kitchen, and at the other for a kind of extension that housed a narrow dining table and four chairs. At the back of the room, set in the curve of the wall, was an open fireplace within a rounded arch, and on one side of this was a steep spiral staircase made of open ironwork, leading upwards to the two tiny rooms and miniature bathroom in the roof space above.

'It's very small,' said Margaret, 'but it has all the basics.'

'It's enchanting,' Beth answered, in a hushed voice of dream. And then, trying to be practical, 'What about the furniture?'

'Oh, that goes with it, if you think it will do. Though, of course, you could always bring some of your own.'

'No.' Beth was firm. 'It's perfect as it is.'

There were a couple of good old rugs on the floor, dark-coloured and glowing with a faded richness, and the small sofa and two equally small armchairs looked lived-in and comfortable, all covered in creamy-coloured linen.

'Well?' said Margaret gently, watching the thoughts chase themselves across Beth's vulnerable face. 'What do you think?'

'I think I'll come,' said Beth, adding humbly, 'if you'll have me.'

Margaret laid a hand on her arm. 'I am so glad.'

Out in the tangled garden, Beech straightened his back again to watch them go. 'I'll get her shipshape,' he said to Beth as she passed, 'afore you come. She'll come together with a bit o' care, given half a chance.'

Beth did not think to ask how he knew she was coming. It seemed part of the magic of this dreamlike place. She merely smiled and murmured, 'Thank you,' as she followed Margaret down the path.

And Beech turned back to look after her, with quiet satisfaction in his rheumy eyes. To him, she was just another wounded creature who had found sanctuary in his gentle hills.

IT TOOK LONGER than Beth had expected to get things sorted out in London. It was difficult to sell the house, and even more difficult to make up her mind what to take with her and what to leave behind. In the end she got rid of all the clothes and personal things she did not want to keep (after much heart-searching) and was left with a small pile of necessities which included her books, all the photos of Robert and Mo that she could find, her violin and set of recorders, and the best of her records, CDs and tapes.

She snapped the suitcase shut and carried it out to the car before she could change her mind. For a moment she stood looking back at the empty house—the bare rooms and the silent garden. Could she still hear an echo of Mo's laughter across the lawn, the sound of his small feet running down the path? Or Robert's deep voice saying, 'Come on, Mo. I'll be the horse.' And Mo, upright and sturdy, riding high on his father's shoulders and laughing . . .

No, she told herself. This will not do. I am going away. I am going to begin again. I must. I know I must . . . Shivering a little, she turned her back on the empty garden, climbed into her car and drove away.

IT WAS GROWING DARK when she got to Ashcombe but the village was still bathed in golden light, and it was almost with a sense of home-coming that she drove along the lane to the little Beehive cottage. Late-evening sunlight glanced off its windows and made gleams of gold on its old stone walls.

She found the key under the flowerpot in the porch, as directed, and went inside. The place looked swept and scrubbed, and shining with polish. Someone had been busy. There was a fire laid in the hearth and a neat stack of small logs tucked in under the stone arch of the fireplace.

She went into the tiny kitchen and found a box of groceries on the table, together with a loaf of fresh, crusty bread, a pint of milk and some brown eggs. There was also a glass jamjar filled with wild flowers—oxeye daisies and scabious, purple knapweed and delicate harebells. As she stood looking round her, touched by these signs of thoughtful welcome, a shadow crossed the window and there was a gentle tap at the open door. She turned and found the old man, Beech, looking in at her.

'Everything all right, missus?' he asked, smiling a creaky smile.

'Yes, Beech, thank you. Did you put the stores there—and the flowers?'

'Aye. Thought they might cheer you up. Flowers is cheerful things, given half a chance.'

'What do I owe you for the groceries?'

Beech shook his grizzled head. 'Nay, Missus Collier fixed all that. She said to tell you she'd be up directly, and you was to ask me if there's anything else you wants.'

Beth smiled at him—and the old eyes blinked a little at the sudden transformation in her pale, shuttered face. 'No, Beech, thanks. You've thought of everything.'

He stood looking at her for a moment and then said in his slow, quiet voice, 'Well, I'll be gettin' on, then. You can usually find me at the school, come termtime, or leave word at the post office. I allus calls in there for messages.' He hesitated and then added as he turned away, 'She's a happy place, this—given half a chance.'

Given half a chance, thought Beth, as she watched him stump off down the path. It seemed to be the old man's catchword—his philosophy, probably. Give everything and everyone half a chance, and they'd be all right. Would she?

A happy place, he had said. Well, it was up to her now to make it true. She could probably do it, given half a chance.

WHEN BETH ARRIVED to take her first special music class, she walked into chaos. One boy was lying on the floor, kicking and screaming in a furious tantrum. He was quite big—about ten years old, she thought—and far too old for tantrums of that kind, but at that moment he was clearly quite beyond reason. Three other boys were fighting in a heap on a pile of mats in one corner. A small knot of anxious girls were watching the action with obvious trepidation, and several other children had seized the noisiest of the percussion instruments, including a bass drum and xylophone, and were making a determined effort to drown the screams of the boy on the floor.

'That's Mark,' said Margaret Collier, who had come in with Beth to see her through the first few chaotic moments. 'He does this every other Monday.'

'Why?' Beth looked down at the wildly flailing legs and purple, outraged face.

'Family split.' Margaret's voice was dry. 'Spends the weekend with his father.'

Beth nodded. 'I see.' It made sense, of course, and she could well understand how the boy's grief and rage had to come out somehow.

She looked round the room and wondered which problem to tackle first. As her glance took in the other children and the array of different instruments waiting to be used, she suddenly remembered little Chloë's voice saying, *'Remember the tubular bells.'* Tubular bells, she thought. Yes, that's it.

She went up to the little group of scared girls and asked them to show her where the bells were kept, and together they got out the long silver tubes and their frame. But instead of setting up in the normal fashion, Beth carried the frame over to where Mark lay yelling on the floor, set the framework half on its side across two chairs and fixed the bells so that they hung down right over the boy's frantically flailing legs. Then, with a gentle push to one of the chairs, she lowered the whole contraption until the silvery tubes made contact with Mark's angry feet.

A wonderful cacophony of chimes rang out, and the rest of the class crowded round to enjoy the effect.

For a moment, Mark went on kicking and screaming, but then he seemed to become aware of the extra noise his feet were making and he paused in mid-scream, took a bewildered, sobbing breath and looked up at Beth in amazement.

'Well done,' said Beth. 'That sounds lovely. Do it again.'

But though he kicked out obediently at the bells again, the heart had gone out of his rage and he got slowly to his feet, looking confused.

Margaret, watching all this with a distinct quirk of amusement touching her stern headmistress demeanour, murmured, 'You'll do, Beth, you'll do,' and went quietly out of the room.

'What we need is an earthquake,' said Beth to the class. 'Do you think you could manage that?'

They looked at her doubtfully.

'Come on,' she urged. 'You could make enough noise for an earthquake, couldn't you?'

'Yes!' said the boy with the bass drum, and began to demonstrate his ability with enthusiasm.

'And a tidal wave,' she added. 'We could use the gongs for that, and the piano. Look, I'll show you . . . And then we want a fire. A fierce fire. How can we do that? You could *dance* a fire, couldn't you? Flames dance.'

She looked at their puzzled faces and smiled. 'You see, there's this story—a true story, about an island and what happened to its people. It all began one hot day in Japan . . .'

Before the class was over, she knew she had got through to most of them. The musical story grew—the noise was tremendous—and the young faces were enthralled.

Later on, she told herself, I'll be able to put on a record or a tape. Something peaceful and quiet. They'll calm down in the end. But, at first, what they need is this. More violence than their own, larger events than they have ever seen, dangers much greater than they have had to bear. Their own lives won't seem so terrible then. And maybe, somehow, I will begin to feel the same . . . Maybe we'll learn together how to accept disaster.

She sat down at the piano and began to play them a tidal wave.

THAT EVENING, Beth went for a walk on the hills. She needed to clear her head of noise and turmoil—both emotional and physical. For she had to admit to herself that she was already involved in the frustrations and anxieties of the children she had been teaching.

But the high hills received her calmly, reducing all her problems to human size, and she found herself walking in blue air on springy turf, looking out at climbing ridges of beech-clad slopes on one side, and the silvery curves of the winding Severn River below. It was still early autumn, and the beech trees had not yet turned to their fiery brilliance of russet and amber, but even so there was a faint wash of gold on the leaves—a hint of changing colour to come in the dying fall of the year.

How little Mo would love it, she thought—and Robert, too. He'd never had much time to stop and stare. But then a curious thought came to her, stirring all her held-down grief into breathless uncertainty. Maybe they can see it all. Maybe, she thought to herself, they are here beside me, and I am just too shut in to my own grief to realise it . . . I can imagine them running down the green curves of these hills hand in hand . . . And if I can imagine it, maybe it is true?

I don't know, she thought. I don't know anything any more. But Stephanie told me anything is possible. I must let them in, if I can . . . And she walked on across the hills, arguing with herself as she went.

As the sun finally sank into a golden haze far in the west behind the Welsh mountains, and twilight began to cast a blue shade over the hills, Beth turned for home and took the path that led through the edge of Swift's Wood on the way down to the village. The primrose afterglow from the sky still made shadows under the trees, so that her feet walked in dappled patterns of green and gold, and it was through this dazzle of gleams and glooms that Beth saw the cottage. It stood alone in a small clearing, the door was open to the quiet evening and the scent of woodsmoke drifted across in a blue haze from its single chimney.

Beech saw her standing there, straightened up from his cluster of cages and stood waiting for her to come forward.

'Good evenin' to you,' he said, mustering his creaky smile. ''Tis a pearly old time for walkin'.'

For a moment, Beth stood looking from the grey stone cottage to the deepening sky beyond, and decided he was right. It was a pearly old time. 'So it is,' she acknowledged and smiled back.

'I wus just feedin' the critturs,' he explained, holding a bucket of scraps out for her to look at.

'Can I come and see?'

The old man nodded briefly. 'Wunt do no harm. So long as you'm quiet, like.'

Beth followed him, feeling she ought to walk on tiptoe. They came first to a small wire pen with a kennel-like box at one end and a heap of golden-brown bracken at the other. At least, Beth thought it was just a heap of bracken, but when they got close she saw that there was a small russet-coloured fox cub curled up asleep on top of the heap. When the cub heard Beech coming, her ears twitched and she leaped to her feet and skittered forward eagerly to meet him, thrusting her little pointed muzzle at him through the wire in ecstatic welcome.

Beech shook his head at her reprovingly. 'Never get you back to the wild, will I?'

'Isn't she pretty!' breathed Beth, enchanted by that small, inquisitive face framed in its soft ruff of baby fur.

'Ar. Handsome is as handsome does,' growled Beech darkly. 'She's too forward by half!' and he opened the cage to let the cub out. It was only then, when she sprang out and made straight for the safe protection of Beech's arms, that Beth saw that she had one very crooked, mangled leg.

'A trap, that was,' muttered the old man, allowing a glint of anger to show in his faded eyes. 'Not allowed, they aren't, but they still puts 'em down, the b—' But he changed that into a sort of snort, in deference to present company.

He let Beth touch the soft fur, and then put her carefully back in the pen with a small handful of food scraps to keep her happy.

'Got an owl over there,' he said, and led Beth over to another, rather taller wire enclosure with an upright tree branch placed carefully inside. There was a wooden nesting box fixed in the angle of the branch and, sitting just inside it, on the enclosed piece of tree, was a large tawny owl, fast asleep with its head sunk down into its shoulders.

'Broken wing,' said Beech succinctly, eyeing the bird with an assessing gaze. 'Can't hunt for herself, see? But her'll get away easy enough when the time comes. She'll go when she's ready.'

'How many other charges have you got?'

The old man laughed. It was a sound rather like a blunt saw on a piece of very knotted wood, but it was a laugh, nevertheless. 'Well now, let's see. There wus two hedge'ogs got run over, but now they're both mendin' they just comes back for food. And then there's Blackie, but he's free to come and go, only he *wunt* go.'

'Who's Blackie?'

For answer, Beech gave a slow, surprisingly tuneful whistle, and almost immediately a cock blackbird with a bright yellow beak flew down and settled on his shoulder.

'Reared 'im,' he told her. 'Fell out of the nest. Never thought 'e'd live, but he did.' He reached up one gnarled finger and scratched the bird's head. 'They tells you not to try to save 'em, but some'ow this one just wouldn't die. And now he wunt go, the varmint.'

The rusty-saw laugh came again, 'Now it's only the reg'lars. There's Juniper, the goat. I keeps her for the milk, see? She'll eat anything, including the washing on the line, if I don't watch her!' He waved one brown hand at an enclosed piece of green grass where one very white goat was tethered and munching happily at a low branch of hawthorn. A good mother, she is—and I'll show you another. Though she's more of a long-termer than a reg'lar.'

He took Beth this time through another wire enclosure to a thick clump of bushes at the edge of the main stretch of beech wood, and put his finger to his lips, cautioning Beth to move quietly.

The old man bent down and lifted one hawthorn branch and one frond of bracken with infinite slowness and care. Then he stood back a little so that Beth could look down. There, on a soft bed of grass and bracken, sat a velvet-coated deer and beside her, curled up very small, was a tiny fawn. The doe looked up at Beech and his companion with big, anxious eyes but she did not move.

'There then,' crooned Beech, 'we won't moither you—you're safe enough here,' and he let the branch slide gently back to cover their safe haven. 'Chased by dogs, she wus,' he said softly. 'Dropped her fawn right there almost on my doorstep, you might say. And there she stayed.'

'Do you feed her too?'

'I do, that. Needs her strength, a nursing mother.' He was leading Beth back towards the cottage now and, as he drew near to the doorway, a sandy-coloured mound of fur lying on the step began to wave a feathery tail. 'That's my Jess,' he said, a hint of extra warmth creeping into his voice. 'And she's going to be a mother too, any day now.'

'Puppies? How lovely.' Beth stooped to touch the gentle head.

'Would you like a cup o' tea?' asked Beech, hardly daring to offer such a thing—but he had to try. He had promised himself he would, if she came. And if she said no, well then, there was no harm done.

He liked the look of the new teacher, though she was sad, of course—very sad and lonely at present, he knew. But that would pass. They had told him at the post office that she had recently lost her little boy, and her a widow as well, poor thing, and all but destroyed with grief, so they had said.

Beech knew about grief, too. He had watched his own wife die, slowly and painfully, of cancer, and nothing anyone could do about it either. And his only son had gone and got himself killed in some far-off war he did not understand . . . But those were old stories now, and the grief had sunk down and gone deep, like a dropped acorn buried fathoms deep in leaf-mould. It was still there, but it didn't hurt any more.

Beth didn't say no to the cup of tea. She saw the sudden brief flick of anxiety in those faded blue eyes and thought to herself, with sudden recognition, Why, I do believe the old man is lonely—just like me. 'I'd love one,' she said, smiling, 'if it's not too much trouble.'

Beech grunted amusement. 'We've fed them,' he grunted. 'Now it's our turn!'

So they sat companionably in the deepening twilight beside the open doorway and sipped hot strong tea out of chipped china mugs until it was almost dark and it was time she went if she was to see her way home. She put her mug down on the step and got to her feet. 'Thanks for showing me round,' she said shyly. 'They're lucky to have you to look after them all.'

Beech shrugged creaky shoulders, but he was clearly pleased. 'Ar, well, I reckon most things mend theirselves in time, given half a chance,' he said. The smile behind the old, hazy eyes was warm and full of quiet understanding, but he did not say any more. He just pointed Beth's way down the stony path to the village, and stood in the deepening shadows to watch her go.

BETH TOOK HER TIME to sort out in her own mind the various children and staff at the school, but each day she notched up a few names. With the children from the extra music class it was easy, for they were so individual with their quirks and hang-ups.

Besides Mark, the Monday tantrum boy, there was Lisa, who hit every blonde in sight and was caught trying to cut off one small girl's golden ponytail. (It turned out her father had gone off with a dizzy blonde bombshell.) There were the twins, James and Ann, who fought everyone who came near or tried to separate them, and refused to do anything at all unless they could do it together. And there was George, who was large and lumbering, older than the others but not yet considered ready to go to the comprehensive school, so he was staying at Ashcombe a year too long. He was mostly slow and quiet, but would suddenly fly into frustrated, violent rages when he smashed everything in sight.

There were others in that special class, too, whose needs didn't seem quite so pressing, but none of them were easy to manage and several of the larger boys were sometimes very stroppy until Beth got tough, and then they looked at her with grudging respect and subsided.

But through all this mayhem the dramatic story of the Japanese island was growing, the noise was slowly turning into something approaching music, and the class—even the worst misfits—were beginning to cooperate. 'I believe we are writing an opera,' she told them. They weren't impressed. But they were getting more and more involved and some of them could sing like angels.

As to the rest of the school, whose different forms she taught from time to time, they were easy to deal with on the whole, and friendly, and the faces were becoming individuals one by one.

Then there was the staff—easier to sort out, as there were fewer, but perhaps not so easy to get to know. There was Bill Lewis, the oldest, known affectionately as Old Bill, who had been with the school for years and taught maths with fierce, old-fashioned discipline. He ruled his own form with a rod of iron but he was, inexplicably, popular with everyone (though the more mischievous boys watched him somewhat warily). Then there was little Miss Brown (no one seemed to call her Ruth), who was birdlike and wispy and looked after the reception class with enormous patience. Her cheerful colleague with the kindergarten, Laura Fredericks, was the opposite—large, positive and friendly, rather like a well-meaning St Bernard. She seemed to tackle all crises with unflagging energy and good temper, and everyone—children and staff alike—called her Freddie. Besides these, there was young Peter Green, yellow-haired and athletic, in charge of a lively form of ten-year-olds, and who also taught games when it was fine and chess when it was not. He was nearly always friendly and approachable, except when the weather spoilt a football match with a rival junior school, or ruined a cricket match just when his side was winning. Sometimes he also joined forces with Debbie Arnold, the fourth-form teacher, who liked taking parties on 'history delving expeditions' and was keen on archaeology and Roman villas.

Beth found them all quite welcoming and easy to get on with. The only thing that puzzled her was that there was no sign of little Chloë Edmondson in any of the classes, and no welcoming word from Stephanie, who had been so keen for her to take this job. On reflection, she supposed they must have stayed on in Greece while they had the chance, and would probably return later in the term.

She was actually thinking about this one evening as she pottered about the little Beehive garden when she saw the headmistress, Margaret Collier, coming up the path.

'How nice,' she said, laying down her fork.

'Are you busy?'

'Not really—I don't know where to start!' She laughed. 'I need Beech to tell me what to do.' She glanced at Margaret's face and added swiftly, 'Let's put the kettle on,' for it seemed to her that Margaret was looking far too grave and troubled for this scented autumn evening.

Together they went inside and Beth made some coffee, wondering with increasing uneasiness what was behind Margaret's silence. Had Beth's unorthodox methods with her special music class been too noisy and chaotic even for her? Was she, perhaps, having second thoughts about Beth's appointment?

Beth carried the cups over to the fireside. Margaret looked up from one of the deep armchairs and took the cup from her gravely. 'Sit down, Beth. I'm afraid I've got some rather awful news for you.'

Beth sat down in the other chair and waited. What else could happen in her life that was awful enough to matter?

'It's about Stephanie,' began Margaret. 'Stephanie Edmondson.' She paused to draw a long, steadying breath. 'I . . . I'm afraid she's dead, Beth. She died in Greece a week ago.'

Beth looked at her in utter disbelief. 'She can't be!' Her voice trailed off as she saw Margaret's sorrowful expression. 'What happened?'

Margaret sighed. 'No one knows exactly. The Greek doctors said it was a brain tumour which caused a massive stroke, and the post-mortem confirmed it.' She shook her head. 'It happened very suddenly. And the worst of it is, Finn was away at the time, inspecting some building site on one of the smaller islands nearby. Chloë sat beside her mother for three days by herself until he returned.'

'Oh, my God.' Beth's voice shook. 'How absolutely dreadful.' She thought of Chloë sitting alone in a silent room beside a mother who did not stir, and shivered. 'Why did no one come?'

'A rented villa, on the main island away from the town . . . Chloë spoke no Greek, so she just sat there.'

Tears stung Beth's eyes. 'How . . .? How has she taken it?'

'That's the trouble,' said Margaret grimly. 'That's where you come in. She won't speak.'

'Won't speak?'

'Won't, or can't.' Margaret shook her head again in helpless sympathy. 'It's the shock, they think. Finn says she has totally cut herself off from everything and she won't even let him touch her. I think she probably blames him.'

'Oh, the poor child.' Beth paused, trying to assemble her own shocked thoughts. 'Will she . . .? You said that was where I come in?'

'Yes, I did. She will have to go into your special class, you see. Finn is bringing her home. Apparently, it has been recommended that she continues her schooling in the normal way. He asked specially if you would be there to look after her. He seemed to think you might be able to get through to her, having been so close to her mother.'

Beth looked doubtful. 'I don't know . . . She might hate me, too, because I couldn't prevent what happened.'

A sudden awful thought came to her, then. If she had gone to Greece with them, as Stephanie had planned, would she have been able to prevent it? Probably not, but at least she could have been there for Chloë and maybe avoided this latest catastrophe. 'Oh,' she murmured, agonised, 'I should have been there.'

Then she began to think back to those strange conversations that had taken place between her and Stephanie in Devon.

'Why?'

'Because I need to know . . . I sometimes wish Chloë would get attached to someone besides me . . . It's dangerous.'

Yes, it was dangerous. Love was always dangerous. You thought life was safe and full of happiness—and then it was suddenly quenched and you were in the dark.

'I wonder,' she said looking into Margaret's face with painful intensity, 'do you think Stephanie knew this was likely to happen?'

Margaret hesitated. 'I don't know. But something our local doctor said when I told him made me wonder. He said it was very sad, but not altogether unexpected.'

Beth nodded, confirming her own thoughts. 'Then she knew . . .' She was suddenly quite certain. 'That's what this was all about.'

Margaret sighed again, and said, 'Well, the child will be home tomorrow, in time for school on Monday . . . Finn thought she would be better occupied, even if she doesn't communicate. I'm so sorry to spring this on you. But I thought you'd rather know about it before you see Chloë in class.'

'Yes, of course.'

Margaret's pleasant voice slowed a little. 'And there's the funeral next week, too. I expect you'll want to go to that—unless you would find it too upsetting?'

'No,' said Beth bleakly, 'it's no good being upset, is it?' No good. Generous, warm-hearted Stephanie, whom she had grown to love in so short a time, was gone, like the other two she loved, and there were no tears left to shed, no words left to say.

But then she remembered Stephanie's gentle voice insisting, *'But I wouldn't have it otherwise. Every moment, every small happening . . . Don't you see? You still have them—all those special moments. You only have to remember.'*

Yes, Stephanie had known then how precious the days with Chloë and Finn were. But she hadn't wept about it and she hadn't been afraid. She had simply rejoiced in the moments she had, and still found the time to offer Beth consolation.

'I'll be there,' she said, 'but I'm not sure Chloë should be.'

'No,' agreed Margaret. 'We'll keep her in school that day.' She was eyeing Beth's startling pallor with some misgivings, but thought it better to keep to practical arrangements. 'Stephanie already had a housekeeper, since they were away such a lot and needed someone to keep an eye on the place. No doubt Finn will keep her on. Mary's kind enough, and very practical, but I don't know how much comfort she will be to Chloë. I should think she'd be way out of her depth with this.'

Beth sighed. 'Aren't we all?'

'I'm sorry, Beth. You must think life is nothing but blow after blow at the moment.'

Beth kept her voice surprisingly steady. 'If we can help little Chloë, perhaps something good may come out of it.'

WHEN BETH SAW CHLOË sitting alone in the corner of the music room, with the rest of the class milling noisily around her, it was difficult to believe it was the same bright-eyed, independent little girl she had known before. The flower face was closed and pale, as if blanched with sudden frost, the flyaway, silver-gilt hair hung lank and flat on her head, and the wide grey eyes looked strangely veiled and opaque. She did not show any sign of recognition when Beth came towards her and did not answer in any way when Beth said gently, 'Hello, Chloë.'

The only time there seemed to be a flicker of response was when Beth mentioned the tubular bells and suggested that someone should get them out. Then, it seemed to Beth's watchful gaze, some faint spark of recollection came into the small blank face, but Chloë did not move or make any attempt to speak. She just sat there, docile and quiet, and let the activities of the class flow round her unnoticed.

But there was one rather curious result in all this hidden, unspoken drama. The tantrum boy, Mark, suddenly decided to take Chloë under his wing. 'It's all right,' he said to Beth, 'I'll look after her.' And from then on he did. He led her by the hand when she needed to go from one class to another. He left her sitting quietly close to the window, and positioned himself beside her or in front of her to fend off persistent intruders asking awkward questions. He joined in the music-class activities himself when asked, but he always kept a weather eye on Chloë's small, lost figure and never left her alone for too long.

Beth was amazed at the transformation. Here was a child who had been almost unbearably sunk into self-centred anguish now suddenly becoming the most thoughtful and sweet-natured boy in her class. Though Chloë didn't exactly respond, Beth noticed that her hand went quite readily into Mark's and she went where he told her without demur.

When the time came for the children to go home Beth wondered if Finn would come to collect his little daughter, but the housekeeper came instead. Beth did not see how she could discuss Chloë's condition in front of the child herself, so she did nothing more than say, 'Do let me know if there is anything I can do.'

Mary Willis was briskish and plumpish and competent, with a cheerful disposition and kind brown eyes that were probably a lot more observant than they let on. She looked at Beth with sudden gratitude, for here was someone who clearly understood what a difficult time she was having. 'Thank you, Miss . . .?' she began, sounding almost shy.

'Halliday,' said Beth, smiling. 'Mrs Halliday—but most people call me Beth.' She watched the shyness begin to recede from Mary's round face as she took Chloë's limp hand in hers and turned away.

Well, I've done what I could, thought Beth. But I wish I could talk to Finn. He ought to know what to do, if anyone does . . . Then she collected her belongings from the staff room and walked the short distance from the school to her little house at the top of the lane.

She was getting to like living in the Beehive, as much as she liked living anywhere at present. It was a welcoming little place, warm and compact, and no trouble at all to keep in order. But even so, going home after school was still an ordeal. The world was terribly empty when she dared to think about it, and the silence of her lonely evenings echoed round her even in those small rooms.

But this time, when Beth got home, she found that she was not alone. The old man, Beech, was in the garden. He was stooping over a tangled flowerbed and patiently disentangling some half-choked late chrysanthemums that were trying to bloom in spite of the couch grass that was smothering them.

He straightened up when he saw Beth, and touched one finger to his unruly thatch of white hair in a curiously old-fashioned salute.

'Arternoon,' he said, and then added in his soft old voice, 'I wus hopin' you'd come—I brung you a tree.'

Beth went across to him, startled. 'A tree?'

'Only a little 'un,' he explained, and then paused, as if the phrase reminded him of something. 'Missus, I heard about the trouble at Edmondsons'—and about the little 'un, Chloë. Really sorry I wus to hear it.' He sighed. 'A lovely lady, Missus Edmondson, if ever there was one.'

'Yes,' agreed Beth slowly. 'She was.'

'That's why I brung the tree,' he said, and stooped to pick up a small flowerpot containing a seedling beech.

Beth looked puzzled. But she put out a finger and touched the green, furled leaf at the top of the tiny sapling.

'I allus plants a tree,' said Beech softly, 'when there's a gap, like.' His smile rested on Beth. 'That way, there's allus something new.'

Beth looked at him with tears in her eyes. It was such a simple philosophy but today, in this sun-gilded autumn garden, it made sense. 'What a good idea,' she said, and smiled at him through a dazzle of tears. 'Where shall we put it?'

Beech pointed to his newly turned patch of earth. 'Her won't block the view here, however tall she gets, and she'll have plenty o' room to grow.' He quietly handed her the pot and a small, shabby trowel.

'What do I do?'

'Just make a hole and put in a handful of this here leaf mould. It'll feel like home, then.'

When the tiny tree with its neat rootball of soil had been transferred to the bed, they stood back to admire their work.

'There!' crooned Beech. 'You'll do nicely now.' And he smiled at Beth again over the head of the little tree.

'Would you like a cup of tea?' asked Beth, remembering how anxiously Beech had offered her one and wanting to return the compliment. It seemed to her, somehow, that a ritual was being established that might be important.

'Ar, I wouldn't say no,' agreed Beech, and followed her politely up the path.

IT WAS LATER that evening when Finn came. He stood in the doorway, looking haggard and grim, and Beth was shocked at the change in him. Gone was the wicked buccaneer's grin, gone was the light of adventure in his blue, sailor's eyes.

'Can I come in?' he said.

And Beth, almost without thinking, put her arms round him and answered, 'Oh, Finn, I'm so sorry,' and drew him inside. But she felt his strong, wiry body stiff and unyielding within her swift embrace, and withdrew at once. Finn was far out on a tide of private desolation—like she had been—and could not be reached at present.

'Yes. Well, now I begin to understand what you have been going through,' he said gruffly.

Beth did not comment on that. She went through to the kitchen and made some coffee.

'How was Chloë when she got home from school?' she asked, bringing in two mugs. 'Did it seem to have upset her at all?'

'No.' Finn shook his head. 'There was no change.' He sighed, and sipped gratefully at the scalding coffee. 'That was really what I came to see you about.' He paused and looked vaguely round the room, not really seeing his surroundings.

When he failed to say any more, she gave him a gentle nudge. 'Tell me what has been happening to Chloë, since . . .?'

Finn rubbed a weary hand over his face. 'Well, nothing really. That's the trouble. When I . . . when I got back from the Spirios site and found them . . .' His voice shook for a moment and then steadied itself. 'Chloë was just sitting there, holding Stephanie's hand, staring at nothing. She didn't seem to be distressed exactly, just blank.'

'Did she know you?'

Finn's face darkened. 'Yes. I think so. Though she didn't speak. But she . . . she shrank away from me as if I was an enemy.' Once again his voice shook, and once again he controlled it. 'She's been like that ever since.'

Beth looked at him in wordless sympathy. Then she said carefully, 'How is she at home? What does she do?'

'Nothing much.' Finn's voice was rough with anxiety. 'She just sits there quite passively with her hands in her lap, waiting to be ordered about. It's so unlike her.'

Yes, Beth thought sadly. It was totally unlike the lively, independent little girl she had known. 'Doesn't she play with her toys, or read or anything?'

'No. Mostly, she sits staring out of the window at the garden. She shows no interest in anything—and positively hates me.'

'Oh, Finn, that can't be true.'

'I'm afraid it is,' said Finn, and once again his hand went up to his face, covering his eyes. 'She blames me for Stephanie's death, and I can understand why. I blame myself, too. I wasn't there when I was needed.' There was a world of self-reproach in his deep voice now. 'Maybe, if I *had* been, I might've been able to save her.'

Beth knew she had to protest at this. Finn must not be left with this dreadful weight of guilt, on top of everything else. 'Finn, there was nothing you could have done to prevent it. You might have protected Chloë from extra stress, but you couldn't have saved Stephanie. You must believe that.'

Finn shook his head. 'I don't know . . . I just don't know . . .'

'There was no indication that anything was wrong, was there?'

For a moment Finn hesitated, and then looked up at Beth with piercing directness. 'Nothing specific, no. But I might've guessed, if I hadn't been so wrapped up in my own affairs.'

'Why?'

'Oh, there were small clues. She had sudden fierce headaches, which she put down to migraine. And she complained once or twice of numbness in her hands. Steph was very practical. She hated anything hampering her fingers . . .' He hesitated again, as if remembering forgotten things. 'And she did go to see her own doctor and was then sent on to a specialist, but she told me it was nothing to worry about.' He paused and then added, in a voice of bitter condemnation, 'And I believed her.'

Beth nodded slowly. It only confirmed her own suspicions that Stephanie had known what was likely to happen—if not when it might occur.

'I always used to think,' said Finn, in a strange, cold voice, 'that something might happen to me—though I didn't worry about it much.' He drew a sharp breath of pain. 'It was only recently that I realised how much Stephanie worried about me. But . . . but it never occurred to me that it might be Stephanie—that something might happen to *her*.' He shook his head again, appalled by his own selfishness. 'And now there's Chloë—and I'm failing her, too.' His eyes glittered with self-contempt as he stared at Beth. 'D'you know, she won't even eat at the same table? Not that she eats much at all these days. I've tried talking to her, coaxing her, or ignoring her and leaving her alone. Nothing seems to register. I don't know what else to do.' He rubbed a weary hand over his sparkless hair in despair.

'That's why I came to you,' he continued. 'Mary Willis is kind enough, but she doesn't really understand the situation.'

'And you think I do?'

A glimmer of a smile touched his gaunt face. 'At least you have an inkling. I just . . . I would be so grateful if you would keep an eye on her.' He looked at Beth with sudden fierce entreaty. '*Please*, Beth, help her if you can. No one understands as well as you.'

Beth was distressed that Finn expected so much of her. 'I'll do anything I can, of course. But I can't promise to be successful.' She was regarding Finn with some anxiety. 'I think it has to come from you, in the end.'

Finn got up, almost violently, and began to pace up and down. 'No. I only make things worse. I'm just an added source of stress—and anger.' He took a deep breath and turned round on Beth. 'That's why I'm going away again.'

Beth was horrified. 'You *can't*! Not now. She needs you, Finn. You're all she's got.'

'She doesn't need me.' His tone was clipped and dry. 'She dislikes me intensely—and she's better off without me.'

Beth looked at him in helpless disapproval. 'I think you're wrong.'

'Probably,' he snapped. 'Everything I do is wrong, as far as Chloë is concerned.' Then he tried valiantly to sound calm and reasonable. 'No, I'll keep out of her way for a bit. She's got Mary, and if you will just . . . just watch over her a little, I think she'll have more chance of recovery.'

Beth shook her head at him sorrowfully. 'Very well. But things are never that cut and dried, Finn. Can't you wait a while and see what happens?'

'No,' he said violently. 'I can't. I can't bear to see her like this—and to know that I'm making it worse.'

Then Beth understood that nothing she could say would make any difference. Finn had to work out his own hurt and grief—and find his own salvation—before he could be any help to his daughter.

'I'll do my best,' she promised. 'But you will have to come back in the end.'

Finn nodded briefly. 'I know that. Just give me time—give Chloë time. And try not to blame me too much.' And he walked away from her out of the door and didn't look back.

BETH WENT TO THE FUNERAL, willing herself not to think of her own past tragic events, and managed to get through the service without becoming visibly distressed. But when Finn, looking taut and grim, invited her up to the house with the other mourners, she gently refused.

'No, Finn, thanks. Chloë's still waiting at the school. I'll take her home and give her some tea. She's better out of the way till this is all over.'

Finn nodded gratefully and said no more.

Back at Ashcombe School the children were preparing to go home, but Chloë was still sitting passively in the classroom, waiting for someone to tell her what to do next. And standing protectively beside her, also waiting, was Mark.

'No one came,' he said, in accusing tones.

'It's all right,' Beth reassured him. 'Chloë's coming home with me today. Just for a while,' she added to Chloë's blank face, in case the idea seemed too alarming.

But Chloë made no protest. She simply looked up at Beth out of grey, sparkless eyes, and allowed herself to be led away.

Mark came with them as far as the end of the school drive, still looking anxious, and Beth turned to him there and asked, 'How are you getting home?'

He shrugged careless shoulders. 'On my own. Mum's at work.'

'I see,' said Beth. 'Well, go carefully.' But a plan was beginning to form inside her head, only she would have to talk to Margaret Collier first. 'Chloë'll be all right now,' she added to Mark, and went off up the path to the Beehive with Chloë's hand in hers.

When they arrived at the cottage she left Chloë sitting in the sunny porch while she fetched some tea and a couple of rock buns she had made earlier. She didn't bother much with cooking these days—since Margaret Collier had wisely insisted that she ate a school dinner every day, there wasn't much need for anything else. But lately people had begun to arrive on her doorstep at teatime with the flimsiest of excuses—she suspected that it was a bit of a conspiracy among the staff and the villagers—so she kept a cake tin full of buns just in case.

First of all it had been little Ruth Brown, fluttery and shy, explaining that she was 'just passing' and couldn't stay long, but in fact staying for nearly two hours of gentle, enthusiastic chitchat about Ashcombe village and the children she cared for in her classes. Then came her cheerful colleague, Freddie, bearing a plate of fairy cakes covered in sickly green icing—the product of her cookery class—chattering happily about nothing in particular and managing to make Beth laugh at her description of the culinary disasters of her class.

After her, it was Peter Green's turn. He told Beth, somewhat bashfully, that he was very good at fixing things, if she had any problems with shelves and such, and asked whether she would like to join the Ramblers on their sponsored walk next Saturday. To this Beth bravely agreed, having determined some time earlier that she must try to accept every invitation offered, at present.

Besides the school visitations, various villagers turned up on different pretexts, bringing small gifts of one kind or another.

'Thought you might like some lettuces . . .'
'I've got too many apples, you see . . .'
'This is local honey from Charlie's bees.'
Beth quickly realised the word had gone round and that everyone was going out of their way to be helpful, but somehow she did not mind. They were so open and friendly about it, and who was she to be proud and stand-offish, anyway? It was clear that her time would be filled with useful activity and cheerful company, if she wanted it—and she rather thought she did at present.

But now it was little Chloë who needed useful activity and cheerful company, and someone patient and observant to watch for any signs of return—and Beth was determined to be that person if she could. Not only for Finn's sake, she told herself, but for Stephanie's, too. She owed it to her to do what she could.

It occurred to her, over the tea and buns, that Chloë might like to see Beech's animals—they might even trigger some response. In any case, Beth felt curiously certain that Beech would be good for Chloë. It was worth a try. So, after tea, Beth took Chloë's hand in hers again and walked firmly up the hill to the edge of the woods to look for Beech.

They did not have to look far. He was stooping over one of his cages, inserting some scraps of food for its eager occupant. When he saw the two of them approaching he stood up and waited for them, not saying anything until they came and stood beside him. Then he turned gravely to Chloë and said, 'I'm glad to see you, little 'un. I've something to show you.' And he led the way over to a new wooden box set down on a spread of fresh straw close to the house.

'There!' he said, and there was a note of pride in his voice. 'What d'you think of that?'

Beth still had Chloë's hand in hers, and now she looked down into the wide, straw-filled box before her. And there, lying peacefully spread out on the straw, was the golden retriever, Jess, and nuzzling close to her in small wriggling heaps was a tawny litter of tiny puppies.

'Oh!' breathed Beth. 'How lovely. Six of them!' and she went down on her knees and stretched out her hand to touch them. 'Look, Chloë! Jess has got six new babies to look after.'

Beech stood looking down with a smile at his favourite animal and two of his favourite people. 'She's a good mother,' he said in his soft, warm voice. 'See, little 'un, they'm very small and new just now—need a lot o' lookin' arter. But she wunt let 'em come to harm.'

Beth was still on her knees beside the pen and Chloë was still standing beside her, but no longer holding her hand. At first she had paid no attention whatever to the new litter, but now something like a flicker of realisation seemed to come into her eyes and she looked down. She stood there for a long time, just staring down at the wriggling puppies, all fighting blindly for their mother's teats, and then, very slowly, one of her hands stretched out towards them.

Beth and Beech looked at one another in triumph. It was the first spontaneous gesture Chloë had made since she came home, as far as Beth knew.

'That's the way,' said Beech gently. 'Go slow, so as not to let 'em get frit . . . Feel how soft they are.'

And they both watched, breathless, as Chloë's small hand actually reached out and touched one warm, squirming body. Every movement she made seemed very slow and hesitant, but her hand did move and linger, and then withdraw carefully to its usual passive position by her side. For a moment she looked up into Beth's face and seemed to be struggling to find words. But then the faint urgency in her expression seemed to fade, and it returned to its look of closed indifference. But Beth was sure from then on that the child really could not speak, and was not, as Beth had vaguely suspected, just staging her own private protest. Whether it was shock or the sheer desolation of life without her mother, Chloë could not help it. She wanted to speak, but somehow she could not.

'There now,' said Beech, in the same soft, reassuring voice. 'It's a start. When you comes again, they'll be bigger and you can pick 'em up.' He glanced again at Beth and a quiet smile passed between them.

Yes, it was a start. And Beth must be content with that. If this was a beginning, maybe the rest would follow in time.

PART III
Yonder?

Finn did not want to go back to the Spirios site, but he knew he had to before he could hand it all over to someone else. He hadn't tried to explain to Beth why he had to go back. It didn't seem possible at the time, and her horrified face only made him feel guiltier than ever at leaving Chloë. He was sure he was right to keep out of his small daughter's way, at least until the initial shock had worn off, but that didn't make him feel any better about it. How could he explain to Chloë that Stephanie's death was not his fault? Especially when he wasn't even sure about that, either? He blamed himself bitterly for not having been there when he was needed. But if he had been, could he have prevented it?

He did not know. Being without Stephanie somehow meant that he didn't know anything any more. All certainty was gone. She had always been his rock—the fixed point on his compass, to which he always returned. Now there was no fixed point—no one to return to, except Chloë, who did not want him.

It was a new experience for Finn, not to be wanted, not to be admired and fêted. Maybe, he reflected, it was good for him, maybe he had taken too much for granted. And Stephanie—brave, uncomplaining Stephanie—had never reproached him, never made him feel selfish and insensitive, which he now realised he was. And it was not only Chloë's blank, pinched face that haunted him, but Beth's accusing stare as well.

So he was going back to Spirios with something like a sense of relief. Out there, in the simplicity of Greek island life, no one would be getting at him. There was a lot of work to do and he would be glad to get on and do it, easing the awful anguish that Stephanie's absence left in his centreless life.

There were difficult problems with the Spirios site. The initial trouble was the actual placing of the hotel complex. The original promoters of the scheme had planned a huge, brash, five-storey complex right in the middle of the island's most beautiful bay. It would also interfere with an archaeological site still being explored by a mixed team of experts from the Athens Archaeological Museum and from several American universities who were putting up the money. Everything was wrong about the scheme but the building work began and a forest of metal struts went up, making the lovely golden bay look like a scrap-metal dump. Then the promoters went bust, the metal struts stayed pointing at the blue flawless skies of Greece, and nothing more was done.

Here, Finn had stepped in and bought the whole concern. He drew up new plans, arranged for all that awful structure to be removed and for the raw, sandy site to be filled in. Instead, a new, separate complex of low-storey buildings was to be constructed round the corner in the next, slightly less spectacular bay. It was a good scheme, and the local villagers were pleased about it and very anxious to help. But before that could happen, Finn had to find a more intelligent site manager and persuade the new, imaginative architect to come down from Athens and oversee the building process.

In the middle of all this, Finn had meant to go back to Athens to fix everything up, but the awful events surrounding Stephanie's death had overtaken him. Now, he knew, he had a lot of arranging to do, various people to placate, and he needed to spend at least a couple of weeks on the spot, making sure that his plans were being put into effect without upsetting anyone else. It would be difficult, requiring tact and good humour, but Finn liked that kind of challenge.

He flew straight to Athens with the plans and arranged with his architect, Theo Koussalis, to meet him on site in three days' time. Then he went down to Piraeus, where he got on a boat for the islands. Finally a caïque from the last port of call on the shipping run took him to the small island where the Spirios site lay waiting for him in the bright Greek sunshine.

It was a little island, with a little port—too small for the Piraeus boat to visit—and only the caïques had a shallow enough draught to pull up at the jetty. This meant that it was not overrun with tourists and the steep, narrow streets and neat white houses of the miniature town were untouched by the taint of Western commercialism.

Spirios was on the far side of the island. Finn did not wait for the island bus or the one and only taxi, but set out on foot. It was no great distance, only four miles across, though the going was steep in places. But he needed the exercise, and the familiar scent of the sun-warmed clumps of sage and thyme, juniper and basil went to his head like wine. So did the gentle warmth of the October sun and the extraordinary brilliance and clarity of the light. He had forgotten how marvellous that light was—how every late wayside flower seemed to glow with colour, every leaf and twig shine with its own incandescence—and the sky, that cloudless burning blue, seemed to reach to eternity.

How Stephanie would have loved it here, he thought. I meant to bring her, as soon as the site was fit to look at and safe for Chloë to run about on . . . I only meant to leave them on the main island for a day or two, until I could go and fetch them . . .

He quickened his stride, trying to walk away from his thoughts. But they pursued him. In Greece, he thought, the Furies are never very far away.

'Kirios Finn, you are back early,' said a voice beside him, and the smiling face of his foreman, Yannis, was looking up at him.

'It is good to see you, Yannis,' answered Finn, and grasped his old friend by the arm. 'How are things?' he asked, as they fell into step together.

Yannis spread out his hands in his usual gesture of comic dismay. 'But dreadful, Kirios Finn, of course. There was rain, and the bulldozers got stuck in the mud. Then the pile-driver broke down.

The taverna ran out of food and the fish did not come in, so the men grumbled . . . But,' and here his infectious smile broke out again, 'the farmer, Andreas, killed some chickens, so everyone was happy.'

Finn laughed.

Yannis's seamed brown face grew grave and his merry brown eyes looked suddenly shadowed. 'I am sorry, Kirios Finn, about your sadness. I would not mention it, but we are all most sorry.'

Finn looked down at his old friend and nodded. 'Thanks,' he said briefly. And they strolled on together to look at the site.

IT WAS A LONG DAY by the time Finn had inspected everything—even the abandoned site in the next bay, which was being filled in and slowly returning to normal—and he was tired and dispirited when he arrived back in the village. It was dusk now, and a small cool wind carried the scent of herbs from the sun-warmed hill above the village, where the little church of St Spyridion stood, to Georgio's taverna at the edge of the shore. Finn stumbled up the steps of the taverna to the little whitewashed room where he usually stayed. He found his bed made ready, a jug of fresh water on the table and a bunch of the wild island flowers in a glass jar on the window ledge.

He looked at the flowers with a faint smile of recollection touching his tight, grim mouth. The red poppies, said to be the blood of the heroes of Marathon, the blue bellflowers, almost as blue as the Aegean skies, and the gold and orange, tightly closed petals of the hawk's-beard that only opened with the sun. He remembered that he had learned his first word of Greek from Georgios's wife, Marina. He had paused to touch a poppy and looked up to find a pair of dark, sympathetic eyes regarding him with approval. Anyone who admired the island flowers merited her approval.

'*Orea*,' she murmured.

'*Orea*?' He did not know the word yet.

'Beautiful,' she translated, and smiled at him. It was the beginning of a love affair, really. Not with the wife of Georgios, though she was pretty, but with her countryside and the deep blue encircling sea.

And here he was again, in the familiar small bedroom above the taverna: plain white walls, the simplest of furnishings, a goatskin rug on the floor, and it felt like coming home.

'Kirios Finn,' said Marina's voice at the doorway, 'I have brought you some tea.' She smiled at him, welcome in her tranquil brown eyes, and held out a steaming cup of green, fragrant tea. 'It will help you to sleep,' she added in a matter-of-fact, no-nonsense tone.

'Thank you.' Finn took the cup from her. 'You are very kind.'

She stood looking at him judiciously for a moment, as if assessing the emotional state of her most favoured guest.

'The island mends sadness,' she said, in careful English. 'But you must wait. St Spyridion takes his time.' Then she turned and went out of the room before Finn could answer.

MARK'S MOTHER, Lucy Reynolds, was youngish, thinnish, harassed and tired. But she had a smile like her son's, warm and genuine when it flashed out. The permanently anxious look in her brown eyes softened a little when Beth explained her mission—that she had come to ask if Mark could go home with her for tea some afternoons after school. She explained also that she had already obtained Margaret Collier's blessing for the project.

'Oh . . . I thought you were coming to tell me that Mark was being unmanageable again.'

'On the contrary,' said Beth, and turned to smile at Mark, who was supposedly not listening from his perch on the sofa in front of the television screen. 'He is actually being extremely cooperative and helpful with a little girl who is in deep trouble.'

Lucy looked astounded. 'That doesn't sound like Mark!'

Beth laughed. 'It may be a surprise, but it's the truth.' She went on to describe how Mark had adopted Chloë as his own special charge, and the effect it seemed to have on his own behaviour.

Lucy listened in silence, a look of painful understanding gradually dawning on her face. 'I'm afraid he is left alone too much,' she confessed. 'When my husband walked out, I was obliged to go back to work . . . He does contribute something *now*—after I went to court to sue for maintenance. But it is somewhat grudging.' She looked at Beth a little grimly. 'And of course it's all tied up with him having what they call "reasonable access"—whether I like it or not.'

'And whether Mark likes it or not?' murmured Beth.

Lucy sighed. 'It's not that simple for him. He misses his father. One part of him wants to go and stay for the weekend but when he gets there, with the new girlfriend in residence and all that, he finds that he doesn't like it, after all. I suppose he will come to terms with it in the end.' There was a question in the light, careless voice.

'Oh yes,' Beth spoke with certainty. 'I think that is beginning to happen already.'

Lucy's smile flashed out briefly. 'You're very encouraging.'

'I think he deserves encouragement. And so does little Chloë.'

Lucy nodded tiredly so that her heavy, straight-cut bob swung round her face. She would be quite good-looking really, thought

Beth, if she wasn't so tired. I wish I knew how to help her.

'Can I take it that you approve, then?' Beth asked, returning to the point of her visit.

'Oh, yes. Anything that helps Mark and keeps him occupied. I can't ever be home much before six . . . It's a long time to have to wait for home comforts, and I don't really approve of latchkey kids.'

Beth grinned and got to her feet. 'I'll fix it for next week.' She hesitated and then added, with sudden shyness, 'By the way, if you are ever at a loose end at weekends, I'm usually there.'

Lucy stared at her for a moment in silence. 'D'you know,' she said, in a curiously brittle voice, 'people are apt to avoid a divorced woman—as if you were some sort of pariah, or a threat to their husbands, or something.'

'Well, I haven't got a husband now,' said Beth, putting on a resolute smile. 'And I'm not sure I know what a pariah is.'

The two women looked at one another and the smile between them seemed to grow.

'Mark,' Beth said as she passed him, 'you're going to help me to look after Chloë. Your mum will tell you all about it.'

'Smashing!' grinned Mark, and turned a neat cartwheel on the living-room floor.

SO, EACH WEEKDAY after school, Beth took Mark and Chloë home with her. She did not mind the encroachment on her free time—why should she? There was too much free time in her life already. The long evening hours still hung heavily on her hands, and there was still that echoing silence to fill—the unceasing ache for little Mo and his laughter, for Robert and his warm protection—to be kept at bay, somehow or other. So it was better to be busy. Her concern for Chloë was very real, and for Mark, too, as he struggled to come to terms with his warring family loyalties and turn himself into a responsible young person.

She talked to them both as she walked home with them, just as she would have done to Mo, pointing out anything that seemed to catch their attention. Mark listened and responded, Chloë did not, though Beth sometimes fancied that the small girl's face was not quite so closed and blank as before.

They ate Beth's buns and drank tea in the garden if it was fine—as it usually was this golden autumn—or on the rare wet evenings they sat round the fire and toasted bread on a long brass toasting fork.

Mark continued to talk cheerfully, and to play Scrabble or do a jigsaw, or even play chess with Beth if she set it up for him. He described every move to Chloë. 'Look, that's my knight, see? And that's my queen . . . If I move it here . . .'

But Chloë did not seem to see the chessboard. Or the jigsaws. The only time she actually made any kind of response was when Beth was showing Mark how to plant some winter pansies in the flowerbed near the front door.

'Look, Chloë, that's a pansy—a yellow one—and here's a sort of red one.' Mark held it out for her to see and waited, bright-eyed and challenging, to see what she would do. And slowly, very slowly, Chloë's small fingers came out and stroked the jewel-coloured velvet face of the flower.

'Would you like to plant this one?' asked Mark, blithely suggesting what Beth had not dared to ask.

But that was too much to hope for. Chloë did not move. She just stood there, looking down, while Mark's strong, competent young hands put the little plant in its place.

'Never mind,' he said cheerfully, 'you can do it next time.'

It was slow, and not always obvious, but by these small signs and tiny victories Beth knew that Chloë was gradually returning to the world she had shut out.

So far, Beth had not taken them up to see Beech, for by the time they had got home to the Beehive and had tea and wandered about the garden a bit, it was usually time to go home. Beth decided to ask Beech if she could take the children up at a weekend, when they could stay a bit longer and look at the animals. And so, the following Saturday, Beech was waiting for them when they arrived by his cottage door and took them, with no preamble, to see his latest arrivals. He appeared to pay no special attention to Chloë, who held onto Mark's hand and followed willingly wherever he led. As for Mark, he was so entranced by all the animals that he just gazed at everything in fascinated silence.

'This here,' said Beech, stooping over a new little cage, 'is a ferret. Got himself caught in a snare, see, and the wire near took his head off, he wriggled so bad.' He took out the long, lithe creature and smoothed its golden-brown fur with a gentle hand. 'But he's mendin' nicely now, see? And not a bit afraid o' me.'

'Where did he come from?' asked Beth, wondering whether the old man himself kept ferrets and did a quiet bit of poaching on the side. Somehow it didn't seem quite in character.

'Boy in the village,' replied Beech succinctly. 'A pet, see? Not used to the wild. Ran straight into a snare. Didn't know as he couldn't trust everywhere to be as safe as houses.'

'Poor thing,' said Mark, and also reached out a hand to stroke the golden fur.

'Mind, there shouldn't have been a snare there,' Beech told him severely. 'Not allowed, them wires—lethal, they are.' He placed the young ferret back in its cage with careful slowness, and put a few scraps of food inside to keep it happy.

'Do you always know what to do?' asked Mark, awestruck at all this unspoken knowledge and expertise.

'Nay, that I don't. Sometimes, if it's bad, I gets the vet out, or I takes the crittur in, if I'm able. There's things I can't do, see, and medicines to give, like . . . If there's bones broken, or a bad wound and they needs antibiotics, I has to get 'em from the vet then.'

Mark nodded sagely.

'Now, this 'un, for instance,' said Beech, leaning down to a wire enclosure where a big grey bird was sleeping. 'She's a barnacle goose, on her way to winter at Slimbridge, where it's safe and warm. All the way from the Arctic, she came, and what did she do? Flew straight into a power line. Near killed herself, she did, and broke a wing an' all.'

'Will she mend?' Mark sounded quite anxious.

'Aye, she'll do fine now. But I got the vet to set her wing. It were too bad for me to handle.'

After that he took them to see the owl, which was close to recovery and would soon be able to hunt again in the wild. 'Another day or two,' he said judiciously, 'and she'll be ready to go.'

But Mark was working something out in his mind, and now he said, in a rather angry voice, 'Is it always *our fault*?'

Beech looked at him gravely and did not misunderstand him. 'Nay, that it's not. Not always.' He considered for a moment. 'Take Blackie, now. That blackbird just fell out o' his nest—an accident, like.' The old, clever eyes strayed now to look at Chloë's closed face, and then at Beth's, where they lingered with reflective gentleness. 'Sometimes,' he said softly, 'it ent nobody's fault. It just happens . . . Animals get sick, just like people. Without warning. You can't go on blaming it on other folks—that don't help to mend 'em, do it?'

There was a silence, while Mark thought about a lot of things that he could not put into words. 'No,' he agreed at last, very slowly, 'I suppose not.'

'Let's have a look at my Jess afore you goes,' suggested Beech. 'The pups are growin' fast.'

He went back to the cottage door, where Jess and her wriggling litter of golden puppies lay in the sun.

Chloë had let go of Mark's hand and was crouching down by herself to look at them, the blankness briefly gone from her eyes.

'Come Christmas,' murmured Beech to Beth, 'they'll be wantin' homes.' He did not say any more just then. But Beth understood him very well.

Yes, it might be just the thing to bring Chloë out of her shell. She would have to talk to Finn about it. Then she remembered that Finn was away and could not be talked to at present. It made her suddenly angry. He ought to be here, she thought to herself.

She looked up to find that Beech had produced two glasses of fizzy lemonade for the children and was offering her the customary cup of tea.

'Can we come again?' asked Mark, who seemed enchanted by all that he had seen.

'Surely,' smiled Beech. 'I'm allus here about now of a weekend, and allus pleased to see you.'

'That's good,' grinned Mark, looking suddenly cheerful. 'Isn't it, Chloë?'

She did not answer, but she put her hand in his without being asked and walked quietly between him and Beth through the tawny woods towards home.

FINN WOKE TO THE SOUND of the tinny single bell of St Spyridion's little bell tower on top of the whitewashed church. He lay for a few moments listening to the sounds of the early morning: a donkey braying and the strident voice of a cock crowing above a comfortable clucking of hens. A couple of women calling to one another across the tiny village street, and the laughter of children as they waited for the island bus to take them to school in the little port.

But the laughter of children brought recollection to Finn's dreaming mind, and he sprang out of bed, determined to get on and do something practical—anything hard and useful that would serve to keep his thoughts at bay.

At one of the taverna tables his foreman, Yannis, was having coffee and a hunk of bread before starting work and he called Finn over to join him.

'You must have coffee, Kirios Finn. You cannot start the day without.'

Reluctantly, Finn sat down beside him. He had a great, almost ungovernable urge to push on and get started, but that was not the way they did things out here in the islands. Like Yannis, Finn broke off some bread and absently dunked it in his coffee while watching the rest of the village preparing for the long day's toil. Several of the women were going into the bakery with their covered dishes of lamb and herbs to be baked for them in the big, slow ovens, for tomorrow was a special saint's day—in fact, St Spyridion's own—and everyone would be eating a festive meal. As he watched, the village priest came out of his house near the little church and joined the queue in the baker's shop. Presently he came out, carrying a long loaf under his arm and, seeing Finn and Yannis, came over to join them.

'Good morning, Father,' said Yannis dutifully.

The old priest nodded kindly and turned to Finn. 'Kirios Finn, I am glad to see you back,' he said gravely. 'But I am grieved at your loss.'

Finn inclined his head, and said briefly, 'Thanks.'

Yannis, with supreme tact, gave them both a swift glance and muttered something about 'getting the men started', then went off down the street to the site.

'It's a good morning for work,' said Finn hopefully, looking up at the flawless blue of the sky.

But the old priest was not to be deflected from his duty. 'The little one—your daughter—she is better?'

'No,' growled Finn, avoiding the priest's gaze. 'I'm afraid not.'

'You have not brought her with you this time?' Was there unspoken criticism in that innocent question?

'No . . . I thought it might upset her . . . even more.' Finn hesitated, and then something compelled him to go on. 'She is better without me at present.'

'But not for ever,' said the priest, and it was not a question this time.

Finn sighed. 'I hope you are right.'

The old priest was looking at him with some concern. 'You are not the only one, Kirios Finn, to blame yourself for the happening.'

Finn looked startled. 'Not the only one?'

'We islanders like to look after our friends—especially a friend like you, Kirios Finn, who brings work to the island . . .' He paused, and then continued with slow deliberation. 'So it was very bad for all of us when something so terrible happened to your family—especially for those on the main island. They felt responsible.'

'But they weren't.'

'No, Kirios Finn. They were not. And you were not. But in the eyes of God we are all one family, are we not? And we must share in each other's griefs and each other's joys, must we not?'

Finn was silent.

'We will all be waiting,' said the priest gently, 'for news of the little one. We will all be praying to St Spyridion tomorrow for your wife, God rest her, for you and for the child, little Chloë. We will all ask that she be well, and you will be together again soon.'

Finn did not dare raise his head, for fear the tears in his eyes would spill out and disgrace him in front of everyone. Life was so simple to these people. Ask Agios Spyridion and the good God to take care of things and all would be well. Stephanie would be all right. Chloë would be all right. Even he, with his load of guilt, would be all right. If only, he thought, if only it was true!

The old priest seemed to know he had said enough. Now he merely patted Finn's shoulder kindly and said, 'You will go home when the time is right,' and then he wandered off down the village street.

Finn looked at Georgios, who was hovering anxiously nearby, and rolled his eyes in comic dismay. 'For God's sake, give me a brandy and let me get to work!' he said.

IT WAS A DAY or two after the trip to see Beech, when Beth was having five minutes' breather between classes, that Mark came rushing into the staff room.

'George is on the roof,' he said. 'He won't come down.'

Beth leaped to her feet and so did the other two staff in the room, who happened to be Peter Green and Ruth Brown. They all rushed out into the playground to have a look and found a small group of children standing in a huddle, gazing up at the steep pitch of the roof. At the top of the ridge, with one arm round a chimney-stack, stood a wild-eyed George.

'How did he get up there?' asked Beth swiftly. 'Can we reach him?'

'There's a skylight in the top attic,' said Peter, and began to run. 'I'll go.'

'No!' Beth followed him urgently. 'He's my responsibility, Peter. I know how to handle him.'

Peter glanced at her over his shoulder but he did not stop running. 'We'll both go, then. Come on.'

The rooms up there were mostly used for stores, or occasionally for extra craft lessons. In the last one, a collection of wooden boxes had been stacked together underneath the open skylight where George had managed to climb out.

Without hesitation, Peter climbed out and reached down a hand to help Beth to clamber out after him.

George saw them coming and began to back off onto the far slope of the roof. 'Keep off!' he shouted. 'Or I'll jump!'

'George,' said Beth reasonably, 'there's no need for this. What's the matter?'

George glared at her, daring her to come any nearer. 'I told you,' he hissed. 'I'll jump!'

'Why?' asked Beth, hoping to get him to tell her what his grievance was and edging a little nearer as she did so. Meanwhile, Peter began to work his way round to the back of the building, hoping to come up to George from behind.

'Why?' shouted George, even more wildly. 'I'll tell you why! They hate me, see? I'm no good. No good at *anything*—and they hate me, all of them.' He backed a little further and Beth saw his foot slide a little on the tiles beneath him.

'Who hates you, George?' she asked softly. 'Who are you talking about?' And she edged a little nearer.

'Everyone!' yelled George. 'All of them!'

'That's not true, George,' said Beth, still sounding reasonable and calm, though she wondered fleetingly if George could be the victim of school bullying of some kind. 'I don't hate you, George. None of us here hate you—so who are you talking about?'

'Them!' screamed George, and took another unwary step backwards. 'Ask *them*! They'll tell you! They'd rather I was dead!' And he teetered wildly on the roof-ridge and began to slide backwards down the slope.

Beth acted then. It was too late for caution. She flung herself forward and grabbed George's flailing arm as he lost his balance and fell sideways, spread-eagled on the slanting roof. Her hands caught one arm and held on, but she thought desperately, He is too heavy. I won't be able to hold him.

'Hang on,' said Peter's voice, from the other side of the chimney-stack. 'I'm coming.'

Beth found herself looking straight into George's mad, frantic gaze, and as she stared the red rage seemed to die in his eyes and he looked suddenly like an ordinary, rather frightened boy.

'Just keep still,' said Beth. 'I've got you. We'll soon have you safe and sound.' She did not dare shift her position but her own arm was beginning to feel as if it was being pulled out of its socket. 'Reach up your other hand,' she told him. 'Try to catch hold of me—can you?'

But George could not move. His hand was clamped on the edge of a tile like a frozen claw and he could not get it off.

'All right,' said Peter, close to Beth now and within reach of George's prone body. 'Take it easy. We've got you.' His arm went round George and held him firmly against the slippery tiles. 'Now, when I say "heave", push yourself up a little. We'll pull you back bit by bit—understand?'

George gulped and tried to nod. But he was too terrified to move his head, let alone anything else.

'Try, George,' coaxed Beth. 'I'm sure you can do it.'

'Now,' ordered Peter. 'One, two, three—HEAVE!'

Peter pushed, Beth pulled, and George at last made an effort and moved upwards.

'That's it!' said Peter, sounding cheerful and approving.

'Well done, George,' Beth encouraged. 'Try again!'

'HEAVE!' commanded Peter, and something in the sharpness of his voice made George obey.

Once again Beth pulled and Peter shoved the boy upwards, and he was suddenly safe again on the ridge of the roof.

'There!' said Peter, breathing hard.

'I knew you could!' smiled Beth. 'Now, all we have to do is wriggle backwards to the skylight.'

In a few moments they were all safely down on the attic floor, where Margaret Collier was quietly waiting for them.

'I think we all need a cup of tea,' she said.

IT WAS WHEN George's mother came to fetch him that Beth began to understand the trouble. Mrs Warner was small and dainty where George was large and clumsy, and she was blonde and pretty where George was dark and plain. She was also, Beth suspected, vain and rather stupid, and George was neither of those. To add to the bitter contrast, she had brought her daughter, George's sister, with her. Germaine Warner was fourteen, small and blonde like her mother, with elegant legs and a supercilious manner that did not make much attempt to disguise her contempt for her bumbling brother.

'What's he done *now*?' she groaned to her mother.

'I asked Mrs Halliday to be here when you came,' said Margaret Collier steadily, 'since she was instrumental in getting George safely out of trouble.'

'Very grateful, I'm sure,' said Eve Warner, not sounding particularly pleased.

'She probably knows more about the cause of his outburst than any of us,' added Margaret, and waited for Beth to speak.

'He said,' Beth told them deliberately, ' *"They hate me. They'd rather I was dead!"* '

Eve Warner flinched, and even Germaine's pert face looked suddenly uncertain.

'I don't know who he meant,' added Beth, looking from one to the other of them with the greatest innocence.

'Oh, the poor boy,' wailed Eve Warner and began to cry.

'There's no harm done,' said Margaret Collier briskly. 'He'll be all right after a good night's sleep.' She paused, and then went on with firm intent. 'But he is rather highly strung, like most clever boys.'

'Clever?' The woman sounded incredulous.

'Oh yes. Very.' Margaret turned to Beth. 'Ask Mrs Halliday.'

Beth smiled. 'One of the most intelligent boys in my class—except when he's upset.'

They did not rub it in any more just then. It seemed to them that they had done enough to help George's cause for the time being. Beth went to fetch a somewhat chastened George, and gave him a swift hug of reassurance before she handed him over to his mother.

'Oh, *George*!' said Mrs Warner, and then somehow could not think of anything else to say in front of Margaret Collier's grave, carefully neutral gaze. She gave Beth one nervous glance and then hurried out of the room with her hand on George's unwilling arm. Germaine followed, looking bored—but she did not say anything unkind to her brother. At least, not then.

'Sit down, Beth,' said Margaret close behind her, 'before you fall down.'

'Thanks,' said Beth, suddenly aware of her shaky legs. 'I don't mind if I do!'

BETH HADN'T REALISED she was so shattered till she got home. She was just settling down with a mug of tea when someone knocked on her door. Sighing, she struggled to her feet and went to see who it was. Peter Green stood in the porch, looking shy.

'I just came to see how you were,' he said.

'Recovering.' Beth stood back to let him come inside.

'It was quite an experience,' he remarked, and began to grin.

'You can say that again!' Beth went back into the kitchen and poured out another mug of tea.

'Have you been down to look at the river yet?' Peter was nothing if not direct.

'The Severn? No. Why?'

'Very soothing.' His grin was somehow infectious. 'Very restful.' He took a cheerful swig of tea. 'There's a nice pub right by the river. Thought you could do with a breather.'

Beth was on the point of refusing, on the grounds of total exhaustion after the day's traumatic events, when she suddenly thought, Well, why not? A peaceful drink beside a slow-moving river sounded very tempting.

'You'd like it down there,' he coaxed. 'Lovely and quiet.'

'All right,' she agreed suddenly. 'Why not? It sounds a great idea.'

THEY SAT PEACEFULLY at a wooden table on a green slope of rough grass with the silver Severn spread out before them. Beth had not realised it was so wide, but the silken water seemed to stretch for miles and the mud flats at the edge made it look even wider.

It was close to sunset now and over all this silvery spread of water the sun, sinking behind the far Welsh hills, laid a patina of gold and rose and a shimmering pathway of fading crimson light from its own bright disc across the smooth stretch of water at Beth's feet.

'Thought you'd like it,' said Peter, sounding as pleased as a magician who had just produced a rabbit out of a hat.

Beth turned to him, smiling. 'You're very clever. It was just what I needed.'

Peter nodded a cheerful yellow head. 'Often come here myself when things get fraught.'

Beth laughed. She couldn't imagine Peter getting worked up about anything.

'Look!' said Peter. 'The birds are going home for the night,' and pointed downriver to where flight after flight of white-winged water birds wheeled and turned in the sunset afterglow before fanning out into flocks and skeins of drifting flights homing in to the west.

'Where are they going?' Beth wondered.

'Mostly to Slimbridge—to the Wildfowl Trust,' explained Peter. 'The tide's coming up fast now. The feeding grounds will be covered.'

Spellbound, Beth watched the bird-clouds grow faint in the west and the incoming thrust of the tide make swirling eddies on the rose-coloured surface of the sleeping river.

'Magical!' she murmured, admitting to herself at last that this was something she was glad to be alive to see. It would have been better if Mo and Robert had been here to see it, too. But even without them it was worth seeing.

'Magical!' she repeated, and smiled at Peter in sudden gratitude.

And Peter smiled back and raised his glass to her, and carefully did not say a single word.

BETH KNEW WHAT SHE WANTED to do about George, and she got busy organising it as soon as she could. She was going to make him the star of the Japanese opera that she was hoping they would perform in front of the whole school and, what's more, she was going to make him so good that everyone, particularly his idiotic mother and sister, would be filled with admiration.

'But I can't sing,' growled George, when she put it to him.

'You won't have to. You are Hamaguchi, the Village Grandfather—the one everyone looks up to and obeys. You are a wise old man, see? You wouldn't be able to sing anyway, but you can speak, can't you?'

'I s'pose so . . .' He still sounded very dubious.

'We'll give you a beautiful long robe—a kimono, they call it—and a long, thin beard. You'll look smashing.'

'I'll look right silly.'

Unexpectedly, Beth found an ally in Mark, who had already agreed to sing the solo part of the young fisherman, Ojotaki. 'Go on, George,' he urged, suddenly appearing beside him. 'Have a go. I'm going to.'

George looked at him suspiciously. 'So what?'

'So it's no worse for you. At least you haven't got to sing.' Mark glared at him with fierce challenge.

For some reason this made George begin to smile. 'Oh, all right,' he said grudgingly. 'But I'll make a proper mess of it.'

'No, you won't.' Beth grinned back. 'I won't let you.'

She went off to tell Margaret Collier about her plan and to enlist her help. 'I know they've never done anything like it before,' she said, trying to sound persuasive and entirely reasonable both at once, 'and they're apt to be unpredictable . . .'

'You can say that again,' agreed Margaret, smiling.

'But I . . . I'd like to try.' Beth looked at her with urgent appeal. 'It would be so wonderful for them to do something really well that everyone else admired.'

'Yes.' Margaret thought about it. 'Yes, it would.'

Beth saw her approval and sighed with relief. 'Then I can go ahead?'

Margaret nodded. 'Of course. Though goodness knows what you're letting yourself in for.'

'If it's a flop,' said Beth slowly, 'you mustn't blame them. It'll be my fault for being too ambitious.'

'Quite so,' agreed Margaret, an unmistakable glint of humour dancing in her eyes.

FINN HAD FORGOTTEN about St Spyridion. His festival did not really start till the evening, but when it did, it erupted with a bang. A volley of firecrackers went off in the street and on the quayside, everyone who could move at all flocked to the little church on the hill, and everyone who could play any kind of instrument played it loudly all the way up the road. In the church the statue of the saint was lifted onto his ceremonial float, bedecked with late flowers, and then the bearers stooped their shoulders to the platform handles and lifted him aloft. Everyone lit a candle and followed the saint in a long, glowing snake of lights down to the village streets below.

Finn had been sitting alone at the taverna, not feeling that he belonged in such joyful festivities, but now the crowd all began to spill out round him into a singing, purposeful mob that would not let him be left behind. Someone grabbed his arm, and someone else thrust a lighted candle into his hand, and several of the children dragged him along, singing and laughing as they went.

The procession wound its way along the front of the village to the edge of the sea and the little jetty with its few small boats. Here the village priest, in his best festival robes and carrying a tall silver cross, blessed the tiny quayside and the fishing boats and the sea itself, which provided them with riches as well as winter storms.

'Kyrios Finn,' said Marina's voice close to him, 'you must have some herbs to give the saint,' and she handed him a bunch of fragrant leaves tied up with yellow ribbon.

Finn smiled at Marina and thanked her in careful Greek, and resolved to watch what everyone else did with their gifts for the saint, and do likewise.

The procession now moved off along the edge of the sea round the small, sandy bay to where Finn's new development was beginning to take shape close to the rocks at the furthest end of the cove. And here the priest signalled to Finn and Yannis, his foreman, to come forward and stand beside him.

'We will bless the new site,' the old priest said gravely, 'that it may bring prosperity and happiness to our village, and not destroy the beauty of our shore.' And when he had lifted his hand and waved his silver cross, the singing rose up louder than ever, and the saint on his flowery platform seemed to nod and smile in the candlelight as the bearers turned round and began to move off in another direction.

This time, the procession left the edge of the shore and wound its way over the hill path to the next bay, where the old building foundations were being cleared away. It was a beautiful bay, long and curving, with very white sand lapped by a gentle surf and surrounded by sheltering rocks beneath shallow ochre-coloured cliffs.

Here the procession stopped again, and this time the priest blessed the bay itself and the sea once again. After all, the sea dominated their lives—and its moods, its fierce tempests and sudden calms, governed all their going out and coming in.

'May the flowers of the field return,' said the priest in his most musical voice, 'and the herbs and grasses of the hills clothe our bay anew . . . And let us also thank Kirios Edmondson that he has returned our land to us,' he added, and various of the villagers clapped their hands in agreement. The singing started up again and the procession moved off, back to the village and the little church on the hill.

When at last the weary saint-bearers desposited their burden back in the church, the singing grew louder still, the candles were all stuck into spikes round the saint so that his gold paint glistened and the people gave him their presents one by one before they left for the more light-hearted festivities in the village below.

Finn, too, went up and left his small bunch of silvery herbs, and was not ashamed to whisper a small prayer. 'Help Chloë to come back,' he breathed, and such was the power of all that faith and homage around him that he found himself almost believing in miracles.

TRUE TO HER PROMISE, the next Sunday morning Beth took Mark and Chloë up to see Beech again.

This time, Beech had some different charges. The owl had gone, and so had the mother doe and her fawn. The fox cub with the injured leg was still there, and Blackie was singing small snatches of song from the nearest beech tree. A Rhode Island hen had hatched her pheasant foster babies and the chicks were tumbling about the straw like small speckled balls of fluff. The puppies had grown, too, and did even more tumbling than the chicks. But in one quiet pen, a hare lay prone in a concealing heap of bracken, and scarcely even moved when Beech came near.

'Shot, she was,' he said, his voice rough with anger. 'Pellets all over the place.' He bent down to smooth the bedraggled fur with gentle fingers. 'We got most of 'em out, but the shock near killed her.'

'Will she get better?' Mark's voice was anxious.

Beech looked down at the hare, and then at the boy beside him, and gave a noncommittal shrug. 'Maybe—if she'm not too frit.'

Mark did not say any more just then. He just stood looking from the sick hare to Beech's seamed, compassionate face. Eventually he spoke. 'Do they ever die on you?'

Beech stopped short. Something about those clear grey eyes disturbed him. He hesitated. 'Sometimes they do, young 'un, yes.'

'Can't you make them better?'

He understood then what was behind the question, and knew he must go carefully now. 'Not always,' he said slowly. 'Sometimes they just don't make it. Sometimes . . . I reckon their time is up.'

'Why?' Mark demanded, and took a tight grip of Chloë's hand. And in that fierce question was a cry of bewilderment and rage against a world that was cruel and unfair.

Beech paused for thought. Go easy now, he said to himself. This is important. And not only for the boy and the shocked little one who cannot speak, either. There's the young woman, too, as full of sadness as all of 'em put together, though she don't say so . . .

'Well,' he began slowly, 'I don't rightly know how to answer that, young 'un, but I reckon it's like this. Some of 'em, like this here fox cub—they has to get knocked about a bit afore they grows up, so's they can cope with the world out there. Wicked ol' place, the world is, young 'un, and you needs to be tough, see, to get through.' He looked into Mark's face enquiringly, and saw the boy nod quick comprehension. Yes, the boy had been knocked about too by life, one way or the other, Beech guessed.

'And in the end,' he went on, 'when you've mostly learned what there is to know and done what there is to do, like—then you're old, like me, and it's nearly time to go home, all natural, like.' He took a long breath into his tired old lungs and wondered if he was making any sense at all to his listeners.

'But there's some,' he went on, and now there was an odd thrill of authority in the old voice, 'there's some as is well-nigh perfect already, see? Not when they're old with the corners knocked off at all, but young, like . . .' His glance strayed to little Chloë's closed flower face and then to Beth's still one, which was watching him with such breathless attention. 'And they be ready to go home much sooner, see? So that's what they do, you see, young 'un—go home where they're safe and free.'

He wasn't sure what 'home' was exactly but somewhere, in his mind's eye, home was a green place where the sun shone and no creature, whether man or beast, was ever frightened or hurt again . . .

'D'you know what I do?' he said, and this time he spoke very softly and gently to those vulnerable faces turned towards him. 'When one of 'em goes home, I goes out and plants a new tree.'

'A new tree?' Mark was straining to understand, and to make it clear for Chloë.

'Come and I'll show you,' said Beech.

He stumped over to his small patch of tilled land at the back of the cottage and pointed to a row of little flowerpots at the side of the path. 'See? This here's a new beech. One day it'll be as tall as that one there—and as gold—but now it's just a twig. And this here's an oak.' He looked into the young faces and added cheerfully, 'Some time, I'll take you to find where the acorns fall. Then you can grow an oak all by yourselves. Would you like that?'

For a moment, Mark did not answer. Then he looked from Beth to Chloë and back again, beseechingly, to Beech, and said in a quiet, clear voice that somehow understood everything, 'I think Chloë would like to plant a tree *now*.'

Beech nodded tranquilly. 'Well then, so she shall. You can choose one for her. Which is it to be?'

Beth stood spellbound beside the old man and looked down as Mark bent over the little pots, pulling Chloë after him to look at them, too. He hesitated over each pot, not knowing which one to choose. The beech seedlings were very green and curly.

And then he saw the right one. 'That one!' said Mark, and as he pointed at a small oak seedling whose leaves were extra bright and extra curly, Chloë's small brown hand reached out and touched the tiny, perfectly shaped leaves with one shy finger.

'Right then, that one it is,' agreed Beech, and his eyes met Beth's in quiet triumph above the children's heads.

He gave Mark an old, battered trowel and showed him where to plant the little tree at the edge of the woodland, where it would have space to grow 'mighty', and helped him to dig a hole in the layer of leaf mould on the forest floor. Mark set the little tree in it, and then patted the earth firmly round it—and Chloë leaned forward and patted it, too.

Beech looked at them then, out of his shrewd old eyes, and said suddenly, 'I reckon they'm all runnin' about out yonder, right as rain, the safe-home ones—all on 'em, out yonder—dancin' about like hares in a cornfield.' And he waved a gentle hand at the golden woodland around them. 'What do you think?'

Mark did not answer but he turned slowly to stare out into the dreaming spaces of the woods. Chloë looked, too, with eyes that hoped to see miracles. She wanted to ask the old man where 'yonder' was. But then she suddenly felt sure she knew. 'Yonder' was out there, just past where you could see, in those bright and hazy places between the trees where the hills grew misty and blue before they reached the sky.

And then Chloë spoke the first word she had uttered since her mother's death. *'Yonder?'* she said, and pointed towards the dazzle of sunlight beyond the trees.

PART IV
Corny

The small breakthrough with Chloë did not develop into a major cure, though there were increasing signs each day of returning awareness. She did not speak very often, only if words seemed imperative, but she was less shut in. She even tried to cooperate with Mark and the rest of the class in the rehearsals for the little Japanese opera, for she had been given the part of Mark's sister in the play.

It was November now, and the trees stood gaunt and dark against the evening sky, with every branch and twig etched in fine tracery, while the ground beneath them was springy and rich with the red-gold of fallen leaves. It was a time for wood fires and lamplight and drawn curtains, and crumpets and toast for tea. What with the weekday teatimers and the Sunday morning visits to Beech, it left little enough time for Beth to be lonely or at a loose end. Especially since young Peter Green had become a persistent Saturday visitor, with always some new excuse or some new place to show her. Beth did not mind. She rather liked his company. He was easy and undemanding, and seemed to like the kind of quiet pubs and wayside cafés in small unpretentious villages that also appealed to Beth.

She was therefore half expecting him one Saturday morning when there came a knock on her door. She went through from her little kitchen, crossed the front room and opened the inner door to the porch. But it wasn't Peter who stood there, it was Mary Willis.

'I'm so sorry to bother you,' she began, almost wringing her hands in her distress, 'but is Chloë with you?'

'Chloë? No. Should she be?'

'Oh dear. Oh dearie me.' Mary looked about to cry. 'Wherever can she have got to?'

Beth put a hand on her arm and led her inside. 'Sit down a minute, Mary, and tell me what's happened.'

Mary took a deep breath of attempted control. 'I left her playing in the front room while I went upstairs to do some hoovering. When I came down, the French windows were open and she was gone.' She looked at Beth with fearful apology. 'I didn't leave her for long.'

'Of course not.' Beth waited for her to go on.

'I went out to look for her in the garden but she wasn't there, nor in the sheds nor the summerhouse. I did wonder if she might've gone up to see old Beech.'

'She might . . . She's very keen on those puppies . . .' Beth said, thinking it out. 'I'll tell you what,' she decided, 'I'll walk up to Beech's cottage and see if she's there. You go on home and wait. She may come back of her own accord, anyway. And a nice warm fire and a good hot meal will be just what the doctor ordered!'

Mary's face lit up. This was something she could understand. Warm fires and hot meals were exactly what she was good at. Together they went out into the grey November day, and while Mary hurried back to the old Mill House, Beth climbed the hill to the edge of the woods and Beech's cottage.

As she reached the top of the path, she saw the old man himself hurrying towards her. 'Missus,' he said, still just remembering that small, polite salute with his hand, 'I'm glad you've come. I didn't rightly know what to do.'

'Why, Beech? Is Chloë here?'

He hesitated a little, and then shook his head. 'Not here, exactly, missus, but not far off, like.' He fell into step beside her then, and led her past his cottage towards the wood.

'I came on her by chance, like,' he explained, and now his old voice sank to a whisper, 'and she looked so . . . happy, like, that I wus in two minds whether to leave her be and go for you, or to stay by her in case of trouble . . .'

Ahead of them the trees grew closer, but just to one side there was an unexpected clearing. It was where the great old beech tree had come down in a storm, its roots dangling over the deep and hidden hollow that its upheaval had left in the sandy soil. And as they came close to it, Beth heard a small voice talking softly to something—talking freely in a quiet, happy way.

Beth leaned over the edge of the hollow to look inside. It was like a cave down there, under the roots of the tree. And curled up on the ground, crooning softly to something warm and wriggling on her lap, was Chloë, with one of Jess's puppies cradled in her arms.

'. . . and you'll grow big and strong,' she was saying, 'and run about everywhere, won't you? . . . I'll take you in the fields . . .'

Beth looked at Beech in a mixture of dismay and relief. Chloë was talking! Not to them, of course. Not yet. But to the puppy she could say anything. And it was clearly of enormous importance to her already—this small bundle of fluff—a release and joy they had none of them anticipated. Now what were they to do?

But Beech was beckoning to her to come away out of earshot. 'I said as they'd be needing homes,' he said, with a gentle smile. 'Seeming she's chosen already.'

'I haven't even got permission from her father,' Beth said. 'And

isn't it too soon to take the puppy from her mother?'

He considered. 'Nine weeks would be better.'

They stood there for a little while, each pondering the best way to approach her, when suddenly they saw the top of Chloë's head appearing above the edge of the hollow. Still cradling the puppy in her arms, she came directly towards them. 'She needs her mother,' she said, quite calmly and clearly, and handed the puppy back to Beech without any fuss at all.

'Well, now,' said Beech, 'let's go and put her back then, shall we?' He took Chloë's hand in his and gave Beth a slow, mischievous wink as he went past with the puppy tucked under one arm. 'You can allus come and talk to her again, can't you?' he said as they laid the wriggling puppy back among her brothers and sisters. 'Then when she'm ready you can take her home,' Beech said. 'But not yet.'

'No,' agreed Chloë gravely. 'Not yet.'

'You'll have to think of a name for her,' smiled Beech, trying to give her something to hold onto.

Chloë looked at the pale gold bundle of fur and then away through the trees, as if remembering something. 'Cornfield . . .?' she said in a questioning voice.

'Dancing about like hares in a cornfield,' remembered Beth and, looking into the old man's faded eyes, knew that he remembered, too.

'Corny?' murmured Chloë.

'Corny would do fine,' said Beech, his voice warm with approval.

'Corny?' repeated Chloë, and bent down to pick up the puppy and have one more look. 'Are you Corny?' And the squirming puppy reached out and licked her on the nose.

'That settles it!' smiled Beth, and Chloë actually laughed.

Then she carefully put the puppy back, got to her feet and put her hand into Beth's, seeming perfectly ready to go home.

Beech watched them go, then turned to his litter of puppies and picked up Chloë's choice to have another look at her.

'You'd better keep it up, young Corny,' he told her. 'I think you're doing the little 'un good.'

IT WAS NOT LONG after this that Beth decided to talk to George's father. She didn't know quite how to engineer this without involving the mother and daughter, too. But here Peter Green proved to be an ingenious ally.

'He's quite good at football,' he said. 'George, I mean. He's got the bulk for it.' His infectious grin flashed out. 'I'm sure his dad would come to watch a game if I asked him.'

'Peter, you're a genius.'

'Thanks,' he said modestly. 'I'll talk to George.'

So it was that Beth found herself on the edge of the cold football pitch at the end of the game, waiting to talk to George's father while the boys were in the changing room.

'Mr Warner,' she said, looking up at the tall, burly man with some trepidation, 'could I have a word with you about George?'

The round, friendly face looked instantly anxious. 'Of course. Is he being a nuisance?'

'No,' said Beth firmly. 'Far from it. He's being a very stalwart and cooperative member of my team.'

The tough red face relaxed and the eyes—brown and warm like George's—began to smile. 'Well, that's good news, at least.'

'Yes.' Beth tried to marshal her arguments into some sort of coherence. 'I think he's much underestimated, your son. He's very intelligent. Especially over maths and anything constructional that requires tricky calculations. Maybe he takes after you?'

Stan Warner laughed. 'Well, I am a builder. I suppose those sort of skills do come into it.'

'He needs someone who understands his kind of ability, Mr Warner. Someone who might give him a bit of praise now and then. I'm afraid the crux of all that roof business—'

'What roof business?'

Beth looked at him in astonishment. 'Didn't they tell you?'

'Who?'

'Your wife and daughter . . .' Beth took a deep breath of outrage. How could they say nothing about it? 'I think I'd better tell you myself, then,' she said, and promptly did.

The effect on Stan Warner was immediate. 'They should've told me!' he growled fiercely.

'It was a near thing, Mr Warner,' said Beth, 'and the reason I'm telling you about it now is that it showed what was bugging George.'

'Yes.' His mouth grew straight and grim. 'So it seems.'

'So, I was wondering if you could—as it were—*counteract* the criticism at home with some extra praise of your own?'

'I'm sure I can do that.'

'And then there's the school play—well, musical drama, I suppose you'd call it,' Beth went on. 'I've given him a leading part and he's doing it very well, surprisingly well . . . I am hoping that you will all come to the performance and clap him like mad!'

'It'll be a pleasure!'

And then they both saw George coming towards them, looking

anxious. 'Well done, George!' said Stan, going over to him and giving him a hearty slap on the back. 'That was a damn good game.'

George looked up at his father in amazement and actually smiled. It was clear to Beth that he was not used to such praise. Then in a stifled, shy voice he said, 'Oh well . . . it wasn't bad . . . ' He added honestly, 'I could've tackled a bit harder. '

Stan winked at Beth over the top of George's tousled head and said judiciously, 'No. Just right. You need to know your strength . . . ' and they went off together, arguing happily.

FINN'S ARCHITECT, Theo Koussalis, came out to inspect the work on the Spirios site and expressed himself satisfied that it was going according to plan.

Then Finn broached the subject of a site manager—pointing out that neither he nor Koussalis could be there all the time and that someone would have to take responsibility.

But here Theo Koussalis surprised him by saying, 'Your foreman, Yannis, seems very reliable. I should think he could handle it, that is if he really understands the plans.'

Finn looked startled for a moment, and then the idea took shape in his mind. 'I *have* been over the plans with him while we were discussing the foundation digging . . .' He looked at Theo searchingly. 'Would *you* be satisfied to leave things in his charge?'

Theo temporised. 'Let's talk to him and see what he says.'

'He's got quite a lot of experience, I believe,' said Finn slowly. 'Though I doubt if he can boast many qualifications.'

'A site manager doesn't need qualifications so much as good relations with his work force,' said Theo crisply. 'And I can keep an eye on things myself from time to time.' He smiled at Finn, offering cheerful reassurance. He was a calm young man with the kind of dark, solid good looks that somehow engendered confidence.

They strolled on down to the site, where the men were already busy pouring concrete. Yannis, seeing them approach, left the little knot of workers and came across to speak to them.

'Yannis,' said Finn, smiling, 'we have a proposition to put before you.' He turned to Theo, instinctively realising that the suggestion would come better from him.

Theo took his cue. 'How would you feel about being site manager?'

Yannis looked astonished. 'Me?' He stared at them both, and then turned to look at the laid-out lines of the hotel complex with an anxious gaze. 'Would I know enough?' he murmured, seeming to ask himself as much as the other two.

Finn smiled. It was that kind of humility that endeared these sturdy island people to him.

'I am sure you would,' said Theo, speaking for Finn as well. 'Why don't we go into the site office and discuss it?'

A large, shy grin came over Yannis's rugged face. 'I would be honoured,' he said.

It was while they were still poring over the plans that the shout went up. Yannis went quickly outside and started running down to the little jetty, accompanied by most of the able-bodied men of the village.

Finn, when he got outside, was amazed at the change in the weather. Five minutes ago, it had been brilliant sunshine and clear blue skies, but now the horizon was inky-dark, the sea was rising into black choppy waves and a fierce squall was sweeping across the surface.

'What is it?' asked Finn, close beside Yannis.

'A boat out there . . .' Yannis pointed a brown finger into the darkness across the sea. 'A yacht in trouble—can you see her?'

Some of the men were already launching the biggest and sturdiest of the caïques and getting ready to go to the rescue.

'We do not have a lifeboat service,' Yannis explained. 'Out here, we make our own.' He was watching the approaching squall anxiously. 'I must go. I am one of the crew.' And he sprang away down the tiny slipway and leaped into the rocking boat.

Finn, after a swift glance of apology at Theo, followed Yannis at a run and leaped on board as well. 'Used to yachts,' he said briefly to Georgios, the taverna owner, who seemed to be the skipper of the caïque. 'Might come in handy.'

The others looked at him with brief, swift assessment and then nodded agreement. They set off into the teeth of the gale. Rain swept across them, whipped up into stinging needles by the wind and waves. Finn was used to storms, and the men beside him seemed used to them, too—but he knew that the caïque was quite likely to turn turtle in such a sea. As for the yacht—what they could see of it between gusts of rain and spray—the white hull seemed deep in the water, listing heavily in the swell, and the mast seemed to be gone altogether.

The caïque was making little headway against the driving force of the wind and tide, in spite of its powerful engine, but it ploughed steadily on, making a half-circle round the stricken yacht so that the actual power of the storm might bring them nearer to its wallowing side. But it was a perilous operation and twice they were swept even further away by an unexpected gust.

'We'll never get near enough,' Yannis murmured, shaking his head.

'Might get a line on board,' answered Finn, and edged his way forward to help uncoil the rope.

They came up suddenly quite close to the ailing yacht, and now Finn saw a couple of dark shapes crouched helplessly on the deck. One, he guessed from his position, was injured but the other seemed more alert and waved an arm.

Finn threw. But the caïque gave a sudden lurch and he missed. Twice more he threw and watched the line fall uselessly back into the sea—but the fourth time it fell across the yacht's heeling deck, and the dark wet shape of the man fell on it and grabbed it. Finn saw him stumble to his feet and manage to lash the rope onto a cleat before another wave broke over the bows. He began to haul the thin rope in until he reached the joined thicker line that would be strong enough for a tow. Lurching wildly on the slippery deck, he managed to secure it to the nearest solid-looking stanchion in the bows. And then, to the horror of the watching crew of Georgios's boat, the sodden figure on the yacht seemed to slide sideways in the retreating wash of the last huge wave, and before he could grab at anything else he was swept overboard.

'Throw a line!' yelled Yannis, and one of the others seized a life belt and flung it overboard. But though it floated on the surface of the boiling sea, the man did not respond. He just lay there, tossed to and fro like a piece of flotsam.

Finn, cursing under his breath at the storm and the helpless vulnerability of inexperienced sailors, stripped off his jacket and his shoes and plunged overboard.

'No!' shouted Yannis. 'Kirios Finn—it is too rough!' But Finn did not hear him. He was a good swimmer, and he knew from experience that the islanders mostly were not. They managed their boats and they fished their seas when they had to—but they did not waste time swimming in the sea like the tourists. They were too busy.

So it was Finn or no one, he thought. And it might as well be him, he had nothing to lose. He struck out strongly, but the waves were very fierce and kept carrying him away from the sodden body in the sea. At last he got a grip on the man's hair and yanked him upwards so that he could breathe, and then reached out to grab the life belt as it floated by. He had just succeeded in getting the rubber ring round the man's body when a sudden lurch of the yacht brought the white-painted side heeling over almost on top of him, submerging him in a flurry of spray and sucking water. He went under, still clutching the man in his life belt, and thought, very clearly and distinctly, This is it. What a fool I am. And then he thought something else, with piercing clarity: I can't drown now. What will happen to Chloë?

He did not hear Yannis shout, or the splash as his devoted foreman plunged in after him, but all at once there was someone else flailing about in the water beside him, and he was coming up for air.

'The line,' gasped Yannis, 'take the line,' and sank like a stone under the next huge wave. Finn didn't know then whether he was rescuing Yannis or Yannis was rescuing him but, somehow or other, he hauled Yannis up again and wound the trailing line round all three of them. Then all he could do was tread water and wait for the crew of the caïque to pull them in.

It seemed to take for ever, but at last he was near enough to the wildly dipping side of the caïque to push Yannis into the strong waiting arms of his friends. Then it was the turn of the unconscious man in the life belt, who was harder to get on board because he was a soaked dead weight. And last of all, the same strong, friendly arms seized Finn and dragged him on board just before another wave smashed over them.

'My God,' spluttered Finn, coughing up half the Aegean, 'some storm!' Then he looked round to see how the other two were doing. Yannis was also coughing and grinning with relief, and one of the crew was working on the prone figure of the second man, trying to pump the water out of his lungs.

Finn thought of the other crouching figure on the slippery deck. He peered out through the sheeting rain and thought he caught a glimpse of something dark still huddled on the slanting deckboards, but he couldn't be sure.

'The line's still holding,' shouted Georgios. 'We'll try to tow her in.' He turned his boat away from the pounding swell and began to let it run with the wind and tide.

Finn looked up at the sky and thought he could see a lightening at the edge of the purple-black storm clouds over the sea. 'Squall's going over,' he said to Yannis, and got to his feet to go and help the others keep the line clear and the brave little caïque afloat.

It was a slow, painful process, bringing the two boats in, but at last the caïque bumped awkwardly against the little jetty and managed to tie up, leaving the stricken yacht lying sluggishly in the deep water some way off.

After that, the island routine took over. A small boat shot across the choppy bay to the yacht to take off the injured man. Someone had already ridden over to the little port on his motor scooter and sent messages to the rescue service. It was still too rough for a boat from the main island to get round the point, but a helicopter would come and ferry the injured men to hospital on the mainland.

Yannis and Finn were plied with coffee and brandy, and slapped on the back by everyone who could get near them, and Theo Koussalis looked at them affectionately and said, 'I didn't realise I was dealing with heroes.'

Yannis laughed and was clearly pleased, but Finn frowned a little and kept his thoughts to himself. That moment of blinding truth about little Chloë had shaken him to the core. He knew now what kind of man he was. He would rather take foolish risks and plunge into boiling seas than face up to his responsibilities. He would rather be seen as a hero, admired and fêted as usual, than go home and look after his own bereft small daughter, who needed him more than she knew how to say.

Tonight, said Finn to himself, I'll telephone home.

THE TELEPHONE LINES were even worse than usual after the storm, but at last Finn got through to Mary Willis and heard Chloë was actually improving and beginning to come out of her shell. He was so relieved by this that he knew he must talk to Beth and find out exactly how the improvement had come about, and how much of an advance it really was. Mary had said something about a puppy but he couldn't catch exactly what she was trying to tell him over the crackling line.

So he went through another long and tiresome wait before he finally heard Beth's voice on the line. He was surprised (and rather shocked, he had to admit) to discover how much the sound of Beth's voice meant to him and what a curious lurch of pleasure it gave to him.

'Finn? Where are you?'

'Still in Greece. But I'm finishing up here now, Beth, and then I'm coming home.'

Beth also felt an unexpected little jolt of pleasure—or was it relief?—when she heard these words. But she did not say so. 'I'm glad to hear it.' She knew she sounded too prim and severe, but she couldn't help it. There was so much she needed to discuss with him about Chloë, and it was impossible to say any of it over this fading, uncertain line.

'Mary says Chloë is getting better. Can you tell me what's been happening?'

Beth sighed. 'She is showing signs of improvement, Finn, but it's been slow progress.' She hesitated, wondering how much to say about

Beech and the boy, Mark, and his staunch protection of little Chloë. 'There's a boy here called Mark who seems to know how to handle her. Very supportive . . . I have them both to tea most days.'

'That's wonderful of you.'

'No,' said Beth honestly. 'It's just practical. Mark needs help, too—and they seem to get on together somehow.' Once again she hesitated, considering. 'And then there's Beech—you remember him?'

'I do, indeed. Nice old fellow.'

'And pretty wise in his way. He's got the two of them interested in his animals. Chloë's particularly interested in one of his retriever puppies.'

'Yes?' Finn sounded almost impatient.

'Well, she went off with it. We found her talking to it.'

'Talking to it?'

'Yes. Exactly. It was the breakthrough we had been hoping for. I don't know why, except perhaps it was something of her own to love and care for, without any connotations of grief or anything.'

'I see.' Finn did see, too, and was ashamed at what he saw. 'Beth,' he said abruptly, 'something happened today that brought me to my senses . . . I'm sorry to have been so dense . . .' He wasn't being very coherent, he knew, but somehow he felt sure Beth would follow him. 'I'll try to find some way to reach her when I get back, but . . . but can I ask one more favour . . . among the many you've already done for me?'

'Of course.' Beth sounded entirely calm and sure.

'It's just . . . I don't know how Chloë will feel about me coming back. Can you . . . could you sort of prepare the way a bit? I mean, I don't want to send her back into retreat just when she's coming out.'

Beth could hear the anxiety in Finn's voice, and knew she must try to reassure him. 'I'll sound her out gently, Finn. She's a lot less fragile now. Some of that sturdy independence is coming back at last.'

'Is it?' There was such hope and heartbreak in his voice that Beth could have wept.

'Oh yes. I think it will be all right. But you must come home soon, Finn. There are a lot of things to talk about.'

'I know.' Finn's voice faded on the line and seemed to grow near again. 'I know there are—and I know I've been avoiding them . . . I'm an awful coward, Beth.'

She smiled a little at that, having a very clear picture of that brave buccaneer striding up the jetty after his famous single-handed voyage. 'I think we all are, Finn, when it comes to human relationships. Stephanie is the only person I've known who wasn't afraid of them.'

There, she thought. I've said it. Sententious and prim it sounds, but it's true. Maybe it will make Finn feel a bit better—or at least make him less shy about his emotions.

'You are absolutely right,' Finn said, sounding suddenly warm and close. 'And I'm coming home. Give . . . give Chloë my love . . . if you can, that is.'

And before she could reply, he had rung off.

THE FOLLOWING SATURDAY morning Beth took Mark and Chloë to see Beech and the animals.

'Yes, you can take Corny out, little 'un,' said Beech, smiling at Chloë and Mark as they bent over the puppies. 'Show her the wide world, like. She'll have to get used to it soon.'

Beth watched them take the golden-haired retriever pup out of its box and set her down a little way off under the trees, where it scampered about chasing leaves and shadows. Then she turned to Beech and said rather anxiously, 'Her father is coming home. She'll be able to have the puppy soon. But I'm worrying about how Chloë will react to her father.'

Beech nodded. 'I dessay we could do summat about that.' He went across to the two children and said cheerfully, 'I got someone new to show you. Bring Corny with you, then,' and he led them a little way down the path to where the grassy hillside met the edge of his own smallholding. Here at one end of the little paddock there was a small lean-to shed. He led Chloë and Mark, with Beth close behind them, towards it. A shaggy grey donkey was standing motionless with its back to the open door.

'This here is Moses,' he said, and laid a quiet brown hand on the rough furry flank. 'And he's mortal sad and lonely, so we've got to be extra kind to him.'

'Why is he sad?' asked Mark, who already realised that Beech was up to something and knew he ought to ask the right questions.

'Well, there's two reasons really.' Beech paused and looked down at Chloë with a speculative gaze. 'One is, he's lost his Jenny—his wife, like. She died at the end of the summer and he can't seem to get over it.' Once again he paused, still with his eyes on Chloë's listening face. 'And then there's the children, see—he misses them, too.'

'What children?' asked Mark.

'Why, on Weston sands,' explained Beech. 'Moses was a riding donkey, see. All summer long, the children came to have rides, and they used to pat him and make a fuss of him, like. Come winter, all the donkeys go to have a rest in some farmer's field and such. I usually has one or two.' He gave the shaggy coat another gentle pat. 'Old Moses here, he's grieving for his Jenny and there's no children to take his mind off things. He needs a lot o' cosseting just now.'

'Cosseting?' said Chloë, very distinctly.

'Ar. Cosseting.' He took Chloë's hand and led her a little nearer to the donkey's warm flank. 'When people miss someone bad, little 'un, they needs a lot o' cosseting. Would you like to give him an apple? Moses likes apples.'

'Yes,' said Chloë, and held out her hand.

Carefully, Beech put the apple into her hand and showed her how to hold it out on the flat of her palm to the velvet muzzle.

For a moment the sorrowful donkey did not move, but then the scent of the fruit seemed to reach him, and he lifted his drooping head a little and nibbled delicately at the apple.

'That's it,' encouraged Beech. 'Try talking to him, little 'un.'

'Moses?' said Mark, close behind Chloë, and urging her on. 'Don't be sad. We've come to talk to you, Chloë and me.'

'And Corny,' added Chloë firmly. 'Look, Corny, this is Moses . . .' and she held the small puppy up to see what a furry old donkey looked like.

Mark smiled in triumph at Beech and asked him for another apple. And when that had been crunched up, both children put an arm round the shaggy grey neck and began to whisper into the twitching, intelligent ears.

Beech and Beth stood a little aside and watched this without comment. But at last Mark said regretfully, 'I've got to go now, Moses. My mum needs some help with the shopping, you see. But I'll come and see you again soon.'

'I'll come too,' added Chloë, not to be outdone. She turned away then, still clutching little Corny under one arm, and went rather unwillingly to put her back with her brothers and sisters.

Beech noted her reluctance with satisfaction. 'You'll be able to take her home soon,' he told her, smiling. 'Missus here says your father's on his way home. He'll need a lot o' cosseting, an' all. Like Moses, he is—sad and lonely.' His faded blue eyes were regarding Chloë with gentle understanding. 'Only, o' course, he's got a little girl of his own to talk to.'

Chloë gazed at him in silence. Then she nodded once, and put her hand firmly into Mark's and started for home.

There was no need to say any more, Beth knew. Skilfully, the old man had prepared the way for Finn's return. Now Chloë had a role to play in his homecoming.

'Thank you, dear Beech,' she murmured, as she turned to follow them down the path.

And Beech just winked and muttered 'Cosseting!' as she passed.

BETH WAS IN TWO MINDS about Finn coming home. One part of her was still anxious about how it would affect Chloë. In spite of the clever suggestion put forward by Beech, Beth was still not entirely sure how the small girl would react. Would she remember that important word 'cosseting' and really want to look after her father? Or would she close up and grow silent and pale again, refusing all overtures? She only knew that she wanted to put things right for Chloë, and for Finn, too. Somehow, she still felt she owed it to Stephanie, and she ought not to fail her. And, thinking about all this, she was troubled.

But another part of her seemed to be unexpectedly relieved and glad that Finn was coming home. She felt a curious warmth about his return into her life, even though she knew that he, too, was still caught in the same inextricable web of grief and loneliness as herself.

Loneliness? That word brought her up short. And she knew she must not try to use Finn to cure her own sense of loss. Or Peter, either. For it was becoming clear to her that young Peter was trying very hard to fill the gap for her and she knew she must not let him. It was too soon to think of any such thing, especially as she had nothing to offer in return.

With these thoughts very much in mind she decided to go off on her own that Saturday and not wait for Peter to come knocking on her door. So she got in her car and drove off to visit the small Saxon church at Elkstone, which someone had told her she must see.

It was a grey late-November morning when she set out, with the hills looking cold and clear and the nearly leafless trees standing gaunt and beautiful against a pearly sky. But when she got to Elkstone a gleam of winter sunlight pierced the clouds and suddenly bathed the ancient stone of the little church in a pale wash of gold.

Inside, it was cool and quiet under the timbered roof, but as she looked up the tiny nave she became aware that the shaft of winter sunshine outside seemed to have got into the church, and the whole of the chancel beyond the double stone arches seemed to be swimming in golden light.

Astonished, she walked slowly towards the shimmer of brightness behind the miniature wooden altar rail, and saw that the small windows set either side were furnished with a special amber-yellow glass which transformed all the light pouring through them to translucent gold, and laid a gentle, glowing ambience on the honey-coloured stone of the walls. It felt to Beth as if she was wrapped in warmth and light, and an extraordinary sense of timeless tranquillity seemed to encompass her.

But when she looked up at the east window above the altar, she saw that this glass was not amber-coloured but blue—the clear and brilliant blue of a Madonna's robe—and the light shone through her blue veil and the plain white wraps of the Child in her arms. It was a simple window and the figure was small and unpretentious. Something about that serene and patient mother, waiting there through the years of eternity, made Beth's own unguarded heart clench with sudden pain. I can't look at you, she thought, a sudden spurt of irrational anger seizing her. The perfect mother and child. How can you stand there, looking so calm and good? How could you bear it, knowing what you knew?

She began to turn away then, but something about the very simplicity of that quiet figure made her pause; the atmosphere of the little church seemed to reach out to her, the radiance of that golden chancel seemed to fill her with a curious sense of acceptance. For the first time since Mo's death—and Robert's death, too, which she had shut away inside her—she could look back to all that past happiness without flinching. And, perhaps, look forward, too, to a life that had to go on somehow, and find a purpose and some kind of peace . . . And for the first time she began to feel that they were not far away, the ones she loved. Not far in this dazzle of gold—she need only stretch out a hand . . .

She stood there gazing for a long time, but at last she turned away from the window and stumbled rather blindly down the aisle into the porch. As she sank down on the stone seat beside the door and closed her eyes against the dazzle of tears, a gentle voice beside her said, 'Are you all right?'

Making a vague effort to collect her flying thoughts, Beth turned her head to the light and looked up. The face she saw before her was long and scholarly—with the parchment-thin frailty of old age giving it a luminous transparency. It was also compassionate and concerned.

'Er, yes,' she answered, somewhat doubtfully. 'I think the atmosphere rather threw me.'

The old man nodded, and sat down beside her companionably on the stone seat. 'It is a bit overpowering.'

Beth glanced at him in surprise. 'You feel it too?'

'Oh yes. I think most people do—especially if they have some private grief on their mind.'

She looked at him in disbelief. 'Does it show that much?'

He smiled at her, and she was astonished at the sudden transformation. The face looked instantly younger and stronger, and somehow happier. 'Only to the initiated.'

Beth's eyes opened wider. She was about to say 'You too?' when she noticed that the stranger was wearing a clergyman's dog collar under his jacket, and her heart sank. Now he will preach at me, I suppose, she thought, like the one who came when Mo died. Stupid platitudes that didn't help at all . . . But he had been kind, so she had better be polite. 'Are you the vicar of this little church?'

'Oh no,' he said and laughed. 'I have long since retired from active work. I'm just a visitor, like you. I come here quite often—and it always gets to me.' He paused, and added in a reflective tone, 'There's something about ancient places of worship—an aura of holiness, perhaps? It seems to cling to them through the ages. Generations of prayer have gone up from these old stones . . .' He paused again and then added with apparent irrelevance, 'Have you ever been to Delphi?'

Beth stirred from her thoughts and looked at him with attention. 'Delphi? In Greece? No, I haven't.'

'It has the same feeling,' he said dreamily. 'Two thousand years of prayer to the ancient gods. The very stones seem steeped in it . . .' He glanced sideways at Beth and smiled again. 'And, after all, I think the concept of the ancient ones was only another facet of the same eternal belief . . .'

'Belief in what?' asked Beth, and there was a real need for an answer in her voice.

'A merciful God?' suggested the soft old voice. 'The power of good?' He looked at her again, and there was understanding in his quiet gaze. 'A life beyond our own?' He hesitated and then added gently, 'We have always searched for such reassurance—all through history.'

Beth bent her head to hide the swift, too-easy tears. 'And never found proof?' she said.

The old man's tranquil stare did not change. 'You can't prove light,' he said. 'But it's there.' He waved a transparent hand towards the little church behind him. 'You can explain the yellow glass and the position of the sun—the warmth of the Cotswold stone in the arches—but can you explain what you felt in there?'

'No,' said Beth. 'I can't.' And she kept her head bent.

'I think they are in all of us,' murmured the old voice, as if speaking half to himself, 'the seeds of eternity . . . binding us all together . . .'

He did not say any more, but sat on quietly beside Beth until she had mastered her tears and began to smile again.

'You are very clever,' she said at last, 'and very comforting. I . . . I don't know how to thank you.'

'Thank Elkstone,' he said. 'It's not my doing. *Remember the light*.' And he walked off down the path, past the ancient, lichened tombstones, and disappeared among the trees.

FINN HAD PLANNED to go straight home from the Spirios site, but there were still a lot of loose ends to tie up if he was going to arrange his working life round his family commitments. He went first to Athens, where he saw a couple of banks and arranged finance for the Spirios development, and then he took a plane to Bonn for more banking talks, and from there, certain at last that he had got everything in order, he rang Beth to announce his return. He did not ring Mary first this time, wanting to be sure that his coming was not going to cause a major upset with Chloë before he spoke to her. He sounded absurdly humble and anxious on the phone, and Beth was touched by his desperate concern to do the right thing.

'It's going to be all right,' she told him. 'Chloë's got a role to play now. You're going to be "cosseted". Beech put the idea into her head. You'll need to play up a bit, Finn, that's all.'

'How?'

'Just be a bit sad and lonely. That's what Beech said you were.'

'He's not far wrong,' admitted Finn, still not quite understanding the situation.

'She needs to be useful, Finn—to feel wanted.'

'Don't we all?' growled Finn, but he was beginning to follow what Beech's skilful suggestion had done for Chloë. 'So you think she won't mind my coming?'

'Mind?' said Beth, realising that Finn needed as much reassurance as Chloë. 'If you handle it right, she'll revel in it.'

Finn sighed. 'Tell me what to do.'

Beth thought for a moment, reflecting how strange it was that this man, who could sail round the world, climb impossible mountain peaks and run innumerable enterprises in far-off places, should sound so humble and shy. 'I think you'd better come here, Finn. At teatime. Chloë and Mark will be here then, so it will break the ice. We can arrange a special tea—she'll enjoy that. And then you can take her home, and she and Mary can fix a special supper!'

Finn laughed. 'It sounds like one long party.'

'Yes,' agreed Beth. 'That's the idea.'

'Shall I . . . ought I to ring Mary and tell her when I'm coming?'

Again Beth thought carefully. 'No,' she said at last. 'I'll tell her—and I'll tell Chloë. That way there's no awkward moments. Just tell me when you *are* coming, that's all!'

'The day after tomorrow,' said Finn, sounding humble again. 'Will that be all right?'

'Lovely.' Beth's voice was warm with approval. 'Teatime. At the Beehive. We'll be waiting for you.'

Finn did not know whether to laugh or cry with relief. So he did neither. He just said, 'Bless you, Beth,' and rang off.

SO FINN CAME HOME. And when he stood in Beth's doorway, looking in on the firelit scene before him, he was suddenly caught in such a wave of gladness that he was almost shocked. Beth, too, was overtaken by the same unexpected surge of feeling, and stood looking at him without quite knowing what to say.

Beth had planned carefully for this meeting, knowing that it was vitally important for Chloë that it should go well. So the fire was warm and inviting, the two children, Mark and Chloë, were crouched in front of it brandishing toasting forks, and the table was laid for tea by the hearth. And yet here they both were, Beth and Finn, almost tongue-tied at their meeting, when they both needed to carry things off with the utmost tact and diplomacy.

But Chloë took things into her own hands.

She walked gravely across the room, and stood looking up into Finn's face for a moment in silence. Then she said simply, 'I'm glad you're back safe,' and led him towards the fire. It was not exactly an effusive welcome, but it told Finn what he wanted to know.

And then the cosseting began. 'We're toasting crumpets,' Chloë told him. 'Are you hungry?'

'Ravenous,' admitted Finn, and somehow everyone was laughing and the dangerous moment was past.

Chloë did not ask any questions or make any demands upon him, but kept him plied with crumpets and rock buns and cups of tea, and afterwards she and Mark challenged him to a game of chess which he skilfully lost. And then it was time for him to take Chloë home, and Chloë suddenly made her first and most important request. 'Can we go and get Corny from Beech now you're back?'

Finn looked at Beth in bewilderment.

'It's the puppy,' she told him, smiling. 'Chloë was just waiting for you to say yes.'

'Then "yes" it is,' agreed Finn, nodding cheerfully so that the firelight glinted on his golden buccaneer's beard. 'But wouldn't Saturday be better? Then you'll be home all the weekend to look after her.'

Chloë saw the sense of that. 'Can Mark and Beth come too?'

'Of course,' said Finn. 'We'll all go.' Then, smiling a little apologetically at the three of them, he added, 'I don't know much about puppies. But I'm willing to learn.'

'Beech knows,' stated Chloë, with sublime confidence.

'Yes,' agreed Mark. 'Beech knows most things.'

'Saturday, then?' Finn was looking at Beth over the top of Chloë's head. 'At Beech's. When?'

'He likes to feed his animals about noon,' volunteered Mark.

Finn looked from him back to Beth. 'Noon?'

'We'll be there,' smiled Beth, and followed them over to the doorway to watch them go.

'That was a splendid tea,' Finn sighed, including them all in his thanks. 'And now for our special supper,' he said to his daughter, playing up like mad as he had been told to do. 'Lead me to it, Chloë!' And they went off side by side down the path.

Beth and Mark looked at each other and smiled like conspirators.

'He's nice,' said Mark, and there was a certain wistfulness in his voice. 'Chloë'll be all right now.'

'Given half a chance,' murmured Beth, unable to resist Beech's catch phrase.

And they both began to laugh.

BEECH WAS INDEED feeding the animals when they arrived, and they all found themselves caught up in the process, carrying buckets of food and bundles of hay. Chloë could barely contain her impatience, but in a while all the chores were done and Beech led them back to the cottage. Chloë ran on ahead to pick up Corny from among the tumbling litter of puppies by the back door. When they came up to her, she was standing there with the bundle of fur in her arms, looking down at her with an expression of such loving delight that Finn's own heart seemed to contract with sudden pain. If only she would look at him like that! But perhaps it would come with time.

'This is Corny,' she said. 'Would you like to hold her?'

Finn took the eager little puppy in his arms and held her up close to his face. 'So you're Corny, are you? Welcome to the family, Corny.'

And Corny, seeming to know that this was an important moment, licked everything she could reach and tried to bury her head in Finn's golden beard.

'She thinks you're as safe as her mother,' explained Chloë. 'Your fur's the same colour!'

And everyone laughed.

Then Finn handed the puppy back to Chloë, and asked, 'Why did you pick the name Corny?'

Beth waited somewhat breathlessly to see whether Chloë would answer, but when she didn't and shot Beth a glance of mute appeal, it seemed better to answer for her. 'I think it's short for cornfield,' she said easily, 'because of her colour.' She paused and then added softly, 'But Chloë will tell you why later on, I'm sure.'

Finn was aware that there were hidden meanings here, but he merely nodded as if quite satisfied with Beth's explanation and said no more.

Beech, too, ignored the conversation and went on to explain a bit more about puppy-handling to her new owners. 'I've bin teachin' her a bit, like,' he said, 'while she was waitin'. She comes to "Corny" now when she's called, and she'll walk a little way on a lead, but her legs is a bit short still for long walks.'

So at last it was all arranged, a price was agreed and Beech gave Corny a last valedictory pat on the head.

'You look after her, little 'un,' he said to Chloë, 'and she'll do you proud.' He looked for a moment as if he was going to give Chloë a farewell pat on the head as well. But instead he winked at her broadly and added in his soft voice, 'Talking and cosseting—that's what's needed. Remember?'

'I'll remember,' promised Chloë, and set off down the path with Corny pulling every which way on her lead.

The others began to follow her, but Finn suddenly turned back to Beech and murmured an extra thankyou, adding, 'I believe I owe you a lot more than the price of one small puppy!'

Beech did not answer but he nodded and smiled, and watched them with tranquil satisfaction as they went down the hill.

PART V
'And Make Another Song'

Finn still had not managed to have any private conversation with Beth, and for the rest of that day and the next he was entirely occupied with Chloë and the new puppy. But late on Sunday evening, when Chloë was at last asleep, Finn left Mary in charge and walked over to see Beth at the little Beehive.

Beth came to the door, looking both startled and pleased to see him, and stood back at once to let him come into the warm and welcoming room.

'I'm sorry to come so late,' he began, 'but I waited for Chloë to go to sleep and it took some time!'

'I can imagine,' laughed Beth, 'with Corny to distract her. Would you like some coffee?'

'Lovely,' sighed Finn, and stretched himself out in the chair that Beth drew up for him close to the fire.

There was silence in the room for a few moments while Beth fetched the coffee, but as she came back into the room he said abruptly, 'You've worked miracles with Chloë.'

Beth handed him his coffee and smiled. 'Not me only. Mary and Mark—and most of all Beech. They all had a hand in it.'

Finn nodded and then asked curiously, 'And where does Corny come into it? Is there something special about a cornfield?'

Beth looked away from him into the fire and she answered, 'Beech got Chloë and Mark to plant a tree. He told them he always did that when one of his animals died. And then he said, *"I reckon they'm all running about out yonder—dancin' about like hares in a cornfield . . ."* ' Beth turned her head then and looked straight at Finn. 'And Chloë understood him. She pointed away through the trees as if she could almost see them . . . and that was when she said her first word, *"Yonder"*.'

'Yonder,' sighed Finn, understanding a whole lot of things in a very short space of time. He was silent again for a while, and then he seemed to recollect that Beth had her own problems to sort out as well as Chloë's, so he said gently, 'And how has it been for you?'

'Me? Oh . . . I struggle on.' Her smile was a little fragile. 'My days are absorbing and people have been enormously kind,' she added, thinking of Peter and the rest of the well-meaning staff.

'But . . .?' pursued Finn.

She sighed. 'Oh, you know it too, Finn. The gap is still huge—one day, perhaps, it will seem less vast . . . I don't know. But in the meantime, I suppose we have to do the best we can.'

She got up then, a little restlessly, to put another log on the fire and fetch some more coffee from the kitchen.

Finn had not answered her this time, but at last he asked slowly, 'What did Stephanie say?'

Beth paused in surprise. 'About Mo and Robert?' Then her face softened as the words came back to her. 'She said, *"You only have to remember."* '

Finn nodded. 'That sounds like her.' He gave himself a rueful little shake of self-contempt. 'I told you I was a coward. She faced up to everything.' Then he seemed to pull himself together and come back to the questions of the day. 'About Chloë . . . what ought we to do about these teatimes with Mark? They seem to be important.'

Beth was ready for that. 'I've been thinking—she'll want to get home to Corny now, as well as you, won't she? Why don't you walk down with the puppy to meet her? That way she'll just get in Corny's exercise while it's still light.'

'What about Mark?'

'Well, as a matter of fact, the rehearsals for the Japanese opera are getting intense just now, so I shall probably want to stay on late with Mark and George and one or two others . . .' She glanced at Finn, all at once alight with enthusiasm. 'They're getting quite good, you know. You will come to it, Finn, won't you? Chloë's in it, too.' She hesitated, and then added honestly, 'I haven't given her a big part, because she couldn't do very much at first. But she's beginning to join in now and she will do anything Mark tells her to!'

Finn laughed. 'He'll have to give me lessons!' Then he grew serious again. 'But I don't think Chloë will like not seeing you after school at all. It seems to me that she has got very fond of you—and so she should!' He looked at her, half smiling. 'So I wondered if you would come over to supper—once or twice a week, or something? I . . . I don't want her to feel cut off from you . . .' He stalled there for a moment, and then blurted out, 'And I'd like it, too—if you'd come?'

Beth grinned. 'Don't sound so humble. I'd love to come.'

Finn let out a gusty sigh of relief. 'Phew! I'm glad that's over . . . I never was any good at begging for help!'

'I think you're doing splendidly,' said Beth. 'You've only got to look pathetic and everyone melts!'

Finn got up then, still laughing a little. 'I'd better go, before you unravel me any further.' But he had done what he set out to do, and Beth too, now, would have an excuse to fill one or two lonely evenings.

Steph, he though, I'm doing what I can. And I have a sneaking suspicion that you planned this all along. But aloud he just said, 'This is a lovely room. I only hope mine will be as welcoming.' And he turned his back on the glowing firelight and went home in the dark.

THE REHEARSALS WERE, in truth, growing intense in the couple of weeks before the performance, and George and Mark were only too pleased to stay on after school. One or two of the girls stayed on too, if they had tricky solos to sing, but the main chorus of Japanese villagers had to be content with the ordinary music classes. George seemed to blossom with the special attention he was getting, and was producing quite an impressive performance as Hamaguchi, the Village Grandfather. He had even found a strange, deep voice hidden somewhere in his gangling frame. Mark's clear treble was as pure and true as a boy's voice should be, and he enjoyed the bit of dramatic acting Beth had given him to do.

But now she realised she had got to organise some scenery, and a bit of lighting, too. But, above all, she needed two more instruments: a tam-tam, and a timp as well, if she could get hold of one.

For the first two problems, she went to Peter. He was practical and reasonably inventive. He would be bound to think of something.

'Peter, could you build us a mountain?'

'Certainly. Everest or Snowdon?'

'Well, more like Fujiyama, really.' She answered his grin with a hopeful one of her own. 'I'm trying to paint a backcloth a bit like a Japanese print—you know, all washy and cloudy, with islands floating in a sea of mist.'

'Sounds wonderful.'

'Well, it won't be, unless you can put a sort of slope for them to climb up in front of it. And then I want lighting for three different things.'

'What things?'

'An earthquake, a fire and a tidal wave.'

Peter scratched his head. 'You don't want much, do you?'

'I know it sounds awful, Peter, but can you do it?'

'Of course,' agreed Peter stoutly. 'Leave it to me.'

Then she went to ask Margaret Collier about the tam-tam and the timp.

'I think you'd better talk to Finn,' said Margaret, smiling. 'He's in charge of the music fund, and I'm sure he'll find the money if you ask him.'

'Will he know where I can get them from?'

'If he doesn't, he'll find out. Nothing daunts Finn when he sets his mind on something.'

Beth nodded, but it was not the picture she had of Finn as he was at present—shy and uncertain. She sighed a little, and said in an unconvinced voice, 'All right, I'll ask him. I shall be seeing him and Chloë tonight.'

Margaret did not miss the hesitation behind Beth's quiet manner, or the fact that there already seemed to be some kind of understanding between Finn and her young colleague, but she kept her own counsel about it, and merely added, with a glint of extra warmth, 'It's a good cause, Beth—you can tell him that from me. You deserve all the help you can get.'

Beth shot her a surprised, grateful smile and went back to work, somewhat reassured. So that night, when she arrived at the Mill House for supper, she had an extra purpose for her visit, which for some reason made her feel less shy and awkward. The old house was ablaze with lights and smelt of beeswax and wood fires, and everything shone with Mary's devoted polishing. Chloë and the puppy came racing together down the hall as Finn opened the door, and the sound of laughter floated out into the cold night air.

It feels alive again, thought Beth, and smiled in genuine pleasure at the change in atmosphere. She looked down at Chloë's small, glowing face and was amazed at the change in that, too.

'Look at Corny,' said Chloë, giggling. 'She's got Mary's knitting wool.'

'Oh, Corny, how could you!' protested Finn, laughing too. 'What on earth will Mary say?'

But Corny merely pranced off a bit further down the hall, wreathed in purple wool, and Chloë ran after her, giggling helplessly.

'Come into the sitting room,' said Finn. 'Supper's nearly ready.' He gave one exaggerated glance of mock despair at Chloë and the puppy, and left them to unwind each other. But his eyes met Beth's and they both smiled with undisguised gladness. It was wonderful to see Chloë laughing again.

'It's a great success,' he said.

Beth nodded. 'I can see that.'

'I can't tell you—' he began, and then shook his head. 'She's a different child.' He went over to the tray of drinks and asked over his shoulder, 'Sherry? Or would you rather have gin?'

'Sherry will do nicely.'

He brought it to her, still smiling. 'There's a lot to celebrate!'

'I know.' Beth lifted her glass. 'To Chloë and Corny—and Beech.'

'And Beth!' Finn added.

This seemed to Beth a good opening for her request, so she said cheerfully, 'If you include me, can I claim a reward?'

'Name it,' grinned Finn. 'The sky's the limit.'

'I want to hire a tam-tam.'

'A what?'

'A tam-tam. An orchestral gong. A huge one. And a timp—a kettledrum—if you can get one. For the school production.'

Finn thought for a moment. 'Why not? It shouldn't be impossible.'

His grin was mischievous now. 'And the impossible will only take a little longer.'

Beth laughed. 'Margaret Collier said you'd fix it.'

At this point Chloë ran in, with Corny skittering about on the polished wood floor behind her, and announced solemnly, 'Supper's ready and Mary says not to let it get cold.'

It was a cheerful meal. Chloë told them proudly that she had made the apple crumble herself, and then admitted, 'Well, Mary helped . . .' Mary confirmed this, and then added, smiling, 'She's becoming a right good little cook,' which pleased Chloë enormously.

Finn did not insist on a specific bedtime at weekends, but now he reminded Chloë that there was still school tomorrow and that Beth would not like her young singers to be yawning their heads off. To Beth's surprise, Chloë took this seriously and turned to her with earnest insistence. 'I *am* singing now, aren't I? He'll be able to hear me, won't he?'

'Of course he will,' Beth reassured her.

'That's all right then.' Chloë suddenly sounded brisk and matter-of-fact. 'Come on, Corny. Bedtime.' She started for the door, and then looked round at Beth. 'I promise not to yawn,' she said solemnly, and went off up the stairs with Corny tumbling up after her.

'I'll come up and say good night,' Finn called after her, and turned back to pour out some coffee. 'She seems happy enough,' he said, and there was sudden anxiety in his voice, 'don't you think?'

'Yes, I do,' Beth said decisively. Then, seeing the uncertainty in his eyes, she added gently, 'What worries you about it?'

He sighed. 'It's just—will it be enough for her—just me here, and Mary and the puppy? She must still miss Stephanie dreadfully.'

'She's beginning to talk to you again, isn't she? You'll soon build up a kind of working relationship.' She smiled at him encouragingly. 'And Corny helps.'

'Oh, yes,' he admitted, smiling a little himself. But then he grew serious again. 'I've decided to work from home now,' he told her. 'I've fixed up an office and phones and faxes and things. It'll be perfectly feasible to run all my projects from here. I needn't go away at all.'

'But you must sometimes,' protested Beth, alarmed at the thought of this restless, adventurous spirit entirely caged at home. 'You can take Chloë with you during the school holidays. Travel would be good for her and I think she'd like to feel part of your working life, Finn. You could talk to her about it, couldn't you?'

'If she'd listen!' Finn laughed a little.

'Try her,' said Beth.

And then they heard Chloë calling to them to come and say good night. Finn insisted on Beth going up with him, and she stooped over Chloë rather shyly and patted the sleepy puppy on the way. She was wary of showing too much affection, of becoming too much involved with Finn and his demanding small daughter, even of admitting to herself her own need of simple human contact in a world grown grey without Mo's loving presence in her life. But before she could draw back, Chloë's arms came up in a warm, strong hug and she whispered into her ear, 'Thanks for coming,' before she let go.

Beth went out of the room rather blindly and left Finn to talk to Chloë alone.

When they had settled down by the fire again, sipping hot coffee, Finn said suddenly, 'Beth, do you feel manipulated?'

Beth did not misunderstand him. 'By Stephanie, you mean? Yes, a little.'

'Do you mind?'

She paused to think it out. 'No,' she said at last. 'Not really. Stephanie saw very far ahead, didn't she? Somehow, this job—which she engineered for me, as you well know—and the problem of Chloë seemed to fall into place naturally. It wasn't forced on me. I'd do anything to help Chloë—that goes without saying. And not only because Stephanie was very good to me . . .' She paused and then added shyly, 'I loved her too, you know.'

'Yes,' agreed Finn. 'I know.'

They did not talk of it any more after that, and presently they got up, warmed by the fire and their companionable silence, and Finn took her home.

AND THEN, ALL AT ONCE it seemed, it was time for the school performance. Peter had been as good as his word and made them a mountain to climb up, and his lighting was in place and magically effective—if the boy in charge of it didn't push the dimmer slides too fast. Finn had found Beth a rather battered timp for the earthquake, and an absolutely beautiful tam-tam whose deep reverberations were almost too soul-shaking to bear. Beth's own misty backcloth seemed to take on a kind of shimmering life of its own under Peter's lights, and the colours of the costumes looked unexpectedly subtle against it.

The cast were ready, and not too nervous—not even George, who looked extraordinarily tall and dignified in his long robe and beard. The audience were in place, the lights in the hall were dimmed, and everything was in order. It was time to start.

Beth took a deep breath and put her hand on the piano keys. Oh God, let them make a success of it, she prayed. It will do them so much good to do something really well and be admired! Then she began.

The Japanese villagers came on, singing about the rice crop, and began to hoe in long lines across the stage, watched over by a benign Hamaguchi, the Village Grandfather.

Then Mark, as the young fisherman, Ojotaki, began his sad song about the missing fish shoals and the empty sea, and the chorus joined in softly with their repeated lament: 'The fish have gone . . .'

'The fish have gone . . . But where they go we do not know . . .' sang Mark, sounding bewildered and sadder than ever.

The light changed then, from the silvery magic of dawn to a flat and sultry yellow. And Mark's voice changed too, from that sorrowful, melting treble to something ominous and full of foreboding. 'The land lies locked and spellbound in the heat. We hear our own hearts beat. O strange, uneasy day. What heavy doom lies on our silver bay?'

The timp began a slow, menacing beat that grew slowly louder. And then the earthquake came. The timp and cymbals thundered, and Beth thundered too on the piano. The lights went dim and the villagers rocked on their feet and fell about the stage in terror, while Chloë clung to Mark's hand and looked just like an authentic frightened little sister.

'Hamaguchi, save us!' cried the chorus, falling on their knees.

Then George, in his new deep voice of authority, commanded: 'Be still, my children. It is an earthquake. But it is far away.'

For a moment there was almost stillness from the frightened villagers, but then all at once Ojotaki pointed over the heads of the chorus and cried: 'The sea! Look at the sea!'

He was answered by the wondering chorus of villagers, whispering in fear: 'The sea is receding . . . It is going away . . . The sea is gone. Nothing is left except the empty crawling bay . . .'

But Ojotaki suddenly pointed again, his voice alight with triumph: 'The empty bay, you say! Look at the fish—the fish! Leaping and tumbling like silver fire!'

And the chorus, wild with excitement now, repeated his words over and over again as they rushed off the stage. In vain Hamaguchi's deep voice rang out, trying to warn them: 'Wait, children of my village, wait till the anger of the earth is done.'

They did not heed him, and their sweet, childish voices floated up to the stage, still singing far away.

Then Hamaguchi began to climb Peter's mountain. Mark followed him, holding Chloë by the hand and letting his voice become sad and puzzled again as he asked: 'What is it, honoured Grandfather, that you fear to say?'

'Look far out, boy,' commanded Hamaguchi, on the top of Peter's mountain now. 'What do you see?'

'I see the bay, all silver grey!' began Ojotaki.

'Look farther, boy, look farther!' commanded Hamaguchi, sounding sterner than ever.

And this time Ojotaki sang, as sweet and true as ever, but even more puzzled: 'I see the sea—the wide and restless sea, tossing and churning, lifting and falling,' and then he screamed. 'Ah!'

(Well done, said Beth to herself, heaving a sigh of relief. That was a splendid scream.)

'Yes, boy, what do you see?' demanded Hamaguchi.

'I see a wave, a tidal wave. High as a hill. Strong as a hurricane. Our people will all be drowned. What shall we do?'

Hamaguchi lifted his hand with his long white staff in it and pointed. 'Ring the bells in the temple! Beat and ring! They must hear us!'

Then Ojotaki ran about, beating all the gongs and bells, but when the villagers still did not hear, Hamaguchi said: 'Quick, boy, fire the rice fields! They will see them burning and come running to help me save them.'

So Mark and Chloë ran about with torches in their hands. 'It burns, it burns!' sang Mark, and beat at the bells and gongs again. Then the girls who were flames danced in, waving their crimson and scarlet scarves, and Peter's lights went red and the fire-flicker wheel began turning so that the whole stage seemed to be on fire, and the chorus came running back.

'Hurry, my children, up the mountain. Leave the rice fields,' called Hamaguchi. 'We have our lives—our lives . . .'

'Our lives . . . we have our lives!' answered the chorus, running upwards round Peter's ramp in terror.

And then the wave came. The voice of the tam-tam rang out, huge and deep and fierce, and the girls who were waves surged up across the stage with their floating blue and green scarves, dowsing the flames, and then retreated, hissing like receding water against the dying reverberations of the tam-tam, until there was almost silence.

'Honoured Hamaguchi, Oji-san, you have saved our lives,' sang the chorus, kneeling.

'But not our village, or our rice!' sang out a doubting voice.

George seemed to stand taller than ever then, and to draw himself up very straight as he said, strong and clear: 'We have our lives, we can begin again.'

And that was the cue for the last, sentimental song that everyone sang. (They've done it, thought Beth. They've got there! You just listen to them, Stephanie! Aren't you proud of them?)

'Though all our little world is wrecked and gone,' they sang, with all their hearts in it. 'We find another way, and make another song.'

And the company lifted their hands then to the audience and sang the last line again: 'And make another song!'

And Beth brought the last chord to an end, and found that she could not see the keyboard. Those wonderful children, she thought. All of them with problems of their own—all singing like angels! But she was not the only one with tears in her eyes. The silence seemed to go on and on, and then the applause began. It roared and surged like the sea. Like her tidal wave.

The cast bowed politely and went off, and came on again. George came forward and the clapping became ecstatic, and someone—was it George's father?—cried: 'Bravo!' Mark came forward next, still holding Chloë by the hand, and the clapping was almost louder. After all, Mark had done most of the solo singing, and beautifully, too. And then the whole cast bowed again, and one of them came down and grabbed Beth from the piano, so she joined them, taking the timp player and the tam-tam smiter with her, and everyone bowed again.

Afterwards George's father came up, and said under his breath to Beth, 'I said I'd clap like mad, come what may, but I never expected anything like this!'

'Wasn't he splendid?' said Beth.

'He was that!' He turned to his wife and daughter beside him, who both seemed to be struck dumb with amazement. 'Wasn't George grand?'

'Wonderful,' said George's mother, suddenly sounding pleased and proud, as any good mother should. 'Simply wonderful!'

Then Mark's mother, Lucy, was there, looking both tearful and happy at once, saying incoherently, 'I can't tell you—I didn't know he could!' And Beth smiled, remembering her first sight of Mark lying on the floor and screaming out his private rage and frustration against all the world.

And last of all came Finn, who had waited patiently till the throng of delighted parents and friends had stopped besieging Beth and there was room to breathe. He simply grasped her by the arm and said, smiling, 'Never was a tam-tam put to better use!'

Beth laughed, and Chloë, who was still clinging possessively to Mark's hand, looked up at her father and said, 'I *was* singing—did you hear me?'

'I heard you,' smiled Finn. 'I heard you loud and clear! It was simply beautiful—all of it!'

'Hear, hear!' agreed Peter, who was standing close beside them. 'Especially my Fujiyama!' and everyone round them laughed.

Margaret Collier had not attempted to say anything to Beth while the excitement was at its height, but now she came over with a cup of coffee in her hand and said, 'I think you'd better drink this before you pass out.'

'Do I look that bad?' said Beth, laughing.

Margaret looked at her judicially. 'For someone who has just broken the sound barrier, you don't look too shattered.'

Beth grinned. 'Was it all right?'

'All right?' Margaret glared at her. 'I wonder if you know what you've done for those children? . . . But yes, of course you do.' She shook her head at Beth, as if words almost failed her. 'Stephanie knew what she was doing when she sent you to us!'

When it was all over and Beth was finally alone and walking back to the little Beehive under the December stars, she found herself thinking almost tranquilly of Robert and little Mo. They'd have enjoyed it, too, she thought. Mo was so musical, he would have loved to join in the singing . . . And then, unexpectedly, she found herself smiling as a new thought came to her: *Perhaps he did.*

SOON AFTER THE PERFORMANCE of *Hamaguchi's Harvest* the school broke up for Christmas and Beth said a temporary goodbye to the rest of the staff.

Peter, of course, insisted on taking her out for a farewell drink before leaving to spend the holidays with his parents. He had the sense not to give her an expensive Christmas present; instead he gave her a handmade mahogany Chinese block to add to her percussion instruments and a toy clown on a stick who turned somersaults when pushed—'To make you laugh when I'm not here.' Beth laughed then and there, but she was touched at the thought behind the little gift. Peter was a lot more sensitive than he made out.

A couple of days later, Finn and Chloë, with Corny gambolling about on the end of a brand-new red lead, arrived at the Beehive with a question to ask.

'Chloë wants to give Beech a Christmas present. What do you think he'd like?'

Beth considered. 'Food for his animals?'

Chloë's smile came out like the sun. 'He'd like that.'

Finn looked doubtful. 'How do we know what to get?'

'A pet shop,' suggested Beth. 'And—I know—ask Mark to come with you. He understands a lot about Beech's animals.'

'Ask Mark,' commanded Chloë, and Corny began running round in circles, chasing her own tail and tying Chloë up in knots. When she had been disentangled, Chloë looked up hopefully at Beth. 'Will you come too?'

Finn looked hopeful, too.

'All right.' Beth gave in to the pleading looks. 'I was going to give Beech a little Christmas cake. We can take that up to him as well.'

They collected Mark and drove over to the town to the nearest pet shop. Once there, Mark seemed perfectly confident about what to buy, and before long Finn was loaded with parcels and everyone was heading back to the car.

'Tell you what,' said Finn, 'let's dump these and go and get an ice cream or something. It's Christmas, after all.'

The day was frosty and bright for once, clear of the grey fogs of November, and the town was alight with tinsel decorations, fairy lights and sparkling Christmas trees. Finn led them all into a cheerful café where Mark and Chloë were allowed to order the fanciest ice creams they could find.

'Beth,' said Finn, looking at her over his cup of coffee and sounding absurdly tentative, 'you will come on Christmas Day?'

Beth sighed. She had known this was coming, and she had also known that she couldn't refuse. Chloë was going to need all the care and kindness she could get this first Christmas without Stephanie—and so was Finn. And so, she supposed, was she, this first one without little Mo, though not the first without Robert. There had been two of those while she struggled to make the day cheerful for Mo, not allowing herself to admit to her own loneliness and grief . . . Well, it looked like being a repeat performance.

'If I can bring Mark and his mother, too,' she said. 'Chloë and Mark get on so well,' she explained, 'and Lucy's lonely, too.'

Finn nodded. It was a relief to have that tacit admission from Beth. They were all lonely. Well, they would all make the best they could of the difficult day when it came.

'I'm not much good at ceremonies,' he admitted, smiling. 'I left all that to Stephanie. But . . . but I'd like it to go right, for the kids' sake.'

'Stop worrying,' said Beth. 'We'll make it positively scintillate!'

So they waited patiently while Mark and Chloë demolished their

Sundae Specials and then drove back to Ashcombe and climbed the hill to Beech's cottage with their purchases in their arms.

Beech saw them coming and stood waiting for them, looking a little apprehensive at the visitation.

'It's all right,' said Beth, smiling at his puzzled face. 'We've brought the animals their Christmas presents, that's all.'

Beech watched gravely while Mark and Chloë laid out the various bags in front of him.

'Those are for Moses . . . and that's for the hens, and that's for Blackie . . .We didn't know what Juniper liked best, so we brought her some broccoli . . .'

They unloaded all their offerings and then went happily with Beech to distribute them to his hungry charges.

When they had finished doing the rounds, Beech said gruffly, 'I got something for you, too. Remember I said as I'd show you where the acorns fell? I come across some yesterday—already sprouting, a few of 'em. Would you like to take a couple home?'

'Yes, please,' said Chloë, sounding very polite. Then she put her hand firmly in Mark's and followed Beech down the path. Beth and Finn glanced at one another and joined the procession through the tall winter trees.

Beech led them to a different corner of the wood where several thick old oak trees stood in a rough circle round a curious open area of short grass, almost like an ancient sacred grove, thought Beth.

'Here,' said Beech, stooping down under one of the oaks, whose massive trunk stood firm and strong above sturdy roots on the forest floor. 'See?' And he pushed aside a few tufts of silvery dried-up summer grass so that Mark and Chloë could look down at the brown leaf mould below. Mark bent down to see what the old freckled hand was pointing at, and Chloë crouched down beside him, even lower.

On the soft ground in the hollow between the upthrusting roots was a small pile of gold-brown acorns, and a few that were already blackened by the winter rains. As they looked closer, they saw that some of them had split open to allow curly pinkish sprouts to escape into the warm blanket of leafy soil around them.

'It be winter now,' said Beech softly, looking down at the children's rapt faces, 'and things look mighty dead and cold, in the main.' He put out one blunt finger and touched a coral-coloured shoot. 'But here, see, spring's already beginning. They'm just waitin' for the sun to shine.'

The two intent young faces looked up at him silently.

'You put one o' they in a pot,' he told them, 'and come spring, you'll have an oak tree.' He smiled at their awestruck expressions. 'Small, mind, but a tree they'll be, no less!'

'Can you spare one?' asked Mark, almost afraid to touch anything so fragile and so miraculous—though he could not put such thoughts into words.

'Surely,' said Beech. 'Come up to the cottage and I'll find you some pots.'

'Can they have one, too?' asked Chloë, looking from Beth to Finn. She was determined that everyone should share in this new magic.

For answer, the old man stooped again, picked up two more pink-fronded acorns and handed them solemnly to the two adults who looked almost as spellbound as the children. 'There!' he said. 'Now we'm all fixed up.' But there was a distinct spark of mischief in his faded eyes.

At the last moment, when everyone had been provided with pots and forest leaf mould, and all the pink shoots had been successfully 'put to grow', Beth suddenly remembered her Christmas cake and handed that over as a final offering. 'Happy Christmas,' she said, and added quietly, so that only Beech could hear, 'and thank you for many things . . .'

Beech nodded, and did not attempt to reply. But the old eyes met hers in perfect understanding.

Corny, meanwhile, had gone back to talk to her mother, but now she came out again onto the grass with a half-eaten paper bag stuck on the end of her nose, and ran off down the path with everyone in laughing pursuit.

Just as well, thought Beth. We were all getting much too solemn. Christmas does awful things to one's emotions . . . But there was no time to be sad now. They had to catch Corny before she ran out onto the road.

BETH DID NOT MUCH LIKE Christmas Eve. It was going to be hard enough just to get through her first Christmas without little Mo, and only the realisation that it was just as bad for Finn and Chloë made her stop feeling sorry for herself and resolve to be as positive and cheerful about it all as humanly possible.

Finn, she knew, was trying desperately hard to be a good father—to buy the right presents, remember the Christmas tree, fill Chloë's stocking and arrange with Mary for all the trimmings of a grand Christmas meal. At least, she thought somewhat bitterly, he has got something to do, and he has got Chloë, while I . . . But she wouldn't go on with that. Better not to look round at the empty rooms of the little Beehive, or remember too much about the loving warmth of those other Christmases.

Finn had actually asked her to come over and help them with their Christmas preparations, but she had refused—partly because she knew Chloë and Finn ought to do this together, it would strengthen the fragile bond that was slowly rebuilding between them. But she had also refused out of a perverse sense of panic because she was being drawn so inexorably into their lives, and Finn was so devastatingly attractive in his new humility. He was already beginning to loom large in her life and she was sometimes a little shocked at the lurch of gladness she felt when he was near.

Of course it was only loneliness, she told herself. It was inevitable, really. They were both alone, both grieving desperately for people they loved. It was too soon, too soon for anything but a grim attempt to get through the days, and much too soon for Finn, who had only been without his beloved Stephanie for four short months. And then there was Chloë, too, whose recovery had come to mean so much to Beth, and who was now beginning to show unmistakable signs of returning warmth and affection—directed almost as much at Beth as at Finn, and where on earth was that going to lead them?

With these restless thoughts pursuing her, Beth decided to go out and walk, even though it was late and dark and there was a bitter frost. The village was still very much awake, though it was after eleven, and many of the windows, curtains open, displayed glowing interiors and sparkling Christmas trees. There were cheerful families getting things ready and wrapping presents—and Beth hurried by, churlishly averting her gaze from all this cosy preparation and feeling guilty for being so ungenerous.

She passed the floodlit church with all its windows aglow with candles and the bells ringing for the midnight service. For a moment she hesitated. Should she go in? Sit comfortably in the warm, among the singing parishioners, rejoicing in the Christmas story? But how could she? It wasn't possible for her to rejoice about the birth of a baby, not this Christmas, not with her own, loving little Mo so cruelly taken from her. I'm sorry, God, she said. I'm sorry—but not this year. Perhaps by next year I will see it more clearly, but now there is too much hurt.

She hurried on, head bent, away from the friendly village up onto the starlit hills. The moon had risen into the cloudless frosty sky and the curving slopes of winter grass looked almost white in its pure cold light. *Almost* white? She paused to look round her in wonder. For it had been foggy for most of the last two days, and now the frost had caught the drifting moisture and turned it all to a winter wonderland of shimmering crystal, and every twig, every blade of grass, every filigree spider's web was etched in silver, sparkling and winking in the moonlight like a thousand jewels.

Drawing a deep breath of enchantment at so much fragile beauty, she began to walk across the crisp, silvered grass.

After a while, when her mind was calmed and her body tired, she came full circle to the hill just above the village. She stood for a few moments looking down at the firefly lights below and the silver hoarfrost on the tree branches in the glow from the distant street-lights. The moon was still bright in the sky and the whole sleeping landscape lay bathed in the luminous whiteness of that glittering frost cover. It seemed almost too pure and pristine to bear.

She was just about to start down the hill towards the Beehive, deciding at last that she must go home and try to sleep, when she found herself looking at the dark figure of a man coming towards her over the pale, glinting hillside. A tall man, whose stride she recognised instantly, and who had been in her thoughts more than she cared to admit as she walked in the frost-transfigured night. Her first instinct was to turn swiftly and escape down the hill before he saw her, but then she saw that it was already impossible to run away for he had seen her and had quickened his stride to reach her, his face under the bleaching moonlight reflecting the gladness of recognition. She could not quench that look with craven retreat.

'What are you doing up here?' she asked, half smiling at him.

'The same as you, I should think.' Finn's voice was strangely rough. 'Walking away from my ghosts.'

'Not walking away from them.' Beth shook her head at him gently. 'More like . . . trying to find a way to keep them with me.'

'Looking for "yonder",' said Finn, and though he also was smiling, his tone was quite serious.

Beth thought instantly of Chloë and looked up at Finn with some doubt. 'Ought you to be out here? What if Chloë wakes up and comes looking for you?'

'She won't.' He sounded quite certain. 'She and Corny were quite exhausted when everything was done. We decorated the tree and hung up the stockings, iced the Christmas cake and helped Mary to stuff the turkey . . .' He sighed, and then grinned at Beth in a rueful, apologetic way. 'Honestly, Beth, we both tried so hard, it positively hurt!'

Beth laughed a little, but she did not miss the ache of sadness behind his flippant words.

'I'm glad I found you,' he went on. 'There's something I wanted to say to you, only somehow it never seems to be the right time and tomorrow will be no exception.'

Beth stood still, looking at him quietly.

He seemed to hesitate, as if not knowing how to begin. At last he laid a deliberate hand on her arm. 'I know you feel a bit pressured. I understand why you fled from our preparations this evening—'

'I didn't exactly flee!'

He kept his hand on her arm and gave it a little shake. 'Be serious—I'm trying to apologise.'

'What for?'

'For dragging you into our lives, whether you like it or not! For making use of you at every turn, for—'

'Be quiet,' said Beth crossly. 'You're talking nonsense.'

'Am I?' He sounded relieved. 'Then, maybe I can dare to go on?' But he didn't for a moment. He was a man more used to actions than words, and these were thoughts that he found hard to express. At last he drew a long, slow breath and began again. 'What I'm trying to say is . . . I know we've been driven into a . . . a closeness we didn't expect, but it means a lot to me, Beth, just now, and I don't want to lose it.' He paused, looking at her questioningly in the moonlight.

Beth did not know how to answer this, so she simply nodded. It meant a lot to her, too. How could she deny it?

Finn sighed again and lifted his hand to touch her hair. It was a gentle movement, quite undemanding, but somehow unexpectedly tender. 'Poor Beth, you've got so much to contend with—without my clumsy approaches!'

She smiled at him a little uncertainly in the sparkling white night. 'It's just that . . .' She paused, sounding shy and tired.

'Yes?'

'I don't know who I am, Finn.' She pushed the hair out of her eyes in a gesture of bewilderment. 'You are an explorer . . .'

'An adventurer,' he corrected grimly, 'who is trying desperately hard to be a father.'

At least you have a role to play, she thought, and a child to live for. She looked up at him with a kind of bleak honesty and repeated, 'I don't know what I am or what I'm trying to be, Finn, or where I'm trying to go . . . Not yet.'

He nodded, accepting it quite calmly. 'Well, then, that makes my request even easier. It's just this,' he went on, sounding almost as shy as she was. 'Couldn't we, in the meantime, not worry about the future, but accept what comfort we can bear and be glad?'

Accept what comfort we can bear and be glad, thought Beth, a strange tide of relief washing over her tired mind.

'Of course we could,' she murmured, and the tears glittered in her eyes and made prisms on the frosted trees.

'And be glad?' he insisted, staring down at her.

She nodded again, not trusting herself to speak.

'Then—happy Christmas, Beth,' he said softly, and drew her close and kissed her under the pure white light of the winter moon.

SOMEHOW OR OTHER, it turned out to be a better Christmas than any of them had expected.

Mark and his mother arrived at the Beehive armed with mince pies and presents before walking over to Finn's house with Beth in time for the midday festive meal. Mark had brought Beth a piece of soap shaped like a fish, to remind her of the fisherman's solo in the school production. Lucy had brought her a new blue teapot because Mark had told her that the old one had been chipped, and she would have gone into lengthy thanks for all those after-school teas if Beth hadn't stopped her.

'I needed the company,' she said, smiling, and then, looking at Mark, she added, 'and so did Chloë.'

So they drank some spicy punch that Beth had concocted, and Lucy began to look less pinched and tired even before they set out for the Mill House.

Then it was cheerful chaos, with Corny tearing up all the Christmas paper as soon as the presents were unwrapped (and sometimes before), and trying to run off with Mary's new scarf and almost fusing the Christmas-tree lights on the way, and Mark and Chloë trying to catch her and prevent any further disasters, amid the general laughter.

Beth had bought a new blanket for Corny. For Chloë she had knitted a red woollen hat and scarf with bobbles on, to match the new boots that Finn had bought her. The present for Finn had been more difficult, but in the end she had found an old-fashioned glass prism in a local antique shop. It was meant to be an ordinary paperweight, which would be suitable for Finn's new home office, but there was something about the light glancing through it that had reminded Beth of Elkstone church and the strange conversation with the old man. *'You can't prove light. But it's there.'* When she gave it to him, he looked from the glinting prism to Beth's face and murmured, 'It's like the moonlight on the frost . . .'

Finn and Chloë had arranged to hand out their offerings from the

Christmas tree. There was a penknife for Mark, and a frivolous powder puff on top of a tin of talc for Lucy, with Finn rightly supposing that she wouldn't buy anything so unessential and pretty for herself. There was a large box of marrons glacés for Mary, because she said they were her favourites. For Chloë, there was a pair of bright red socks to go with the red walking boots, and a dolphin-headed carved shepherd's crook from Spirios. And for Beth, he and Chloë had found a small wrought-iron Japanese lantern with a candle inside, to remind her of *Hamaguchi's Harvest* and the children's own special triumph.

After all this excitement, it was time for turkey and plum pudding, and Mary and Chloë carried in the food together, both of them beaming with pride.

'She seems to enjoy it,' murmured Finn, worrying as usual about whether he was expecting too much of his small daughter.

'Cosseting, remember,' Beth replied, in an equally low voice. 'It's important to her, Finn. Don't try to stop her.'

He nodded understanding and raised his glass. 'To the cooks,' he said. 'God bless 'em!'

Corny blessed them too, when the scraps came her way at the end of the meal. She looked up at everyone with the utmost devotion and made it plain that everything was entirely right with her world, especially when there was turkey for lunch.

Presently Mark and Chloë demanded to take Corny for a walk, so the whole party decided to go with them, leaving Mary to build up the fire and mutter about Christmas cake.

It was very cold outside, and still a glittering world of white hoarfrost, hanging like lace on every tree branch and edging each blade of grass with silver fire.

'Oh, isn't it pretty!' said Chloë, and ran off with Mark and Corny. Her bright red boots and woolly cap stood out against the sparkling frosted grass and made Finn smile.

'She looks like an elf,' he said, and Beth and Lucy smiled too as Chloë's laughter floated back to them.

'I'm so glad she's well again,' said Lucy impulsively.

Finn looked at her with sudden gravity. 'Your son, Mark, had a lot to do with it, I'm told.' Then his serious glance lightened as he saw the children turn and begin racing back towards him, with Corny at full stretch on her smart red lead. 'Anyway,' he said, before Chloë had quite reached him, 'I'm enormously grateful.'

Lucy did not reply to this, but somehow Finn's quiet word of praise seemed to soften her face and make her look much younger.

'Time for tea,' announced Finn. 'Though I doubt if I can eat any more!'

'But Mary and me's made a cake!' protested Chloë. 'You must eat some of it!'

'I'll try,' groaned Finn. 'And I'm sure Corny will help.'

Corny looked up with liquid eyes and indicated, with wildly wagging tail, that she would be happy to oblige.

The absurd cheerfulness seemed to continue without being forced, but Beth suddenly found herself beginning to feel extraordinarily tired and was glad when Lucy and Mark decided they ought to go home. At this point, however, Chloë, who up till now had been extra sunny and cooperative for Christmas Day, suddenly became mutinous. 'I want Beth to stay and say good night,' she demanded.

Beth had already begun to feel trapped in all this family cosiness, and now a screaming claustrophobia threatened to overwhelm her. You're not Mo! she wanted to yell. You're not Robert! You're none of you the ones I want! Why can't you leave me alone? But Chloë was looking up at her with eyes that were growing dark with unshed tears and she could not refuse them.

Then Mark, speaking in the curiously adult voice of one who had tried many times to defuse family rows, said mildly, 'Where does Corny sleep?'

'Upstairs with me,' said Chloë, and the tears were getting nearer.

'Well, I want to say good night to Corny,' he told her briskly. 'So hurry up and we'll *all* come up.'

Chloë just looked at Mark's calm, cheerful face and went without a word. In a remarkably brief time she called down to them, and they all trooped upstairs to say good night. Beth understood very well why the child was making such a ceremony out of it, trying desperately hard to fill the gap where her mother should have been. And, she suspected, Lucy understood, too.

So Mark hugged Corny and gave Chloë a brotherly tap on the head. Lucy looked shy but accepted Chloë's lifted face for a Christmas kiss. Beth, feeling a dreadful reluctance and guilt, leaned down and allowed those warm young arms to cling round her neck.

'It's been a lovely day,' whispered Chloë in her ear.

And Beth knew she could not reject the appeal in that anxious voice. 'Yes, it has,' she said. 'Simply lovely,' and hugged her back. And then she fled downstairs.

Then there was the difficulty of saying good night to Finn, but here Chloë's bunch of mistletoe in the hall came in handy. Finn—being the only man in all their lives—kissed Lucy, leaving her all rosy and laughing, ruffled Mark's hair with genuine affection and kissed Beth in another cheerful smother of laughter.

'I could run you home in the car?' he suggested.

'No,' said Beth. 'We'll walk. It's a lovely night.'

They went out into the porch and stood looking out. The frost was holding, and the trees still looked dressed in diamond lace.

'It was a lovely day,' repeated Lucy, looking up at Finn with gratitude shining out of her. 'Thank you so much.'

Beth said nothing. But Finn did not seem to notice, or if he did, he ignored it. He just looked at Beth and smiled, and murmured obscurely into the frosty night, 'The magic is still there.'

CORNY WAS IN THE DOGHOUSE. That is, she was in disgrace, but as there was no kennel to be banished to, she merely crept upstairs and hid under Chloë's bed. She knew she had done wrong, or at least she knew she had been shouted at and, since it hurt her sensitive soul to be scolded in loud voices, all she could do was hide.

First of all, it being so bitterly cold outside, Chloë hadn't stayed with her long enough in the garden, so she had been obliged to come in before she was ready and that meant she simply had to make a puddle somewhere in the house. She had thought the best hall rug was a good, open spot, but Mary had disagreed. Loudly. So she fled upstairs. She was only passing Finn's door, she knew she was not supposed to go in, but there was this long, dangerous-looking snake thing hanging from a chair and she thought she'd better kill it before it did any harm. It tasted of good chewable leather, and though the metal bit at the end wasn't edible the rest was.

'Corny!' shouted Finn. 'That was my best leather belt. It's a good thing you've eaten it or I'd have used it on you!'

His voice sounded fierce, but somehow Corny didn't think he was really very angry. In fact she thought he might be laughing inside, but she fled all the same. This time she went into Finn's other room where there were lots of bits of paper and machines that went clack, and there was one in particular that kept on spewing out long thin strips of paper into a sort of tray thing just below. The paper kept falling off the edge and Corny thought she ought to give it a tug or two and see if she could tidy it up a bit. It didn't get any tidier, in fact it got a lot worse, but it was a lovely game, anyway.

'Oh, Corny!' shouted Finn. 'What *have* you done now? Look at the mess! Get out of here, you little horror!'

Corny got out, rather fast, and went and hid under Chloë's bed. She couldn't seem to do anything right, somehow.

When Chloë heard Finn shout, she left the sitting room where she'd been drawing and went into her bedroom. She rescued Corny from underneath the bed and sat down on top of the duvet with the puppy in her arms. 'It's all right, Corny,' she told her in a soothing voice. 'He's not really cross. We'll go and say we're sorry.'

Corny licked her hand and wriggled a bit closer. She was glad someone still liked her. Chloë could see she was still a bit hurt by all the shouts, so she held her tight and carried her out of the room, meaning to go and talk to Finn about it. Perhaps if she reminded him that Corny was still only very little—eleven weeks wasn't very old—he would forgive her. She only needed a pat on the head to make her feel all right again.

But Finn was talking on the phone when Chloë got to the door and she hesitated just outside, not liking to interrupt.

'No,' he was saying, 'it isn't any good. I can't keep her.'

Chloë froze, and went on listening in horror.

'My life has no room in it now for such distractions,' he continued. 'I'll have to get rid of her . . . What? No, I won't change my mind. She's only an unnecessary burden—with too many unhappy associations. She'll have to go.'

The tone of his voice was crisp and decisive and brooked no argument. Chloë knew that voice—and, like Corny, when trouble was brewing her instinct was to hide. Clutching her beloved puppy tightly in terrified arms, she turned and fled.

Finn had vaguely noticed a flicker of movement outside the door as he talked on the phone, but he hadn't worried about it. Chloë and Corny came and went more or less as they chose. It was enough for him that they were happy together, and Chloë was continuing to blossom in the puppy's cheerful company. So he went on working for an hour or so, and then became aware that the house seemed unusually quiet. There was no scampering of small feet, no laughter on the stairs—in fact, nothing at all.

He got up and went to look in Chloë's room. It was empty. So was the little sitting room where she had been drawing.

He went downstairs to speak to Mary. 'Have you seen Chloë?'

'No.' Mary was cooking, and pushed the hair away from her flushed face. 'I thought she was with you.'

Finn frowned and turned away. 'I expect she's upstairs somewhere.'

But she wasn't. He searched every room in the house and there was no sign of her at all. 'Perhaps she's in the garden,' he said to Mary, and it was only then that he looked out of the window and saw the snow. It wasn't just a few flakes falling but a solid white sheet pouring out of a leaden sky and slanting in a vicious curtain before the fierce northeast wind. 'My God!' he said. 'Surely she wouldn't be out in that?'

Mary also looked out in horror. 'I hope not,' she said fervently, and began to pull on her boots.

They searched the garden and the summerhouse, the potting shed and every hidden corner. But there was no one there. By now the snow was falling so fast that any small footprints would soon be covered, and Finn could find no trace of any, except a few vague depressions near the dry-stone wall that bordered the field.

He turned back to the house, shaking his head in puzzled disbelief. 'But I can't think why—in this!'

Then, all at once, the sound of his own voice talking to Theo Koussalis in Athens came back to him, and the words he had said took on a terrifying significance. 'Oh, dear God,' he muttered, 'I believe she thought I was talking about Corny.'

Mary looked at him, uncomprehending, but he didn't wait to explain. He went into the hall and rang up Beth.

When the snow began, Beth had made a quick dash to the village shop for extra supplies, knowing that her lane was very likely to get silted up in a heavy snowfall. When she got home again, her phone was ringing; she dropped all her parcels on the floor and hurried to answer it. It was Finn—but a Finn she scarcely knew. His voice was rough with anxiety, his tone sharp and desperately upset.

'Beth? Is Chloë with you?

'Chloë? No. Should she be?'

'No. She shouldn't. She should be here, but she's not.' He drew a shaking breath. 'Beth . . . I . . . think she may have run away.'

'Run away? Why?'

He made a despairing, anguished sound. 'I was talking to Theo Koussalis about getting rid of *Dancing Lady* . . . I think Chloë may have overheard and misunderstood . . .'

'What exactly did you say?'

'I said . . . "I can't keep her . . . I'll have to get rid of her . . ." and something about . . . "an unnecessary burden with too many unhappy associations", or something. She could have thought—'

'Yes, she could,' agreed Beth grimly. And then returned to practicalities. 'Where have you looked?'

'Everywhere. I don't know what to do. Can you think of anywhere she might go?'

Beth thought hard. 'She might have gone up to see Beech. She's done it before. But it would be pretty difficult in this snow.'

Finn groaned. 'I'd better go up there and see.'

'Finn, what was she wearing? Was she wearing those red boots? And her red bobble hat? You'd see them very clearly in the snow.'

'Yes,' he breathed, 'you would. Hang on, I'll go and look.'

The line went silent and Beth waited, picturing in her mind a frightened little girl, clutching her beloved puppy in her arms, struggling through the snow.

'Yes, you were right,' said Finn's voice, close in her ear. 'She's taken the red boots and your red hat and scarf, and'—his voice almost cracked here—'and her shepherd's crook . . . She must have meant to walk a long way.'

'Don't jump to conclusions.' Beth's voice was crisp and practical. 'Tell Mary to keep up the fires and lots of hot water. I'll meet you up at Beech's cottage.'

'But Beth, is it safe for you to go out? There's a blizzard blowing.'

'Chloë's out in it,' snapped Beth. 'I'll see you up there,' and she rang off before he could make any further protest.

She put on all the thickest clothes she possessed, with two pairs of socks inside her Wellington boots and, as an afterthought, filled a Thermos with hot sweet tea. Then she found a walking stick to help probe the drifts and set out into the storm.

It was blowing a furious gale by now and the snow was driving across the hills almost horizontally in a blizzard of blinding whiteness. She plodded on against the wind, pausing from time to time to look round at the snowy hillside in the vain hope that she might see something red bobbing about ahead of her. But there was nothing in all that shrieking inferno but snow and more snow, and the dark shapes of trees cowering before the wind.

It seemed to take an age of climbing and fighting the relentless gale before she saw the final slope of the hill leading to Beech's cottage. As she approached, she saw the bent figure of Beech himself stooping over his pens and cages, battening everything down against the tearing northeaster. He straightened up when he saw her and came hurrying towards her, instantly aware that something was wrong.

'It's Chloë,' gasped Beth, against the wind. 'She's gone missing again. I suppose she's not with you?'

He shook his head, looking grave and concerned. 'Nay, I've not seen her. You'd best come inside and tell me about it. 'Tis a bad day for a little 'un to be out.'

He led Beth into the cottage, kicking the door shut behind him with a snowy boot. He took one look at her and hastened over to his old-fashioned range, on which a blackened kettle was hissing quietly.

'A cup of tea wunt do no harm,' he said. 'Why did she go off, then? What frit her?'

Beth sighed. 'I'm afraid it was something Mr Edmondson said. She misunderstood and thought he was going to get rid of the puppy.' Or even get rid of Chloë herself? Beth wondered painfully, knowing how insecure and uncertain of her father's affections the child was.

Beech nodded slowly, busily thinking about Chloë's possible whereabouts. 'If she wanted to hide Corny, she might go back to that old tree where I found her afore,' he said. 'Remember?'

'Yes,' agreed Beth. That certainly made some kind of sense. 'Is it far? Could you find it in this blizzard?'

'Nay, 'tis not that far,' he told her. 'We can reach it through the woods.' He stared out of the window, assessing the state of the storm. 'But we'd best hurry—'twill be dark early.'

'Finn is coming,' Beth explained. 'He'll be here in a minute or two. It's a bit further from his house.'

Beech nodded and went across to his dresser where an old storm lantern hung on one of the hooks. He reached it down and lit it, and then looked round for a blanket.

'I've got a Thermos of tea as well,' said Beth.

'Good girl,' said Beech, as if he was talking to one of his frightened animals. Then he saw the tall figure of Finn Edmondson silhouetted against the snow, and went out to meet him.

'Is Beth here?' asked Finn at once, anxiety deep in his voice, and then smiled with relief when he saw her coming out behind Beech into the snow.

'Best get on then,' said Beech, not waiting any longer or wasting any words on explanations, and he set off into the woods at once.

Finn grasped Beth's arm for a moment in a hard, grateful grip. 'My God, I'm glad to see you,' he muttered. 'I never should have let you come out in this alone.'

Beth grinned at him through snow-caked lips. 'You couldn't have stopped me,' she told him, and ploughed gamely on at Beech's heels through the deep, drifting snow.

Beech had moved with surprising speed through the darkening woods and both Finn and Beth had found it quite hard to keep up with him, but now he slowed a little and seemed to cast round him as if not quite sure of his direction. The snow had changed the landscape, making it hard for him to recognise the landmarks he knew. But at last he gave a quick affirmative nod and set off again among the brooding dark trunks of the massive beech trees. He was near his destination now.

Finn and Beth pressed close behind him, breathing hard with the exertion, and Beth noticed that even Beech's hillman's stride was slower and his breathing was sounding ominously wheezy in the piercing wind.

But before she could begin to worry about the old man, he stopped suddenly and pointed downwards. There was a large drift where the fallen beech tree had lain, and the snow seemed to have entirely filled the deep hollow beneath the upended roots. Beth's heart sank when she saw it, for surely no little girl could be crouching down there under all that weight of snow? But even as she thought that and stooped to look further, she saw what Beech had seen—a flash of something red protruding from the snow.

'Oh, God,' said Finn, 'she's gone to sleep in the snow!' and he began to scramble down into the hollow, afraid of what he might find.

But Beth forestalled him, leaping down past him and saying urgently as she did so, 'No, Finn. Let me. She may have—' Gone back into retreat from Finn himself, she had been going to say, but she knew that she could not. It would hurt Finn too much.

The child was curled up in a tight ball of misery, with the puppy wrapped inside her coat for extra warmth. At first Beth could not tell if she was unconscious or merely so cold and scared that she could not speak. But it looked as if the two small creatures had somehow kept each other warm, huddled together under the snow, for both of them stirred and opened snow-fringed eyes when she shook them.

'Chloë,' she said, and wrapped her own arms tight round her for instant comfort. 'It's all right. There's nothing to worry about. It was the boat—*Dancing Lady*—Finn was talking about. The *boat*, do you understand? Not Corny. Not anything to do with you. Finn wants to get rid of the boat—that's all.'

She repeated it again several times, holding Chloë very tight in her arms until she felt the tension begin to drain out of the small, weary body and Chloë's own arms slowly came up and wound themselves round her neck.

'Not Corny? . . . Not me?'

'*Not* Corny. *Not* you. Not anyone here,' repeated Beth. 'How could you think such a thing? Your father's been nearly out of his mind with worry—and so have I. Now, let's go back with Beech and get warm.' Talking gently, cajoling and coaxing, Beth got Chloë out of her nest of snow and handed her up to Finn's outstretched arms.

'Oh, darling,' he whispered into the tangled hair under the little red bobble hat, 'thank God you're safe!'

Beth climbed out then, carrying the bewildered puppy, and Beech came forward to wrap the rugs round both of them.

'She'd better have that tea,' he growled, 'afore we sets off again . . . The cold can kill, if it ent checked.'

Beth agreed, and managed to unscrew the top of the Thermos with frozen hands. 'It's the first time I've had a picnic in a snowstorm,' she said, and held the plastic cup for Chloë's nerveless fingers to grip.

'Best get back now,' said Beech. 'It's near dark.'

And it was. The snow was still whirling but night was closing in and it would be hard going even to get back to Beech's cottage. We'll have to stay there for the night, thought Beth. We'll never get Chloë down to the village through this. She could see the same thought in Beech's eyes, but he merely nodded his head at her and murmured, ''Twill be all right,' as he picked up the lantern to lead the way.

It was a long hard slog back to the cottage and they were all exhausted by the time they got there. As soon as they were inside, Beech went into action. First of all, he pulled out the damper in his old range so that the fire began to roar up the flue and grow red and hot through the bars. Then he dragged an old tin bath in front of the glowing fire and began to fill it with hot water.

'A bath by the fire,' he said to Chloë, smiling, 'like my ma used to give me when I wus a little 'un. Now, you just get yourself in there, while I go and fix some soup.' He winked at Beth and stumped off into his back kitchen.

Finn stayed to help Beth with the bath, to which Chloë submitted with a rather alarming docility, but as soon as she was dressed again and wrapped in blankets by the fire, Finn announced that he must try to telephone Mary.

'Where from?' asked Beth, alarmed. 'You'll never get down to the village in this.'

Finn looked obstinate and started shrugging himself into his coat again. 'Mary will be going mad with worry down there. I've got to do something.' He turned to Beech, who was busy handing out mugs of hot soup.

The old man considered the question calmly. 'Dan Briggs would be nearest, down at the farm.' He looked at Finn doubtfully. 'You'd probably make it to there—if the fields aren't too drifted up.'

'You drink that soup first,' ordered Beth. 'It'll keep you warm on the way. And don't you dare be long! We need you here.'

Chloë looked at him out of drowsy, shadowed eyes and echoed Beth's words in a small, shy voice: 'Don't be long.'

Beech also began to put his coat on again, but Finn protested at this. 'No, Beech, you've done enough. I can manage.'

'I'll see you to the field gate,' insisted Beech, sounding as unruffled as ever. 'You can see the lights from there, if the snow'll allow.'

They went out together into the howling storm and, by the time Beech got back inside, Chloë was on the verge of sleep. She sat up with a start when the door banged shut against the wind, and asked in a scared voice, 'Is he all right?'

'Surely.' Beech's soft old voice was full of comforting certainty. 'He's a big, strong man, your father. He won't be moithered by a bit o' snow.'

Chloë burrowed her head against Beth's shoulder in relief, but instead of settling down and going to sleep, she suddenly began to cry.

In all the time that Beth had known her, she had never seen Chloë cry. In the sunny days with Stephanie there had never been any need—and when she was at her most shocked and grief-stricken she had seemed too remote and cold to cry at all. But now, suddenly, the floodgates were opened and she wept in Beth's arms as if she would never stop.

'I thought . . . I thought . . .' she sobbed.

'I know what you thought,' said Beth, holding her close. 'But it isn't true—you know that now.' She brushed a gentle hand over the tangled hair and hot, flushed little face. 'He loves you very much.'

'And Corny, too?'

'Of course, and Corny, too.'

But Chloë was still not quite convinced. 'What's a *burden*, Beth?'

'Not you, anyway,' replied Beth firmly. 'But a boat like *Dancing Lady* could be, if you didn't want to be bothered with it any more.'

Chloë was silent then, trying to work it all out, but the helpless sobs still shook her. 'He might want her, if he didn't have to stay here with me.'

'No.' Beth was quite definite. 'He doesn't *have* to stay with you, Chloë. He came home because he wanted to. I think he needs you more than you need him at the moment.'

'Does he?' It was a new thought to Chloë, and as she began to consider it the sobs at last subsided. 'I'm sorry I ran away,' she said, in a small contrite voice, and leaned back wearily in Beth's arms.

'It's all right,' murmured Beth. 'Everything's all right now.' But before she had finished speaking, Chloë was asleep.

Beech had tactfully gone upstairs to potter about the cramped attic space, wondering where to put his unexpected guests. The upper floor of the cottage was divided into two tiny rooms, but they were icy cold and the one Beech didn't use hadn't got a bed at all, only an ancient horsehair sofa.

Now he came downstairs quietly and put a cautious face round the door. When he saw that Chloë was asleep, he came over to stand by Beth and spoke softly in his gentle old voice. 'I reckon it's too cold upstairs for the little 'un, after what she's bin through. There's an old settee up there. If her father'd help bring it down, like, when he gets back, we could put it close to the fire and she could stay warm all night, if you could make do with the chairs?'

Beth smiled at his anxious expression. 'That sounds perfect, Beech. But where do you sleep?'

'Up there,' he said, jerking a thumb skywards.

'In the cold?'

'Nay, I allus sleeps up there,' he said reasonably. 'I'm used to the cold, see? But the little 'un—and probably you as well—you're used to heated rooms and such.'

'At least stay by the fire a bit, Beech. You've had no time to get warm yet. It would never do if you got sick. What would your animals do?'

That was an argument that the old man couldn't resist. He sighed, shot Beth a faintly humorous glance and sat down in the other chair by the fire. He had to admit he was tired when he thought about it, and the warmth of the fire made him want to close his eyes.

'Why does everyone call you Beech?' asked Beth. 'Why never *Mister* Beech?'

He shrugged cheerfully. 'Nay, I've never been much of a mister. I was 'prenticed to a gardener when I was fourteen, see? And it was Beech, come here, Beech, go there, Beech, bring me that spade, and it sort of stuck.'

'Didn't you mind?'

He grinned. 'Nay, I liked it. Sounded kind of manly. And anyways, I've allus had a soft spot for beech trees.'

Beth laughed, but before she could think of another way to detain him, he was on his feet again.

'I got another lantern out back,' he said. 'I reckon I'll put it on the field gate—then he'll see his way home.'

Beth had been getting increasingly worried about Finn out there in the blizzard but she had not liked to say so—or to admit, even to herself, how much Finn's safe return mattered to her. But now she said, as casually as she could, 'How long is he likely to be?'

Beech shook his head doubtfully. 'Nay, 'tis no great distance . . . but snow is slow-going stuff. He might be an hour or so.'

Beth sighed. He had already been an hour or so, and the wind was still howling out there, the snow was still falling on the shrouded hills.

But Beech is right, she told herself, Finn is big and strong and used to hardship. This little adventure would be nothing to him.

Beech went out through the door and Beth sat on alone, waiting for the sound of footsteps on the path. And presently she did hear them—not one set of footsteps but two—and Finn's deep voice answering Beech's soft one as they reached the door.

'Here I am!' he said, shaking the snow off his shoulders and dropping two heavy-looking bags on the floor. He turned to Beech, smiling, but Beth could see that even he was looking exhausted now. 'Mrs Briggs sent you up some provisions for your uninvited guests.'

'What's it like down there?' asked Beech, eyeing the heavy bags on his floor with interest.

'Pretty bad,' admitted Finn. 'Dan Briggs says all the roads are blocked and they won't get a snowplough through till tomorrow morning at the earliest.'

'Did you get hold of Mary?' asked Beth.

'I did. She was mightily relieved.' Finn looked down at Beth cradling the sleeping Chloë in her arms, and his face softened. 'You must be tired,' he said softly. 'We'll move that sofa down in a moment. Beech has told me all about it.'

Beth looked up at him and found that she was so glad to see him that she couldn't speak at all.

Presently, the old horsehair sofa was brought down and put by the fire and Chloë was gently transferred to it, still wrapped in blankets. She scarcely stirred and neither did Corny, who had fallen asleep in a warm corner out of harm's way. Then Beech brought in a pot of tea and some of Grace Briggs's bread and cheese, and though both Beth and Finn thought they were too tired to eat, they found that they were not, after all.

'Will you be all right now, down here?' Beech enquired.

'We'll be fine,' Beth assured him. 'But have you got enough blankets left for yourself? Haven't you given them all to us?' She was still worried about the old man upstairs in the cold.

'Nay,' Beech laughed. 'There be plenty o' they. My missus was a great hoarder o' blankets. Cupboards full, she had.' He gave an impish smile and added, 'I uses 'em for the animals, too. She'd have a fit if she knew!'

He hovered for a moment, waiting to see Beth smile, and then said, 'Well, then, I'll leave you to it . . .' and stumped away up the stairs.

Finn stretched his long legs out towards the fire, lay back in his chair and sighed. 'He's a wonderful old man. I don't know what we'd have done without him today.'

'I tremble to think,' agreed Beth. But her voice was slow and vague. Exhaustion was catching up on her, that and the warmth of the fire.

Finn smiled at her dreaming face, and then leaned forward once more to have a look at Chloë. 'Do you think she's all right?'

'Yes.' Beth roused herself enough to sound firm. 'She's not too hot—or cold. Her breathing sounds all right. I don't think she'll suffer any ill effects.'

'She looks a bit flushed.' He sounded absurdly anxious.

'That's because she's been crying,' said Beth, and went on to tell Finn what had been going on in his daughter's mind.

He shook his head sadly. 'I'd no idea . . . how could she know about *burdens*?'

'She understands a lot more than you give her credit for.' She looked at him straight. 'You must talk to her, Finn.'

Finn looked at her tired face. 'Of course I'll talk to her,' he said softly. 'But now you must go to sleep. You've done more than enough for us today.'

IN THE MORNING, when they were just finishing an enormous breakfast that Beth and Beech had cooked between them, there was a loud, cheerful knocking on the door. Beech opened it and found the two Briggs boys smiling at him on the snowy step.

'Mornin', Beech,' said the tallest. 'Our dad sent us up to see if you was all right.' His bright, inquisitive glance took in the family party round the table and he spoke now to Finn. 'And he said to tell you the snowplough's been through and he's got the Land-Rover out. So if you can get down to the farm, he'll run you all home.'

'And we've brought the sledge for the little 'un,' added the other boy, smiling even more broadly.

'Makes sense, that does,' approved Beech. 'Her legs are mighty short for this snow.' He looked enquiringly at the boys. 'How was it coming up?'

'Pretty deep,' said the eldest. 'Dad says you'd best go round by the farm till it's cleared up.'

The old man nodded, and he and Finn went out with the boys to have a look while Beth got Chloë into her coat and boots, then rescued Corny from the back kitchen where she had been visiting her mother, Jess.

'Afore you go,' said Beech, standing in the doorway, 'I wants to show Chloë something.' And he beckoned to them all to follow him over to the animal pens.

'Here,' Beech said, and stooped down by the last wire enclosure, where Beth knew he kept the injured hare. 'I want you to let her go.'

'Now?' Chloë protested. 'In the snow?'

The old man smiled at her. 'Hares don't mind the snow. They can run in it, light as feathers, and they can curl up small somewhere in a hollow, like you did, and keep quite safe and warm.' He looked down at the wary, nervous creature with her sensitive, twitching ears laid back almost flat against her head in fear. 'But she'm ready to go, little 'un. She needs her freedom, see? It's time she was away.'

'But what will she eat?' asked Chloë anxiously.

'She'll burrow down and find the grass,' Beech explained. 'And the snow's less thick under the trees where the roots are . . . She won't starve.'

Chloë nodded then, seeming satisfied.

'Keep still now,' ordered Beech. 'If we all of us keep still when I opens the cage, she'll go easy and not be frit.' He stooped and gently lifted the wire gate at the end of the pen. 'Come on, now, my lovely,' he crooned to her in his gentle old voice. 'Time to go.'

For a moment the anxious eyes looked into his and the hare kept quite still, but her nose was already scenting the wind. Then, cautiously, she moved, and the black-tipped velvet ears lifted to catch the new sounds of freedom on the snowy hillside. Just for one more breathless second she hesitated, and then she was out of the cage and streaking away across the snow. But she did not immediately disappear from view. Instead, she began to make curious zigzag patterns on the snow with her dancing feet, leaping in the air in a sudden ecstasy of free flight. Once, twice, she zigzagged, her feet flying over drift and hummock and curving slope, until she was gone.

'There she goes,' said Beech softly. ''Tis not only cornfields they dances in, see?' he said.

None of them answered but they all understood him, even Chloë. But now it was time to go themselves, and Chloë put her arms round the old man's neck and said, in her best manners, 'Thank you for having me. It was a lovely breakfast!'

Finn and Beth scarcely knew how to thank Beech—for it was clear to them both that he had probably saved Chloë's life yesterday, by knowing where to look for her. So Beth followed Chloë's example, and simply put her arms round the frail old shoulders and hugged him hard, and Finn added his arm to the general embrace and growled, in his deepest voice, 'Bless you for all you've done!'

The merry boys settled Chloë on the sledge and then they were away, with Finn keeping up beside them in case Chloë fell off and laughing as his feet fell into drifts and potholes in the powdery snow.

Beth came on more slowly, watching the cheerful procession with curiously misted eyes. She stopped for a moment on the hillside and looked round her, still seeing in her mind's eye the dancing hare before it streaked away into the distance.

Are you out there, Mo? she asked. You and Robert? Dancing about like the hare in the snow? . . . There were other children below her now, on the slopes near the farm, sledging and snowballing, tumbling and laughing in the sun. And among those dancing figures on the snowy slopes, did she see another small one she knew? . . . The light was very dazzling on all those pristine crystals, setting the whole brilliant world a-shimmer . . . It's all right, then, she told herself, suddenly sure of it—sure of the rightness of everything in this new white world. Be happy, little Mo, be happy, my tall Robert. Keep dancing . . . I know you are with me now.

'Are you coming?' called Finn.

'Are you coming?' echoed Chloë.

They had reached the edge of the slope above the farm and they waited there, holding out their arms to catch her if she ran too fast and laughing up at her in the sun.

'Yes,' answered Beth. 'I'm coming.' And she began to run through the snow.

PART VI
The Green Leaf

After the snow came the thaw, and with it the doubts. From the euphoria of Chloë's rescue and the relief that everyone was safe, and the wonderful sense of rightness and certainty that came after, life ground down to the anxieties and problems of day-to-day existence, and it wasn't easy.

Finn had black moods when self-reproach and a kind of helpless rage almost swamped him. He would shut himself up then in his study and try to work, and neither Chloë nor Beth could get near him.

And Beth herself still had moments of panic when she felt drawn into their lives more swiftly and finally than she wanted to be—moments of guilt when she thought, What about Robert and Mo? How can I let them be crowded out by these two demanding people? How can I desert them? She was very torn, very confused.

At last the tensions between them suddenly blew up into a major row and Beth was horrified to hear herself shouting at Finn, 'You're turning into an introspective, self-pitying wimp!' And Finn, shouting back, called her a self-righteous prig and told her to stop preaching at him.

They looked at each other, appalled. But it was Finn who relented first. 'I'm sorry, Beth,' he said, holding out a hand to her in contrite appeal. 'It's my guilty conscience speaking.'

'That's what I'm complaining of,' retorted Beth. 'You have absolutely no reason to feel guilty—and you *must* stop it, Finn. It's destroying you—and it upsets Chloë, too.'

'I know,' he said heavily. 'I know.' He managed to summon up a bleak smile. 'And you have every right to lecture me.'

'No, I haven't,' Beth told him. 'You've got to work this out for yourself.' And she turned away, determined to escape from Finn's house and his private demons to a more neutral place where she could deal with her own.

'Where are you going?' Finn's voice was suddenly sharp with anxiety.

'Just home to the Beehive.' Beth's voice was weary. 'I . . . I think we both need some space, Finn.' She looked up at him, also trying a tired, bleak smile. 'I just need time . . . and so do you . . . don't fret about it.'

'I'm sorry,' he said again, speaking gently this time. 'I didn't mean to pressurise you. Just . . . just come back soon. I mean, as soon as you can . . .'

Beth simply turned back and kissed him quietly. '*Wait*, Finn,' she said, her voice soft with more love than she knew. 'Wait . . . It will be all right.'

And she went then, very firmly, and did not look back.

So she was alone at home that weekend morning when Mark came knocking on her door. Since Christmas she had not seen so much of Mark as before and she felt a bit guilty about that, too. Really, she told herself crossly, it was absurd to be so riddled with guilt about everything—she was just as bad as Finn. But the rift with Finn lay like a bruise on her mind and she knew she ought to resolve it soon.

'Mark,' she said, smiling. 'I'm glad to see you. Come in.'

But he shook his head. 'No. I want you to come with me.' His voice was sharp and urgent. 'It's Beech . . . I think he's ill.'

'Wait while I get my coat,' said Beth at once. 'You can tell me about it on the way.'

They set off together to climb the hill to Beech's cottage and Mark at once launched into half-apologetic explanations. 'I've been going up to help with the animals on my own a bit.' He glanced sideways at Beth. 'I mean, Chloë's got her dad back now . . . She doesn't need to go and see Beech so much.' There seemed to be a faint question in his voice as if he was not sure he had done the right thing.

Beth nodded. And felt even more guilty. Had Mark missed Chloë and the cheerful Saturday-morning outings?

'But today when I went up,' Mark continued to explain, 'there was no one about.' His concerned young face turned to hers in anxious appeal. 'So I went to the cottage but I couldn't make anyone hear. Jess was outside, whimpering to get in. She made quite a fuss so I looked through the window . . .'

'And?' Beth felt his hesitation and knew she had to get past it.

'Well, Beech was there, all right—kind of lying back in one of the chairs. And he was coughing a bit, so I knew he wasn't asleep, but he didn't seem to see me.' He hesitated again, and then went on with a rush, 'I . . . I didn't like the look of him much, so I came for you.'

'Quite right. If he's ill, he'll need help.' Beth glanced at the boy with renewed appreciation, and then concentrated on climbing the hill as rapidly as possible.

Again there was no reply when she knocked at his door, so she lifted the latch and walked in, with Jess slipping in behind her. The old man lay in his chair, breathing fast and wheezily, and scarcely seemed to notice her coming in.

'Beech,' she said, giving the frail shoulders a little shake to recall him, 'how long has this been going on?'

He stirred and opened bleary, dilated eyes. 'Missus?' He seemed almost embarrassed at being found in this collapsed state and tried to sit up in his chair.

'No,' said Beth firmly. 'You stay there. Mark and I will see to everything . . . Just lie back and relax.'

She was a little alarmed when the old man did just that, too tired even to resist being ordered about. Beth noticed then that his breathing was very rapid and shallow, with an ominous catch in it. I'll have to get the doctor over here, she thought as she went into action. 'Mark,' she called. 'Can you find some logs? We've got to get his fire going.'

Mark wasted no time in answering and shot off round the back of the cottage to the log pile. Meanwhile, Beth had made some tea on the old electric cooker in the back kitchen, and she also found a tin of soup which she emptied into a saucepan to heat. Soon, Mark and she between them had the old range roaring up the flue. Beech stirred as the warmth began to reach him, and obediently clasped his hands round the mug of tea that Beth held for him.

'Drink a little,' she coaxed. 'It'll warm you up.'

He took a sip then, and managed a creaky smile. But with returning awareness came the anxiety. 'The animals?'

'Mark will see to them. He knows what to do.'

Once more a faint smile touched him, but a fit of coughing suddenly quenched it and Beth was shocked at how much it shook those bent old shoulders.

'Beech,' she said, 'I think you need a doctor.'

'Nay,' he mumbled, ''tis only a cold.'

'It is *not* only a cold,' she told him severely, 'and you know it.'

For a moment the faded, rheumy eyes seemed to glare defiance, but then they clouded a little and he shook his head in helpless denial. But he didn't say any more.

Beth went outside and sent Mark off to Mrs Briggs at the farm. 'She will know who to send for,' she told him. 'Just tell her what's happened and I'm sure she'll help.'

Once again Mark ran off, wasting no time on words. Beth went back and managed to persuade Beech to spoon down a little soup. But it obviously tired him and he soon laid down the spoon and leaned back in his chair again, with one hand resting on Jess's head as she lay curled up beside him.

Beth thought the best thing to do then was to tidy the cottage a bit, as quietly as she could. But presently the old voice spoke from the chair by the fire in a curiously flat and tranquil tone.

''Tis no great matter . . . at my age.'

Beth stopped in her tracks. At first she thought it was the faint reproach of an old man who felt ill and neglected. But then she realised that it was no such thing. It was a simple statement of fact, as he saw it. He was old, and if he was near to death it was no great matter.

She went across to his chair, drew up a stool and sat down beside him, taking his hand in hers. 'It may be no great matter to you, Beech, but it is to your animals, and to Chloë and Mark, and to me.'

His cloudy eyes rested calmly on her face. 'Nay, 'tis the natural way of things . . . I told 'em, remember? When you've got most of the corners knocked off and done all you can—'

'Yes,' Beth interrupted firmly. 'But you haven't, not by a long chalk. There's Chloë, for instance. How would she feel if you go off chasing hares in cornfields? She'll think it's all her fault for getting lost in the snow.'

Beech shook his head slowly, only half convinced. 'I'm tired, Missus,' he said, and again it was not a plaint but a simple statement of fact. ''Tis time I had a rest.'

Beth simply looked at him and shook her head, deciding not to argue any more for the moment. Probably it was the bronchitis talking, she told herself, and Beech's own sturdy spirit would revive when he felt better. So she sat on beside him, saying nothing, and waited for the doctor to arrive.

And presently he did, accompanied by Mark and Grace Briggs, who had brought another bag of useful stores with her.

Dr Forbes was oldish and kind, and he knew his villagers and their ways pretty well. He knew that Beech was fiercely independent and that the idea of hospital simply appalled him. 'Well, my friend,' he said, after listening to the sounds in the old man's chest with careful attention. 'I've brought you up some antibiotics, and you'd better take 'em. That chest of yours sounds like the church harmonium being sat on.' He grinned at the old man's obstinate face and added, 'You be good now, and do as you're told for once, and we'll soon have you on your feet again.' He winked at Beth, snapped his bag shut and followed her outside to have a quiet word.

'How bad is it?' asked Beth anxiously.

'Bad enough. But the old boy's tough. He's done this before and come through all right.' Dr Forbes smiled and patted Beth's arm. 'I'll get Sally—the district nurse—to come up and bully him!'

'I can come up in the evenings after school,' Beth told him. 'But mornings would be difficult . . .'

'I can do mornings,' said Grace Briggs's cheerful voice from the doorway. 'I'm up at five for the farm, anyway.'

'And I can feed the animals,' volunteered Mark.

'That's settled, then,' nodded Dr Forbes, smiling at them all. 'I'll be up myself to keep an eye on him . . . With all that tender loving care, he should do all right!'

THEY KEPT IT UP for two worrying weeks, disregarding Beech's protests, and by that time the antibiotics were beginning to work and the noises in Beech's chest sounded a little less frightening. But the old man did not seem to recover any of his old vitality and remained curiously listless, with his eyes far away and full of smoky dreams. He did not even seem to be much concerned about his animals, but merely nodded when Mark reported progress, and murmured, 'Good lad,' and left it at that.

As soon as word got round about Beech's illness, there was a touching procession of children from the village, bringing him soup and pies from their mothers, small offerings of cakes and sweets from the village shop, and sprigs of winter jasmine and bright-berried holly from their cottage gardens and the hedgerows on the way. Beech accepted their offerings quietly, seeming a little bewildered by all this attention, but the dreamy distance did not quite leave his faded eyes even when he smiled at the shy young faces at his door. Come back! thought Beth, almost wanting to shake him. Come back, Beech! Stop dreaming. You are needed here!

So far, she had not told Chloë or Finn about the old man's collapse, and she had given Mark strict instructions not to do so either. She wanted to be sure that Beech was really on the mend and back to his cheerful, optimistic self before she dared let them know what had been happening. It had meant, of course, that she had not had time to go over and see Finn at all during these weeks of anxiety, and the rift between them remained open and unresolved. But since she had asked Finn so desperately for some space, she supposed he would respect her wishes and accept her continuing absence to be exactly that—a need for space—and not make any attempt to contact her.

Peter Green, on the other hand, had no such scruples and, when Beth had refused several invitations to go out for a drink, he demanded to know why.

'Beech is ill,' she explained, 'and I've been going up there most evenings to give him a hand.'

Peter's cheerful face looked concerned. 'I'm sorry to hear that. Can I help?'

Beth smiled. 'I think it's all under control,' she said carefully. 'They've worked out a sort of rota system, and Mark's been very good with the animals.'

'Well, at least I could chop up some wood or something,' he insisted. 'And then I could buy you a drink on the way home.'

Beth sighed. 'You're incorrigible! All right . . . I'm sure I can find you something useful to do up there.'

So after Beth had got Beech some supper and Peter had banked up the fire and fetched in some more logs, they found themselves going companionably down the path to the village pub.

Finn saw them come in, laughing, from the cold outside, and watched them morosely as they settled down at a table across the room. Now, as Peter went to the bar to order drinks, he looked up and smiled at Beth faintly but made no move to go across and speak to her.

When she noticed the tall figure sitting alone in the corner she did not know what to do or how to ignore the wild racing of her heart. I want to go over and talk to him, she thought. He looks so gaunt and grim. What has happened to him? If this is what not communicating does to him, it can't be right. Can it?

But Peter had come back with the drinks and was looking at her curiously. 'What is it? You look as if you've seen a ghost.'

She tried a wan smile. 'Not a ghost, exactly. It's Finn Edmondson.'

'Oh.' Peter put down the drinks. 'Shall I ask him to join us?'

'No!' Beth sounded absurdly fierce. 'No,' she repeated more calmly. 'And if he comes over, don't tell him about Beech.'

'Why not?' Peter was nothing if not forthright.

Beth looked at him helplessly. 'It's a long story—I'll tell you later.' But her eyes kept returning to Finn, longing to bridge the aching chasm that seemed to yawn between them.

Finn, however, was not going to prolong things. He finished his drink rather too quickly and got to his feet. Then, with careful deliberation, he came over to speak to Beth on his way out. 'How are you? We've missed you.'

'I . . . I've been busy,' said Beth, trying desperately to hold herself back from launching into justifying explanations.

'I can imagine.' Finn's voice was dry. 'Well, come and see us, when you have time to spare.' He nodded coolly at Peter, avoided Beth's eyes and strolled out with studied nonchalance.

Beth stared at his retreating back, with a face grown suddenly ashen, and could not say a word.

Peter watched her quietly but made no comment. A little later on he fetched her another drink and said abruptly, 'Why mustn't he know about Beech?'

Beth had more or less pulled herself together by this time, and now she told Peter about Chloë and the snow, and about the absurd cloud of guilt that hung over both father and daughter and how hard it was to disperse . . . And if, in the process, she told Peter a bit more than she realised about her concern for the two of them, he was much too kind to remark on it. Looking at Beth's expressive face he drew his own conclusions and stoically put away a lot of private dreams.

It was only when he left her at her own doorstep that he decided to speak. 'Beth,' he said, 'the winter's nearly over. It's time you got your act together. You can't go on living in the shadows for ever.'

She looked at him in astonishment. But before she could think of any reply, he had stooped swiftly and kissed her and had gone away down the path in the dark.

IT WAS ONE MORNING soon after this that Beth suddenly noticed the little green shoot. She had left the flowerpot with the planted acorn in it on the kitchen windowsill where it could catch the sun, and it had remained there all the winter, with its dark leaf-mould surface undisturbed. But now, all at once, there was a thin green shoot thrusting up to the light, with two perfect young oak leaves at the top of the stem.

I must show Beech, she thought. Perhaps it will make him want to come back . . . I wonder if Finn's or Chloë's has come up yet? . . . And whether they'll be wanting to show it to me, just as I want to show it to them? . . . But that must come later, she told herself sternly. Beech must come first.

She went up in the morning this time, since it was the weekend, and found the old man still in his chair but bathed in a shaft of pale winter sunlight.

'Look, Beech,' she said, holding out the little tree in its pot, 'it's happened—just as you said it would.'

The old faded eyes looked from the transparent green of the new leaves to Beth's face, and the cloudy distance was suddenly gone from his gaze. 'Well now,' he said to that ardent face beside him, 'seems like spring's on its way . . . 'Tis time for new beginnings.'

'Shall I leave it here for you?' asked Beth.

He paused, and then smiled at her 'Nay . . . Take it with you. There's maybe someone else you ought to show it to . . .'

Beth did not misunderstand him. The old man knew too much about her and it was no good dissembling. 'Do you think . . .?'

'Go and see,' he said, with a faintly impish smile. 'Like I said, spring's on its way . . .' And he gave her a real, Beech-like mischievous wink.

Beth turned away, with the little oak tree still in her hands, and went down the path at the edge of the trees. But she didn't go home the usual way. Instead, she took the steeper track that led down to Finn's house at the other end of the valley.

The pale winter sunshine had strengened a little as the morning wore on, and now there was a hint of warmth in it and an extra patina of bright gold lay on every twig and fallen beech leaf. Beech is right, she thought. Spring's on the way. She began to notice as she walked that there were already hints of new green among the winter tangle of grass and bracken, and suddenly she came upon an early primrose struggling to flower.

Somehow, the sight of the small, pale flower, with its face lifted bravely to the sun, made Beth's own anxious heart stir with hope. All the warm feelings of certainty that had swept over her that joyous day in the snow, when she had called out 'I'm coming,' to Finn and

Chloë, waiting for her below on the snowy slopes, now came sweeping back. The agony of dark doubt that had kept her away from them these last weeks suddenly seemed to dissolve and disappear. It was going to be all right—she felt sure of it—and somehow Mo and Robert were caught up in this sense of renewal, too.

You are alive again, like me, she told them, smiling a little to herself in the strengthening sunlight. Aren't you? . . . Can you feel the spring coming, too? There'll be more dancing in cornfields than ever, then, won't there? . . . And she went on through the faintly greening woods, growing slowly more certain of her direction and her future with every step in that bright, glowing new world of early spring.

There was even a thrush singing, high up in a tall beech tree, to light her on her way. 'Be quick!' he sang. 'Be quick! Spring's on its way!' Beth smiled up at him, shading her eyes against the dazzle of sunlight, and almost fell over the silent figure of Finn sitting with his back to her, gazing away through the woods at an unbearably empty world.

'Finn!' she said, sudden wild gladness surging through her, and she carefully set down the little oak tree before him, and then her arms went round those stiff, lonely shoulders, drawing him close.

'I thought you said you wanted some space,' he growled, not looking round.

Space? she thought. With all these deep woods and wide hills around me? . . . Space for Mo and Robert—for Finn and Chloë—for Beech and his animals . . . and for me? What more could I want?

'This is all the space I need,' she said, and laughed in the sun.

ELIZABETH WEBSTER

It was tragedy in her own life which prompted Elizabeth Webster to tackle such a heartbreaking subject as the death of a child. 'I lost my own son when he was two years old,' the author, now in her seventies, recalls. 'It was so traumatic for all the family, particularly my other three young children. It was a long while ago but it's taken me all this time to get to a stage where I felt able to write something which might be of comfort to others who are coping with bereavement. It's something people find so hard to talk about.'

Elizabeth Webster has never been afraid to tackle difficult subjects in her writing, always starting with a theme that interests her and then developing the characters and plot. In the past she has explored such demanding themes as wife-battering in *The Flight of the Swan* and environmental conservation in *Dolphin Sunrise*, always with the same ability to move the reader through sympathetic characters.

Turning to novel-writing relatively late in life, Elizabeth Webster can't remember a time when she hasn't been writing. 'I wrote plays for the other children when I was at school, and then when I started teaching myself I wrote plays for my pupils.' Music is another field in which Elizabeth Webster has been keen to compose her own material. The Japanese opera in *The Acorn Winter* is one she wrote and has staged many times with local children. 'Music means a lot to me. It's important because it can reach all sorts of people, especially disturbed children, like the ones in *The Acorn Winter*.'

Luckily for all her readers, Elizabeth Webster is hard at work on her next novel. And the theme? 'Well, it's inspired by the Bible story of the Good Samaritan,' she admits, 'but for more than that you'll have to wait and see.'

The SURVIVOR

The True Story of the Sinking of the *Doggerbank*

by HANS HERLIN

Translated from the German by John Brownjohn

When the German blockade-runner, *Doggerbank*, was torpedoed in the middle of the Atlantic, of the original 365 men on board only 14 survived. Adrift in a small dinghy with no food, no water, and a makeshift sail, their chances of survival were minimal.

Indeed, only one man lived to tell the tale. This is the story of that survivor—Fritz Kuert—who was determined to learn the answer to one burning question. Was the submarine that torpedoed his ship a German U-boat? He owes it to his shipmates to find out the truth.

Prologue

The city and lake of Geneva were shrouded in white, vaporous mist on January 16, 1944. It had started to snow towards midday, and fat snowflakes were drifting across the railway tracks leading into the Gare du Cornavin. All that could be seen of the name on the station signboard were Geneva's last three letters: '. . . ÈVE'. The hands of the clock were obscured by a coating of snow and ice.

Men and women wearing Red Cross armbands shivered as they stood waiting at two trestle tables, hot coffee steamed in big aluminium pots, Swiss soldiers stamped a little warmth into their feet on the crusty snow. The two prisoner-of-war specials were scheduled to arrive at 3pm.

As usual when an exchange of prisoners was to take place, the Red Cross had notified the Swiss military authorities and the German and American consulates. The American POWs had been brought to Konstanz from various camps in Germany; their German counterparts from the USA had been shipped across the Atlantic and put aboard a special train at Marseilles.

There was a shrill, piercing whistle in the distance: the train from Konstanz. It halted outside the station, just visible through the whirling whiteness.

Two men in black, fur-trimmed overcoats identified themselves to the sentries. The Swiss examined the German diplomats' papers politely but coolly. The American consular officials had earlier received a far more cordial reception.

The platform vibrated underfoot as the train from Konstanz pulled in. The tender of the German locomotive bore the regulation Propaganda Ministry slogan WHEELS MUST TURN FOR VICTORY! but this had been tactfully painted over for the occasion. The taller of the two Germans, whose cold-reddened cheeks were adorned with duelling scars, said, 'Our own boys should be arriving any time now.'

Doors burst open all along the train and eager figures jumped down onto the platform, filling the air with loud, exuberant American voices. The Swiss sentries hustled them back inside and closed the doors. The women with Red Cross armbands progressed from carriage to carriage with their aluminium coffeepots and cardboard cups.

The man with the scars produced a list of German POWs from the cuff of his overcoat. It was several sheets long and comprised 417 names. One entry on the third sheet was underlined in red: Surname Kuert, given names Fritz, Louise, August, Otto; born August 7, 1918; place of birth Lünen, Westphalia; nationality German; rank boatswain; last-known address, PW 2000 NA, Valley Forge PW Camp.

'That's our man. We don't have a personal description, but they'll call the roll. What we need is a decent photograph of him, so get ready with your Leica.'

'Why are they so keen on him?' asked the shorter of the two men, who had a camera dangling from his neck. 'Did he shoot his mouth off to the Yanks?'

A dark plume of vapour rose from the locomotive's smokestack. A coupling fell with a crash. The locomotive moved off, two armed sentries on the running boards. 'His ship was sunk,' the man with the duelling scars said tersely. 'He's the sole survivor.'

'What ship was that?'

'The *Doggerbank*.'

The locomotive disappeared into a flurry of snow.

'The *Doggerbank*?'

The man with the scars didn't reply. He set off along the train. The carriage windows were filmed with condensation. The wind whipped loose snow off the roofs onto the platform.

The snow-encrusted train from Marseilles had pulled into the platform alongside. The stretcher cases made their exit first, thickly swathed in blankets. Little puffs of frozen breath issued from their lips as Red Cross attendants carried them over to the train with the misted windows. The American POWs had vacated it and were waiting behind a rope strung across the platform. Silently, the other Germans emerged from the Marseilles train and stood in line at one of the tables, where Red Cross officials checked their names on a list.

Two prisoners approached the table. One was thin and pale, with the fixed gaze of a blind man. 'Kürzinger,' he said, 'Josef.'

The other man, who was guiding him, wore a strange mishmash of uniforms: a long U-boat greatcoat, a thick white woollen scarf, and the cap of a master in the merchant marine. His face was framed by a luxuriant beard. When he spoke, he displayed five gold teeth. 'Kuert, Fritz,' he said, 'boatswain.' He made a civilian impression, in spite of his peculiar uniform.

'Next!'

The man named Kuert led his blind companion over to the train, helped him onto the step, handed him his suitcase. Once on board, he turned and looked back. One of the men in dark overcoats had raised his camera. He clicked the button, wound the film on, and clicked the button again. Kuert gave an automatic smile into the camera and said, 'Do I get a copy?'

The men in the fur-trimmed overcoats headed for the exit. Names were still being called out behind them. A railwayman was making his way along the platform, freeing frozen brake shoes with a long-handled hammer.

'Well?' said the man with the duelling scars.

'He didn't seem to mind being photographed. He actually smiled for the camera.'

Outside in the Place du Cornavin their driver was waiting for them. Newspaper sellers were shouting the headlines of the evening editions. The Germans' faces turned to stone.

'Red Army breakthrough on the Vistula!'

'German Ardennes offensive halted!'

The two diplomats sat stiffly in the back of the car. They didn't look at each other, merely stared out at Geneva's broad, brightly lit streets.

The long line of carriages left the station and disappeared into the murk. Kürzinger and Kuert were installed in window seats. The lake made a brief appearance, wreathed in mist.

'The lake's on our left,' Kuert said. 'Looks like grey soup. You can hardly see a thing.' He had grown accustomed to describing everything for the blind man's benefit. The compartments were hushed. Apart from the footsteps of an occasional passer-by in the corridor, nothing could be heard but the sound of the speeding train. Dark shapes loomed up on the right: mountains.

'Just think,' said Kuert, 'you'll be home by tonight.'

'With luck.' Josef Kürzinger came from Radolfzell, a small

German town near the Swiss border. He had been a schoolmaster there before the war. Wounded by a shell splinter during the North African campaign, he would never see again. 'Sure you won't come with me?'

'I've got to get this business settled first,' Kuert said. There was little the two men didn't know about each other. They had occupied adjoining beds in the hospital ward in Philadelphia.

Kuert felt for the haversack slung around his neck, his only piece of luggage. His hands were badly scarred. He leaned forward as though the other man could see him. 'First, I've got to find out exactly what happened. I want to know who sank us.'

'You'll talk yourself into a whole heap of trouble,' said the blind man.

'I'm the only one left—the only one out of three hundred and sixty-five!'

'Asking awkward questions won't bring them back to life.'

'I promised! I've got to speak for them. No one else can.'

The shadows lengthened, gradually immersing the compartment in gloom. All that broke the silence was the monotonous clank and rattle of the wheels.

'At least give me the diary,' the blind man said eventually. 'It'll be safe with me.'

They had written it together. Kuert had told Josef his story in the hospital, and the schoolmaster had advised him to put it down on paper, all of it, from first to last.

'Be sensible, Fritz. They'll put the fear of God into you.'

'I don't scare that easy.' Kuert couldn't imagine ever being scared again, not after what he'd been through. He brought out the notebook in its oilskin wrapper and weighed it hesitantly in his scarred hands. 'Promise me.'

'I won't let it out of my possession. I'll keep it till you need it.'

Kuert put the notebook in the blind man's suitcase and returned to his corner seat. It was now almost dark outside. The ceiling light had come on. They said no more.

Kuert dozed fitfully until Josef shook him by the knee, then sat up with a jerk, shivering despite his submariner's greatcoat. 'Don't tell me we're there already?'

'Listen!' A wry smile had appeared on the blind man's face.

Kuert could hear voices. More precisely, a tone of voice he had never thought to hear again. He lowered the window—Konstanz. They were back in Germany. Pinpoints of light came bobbing along the darkened platform. He recognised the German MPs by the metal gorgets on their chests. One of them came to an abrupt halt outside the window.

'You, there! Are you crazy? Douse that light!' Kuert pulled the blind down fast. Outside, the raucous voice went on. 'Anyone'd think they'd never heard of the blackout.'

Kuert lifted Josef's suitcase down off the rack. The blind man was still smiling. 'We're home all right,' he said.

A FORTNIGHT LATER Boatswain Fritz Kuert was escorted to the admiral's office by two naval ratings.

It was a dismal day. The snow descending on the barrack square at Buxtehude, headquarters of Naval Operations, turned to grey slush as soon as it touched the ground.

Kuert waited outside in the passage while one of the seamen announced him.

'Boatswain Kuert of the *Doggerbank*, sir.'

'Send him in.'

Kuert marched in and saluted.

The admiral indicated the chair in front of his desk. He took a file from his flag lieutenant. 'I'll see this man alone,' he said. He had peculiarly bright, pale blue eyes, and his hair was white with a yellowish tinge. The flag lieutenant and the seaman left the room.

The admiral leaned forward. 'I want us to be absolutely frank with each other,' he said, doing his best to strike a genial, paternal note. 'Nothing we say leaves this room, is that clear?' He opened the file and smoothed the sheets with his palm. 'Unpleasant business, this. I'm anxious to dispose of it as quickly as possible.'

Kuert said nothing. *The bastards sank us!* he thought. It occurred to him that those were the first words Stachnovski had uttered when he fished him out of the water after they were torpedoed, but he kept the thought to himself. He could feel the heat of the cast-iron stove on his back. His throat was parched, constricted. He transferred his gaze to the rows of medal ribbons on the admiral's chest. He had an urge to shout, to bawl out everything he'd meant to say, but he couldn't get his tongue to work. 'It's because of my shipmates, sir, that's all.' That was as much as his anger and agitation would allow him to say.

'How old are you, Kuert?'

'Twenty-six, sir.'

'Old enough not to go around telling wild tales and asking foolish questions. You're a serviceman, after all.'

'I've never been a serviceman.'

'What do you mean?'

'I'm a merchant seaman, sir. The merchant marine may be on attachment to the navy, but we're an outfit of our own.'

The admiral shook his head. For the first time, his voice became tinged with annoyance. 'We're all servicemen these days.' He picked up his glasses but didn't put them on as he leafed through the file on his desk. 'We investigated this matter thoroughly.' He looked up. 'At first we couldn't account for the *Doggerbank*'s disappearance. Then came word that a survivor had been picked up. It wasn't until that Spanish tanker fished you out and took you to Aruba that we knew for sure she'd been sunk.'

Kuert sat there stiffly, expectantly. He was becoming less and less mindful of his surroundings. He was more than ever conscious of the presence of his dead shipmates. He felt himself to be their representative, their spokesman—the sole surviving witness.

'We checked the date,' he heard the admiral say. 'Only one of our submarines reported a sinking on March 3, 1943, and that was *U43*. We summoned the captain to Berlin. After questioning him, we were forced to conclude that—' He broke off. 'What's the matter?'

'So it's true!' Kuert gripped the edge of the desk. 'It *was* one of ours! Who was the captain? Who did for us? What's his name?'

The admiral had turned pale. 'I assumed you already knew,' he said sharply, 'from the way you've been spreading the word.'

'We had our suspicions, but we weren't sure, any of us.' Rage and despair at the others' death had loosened Kuert's tongue. 'He didn't stop to rescue a single one of us! Who was the swine? Who pumped three torpedoes into us and then made himself scarce?'

'Pull yourself together, man!' The admiral's face had stiffened. 'The case is closed. Our inquiry absolved the U-boat commander of all blame. He acted under a misapprehension, a regrettable misapprehension. If you'll take my advice . . .'

As he listened to the admiral, it occurred to Kuert that they were talking at cross-purposes. Three hundred and sixty-four men had died a miserable death. Some of them had been drowned or burned alive, others had abandoned all hope of rescue and killed themselves. *A misapprehension.* Was that all? An official report, a few sheets of paper, a figure: 364, one more item in a mass of statistics? And he was expected to keep his mouth shut.

The words came out without his realising it or grasping the enormity of the situation: an insignificant boatswain in the merchant marine was crossing swords with an admiral in Naval Operations. 'So that's what wiped out the crew of the *Doggerbank*, a misapprehension! Stop hedging and tell me his name!'

The admiral straightened up. 'That's enough!' he snapped. 'God Almighty, man! The fate of our country is hanging in the balance, and you have the effrontery to put your personal concerns first! I had hoped we could settle this matter between the two of us. I can understand your speaking out on behalf of your shipmates, but—' He pressed a buzzer. 'I'm sorry, Kuert, you've only yourself to blame.'

Half an hour later he was escorted back across the barrack square, not by naval ratings this time but by two men in the grey-green uniform of the *Sicherheitsdienst*, the Security Service of Himmler's SS. The snow was falling more heavily, but it still hadn't settled. The interview with the admiral seemed unreal, as if it had never taken place. His neck was at stake now, and the realisation had galvanised him. At least he had learned one thing, the number of the submarine: *U43*. It wouldn't be hard to discover the captain's name.

They escorted him into an austere, sparsely furnished office. The man behind the desk said nothing, just pointed to the chair facing him. The collar of his uniform tunic was open. In addition to the 'SD' badge on his left sleeve, he wore shoulder straps adorned with two pips. Kuert didn't know what grade the pips denoted—but the man's rank was unimportant. His smooth, bland face and inscrutable expression, neither hostile nor friendly, were sufficient identification. He simply sat there, regarding Kuert with almost clinical interest. In front of him lay the file that had been on the admiral's desk.

A typewriter could be heard in the adjoining room. The man behind the desk got up and went over to the door.

'How's it going?'

'Nearly finished.'

'Bring it in as soon as it's ready for signature. He's here.' The SD man returned to his desk and stood looking down at Kuert. 'I've read the report. Twenty-six days adrift in the Atlantic without food or water. You must have been tough to survive.' His voice was like his face, bland and unemotional. 'When did the Americans first interrogate you?'

'At Aruba.'

'How much did you tell them?'

'There wasn't much to tell.'

'Enough for the BBC to report that the *Doggerbank* had been sunk by a German submarine.'

This was news to Kuert. He flinched as if an unseen chasm had yawned at his feet. Tense and wary now, he hesitated before speaking again. His instinct for self-preservation was functioning again. It had saved his life more than once. 'They must have figured it out for themselves. It can't have been that difficult. Maybe they picked up some radio messages. They couldn't have got it from me, anyway.'

'Really? Why not?'

'Because we didn't know the sub was one of ours. I only found out myself half an hour ago. We had our suspicions, but that's all.'

'And you aired those suspicions?'

'No. Who's going to admit his ship took three torpedoes from a friendly submarine?'

'Smart as well as tough, eh? The fact remains, the BBC did broadcast that report. Supplying the enemy with information capable of being used to the detriment of the Fatherland. That's one interpretation of your conduct. Men have been executed for less.'

The SD man hadn't raised his voice. His slightly parted lips were set in a frigid smile. The typewriter stopped clattering next door; the clerk came in with some typewritten sheets and handed them over. The SD man took them from him with barely a glance and spread them out on the desk. He unscrewed the cap of an ink bottle and pointed to a pen. 'Perhaps you'd like to sign these,' he said, 'being as smart as you are.'

It wasn't a lengthy document. He, Fritz Kuert, solemnly undertook never to discuss the circumstances of the *Doggerbank*'s sinking. Date, place and a dotted line for his signature.

Kuert took the pen and signed. It was only a scrap of paper, after all. If he could survive twenty-six days in an open boat, he could survive this too.

'Now do I get to go on leave?' he asked.

'We'll be needing you for a little while longer, Kuert. We've got a few more questions for you.'

'But—'

'Consider yourself under open arrest,' the SD man cut in. 'You're a bit *too* smart for my liking, Kuert, and it's easy enough to sign a piece of paper. Your case has been referred to us, so we want to wrap it up for good.'

A WEEK LATER he was taken under guard to Jachmann Barracks at Wilhelmshaven. He remained under open arrest but was free to move around inside the barracks themselves.

Here he was subjected to further interrogation by SD personnel. They kept harping on the broadcast from London, and their questions always followed the same pattern. How much had he told the Americans? How could he have known it was a German submarine that sank the *Doggerbank*? With whom had he discussed the matter?

Escape was Kuert's sole preoccupation, and after three weeks an unforeseen opportunity presented itself.

The air-raid warning had sounded that night, as it so often did, but Kuert could not be induced to take refuge in the shelter. Air-raid shelters were for landlubbers. He was every inch a seaman, and experience had taught him that a seaman's chances of survival were worse below deck. The few extra seconds required to reach the open air in an emergency could spell the difference between life and death.

Tonight, having stationed himself in his usual place near the door when the air-raid siren sounded, he was accosted by an unknown petty officer.

'I've been hoping for a word with you. You must have known Werner Gernhöfer. He was with you aboard the *Doggerbank*.'

The petty officer was a man in his forties. His broad, weather-beaten countenance inspired trust, but then if the SD were setting a trap, this was just the type they would let loose on him.

'How did you know about the *Doggerbank*?' he asked warily.

'These things get around,' said the petty officer. 'I'm not being nosy, you understand. It's just that, well, Werner was a pal of mine. His wife and parents are living here in Wilhelmshaven.'

They'd be bound to have some civilian clothes, Kuert reflected. He wouldn't stand a chance in this naval uniform they'd made him wear. If he wore civvies he might just get away with it.

'All they received was a brief notification,' the petty officer went on. 'It simply said the ship went down with all hands. I told old man Gernhöfer about you. He'd like to meet you.'

'I'm confined to barracks.'

'So I gather,' said the petty officer, 'but let me worry about that.'

'All right, you're on.'

'Fine, see you this time tomorrow night.'

His misgivings revived as soon as the man had gone. They remained with him all the following day. The petty officer turned up just before eight. Kuert followed him in silence. It was only a hundred yards across the barrack square to the guardhouse. His companion nodded to the sentries. Then they were outside.

IT WAS A MODEST HOUSE situated in a side street. Werner Gernhöfer's wife and parents had assembled in the living room. Spread out on a table were photographs of Werner. Kuert was prevailed on to tell them about the *Doggerbank*'s last voyage. He described the crossing-the-line ceremony, their arrival in Japan, the time they had spent in Yokohama while the ship was taking on cargo, the judo lessons, the craze for gold teeth. He showed them his own five gold teeth engraved with dragons' heads. He recounted incidents he had almost forgotten, embellishing them to avoid having to tell the truth.

The two women sat there, outwardly composed, but their composure was only a thin veneer superimposed on grief and despair. One ill-judged word, and they would both have burst into tears.

At last the petty officer came to his rescue. They must go, he said. They had to get back before the sentries changed.

Gernhöfer's father saw them out. He shut the living-room door behind him. 'How did Werner die?' He stood there, a white-haired man leaning on a stick. 'I'd sooner know the truth.'

Kuert told him, but only in broad outline. He embellished the facts yet again.

'Werner made it into the dinghy. He was one of the first to die. Of thirst and exhaustion. The first to go died easier than the rest.' Kuert's thoughts kept returning to the clothes. He had to ask about the clothes.

'I wanted to beg a favour,' he said eventually. 'I need some civvies—a jacket and a pair of trousers. I'll return them to you.'

The old man limped over to a cupboard, leaning on his stick. 'Take whatever you need. You're just about Werner's size. His things ought to fit you.'

Kuert selected a jacket and a pair of slacks. The old man brought him some wrapping paper and a piece of string. At the front door he said, 'They're not to be trifled with, those people. I hope you make it, my boy.'

HIS CHANCE TO ESCAPE came three days later, when Allied bombers launched their heaviest raid on Wilhelmshaven to date. He was at his usual post in the entrance to the barrack block. The sirens were wailing. Searchlights groped their way across the low cloud cover, antiaircraft guns opened up. The crump of falling bombs, distant at first, drew nearer. Then a stick of five straddled the barracks. The force of the explosions sent Kuert sprawling. He scrambled to his feet, dashed to his room and put on the civilian clothes. He concealed his uniform under the mattress and made his way outside.

The bombs had completely flattened the guardhouse beside the gates leading to the main road. A building was on fire nearby. He set off at a run, oblivious of everything save his single-minded determination to get out of the city, out on the open road. He ran, panting hard, through the blazing streets.

At last he paused in a field. The thunder of the antiaircraft guns had died away, the sky behind him was crimson. Darkness closed in, strangely still and menacing. All he could hear was the distant hum of departing bombers high overhead.

By day he slept in isolated haystacks or woods; at night he trudged on, keeping to the minor roads. He reached Hamburg on the morning of the fifth day. He was now on familiar territory, having often signed on at Hamburg in the past. He waited for nightfall before making his way to the house in Sierichstrasse.

He was in luck. Harry Purrmann, a seaman like himself and thoroughly trustworthy, was at home. They had sailed together many times. But Purrmann couldn't hide him. His ship was sailing in the morning, and the landlord was an enthusiastic Nazi, a snooper. Purrmann went off in search of somewhere Kuert could lie low.

He was back within a couple of hours. 'I've got just the man, a ship's engineer, but he'd like to take a look at you before he decides.'

A fourth-floor flat in Jungfrauenthal, a Hamburg suburb. Hugo Schulz looked Kuert over and asked a few questions. Then he nodded: the fugitive was welcome to stay.

They fixed him up a bed in the roof space. There were air raids almost nightly, but he had to remain there. He couldn't afford to show his face or leave his hiding place, not ever.

Sometimes his meals were brought to him by a girl. Sometimes, though only for a few minutes, Schulz himself came bearing the latest news of the Allied advance. Kuert spent the rest of the time alone, alone day and night with his memories of the *Doggerbank*. He would awake in the small hours, haunted by horrific visions. And, as he lay there in the darkness, his shipmates would come alive once more.

PART ONE

The Ship

He had never forgotten the morning he first saw the *Doggerbank* in mid Atlantic. The date was June 23, 1942, the place a rendezvous codenamed 'Nelke' (Carnation). It was there, southwest of the Cape Verde Islands at 13°N, 26°W, that the *Charlotte Schliemann*, a tanker laden to the gunwales with fuel oil, spare parts and provisions, had been replenishing some U-boats.

Boatswain Fritz Kuert could still remember every detail of that fine, windless morning: the pots of mouse-grey paint with which they were daubing the *Charlotte Schliemann*'s wireless office, the dark blue sea with its long Atlantic swell, and the moment when the ship emerged from the haze that veiled the horizon like a gauze curtain.

Off-watch members of the tanker's crew lined the rail as the vessel slowly approached. Kuert had joined the two forecastle lookouts, who were observing the new arrival through binoculars.

'Hey,' said one of them, 'what a shabby old tub!' Kuert would have asked to borrow his glasses, but he still felt like an outsider aboard the *Charlotte Schliemann* and had few friends among the crew. The tanker had inspired him with instant dislike.

The 'shabby old tub' drew steadily nearer. Kuert would have guessed her to be a British boat from her silhouette, which displayed a typically flush deck-line running from stem to stern. The approaching vessel had clearly been a long time at sea. They'd given her a lick of grey paint at some stage, but the original paintwork was showing through: black on the hull, canary yellow on the upperworks. The bow bore no name that he could see, nor was there any port of registry visible on the stern. The odd-looking vessel's approach hadn't signalled a call to action stations, however, so he concluded that the *Charlotte Schliemann*'s skipper must be expecting her.

She went astern and stopped, riding the long swell barely a cable's length away. Kuert saw a signalman on the wing of the nameless vessel's bridge flash a message, heard an engine start up. Moments later a launch rounded the black and grey bow.

Kuert was standing near the accommodation ladder when the launch made fast to the side of the *Charlotte Schliemann*. As soon as the officer from the strange ship came aboard he hailed the young seaman who had remained in the launch. The youngster was wearing white ducks and an open-necked white shirt, the hot-weather uniform of the merchant marine. His thin, pale face had never seen a razor. A ship's boy probably, sixteen at most.

'Hey, what ship are you?' Kuert asked.

'Us?' The youngster glanced back over his shoulder. 'We're the *Doggerbank*.'

Kuert was a good judge of his fellow seamen. From the way this one had looked at his ship and the way his eyes lit up, he could tell that the *Doggerbank* was a good ship despite her shabby exterior.

'Foreign-built?' Kuert asked.

'British,' the young seaman replied. 'Captured in the Indian Ocean a year ago. Used to be the *Speybank*. Now she's the *Doggerbank*.'

'Any more of you from the merchant marine?' Kuert asked.

'The whole crew.'

'Who owns her?'

'Hansa.'

Kuert stared fixedly at the ship as she rode the swell. He absorbed her every detail: the bridge superstructure, the two masts, the derricks, the lifeboats, the gun in the stern, the men leaning on the rail.

'Who's your skipper?'

'Our captain? Schneidewind.'

'Paul Schneidewind? Of the *Tannenfels*?'

'Could be. Nearly all our lot are former Fels-folk.'

The *Tannenfels*, *Geierfels*, *Freienfels* and *Reichenfels* were all Hansa ships in which Kuert had sailed in the past. He continued to gaze at the *Doggerbank*. He now saw her with other eyes: to him she seemed beautiful beyond words.

'Who's your mate?' he asked.

'Karl Gaides.' The boy looked at him curiously.

'What about the cargo master?'

'His name's Johnny Jahr.'

'And the cook?'

'Our cook—' started the boy.

'Don't tell me: Jan Bahrend! The best-loved, most-hated cook on the Atlantic run. Still got a thing about sauerkraut, eh? That only leaves Papa Boywitt and Polack Stachnovski.'

'They're all on board.'

'The whole bunch? You don't say!' The floating slum had metamorphosed itself into the finest vessel Kuert had ever set eyes on. 'Are you the ship's boy?'

The youngster nodded. 'My name's Waldemar Ring.'

'Right, Waldemar: as soon as you get back, have a word with one of them, preferably Karl Gaides or Johnny Jahr. Tell them this is the lousiest berth I've ever had. No laughs, no kindred spirits. They've got to get me off this tub. I want out, understand?'

'I'll try. What name shall I say?'

'Tell them "For Fatherland and *lire*".' That had been their slogan in the days when they were paid in Italian currency for ferrying troops and equipment from Italy to the North African front.

' "For Fatherland and *lire*"?'

'Yes, lad, and I'm Signor *Lire* in person.'

An hour later Johnny Jahr came over in the launch; three hours later the *Charlotte Schliemann*'s second mate sent for Kuert and announced that Captain Schneidewind urgently needed a boatswain and had asked the skipper to let him go. 'They seem to think pretty highly of you,' the second mate added rather sourly.

Kuert stifled a retort and just waited for his papers. Then he packed his things. The most important item was a homemade survival kit. It always lay ready to hand at the foot of his bunk, a broad belt of stiff sailcloth with a clasp-knife and canteen attached, the latter permanently filled with rum. He donned the belt every night before turning in and wore it whenever things got hairy.

Kuert buckled on his survival belt, picked up his suitcase and headed for the accommodation ladder.

He stood with his legs braced apart as the launch cut through the long swell, ducking to avoid occasional showers of spray. All his attention was centred on the *Doggerbank*. They threw a line and a Jacob's ladder over the rail. He was halfway up the ladder before the boat had even made fast.

THEY HAD ALL TURNED OUT to welcome him: Karl Gaides, the *Doggerbank*'s mate, wearing shorts and stripped to the waist, a walking museum of the tattooist's art; 'Polack' Stachnovski, reddish-blond but still beardless except for a few sparse hairs between his chin and lower lip; Jan Bahrend, the cook with German and American nationality, elegant as ever in his silk shirt and starched chef's hat; and Karl 'Papa' Boywitt, the silent, self-effacing trawlerman. The rest were new to him.

Their faces were grey, the faces of men long at sea, weary and lined with many days and nights of nervous tension.

'Oh, rats,' said Jan Bahrend in English, 'if it isn't Signor *Lire*! All we needed.' He beamed all over his face.

'Fritz!' Stachnovski gripped Kuert by the shoulders, spun him around, scrutinised the survival belt. 'It's our Fritz all right, complete with all the trimmings.'

Karl Gaides stepped forward and put his hands on his hips. 'Boatswain Kuert,' he said in an assumed voice, 'what are you doing here again?'

It was a perfect imitation of someone familiar to every merchant seaman in the Mediterranean: Commander Koch of the maritime personnel office at Naples. Koch, who was responsible for crew allocation, had eventually assigned Kuert to shore duties because he had been sunk four times in the space of a year. Four of the ships in which he had sailed had been torpedoed by enemy submarines or bombed by enemy aircraft. His former shipmates had witnessed the scene in the personnel office which Gaides was now re-enacting.

Gaides threw up his hands. 'I'm not letting you set foot in another ship, Boatswain Kuert! Out of my sight, I never want to see you here again! Every ship I assign you to goes down.'

'No more ships for you, Boatswain Kuert!' Stachnovski yelled. Then they all crowded round, shook his hand, bombarded him with questions. Standing there in their midst, with their friendly laughter ringing in his ears, he felt at home.

Later he discovered that in the crew's eyes the *Doggerbank* had become a legend, a lucky ship capable of the most foolhardy exploits and commanded by a skipper who was a credit to his profession: Paul Schneidewind, a man seemingly without nerves, forever spick and span in his merchant-marine tunic with the captain's four rings, as if it were still peacetime. He was liked and respected for his imperturbability, his lack of rank-consciousness and the way in which he combined tolerance with discipline.

On June 27, 1942, four days after Boatswain Fritz Kuert had transferred from the *Charlotte Schliemann* to the *Doggerbank*, Captain Schneidewind received a signal ordering him to Japan. In August the *Doggerbank* reached Yokohama and underwent a refit.

On November 30 an explosion had devastated a German ship berthed at Yokohama, killing 56 and injuring hundreds of men. The *Doggerbank* had taken all the walking wounded on board before sailing. There were over 200 of them, so the *Doggerbank*, with a normal complement of 109, was carrying a total of 365 men.

She left the Japanese port on December 17, having been converted into a blockade-runner, one of the lightly armed vessels that sneaked past Allied naval patrols carrying cargoes essential to the German war effort, mainly raw materials. Thereafter she put in at Kobe on December 19, Saigon on December 30, Singapore on January 7, 1943, and Batavia (now renamed Jakarta) on January 10. At all these ports the *Doggerbank* took on valuable items: fats, oils, precious metals, crude rubber. Then, fully laden, she set off on the long and perilous voyage home. Her destination was the port of Bordeaux, over 10,000 miles away.

The *Doggerbank* rounded the Cape of Good Hope and successfully negotiated the Atlantic 'narrows' between West Africa and Brazil, an exceptionally hazardous sea area patrolled by Allied aircraft.

At the end of January the ship was overflown by an American Liberator. The crew spread a Union Jack on deck, and the imposture worked as so often before. By the third day of March 1943, the *Doggerbank* was nearing the Azores. Thanks to fine weather and favourable currents, she had made better time than on the outward voyage. Not a masthead, not an aircraft was in sight. The sparkling, dark blue sea revealed no sign of life.

THE WATCHES HAD CHANGED at noon. The lookouts silently manned their posts. At 12.10 Seaman Richard Binder looked down from his perch on the foremast crow's-nest, sixty feet above the deck.

'Nothing in sight!'

The crow's-nest lookout had reported nothing else for the past week, ever since they crossed the Equator, but everyone knew that appearances could be deceptive. Here in the North Atlantic the risk of being detected by enemy aircraft was many times greater than it had been further south.

No one knew that better than the skipper. Paul Schneidewind had been on the bridge for hours. As he swept the horizon yet again with his binoculars, he couldn't banish the thought of what might happen at any time. Visions of sinking ships and drowning men preyed on his mind and had left their mark on his face, which was strained and hollow-cheeked with fatigue. He was in his early forties but looked ten years older.

'This weather isn't going to hold.' Langhinrichs, the first officer, was standing beside the captain with a signalman and lookouts close at hand.

A few pale feathery clouds were gathering in the west. Schneidewind lowered his glasses and nodded silently. There was nothing to be heard but the pounding of the engines and the hiss of foam along the hull.

'We're getting pretty near the Azores, sir,' said Langhinrichs. 'How soon do you think we'll pick up our escort?'

They were rapidly approaching the sea area where a German submarine had been instructed to assume protection of the ship and her precious cargo. The *Doggerbank* was to make for Bordeaux across the Bay of Biscay, an exceptionally dangerous part of the voyage.

'Today or tomorrow, I reckon. Keep your eyes skinned.' Schneidewind nodded to the lookouts and retired to the chart-house.

'Course zero-three-five,' the helmsman reported. Hans Hencke was a beanpole of a man at least six foot six inches tall.

'Very good.' Although every British ship bound for England from West Africa steered this course, Schneidewind's choice of route was deliberate. The *Doggerbank* not only behaved like a Britisher; she really was one, in a sense, having been built on Clydeside in 1926 and named the *Speybank*. Over the years the yard had turned out seventeen ships of the same class, vessels as alike as peas in a pod, so Schneidewind had a wide variety of genuine names to choose from. This capacity for disguise was his ship's greatest asset, and one that had many times saved her from destruction.

LEFT: The proud Kuert parents with their baby son Fritz in 1918.

RIGHT: Fritz Kuert at the age of six.

BELOW: Fritz Kuert at the helm of the *Brake* in 1938.

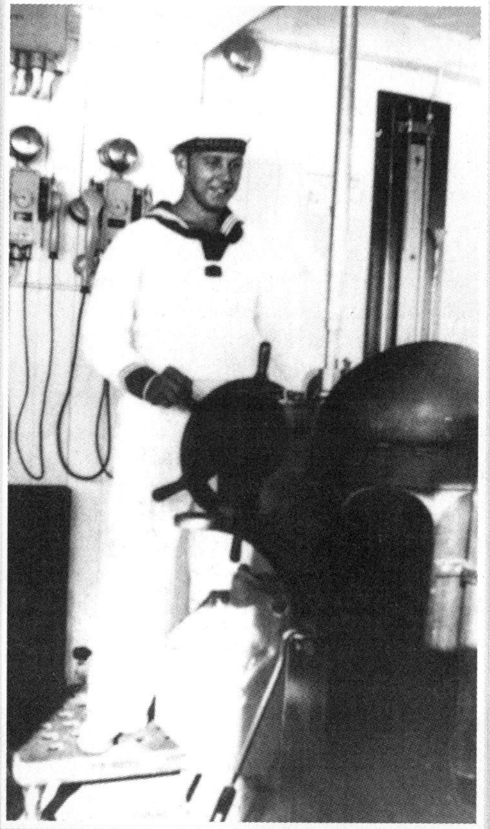

ABOVE: Fritz Kuert as boatswain of the *Charlotte Schliemann* at Las Palmas in 1942.

The crow's-nest lookout, who had orders to report every ten minutes, sang out his ritual 'Nothing in sight!'

It was 12.20pm, ten minutes before the submarine surfaced.

BOYWITT HAD GONE AFT to his quarters above the tiller flat, which he shared with Karl Gaides, Stachnovski, Jan Bahrend and Kuert.

'Have you eaten yet?' Kuert asked him. At twenty-five, he was the youngest of them.

Boywitt shook his head. 'Not hungry.' He stretched out with his arms behind his head and stared into space. They didn't call him 'Papa' for nothing. Older than all of them except Bahrend, he was a quiet, taciturn man who kept himself to himself. He said his prayers night and morning, kneeling beside his bunk as if he were quite alone, but no one would ever have dared to tease him about it.

'I'll bring you something,' Kuert said.

It was the usual Saturday midday meal, smoked ham with sauerkraut and fried potatoes. When Kuert returned with two helpings, Stachnovski rolled over on his bunk and stuck his hand out.

'I'll have that.'

Kuert cocked an eyebrow at Boywitt, who nodded.

'He's welcome to it.'

Having wolfed the lot, Stachnovski put the tin plate on the floor beside two others. He was permanently hungry, however much he ate, but he never gained a pound.

'How I hate sauerkraut!' Jan Bahrend thrust his plate aside in disgust with his foot. 'Damned cabbage-guzzlers,' he said, and then, switching into English: 'nothing but damned kraut-eaters!'

Other German seamen tended to garnish their native tongue with snippets of English, whereas Bahrend spoke English garnished with snippets of German. He had spent thirty years of his life in America, and had acquired US citizenship. Not far off sixty by the time the Second World War broke out, he had made an impulsive and adventurous return to his native land.

Jan Bahrend's stint as the ship's cook had been terminated at Yokohama. It wasn't that he couldn't cook. He had owned a restaurant in New York. The trouble was that Bahrend couldn't make do with anything less than a superabundance of all ingredients, so the meagre, carefully computed rations aboard a ship like the *Doggerbank* had defeated him from the start. He had produced the most sumptuous meals, but only for a week or two. After that Bahrend had used up the bulk of his stores.

Replaced as cook by Schneidewind because of mutinous mutterings among the men, Bahrend was now an ordinary seaman. Even though the skipper let him continue to draw cook's pay, the demotion had badly wounded his self-esteem.

'Know something?' he said. 'When we get to Bordeaux I'm going to cook you a meal fit for a king. Thirteen courses, that's a promise!'

'For God's sake stop talking about food!' said Stachnovski.

He had gone over to Gaides's bunk. He was wearing a pair of Russian leather riding boots acquired in Japan and a huntsman's green jacket over his bare chest, on which a tattooed representation of the *Doggerbank* was faintly visible.

'Fritz did a rotten job on me,' he said. 'It didn't last. Three weeks, and there's almost nothing left.' For want of suitable ink, Kuert had tattooed Stachnovski's chest with engine-room soot. It looked quite good at first, but it had soon begun to fade. Stachnovski gazed admiringly at the tattoos on Gaides's torso. 'The fellow who did those,' he said, 'was a real artist.'

'I'll get you some decent soot next time,' Gaides told him. 'You used the wrong kind.'

Stachnovski turned to Kuert. 'You must have another go at it before Bordeaux.'

'Bordeaux?' Bahrend said. 'I wouldn't be so sure you'll see it again. Did any of you catch sight of Fujiyama when we sailed?'

Nobody spoke. They looked at him as he sat there, a tall, cadaverous figure with bushy grey eyebrows and pendulous cheeks. No one knew how seriously to take Jan Bahrend when he embarked on one of his yarns. Most of them were grim, sinister tales, all of which ended with their ship being sunk by torpedoes. His stories were popular nonetheless, especially the ones about his years in America. People would listen to him holding forth for hours on end, always with such an earnest, melancholy expression that they could never be certain whether or not he was pulling their leg.

'You know what the Japs say,' he went on. ' "He that sees the Sacred Mountain when he sails will come home safe." I didn't see it. Did *you*?'

They all preserved an uneasy silence. Already hot and stuffy, the air in their quarters seemed suddenly more so.

Abruptly the cramped compartment was filled with the sound of the ship's klaxon sounding action stations.

KUERT BUCKLED on his survival belt as he ran. The klaxon was still blaring when he reached the deck.

He could see Captain Schneidewind and his officers standing on the bridge with their glasses levelled. He himself could detect nothing on the mirrorlike surface of the sea.

When the klaxon died away he heard the crow's-nest lookout call, 'Still at green one-zero. Hard to make out at this range. Small vessel, no smoke. Could be a submarine, sir!'

Langhinrichs glanced at Schneidewind. 'What do you think, sir? Could it be *our* boat?'

Schneidewind took a quick look round. Gernhöfer had cleared his gun for action in the stern, and the pair of quadruple 20mm cannon flanking the bridge were fully manned.

He gave his messenger some steering orders for the helmsman, and they headed for the submarine in a wide arc that would put the *Doggerbank* down-sun of it.

'They must be fast asleep,' said Langhinrichs. He glanced back at the stern, where the 105mm gun was now trained on the stationary vessel. 'We could blow them out of the water.'

Lieutenant Fischer, who had joined them on the bridge, said, 'That's a German boat, no doubt about it. I know the class.'

Still no sign of life aboard the submarine. It lay there, glinting in the sunlight, like a ghost ship.

'Make the recognition signal,' Schneidewind said.

The German war ensign was run up the mainmast and an anchor ball displayed in the bow. A Manila rope with eight red fire hoses suspended from it was strung between the aftermast and the wireless room.

'Think they've got the message, Captain?' Langhinrichs looked back into the sun, which was high in the sky. 'Surely they must have spotted us by now?'

Schneidewind turned to the signalman. 'Aldis, please.'

The man hurried back with it. Schneidewind could sense them all watching as he climbed to the monkey island atop the chart-house. The old Morse signal lamp was part of the *Doggerbank*'s legend. Schneidewind had used it to bluff his way past a British cruiser when ordered to heave to and identify himself.

'WHAT SHIP?' the cruiser had signalled.

'BRITISH INVERBANK FROM NY BOUND DURBAN.'

He had played the same trick time and again. Once, having inadvertently found himself at dawn in the middle of an Allied convoy, he had spent the entire day in the guise of a British ship. On another occasion, using the same cover, he had taken his ship into the heavily guarded roads of Cape Town and laid enough mines to render that important Allied naval base unsafe for several months.

Almost lovingly, Schneidewind raised the lamp and signalled: 'WHAT IS WRONG? DO YOU HAVE ENGINE TROUBLE? CAN WE ASSIST?'

No reply.

Schneidewind could sense the others' eyes upon him. The fact that his men trusted him so implicitly only heightened his sense of responsibility. Only four lifeboats and four life rafts between 365 men! He considered the matter soberly, without panic, but could not suppress an uncharacteristic pang of fear. Whatever his decision, it was his alone to make. He couldn't check by radio with Naval Operations I, the section responsible for his ship: the British and Americans had Direction Finds stations all along the African coast and were able to plot a ship's position in minutes and with deadly accuracy.

Schneidewind wondered if this would prove to be the voyage on which his proverbial good luck finally ran out.

Back on the bridge he handed the lamp to the signaller and turned to the helmsman. 'Half ahead. Steer zero-three-five.' It was their original course.

Hencke repeated the order. 'Course zero-three-five.'

Schneidewind turned to Langhinrichs. 'Keep the men at action stations.' It was now 13.00. Half an hour had elapsed since the submarine was first sighted. He raised his binoculars. The submarine slowly receded until there was nothing in sight but sea, until the whole incident seemed an illusion.

Three hours later, at 15.55, the lookouts made another sighting. It wasn't the same submarine, but they were never to know that, any more than they knew that the *Doggerbank* had entered a sea area in which a group of seven U-boats was preparing to attack an Allied convoy.

None of the U-boats was expecting the *Doggerbank*. None had been informed of the recognition signal prearranged with Naval Operations. They were lying in wait for prey.

The sea area into which the *Doggerbank* was heading was not the traditional U-boat hunting-ground. That was the North Atlantic, whose principal supply routes were used by convoys from the United States to Britain and from there to Murmansk by way of the North Cape. At this stage, however, the U-boats in the North Atlantic had ceased to be the hunters and became the hunted. The defensive measures employed by the convoys' naval escorts had steadily improved, the U-boats were becoming obsolete. From October 1942 onwards, therefore, more and more German submarines had been withdrawn from the approaches to the British Isles. It was hoped that new improved U-boats with better weapons systems would soon be operational. Meanwhile, the focus of U-boat operations was shifted further south. Other U-boats were dispatched to the Mediterranean, where Germany's Afrika Korps was being hard pressed in Tunisia, their task being to halt, or at least disrupt, the flow of Allied supplies and reinforcements.

On February 27, 1943, the German Admiralty received intelligence of a westward-bound convoy. On March 1 a group of seven U-boats, the 'Tümmler' Group, was instructed to form a patrol line, or cordon, southwest of the Azores. The seven boats stationed themselves at intervals of thirty miles on a north–south axis, thereby covering the 180-mile stretch through which the convoy was likely to pass. The U-boat at the southern extremity of the patrol line, *U521*, was in all probability the one sighted on March 3 by the *Doggerbank*.

A copy of *U43*'s war diary, now preserved in the archives of the British Admiralty, records the time of the sighting as 17.00, broad daylight in other words. This fact has an important bearing on any assessment of subsequent events.

When the U-boat captain, Lieutenant Hans-Joachim Schwantke, sighted the *Doggerbank*'s faint plume of smoke through his binoculars, *U43* was some ten miles away. She was the first ship *U43* had sighted for weeks, and Schwantke left his place in the patrol line without a moment's hesitation. Proceeding on the surface, *U43* made its way towards the plume of smoke.

U43 was a celebrated, almost legendary submarine. Its previous commander had been Captain Wolfgang Lüth. During his active service he had sunk 46 merchantmen totalling over a quarter of a million tons, a destroyer and an enemy submarine. He had also torpedoed and damaged two battleships.

Hans-Joachim Schwantke, a native of Upper Silesia and twenty-five years old at this time, had inherited *U43* from Lüth in March 1942. Thereafter, luck seemed to have deserted the U-boat.

U43 had sailed from Lorient on January 9, 1943. Late in January *U43* and several other German submarines were deployed against Convoy UC1. The engagement lasted four days. *U43* had not only been unable to attack; it had sustained minor damage from depth charges. After two whole months at sea, its tally of torpedoes was still intact. Schwantke needed, indeed craved, a success.

The ship's masts were now clearly visible from the U-boat's bridge. Schwantke and his men scanned the horizon for other vessels.

'She seems to be on her own,' said the officer of the watch. The lookouts called the bearings down through the hatch. Below, the quartermaster sat over his charts, working out the ship's course. Finally he called up, 'Target's course northeast, no zigzag, speed approximately twelve knots.'

Did Schwantke never stop to wonder what a lone ship was doing in this sea area, let alone steering a straight course? Allied ships usually zigzagged their way across the Atlantic to make it harder for German submarines to attack them.

U43 was now so near that the ship's silhouette showed up crisply in Schwantke's binoculars. He recorded his observations. 'Vessel of 7,000 to 10,000 tons. Flush-decked. Foremast between hatches one and two. Bridge amidships, mainmast between hatches four and five.'

The details were passed to the officer of the watch, who had gone below and was consulting Lloyd's Register. Nothing broke the silence on the bridge until the man in the hatchway straightened up. 'Officer of the watch reports she could be the *Dunedin Star*, sir. Or a Blue Star liner. Almost certainly British.'

Schwantke passed his orders below. The bow-wave rose higher. *U43* was drawing ahead so as to gain bearing on the target and torpedo her at right angles to her course. This the U-boat could only do on the surface, its speed when submerged being insufficient. Schwantke was attacking by the book.

The unknown ship made no attempt to zigzag. Quite unsuspecting, she continued to hold her course, almost in the U-boat's wake. Would Schwantke realise his mistake at the last moment? Would something make him think twice? The ship's course? Her crowded deck? The red fire hoses suspended aft?

But Schwantke had no reason to suspect that this ship was a German blockade-runner. Sea areas in which such vessels were expected were declared no-go areas, which meant that U-boat commanders were debarred from attacking unescorted ships in those waters. Besides, a blockade-runner's expected position was notified several days in advance for safety's sake.

U43 had received no such notification.

THE SUBMARINE WAS ploughing along some two miles broad on the *Doggerbank*'s bow. Dusk was falling, but it was still light enough for the naked eye to discern its wake from the ship's bridge.

Any doubts Schneidewind may have entertained about the submarine's nationality had evaporated. It was a U-boat right enough, but why hadn't it acknowledged his original signal? For that matter, why didn't the boat identify itself even now?

Schneidewind, who knew nothing of the 'Tümmler' Group's seven U-boats, could only conclude that he was dealing with one and the same submarine. As for the staff officers of Naval Operations I, the section responsible for blockade-runners, they knew about the seven U-boats but were ignorant of the fact that the *Doggerbank* had reached the same sea area eight or nine days earlier than estimated. A signal had been sent to her captain on February 14, warning him not to cross the Equator before March 5, and it was taken for granted that this order had been received.

Schneidewind raised his glasses and took another look at the submarine. He was smartly turned out as usual. The peaked cap was snow white, the blue tunic with the four gold rings unmarred by a single crease. The others were awaiting his decision. At last he nodded to the first officer. 'You can secure the lifeboats.'

The faces around him relaxed. 'Aye aye, sir,' said Langhinrichs. 'What about the recognition signals?'

Schneidewind glanced at the eight red hoses suspended from the rope between the wireless room and the aftermast. 'Leave them where they are,' he decreed.

'And the guns?'

'The gun crews can stand down, but keep the lookouts on their toes.' He nodded to the others. 'I'll be in my cabin if I'm needed.'

THE SUBMARINE *U43* was still ploughing along. The *Doggerbank* was right in its wake. Kuert went below as soon as he had attended to the lifeboats. On his way to the galley he caught snatches of conversation. There was only one topic: their imminent homecoming.

Seamen being superstitious, this subject had so far been taboo. But now that the U-boat had appeared they all felt home and dry.

On his way aft Kuert bumped into Waldemar Ring, the ship's boy. Waldemar, who had joined the ship as a fifteen-year-old, looked little older now. He was a scrawny youth with spindly arms, and not much more than five foot tall. 'Hey, Fritz,' he said, 'do you realise? Another week and we'll be in Bordeaux. Just think, only another week!'

'You can hardly wait, eh?'

Waldemar looked down at the grey fox terrier winding around his legs. He and Leo, the ship's dog, were inseparable.

'I've been meaning to ask you something, Fritz. Do you think she'll write to me?'

Kuert could see, even in the dimly lit passage, that Waldemar's cheeks were crimson. Everyone on board knew the story of the ship's boy and Hanako.

Hanako was a Japanese girl, a prostitute in a Yokohama brothel. It was Stachnovski who had persuaded Waldemar to accompany him there, Stachnovski himself having run out of money to spend on whores. That was how Waldemar had met Hanako and fallen in love with her, although all he had done was sit there gazing at her and holding her hand.

'Sure she'll write to you,' Kuert told him.

'You really think so?'

Kuert eyed the little youngster with a trace of compassion. 'There could even be a letter from her on board, if she handed it in at the dockyard gates before we sailed. You'll get your letter when we reach Bordeaux, you'll see.' He didn't know why he was lying to the boy. It was unlike him.

'Stachnovski's looking for you,' Waldemar said, blushing even harder.

When Kuert entered the compartment above the tiller flat, Stachnovski was peering through the porthole. The *Doggerbank* was gliding almost silently, so it seemed, into the dusk. Kuert unbuckled his homemade survival belt and returned it to its usual place at the foot of his bunk. Taking off his lightweight leather shoes, he put them back in their box. The threat had receded. Besides, his nose for danger had never failed him in the past.

Stachnovski pointed to the faded tattoo on his chest. 'You've got to do me again, Fritz, for Bordeaux.' He indicated Gaides, who was lying on his bunk. 'He says you used the wrong kind of soot.'

'I'll mix you some more,' Gaides said. 'It won't fade this time, believe me. Waldemar, go and get some more soot.'

Kuert fetched the tattooing needles and the stencil of the *Doggerbank* in outline. Stachnovski held it up against the light on the deckhead. 'Lovely ship, isn't she? Could you do me a U-boat as well?'

Jan Bahrend was perched on the edge of his bunk. 'Know something?' he said solemnly. 'I don't like the look of that damned submarine. I don't like it one bit.'

He stretched out on his back with his knees drawn up. The bunk was too small for his lanky frame. No one spoke for a while. The air was filled with the monotonous, unchanging throb of the engines. Quite suddenly, Bahrend went on, 'We've had some good times together, haven't we? We've made it so far, but for how much longer? We've been too damned lucky. It's too good to last.'

Silence.

Waldemar Ring appeared with a tin mug of engine-room soot. Gaides, who had sent him for it, sat up in his bunk. 'OK, I'll fix the stuff so it holds, Fritz, but tattoo him somewhere else. I value my peace and quiet. If he hollers the way he did the last time . . .'

He broke off. The loudspeaker on the bulkhead had crackled into life.

It was nearly three months since Schneidewind had addressed the crew. They were well trained, and there hadn't been any untoward incidents. Everyone froze as his voice rang out, calm and composed as ever.

'We are now being escorted by a friendly submarine, but we must remain alert. I know I can rely on you to do just that.

'We shall soon be reaching our port of destination. I shall see to it that half the crew go on leave immediately. The rest will take their turn when the others are back. That's all.'

'Come on,' Stachnovski said, relieving Gaides of the mug of soot, now mixed into a paste. 'We'll be in the forecastle if you want us.'

Kuert picked up the stencil and needles and followed him out, leaving his survival belt and lightweight shoes at the foot of his bunk. Nothing could happen now, he felt sure, not on this voyage.

UP ON THE BRIDGE of *U43*, Hans-Joachim Schwantke turned to the officer of the watch. 'We'll attack from dived, just in case she isn't as unescorted as she seems. Let's go.'

Darkness seemed reluctant to fall, as if in league with the unknown ship astern of them, but they couldn't wait any longer. As part of the 'Tümmler' Group, *U43* had received a signal ordering it to close the convoy. If Schwantke was going to attack the lone ship at all, he had to do so now.

He waited until the last man had disappeared through the upper hatch, feeling a mixture of determination and anxiety. Determination to sink the ship at all costs, anxiety lest there was something suspect about the situation. It might be a trap. His instructors at Flotilla had repeatedly warned him against decoys, lone ships sailing in sea areas commonly traversed by enemy convoys. Armed with depth charges and the most up-to-date defensive aids, they were commanded by experienced British naval officers.

The ship, her dark shape standing out against the paler skyline, acquired a sudden look of menace. Schwantke secured the upper hatch. Moments later he heard the waves breaking over the forecasing.

U43 went to ninety feet and levelled off. There was no sound but the gentle hum of the electric motors. The U-boat had turned and was slowly manoeuvring into an attacking position.

The hydrophone operator called out a long string of bearings.

Schwantke put up the periscope. 'Course still zero-three-five,' the quartermaster reported.

Schwantke's misgivings revived. He found the ship's unruffled behaviour disquieting. 'Periscope depth,' he said.

Tilting his cap back, he peered through the eyepieces. The ship's dark silhouette was growing steadily broader.

'Flood tubes one to three,' Schwantke ordered. As if he felt it necessary to explain why he was so hell-bent on putting three torpedoes into the ship when one would have been sufficient to seal her fate, he added: 'Better make absolutely sure of her.'

TATTOOING WAS WELL UNDER WAY in the forecastle. The younger seamen, who had gathered round to watch, were highly amused whenever Stachnovski grimaced with pain.

'Are you making a decent job of it this time?' He was seated on a stool, stripped to the waist and holding the stencil against his chest while Kuert knelt in front of him. 'Ouch!'

'Keep still!' Kuert dipped his needle in the black paste and continued to puncture Stachnovski's skin through the stencil. 'Pity you don't have a bit more flesh on your ribs. I've never known anyone eat so much and stay so thin.'

'Just do me a nice ship,' Stachnovski said.

'Don't worry,' Kuert told him, 'the girls'll love it.' They were all in high spirits and making preparations for their homecoming.

Kuert caught sight of Waldemar Ring in the bulkhead doorway with Leo, the ship's dog, nestling against his legs.

'That reminds me, Polack,' he said to Stachnovski, 'keep an eye on young Waldemar. He's dead serious about that Japanese tart.'

'Nice girl, Hanako,' said Stachnovski. 'Took a real fancy to him.'

'Yes, but he's expecting her to write to him. Damn it, Polack, you dragged him off to that whorehouse. It's up to you to look after him.'

'I'll ask the skipper to send us on leave together. How would that be?' Stachnovski said. 'We come from the same part of the world. He's from Hindenburg, I'm from Beuthen. I'll take care of the lad.'

For a moment Kuert remembered the sensation he'd had when coming aboard the *Doggerbank*, the feeling that he was at home.

'Hey,' said Stachnovski, 'you're daydreaming.'

Kuert carefully removed the stencil.

'Finished?' Stachnovski enquired. 'How does it look? Good?'

Kuert nodded.

Stachnovski rose and squinted down at his chest. 'Anyone got a mirror?' he demanded of the forecastle at large.

IN *U43*, THE FORE-ENDS reported that the tubes were ready for firing.

'Range one thousand metres.' Schwantke could detect no lights on his target. She had darkened ship but was holding her course.

It was deathly quiet aboard the U-boat. Every member of the crew knew his job. Silent routine had been ordained and the men were padding around in their stockinged feet. The hydrophone operator sat hunched over his equipment. The radio had already been tuned to the 600-metres international emergency frequency in case they could pick up the ship's distress signal and learn her name when they surfaced after attacking.

It was 20.55 when the bow-caps over the torpedo tubes swung open. Schwantke clamped his eyes still tighter to the eyepieces, then slowly raised his arm. Everyone waited for his signal.

KUERT WAS STANDING beside Stachnovski, who was inspecting the completed tattoo with the aid of a hand mirror. They were at the foot of the forecastle ladder, twelve steps down from the main deck.

Waldemar Ring was on his way from the galley to the captain's cabin with some coffee for Schneidewind. He hurried to ensure that the skipper's coffee didn't go cold before it reached its destination.

Karl Boywitt, the former trawlerman, was bound for his favourite spot, the monkey island. He would spend long hours sitting up there all by himself, gazing at the constellations. He dreamed that he was back in his fishing boat off the Baltic coast.

Captain Schneidewind was standing beside the helmsman. He stared through the big window at the darkness ahead. There was nothing to be seen but inky water. The night was chill, fraught with potential danger. An insidious sense of foreboding pervaded him.

He turned away. The coffee he had ordered would do him good. Maybe a bath. A clean shirt and a shave, too. His cabin was just below. He reached it and started to open the door.

SCHWANTKE LOWERED HIS ARM, signalling the torpedo officer to open fire. He heard the firing lever being depressed.

U43 jolted as the bow torpedoes left their tubes. Schwantke pictured them speeding through the water, three steel sharks with minds of their own, beyond recall.

A voice behind him began counting the seconds to impact.

A MUFFLED EXPLOSION shook the *Doggerbank*. Kuert knew at once what it meant: torpedo! Instinctively, he dashed to the ladder and scrambled up the iron steps. He heard someone shout 'Torpedo!' in his ear, then realised that the voice was his own, realised that he was yelling as he ran across the deck, blundering into dozens of other men who were desperately trying to reach the rail.

He hadn't gone more than a few yards when a second torpedo hit the *Doggerbank*, ripping her open amidships. The explosion sent him flying. He was showered with sea water by the geyser that erupted alongside the ship and came pattering down on the deck.

He lay there for a moment, half-stunned. The ship's engines had stopped. She was losing way and developing a heavy list. Dim figures were staggering past him and jumping overboard.

The sight of them brought Kuert to his senses, recalled a lesson drawn from past experience: the first to jump seldom stood a chance; they were usually sucked down by the undertow. One's best aid to survival was the wreckage of a ship, the hatch covers, crates and baulks of timber that floated to the surface when the vessel foundered. And then it occurred to him that one of his duties was to launch a lifeboat.

He crawled across the canting deck on his hands and knees. Terrified screams rang out nearby. They were coming from Compartment No. 3, just abaft the bridge, where over a hundred men were accommodated in twin-tier bunks.

He saw it at once: the heavy iron ladders leading down to the tween-deck had come unshipped and cut off the men's escape. The compartment was in darkness except for some emergency lamps, but he had no need to see anything. The piercing cries for help were revealing enough. Hundreds of tons of water were pouring through rents in the hull, bulkhead doors bursting open, men trampling each other to death as they strove to escape the swiftly rising water that was imprisoning them in an iron tomb. They hadn't a hope. They would drown like rats in the flooded compartment and go to the bottom with the ship that was inexorably dragging them down with her. There was nothing he could do for them.

He turned away and staggered on like a blind man. *I must get to my boat.* He clung to that thought.

The third torpedo struck the ship just as he reached the lifeboat, hanging from its davits at an angle. Kuert couldn't free the pins that held the ropes. He wrenched an axe from its clips on the rail and hacked away at the retaining ropes, but it was no use. The ropes were of steel, and it took him six blows to sever the first of them. He knew he would never free the boat. He saw the ship's bow begin to rear up against the night sky. He threw the axe away. When he turned to look, the base of the mainmast was already awash. Aware that the end was near, he felt an overpowering determination to survive. The dinghy! Of course! They'd taken it aboard in Japan. It was there on the boat deck, and it wasn't lashed down!

The water almost overtook him. He could already hear it gurgling close behind him as he reached the little craft. There was only one thing for it: he just had time to insert his hands in the loops of the grab rope that ran round the hull.

Water engulfed the boat and the man clinging to it. The iron foremast shot towards them. Kuert felt the grab rope cut into his wrists. The mast flashed past like a knife, missing him by inches. His next conscious sensation was of being under water.

Everything went black. Something was constricting his chest, squeezing the breath out of him. His head threatened to burst. He couldn't feel his arms or legs. His limbs might have been torn from his body. *This is it!* He found the prospect of death less terrifying than novel and wholly unfamiliar.

The undertow of the sinking ship sucked the dinghy down, and him with it, to a depth of some thirty feet. Recalling those moments in afterlife, he felt that there was only one thought which his fear of death had failed to suppress: *Hang on. Hang on to the dinghy. A boat will rise to the surface quicker than a man.*

The pressure lessened as the dinghy shot to the surface like a cork. His limbs were suddenly restored to him. Kuert removed his hands from the loops in the grab rope. His wrists felt as if he'd broken them. He got his arms over the gunwale and clung to it. His body heaved convulsively as he hung there, vomiting up the water he'd swallowed.

A strange silence surrounded him. The dinghy had righted itself keel down. It was full of water, but it floated. He raised his head and peered into the darkness. Their ship, their legendary, happy ship. It was like a dream, a dreadful hallucination: the *Doggerbank* had all but disappeared. Her bow pointed skyward, seemed to hang there for a moment, and slid beneath the surface with the inexorability of lead melting in a crucible.

Kuert could feel her dying ripples gently rock the waterlogged dinghy as he hauled himself aboard.

THE NIGHT SEEMED less dark now; it had paled to a grey, nebulous twilight. The dinghy rode the long swell without a sound. Kuert could hear no cries for help. The silence was strangely profound and all-enveloping.

His wrists were bleeding, lacerated by the rope. He groped for a handkerchief, only to find that he was naked except for a singlet and a pair of silk underpants bought in Yokohama. His trousers, shoes and socks were gone, torn from his body.

The survival belt! It occurred to him only now that he wasn't wearing it. Why on earth not? Why had he left it on his bunk together with the canteen and clasp-knife? Hadn't the klaxon sounded? No, that was at noon. The U-boat! Schneidewind's announcement over the public address system, the exuberant atmosphere on board.

Suddenly his thoughts turned to the others. He listened intently, but the darkness and silence persisted. He might have been the sole survivor.

Knee-deep in water, he searched the dinghy from stem to stern. It had possessed a mast, a sail and a pair of oars, but there was no sign of them. Only the tiller and rudder remained.

You've got a boat. You're alive and you've got a boat. Everything else can wait.

KUERT BECAME AWARE of sounds for the first time. They steadily increased in volume. The pressure on his eardrums was easing. He shook his head like a wet dog, and it was as if someone had removed plugs from his ears. From one moment to the next the darkness around him ceased to be hushed and lifeless. Cries for help were audible on every side. He simply hadn't heard them before.

He cupped his hands to his mouth.

'Over here!' he shouted. 'Over here, I've got a boat!'

A figure swam out of the gloom. All he saw at first were two arms hooked over the gunwale.

'The bastards sank us!' said a voice.

'Careful,' Kuert said, thinking clearly again. 'Climb in over the stern. We don't want to capsize.'

The face was thin and bloodless, the forehead plastered with strands of wet hair.

'Is that you, Polack?'

'Fritz, by God!' Stachnovski gasped. 'Fritz, you're alive!' His sodden shirt gaped open, revealing the fresh tattoo on his bare chest.

'How did you manage to get out?'

Stachnovski shook his head. 'Search me.' He went on shaking his head, but not at the fact of his survival. 'What happened to the ship, Fritz?' He peered into the darkness. 'My lovely ship.'

They huddled together in the stern sheets. Cries for help could be heard all around, some faint and distant, others closer at hand. Abruptly, Stachnovski straightened up. He glared into the darkness and shook his fist. It was a helpless, impotent gesture. 'How could the bastards do that to my ship!' He couldn't go on. His eyes were filled with tears.

U43 BROKE SURFACE. Schwantke himself opened the upper hatch and came out on the bridge. The lookouts took up their posts around him. He levelled his night glasses.

The U-boat captain still retained a vivid picture of the ship's last moments as he had observed them through his periscope. Barely eight minutes had elapsed between the instant when she was almost obscured by the first huge waterspout and her final descent. Schwantke had watched the spectacle, fascinated. His first kill. He was still surprised at how easy it had been, but still suspicious. He had kept the site of the sinking under surveillance for an hour before giving the order to surface at 21.58.

'We'll take one more look,' he decreed.

U43 headed for the spot at slow speed. The men on the bridge soon sighted some wreckage. The port lookout was the first to report. 'Men in the water, sir.' They were dead. They floated past at close range, face down in the water. Schwantke stopped engines. Cries for help could be heard in the silence that followed.

'You speak a bit of English, Number One,' Schwantke told the officer of the watch. 'Get down on the forecasing and question them. I want the name of their ship!'

The first officer had already started down the ladder when he paused. 'Shall we fish someone out?'

There was a long silence. Schwantke, leaning over the bridge casing, stared down at the water that had closed over his kill. He had already taken a risk, chasing after an unescorted ship when his duty was to maintain station in the patrol line.

'Find out her name, that's all,' he said finally.

THE TWO MEN in the dinghy had started to bail, but it was a hopeless task with their bare hands alone.

Someone shouted for help nearby. They shouted back and listened until they heard the sound of someone swimming. It was Waldemar Ring. The youngster burst out sobbing when they hauled him aboard. Like Kuert, he was wearing only his shirt and underpants. He'd jumped from the bridge, he told them eventually. Had he seen Schneidewind? Yes, he'd last seen the skipper emerging from his cabin, carrying a sea bag. Ship's papers, probably.

The sixteen-year-old was shivering with cold and shock. The eyes in his thin face conveyed a mute appeal, as though he expected them to reassure him that all would be well.

'We'll be OK,' Kuert told him firmly. 'We've got this boat. Someone'll pick us up sooner or later.' The words sounded ludicrously hollow, and he knew it. Did he believe them himself? It didn't matter. All that mattered was to do something. He turned to Stachnovski.

'You go up forward, Polack. There's plenty of flotsam around. See if you can salvage something useful.'

'And look out for Leo!' Waldemar said eagerly. 'He jumped in after me, but I lost sight of him. Please!' When Stachnovski went forward the boy waded after him and cowered down in the bottom of the boat, waist-deep in water. Stachnovski scanned the surface.

Papa Boywitt came aboard soon afterwards. He'd been drifting on part of a hatch cover when he sighted the dinghy and paddled towards it. Kuert helped him over the stern.

Boywitt had also lost his shoes and trousers, but he was still wearing his blue seaman's jacket with the brass buttons and his cap. He wrung it out before speaking. 'Got the sail?'

'No sail, no mast, no oars, nothing,' Kuert replied.

'First thing to do is get the water out of her.' Boywitt was calm personified. He proceeded to use his cap as a bailer.

It was good having Boywitt aboard, Kuert thought. Boywitt was a fisherman, an expert on small craft. There was room in the dinghy for eight or nine men, but much would depend on who they were. If they hoped to survive they needed experienced, imperturbable types like Boywitt. He was probably the only one of them that knew the *Doggerbank*'s position when she went down and where to make for when it became light.

Boywitt was still bailing with his cap when they came across the tarpaulin. Prevented from sinking by a bubble of trapped air, it drifted towards them like a big black jellyfish. It was a sizable sheet, maybe fifteen feet square. They had some difficulty in hauling it into the boat, and Kuert had even greater difficulty in tearing the tough, tarred canvas with his bare hands. He managed to detach a piece some three feet square. Then, each holding two corners, he and Boywitt proceeded to use it as a bailer. But the dinghy was still half full after an hour's hard work.

They could hear Stachnovski cursing all the time. He kept fishing things out and throwing them back. 'Hell and damnation,' he would growl, 'still nothing edible!' He was so obsessed with the thought of food that on one occasion they only just prevented him from jettisoning a length of rope.

'Nothing gets thrown away in this boat.' Kuert snatched the rope from his hands. 'Anything may come in handy, anything at all.'

Stachnovski continued to scan the surface and curse, but from now on he consulted them whenever he found something. 'A crate. Empty. Want it?'

He fished out an empty 105mm shell case, miraculously bobbing in the sea open end up. It held around a gallon and made such an ideal bailer that they soon emptied the dinghy. Stachnovski's search yielded more lengths of rope and rope ends. Then they found three oars in quick succession. Boywitt stood one of the oars on end and inserted it experimentally in the hole in the dinghy's central thwart. It fitted.

'We'll take two oars,' he suggested, 'lash them together, and there's our mast. The other one we can use as a spar, and the tarp will make a sail. No point in hanging around.'

Kuert nodded. He was gladder than ever to have Boywitt on board.

Now that the boat was higher in the water they could hear the gentle, persistent lapping of the sea against its sides as it rode the swell. But Kuert was conscious of another sound as well. He cocked his head and listened. It was a faint hum reminiscent of a diesel engine. The submarine? The sound died away. He couldn't be certain, so he refrained from saying anything.

He got the ropes and the tarpaulin ready.

'Right,' he said, 'let's get started.'

U43'S FIRST OFFICER was still down on the forecasing. Schwantke couldn't see him clearly from the bridge, but he could hear him calling. 'What ship? What ship are you?'

The cries for help issuing from the gloom seemed to be growing louder. Schwantke thought he identified the language as English.

How many of the *Doggerbank*'s 365 men had survived the sinking of the ship will never be known, but it is probable that about one-third of them were still alive at this juncture and could have been saved. However, no one in *U43* seemed to doubt that the ship in question was British.

The first officer continued to hail the survivors from his post on the forecasing. A piece of wreckage struck the outer hull with a dull thud. 'Hurry it up,' Schwantke called, 'we've got to get back!'

The first officer climbed back up the conning tower. 'Well,' said Schwantke, 'any luck?'

The first officer shrugged. 'Nothing definite, skipper. I heard someone shout something. Could have been the name of a British ship.'

'The *Dunedin Star*?' That was the only clue, the resemblance between their victim and the type in Lloyd's Register.

'I couldn't say for sure.'

Another piece of flotsam nudged the hull. The cries for help grew louder.

'Life raft on the port beam, sir!' one of the lookouts reported. 'Quite a few men aboard.' His voice rose. 'A couple of them have dived in! They're swimming towards us. Can't be more than twenty yards away!'

Schwantke gave an order, and the U-boat went astern. As it left the wreckage and the life raft behind, Schwantke looked back at the site of the sinking through his night glasses.

Why hadn't he picked someone up? There were no formal instructions against doing so, especially as it was dark and they were in no danger of detection from the air. *U43*'s war diary expressly states that Schwantke was afraid the wreckage would foul his propellers, but that seems a dubious pretext. His conduct remains inexplicable to this day.

U43 rejoined the 'Tümmler' Group at 10.30. Its immediate neighbour in the patrol line, *U66*, flashed a recognition signal. *U43* acknowledged the signal in kind and reported its success. The response came flickering through the darkness: CONGRATULATIONS.

PART TWO

The Boat

They'd been hard at it all night. By the time the grey light of dawn washed over them, the makeshift sail was ready. Boywitt hauled the square of tarred canvas up the mast. It was on the large side for such a small boat, and they quickly picked up speed once the wind came.

Kuert had taken the tiller. He tried a couple of turns, and the little craft obeyed.

'We're sailing!' he cried. 'My God, Papa, we're sailing!' He bent down and called to Stachnovski under the sail. 'Keep an eye open for wreckage, Polack. Maybe we'll come across some of the others.'

But they had drifted during the night, and there was nothing around them now but sea, a grey expanse illumined by the eerie half-light in the east. The clouds hung low, as leaden as the water.

The feel of the tiller was a comfort. Kuert was far from downhearted. Whenever he was assailed by memories of the sinking, he suppressed them and concentrated on the present. He had weathered the night's ordeal remarkably well. It surprised him how little he felt the cold. *I'm in good shape. I've been sunk before now with plenty less flesh on my bones.*

'Easy!' called Stachnovski. 'Look! Over there, to starboard. Are they alive?'

Kuert, who had already spotted the bobbing heads, steered in their direction. He counted seven of them, all floating face down. Nothing could be seen of the men but their life jackets and their hair, which had fanned out like fine seaweed.

Boywitt raised a hand and touched his forehead, chest and shoulders in turn. His lips moved as he crossed himself.

They found more dead bodies. They also found four survivors.

The first to be hauled aboard by Stachnovski was the gunner's mate, Gernhöfer, a man in his forties. He was in the last stages of exhaustion. Next came Klockmann, the officers' steward. Only just twenty, Klockmann was a hefty young fellow who was little the worse for his night in the water. The last two to be fished out were Bergmann, an apprentice engineer, and Lofty Hencke, the helmsman.

The little craft rode lower in the water with eight men on board. They had stripped off whatever they were wearing in the way of shirts and jackets. The sun, which had now come out, was a welcome sight. An hour went by. No wreckage, no more dead bodies or survivors.

Eight men. We can pick up another three or four at most. And then? There was only one thing for it: they must make for the nearest land. But where was it?

Kuert leaned towards Boywitt and lowered his voice so the others wouldn't hear. 'Know anything about navigation?'

Boywitt looked down at his hands, which were holding the rope attached to the sail. 'Not enough. Only the skipper would know.'

Stachnovski crawled aft beneath the sail. His face, thin enough at the best of times, was a hollow-cheeked shadow of its former self. Immersion in sea water had inflamed the fresh tattoo on his chest, Kuert noticed.

'Reckon there's still a hope of finding one of the lifeboats?' Stachnovski asked.

'Yes, if they managed to launch one.'

'And if not? You know what this means, don't you? We're done for, Fritz. Not a bite to eat, not a drop of drinking water . . .'

Kuert cut him short. 'Get back to your place,' he said. 'And give your brains a rest. It doesn't do to think too much, not in a situation like this.'

I ought to know. None of the others had experienced a sinking. He had, more than once, and one thing he knew for sure: thinking was poison. It sapped your strength. *Keep your eyes open, remain alert, but don't think, or, if you do, no more than a minute ahead.*

'THE SUB!' THE VOICE was that of Stachnovski, crouching at his lookout's post in the bow. 'I saw its periscope!' He pointed into the sun, and for a moment Kuert yielded to the same delusion. He was incapable of speech or movement.

'It's a life raft,' Papa Boywitt said eventually. They could all see it clearly now: the *Doggerbank*'s big inflatable was wallowing in the swell. What Stachnovski had mistaken for a periscope was merely an oar with a shirt fluttering on the end.

Kuert steered for it until he could see over the life raft's bulbous sides and make out the figures, at least thirty of them, huddled together on the bottom. Another thirty or forty men were in the water, hanging onto the grab rope.

Kuert turned the helm into wind when the dinghy came to within a hundred yards or so. Boywitt gave him a look of enquiry.

'If they all decide to make a dash for it, they'll capsize us,' Kuert said. 'We'll stay within hailing distance.'

'The skipper!' Stachnovski yelled. 'He's there on board!'

Kuert thought he glimpsed Schneidewind's white cap and blue tunic. Cautiously, he brought the dinghy in closer.

'Who's in charge?' It was Schneidewind's voice right enough.

'Boatswain Kuert, sir!' The words came out quite naturally, although Papa Boywitt was older.

'How many of you?'

'Eight.'

'Seen any lifeboats?'

'We've looked everywhere. Not a sign of them.'

There was silence for a while. Then Schneidewind called, 'We've got to find a boat. This thing's leaking, and there are too many of us. Go on looking and stay in touch!'

Kuert stared across at the white cap. He wasn't thinking of the rest, only that they needed a man capable of navigating in mid-ocean.

Leaning forward, he cupped his hands around his mouth. 'How about joining us, Captain? We need a navigator, sir. Maybe we'll find a lifeboat quicker that way.'

He kept his eyes glued to the life raft, poised to sheer off at a moment's notice. 'Very well,' Schneidewind called at last, 'stand by to pick me up.'

Kuert saw him climb over the side and lower himself into the water. 'Polack, get ready to grab him.'

The two craft were only some twenty yards apart by now. Schneidewind struck out for the dinghy and Stachnovski hauled him aboard. Kuert put the tiller hard over and the others ducked as the sail flapped and filled again.

Practice makes perfect, Kuert told himself proudly. Besides, their chances were even better now they had the skipper on board.

Schneidewind seated himself in the stern and took the helm. He was still in his sodden uniform, the only man on board to be fully clothed. He looked up at the sail, then at his eight companions.

'What happened to your lifeboat, Kuert? How come you didn't manage to launch it?'

Kuert had relinquished his place at the helm and was seated facing Boywitt in the bottom of the boat.

'No time, sir.'

'And you didn't see what became of the others?'

'I doubt if they got away either.'

'We'll take another look,' Schneidewind said. 'There are over seventy men in and around that life raft, and it's leaking badly. They're pumping in relays, four men at a time, but the water's gaining. They may last the day, but not another night.'

He removed his uniform tunic. Boywitt took it from him and hung it up to dry. Schneidewind surveyed the others. 'Did any of you see the submarine?'

They all shook their heads in turn. No one spoke.

'Some of the fellows on the life raft said they saw it,' Schneidewind went on, 'last night, after the sinking. Binder was there.' Richard Binder was one of the *Doggerbank*'s helmsmen. 'He said they swam towards it and shouted for help. According to him, someone aboard the submarine asked the name of the ship—in English.'

'Did they pick anyone up?' Kuert asked.

'Binder says no. They got to within a few yards of the boat, but as soon as they were spotted it backed off.'

The wind freshened and the dinghy put on speed. Schneidewind devoted his attention to the tiller.

THEY QUARTERED THE AREA all day long, coming across widely scattered pieces of wreckage and more bodies floating face down in life jackets. They found no lifeboats, but eventually, when the light had already begun to fade, they sighted a raft from the *Doggerbank*.

The clumsy craft consisted of a wooden deck supported by two big galvanised drums that kept it well clear of the water. Perched on the deck were Henry Schaper, one of the ship's engineers, a stoker named Thielmann, and, unnoticed until Waldemar Ring gave a sudden shout, Leo, the ship's dog. The grey fox terrier leaped into the dinghy and onto Waldemar's lap, where it whimpered and licked his face before cowering between his legs.

Schaper and Thielmann clambered aboard and, on Schneidewind's instructions, took the raft in tow. There was room on it for a good twenty men, so it held out the prospect of safety for at least some of those in the life raft.

Although Schneidewind reckoned that they must be in the vicinity of the life raft, they sailed far into the night without making contact. They shouted repeatedly, but there was no response.

Schneidewind eventually abandoned the search. Boywitt lowered the sail and they drifted with the two craft made fast to each other so that the dinghy lay in the lee of the raft.

The wind had strengthened. Kuert, who had retained his place beside the skipper, was feeling the cold for the first time. The other nine were stretched out in the bottom of the boat with the remainder of the tarpaulin over them. They lay huddled close together for warmth on the hard wooden ribs.

Around them were the noises of the night, the incessant slap of the waves against the hollow drums supporting the raft, the occasional cough or muffled curse of a man stirring in his sleep, the monotonous murmur of Boywitt saying his prayers.

Kuert dozed with his head propped on his knees, shivering in the icy wind. Whenever he looked up he could see the skipper seated motionless in the stern, back in his uniform tunic. The brass buttons gleamed, the white cap caught the fitful moonlight that bathed one side of his face. He sat there stiffly, erect and alert, waiting for daybreak, and Kuert waited with him.

THE MORNING of the second day after the sinking was as bleak and depressing as the night had been. The sea was rougher. The eleven men in the dinghy awoke one by one, stiff-limbed and shivering with cold. They looked in silence at the flecks of white foam on the waves, the grey sky overhead.

It was Schneidewind who roused and heartened them.

'Look lively! We've got to find that life raft.'

Boywitt raised the sail, and they got under way with the heavy raft in tow. They made even slower progress than the day before, thanks to the waves that were buffeting them about.

Stachnovski was the first to sight them: a sprinkling of black dots bobbing on the wave-crests. When the dinghy drew nearer, they proved to be the heads of several swimmers battling desperately against the heavy sea.

'Four,' Kuert counted. 'Only four of them.' They were near enough now for their faces to be recognisable. 'I can see Binder, and Bahrend.'

Schneidewind, sitting motionless at the helm, was unable to repress a momentary look of dismay. 'My God! They were with me in the life raft. Only four of them?' They scanned the sea for more survivors, but in vain.

The four were hauled aboard one by one: Binder, an able seaman, twenty years old; Heller, nineteen, another of the naval ratings transferred to the *Doggerbank* at Yokohama; Schuster, also little more than nineteen, a slim, silent youth; and Jan Bahrend, the ex-cook. They lay in the bottom of the boat, utterly exhausted, with grey, gaunt faces.

Kuert bent over Bahrend. He gripped him by the shoulders and shook him gently. 'What happened?'

Bahrend brushed the question aside with a gesture so pathetically weary and resigned that it tugged at Kuert's heart. He pointed to Binder. 'Ask him. He'll tell you.'

'What happened to the life raft?' Schneidewind demanded.

'It's gone,' Binder said haltingly.

'What do you mean?'

'Last night. Someone said you'd pushed off and left us in the lurch. That started it.' Binder buried his face in his hands. He'd always been known on board for his high-pitched, almost girlish laugh. No one had known how seriously to take him. 'The men at the pumps gave up. They said it was pointless. A few of the others, the ones in the water, let go and drifted away. Then Fischer shot himself.' Fischer, a naval lieutenant, had joined them at Yokohama.

Schneidewind seemed to have aged ten years. He looked an old, beaten man. 'He had a gun?'

Binder nodded. 'An automatic. It was in a waterproof pouch round his neck.'

Schneidewind's hand went to his chest. Kuert noticed the movement but gave it no particular thought at the time.

'Well, go on,' Schneidewind said.

'It was Fischer that set them off. The men around him must have got hold of his gun. They went crazy. We heard eight shots.'

Schneidewind's face was a mask. He shut his eyes for a moment as though insulating himself against reality. Then he surveyed the little boat and his fourteen companions, all that remained of the 365 who had sailed from Yokohama.

'We all lost our heads. Everyone panicked after that,' Binder went on. 'Some jumped in and swam off rather than prolong the agony. The rest of us stayed aboard the life raft, but it didn't take long to sink with no one working the pumps.'

'And you're the sole survivors?' Schneidewind asked.

'We were the only ones with life jackets.'

It was quiet in the boat. All eyes turned to Schneidewind, every face registered a mixture of dread and foreboding. The death of the others was suddenly forgotten, unreal. They were afraid for themselves. Did *they* stand a chance?

Their concerted gaze seemed to galvanise him. 'There's only one thing for it,' Schneidewind said eventually. 'We must make for land.'

They stared at him. Fifteen men in a dinghy with barely a foot of freeboard, they were hundreds of miles from land; they had no compass, no food, no drinking water.

'We're nearer the Azores than anywhere else,' Schneidewind went on, 'but our chances of getting there are slim. We'd have the wind against us. Besides, it's colder in the north. The Azores are out.'

The sun pierced the clouds for moments at a time, but it gave little warmth.

'The Bahamas? Too far north, given the prevailing wind.' Schneidewind fell silent. Finally, as if his mind had been made up from the outset, he said, 'Our only hope is South America.'

'In this cockleshell?' Stachnovski demanded. 'With nothing to eat? Without any water?'

'It won't be easy,' Schneidewind said, 'but we'll have a following wind, and it's better to try than do nothing. Our route will take us across at least seven neutral shipping lanes. Besides, the further south we go the warmer it'll get. Three weeks, if all goes well.'

Three weeks in this dinghy, thought Kuert, but all he said was, 'What about the raft, sir?'

The raft was wallowing alongside like a secure little island, virtually unsinkable even in the most violent of storms. All fifteen of them could easily have found room on board. It was a diabolical decision, and Kuert felt glad it wasn't his to make.

'We'll have to set it adrift,' Schneidewind decreed. 'We wouldn't make more than three knots with that dead weight in tow, and we've got to sail as fast and as far as we can.'

He inserted a hand in the pocket of his uniform tunic. It emerged

LEFT: Fritz Kuert at the time of his transfer to the *Doggerbank*.

RIGHT and BELOW: Paul Schneidewind, captain of the blockade-runner *Doggerbank*, formerly the British ship *Speybank*.

BELOW: *U43*, the German submarine that sank *Doggerbank* off the Azores in 1943, believing it to be a British ship. Of the 365 German seamen on board, all but one perished.

holding a silver-sided pocketknife. 'Preserve the towrope, Kuert. You never know when it may come in handy.'

Kuert hauled the raft in close. The knife had only one blade, and it was blunt by the time he finally severed the rope.

'You keep it,' Schneidewind told Kuert when he made to return the knife. Kuert's hand closed over it. The feel of the knife gave him a curious sense of satisfaction: he possessed something denied to everyone else on board. He rolled it up in the elastic waistband of his underpants. The raft drifted away.

'Two men stand by to bail,' Schneidewind ordered. 'Stachnovski and Hencke, you kick off. The rest of you distribute your weight evenly. Lie down in the bottom of the boat. You'll be warmer that way. Keep still and try to sleep. Save your strength.' He gave Boywitt a nod.

Boywitt raised the sail, Schneidewind took the helm.

It was midday, forty hours after *Doggerbank* went down, when her skipper brought the dinghy on course.

Kuert sat at Schneidewind's feet in the stern sheets. The space was so cramped that his knees brushed those of Boywitt, who was sitting opposite him.

His sense of satisfaction at having the knife persisted. He cut two notches in the gunwale, one for each day, and put the crumbs of wood in his mouth. He chewed them slowly. That was something else the others didn't have.

The wind had strengthened still more. They were sailing with it and the current. Although the sun appeared from time to time, the air remained chill. Kuert relieved Boywitt at the sail every two hours. The bailers, who sat beside the mast, were also relieved at two-hourly intervals. Schneidewind alone retained his place at the tiller. The tension had left his face, which now wore a calm and confident expression.

Darkness fell. The slap of the waves against the sides of the boat and the creak of the makeshift rigging took on an eerie note.

'Take over, Kuert,' Schneidewind said at last.

Kuert cautiously slid into position on the stern seat and took the helm. He glanced at the sail.

'The sail stays up,' Schneidewind decreed. 'We'll have to keep going night and day.'

The sky, which had cleared, was frosted over with stars.

'See the Great Bear, Kuert?' Schneidewind pointed over his right shoulder. 'Always keep it just abaft the starboard beam.' Schneidewind's voice was calm and composed. 'Then we can't go wrong.'

KUERT CUT ANOTHER NOTCH in the gunwale, the third. Schneidewind had relieved him at the tiller as soon as dawn broke, Boywitt was handling the sail. The others stirred and sat up, but one look at the overcast sky sent them back into the relative warmth of the tarpaulin.

Whenever Kuert wasn't at the helm he tried to sleep, but hunger proved stronger than fatigue. His head emptied of all else when he thought of food. His whole body was crying out for something to eat.

Neither Boywitt nor Schneidewind spoke, although he could distinctly hear their stomachs rumbling. It wouldn't be long before someone started talking about food. He guessed it would be Stachnovski.

It was, in fact, Jan Bahrend who first broached the subject. He sat with his back propped against the mast, his favourite, jealously guarded spot. Bahrend's dissertation roused the others from their lethargy. He lectured them on spring chicken à la turque, stuffed turkey, duck with melon. He recounted where he had sampled those dishes, where the finest birds were to be found, how they were prepared.

Even as he listened to Bahrend, Kuert knew it was a mistake to let him go on. It would only aggravate their hunger, making it more agonising and harder to bear, but he listened avidly just the same. Looking back on it later, Kuert decided that hunger was his worst torment in the three days that followed, the third, fourth and fifth days after the sinking, far worse even than thirst. It was on the morning of the fifth day that hunger very nearly overturned the boat.

At dawn Stachnovski crept up on Waldemar Ring and tried to wrest the dog away from him, cursing and shouting at the top of his voice. Waldemar not only resisted fiercely but ended by biting him. Kuert managed to separate them. Stachnovski stared down at the blood oozing from his bitten hand. Waldemar, still nursing Leo in his arms, was crouching in the bottom of the boat.

'That dog's no use to anyone,' Stachnovski snarled. 'It's in worse shape than we are. I say we butcher the brute. We could drink its blood.'

'There's nothing on that dog but skin and bone,' said Hencke. 'Let's butcher Stachnovski instead. Hands up those in favour!'

For an instant no one knew if he really meant it. Stachnovski cowered away. His eyes widened, and he raised his hands defensively.

Kuert gripped him by the shoulders. 'Come on, Polack!' he entreated. 'What's the matter with you? Don't give up. We'll all be done for if we don't pull together.'

Stachnovski emitted a sudden laugh, a despairing, half-demented bark of laughter. 'Jan had better stop it, that's all. I can't stand it when he goes on about food.'

There was no more talk of food from Bahrend. The incident seemed quickly forgotten. But they weren't the same men. It was as if each of them had crossed an invisible barrier beyond which different laws prevailed.

Schneidewind, still wearing his captain's white peaked cap, sat at the helm. He had taken no apparent notice of the incident and passed no comment. All his attention was on the clouds, the sail and the sea.

The weather steadily deteriorated. Waves broke over the dinghy. They had to bail incessantly in teams of two, relieving each other every half-hour because that was the limit of their endurance. Schneidewind refused to take in sail. He headed straight on through the storm until even Boywitt counselled caution. The skipper's only response was a shake of the head.

And that was how they passed the night and the following day and night, sailing and bailing, bailing and sailing . . .

The wind dropped at dawn on the seventh day. The sky was heavily overcast, and from time to time they sighted dark curtains of rain descending in the distance. Awakened by Stachnovski, the men had spread the tarpaulin in the bow in readiness to collect it. They gazed longingly at the clouds and whimpered for water. Their lips were cracked and swollen. For hours the clouds rolled on ahead of them, but it was not until nightfall that deliverance came. They sailed into a heavy downpour. Even while the rain was filling the tarpaulin, the men plunged their faces in it and drank like horses at a trough.

Kuert had lowered the sail. Boywitt helped him to rinse the salt-encrusted canvas and collect some rain. Then he drank, gulping down great mouthfuls of it. When he paused to catch his breath, he became aware that the men around him were groaning with delight.

He drank till his belly was bulging. But no sooner had he changed places with Schneidewind than he was suddenly terrified that the rain would stop before he could take another drink. He darted forward as soon as Schneidewind resumed his place in the stern. Who could tell when it would rain again?

He filled the shell case and stowed it under the stern seat. Then, with the remainder of the fresh water in the sail, he sluiced his face and the suppurating weals on his wrists, which had never healed.

They set sail again and Schneidewind brought the dinghy back on course. The rain had soaked them all to the skin. At first, Kuert had found it a gloriously refreshing sensation; now, all he felt was the cold. And after an hour his thirst returned.

EARLY THAT MORNING—it was the eighth day, and another gale had blown up—Kuert distributed the water. Everyone got some, even the dog. The shell case was half empty by the time it had gone the rounds.

Kuert watched the others as they drank. Stachnovski was very quiet now. He'd stopped swearing. Bahrend, too, had lapsed into silence. His flow of anecdotes had dried up. The inveterate pessimist and yarn-spinner just sat there in a stupor with his back propped against the mast. He didn't even duck when the heavy seas lashed his face with spindrift.

Kuert had noticed a faint whiff of lemons a couple of nights ago. He thought it was a figment of his imagination until he spotted something in Schneidewind's hand: a small tube of ointment. Every night the skipper would squeeze out a little of the tube's contents and rub it into his face.

They no longer spoke to each other. Each was alone, enclosed in a strange cocoon of silence. They seemed to have forgotten that they had once sailed together in a ship named the *Doggerbank*. They had forgotten the war, the submarine, even, perhaps, the past. Stachnovski, who was Stachnovski? And Boywitt? He'd once known something about Boywitt, but he couldn't remember what. Who was he himself?

He counted the notches, ran his finger over them. Five and three, eight in all. Eight notches. That meant today was, yes, Sunday. They'd been in the boat for a week.

Schneidewind had said it would get warmer. To Kuert it felt colder. Schneidewind had said they would cross some shipping lanes, but they hadn't sighted a single ship. He experienced a sudden pang of doubt. Would he fail to stay the course? Even to consider such a possibility was crazy, the beginning of the end. The thought was draining his last reserves of energy. He thrust it aside.

At nightfall he took over the helm from Schneidewind. Till now he'd always done so without a word, but this time he spoke. It surprised him how normal his voice sounded. 'How far do you think we've come, sir?'

Schneidewind replied without hesitation. 'Eight hundred miles, by my reckoning. Maybe a bit more. We should soon be crossing the Tropic of Cancer.'

'Are we halfway there yet?'

'Not quite.'

Not for the first time, Kuert wondered where the skipper got his quiet confidence. What was his secret source of supply? Could it be that little tube of ointment? The scent of lemons? Not wanting to be overheard, he lowered his voice. 'What are our chances, sir?'

'Remember what I told you about the Great Bear,' Schneidewind said. He had lowered his voice too. 'Always keep it a few degrees abaft the starboard beam. Remember that, Kuert, just in case.'

There was silence for a while. Schneidewind hadn't really answered the question, he'd evaded it.

'I keep wondering,' he went on. 'I ask myself, time and time again, if it was my fault. That submarine, Kuert, I was so certain it was one of ours. Maybe I was too damned certain.'

Kuert saw it now: the skipper's composure was just a façade. Behind it lay a world of doubt and self-reproach.

You mustn't give way to doubt, Kuert told himself. The submarine's nationality didn't matter at present. All that mattered was here and now. 'Do you really think we'll make it, sir?' He'd been wanting to ask that question for days now.

'A few of us may, with luck. The Great Bear, keep it just abaft the starboard beam. Remember that.'

I will. Even if only a few of us make it, I'm going to be one of them.

Hours went by. He was sitting there at the tiller, leaning on it. His neck was stiff, the arm resting on the tiller felt like a lifeless block of wood. His mouth was parched. He thought of the water in the shell case beneath the stern seat.

A sip, just a sip. No one'll notice if I take a sip.

To sleep, if only for a second or two! To shut his eyes! He gave a start: he'd dozed off for a moment. The tiller had escaped his grasp and the boat was heeling dangerously.

How do you hope to make it if you don't pull yourself together?

He scooped up some sea water in his palm and splashed the back of his neck, repeating the process whenever fatigue threatened to get the better of him.

THE RAINWATER in the shell case had turned brown with rust overnight. Kuert passed it round as soon as it became light.

Jan Bahrend shook his head when the container reached him. 'Someone else can have my share,' he said. 'Give it to Stachnovski or the skipper, anyone.'

Weary though he was, Kuert sensed that something was wrong. Something in Bahrend's tone and manner gave him pause for thought. The ex-cook's shoulders seemed narrower. The life jacket that had once fitted him snugly now hung loose. 'No arguments, Jan,' Kuert told him. 'Everyone bails, everyone gets his ration. Come on, drink up. Who knows when we'll get some more?'

'I don't want any water, Fritz, and I don't want to do any more bailing either.' His gaunt face, with its frosting of grey stubble, became animated. 'Why not drink it yourself? You can have my ration.' He eyed Kuert. 'If anyone makes it, you will.' His voice sank to a confidential whisper. 'We can't all survive, there are too damned many of us. Did you see Fujiyama when we sailed? Didn't I tell you what the Japs always say? I told you our number would be up in the end, didn't I? Didn't I tell you about Fujiyama?'

Kuert stood there with the shell case in his hand. He didn't know what to do, he knew only that he had to do something to overcome the mumbled objections of this ageing man. He tried to thrust the shell case into Bahrend's hands, but he wouldn't take it. 'You have it,' he said. 'You stand a chance. It'd be wasted on me.'

Shared out among the rest, Bahrend's ration provided another swallow apiece. Kuert felt drained of energy afterwards. He returned to his place in the stern, aware of Bahrend leaning motionless against the mast.

All at once the boat heeled over. Startled, Kuert saw a tall figure poised on the gunwale. It was already too late to do anything. Bahrend simply let himself fall overboard. He toppled into the sea slowly and stiffly, like a felled tree.

Water came pouring over the gunwale. Even as Bahrend drifted astern, two men automatically began to bail it out.

Schneidewind had turned pale. His lips twitched. He looked from Kuert to the man in the water, then back at the sail. Finally he shook his head. 'We can't go about,' he said, 'not in this sea.'

Boywitt was praying.

Let him die, Kuert thought. *Be merciful, let him die quickly!* Men kept afloat by life jackets died no easy death. They might drift for a day, two days . . . If Bahrend had been seeking a quick, easy death, he couldn't have done worse.

Boywitt was still praying. The skipper sat there like a marble statue.

'Amen,' Boywitt murmured, and crossed himself.

Schneidewind said, 'We'd better be on our guard, Kuert. The boat could capsize, and then we'd all be done for.'

Kuert was grateful for those words. At least the skipper's head was clear. He didn't want to think of Bahrend.

It took a while to bail out the water. Kuert had the impression that the dinghy was riding marginally higher in the water. A good thing, good for the rest of them.

Jan Bahrend? He had simply been a person who wasn't there any more. The only thing that scared him was the question—when would it be his turn?

THE NEXT MORNING brought storm-force winds and fifteen- to twenty-foot waves. Kuert cut his daily notch, the tenth.

He slept whenever he wasn't handling the sail, but not even sleep had the power to confer oblivion. Even in his sleep he was aware of the dinghy's wild cavortings and Schneidewind's tense face as he grimly strove to keep it running before the wind.

They capsized at about midday. The sail collapsed with a fluttering sound.

They were pitched into the sea like so many dolls. Kuert tried to catch hold of the grab rope, but the waterlogged dinghy, which had sluggishly righted itself, was rotating on its axis like a piece of driftwood. He could hear the others' cries. They were in the sea all around him, struggling to remain in the vicinity of the boat, squandering their strength by shouting and striking out wildly.

He saw Schaper, Hencke and Bergmann trying to scramble aboard the dinghy amidships. He was about to swim towards them and do likewise when his instinct for self-preservation deterred him. Knowing what would happen, he trod water and waited. The boat capsized once more, submerging the three men beneath it. They didn't reappear.

Looking around, he made out a white dot among dark waves. The skipper's cap! The sight smote him like an electric current. Anything but that, he thought. He swam towards the cap, only to find that Schneidewind was still wearing it.

'Tell them to distribute themselves fore and aft,' he gasped. 'We've got to hold her steady.'

Kuert passed the order on, shouting to make himself heard. He swam towards the boat, followed by Binder and Klockmann. 'Now!' They caught hold of the grab rope.

'Who's up forward?' Kuert shouted. He could see three figures but they were shrouded in spindrift.

'Stachnovski and Boywitt,' Binder said breathlessly, 'and the youngster, Waldemar.'

Three plus themselves and the captain made seven. *Only seven now*.

Seven were missing, seven plus the dog. Kuert remembered seeing the animal paddling confusedly away from the boat.

The dinghy had steadied now that their weight was evenly distributed fore and aft. Only seven of them: Schneidewind, Binder,

Klockmann, Stachnovski, Boywitt, Waldemar and himself. Were they the handful destined to survive?

'The rudder!' The cry jolted Kuert out of his reverie. It was Schneidewind who had noticed that the rudder was gone. And then the full truth dawned on him. The mast had also been carried away. So had the sail and the remains of the tarpaulin. The shell case, too, was bound to have disappeared. He didn't know how much time had elapsed, a few minutes or an hour, before he heard Schneidewind say, 'It's no use. We'll never get the water out of her.'

He stared at the boat. The skipper was right. No rudder, no mast, no sail; what hope did they have? He was thinking quite clearly. Perhaps it was the chill of the sea that induced such lucidity. All that surprised him was his refusal to give up. His decision to keep going to the bitter end dated from some time in the past, he couldn't remember when.

The seven men clung to the grab rope and drifted. It was all they could do. Hours went by and the light began to fade. 'We won't last the night,' Schneidewind said. 'Not a hope.'

Kuert was in the water beside him. 'This storm can't last for ever. We'll get her shipshape again once it blows over.'

'We're in the Tropics now,' Schneidewind said. 'In these latitudes, storms don't always blow over so quickly. No, we don't stand a chance.'

Kuert looked at Schneidewind. He needed him. Schneidewind was his compass, his navigational aid. He could do without any of the others, but not Schneidewind.

'Klockmann,' he said, 'give me a hand.' They gripped Schneidewind by the seat of his pants and boosted him over the gunwale. He didn't resist.

'Listen to me,' he said. 'You must all decide for yourselves. As far as I'm concerned, it's over.' Schneidewind's eyes convinced Kuert that the man was in deadly earnest.

He saw the skipper reach inside the neck of his sweater and feel for something. The gesture was a reminder of the moment when Binder had told them about the suicides on the life raft. Now he understood.

Schneidewind produced an oilskin pouch from under his sweater. The waterproof container was suspended from his neck by a thong, and the object inside it, clearly identifiable by its shape, was an automatic pistol. His face, emaciated and sprinkled with grey stubble, was as expressionless as his bloodshot, inflamed eyes. 'I'm going to make an end of myself while I still can.'

Kuert stared at the pouch. He couldn't let it happen. He must put up a fight for Schneidewind's survival; he needed him.

'At least wait till morning. The weather may improve.' He had to shout to make himself heard above the roar of the wind. 'Even if it doesn't, we'll bail her out somehow. At least wait till morning!'

Schneidewind shook his head. 'We haven't a hope. None of us will ever reach land.' He fingered the pouch. 'This is the best way out.'

No, Kuert told himself, *no, no, no!* He was incapable of any other thought. Schneidewind's resignation appalled him. The captain of the *Doggerbank* had always been so calm, so courageous and confident, a man who would never break, never give up. Was he right to give up now? *No, no, no!*

Schneidewind had taken out the automatic. Kuert stared at the oily black metal and the pallor of the captain's skin. For a moment he debated whether to knock the gun flying or push him off the thwart.

Then he felt Schneidewind's free hand on his shoulder. 'That wouldn't change anything, Kuert. Believe me, what's in store for us would be worse. It's easier to die now than . . .'

Kuert reasoned with him. He begged and pleaded, simultaneously realising that it was useless. Schneidewind's mind was made up, he knew, and the fact that nothing could change it robbed him of any further value.

The boat gave a sudden lurch. Stachnovski had swum aft, and hitched one leg over the gunwale. 'What's going on?' he demanded. He had spotted the gun in the skipper's hand and was staring at it fixedly. 'Is he planning to shoot himself?'

Schneidewind spoke before Kuert could reply. 'We're done for.'

'Just a minute!' Stachnovski yelled. He made an unsuccessful grab for the gun, lost his balance, and went under. Surfacing, he clung to the gunwale with both hands. 'You can't do that, Captain. Let us go first. We've just as much right to that gun as you. If you're going, take us with you!'

Let them, thought Kuert. *If they want to kill themselves, let them! I don't need anyone. I've got to get away from them, or they'll end by infecting me with their mania for self-destruction.*

'This was our boat, Captain. We didn't have to pick you up, so you owe us. If you're going to end it all, we will too.' There was no fear in Stachnovski's expression, just a mute plea to end his sufferings. 'Please . . .' The word issued from his cracked lips in an almost inaudible whisper. 'Go on, shoot me.'

Waldemar had swum aft too. He clung to the grab rope, his body racked with sobs. 'Don't leave me behind,' he whimpered.

No one had been paying any attention to Binder, one of the four survivors from the life raft. 'If I've got to die,' he said suddenly, 'I'd sooner drown.' He let go of the grab rope and swam away from the boat. He swam powerfully, with a sudden, unaccountable burst of energy, and ploughed through the waves until he was out of sight.

For a moment the others simply clung to the grab rope, too shocked to move. Then Stachnovski started to plead again, and Klockmann, too, was imploring Schneidewind to shoot him.

'Wait, all of you!' Kuert shouted. 'Let's wait till morning. Don't do it, Polack!'

But Stachnovski thrust him violently aside. 'Please, Captain!'

Kuert saw Schneidewind take aim. He turned away, overcome with horror, and swam for the bow. He was scared, afraid of weakening. It occurred to him that he might soon be alone.

He could see Boywitt clinging to the bow. *He's the only one left*, Kuert thought. *Without him, I'd be all on my own!*

The first shot rang out before he could reach Boywitt, who had left his post and swum to meet him. Kuert pushed him back, propelled him towards the bow again. 'Don't be a fool, Papa, we'll make it. I promise you. Papa! Don't leave me!' They heard a second shot, followed almost immediately by a third. 'Please, Papa! I promise you we'll make it!' He kept repeating the words like an incantation. The shots meant nothing, simply that the others weren't there any more. They were dead, but not even death was a reality. Boywitt was the only reality. His life depended on him now.

'Let go of me,' Boywitt said. 'We're finished and you know it. If the skipper thinks so . . .'

The sail! Kuert thought. What was it about the sail? Something important, but what?

'The sail's still there!' he said, surprised to hear himself speak with such conviction.

'The sail? How can it be?'

'Because we made it fast. Of course! We secured the mast and the sail to the boat.'

Boywitt shook his head. 'The skipper would never give up if we still stood a chance, not the skipper.'

'We'll make it, Papa! We'll make it, the two of us! Stay with me and I'll get you out of this.' *You've got to convince him, you've got to! You need him!* 'We've stuck it for ten days. Why give up now? Nobody would ever find out how we died. Your wife would never know. And what about your son, Papa? Who's going to teach him to sail and fish?'

'Stop it, Fritz, please!' Boywitt shouted. 'All right, I'll stay, I promise I'll stay. I mean, if you really think we'll make it.'

A sudden sound transfixed them: Schneidewind was laughing to himself. It was Kuert who broke the spell. 'I'll have another word with him,' he said. 'It's worth a try. Stay here and hold the boat steady.'

Alone now, Schneidewind was sitting on the thwart with the gun still in his hand. The others weren't there any more, but the knowledge that they were dead left Kuert strangely unmoved. His horror had subsided.

'Boywitt's staying, Captain,' he said. 'We're going to try to make it. Why not come with us, sir?'

'It's too late, I've had enough,' Schneidewind replied in a low, flat voice. 'Too many men have died . . . Too many—a whole crew . . .'

'We've still got the sail and the mast.' In Kuert's mind, this had now become an established fact.

Schneidewind looked down at him and shook his head. 'The Great Bear, Kuert.' His tone was suddenly matter-of-fact. 'Remember what I told you: the Great Bear, keep it just abaft the starboard beam.'

He put the pistol back into the pouch and waded aft to the stern seat. He wound the rope that had been used to tow the raft and knotted it round his chest.

'This is the most I can do for you,' Schneidewind said. 'You can use me as a sea anchor. It may help to keep the boat steady.'

He took the pistol out of the pouch again and, perched on the transom, put it to his temple. Then he said, with total serenity, 'If you want the gun, you'd better look lively.' They were his last words.

He squeezed the trigger. The report was followed by two splashes, the first as the automatic fell into the waterlogged boat, the second as Schneidewind's body toppled over backwards into the sea. Kuert made no attempt to retrieve the gun. He had a terrible suspicion that the feel of the smooth, cold metal might prove too great a temptation.

He made his way back to the bow. Boywitt was praying again.

'We'll climb aboard,' Kuert said. 'You here, me in the stern. Easy does it. If we capsize again, we're done for.'

He swam aft. The rope Schneidewind had knotted round his chest was slanting down into the water from the transom. It was taut, he noticed, but the sight aroused no particular emotion in him.

He signalled to Boywitt and climbed in over the stern, then waited until he saw the older man crouching in the bow. 'Easy, Papa! One step at a time!' They waded towards each other, keeping their centre of gravity low to avoid overturning the waterlogged boat.

They found the buoy rope and hauled it in. When the mast and sail were floating alongside, they manhandled them cautiously over the gunwale.

'What did I tell you?' Kuert was too tired to feel triumphant. He felt for the knife rolled up in the waistband of his underpants and cut a square piece out of the sail. Then they started bailing. They bailed for hours on end, taking it in turns, but to no effect. Any water they removed was quickly replaced by the waves that broke over the boat. It was the first time Kuert came close to giving up.

Boywitt didn't run out on you! You made him a promise. You can't give up now.

In the end they stopped bailing and lapsed into a kind of stupor, but even in this half-sleep they clung to the thwart and each other. It was all that kept them from being washed overboard.

ROUSED BY THE COMING OF DAWN, they sat up. The sea was no calmer, the sky still heavily overcast. The night had been starless, Kuert remembered.

He began the day as he had begun all its predecessors, by cutting a notch in the gunwale, the eleventh. He gave Boywitt the little wedge of wood to chew. They bailed all day long, to no avail. By nightfall they could think themselves lucky the dinghy hadn't overturned.

The storm subsided during the night. They started bailing again. This time they could see the water level sinking. The sight spurred them on, although they were both so weak that they flopped down exhausted every few minutes. The twelfth day, the twelfth notch. They didn't succeed in ridding the dinghy of water entirely, but the bow and stern sheets were dry.

They set sail around midday. They reduced the mast to one oar and trimmed off part of the sail. Now that there were only two of them, the reduced sail area was quite adequate.

The worst thing was the loss of the rudder. To keep the boat on course they were obliged to hold the second oar over the stern with one hand and guide it with the other, an effort that sapped what little strength they had left.

Darkness fell, but no stars, no Great Bear, could be seen. Dawn broke, and there was nothing in sight but sea and sky.

Boywitt, huddled in the bow, kept moaning and begging for water. Kuert tried not to hear him. The old fisherman's appeals for water were gradually eroding Kuert's strength, his will to survive.

It was then, on the morning of the thirteenth day, that he first saw the sharks, only fifteen or twenty feet astern. Boywitt must have noticed them too, because he suddenly fell silent. Kuert could see their dorsal fins jutting from the water. He counted two big fish and four smaller ones. Uneasily, he watched them following the boat. Blood, he thought vaguely, they're drawn to the scent of blood. His eyes fell on the towrope slanting down into the water. So that was what had attracted them!

The best policy would have been simply to cut the rope and let the corpse fall astern, taking the sharks with it, but Kuert was reluctant to sacrifice a few feet of rope. It might come in useful.

His hands were raw, but he grasped the rope and hauled it in. It surprised him how easily it came, until he saw what was on the end. Schneidewind's corpse had been horribly diminished. The arms and legs were gone. Kuert went numb with horror at the thought that the sharks had been there during the night, only a few feet away.

He let the mangled remains flop back into the water and cut the rope. *That's six feet of rope I've lost*, he thought. The mutilated corpse meant less to him than the loss of the rope.

No sign of the sharks any more. *But they'll show up again. They never tire, never give up. All they have to do is follow us. They know they'll get us in the end.*

It did him good to hate them. Hatred galvanised him, gave him renewed strength. It was good to know that the boat was their only protection. *Or our coffin.*

He stared at the rope in his hands. *Do something!* he commanded himself. *For Boywitt's sake, for your own. For Schneidewind, Bahrend, Stachnovski, young Waldemar. Do something!*

He crawled to the bow and took out the pocketknife. 'We're going to make ourselves a rudder, Papa.'

'A rudder?' Boywitt stared at him incredulously. 'How?'

'We'll do it, Papa. We're going to make ourselves a rudder, and we're going to make it home.'

'Water, Fritz! Just a mouthful!'

Kuert began cutting the forward thwart in half with the knife. Working carefully to avoid snapping the blade, he progressively deepened the incision until the thwart broke under his weight.

The hardest part was extracting the two nails at either end of the thwart. It took him several hours to extract one pair of nails. The other two were easier to get out using the board as a lever, but he had to be careful: he would need them.

By the time the light began to fade, the fruits of his day's labours were as follows: the two halves of the forward thwart; four two-and-a-half-inch nails; a length of rope; and a makeshift tiller cut from the thwart that held the mast.

He was exhausted, so much so that he feared he might collapse at any moment. But he worked on long after nightfall, until the rudder was finished at last.

Next morning he cut the fourteenth notch. Then, with Boywitt's help, he installed the rudder. It fitted perfectly.

He felt proud of himself. And of Boywitt. And of the fact that they made such a good team. His hands were bleeding and covered with suppurating sores. He sluiced them with sea water. *They'll heal*, he told himself. *The less you think about them, the sooner they'll heal. All you've got to do is keep your wits about you and sail, sail like the skipper said. You're the skipper now!*

THE WEATHER HAD IMPROVED. The sun was shining, but he felt no warmer. He was made up of separate parts, all of them agonisingly painful: torn hands, oozing sores, throat swollen with thirst, eyes smarting and half blinded.

Now that they had a rudder they could sail again, but half an hour at the tiller was enough to drain him of energy. He would simply stretch out in the bottom of the boat, and Boywitt would crawl aft and take over. Then came his turn again, then Boywitt's. No words were exchanged. To speak, to move their cracked, raw lips, would have been too great an effort. For all that, it was good not to be alone. Being alone would have meant surrender and death.

Boywitt had stopped begging for water, aloud at any rate, but his eyes craved it incessantly.

The fine, sunny weather persisted, the trade wind blew steadily.

Towards noon on the fifteenth day, while Kuert was asleep, Boywitt lowered the sail because the wind had become too strong. When they came to raise it again they almost failed. They would have to risk leaving it up; they had no choice.

On the night of the seventeenth day Boywitt heard, or claimed to have heard, the sound of a ship's propellers.

Kuert didn't believe in Boywitt's ship. All he believed in was the wind. And so they sailed on as the wind, sun and stars dictated.

On the eighteenth day Boywitt failed to relieve Kuert at the helm. Although it was his turn, he lay in the bow without stirring. Kuert lashed the tiller and crawled over to him. To stand up and walk was out of the question; he crawled on his hands and knees.

'Time to take over, Papa.' Every word was a painful effort.

Boywitt gave a start. 'I don't have the strength, Fritz. Give me some water, please.' He was weeping dry-eyed. The sight of him wrung Kuert's heart. His face was nothing but skin and bone and sores. 'Why won't you let me drink some sea water, Fritz? A mouthful wouldn't hurt, surely?'

This time Kuert was alarmed. 'It'll kill you, Papa. Sea water will do for you.'

But Boywitt wouldn't be silenced. His pleas sent Kuert wild with thirst. He couldn't bear to hear them any longer. Leaving him huddled in the bow, he crawled back to the tiller.

That afternoon Boywitt started singing. Kuert was amazed at the sudden steadiness and clarity of the old fisherman's voice. He sang hymns, most of them unfamiliar to Kuert.

Boywitt continued to sing all afternoon, pausing only when exhaustion got the better of him. The words eventually became unintelligible. The melodies degenerated into a monotonous singsong interspersed with ever-lengthening pauses. The singing didn't trouble Kuert at first, but in the end, afraid that Boywitt was cracking up, he couldn't stand it any longer.

He crawled back to the bow. 'Come with me, Papa.' He put an arm round Boywitt's shoulders and hauled him aft. It was only now, with the other man close beside him, that he realised how scared he was of solitude.

'I'm sorry, Fritz,' Boywitt muttered, 'I'm just a burden to you. Leave me be.' A little while later he even offered to take the helm.

Kuert shook his head. *I've got to pull him through*, he kept telling himself. He began talking to the old fisherman. What did he know about his background? What had he told him?

There was his fishing boat. It had a red sail, Boywitt had confided. That sail was known all along the coast. So Kuert talked about the boat with the red sail, that and anything else that came into his head. Boywitt grew calmer, so he talked on. It never struck him that his words were barely coherent . . .

WHEN HE EMERGED from his torpor the next morning Boywitt was no longer beside him. He had resumed his place in the bow and was lying there with his face pillowed on his arms. He wasn't asleep, though. When Kuert crawled over to him he slowly sat up. His expression had changed. Kuert stared at the face that was, yet was not, Karl Boywitt's. Then he caught a whiff of his breath and knew at once what had happened.

Boywitt's mouth was open. The lips were grey, and white crystals were adhering to the corners of the mouth and the grizzled beard.

'What have you been up to, Papa?' Kuert gripped Boywitt by the shoulders. 'You've been drinking sea water!'

'I couldn't take it any more, Fritz.'

Kuert began to weep with anger at Boywitt's stupidity, with despair at having failed to preserve him from it. *Why didn't you take better care of him?*

Kuert let go of him, unable to endure their physical contact a moment longer. He left Boywitt and crawled back to the tiller. The thought was steadily becoming clearer and more distinct: *He's been drinking sea water. He won't be with you much longer.*

That afternoon Boywitt started to sing again in a hoarse, sobbing voice. During the night, while Kuert was asleep, he drank some more sea water. Kuert, who could tell this was so when morning came, knew that he would soon be alone.

He added a notch to the others in the gunwale and tried to count them, but they swam before his eyes. He ran his finger along them like a blind man: nineteen. *Nineteen days.*

The wind had dropped. Seated in the stern, he glided on through that profound, illimitable silence.

Keep going, he told himself. *If you want to see land again, keep going.*

THE RAIN CAME AT NOON on the twenty-first day. Boywitt had been lying slumped in the bow for two whole days and nights. Kuert had left him undisturbed. The eighteen feet from the stern sheets to the bow were too much for him. He needed all his remaining strength to sail the boat.

He felt no elation when the heavens finally opened. He sat there, a prey to indecision. If he wanted to drink he would have to lower the sail, but he was afraid to do so.

At length he crawled forward, lowered the sail and spread it out to catch the rain. Boywitt didn't move, but Boywitt was the least of Kuert's concerns as he rinsed the salt off the canvas and spread it out. His raging thirst preoccupied him to the exclusion of all else. Not a morsel of food had passed his lips for twenty-one days, and it was twelve since his last few mouthfuls of rusty water.

The rain was terribly slow to accumulate in the canvas trough. Kuert lapped it up greedily as soon as an inch or two had collected. He must have drunk at least a bucketful before it occurred to him that Boywitt hadn't moved.

He hauled himself to his feet by the mast and clung to it. 'Papa! Come on, it's raining!'

The old fisherman didn't stir. He was lying in the bow with his face upturned, eyes shut and mouth open. He might have been asleep.

Kuert climbed unsteadily over the thwart and knelt down beside

RIGHT: Members of the *Doggerbank*'s crew, photographed while on leave at the Japanese resort of Hakone in September 1942. The following were in the dinghy with (1) Fritz Kuert: (2) Richard Binder, (3) Polack Stachnovski, (4) Bernard Thielmann and (5) Hans Henke.

LEFT: Once the survivors were in the dinghy, they managed to salvage tarpaulin, a length of rope and three oars from the flotsam, all of which they used to fashion a makeshift sail.

RIGHT: When sighted by the Spanish tanker, the dinghy was 1,600 nautical miles from the spot where the *Doggerbank* had sunk.

BELOW: The dinghy's original rudder was lost when the boat capsized, but Fritz Kuert, not willing to give up hope, fashioned a new rudder from part of the forward thwart.

4
5

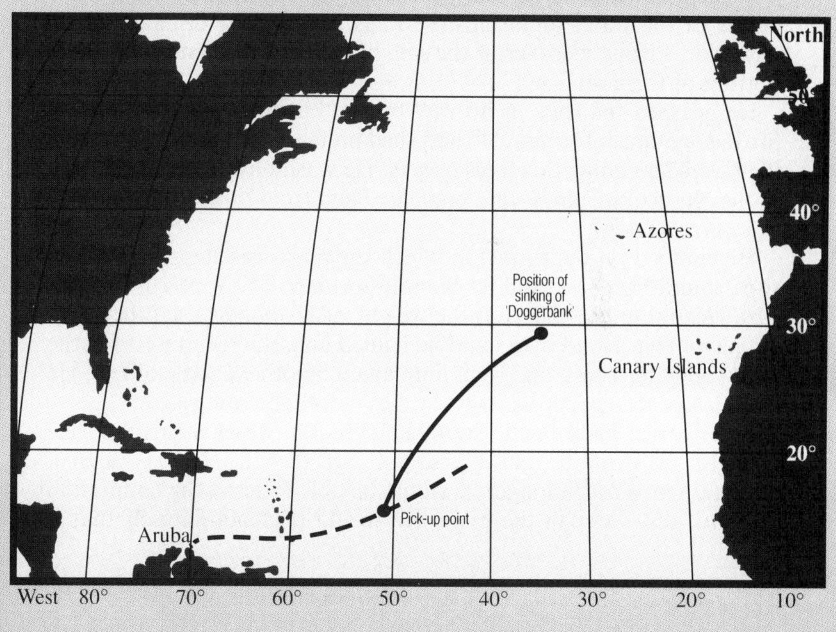
North
40°
Azores
Position of
sinking of
'Doggerbank'
30°
Canary Islands
20°
Pick-up point
Aruba
West
80°
70°
60°
50°
40°
30°
20°
10°

him, bent over him. Boywitt's cracked and bloated lips were quince-yellow. Pus was seeping from the corner of his mouth. Kuert gave a shudder and briefly averted his eyes. 'Papa, why did you have to drink that stuff? I told you it would kill you. Now it's raining. Come on.'

Boywitt made no sound as Kuert put a hand beneath his back. His head lolled sideways, his arms hung limp. Kuert knew he was dead, but he refused to accept the fact.

He crawled back to the sail and drank some more, half expecting Boywitt to sit up at any moment and join him.

At least I've got enough water to last me now.

It took a while to dawn on him that he had no receptacle of any kind. If he wanted to sail on, he would have to jettison the water, all that glorious water for which he'd waited so long.

It was an inhuman decision that confronted him, and he had to make it alone.

He sobbed silently, feebly, as he wrestled with the problem. He stripped off his ragged clothes, scooped up some water in his palm and emptied it over himself. Cuts and abrasions covered his entire body like leprosy. Every little scratch was festering from exposure to sea water. The skin was broken in innumerable places. He sluiced his wounds, conscious all the time that he was only postponing an inescapable decision.

You've got to keep going.

What if he emptied the rainwater into the boat? There were a few inches of sea water amidships. Perhaps it would be drinkable if he diluted it. Lifting a corner of the sail, he emptied its contents into the bottom of the boat.

He grasped the rope in his raw hands, but the weight of the sail proved too much for him. He had shed no tears for Boywitt, but now they were streaming down his cheeks. He wasn't aware of them, only of the physical weakness that prevented him from raising the sail. *You can't give up now.*

He climbed on the thwart in which the mast was stepped, tied the rope round his chest, and let himself go limp. The rope cut into his ribs, lacerating the skin, but the weight of his body raised the sail a couple of feet. Hand over hand he hauled himself erect, resecured the rope round his chest, and went limp again: another couple of feet. He had to repeat the process several times before the sail was set.

Afterwards, back in the stern, he eyed the water at his feet. He thought of Boywitt and his salt-seared throat. He was scared, uncertain how much longer he would be able to resist the temptation to drink the water in the bilge. He would persuade himself that it wouldn't harm him. In the end, he would drink it.

He secured the tiller and crawled forward. Taking the little square of canvas they had used as a bailer when the boat capsized, he emptied the bilge.

HE SAILED ON with the dead man still aboard. He cut his notches in the gunwale, slowly chewed the fragments of wood. The days and nights seemed indistinguishable. He never left the stern seat now. He would doze off, be jolted awake by some movement of the boat or the sail, and return to the present for another spell. His mind still rejected the fact of Boywitt's death. Was he really dead? At any rate, he was grateful for the continued presence of the figure in the bow.

But he was soon compelled to accept the truth. The sun had been beating down on the boat ever since the day the heavens opened, and the stench from the bow was becoming more and more intolerable. He long resisted the thought of consigning Boywitt to the sea. It seemed a form of betrayal. Besides, there were the sharks. They had never ceased to shadow the boat.

On the twenty-third day the stench became so bad that it forced his hand. He waited until dusk, Boywitt's favourite time of day, the time when the first stars appeared and he would sit on top of the *Doggerbank*'s monkey island.

'I've no choice, Papa.' Kuert found it quite natural to speak the words aloud. 'I wanted you to be there when we sight land, but I don't have any choice. Please forgive me.'

Taking hold of Boywitt's legs, he heaved them across the gunwale and rolled the rest of him overboard. He watched the motionless body drift away. The sharks darted forward at once, snapping at its extremities. Fighting over Boywitt's meagre remains, the big fish fell astern. Kuert watched them across the widening expanse of water. He felt very alone.

IT HAD BECOME A HABIT, suffering from thirst, enduring pain and fear. The worst of it was, nothing happened. He was alone, utterly alone. Even the wind deserted him. By day the sea was like glass, the sail hung limp as a shroud. At night a gentle breeze would spring up, so that was when he made progress. He was still on course. He kept the Great Bear just abaft the starboard beam, as the skipper had instructed him. During the day, when the wind dropped, he simply drifted. The sharks were still following.

Towards noon on the day he cut the twenty-fourth notch, the sharks startled a shoal of flying fish, one of which collided with the sail. It skimmed through the air on its gossamer fins, hit the canvas, and dropped into the bottom of the boat.

He pounced on the wriggling, flapping creature, which was no bigger than a herring, and twisted its head off. He sucked the blood that oozed from the gills. He didn't feel hungry, but he commanded himself to eat; he needed energy. Flying fish were a delicacy, he remembered Bahrend saying. He bit off a chunk of flesh, chewed the mouthful and tried to swallow it, but his throat was too constricted. He spat out the skin and put the remainder of the fish on the thwart to dry. The heat intensified his thirst. The sun was blisteringly hot. Almost directly overhead, it beat down upon him without mercy. Sweat ran into his eyes like molten lead. He seemed to see everything through a film of salt.

That afternoon he couldn't stand it any more. He crawled to the mast on all fours. He knew he would never manage to raise the sail again, but he didn't care, he had to have some protection from the sun. Everything swam before his eyes as he released the rope.

He draped the sail over the bow, crawled into its shade, and stretched out on the spot where Boywitt had died. The slight upward sweep of the bow created the most comfortable place in the entire boat. It was wonderful just to lie there after so many days at the tiller, just to lie there with the sail overhead, dozing lethargically.

THE TWENTY-FIFTH DAY DAWNED, and still he lay drowsing beneath the sail. Sometimes he watched the sharks swimming alongside. He could make out their steel-blue backs just below the surface. Sometimes he was awakened by a faint vibration as they dived beneath the boat. He had lost all fear of them. On the contrary, he was happy to have them there, occupying his thoughts. They were now his sole companions. What superb swimmers they were, even the young ones, tireless and tenacious!

He had heard of boats being overturned by sharks, but he felt sure these creatures meant him no harm when they made for the cool depths beneath the hull. Like him, they were merely seeking shade. He would be roused, time and again, by the sound of their tails lashing the water before they dived. He would feel a tremor run through the hull beneath him, turn his head, and see them break surface on the other side, their sleek bodies momentarily burnished silver by the sunlight.

HE NO LONGER KNEW what day it was. He had cut another notch that morning, the twenty-sixth, not that he was capable of counting.

His strength was almost gone, and he knew it. One day they would find him, a nameless corpse adrift in a nameless boat.

Holding the knife, he rolled over on his side. His bones seemed close to snapping every time he moved.

Slowly, letter by letter, he carved some words into the wood: name, nationality, place of birth, last ship. *You've got your coffin now, a big one all to yourself, complete with your name on it. Nothing more to do but wait, wait and see what it's like to die.*

That was when he saw the bird. It was hovering high overhead, immensely high, with dark, outspread wings. Was he only imagining it, or did the bird have some connection with death?

He could hardly breathe. He lay on his back and stared up at the sky. The bird had begun to gyrate. It described one sweeping circle, then another, then hovered on dark, motionless wings.

He stared at it transfixed, conscious of the pulse throbbing in his throat. The sight of the bird tormented him. It meant something, but its significance eluded him.

The sun was at its zenith. It showered down on him like incandescent rain. He crawled back under the sail.

Only the sharks were there now.

The sharks? No shark would produce that peculiar pounding in his ears. Perhaps it was another harbinger of death, like the bird.

The sound grew louder, its rhythmical churning more distinct. He could think of only one thing that made such a sound: the propellers of a ship in ballast.

PART THREE

The Survivor

The date was March 29, 1943, a Thursday. It was twenty-six days since the sinking of the *Doggerbank*. When sighted by the Spanish tanker, the dinghy was 1,600 nautical miles from the spot where the ship had gone down.

Sailing under the neutral flag of Spain, the *Campoamor* was owned by CAMPSA, the national petroleum monopoly. The 10,000-ton ship had left Barcelona two weeks before, on March 15, 1943, with orders to pick up a cargo of Venezuelan petroleum. She was due to reach her destination, the island of Aruba in the Lesser Netherlands Antilles, in three days' time.

The second officer of the *Campoamor* had come on watch at noon.

The day was very hot and almost windless. A dozen sharks were gambolling in the distance. The second officer watched them for a while. The sight of so many sharks so far out to sea puzzled him. At length he turned to the messenger and told him to fetch the captain.

When Joaquin Diaz appeared on the bridge, the second officer indicated a spot off the port bow. 'Sharks, sir, a lot of them, and all sticking close together. What do you make of it?'

Captain Diaz borrowed his binoculars. It was certainly unusual to see so many so far from land, but where was their prospective prey? There were no other vessels in sight.

Then, quite suddenly, he spotted the boat, a dinghy. But for the sharks, the two men realised later, they would never have noticed it.

Through the binoculars, Diaz made out a stumpy mast stepped amidships. There was no sail, just a tarpaulin draped over the bow, and no sign of anyone on board. The dinghy's bow bore no discernible name.

'Derelict, from the look of it.'

The *Campoamor*'s course had brought her closer to the boat, which now lay almost abeam. It drifted slowly nearer, still escorted by its attendant sharks.

The second officer looked at Diaz enquiringly. The captain hesitated. He could ill afford to lose any time. It had been a long voyage by way of their prescribed route across the Atlantic, a special shipping lane reserved for neutral vessels, and he was hoping to pass Martinique and enter the Caribbean at daybreak. On the other hand, the sharks' tenacity suggested that the boat contained human prey of some kind.

It was the sharks that finally persuaded him. 'Stop engines,' he ordered, 'and send Carducho to me.'

The *Campoamor*'s boatswain was a giant of a man. 'Get down there and take a look,' Diaz told him. 'You know the form, Carducho; no clothing, no bits and pieces, nothing but the man himself, if there is one. Don't touch more than you have to. I don't want any disease on board.'

THE STRANGE SOUND had stopped. Even the sunlight, which had rendered the canvas above his head translucent, was blotted out. He lay there in the sudden gloom, at a loss to understand what had happened. He tried to sit up, but he was too weak, so he raised his hand and pushed the sail aside. The big, dark shape was right alongside. It towered over him like the side of a ship.

So you still believe in miracles, he thought vaguely. He peered at the dark wall looming above him. *Rivets, portholes.* The dinghy was bumping against *metal.*

That bird, it had looked like a hawk. That was it! A hawk, a land bird, so land couldn't be that far off. The churning noise had sounded like a ship's propellers and the dark shape resembled a ship's side. And that thing up there? Red-yellow-red: a Spanish flag? He tried to shout, but all that issued from his lips was a hoarse croak.

He must have lost consciousness for a moment or two, because his next recollection was of foreign voices and a man stepping over the thwart; a huge, muscular man stripped to the waist. The man took a clasp-knife from the belt of his trousers and bent over him. He would never forget that expression. The stranger's eyes conveyed such horror and disbelief that Kuert knew he was safe. Then he passed out once more.

Diego Carducho, the *Campoamor*'s boatswain, took his clasp-knife and divested the man in the dinghy of his ragged garments, a pair of underpants and a singlet riddled with holes. His body was a mass of cuts and sores.

The men on deck had started to lower a boatswain's chair, but Carducho waved it away and called to them to lower a net instead. Carducho examined the dinghy. The interior was white with encrusted, sun-baked salt. The stern seat was stained, possibly with blood. The dried remains of a fish were laid out on the thwart. Carducho shook his head incredulously when he discovered the twenty-six notches in the gunwale. The knife used to cut them had fallen out when he slit the castaway's underpants.

Picking up the naked body, Carducho deposited it in the net and gave the signal to hoist away. Then, having set the dinghy adrift again, he climbed back up the ladder.

Captain Diaz, standing at the rail with several of his crew, looked on as the man from the dinghy was gently lowered to the deck, and lay there like a stranded fish.

Carducho disentangled him. The castaway lay slumped on the deck, a human skeleton with a month's growth of beard and a body covered in suppurating sores. The men of the *Campoamor* recoiled at the sight of him. One by one they raised their hands and made the sign of the cross. Carducho picked up the man's limp form—he was easy enough to lift—and carried him below to the sickbay.

Afterwards, back on the bridge, Captain Diaz watched the dinghy fall slowly astern. The sharks had disappeared.

The castaway was still unconscious when Diaz called the sickbay a little while later.

U43 WAS RETURNING TO BASE after three months on patrol in the Atlantic. On the morning of March 31, 1943, the French coast near Lorient loomed out of the morning mist. Barrage-breakers had already taken *U43* under their wing and were guiding it through the minefields that screened the big U-boat base.

Lieutenant Hans-Joachim Schwantke, *U43*'s skipper, was standing beneath the single pennant flying from the half-extended periscope—one only, signifying only one ship sunk. Unlike the rest of the U-boat group to which he had been assigned, whose convoy operation had ended in failure, he had been lucky to sink at least one ship, a British vessel of almost 10,000 tons, his very first kill.

He was glad when *U43* finally glided into its shadowy pen. For the first time in three months, he could feel safe from enemy bombs and depth charges.

Schwantke was in absolutely no doubt that the unescorted ship he had sunk was British. Like all U-boat commanders, he had to present himself at the headquarters of the BdU (Commander in Chief U-boats) and render a personal account of his latest patrol. On the strength of his report, and of the entries in *U43*'s war diary, the BdU's staff were equally convinced that *U43* had, on March 3, 1943, sunk a ship of the *Dunedin Star* class.

Of the *Doggerbank* there was no trace. Press reports and information received from agents based in foreign ports had yielded no news of her. Although there was a chance that the *Doggerbank* had been seized by an Allied warship, it was more probable that she had been sunk. If so, how and where had it happened? As yet, it occurred to no one that there might be a connection between the *Doggerbank*'s disappearance and the sinking reported by the commander of *U43*.

Schwantke was decorated with the Iron Cross First Class and promoted Kapitänleutnant (lieutenant senior grade).

A SMALL CABIN on the upper deck of the *Campoamor* had been set aside as a sickroom. It was hot and stuffy, and the castaway was lying on the narrow bunk naked except for the dressings that covered the worst of his cuts and sores.

Captain Joaquin Diaz had been standing beside the bunk for some time. The man was restless. Unintelligible sounds issued from his swollen lips as he tossed and turned. He had wasted away to a skeleton. Carducho had counted twenty-six notches on the dinghy's gunwale. Incredible, with no food or water on board. There was a strong possibility that they had rescued the man only to have him die on their hands.

'Has he drunk anything?' Diaz asked.

Carducho, who had been keeping watch over the castaway since picking him up, shook his head. 'I tried spooning some broth into him, but he brought it all up.'

Diaz stared at the tattoos on the man's arms. They were oozing where the salt had eaten into them. 'I will send out another SOS,' he said.

The *Campoamor*'s crew was too small to warrant a ship's doctor. As soon as the castaway had been picked up the tanker's radio operator had sent out an 'SOS–sick man on board', and a number of ships carrying doctors had replied. The *Campoamor* had reported the castaway's condition and received medical advice.

Diaz was puzzled. Carducho had found the man's name and nationality—German—carved into the boat's timbers, but how had he got there? German ships avoided these latitudes, which were heavily patrolled by the US Navy. There were one or two German submarines around, but the dinghy could hardly have come from a U-boat.

The unconscious man's lips were moving. Diaz bent over him, but all he could distinguish was '*Wasser*'.

'Maybe you should try him with plain water,' Diaz said. 'A spoonful of water with a few drops of brandy or rum in it.'

THE SMELL OF RUM brought him round. *You're dreaming*, he told himself, but it persisted: the unmistakable smell of brown rum. A light was burning in the cabin; yes, it was a cabin. A giant of a man was seated beside his bunk with a bottle of rum and a tumbler with a spoon in it. Kuert was thirstier than ever, thirstier than on any day in the dinghy. If he'd had the strength he would have snatched the bottle from the man's hand. He watched him pour some rum into the tumbler, barely enough to cover the bottom, and half fill the glass with water. One hand helped him to sit up, the other raised the glass to his lips.

He reached for it avidly, scared that it might be removed at the last moment. Even the touch of the glass on his lips hurt like hell, but he drank, swallowed; and gave a croak of pain. The rum burned his throat like fire, burned his stomach as well. He writhed and moaned, but he didn't vomit.

More. I've got to get at that bottle. He lay there, half asleep but obsessed with the thought. Then he noticed that he was alone. *The rum bottle.* He'd seen where the man had put it, in a kind of medicine chest. How to get at it, though? He tried to sit up, but without success. Rolling to the edge of the bunk, which wasn't very far from the ground, he fell off and landed with a crash. He lay there for a moment, gathering his strength. Then he crawled to the cupboard on all fours, opened it and picked up the bottle in both hands, barely able to support its weight.

They found Kuert on the floor with the bottle beside him, picked him up and put him back in his bunk. Then he slept soundly, without stirring or talking in his sleep, for twenty hours, twenty solid hours during which they could hardly tell if he was still breathing.

His aches and pains smote him with full intensity when he awoke, but his mind was quite clear. He learned the ship's name and its destination, Aruba.

He drank a cup of beef broth and managed to keep it down. He was too weak to stand or walk unaided, but he managed a few steps with the help of the boatswain and a steward.

There were some bathroom scales in his cabin. Supported by the two men, he weighed himself. In normal times he weighed 180 pounds; now he was down to 80. His worst moment came when he caught sight of himself in the mirror on the inside of the locker door, a skeletal figure covered in sores. He looked at the figure without at first recognising it as his own.

The face was hollow-eyed and spectral, the once-broad shoulders drooped, the collarbones protruded. The entire body was leprous with cuts and sores, and the skin was as scaly as a herring's.

At no time in the dinghy had he felt as wretched and helpless as he did now, in front of that mirror. He would never pull through, he told himself. He would never get back on his legs. He began to weep uncontrollably. His body shook like that of a man in a fever as the other two helped him back to his bunk.

THEY SIGHTED ARUBA two days later, on April 1. At noon the *Campoamor* stopped engines and anchored in the roads outside the oil port of Oranjestad. The castaway had been installed in a reclining chair on deck, where he lay swathed in blankets despite the heat. Too weak to walk unaided, he had been helped on deck and over to the chair by Carducho and another man.

Kuert could see the port from his vantage point on deck. A boat emerged from the harbour and headed for the *Campoamor* in a wide arc. It was a pilot boat flying the Dutch flag. He watched it until the ship hid it from view. Then he transferred his gaze to the place where the pilot would come aboard.

The pilot soon appeared, but he wasn't alone. Following him were three men in US Navy uniform. One was an officer, the other two wore MP armbands and carried submachine guns. They disappeared in the direction of the captain's cabin.

Kuert looked at Carducho, who was standing nearby. The Spanish boatswain shrugged his shoulders: the island of Aruba was Dutch territory, but the Americans, who maintained a substantial base there, ruled the roost.

'You won't hand me over, will you?'

The boatswain didn't answer.

'The captain promised he'd take me back to Spain.'

Kuert had been counting on it, though the prospect of an Atlantic crossing in the *Campoamor* filled him with dread. At some stage he had vowed never to set foot in another ship, but his desire to return to Germany was too strong. It had to do with the sinking of the *Doggerbank* and the submarine that had sent her to the bottom.

The captain of the *Campoamor* had questioned him about it, naturally. He vaguely remembered the interrogation. What was the name of his ship? The *Doggerbank*. Outward bound from where? Japan. Her cargo? Crude rubber, for the most part. Where had she been sunk? Approximately 36°N, 34°W. That was over 1,600 miles away! How had the ship been sunk? Torpedoed.

Kuert had a sudden thought. 'Did the captain send off a signal about me?'

'Yes. An SOS, because we don't carry a doctor,' said Carducho.

'Anything else?'

'He said we'd picked you up, and so on.'

'My nationality?'

'It's customary.'

'And the name of my ship? The place where she went down?'

'Possibly, but that's customary too. What else could we do? We're a neutral ship.'

Of course! That explained the presence of the Americans.

A seaman appeared at Kuert's elbow: Captain Diaz would like a word with him. Carducho and the seaman helped him to the captain's cabin. The two naval MPs were standing guard outside. As soon as he entered he could tell from the captain's face that his suspicions were well founded.

The American officer, it transpired, was a doctor. He barely glanced at Kuert, then turned to Diaz. 'You can't possibly keep this man on board. He needs proper medical treatment in a hospital ashore. He could die on you. Think it over. I'll be back in an hour.'

Joaquin Diaz didn't speak for a while after the American had left

ABOVE: Fritz Kuert's children, Karin, Fred and Brunhilde.

BELOW: Grand Admiral Dönitz, Commander-in-Chief U-boats, signed this photograph for Fritz Kuert, former boatswain of the *Doggerbank*, when the latter visited him in 1961.

BELOW: The Italian freighter *Savoia* after being bombed off Brindisi in 1941. Boatswain Fritz Kuert survived four sinkings in vessels of this kind, which were used as supply ships for the Afrika Korps.

ABOVE: Fritz Kuert, sole survivor of the *Doggerbank*, after his release from an American prisoner-of-war camp in January 1945.

the cabin. 'Perhaps it really would be best,' he said at length, 'for your own sake.'

'But I'm doing all right.'

'They can force my hand. We're a neutral ship, of course, but they'll make difficulties. They won't let us take on oil. They won't provision us or give us any drinking water or fuel. There are plenty of options open to them.'

He wasn't just making empty excuses, Kuert could tell. 'You mean they've asked you to hand me over?'

'More or less, yes.'

He started to weep. His knees buckled, and he would have collapsed if they hadn't caught him in time. It didn't really matter what became of him. He was weary, infinitely weary. Even as he stood there, he felt himself falling asleep on his feet.

He was roused by the sound of a siren. For a moment he thought he was in an ambulance, but when he opened his eyes he saw that he was still on board ship and back in his bunk. Carducho and the signal officer were there. The wail of the siren grew louder, then died away.

'The Americans?'

Carducho nodded.

Kuert was ready. He had no need to pack; all he possessed was a borrowed pair of trousers, a borrowed shirt and his life.

Once on deck, he saw an olive-green van adorned with a red cross on a white background parked on the quayside. Flanking it were two Jeeps, and standing beside them were four armed US marines. And all, thought Kuert, for the sake of one feeble, exhausted German seaman.

Captain Diaz was waiting for him at the head of the accommodation ladder. Most of the tanker's crew were there too, just as they had been when he was hoisted aboard in the net three days earlier. They stepped aside as the captain came up to Kuert and kissed him on both cheeks.

Two medical orderlies were ready with a stretcher. He didn't resist when they lifted him onto it. It was only a few steps to the ambulance, but the rocking motion made him feel sick and dizzy. He shut his eyes as they slid him into the interior.

The doors closed, enveloping him in gloom, and the ambulance set off. His sickness and dizziness returned. That rocking motion. Where was he? Then the siren started wailing and his mind cleared: Aruba, an American ambulance, two Jeeps. What a performance! He almost felt like laughing, but he didn't delude himself: he might be bound for hospital, but he was, to all intents and purposes, a prisoner of war.

AN ENCIPHERED RADIO MESSAGE from Spain broke the news. It was only a routine report from the naval attaché at the German embassy in Madrid, but it enabled the German Admiralty to solve the mystery of the *Doggerbank*.

According to the signal from Madrid, a Captain Joaquin Diaz had made the following deposition on his return from a voyage to Venezuela: the *Campoamor* had picked up a castaway adrift in a dinghy. The man had given his particulars as Boatswain Fritz Kuert of the German merchant marine, last ship the *Doggerbank*. On March 3 of the same year, southwest of the Azores at a spot some 36°N, 34°W, his ship had been sunk by a submarine. The Dutch and US authorities at Aruba had requested that the said Kuert be turned over to them, and their request had been granted.

The report reached Berlin, where it was evaluated by Abteilung Seekrieg I, or Naval Operations, the department to which responsibility for all German merchantmen and auxiliary cruisers had been assigned for the duration of the war.

Late in 1942 Naval Operations had launched a major blockade-running operation which would, it was hoped, transport a total of 140,000 tons of dry goods and 70,000 tons of vegetable oils to Germany from the Far East. The *Doggerbank* was one of the vessels engaged in this operation and one of the first to be expected back from her long and circuitous voyage. She was thus a particularly valuable ship, not only on account of her cargo, but also because her captain's debriefing report promised to be highly informative. In the event, the *Doggerbank* never reached Bordeaux, her destination.

The staff officers at Naval Operations had been debating the *Doggerbank*'s whereabouts for weeks. The signal from Madrid disposed of that question, but it failed to reveal exactly what had happened. As for the date of the sinking, March 3, 1943, the German Admiralty found this puzzling because the *Doggerbank* was not assumed to have made such good progress. Most puzzling of all, however, was the report that she had been sunk by a submarine.

No enemy submarine had claimed a sinking on that day, and the enemy would scarcely have neglected to report such a success. Enquiries were made at Section OP, Operation Atlantic, of Naval Operations. A check was run on the records at HQ C in C U-Boats, situated in the Hotel am Steinplatz, Berlin-Charlottenburg. A sinking on March 3, 1943, southwest of the Azores? The war diaries of Germany's own submarines were examined as a matter of routine. Had any U-boat reported such a sinking?

Only one had done so: *U43*, commanded by the newly promoted

Kapitänleutnant Hans-Joachim Schwantke. However, Schwantke had reported sinking a British ship, the *Dunedin Star*, or at least a ship of the same class, and his claim was finally confirmed.

But now? For the first time, C in C U-Boats' chief of staff began to have doubts. The *Dunedin Star* outweighed the *Doggerbank* by nearly 3,000 tons. Could Schwantke's estimate have been so wide of the mark? The date of the sinking, as reported by the captain of *U43*, was identical to that cited by the *Doggerbank*'s sole survivor. The same applied to the ship's position when sunk. Wasn't this one coincidence too many? The castaway was unavailable for questioning. Where was Schwantke, out on patrol again? No, still on leave.

Schwantke was summoned to Berlin, together with all members of his crew who had been on the *U43*'s bridge when it surfaced after the attack. By now it was May 1943, over two months since the *Doggerbank* went down.

The naval officers assigned to the board of inquiry soon ascertained the truth. They found after renewed questioning 'that *U43* had, in fact, sunk the *Doggerbank*. The captain's evaluation of her class and size was very inaccurate, with the result that his war diary entries could not at first be reconciled with the *Doggerbank*.'

In view of all these facts, should the captain of *U43* be court-martialled? Was Schwantke guilty, and if so of what? No one had warned him to look out for a blockade-runner. He had violated no ban on attacking lone merchantmen, nor had he broken any regulation by failing to pick up a survivor, even though this might have enabled him to rescue a considerable proportion of the *Doggerbank*'s crew.

But there was yet another consideration. At this stage of the war, when German U-boat commanders were putting to sea in obsolete, ill-equipped boats, patrolling the Atlantic was a form of living hell. The heavy losses incurred by the U-boat section necessitated that Schwantke reassume command of *U43*. This being so, it would be preferable not to burden him with the information that he had sunk a German ship.

So the file on the sinking of the *Doggerbank* remained closed. Relatives of her 364 dead received the following brief communication: 'Precise details cannot be divulged for reasons of security. We are at war, and any information that may imperil ships or their crews must be withheld.'

SCHWANTKE HAD RETURNED to Lorient to make his boat ready for sea. *U43* departed its base on July 13, 1943.

Schwantke did not receive his full orders until he was at sea. He was instructed by radio to proceed to West Africa and mine the waters off the Nigerian port of Lagos, a major Allied transshipment point.

It was quite coincidental, nothing more, that on July 30, seventeen days after leaving Lorient, Kapitänleutnant Schwantke's boat reached the area southwest of the Azores where it had sunk the *Doggerbank* on March 3.

The weather was fine and sunny, as it had been then. That morning *U43* had rendezvoused with *U403*. In addition to mines for the Lagos operation, *U43* was carrying extra fuel for *U403*. Once *U403* had taken on oil for its diesel engines, the two captains exchanged a final salute. Then *U43* cast off and got under way.

The sea was calm and deserted, but appearances were deceptive. *U43* and *U403* had already been spotted. An enemy aircraft, a Wildcat from VC29 Squadron, had detected both U-boats with its new short-wave Direction Finds equipment. It had taken off from the US aircraft carrier *Santee*.

The Wildcat, up-sun from the U-boats and a considerable distance away, escaped detection by their lookouts. The pilot had radioed the *Santee*, which promptly dispatched two Avenger bombers. The Avengers were duly guided to their quarry by the Wildcat.

The Wildcat made the first pass. It dived on the U-boats out of the dazzling sun. The pilot saw figures running to man the guns, but they never got there. Machine-gun bullets slammed into the casing and whipped the sea into a lather, mowing down the gun crews like a scythe. As he pulled out, the pilot saw those who were still alive running back to the conning tower.

Both submarines proceeded to dive.

U403 escaped with minor damage, but it escaped for the time being only. One week later, having been hunted without respite, it was cornered and sunk.

Not so *U43*, Schwantke's boat.

The second Avenger, piloted by USN Lieutenant Robert F. Richmond, was still two hundred yards from the U-boat. The forecasing was already awash when the Avenger released its pair of bombs and a 'Tido', or homing torpedo.

Richmond pulled out and observed the submarine through his side window.

What happened next was so unexpected, so terrible a spectacle, that he couldn't at first account for it. *U43* blew up like a gigantic firework, debris flew in all directions, flames shot into the air. The series of explosions went on and on. The turbulence was so extreme that Richmond was hard put to it to keep his Avenger airborne.

When he flew over the spot a minute later, nothing could be seen but a big, spreading patch of oil. The truth dawned on him at last: mines! The U-boat must have been carrying mines; it was, in effect, a floating ammunition dump.

The date was July 30, 1943. *U43* and its crew had survived the men of the *Doggerbank* by less than five months.

And this time there was no survivor to tell the tale.

FRITZ KUERT, THE CASTAWAY from the *Doggerbank*, had been an American prisoner in the Lesser Netherlands Antilles for nearly three and a half months.

His condition for the first few days was relatively good, but it hadn't lasted. He suffered a relapse and developed pneumonia. His sea-water sores, which refused to heal, continuously oozed and suppurated. His heart and his immune system had been weakened.

It was six weeks before he could walk unaided, and he was slow to put on weight in spite of ample food and regular vitamin injections. Because of his condition, they decided to take him to the USA, to a hospital in New Orleans.

In New Orleans the *Doggerbank*'s sole survivor had suffered another relapse and was lying in the isolation ward of the military hospital, stricken with typhus. His condition remained grave for three months, then improved. He was transferred to Interrogation Camp No. 6, a secret facility, also known as 'Meade', that formed part of the Fort George prisoner-of-war camp. He was grilled by the Americans and British in turn, but he stuck to his story. Then, in October, the interrogations suddenly ceased. It was clear that his story had been corroborated by information received from other sources: the *Doggerbank*, formerly the *Speybank*, had been sunk by a German submarine! For Boatswain Fritz Kuert, this was his first confirmation of a fact he had always thrust to the back of his mind.

His next ports of call were Fort Myers and the hospital at Valley Forge. Then, midway through December 1943, he was informed that his name appeared on the list of prisoners earmarked for exchange. Who in Germany had put him on it? Who considered him, a humble boatswain, important enough to be released?

Just before the turn of the year he boarded the *Charles A. Stafford*, a ship on charter to the International Red Cross. Her port of destination was Marseilles. From there he and the others would travel by train to Geneva to be exchanged for American prisoners of war. Then Germany. That was where he would finally learn the whole truth, but to what end? What would it avail him? More particularly, what would it avail his former shipmates? Schneidewind, Stachnovski, Bahrend, Waldemar, Papa Boywitt? What motivated him? Simply the thought that he was the *Doggerbank*'s sole survivor, and that he alone could ascertain the truth on the others' behalf.

That thought was uppermost in his mind throughout the crossing.

That and fear. The neutral ship was brightly illuminated, but it was still wartime. Despite the cold, he spent the days and nights on deck, never leaving the vicinity of the lifeboats. And, just as Jan Bahrend used to do, he kept a weather eye open for submarines.

Epilogue

A November day in 1961. More than eighteen years have passed since the *Doggerbank* went down.

Kuert has an appointment in Aumühle, on the outskirts of Hamburg. A road lined with imposing mansions, one of them being Dora Specht Allee 1. It sounds like an encoded U-boat signal, and the man who inhabits it was formerly, at various times, C in C U-Boats, Commander in Chief of the German Navy, and the Greater German Reich's last head of government: Grand Admiral Karl Dönitz.

It is 11am. Fritz Kuert, erstwhile boatswain of the *Doggerbank*, is on time, but he hesitates briefly. What is he doing here, over eighteen years after the event?

Kuert waited out the end of the war in his Hamburg hiding place. There were no ships in which he could have sailed. He returned to the parental home and obtained a job at the colliery where his father worked, a job above ground though, because of his poor health. He helped to rebuild his parents' bomb-damaged house, got married, and fathered three children. He had survived.

But then came the letters. From Papa Boywitt's wife, Schneidewind's family, Stachnovski's mother, Binder's sisters . . . Having learned that one member of the *Doggerbank*'s crew was alive, they begged him for information, for the truth that had never come out. He wrote back. His memories revived, and so did his urge to investigate anew. He tried to locate Schwantke and discovered that the captain of *U43* had survived his victims by only a few months. So why? What was he doing here?

Dönitz, an affable, white-haired old gentleman, answers the door in person and conducts him to the drawing room. Before Kuert can say a word, he brings out a scrapbook filled with press cuttings. The *Doggerbank*? No, Nuremberg, his trial for war crimes, his years in

Spandau Prison. He speaks of the cruel injustice he suffered at the hands of the Allies.

Kuert listens, looks at him, and wonders why he came. All the questions he has been meaning to ask seem pointless, now that he's face to face with this man who talks only of himself, of the wrongs and false accusations that *he* has had to endure.

'It's about the *Doggerbank*,' says Kuert. That, after all, is the reason for his presence.

Dönitz shakes his head. Heavens, it's so long ago. Of course he remembers the incident, naturally he does. A 'distressing business', but it was wartime, don't forget, and 'you can't make an omelette without breaking eggs . . .'

Listening to him, Kuert is struck by the realisation that they're talking about entirely different things. Three hundred and sixty-four men died a miserable death, but their only memorial is a number, a small and insignificant item in the war's great balance sheet.

'We'd probably have court-martialled them, Schneidewind and Schwantke, and acquitted them both. A regrettable combination of circumstances.'

It's pointless to linger, pointless to listen to him any longer.

The two men rise. Dönitz goes over to a writing desk and produces a postcard-sized photograph. 'I've only a few of these left.'

An official photograph from the great days of the Third Reich: Dönitz in his grand-admiral's uniform, complete with orders and decorations.

He unscrews a fountain pen, scribbles a dedication: 'To Fritz Kuert in kind remembrance, Aumühle, November 17, 1961', and signs it.

Kuert takes the photograph.

In kind remembrance.

What he feels, for the very first time, is hatred, burning hatred for those who sacrificed the lives of his shipmates to no purpose, and mingled with that emotion is a sense of utter hopelessness. He takes his leave.

It has started to rain. He walks off down the road, which is paved with wet leaves. He doesn't look back.

He waits at the station. He has two more appointments scheduled for today, both with retired admirals. He will not keep them.

The train pulls in. He boards it. He knows he won't ask any more questions, but he also knows he'll never be free of being the sole survivor of the *Doggerbank*.

HANS HERLIN

Hans Herlin belongs to the generation that experienced the terrors of the Second World War at first hand. At the outbreak of war he was only fourteen years old but by 1944, when the Allies were closing in on Nazi Germany, he was old enough to fight. 'I was called up and given brief air-force training with eight other young men,' the author remembers. 'But because of a TB infection I was put into a military hospital and so didn't see active service. My eight comrades, all seventeen- to nineteen-year-olds, were shot down on their first mission.'

After the war Hans Herlin became a journalist, receiving excellent training on the prestigious periodical *Stern* and gaining solid experience as an investigative journalist. It was in the 1960s, while researching a series of articles about U-boat captains for *Stern*, that Hans Herlin first came across an account of the sinking of the *Doggerbank* and got to know Fritz Kuert. 'His story gripped me,' acknowledges the author. 'I suggested to Kuert that we make a book out of it and he agreed. He spent several hours telling me about his life and the dreadful fate of the *Doggerbank* and I recorded it on a tape recorder.' Herlin also took great care to verify Kuert's information, examining the transcripts of the official inquiry and interviewing the surviving members of *U43*'s crew, who had left the submarine prior to its final patrol.

Hans Herlin's one regret is that Kuert did not live to see his memorable story published in English. He died on July 27, 1986.

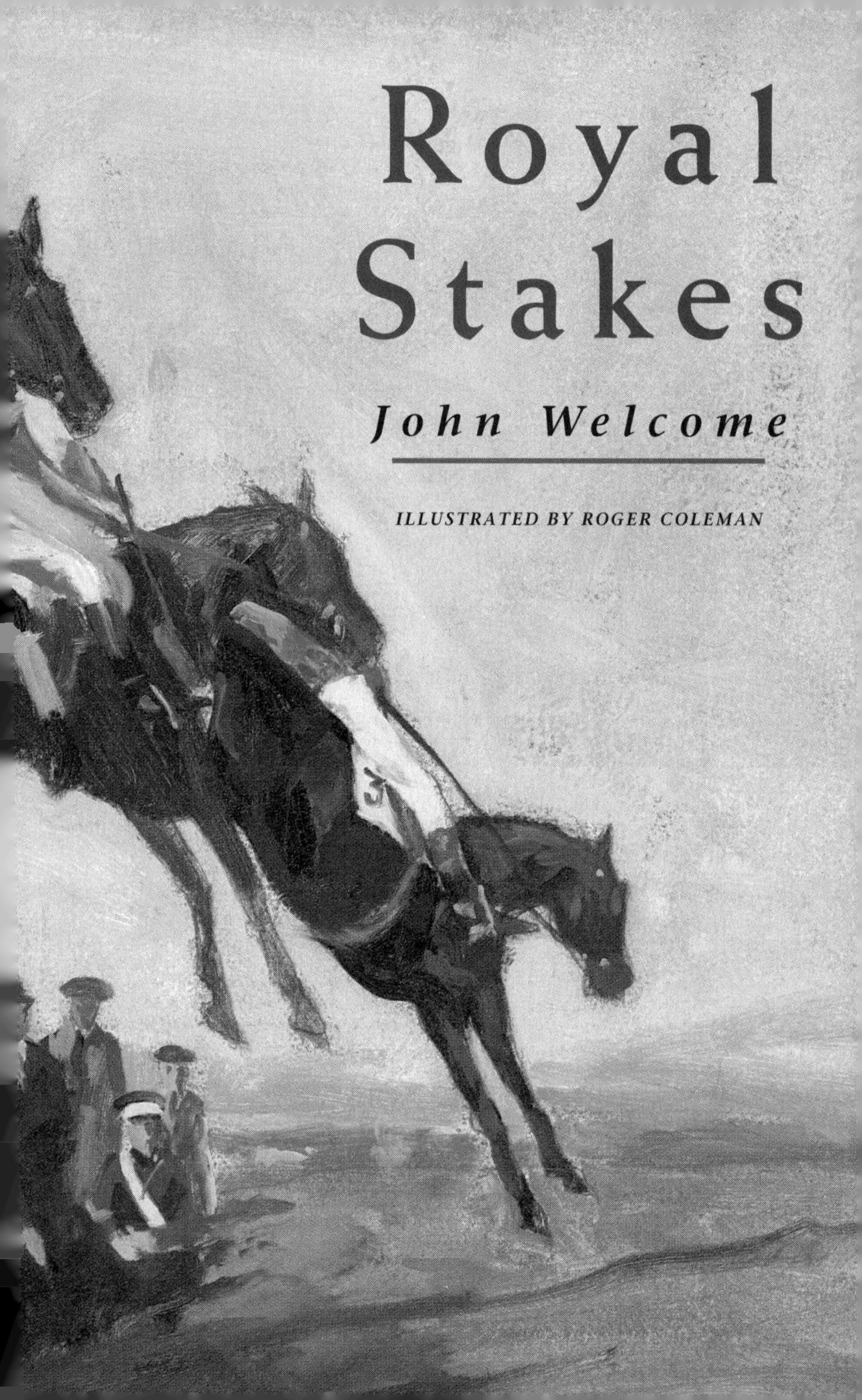
Royal
Stakes
John Welcome
ILLUSTRATED BY ROGER COLEMAN

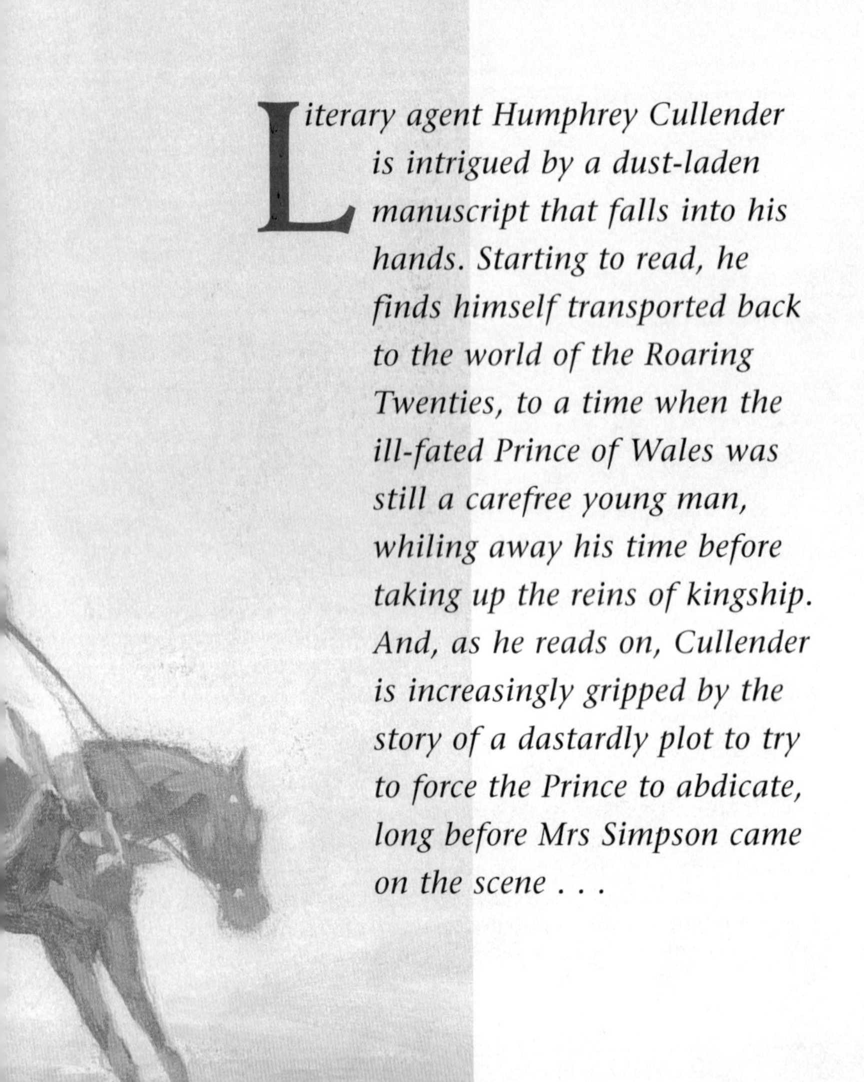

Literary agent Humphrey Cullender is intrigued by a dust-laden manuscript that falls into his hands. Starting to read, he finds himself transported back to the world of the Roaring Twenties, to a time when the ill-fated Prince of Wales was still a carefree young man, whiling away his time before taking up the reins of kingship. And, as he reads on, Cullender is increasingly gripped by the story of a dastardly plot to try to force the Prince to abdicate, long before Mrs Simpson came on the scene . . .

Prologue

About a year or so back we were having trouble with one of our authors or, rather, he was having trouble with his writing and desperately looking to us for help. I'd better explain before I go any further that my name is Humphrey Cullender and I am a literary agent, a partner in the firm of Cullender and Colton and the author in question, Max Melville, who wrote stirring tales of the Second World War on sea and land, had done very well for both himself and us—until now. He had dried up, he said, and was suffering from writer's block. His contract provided for his delivering his new novel in two months' time and he had scarcely started it. In fact he had run out of ideas after about ten thousand words and had already torn up two drafts of that. What on earth was he to do?

My partner and I discussed it and it was decided that I should go over to see him. He lived on the west coast of Ireland and to tell the truth I was not looking forward to the trip as I thought there was very little help I could give, but he was a valuable client who'd been paid a whopping advance, so it was up to us to help him if we could.

When I arrived he told me that his mind was clogged up, and inspiration would not come. I made reassuring noises and suggested that he make his mind a blank for a bit and that somehow the flow would return. It all worked out in the end and the third of his books was his best; but that has little to do with what came out of my visit.

Towards its end we were sitting on his terrace looking down to the waters of the bay when Melville suddenly said, 'Good of you to take the trouble to come over, Humphrey. Wish I could do something in return. Tell you what, why don't you go and see Dermot de Lacey down the bay? His father died recently and he's winding up his affairs. I knew the old boy quite well: he must have been nearing ninety but he had all his faculties. He mentioned he was writing a book, something to do with some sort of racing sensation in the family.'

The old saying that everyone has a book in him is a fallacy which has been proved many times over, and goodness knows how often have those dreaded words: 'I've written a book, care to have a look at it?' been dropped into an agent's ear. It was more than likely, I thought, that this would be a dreary sludge of ill-digested reminiscence fit only for the slush pile.

'Dermot has found the typescript,' he went on. 'There's something about the Duke of Windsor when he was Prince of Wales in it, I believe. They went hunting and racing together back in the twenties. No harm looking, is there? I'll go and phone him now.'

Without giving me time to refuse he shot off inside to the telephone. In a few minutes he was back. 'You're bidden to lunch tomorrow,' he said. 'Twelve o'clock. It's a couple of miles down the road.'

I'm bound to say that it was in no very sanguine mood that I pulled up before the de Lacey bungalow next day. Dermot de Lacey was in his late forties, tall and angular, greying a little at the temples. The first thing I saw when he brought me into a spacious living room was a pair of framed photographs. One depicted two men in steeplechasing jerseys smiling at the camera in a parade ring, the other of the same two hacking home from hunting. One of them was unmistakably the young Duke of Windsor looking boyish and happy, the other I presumed to be de Lacey's father. Both were signed across the corner EDWARD P.

'Yes,' de Lacey said, following my glance as he mixed me a king-sized gin and tonic. 'That's my father with the Prince, or HRH as he always called him. His Royal Highness. I'd better explain that I don't know the first thing about racing. I was a dreadful disappointment to my father who wanted me to follow in his footsteps.'

'It often happens,' I said noncommittally.

'He'd ridden over two hundred winners,' he went on. 'And he was proud of it.'

'What about the book?' I said.

'It's there.' He pointed to two blue-bound folders lying on a side table. 'I found it in a drawer after he died. We knew he was writing it, of course. You see, my grandfather ran into trouble, racing, back in the twenties. It was never really referred to in the family when I was growing up—if it was mentioned at all, it was just called "the trouble" but it did rather hang over my grandmother and to a certain extent my father. He said it was a bit of unwritten history that ought to be told.'

'Did that concern the Duke of Windsor?' I asked.

'It did. You'll find it all there. He knew him well as a young man and he never lost his admiration for him.'

'He took his time about telling it,' I said.

'Well, he'd lived a full life and it was only late on that he came to live here and to put it all down. Then he said he had to wait until people in it were all dead. But he insisted that it was worth doing. I wonder what you'll think of the manuscript. It's redolent of the twenties. My goodness it was a different world then, wasn't it?'

'I'll tell you the truth when I've read it,' I said. 'That's my job. I hope you won't be offended if I don't think it's up to scratch.'

'Of course not,' he said. 'I don't know whether you'd care to take the folders away, or start on them here, before we have lunch. I can leave you alone. I've lots to do going through things and I expect you'll be able to reach a verdict pretty quickly.'

I had the idea that Max Melville's writing cylinders were beginning to fire again and he would be happy to have me away for a while. 'Thanks,' I said. 'I'll do that if I may.'

Settling myself in an armchair and with no very great expectation I picked up the first of the folders and began to read.

Chapter One

When my father was warned off the Turf, I, Danny de Lacey, was in my last year at school. The warning-off was the result of one of those doping cases which took place years before the stewards relaxed the rule placing absolute responsibility on the trainer if one of his charges was tested positive for dope. My father had a winner at Ascot who was tested, traces of a prohibited substance were found and that was that. The penalty then was mandatory and he had to go.

He had been hit hard by the decision as you may imagine. It didn't break him for he was not the sort of man to be broken by misfortune; instead he was determined to find the real culprit and why it had been done. To that end he hired a firm of private detectives and they quickly came to the conclusion that it was an inside job.

My father trained at Newmarket, with forty horses in his care. He trained for and mixed with several members of the Jockey Club and other swells, and he had a devoted staff, all of whom had been with him for years. Just before Ascot some sort of gastric infection had scourged the human element in the stable and he had been forced to take on three temporary stablelads.

The permanent staff were cleared and suspicion focused on the three temporaries. They had gone, of course, but the enquiry agents found two of them in different stables and satisfied themselves of their innocence. The third had disappeared. They managed to trace him to Liverpool where he had taken a boat to America and there they lost him—irrevocably. The two other temporaries testified that they knew nothing about him or his background and that he had left before they did, once Ascot was over. There was, too, a suspicion that the name he gave when he was taken on was not the one he had been christened with. All the evidence pointed to the fact that he had been paid to do the job by someone with a grudge against my father, but in any event the trail had run cold.

Then my father had had his stroke. He had received a message, my mother told me, to meet someone who could give him information about the doping. He was told to go to the Royal Albion Hotel at Brighton on the eve of Brighton races, where he would be telephoned to arrange the meeting. He had left home optimistic, but the next thing my mother heard was that he had been found unconscious, in his car near Beachy Head, having suffered a stroke. (He had, although I was unaware of it at the time, suffered from high blood pressure.) My mother had endured the shame and indignity of the warning-off, and now this second tragedy was a terrible blow to her.

Here I think I had better say something of my parents. My mother was a cold, hard, determined woman. She was one of the best horsewomen across Leicestershire when my father married her and that was not a crown she was prepared to surrender by rearing a brood of 'snivelling brats'; she had one child, myself, and after that my parents occupied separate rooms and to a large extent went their own ways, though there remained a bond of interest and affection between them. So when the crash came she took it as a personal humiliation and withdrew to our house in Ireland, hunting with the local pack which she found 'drearily provincial' and drinking more than she should. By this time I had begun my first term at Oxford where I, too, found myself the object of curious glances and snide remarks about my father.

My father was tall and lean. He trained at Madagascar House, Newmarket, where he lived during the flat season. In the winter he hunted from Melton and in Ireland. Some time before I was born an aunt had left him Kilbarry House in Westmeath. He loved it and it was where I was brought up. My father spent the early part of the hunting season there. Later, after Christmas, 'when hounds really begin to run' he would go to Melton where he mixed on even terms with the swells and cut most of them down, too, over their own country. It was that ability to ride in front and stay there which brought him into close acquaintance with the Prince of Wales, who was also hunting from Melton then.

When he was at Kilbarry he took immense pains with my introduction to hunting and racing. We were both lucky in that, unlike some children of horse-mad parents, I loved it from the start. He mounted me on the best, by which I don't mean putting me up on some flashy brute that cost a bomb, but choosing something that could jump safely and would carry me over anything. I can see him now—he loved to be up with hounds—looking back to see if I was all right, teaching me by his example to have an eye for country, to know what the hounds were doing and to take my own line. And afterwards at tea before a log fire I can see him, too, his long legs stretched towards the flames, talking to me as if I was his equal, discussing the hunt, the fences we jumped and the way we and the fox had gone. And it was the same when I started to ride in point-to-points. Whatever success I later achieved as a GR, or gentleman rider (we called ourselves that in those days), I owe it to him. No wonder that I was desolated by his stroke and the thought that he would remain a hulk, unspeaking, unable to move, cared for by nurses in an upstairs room at Kilbarry for as long as breath was left in him.

In a way, it came as no surprise when my mother summoned me home from Oxford. I found her in the library at Kilbarry; she had just come in from hunting and was standing in front of the fire, still in her habit, a whisky and soda in her hand, tall, angular and handsome. 'I'm taking you away from Oxford,' she said abruptly. 'Sit down. I want to talk to you.'

It was then that she told me the full details of my father's warning-off, his struggles to nail the culprit and the suspicious circumstances surrounding his stroke. 'When the warning-off notice appeared in the *Racing Calendar* I went to stand by him,' she said. 'We had dinner together in London and he told me he was certain he had been framed. He wouldn't elaborate, he said it was as well I didn't know too much, that that might have been his trouble, that he knew too much and there were those in high places who wanted to ruin him. He was remorseful, saying he felt the shame he had brought on us both but he was damned if he was going to lie down under it.'

'Is that why he employed the detective agency?' I asked.

'Of course, and when they found out about that third lad disappearing he was more than ever convinced. "Shipped out," he said. "I wonder who paid for his passage." '

My mother stared into the fire. 'He came back here, you know, during that awful time,' she said. 'He thought of suing the Jockey Club for their wording of the warning-off notice, and bringing everything into the open, but he decided not to. "It would mean involving someone I owe both loyalty and friendship to," he said. "And I will not do it." '

'I suppose he meant the Prince,' I said.

'He must have done, though always in this affair he spoke in riddles. He did murmur something about a plot against the Prince, but I could tell that he was holding something back. He said all along, too, that he didn't want his troubles to involve you and me. But talk of a possible libel action was freely bandied about in hunting and racing circles. There was even a paragraph about it in a gossip column. I don't know if it is a coincidence, but shortly after that your father got the message to go to the meeting in Brighton. You know what happened then, or, rather, you don't because nobody does.'

'Are you telling me the stroke wasn't a pure accident?'

'I'm sure of it. There were marks on his body which were never explained. Someone wanted him out of the way and didn't care how. And he can't tell us and never will.'

'But, Mother, who?'

'That stablelad who disappeared, he must know something. Whoever set up the whole thing must have had resources and power and covered their tracks well. But it was at Melton that it all began. He said as much. The truth lies there, or some of it anyway. I want you to go to Melton and see what you can find.'

Melton! My heart leaped at the very words—Melton Mowbray in High Leicestershire, the mecca of all hunting people. But Melton without horses offered no prospect at all. My father's string had all been sold and dispersed. 'But how—' I wondered aloud.

'I want you to keep your eyes and your ears open. There's bound to be talk. Someone there knows more than he, or she for that matter, is letting on. There's a friend of your father's, a Captain Terrier, he was veterinary officer of your father's regiment and he's now looking after the remounts at Melton. He's always on the lookout for civilian rough-riders. I've written to him. He'll give you a trial.' She left me in no doubt that she did not expect me to let her down. 'I've told him,' she went on, 'that I want you to get experience in both riding and veterinary. He knows nothing of your real purpose. You'll be unpaid because if you ride for hire you won't ever be able to ride races or point-to-points as an amateur again. I'll make you a sufficient allowance to cover all that.'

It was a marvellous opportunity. At that time of my life there was nothing else I wanted to do save spend my time with horses. I'd be right on the inside, and perhaps there would be the chance of a hunt with one of those splendiferous Shire packs of which I had so often heard my father speak. Oxford would have to be abandoned, but I had not been up long enough to make firm friendships and I was eager to be off for wider horizons. 'When do I start?' I asked.

'As soon as you can get onto the mailboat,' my mother said.

Chapter Two

The remount depot at Melton had the responsibility for supplying the army with fresh horses. There would be seventy or eighty of them at any one time, divided into troopers and those likely to make officers' chargers. The better ones went to the cavalry and the Horse Guards; but in the cavalry there were racing regiments and polo regiments and to some extent the chargers had to be suited to the requirements of each. The depot was situated outside the town in a 300-acre farm where the offices and tie-up lines were. There was, too, a large paddock with a jumping lane down one side and a set of schooling fences. Standing by the gate when I arrived was a man who introduced himself as Captain Terrier. Below medium height, he had a knowing eye behind thick glasses, a humorous quirk to his mouth, and a general air of briskness and efficiency. After greeting me he looked me up and down, nodded and said, 'Come to ride, have you? All right, let's see you do it.'

I had a feeling I was being set up for something as I noticed a slight smile on Captain Terrier's lips. A common-looking horse was brought up and I approached him warily.

'Walk him round, out of the gate, bring him back, canter, and then take him down the jumping lane,' Captain Terrier instructed me.

The big trooper was a rotten mover, and as we approached the gate I felt him tighten himself under me. I guessed then what was coming: he was going to veer to one side. Three strides from the gate, before he had time to do anything, I let him have one, hard, down the shoulder. He gave a snort of surprise, shook his big ugly head and walked out as quietly as a kitten. From trotting a little way down the path I turned, brought him back and put him into a canter round the paddock. He sent up a few signals before entering the jumping lane, but by that time I had him where I wanted him and he lumbered over the obstacles effectively if not prettily.

'That's enough,' Captain Terrier said when I pulled up beside him. 'Get down now and come along and meet my chief.'

Colonel 'Pirate' Probert had lost a leg in the war and had been given the job of commanding the remounts at Melton. He had acquired his nickname because he had a piratical air, accentuated by the rolling gait caused by his artificial leg. He was no respecter of persons, nor inclined to suffer fools gladly. He ran the remounts as if they were a feudal fief of his own and woe betide anyone from the War Office who tried to interfere with him. But there was kindness and sympathy behind his appearance, and if you did your job for him, he would go to lengths to help and encourage you.

'New recruit, Colonel,' Captain Terrier said, saluting, as he brought me into his office.

The colonel gave me a piercing stare from a pair of unblinking grey eyes. 'You're Dick de Lacey's boy, aren't you?' he said. 'Well, if you're half as good as your father, you'll do, but we can't pay you anything. If we did you'd lose the right to ride as a GR.'

'My mother has explained that to me, sir,' I said.

'How is she? Hunting away, I hope.'

'Yes, sir. But I think she misses the Shires.'

'Once here, never forgotten,' he said. 'You'll be acting, unpaid supernumerary rough-rider,' he went on. 'Be on parade at eight thirty tomorrow. Good luck.'

So I started with the remounts and loved every minute of it. My goodness, it was an education for anyone who wanted to work with horses. It was the task of the civilian rough-riders to take them out in batches of five or six a day and get them going. I was a bit apprehensive at first that the other riders would resent my presence, but in the event they made me welcome, showed me the ropes and were generally helpful. From them I learned that the 'Pirate' and 'Captain Pat' (as Captain Terrier was universally known) were expected to hunt the officers' chargers, on the good old theory that hunting was the best possible training for horse and man in any future war. They made good use of that theory, culling the best of the drafts for themselves and, as I was told with many a nod and wink, it was usually well after the hunting season finished that these were passed on to the regiments. Some of the real stars remained at Melton for several seasons and even ran in point-to-points.

At the time I joined, Captain Pat had found something quite special, a small mare called Dainty. Captain Pat could ride all right, and on her he had shown the Meltonians the way on more than one occasion, so much so that he had made quite a name for himself and her. It was, in fact, through her that something happened which was to change my whole way of life.

It was a dark, misty morning, I remember, and there was a sort of stir and bustle in the yard when I arrived.

'HRH is coming,' Captain Pat greeted me. 'Says he wants to look over our lines. I know what he wants,' he said, turning to Pirate who had just joined us. 'He's after my mare. If he gets her he'll break her up like he does the rest of his horses.'

'It'll be treason or something like it if you try to refuse,' Pirate said.

Captain Pat looked at his watch. 'We'll see,' he said. 'We've about half an hour.' They moved away towards the line of brick-built stables where Dainty was housed.

I wasn't down to go out with the first lot and I hung around to get a glimpse of the man who had been my father's friend. It was just about half an hour later that he came into the yard. He was wearing a very well-cut tweed overcoat and one of those wide-brimmed caps which a later generation were to refer to as 'gor-blimeys'. He walked with the brisk, springy step which was characteristic of him and, as I later learned, of his way of life, for he was a restless man, always wanting to move from one experience to the next. At his shoulder was Major 'Flinty' Westcough, his aide-de-camp, best friend and Master of Horse. It was my first sighting of Flinty, too, though I had already heard much about him, how he was frowned on by the Establishment and how the Prince relied on him for good company, good cheer and good advice on their horse-buying expeditions.

'Good morning, Captain,' the Prince said, extending his hand as Captain Pat saluted him. 'Bloody awful weather, isn't it?' Then he lost no time in coming to the point and that was another of his ways as I was to discover. 'We've come to have a look at that little mare you've been cutting us all down with, Captain,' he said. 'I'm a spot short of horses at the moment and from what I hear she might suit me down to the ground—eh, Flinty?'

'That's so, David,' Flinty said, and I noticed his easy use of the first name. I saw, too, how his glance darted about, sizing everything up, even lingering on me for a moment before passing on.

'Very well, sir,' Captain Pat said. 'But I'm afraid—' He led the way towards Dainty's box.

I was intrigued by that last sentence and I followed at what I hoped was a respectful distance. The door of the box was opened and the two of them filed in, followed by Flinty. They were out again in a moment or two, a look of disappointment on the Prince's face. 'Well, Terrier, can't be helped, I suppose,' I heard him say.

'Yes, sir, I'm very sorry but she must have got a bang on the tendon that day from Barkby Holt,' Captain Pat replied. Then the Prince and Flinty moved off, got into their car and were driven away.

As soon as they had gone I made a beeline to Dainty's box. Inside the mare was standing contentedly. On her near fore was a large yellow blister—or what looked like one. Going nearer I was bending down to examine it when I heard a voice behind me. 'It's odd, you know,' Captain Pat said. 'These injuries often show themselves when you are least expecting them.'

I straightened up and turned to look at him. If his tongue wasn't in his cheek it was as near in it as makes no matter. 'A slight mixture of paste and paint often effects the cure,' he said then. Our eyes met; there was more than a suspicion of a twinkle in his, and I think it was from that moment that my real friendship with Captain Pat began.

THE FRIENDSHIP GREW steadily as the days progressed. Captain Pat was a bachelor who lived alone. Although he and Pirate were firm friends, Pirate had his wife and family nearby, and also mixed with the swells and the Braden Lodge set at the country club which was their home from home. Captain Pat told me that he did not aspire to that lifestyle nor could he afford to since he lived on his pay or, as he said, tried to. Though he loved his work I think he was lonely and longed for someone to talk to. He had, I discovered, stayed with my parents at Kilbarry on one or two of his horse-buying expeditions to Ireland, when I was away at school. 'Your father,' he said, 'was a fine trainer and a fine man and a hell of a fellow to ride to hounds.' He looked at me under his glasses in a manner which I later christened his 'wise old owl' expression. It was as if he was expecting me to say something, giving me the opportunity to broach a subject he was unsure of opening up himself. I took it.

'My mother,' I said, 'thinks that there was more behind the warning-off than ever came out at the hearing.'

He hesitated a moment. 'She's not the only one,' he said slowly. 'Things are going on in high places. Pirate knows more than I do, for he mixes there and I don't, and he's let a word or two drop here and there. This place, you know, is full of gossip and intrigue. Some say HRH doesn't want to be King. Others have it that it would be as well if he isn't. I don't know, I'm only a vet and a bit of an outsider. But your father was very close to him . . . Now, I've said enough, probably too much. Come on, let's get these horses out.'

Two days later he went down with flu and a day after that I was summoned to his bedside. He was sitting up wrapped in a flannel dressing gown, very red in the face. 'I've been thinking,' he said between bouts of coughing. 'That little mare of mine isn't doing herself any good shut up and eating her head off. She needs a hunt and you'd better take her out tomorrow.'

'But,' I said, 'that blister—what about the Prince, what will he say?'

'He's away in South Wales or somewhere opening something.'

My heart leaped—a day in the Shires on a known performer, what an offer! 'Gosh,' I said, 'I'd love to, but are you sure?'

'If I wasn't sure I wouldn't be giving her to you, would I? But now listen to me a minute. We're semi-professionals, somewhere between the rough-riders and the nobs, so you need to take care. That little mare'll carry you anywhere and you can put her at anything, but don't push on or barge at gaps or gates. It's all too easy to do in that big crowd when you're aching to get a start. But they're very jealous. If you do you'll be damned out of your boots and remembered for it.'

'I'll try,' I said.

'You'd better. There may be the best part of three hundred people out, and that's where the pressure at the start comes from. But you'll find that out of that lot only about thirty or forty have a real go. Don't jump on anyone. Enjoy yourself.'

I went out walking on air.

Captain Pat's words had not really prepared me for the size and swagger of a Shire field, so I gave a gasp of astonishment when I arrived at the meet the next day. It was a clear and brilliant morning with a touch of frost in the air, just such a day as to heighten the anticipation, stir the nerves and set the adrenalin flowing. Everywhere there were red coats, many of them swallowtails with aprons worn beneath them to preserve the pristine perfection of the white breeches, top hats shining and ironed to the *n*th degree, ladies in faultless habits and toppers being put up by grooms as smartly turned out as themselves. All of them hailed each other with cries of familiarity which made me feel more of an outsider than ever. And my word, the horses! Ninety per cent of them were big blood horses, all full of quality and ready to adorn a Sir Alfred Munnings picture.

Coming from rural Ireland it almost struck the sight from my eyes as I lurked inconspicuously at the back, drinking it all in. And then something happened which drove all other thoughts from my mind.

A car drove up and there was a little buzz of anticipation as a door opened and an unmistakable figure stepped out. The Prince of Wales had either changed his appointments or returned from South Wales sooner than expected. There was very little I could do about it save make myself even more unobtrusive. The Prince was immediately surrounded by a press of admirers and those anxious to enjoy even for a few minutes the glitter and glamour royalty reflects. It was unlikely, I thought, that I would come to his notice, and I wasn't going to sacrifice my first chance of a day in the Shires.

Almost immediately after the Prince's arrival we moved off. I was later to learn that he detested hanging about at the meet, 'coffee-housing' with sycophants, and that the Master and hunt staff knew this. He was impatient to get down to the serious business of riding the legs off his contemporaries in the first flight and, unfortunately, off his horses too, which explained Captain Pat's reluctance to let him have the little mare. He was a competitive man and this was, I think, one of the reasons that riding fast over fences and pitting his wits against his fellows so much appealed to him. There is no doubt he truly loved his hunting.

I took good care to keep to the back of the field as we crammed down a laneway. The first draw was a spinney set on the slope of a hill. The whole three hundred of us were penned up below it and behind the field master standing at a gate at the head of the lane. Then, as the draw progressed, we were allowed to file out and spread across a hundred-acre field.

I was just about the last out of that gate, praying all the time that the hounds would not find a scent before I got clear or I would be lost in the press. The moment we reached the turf the little mare's ears went forward. She knew where she was and I could feel her excitement mounting under me. Through those ears I had my first view of that unending sea of galloping grass divided by big, black uncompromising fences, the very sight of which made my pulses quicken. Then the hounds found the scent. There was a screech from the whipper-in at a far corner, his hat held high. In a second, or so it seemed, hounds were out driving forward in a dappled cloud, their music a clarion cry in the clear, frosty air.

'Hold hard! Hold hard, damn you! Give them room!' came from the field master behind his uplifted hand as he admonished two swallowtailed thrusters. Out on the right I felt my way forward, keeping a wary eye on that uplifted hand. As hounds topped the first of the fences below and in front of us, he dropped it. 'Now you can go, those that want to,' he called out, at the same time catching hold of his own hunter's head.

The line surged forward and I let the little mare go. I had already picked a place in that first fence. The mare jumped into her stride and we were off. At first the sheer pace of the thing, compared with the sedate way we hunted over banks in Ireland, took my breath away. We were at the fence almost, it seemed, as soon as we had started. A regiment could have jumped it abreast. I steadied her. She shortened her stride and then—flip!—it flashed beneath us. We were over without a pause and galloping on towards the next, which went beneath us in the same effortless fashion.

I can still recall the thrill of that first hunt in Leicestershire. It was the most exciting thing I had ever done. In front was the clamour of hounds running straight and hard, under me was the mare who knew her business better than I did. She never touched a twig as she flicked those big, black fences behind her.

For a full twenty minutes we were at it as hard as we could lay legs to the ground. Then, mercifully, they checked. Looking around me I saw the truth of what Captain Pat had said: apart from the hunt staff there were only about ten of us up. Among them was the Prince and I noticed that he rode shorter than most, almost a steeplechasing seat, and that he had his horse in a snaffle rather than a double bridle. I noticed, too, that there were one or two glances cast in my direction, wondering no doubt where I had come from in my old black coat and bowler hat. The Prince, I was grateful to see, was concentrating his glance on hounds and what they were doing. And he was right, for hardly had they checked than they had the scent again and were driving forward.

They hunted a trifle more slowly now and not quite so straight. Even so the pace was strong enough. The mare hadn't been out for the best part of a week and the check had barely given her breathing space. That burst had taken something out of her, and when I saw hounds swinging left-handed, I thought I could cut a corner. Turning, I jumped a fence almost at right-angles. Hounds were breasting a slight rise a field in front of me. Separating us was a stout post and rails with a boggy take-off and a fearsome drop and ditch beyond it. The mare was tiring; I couldn't risk breaking her up and I remembered one of my father's admonitions that one should have sense as well as courage. As these thoughts went through my mind, I saw that another rider had jumped the fence behind me and was cantering towards the timber.

'Don't go there,' I called out instinctively. 'You'll break your neck.'

'It's my bloody neck, isn't it?' was the reply, and as he launched himself at the fence I saw that the rider was none other than the

Prince of Wales. His horse was foam-flecked and I guessed pretty well beat like the rest of us but, driven into it, he rose gallantly enough. The next moment there was an almighty crash and then, before my horrified eyes, I saw a riderless horse galloping away. Of the heir to the throne there was no sign.

It is difficult to describe my thoughts at that moment. No one else had followed us; hounds had disappeared and so, for all I could see, had the rest of the field. I was alone with the Prince, apparently knocked out at the bottom of a ditch, from which a fearsome fence separated us.

Fortunately a fence to the left presented no such problems. I jumped this and found that a convenient gate would let me out into the field. The Prince was half sitting, half lying on the side of the ditch, a hand to his shoulder and his face a grimace of pain. 'Are you all right, sir?' I asked as I jumped down from the mare.

'It's my blasted collarbone,' he said. 'It's gone again.' Then he looked at me. 'I've seen you before,' he said with the instant recall which seems a prerogative of royalty. 'I've seen that mare, too,' he went on, while thoughts of the Tower of London raced through my mind. Then, suddenly, he began to laugh. 'Convey my compliments to Captain Terrier,' he said. 'And tell him I hope his camouflage is as successful in war as in peace.'

Just then, mercifully for me, there was the sound of horses approaching. It was the faithful Flinty who had caught the Prince's horse and come back to look for him. He jumped down and, throwing the reins to me, walked towards where the Prince was. 'What happened, David?' he asked.

'Collarbone gone,' was the reply. 'Taking on something I shouldn't on a tired horse. The youngster here warned me.' He gave a rueful grin as he nodded in my direction.

For the first time Flinty recognised my existence. Turning to me he snapped, 'Don't stand there gawping, boy. Take off your stock and I'll make a sling for His Royal Highness.' He did, too, very neatly and effectively when I ripped it off thinking at the same time how cleverly he had avoided having to disturb his own beautifully tied neckcloth.

The Prince insisted on being put up on his own horse again and they moved off, but not before Flinty had hissed at me, 'Keep your mouth shut about this or it will be in all the papers tomorrow.'

I followed at a respectful distance and found that a cluster of farm buildings let us out onto the road where our ways parted. There was no hope now, I realised, of getting back to hounds with the pace they ran. Consoling myself with the thought that it would be time for second horses anyway and I hadn't got one, I made my way slowly back to Melton.

Next morning I was with Pirate discussing arrangements for the day, telling something of my adventures and wondering if the Prince's recognition of the mare would have any repercussions.

'I shouldn't worry on that score,' Pirate said. 'Say what you like about him, and some do, he's a sportsman.'

Scarcely had he said this when a car drew up and Flinty strode into the yard. 'Where's that brat who picked up HRH yesterday?' he demanded in his usual arrogant way.

'He's here beside me,' Pirate said shortly.

'He wants to see you,' Flinty barked at me. 'Braden Lodge. Six o'clock. Make sure you're on time.' He nodded to Pirate, turned on his heel, and strode out of the yard.

'Bloody man,' Pirate said under his breath. It was obvious that there was no love lost between him and Flinty.

Here I think I should say a word about Flinty because I came to like him where many didn't. I know what they said of him (bounder and cad were two of the words used) but he was a royal favourite and royal favourites down the ages have never been greatly loved. It is true that Flinty's antecedents weren't of the bluest of blood, as desired by the starchier members of the court, and it's true, too, that he could be arrogant and off-putting, but I believe that much of that arrogance came from an inner insecurity. Once he accepted you he was fun to be with, and, my goodness, Flinty knew horses, and how he could ride them! He could cut them all down across Leicestershire and that didn't endear him to the courtiers either.

'A horse-trading Indian cavalryman, the worst of all types,' I once heard one of them describe him, and there was something in the horse-trading bit at least, for he bought most of the Prince's horses for him and I've no doubt he took his cut on those deals. But I reckon he deserved it, for he kept at bay those predators anxious to stick the Prince for big money, and I never heard he got him a wrong 'un.

As instructed, I presented myself at Braden Lodge at six o'clock that evening. It is not every day that a naive twenty-year-old from the depths of the Irish countryside is introduced to royalty, and I was nervous. Pirate had given me a briefing. 'When you're introduced, don't bow from the waist like an alderman, he hates that. The way to do it is from the neck, it's a sort of half-bow, half-nod. Here, I'll show you—' When I had practised this in front of a mirror and thought I had it right, I put on my dark suit and hoped I would pass muster.

A special suite of rooms with a separate entrance had been built onto Braden Lodge for the Prince. A manservant opened the door and let me in.

The Prince's suite was on the first floor. Flinty met me at the head of the stairs, introduced me and I made my nod. HRH was sitting in a chair by the fire, in casual clothes—whipcord slacks, an open-necked shirt with a polka-dot silk square loosely knotted about the neck, a fair-isle sweater and a hacking jacket, one sleeve of which was empty. With his free arm he waved me to a chair opposite.

My first impression was of a pair of blindingly blue eyes, my second of a personality that hit you the moment you entered the room. This, allied to his quick smile and the instinctive ease of manner that went with it, made me think that here was the most vital and attractive human creature I had ever met.

'De Lacey, eh,' he said to me. 'Any relation to Dick de Lacey?'

'His son, sir,' I said.

'Well, I'm damned. No wonder you can ride. The only thing I ever saw of him in a hunt was his back and you look to be following in his footsteps. Several people were asking who you were. Did you give Captain Terrier my message?'

'I did, sir.'

'I hope he's duly ashamed of himself.' He laughed, and then added, 'I'll have that mare off him yet.' Scarcely pausing, he said, 'Give the boy a drink, Flinty.'

Flinty crossed to a side table where every imaginable bottle and drink was laid out. There was a huge silver cocktail shaker with which he busied himself. 'White lady all right?' he said to me.

It was the cocktail era: mixed drinks were the fashion then. I had little experience of them, but I could scarcely refuse. A brimming glass was placed before me. It tasted delicious, though I warned myself to be careful of its effect. HRH had a whisky and soda.

'Your father,' he said, sipping his drink, 'was very harshly treated. The Jockey Club should think again about that rule, but I sometimes wonder if they ever think.' It was, I thought, an indiscreet remark to make to the victim's son on first acquaintance, but as I was later to realise he was never discreet, which did not increase his popularity in certain court circles. He had a peculiar, rather rasping voice, utterly unlike the usual upper-class English accent with its clarion notes and tones, and I listened entranced as, finishing his drink and demanding another, he went on chatting to me as an equal. That was one of the greatest things about him, he never patronised, never talked down whoever you were. 'Ireland,' he said. 'Tell me about hunting there. I've always wanted to have a go over the banks, you know. I've heard so much about it and it sounds the greatest sport. Your father was to arrange it for me, until the stiff-necks stepped in and said it was too dangerous. Someone would take a pot shot at me. All damn rubbish.'

'It's real fox-catching,' I said, 'and there aren't big fields to get in the way. I don't think, though, from what I saw yesterday, that it's as exciting as it is here.'

He laughed again. 'Excitement, is that what you're looking for? And I made you lose that hunt. We must do something for you then. I'll be out of action for a bit, so you must hunt one of my horses for me. He can hunt Pepperpot tomorrow, Flinty. See to it, will you?'

At that moment the telephone rang. Flinty picked up the receiver, listened attentively for a minute or two and then, covering the mouthpiece with his hand, turned to the Prince. 'It's Marston,' he said. 'Do you want to speak to him?'

The reply was a vehement shake of the head. 'No. Not under any circumstances. I suppose the old fool has heard of my break and is trying to make what he can of it.'

'That's just what he's up to,' Flinty said and, turning again to the phone, said, 'I'm sorry, Lord Marston, he's not available at the moment. No, it's not a bad break, I assure you, just one of those things that happen. Yes, I'll tell him.' He put the phone down.

'Wants me to stop riding to hounds I'll be bound,' the Prince said.

'That's about it,' Flinty answered.

'Damned old fool,' the Prince said. 'He's one of the interfering gang at the court. They don't want me to live. What they want is a tailor's dummy while they pull the strings.'

The Prince got up and began restlessly to pace the room. 'If they'd only leave me alone,' he said. 'And allow me to lead my own life. They don't want me, that's the truth of the matter.' Then, suddenly turning to me, he went on, 'Your father wasn't like that. That's why they had no use for him.'

After another minute or two there was a nod from Flinty and I knew I was dismissed. I walked home slowly, thinking of the prospect of hunting a blood horse belonging to royalty.

Chapter Three

Next morning Flinty called for me in the open, boat-bodied two-seater Rolls which was HRH's personal conveyance and which only he besides its owner was permitted to drive. I climbed in beside him and we drove off at a high speed along the traffic-free roads. 'You've no idea of the hit you've made,' were his first words to me. He had evidently decided to be amicable. 'You're in luck,' he went on. 'He likes you. Play your cards right and there's no knowing what he'll do for you. He likes chaps with fire in their bellies, not those mealy-mouthed miseries at court. You heard him last evening about Marston.'

'Who is Marston?' I asked.

'He's the grand vizier, the leader of the crowd who don't like him or don't want him for that matter. They're trying to mould him to their image and he won't have it.'

My thoughts were wandering from the Prince and his problems. They were centred on the coming day. 'This horse Pepperpot,' I said. 'What's he like? Is there anything I should know about him?'

'You're in luck again. He's a bit of an old sheep unlike a lot of HRH's which take a pretty good hold. He wants some kicking along to get him going, but once he wakes up he'll gallop till kingdom come.'

By this time we were meeting signs of a hunting morning. Grooms leading horses were on the grass verges and smart cars were beginning to fill up the roads—horse boxes and trailers were virtually unheard of then. The Rolls was instantly recognised and people pulled aside to allow us to pass.

Flinty drew up beside where the Prince's grooms were holding the horses. Once out of the car he busied himself taking off his fur-lined overcoat and donning his swallowtails. I'm bound to say he looked magnificent in them for he had the figure to carry them and the hawklike face to set the whole thing off under the gleaming topper.

I walked over to where the grooms were holding the horses. When I asked for Pepperpot they eyed me superciliously in the way royal servants can do, as if they could scarcely believe that this nondescript creature was going to ride one of the horses in their care. Then one of them nodded to another, who brought the horse forward. Looking at him, I almost gasped in delight. He was a big, rangy, blood hunter, a dark bay, the best of all colours. He was about as unlike Captain Pat's Dainty as a horse could be and despite what Flinty had said I wondered would I hold him among all that thundering crowd once they got going.

As I was settling myself in the saddle I saw that one of the field had detached himself from a group and had come to a halt a few yards away from me. He was a handsome sort of chap with a clipped moustache and something of a presence about him. 'Saw you out a day or so back,' he said. 'You're young de Lacey, aren't you?'

'That's right,' I said, wondering what was coming next.

His stare mellowed considerably. 'Hm. I hope we have a fox for you. He'll carry you well,' he said, transferring his stare to Pepperpot. 'One of HRH's, I see,' he added as he moved away.

Slightly mystified by the approach I watched him go, resolving as I did so to ask Flinty about him, but almost immediately we were moving off.

It wasn't, as it happened, a very brilliant day's hunting. During the morning we hung around without finding, and all about me I could hear murmurs complaining of slowness in the huntsman and lack of foxes, and more than one of them cursing fractious horses playing up, all of which made me glad of Pepperpot's gentlemanly behaviour. I noticed, too, that those who recognised Pepperpot were inclined to make way for me at gates and gaps.

Round lunchtime the field began to thin as boredom took hold and the rich and ritzy members conserved their energies for a better day. It was beginning to rain when hounds were put into a thick wood. I was at a loss which way to go when Flinty came up to me. 'Follow me,' he said. 'I know this place. With any luck we'll be there when he breaks.'

He led the way round a corner of the wood. We jumped a small set of rails and hardly had we done so when hounds opened. I saw Flinty cock an ear, listening. There were only about six of us there, one of whom was the man who had spoken to me at the meet. Suddenly, silently, a big dog fox slipped across the fence bordering the wood and sloped away across the grass. The next second hounds were out and, after them, the huntsmen. None of us cared where the field master was; we had it to ourselves and, by golly, we were off!

Instantly Flinty was into his stride and away. So were the rest, and I saw what Flinty meant when he said Pepperpot took a while to warm up: they were all over the first fence, before he had caught hold of his bit. 'Come on, you old devil,' I said to him and gave him a couple of backhanders. The result was immediate. He stood back and jumped that first fence so big he nearly had me off. Then he started to gallop, and what a gallop it was! Those long strides of his seemed to devour the ground. This, I realised, was the real thing, a true Leicestershire horse all blood and quality, the sort you dream about and the dream comes true.

I suppose we ran for the best part of twenty-five minutes when hounds lost the scent in sheep stain and we lost our fox. Only four of us finished it, the others having come to grief somewhere. All I knew was that I had been carried by one of the living best and I longed for the chance to do it again. Here was something special—a surge of supreme power behind the saddle that almost gave one the feeling of flight as one took off into space.

One of those who had finished was the man from the meet and I saw him go up to Flinty and speak to him. When we were back in the car I asked Flinty who he was.

'Roger Gretton,' Flinty answered. 'He's a member of the old guard, one of the few of them who hunt, incidentally. He wanted to know how you got hold of HRH's horse and what the devil you were doing here. What the devil *are* you doing here, anyway?' he said.

I was tempted then to confide in him, but some innate caution restrained me; I had been sent to look, listen and confirm, and I was still feeling my way in a very strange land. 'I'm here to learn about handling horses and something on the veterinary side,' I said. 'Captain Pat was the vet in my father's regiment.'

He gave me another sharp look as the Rolls purred contentedly along. 'Hm,' he said. 'Your father and Roger weren't exactly soul mates.' Then he changed the subject. 'You're bidden back to tea now. And HRH will want to know how the horse went and pretty well every fence you jumped, I shouldn't wonder.'

He was in the same chair as the night before but this time there was someone else with him. I'll never forget the first time I saw them together. She was standing beside him, her hand on his shoulder, a tall girl with a mass of russet hair, an oval, open face and a friendly smile. She was dressed in a tartan skirt and a twin-set, a rope of pearls at her neck. She moved with the easy grace of, I thought, a tigress—there was something vibrant about her which matched HRH's own electric personality. Between them they seemed to bring an extra dimension of light and brightness to the room. Such was Lady Valerie Spenlove, always known as Lady Val, and from the moment of that first meeting with her I was entranced.

I had heard something about her from my mother. A lot of nonsense has been written about the Prince of Wales's sexual prowess or lack of it, some alleging that he was all but a neuter, others that he rivalled his grandfather as a sexual athlete. The truth, as usual, lay somewhere in between, but that he liked women there was no doubt, and then Lady Val was the chosen one. She had plenty of money, and was considered to be one of the best horsewomen in the Shires, rather as my mother had been a generation before her, and I think my mother was jealous of her though she tried not to show it.

The money and the title came from her father, an ironmaster who had done well out of the war and who had died a year or so back leaving Lady Val, his only child, to inherit his fortune and the landed estate, Huntercombe, he had bought with it. He had also bought an earldom from Lloyd George, with the munificent donation he had made to that shifty gentleman. It was one of the few earldoms Lloyd George had sold and Spenlove had been known as 'Lloyd George's earl' and was looked down on in the highest sporting circles, despite the success which his steeplechasers—two Grand Nationals and an early Gold Cup—had brought him. His beloved daughter, Lady Val, had been brought up with horses and had proved she could out-ride most if not all of those who laughed at her and her father. She took some awful falls in proving just that, and it was rumoured that the Prince had first made her acquaintance when pulling her from under her horse after one of them. At Huntercombe, which numbered amongst its other attractions a swimming pool and a private golf course, she entertained him and his friends discreetly if lavishly. Whenever her liaison with the Prince began, it was in full flight when I first came into their circle.

'Well, who won the hunt?' were HRH's first words as soon as we entered the room.

'He did, sir,' I said, nodding towards Flinty.

'That's Mastermind,' the Prince said. 'We haven't had him long. What about Pepperpot? How'd he go?'

'Like a dream,' I said. 'I've never ridden one like him.'

'He's one of your favourites, isn't he, David?' Lady Val said.

'Came from Ireland originally,' the Prince said. 'Your father got him for me.'

'Only four of us in at the finish,' Flinty said. 'De Lacey here, and Roger Gretton was another. Going quite well, for once.'

'I thought he was at Windsor,' the Prince said thoughtfully.

'No. He's here, keeping an eye on things,' Lady Val said.

'You could be right,' Flinty said. 'He came up to me at the end wanting to know what young de Lacey was doing and how he came to be riding one of your horses, David.'

'The devil he did. Damned impertinence and I'll tell him so the next time I see him. Now, what about that tea?'

Lady Val crossed to the fireplace and rang a bell. Two men-servants brought it in on silver dishes: there were poached eggs and toast and scones and gentleman's relish, crumpets and fruitcake, all of which HRH ate sparingly while I, who was ravenous, tried to restrain myself. Lady Val thoughtfully pressed me to eat. 'Come on, we'll have a go at this cake,' she said.

Soon the Prince left his chair and began to pace restlessly up and down the room. 'Curse this damn break,' he said. 'I'm a prisoner here. I can't even play squash. They say it'll be another week before I'm out again with hounds.' He picked up a copy of the *Tatler* and began idly leafing through the pages. 'There's a photograph of Roger here chatting to Marston at a wedding,' he remarked. 'I didn't know they were all that close.'

'Roger likes to keep near the seats of power,' Flinty said. 'He was out that day you got hurt, you know. I'll bet he was on the telephone to Marston the moment he heard of it.'

They were talking quite uninhibitedly in front of me. Slowly, I was being drawn into their circle, and Lady Val's next words appeared to confirm this. 'He's devious,' she said to me. 'If he's interested in you, Danny, look out.' Her eyes followed the Prince's every move, and she watched as he showed the magazine to Flinty and then threw it down. As their eyes met he smiled and then laughed. 'A pillar of the Jockey Club and mischief-maker in chief,' he said.

They turned then to other personalities of whom I knew nothing, while I munched away at my tea and looked about the room. Over the chimneypiece was a Munnings picture of the Prince on Forest Witch, with below it some silver racing trophies, together with two photographs of his more spectacular falls, which I thought sporting of him to have put there. Two deep sofas faced the fire, there was a Chippendale writing desk, and a side table with signed photographs, trinkets and silver cigarette boxes. It was a typical, comfortable bachelor's apartment without any frills.

When the time came for me to leave, Flinty followed me onto the landing outside the door to the Prince's suite. 'You'd better dine with me tonight,' he said abruptly. 'Here, at the Lodge. I'll book you in. Black tie, of course.'

I almost said: 'I'll try not to let you down,' but I didn't, and after my bath I tied the double-ended black tie with particular care; the tie went round a wing collar on top of a stiff shirt front held in place by a set of studs from Asprey's which my mother had given me. HRH at that time had not made the sensible soft shirt front with dinner jacket acceptable and fashionable.

Flinty met me in the hall of the Lodge and brought me into the bar. It was a long, well-proportioned room, which I imagine had once been one of the reception rooms of the mansion. Flinty led me to a table where a waiter hovered around, and ordered two cocktails.

When these had been brought and we were sipping them, one of the crowd round the bar came over to us. He was a small man with a round, rather simian face, very broad shoulders and the torso of a

prize fighter. Flinty introduced us but in fact I recognised him from his photographs in the illustrated papers, usually being led in on the back of a winner. He was the Honourable Rupert Carleton, one of the leading amateurs of the day.

'Surprised to see you here,' Flinty said.

'Just back from Ireland. Seen this?' He reached into an inside pocket and took out a press cutting which he passed to Flinty. Flinty glanced at it, frowned, and then handed it to me.

It appeared to be a drawing from an Irish comic paper, showing the King and Queen in formal robes and crowns, breakfasting together. Beneath was the legend:

> THE KING: 'What's the matter, my dear? You look upset.'
> THE QUEEN: 'It's Eddy. He's sulking. He's on his high horse again.'
> THE KING: 'Good heavens! Tell him to get down immediately. Else he'll fall off!'

'Doesn't help the image, does it?' Carleton said as he took the cutting back. Flinty made some noncommittal reply and Carleton turned to me. 'Staying here long?' he said.

'That depends on how long Colonel Probert and Captain Terrier are prepared to put up with me,' I said. 'I'm supposed to be learning.'

He gave me a hard look. 'I should have thought you'd have been better in a racing stable,' he said. 'With your connections—' he let that thought hang in the air, and then added, 'though Flinty will teach you a thing or two, I have no doubt.' With that he turned away.

Flinty and I finished our drinks and went into dinner, Flinty, it seemed to me, in an unusually thoughtful mood.

Unlike the bar with its modern trimmings, the dining room at Braden Lodge had been left much as it was. The walls were panelled and the tables with shaded lights on them were set far enough apart to ensure privacy. Flinty had arranged for one in a corner near a curtained window. 'You see,' he said as we sat down, obviously referring to the cutting Carleton had shown us, 'they don't want him and they'll do all they can to discredit him. That bloody drawing will go round everywhere. Rupert will see to that. If they only knew him as well as I do they'd realise he doesn't want all this royalty claptrap either. He's happiest living in the country, hunting and riding races. He'd like to be squire of a couple of thousand acres with a stable full of blood horses.'

'But some day, surely, he'll have to take on all this royalty claptrap as you call it,' I said.

'I suppose so.' Flinty squeezed lemon over smoked salmon.

'Are you telling me that there are some who won't have him?'

'They may have to but they won't like it. Your father knew that. As long as they don't take steps to prevent it—'

It seemed that by keeping my ears open I was learning more every day. But then Flinty suddenly changed the subject. 'How many winners have you ridden?' he asked. 'HRH told me to find out.'

'Six,' I said.

'That's not bad for a start. Over banks, I suppose?'

'Yes. Does it matter?'

'Not much. But there is a difference. You've ridden work—exercised horses—done any training?'

'Yes, quite a bit. What is all this?'

'I'm not sure myself. Sometimes he keeps his cards very close to his chest. He was fond of your father and he's furious with the Jockey Club, half of whom he says have never been on a horse. He likes you and he has a way of taking people up. He likes his own way and by and large he sees he gets it. How could he not—all those tours and that adulation and then everyone here chasing him. Val at least is good for him, as long as it lasts . . .' He looked up at me. 'You know, what he'd like above all to be is a GR. He sort of idolises chaps like Jack Anthony and Harry Brown. It'd give him more pleasure to win the National Hunt Chase at Cheltenham than three kingdoms.'

We were drinking champagne by this time, and I was, I think, emboldened by the wine when I asked him, 'But is he good enough? Would he ever make the grade?'

'Why not if he had the stuff under him? It's true he's so hasty he can never ride a waiting race, but you've seen him out hunting. He's unstoppable and, as an old rough-rider said to me once, "It's them what gallops as gets there." But they're trying to stop him riding in point-to-points. They'd never wear him having a go under Rules and he knows it. He's a sweet man, really.'

We went on sipping our wine. It was damn good stuff and went down smooth as silk, but then everything about Braden Lodge reeked of money. I looked about me at the well-fed faces, the beautifully cut shoulders of the dinner jackets, the jewels and décolletage of the women, and heard the tinsel trickle of laughter as some outlandish exploit was recounted. I saw, too, the hovering waiters eager to obey each beckoning finger.

The laughter at a nearby table was louder than the rest and I glanced across. It was an all-male table and Rupert Carleton was one of their number. After a minute or two they pushed back their chairs and began to leave the room. As he passed us Carleton paused and, looking at me more than Flinty, said, 'Poker tonight. Care to sit in?'

'I think not tonight, thanks,' Flinty said, frowning. I took his frown as a cue and also shook my head.

'We'll be in the card room if you change your mind,' Carleton said as he left us. 'Long sitting, too, I'd say.'

'Do you play cards?' Flinty asked me when they had all gone.

'Not really,' I said. 'Family stuff sometimes, at home.'

'Hardly a preparation for poker at Braden Lodge,' he said. 'Take my advice—don't. Here be dragons as they say.' He threw his napkin on the table and we went out for coffee.

I walked back to my rooms that evening, my thoughts in a whirl. I didn't feel like sleep and I knew I should communicate with my mother to tell her how much had happened since I had arrived and what I had learned. There were no cross-channel telephones in those days so, marshalling my thoughts as best I could, I got them down on paper. I told her about my meeting with the Prince and Flinty and Lady Val, and I said I had the impression something was going on, I didn't quite know what, and were there any further instructions she would like to give me? That done I went to bed and, full of good champagne, slept the sleep of the young and healthy.

Chapter Four

It was two or three days later that things began to happen. A big, rangy horse with quality about him had been picked out by Captain Pat and Pirate from a batch which had been sent over by one of the leading Irish dealers. Horses that have been accustomed to jumping banks often take time to acclimatise themselves to fences and usually have to be rousted up a bit, but for some reason this fellow, who was called Rockalong, had reversed the process and was proving himself something of a tearaway. The moment he saw a fence he made a dash at it, and he had already dumped one of the rough-riders good and proper. He could gallop, though, and I think Captain Pat had his eye on him as a hunter or point-to-pointer if they could get him right.

I was standing in the yard that morning talking to Captain Pat, who loved a bit of gossip.

'Mixing in high society already, aren't we?' he teased, giving me that wise old owl look from under his glasses. 'How is your pal HRH these days? Has he forgiven me yet?'

'I think he regards it all as a great joke,' I said with a grin.

'He's a sportsman.' How many times was I to hear that word used about him? 'If we can only keep him here doing what he wants to do. And you, dining with Flinty at Braden Lodge. In two years I think I've only been in the place twice. How did that go?'

'He was charming,' I said. 'Cocktails and champagne. He's devoted to HRH.'

'So well he might be. HRH has made him. Oh, he can be good company, the best, when he likes. And he's done HRH well over his horses. No doubt about that, whatever people say.'

'Lady Val was there at tea,' I said. 'She's a stunner.'

'She's the best thing that ever happened to him. I dunno, though, can she hold his roving eye?'

At that moment the first lot passed us, Rockalong among them. 'We must get that fellow right,' Captain Pat said. Then he thought for a moment. 'You'd better take a turn on him. Horses seem to go for you. School him tomorrow morning. I'll put your name in the book.' He gave me another of his half-mischievous glances and went off.

Next morning I saddled up the big horse and brought him out. There was no doubt about his strength: a massive shoulder stretched in front of me and plenty of power came from those great loins. I could see why my two mentors had fancied him.

A few other ranks gathered round to see the fun. Actually Rockalong went easily enough as I took him in a quiet canter round the field to settle him down. He came back to my hand as I asked him and I began to wonder if the tales I had heard were not exaggerated. Just to make sure I went round again. Captain Pat had stationed himself beside the second of the schooling fences. 'Come along,' he called when I reached the top of the field again. 'Don't hang about.'

It was as if the big horse had heard him. Once I presented him at the first fence he took off. He didn't—quite—take it by the roots, but he did the next best thing. It was only his strength that saved him and, somehow, I remained in the saddle. The schooling fences were well spaced out, and I had time to restore myself and catch hold. For a moment, I thought I had him in my hand. I was wrong. His head went out and his feet drummed on the ground. Then, suddenly, I saw Captain Pat give a start and peer at the fence. Taking a step back he threw out his arms at the same time shouting at me, 'Pull out! Pull out!'

Nearly knocking him down in the process I just managed it. But the extraordinary thing was that having swerved away from the fence Rockalong dropped his bit, came back to a canter and trot like, as Flinty would have said, an old sheep.

Captain Pat was standing at the back of the fence, staring at it fixedly. 'Look at that . . .' he said, pointing.

Following his finger I saw, stretched between the uprights of the fence about six inches from the top, a piece of wire, tautly strung.

'If you'd hit that at the pace you were going you'd have broken your neck more'n likely,' Captain Pat said. 'And what's more it didn't get there by accident.'

The colonel was sent for and soon came striding along in his masterful way, followed at a respectful distance by the other rank who had been told to get him. 'Well, then, what is all this?' he demanded.

'I think you'd better see what's been done to this fence, Colonel,' Captain Pat said, indicating the wire as he spoke.

Pirate looked hard at the wire and then ran his finger over it, testing its tension. After standing thinking for a few moments and stroking his chin, he went back a few paces and surveyed the fence. 'I see,' he said thoughtfully. 'You'd both better come to my office. In the meantime you, Wilson'—he hailed the other rank—'stand by this fence and don't allow anyone to approach it without my express authority. Understood?'

'Yes, sir.'

It was all beginning to be horribly formal and rather frightening. Once in Pirate's office it became more so. He took his seat behind his desk. 'Sit down, boy,' he snapped at me. 'Now, Terrier, tell me what happened.'

I found a chair and listened. When Captain Pat had finished Pirate sat back in his chair, directing his unblinking gaze at me. 'There has obviously been an interference with His Majesty's property with the intention of inflicting bodily harm—or worse. You're a civilian, de Lacey. Do you want the police called in or are you prepared to allow the military to handle it?'

All sorts of things shot through my mind. The most important was that I definitely did not want any interference from the police which might lead to awkward questions as to my being here, for all I knew bringing up the affair with my father and even dragging HRH into it.

'I'll leave it to you, of course, sir,' I said.

'Very well. Have you any idea who could have done this?'

'None whatsoever, sir.'

'Who knew you were schooling Rockalong this morning?'

'His name was in the book,' Captain Pat put in. 'The whole place knew it.'

Pirate frowned. 'I'll see Sergeant Major Gleeson first,' he said. 'Get hold of him, Terrier, will you?'

Captain Pat left the office and a minute or two later returned with the sergeant major. Saluting in fine regimental style and with great stamping of feet, he stood to attention before us.

'All right, Gleeson,' Pirate said. 'Stand easy. I just want to ask you a few questions. It's about what happened schooling this morning, though I expect it's around the place already.'

'I have heard something, sir. May I say I'm glad the young gentleman wasn't hurt, sir.'

'So am I,' Pirate said grimly. 'You are aware then, that someone strung a wire below the top of the second fence just where it would catch a horse and turn him over. When was the last time any work was done on those fences?'

'Two days ago, sir. They were built up again after that Rockalong made a hash of them. They haven't been schooled over since.'

'I'll want to see the working party. In the meantime, have you any idea who could be stupid or malevolent enough to do this?'

The sergeant major thought for a moment and then shook his head. 'No, sir, I haven't. I can't see anyone here doing a thing like that.'

'Were there any strangers about yesterday?'

'None, sir, that I saw. There was Mr Gretton if you remember, sir, but he saw you himself. Oh, and that Major Westcough, sir.'

'Major Westcough, eh? What did he want?'

'I think he said he wanted to see Mr de Lacey, sir.'

'Thank you, Gleeson,' Pirate said. 'Get that working party rounded up, will you? I'll send for them when I'm ready.'

When the sergeant major had left, Pirate tapped his teeth with his pencil and looked at me appraisingly. 'Flinty,' he said after a pause. 'He's become rather a pal of yours. Any idea what he wanted?'

'No, sir,' I said. 'He didn't say anything to me about coming round.'

'I wonder,' Pirate said reflectively. 'Very well, you two.' We were effectively dismissed.

Once outside I turned to Captain Pat. 'You don't suppose he really thinks Flinty put that wire there, do you?' I said.

'When he goes all broody like that no one knows what he thinks,' Captain Pat said. 'He doesn't like Flinty and that's the truth of it, but what reason on earth would Flinty have for doing it? He could have seen your name in the book, though.'

'So could Gretton or a hundred others if it comes to that.'

'If you ever see Roger Gretton stooping to menial work, go and have your head examined. He can't even put a saddle on a horse.'

We spent the rest of the day working with the Irish batch of horses. When I got back to my rooms that evening there was a letter waiting for me from my mother. She had been fascinated, she said, by my letter.

I remember Flinty well, she wrote. *Your father was one of the few who liked him and had a good word for him. Reading between your lines I think it would be worthwhile now seeing those private detectives again. Your father knew too much about something or someone. We never found out all we should have done about that stablelad who disappeared. It was shortly after that your father got the message and had his stroke.* She went on to give me instructions. I was to phone the firm of detectives for an appointment. They were called Ormsby and Little and operated out of Newmarket, apparently specialising in racing matters. Major Ormsby, the senior partner, was the man who had dealt with my father. My mother had already written to him telling him I would be calling, and guaranteeing him his fees. *Remember,* she concluded, *don't trust anyone, not even Flinty, too far. Your father said that although he liked him and found him good company he was always on the make. I'm not quite sure what he meant by that but perhaps you'll find out! Your affectionate Mother.*

The tragedy which had come upon us had, I realised, at least brought my mother and myself closer together. I read her letter again. The peremptory instructions were there, but a note of humour and affection had crept in, though she could not yet bring herself to use the word 'love' towards me; it was still 'your affectionate Mother'.

NEXT MORNING I telephoned the detective agency and made an appointment with 'Major Charles', as his secretary referred to him, for two days away. I had no car of my own but Captain Pat had told me that I could use his when he did not want it for himself, and when I asked for the day off and the loan of it to go to Newmarket he agreed readily. He wanted to see someone in Melton, he said; he would drive me there and I could take the car on to Newmarket, leaving him to find his own way back.

I spent much of the intervening time thinking how I should approach my interview with Major Ormsby. My mother had told me that my father had kept no written records of his or the detective's research, almost as if he did not want any account of it to be available to others to read. There was one record, however, for all to see, and that was the warning-off notice which had appeared in the *Racing Calendar*. My mother had given a typed copy of it to me; I didn't much care for reading it and being reminded of that blackest of all days, but now thinking it might give me some sort of line on what to say at the interview, I took it out of my writing case and read it. As I did so one name hit me between the eyes.

> The Stewards of the Jockey Club, Lord Wilberton, the Marquess of Farnborough and A.R.J. Gretton (acting for Lord Benby), were satisfied that a drug or stimulant had been administered to a horse in the care of Lieut-Colonel D.R. de Lacey for the purpose of affecting his performance in a race and warned Lieut-Colonel de Lacey, the trainer of the horse, off Newmarket Heath.

When I had read the notice first I had paid little attention to the names of the stewards. I did now, though—A.R.J. Gretton. Could it be he who had enquired about me out hunting and whom Lady Val had branded as devious? Could A.R.J. Gretton, for reasons best known to himself, have been influential in swinging the verdict against my father? No, I told myself, that theory did not hold water since the disqualification was automatic under the rules, but, as I read it again, I realised that the notice merely stated the bare facts and left the implication open that my father was concerned with the doping. Could Gretton have had something to do with the drafting of the notice with the intention of discrediting him, and if so, why? And what had Gretton been seeing the Pirate about the day before that wire was stretched?

All these things were still in my mind when I met Captain Pat on the appointed morning. His car was one of the early 'square radiator' Morrises, a two-seater with a dickey behind. Like many of his generation he regarded the motor car, literally, as a horseless carriage, knowing nothing and caring less about what went on under the bonnet. That morning we had gone a mile or so when there was a splutter and cough and the engine died. We freewheeled slowly to a stop. 'Damn thing,' Captain Pat said. 'What's wrong with it now?'

I leaned across him to look at the fuel gauge. It was registering empty. 'They go better if you put petrol in them,' I said.

'What? Oh, I see. Well, what now?'

'I'd better walk back and get a tin.'

I was opening the door to get out when a car drew up alongside us and a voice called, 'In trouble? Can I help?'

It was a silver-blue Riley runabout, a low-slung, graceful machine, and behind the wheel, setting it off as if it had been designed for her, sat Lady Val.

'We're out of petrol,' I said.

'That's easy. I'll send someone along to fill you up.'

'Could you, please,' I said. 'I've an appointment in Newmarket and I don't want to be late.'

'You're in luck then. As it happens I'm going to Newmarket myself. I'll take you there. What about you, Pat?'

'I'll be all right,' Captain Pat said equably: nothing ever really fazed him. 'Just send someone out when you pass a garage.'

'Hop in then, Danny,' she said.

There was no passenger's door on the Riley and I literally hopped in beside her. She let in the clutch and we were off. She drove like the wind with the lightest of touches on the wheel, and the gear changes, which weren't all that easy in the days before synchromesh, went in like butter. I watched the hedges fly past, quite happy to sit silent in her company.

'The little man and Flinty have gone off horse-buying,' she said. 'He enjoys that, thank goodness, and he's not a bad judge of a horse, either. He's a bit like a caged lion, grounded as he is since you broke his collarbone.'

'*I* broke it!' I protested indignantly. 'He did it himself, taking on that awful place. I told him he'd break his neck and he took no notice. I didn't know who he was then.'

She laughed. 'The point-to-points are coming along and he'll be mad for them however much they try to stop him,' she said. 'He should have been born a commoner—well, a duke, perhaps, with vast estates. You're lucky, he likes you and he wants to do what he can to make up for what the Jockey Club did to your father. He doesn't much care about the Jockey Club and flat racing bores him rigid.'

'He seems to me one of the most vital and wonderful people I've ever met,' I said.

She sighed. 'If he'll only stay that way,' she said, and then, almost fiercely: 'They say Flinty isn't good for him, but he is, he keeps him human. He makes him laugh. If he was led by those stuffed shirts Roger Gretton and Marston he might get pompous himself. Oh, I know he's spoilt, all you men are spoilt, especially elder sons. Are you an elder son?'

'No,' I said. 'I'm an only child.'

'Then I suppose you were always given the best to ride, that's why you can ride cross-country. But you had a bit of trouble schooling the other day, didn't you?'

'How did you know that?' I said.

'Everyone knows everything in Melton. Whoever did it, it was a dirty trick,' she said, and then: 'What brings you to Newmarket?'

Sitting there in that tiny car with her, spinning along the empty roads, isolated, almost as if in a time capsule, intimacy enveloped us. I felt an overwhelming desire to confide in her. Also, I wanted in some way to impress her. Besides, I rationalised, she had mentioned my father sympathetically and she might be a useful ally.

'I'm going to see a detective,' I said, 'about my father. My mother and I want to clear his name. He didn't dope that horse.'

'But no one who knew him believes that he did.'

'That's not enough. The Jockey Club in their notice didn't make that clear.'

'And you think the detectives can find proof he didn't?'

'They're the people my father employed, Ormsby and Little. I want to find out just how far they got.'

'Well, good luck to you.'

By this time we were on the outskirts of Newmarket. She dropped me at the head of the High Street, saying she had to go out to one of the studs. After agreeing to meet later at the Rutland Arms, I made my way to Messrs Ormsby and Little. A brass plate with their names upon it and nothing else, set into a wall beside a Georgian doorway with a fanlight over it, told me I had found them.

There was a stairway facing me at the end of a narrow hall. An arrow pointed peremptorily upwards and I followed it. At the top was a landing with a glassed-in box of an office at its back. Inside this sat a sour-looking puss with drawn-back black hair and heavy horn-rimmed spectacles. When I stated my business she said Major Charles would see me shortly, and indicated a door on the left marked WAITING ROOM. I opened this and went in. It was airy and well furnished with leather chairs and an octagonal table in the centre, on which were stacked orderly piles of the usual illustrated papers. Major Charles didn't seem in any great hurry to interview me and after reading the runners and riders in the dailies I got up and wandered over to the windows overlooking the High Street.

As I watched the passers-by I saw two whom I recognised on the farther pavement. They were Rupert Carleton and Lady Val, talking animatedly as they walked along. Just at the edge of my vision they stopped and appeared to confront each other. Then the door opened and sour puss indicated that Major Charles would see me now.

His office was on the other side of the landing. At my entrance he rose, extended a hand, and motioned me to a chair in front of his desk. He had a cropped military moustache and a round, smooth face, entirely unlined, which gave him an air of innocence. But the first thing I noticed about his appearance was that he was wearing a bow tie. In those days bow ties were frowned upon as being rather raffish and bohemian. This may have been partly due to the fact that Winston Churchill always wore one and Winston then was heartily mistrusted by the upper echelons of conservatism as a slacker and an adventurer. It didn't, however, put me off: those upper echelons had done my father no good and to me it seemed to make Major Ormsby more human and approachable.

'Sit down and tell me your troubles,' he said. 'What can I do for you?'

'It's about my father,' I said. 'You acted for him trying to find out who the real doper was in the matter of his warning-off.'

'Oh yes, I've heard from your mother. How is he, by the way?'

'It's hopeless I'm afraid. We don't know how long it will be but he is not going to recover.'

'How terrible for him and for you both. I liked and admired your father. I'll do anything I can to help.'

'We want to find out who did dope the horse and to clear my family's name,' I said. 'I believe suspicion fell on three temporary lads in the stable before Ascot. Two of them were cleared but the third disappeared very quickly to America. Has anything been heard of him since?'

'Nothing. Despite all our best efforts and those of our agents on the other side we were unable to trace him.'

'Do we know his name? He must have given one, even if it was false.'

'The name which he gave when he was in your father's employment was Vincent Rossiter. As you say, it was probably false.'

'Was any check made about him from my father's stable before they took him on?'

'We looked into that. Things were in a bustle before Ascot but he told your father's secretary that he'd been with Jimmy Connaughton. I don't know if you know, but Jimmy Connaughton's stable has a floating population of lads. He goes over to Ireland, hires them by the boatload for a pittance, and he either fires them or they leave in a few months and he gets another lot in. The head lad told your father's secretary he didn't remember much about Rossiter but he thought he was good with handling horses.'

I approached my next question with some caution. 'Did you ever suspect,' I said, 'that someone might have been behind Rossiter, someone with a grudge or other motive?'

'That thought crossed my mind and I mentioned it to your father but though he didn't dismiss it out of hand he seemed reluctant to discuss it. Find Rossiter first, he said. It struck me then as a little odd.'

'Did you know that he got a mysterious telephone call to meet someone in the Royal Albion Hotel at Brighton who could tell him who the real culprit was, and that it was on the trip to meet him that he had the stroke? He was found in his car near Beachy Head.'

He sat up. 'No,' he said. 'I wasn't told that. You see, after the stroke, I could of course get no further instructions from him. Your mother was too upset making the necessary arrangements, and then the whole thing petered out. But it was an unsatisfactory enquiry. And what you tell me now leaves even more questions unanswered.'

'Is there any way of identifying Rossiter if he turned up again?'

He opened a file that lay on the desk in front of him. 'We do have two photographs,' he said. 'But I'm afraid you won't find them of much assistance.' He took the photographs from the file and passed them across the desk to me. The first was a group picture of the whole staff at Madagascar House taken, I guessed, just before that fateful Ascot. At the back one head and shoulders was ringed, but Vincent Rossiter had so positioned himself that most of his features were hidden by the lad next to him. The second was of two lads larking about. They had their arms about each other's shoulders and this time the features were clear.

'Do you know who took this?' I asked, holding it out to him.

He looked down at the file again and then said, 'One of the other temporary lads, I believe. The two others were Norman Graham and Timothy, known as "Ginger", Elton.'

'May I keep these?' I asked.

'You may indeed. Technically they are your mother's property. Do you mind if I ask what you intend to do now?'

'I thought I'd search for those two lads to find if they could help in any way. Have you any idea where they are now?'

'As I say, the enquiry lapsed. Hold on though—' He riffled through the file. 'Yes, here it is. One of my assistants saw it in a paper and put it on file. Graham was killed in a motor accident a month or so back, and Elton is with Rodney Barker and getting a few rides.'

I rose to go.

'If I can be of any further help,' he said, extending a hand, 'don't hesitate to call me. Your father and your family have had a raw deal.'

I left thinking I had found another friend.

WHEN LADY VAL dropped me back that afternoon I found Captain Pat waiting for me. 'The colonel wants to see you,' he said. 'Blessed if I know what it is, but it must be something official, he's got his orderly-room expression on.'

We trooped along to Pirate's office and went in. He was behind the desk with a sheet of paper in front of him. 'I've received this among other rubbish from the War Office through the director of remounts,' he said, and proceeded to read: ' "The practice of employing unpaid voluntary civilian labour in the remount lines is to be deprecated and if any such exists it should cease forthwith." '

'It looks as though you'll have to go, Danny,' Captain Pat said.

'Go?' Pirate said. 'I'm damned if he does. Someone's arm is being twisted.'

'But what can you do?' Captain Pat said.

'I'll show you.' Pirate took the sheet of paper, tore it into four pieces and dropped them into the wastepaper basket. 'Never got it,' he said. 'Must have got lost on the way. Carry on.'

Once outside we walked a few paces and then I said, 'Will this cause any trouble for the colonel?'

'I shouldn't think so,' Captain Pat said slowly. 'He's seen off other commands before and got away with it. On the other hand, this one seems to come from very high up. There's something going on we don't know about.' He walked on a few paces and then stopped to peer at me owlishly from under his glasses. 'I'm due a trip to the West Country to look for black horses, for the Life Guards,' he said. 'You'd better come with me. It's part of your education.'

'And it'll get me out of the way,' I said.

'It mightn't be any harm in case they send a major-general down, and I've a share in a runner at Plumpton, too. We can look in there on the way back.'

Plumpton, I thought, would do nicely for what I had in mind. Back in my rooms I found the *Sporting Life*. A glance at the fixture list told me Plumpton was the only meeting on that day next week. If Elton was in the jumping game now, and it wasn't at all unusual for a lad to progress to a jumping stable and pick up a few rides, he would almost certainly be there, and if so he might well be able to help me with more information about the elusive Vincent Rossiter. If the file on my father was closed, well, I was about to reopen it.

Chapter Five

My friendship with Captain Pat flourished during that week we spent in the West Country. We talked together of all sorts of things. He was a fund of stories, many of them of his time in India and his racing there; but it wasn't until the night before we were due to make our way back to Plumpton that we touched on my affairs. We had dined at an inn high up in the Quantocks and as it was our last night we treated ourselves to an extra glass of port.

'What do you know of Rupert Carleton?' I asked him.

'He's an upper-class thug,' was the prompt reply. 'He had to leave India in a hurry. He lives on his wits and his gambling and gets away with it because of his connections and the fact that he's a bloody good rider. Why do you ask?'

'That night I dined with Flinty at Braden Lodge he seemed more than a bit interested in me, and when I was at Newmarket I saw him deep in conversation with Lady Val. I didn't think they'd be soul mates, somehow.'

'Why not?'

'It's just that, I don't know—Lady Val is too damn nice for him.'

He looked me straight in the eye. 'Take care,' he said. 'You're moving into deep waters, my lad. That wire didn't get put into the fence by accident, and that letter to Pirate was written by someone with power behind him. The two things add up to rather more than a coincidence.'

'It's all to do with my father,' I said hotly. 'The doping and the warning-off. He was framed. I'm sure of it.'

'I was never happy about that warning-off,' he said. 'And a lot of others weren't either.'

'There was talk of a court action,' I said, 'and the press took it up. My mother said one of the gossip columnists had a piece about the possibility of revelations coming out and reputations being tarnished if it came on.'

'Power,' he said. 'It's all about power, and when those in high places feel their power threatened they can be uncommonly ruthless.'

'I don't think HRH could have had anything to do with it.'

'Of course not. He's to be the loser in whatever game they're playing. You know, I was at a dinner party not so long ago, a very grand dinner party. I was only there representing Pirate who couldn't make it. Over the port they started discussing HRH. There's one old boy at court, Lord Esher, he's the sort who knows all the secrets, and one of the grandees quoted him: "The boy is a Stuart not a Brunswicker," is what Esher said. It stuck in my mind and I've often thought of it since. Esher is no fool. Those few words sum HRH up.'

'Another Bonnie Prince Charlie,' I said.

'You've put your finger on it.'

'I saw the detective my father hired to try to find the real culprit in the doping,' I then said. 'That's what I went to Newmarket for.'

'Did he help?'

'Not much, but he gave me the names of the temporary lads who they thought might be in the ramp. Rossiter, the chief suspect, went to America and disappeared. One of the others is riding now and I thought I might track him down at Plumpton tomorrow.'

'Who was the detective?'

I was anxious to learn more of Major Charles Ormsby and Captain Pat knew everyone. I guessed he would know enough to tell me what I wanted. 'His name is Major Charles Ormsby of Ormsby and Little,' I said. 'I thought I could trust him,' and I added, I hardly knew why, save that it had stuck in my mind, 'he was wearing a bow tie.'

'Charles Ormsby,' he said immediately. 'He was in the Sixteenth. There wasn't enough action for him in the cavalry and he transferred to the tanks, got a DSO and was badly wounded at Cambrai. He went into Intelligence when he recovered, and after he came out set up that enquiry agency. He doesn't take divorce and picks and chooses his clients. Yes, you can trust him.' He chuckled. 'Despite the bow tie. And he'll take up a case from anybody if he believes them and damn the consequences. He's mixed it with the authorities once or twice.'

'Maybe he'll have to do it again,' I said.

PLUMPTON RACECOURSE in those days was not noted for its amenities. I forgot who it was who said that the only place you could really see the racing from was standing on the waterbutt outside the weighing room, but in any event my main object was to find Ginger Elton. Having checked with the number board that he hadn't a ride in the first, I made my way to the weighing room. At the door I asked the attendant if a jockey of that name was about and, if so, would he come out to me. In a few minutes he was back, accompanied by a freckle-faced youth whose mop of red hair told me that this was indeed the Ginger Elton I was looking for.

'Got a ride for me, Guv?' he said cheerfully.

'No,' I said. 'I'm afraid not. Look, my name is de Lacey. I'm the son of Colonel de Lacey who was warned off. I'm trying to find who did dope that horse. I was wondering if you could help me.'

His face fell. 'Gawd,' he said. 'Not all that again. 'Asn't there been enough with those tecs questionin' me? I didn' 'ave nothin' to do with it.' He turned to go.

I put out a hand. 'Hold on for a minute, please,' I implored. 'No one thinks you had anything to do with that doping. All I want is to ask you about Vincent Rossiter.'

'That bastard,' he said succinctly. Then he thought for a moment. 'They did your dad proper, didn't they? I only worked for 'im for a bit, but 'e was as good a guvnor as I've ever 'ad. An' because of it all I've 'ad trouble gettin' work, people thinkin' I was mixed up in it somehow—'

'Then you will help?' I said. 'I'll make it worth your while.'

'You're on, Guv. I've a ride in the next. Meet me after the third, round the back of 'ere.'

I watched the next two races, in a fever of anticipation and impatience. I saw enough to tell me that young Ginger Elton could ride. He had a nice style, rode with a long rein, sat still and finished fourth. Afterwards, when I got round to the back of the hut which served as a weighing room, Ginger was there waiting for me. In those days riding fees for a jumping jockey were in the region of two or three pounds a ride. One thing my mother hadn't kept me short of was money, and I had two of those crisp, old-time white fivers ready for him.

'Thanks, Guv,' he said as he put them away. 'Now what?'

I took out the two photographs I had got from Major Ormsby and showed them to him. 'Is that Rossiter?' I asked.

He examined them, paying particular attention to the snapshot of the two lads larking about. 'I took that,' he said, holding it out. 'That's 'im.' He pointed to the ringed figure. 'I remember now, it was after a footer match. 'E saw me snappin' it, said 'e wished I hadn't, 'e 'ated 'avin' 'is picture taken. I didn't put much notion on it at the time, but later on when 'e asked me 'ad it been developed and could 'e have a look at the negative I did think it a bit strange.'

'Did he get it?'

'Nah. We fell out, like, after that. 'E was always a bit of a show-off and it was about then 'e started to throw money around. We pulled 'is leg about the money and 'e didn't like it when we told 'im it must 'ave bin a mighty touch and why 'adn't 'e let us in on it. "Touch," 'e said, "what do you think? I'm in with the nobs now", or somethin' like that.'

'You're sure he mentioned the nobs? Did he say who they were?'

'Nah. We thought 'e was just talkin' big, but now you're askin' I remember 'e went up to Lunnon one time and it was when 'e came back that 'e was in the money.'

'And was this just before Ascot?'

'That's right. We were only there with your guvnor for a bit, before the regular lads came back.'

'Did you ever find out anything about him? Where he came from?'

'Nah. 'E clammed up about 'imself but 'e liked to play the big fella just the same.'

'Did he dope the horse?'

'If 'e didn', who did?'

'Would you know him if you saw him again?'

'Sure thing. I'd know 'im all right.'

'One other thing,' I said. 'The doped horse, Bloemfontein. They don't dope test every winner. Did you ever hear of any reason given why they tested him?'

He scratched his head, looked at me and said, 'I dunno. I remember there was a bit of a buzz in the weighing room—someone, I dunno who it was, said 'e 'eard there was a tip-off.'

'I see. You don't know who gave the tip-off?'

'Nah.'

I didn't think I'd get anything more from Ginger Elton. 'Thanks,' I said, and extracted another of my mother's fivers, at the same time taking out one of my cards from my wallet. Writing my Melton address and the phone number of the remount depot on the back, I handed it and the fiver to him. 'If you hear anything at all that might be of help, get in touch with me there,' I said. 'There'll be a few more quid in it for you.'

'I 'ope you find the bastard, Guv, and nail 'im. And if you're ever in the way of gettin' a ride for a jockey, remember me, will ya?' Then he was gone.

A tip-off, I thought. Who, I wondered, would be the recipient of the information? The stewards of the day? All of them or just one of them? I resolved to ask Captain Pat. I told myself I must not draw him too deeply into this thing as he had his own future in the army to think of. All the same it could not do him any harm to ask him that one question. Meeting him shortly afterwards, I did.

'If it was a tip-off,' he said, 'it would probably be to the stewards of the day. I'll look 'em up in the *Calendar* and find out who the chairman was; it could have been made to him, though whether he'd tell you anything about it is another matter.'

At that moment I heard a familiar voice hailing me, and I turned to see the tall figure of Flinty striding across the grass towards me. 'I want a word with you,' he commanded as he came nearer. 'Where the devil have you been?' The 'word' clearly did not include Captain Pat, who made himself scarce, and it was easy to see how Flinty's overbearing approach made him so unpopular in many quarters.

'I've been looking for black horses with Captain Terrier,' I said.

'You might have told me you were off on a buying spree,' Flinty complained. 'Now listen to me—HRH wants you to ride to work tomorrow morning very early. It's a secret. No one is to know, not even your pal, Terrier. Understand? I'll call for you.' He nodded and walked off.

MY ALARM CLOCK woke me before first light next morning. I pulled on jodhpurs, a high-necked yellow polo jersey and a hacking jacket, and, shortly after I had washed and shaved, Flinty was at the door in his 4½-litre Bentley. The great green battle cruiser of a car had a distinctive romantic rumble from the exhaust you could hear a mile away. They were all the go just then among the rich and sporty.

We seemed to drive for miles while Flinty talked. 'Much has happened while you were away,' he said. 'First of all the little man has heard of that drawing Rupert was bandying about, and he's bloody furious. Things weren't improved by that ass Marston coming down and reading the riot act about his riding in races. Then he went on about the broken collarbone, even though HRH pointed out that happened hunting, not racing.'

'How is the break?' I asked.

'It's mended, but he had it all done up in an elaborate sling when Marston was here. "How can I ride in a race when I'm like this," he kept saying, and that was about all the change Marston got out of him. He was hanging about the remounts too.' Flinty changed gear, double-declutching expertly, making the big engine give out one of its more exciting rumbles as he swung her round a tight corner.

'Who was? Marston?' I asked.

'That's right. I gather Pirate saw him off, whatever it was about.' Flinty looked sideways at me as if expecting me to say something but I kept my silence. So someone had come down, I thought. It had been wise of Captain Pat to take me away.

'Those who meddle with old Pirate do so at their peril,' Flinty said. 'Ah, here we are.' He turned the big car through a narrow gateway and we bumped up a lane that petered out at the edge of a hundred-acre field.

When we came to a stop I looked about me. Down one side ran a line of schooling fences which looked as though they had not been used for some time. The rest was good galloping grass. Above us was a little knoll with a few scattered trees at its crest: beyond and all around was the rolling grassland of the Shires. Nearby a groom held three horses, one of whom I recognised as Pepperpot; drawn up beside them was HRH's Rolls. Its doors opened and HRH and Lady Val emerged. There was no sign of a sling on his arm now, and Flinty said quietly to me, 'Now you see why he wanted this kept quiet.'

We gathered in a little group round Flinty. 'You'll ride Pepperpot,' he said, jabbing a finger at me. 'It's about a mile round. You and HRH will go round three-quarter speed. When you come to the last bend, Lady Val will jump in and the three of you come back as fast as you can.'

As I approached the horses I noticed that someone had been shoving some work into Pepperpot. He looked leaner and harder than when I had hunted him. They must have something in mind for him, I thought.

The others moved towards their horses, Flinty legged me up on Pepperpot and we set off. Pepperpot surprised me by jumping into his stride far more quickly than I had expected and, once there, it took me all my time holding him. Round we went. The two big horses held by us stride for stride on the springy turf. I thought, How wonderful to have the chance of doing this, and in this company, with the thud of hoofs coming up and the wind whipping past my ears, all of it in the pearly light of an early morning in Leicestershire.

When we turned for home Lady Val jumped in. With that the three of us set sail. I thought for a moment they were going to lose me, for Pepperpot didn't quicken with them. Then, almost you would say in his own time, he put his old head down and really began to gallop. He drew abreast of the Prince and left him there; with Lady Val leading us a length or so we passed Flinty, who was standing by the cars.

'Jolly good,' the Prince said as we pulled up. 'The old boy can still go a bit, can't he?' Then he seemed to catch sight of the schooling fences for the first time. A light of pure mischief came into his eyes. 'Come on,' he said. 'Let's have a go.' With that he turned his horse at the first of the fences and set him alight. Willy-nilly, I followed.

The horses were steamed up. It was a piece of madness really, it wasn't schooling at all, it was a helter-skelter dash. We flew down the line, Pepperpot stretching himself and gaining lengths in the air. They were weak fences and far from suitable for our horses. To this day I don't know how we didn't wreck them, but that was HRH all over. When his blood was up he'd take on anything. As we pulled up he turned to me, flushed, happy and laughing. 'What fun!' he said. 'What splendid fun!'

We walked the horses slowly back to where Flinty was standing looking thunderous. 'That wasn't on the agenda,' he greeted us. 'Racing flat out over those rubbishy fences, of all the bloody silly—'

'They enjoyed it as much as we did,' HRH said, slipping to the ground and pulling up his irons.

'Maybe, but one knock and they'd be out for the whole season.'

HRH was not in the least abashed, though I had the feeling that only Flinty could have got away with thus admonishing the heir to the throne. Lady Val came over to me. 'He's an old darling, isn't he?' she said as she patted Pepperpot. 'He goes for you too, he doesn't for everybody. We wanted to see if he'd quicken. That four-year-old of mine has been placed on the flat.'

I thought to myself that I'd been on trial too and hoped that I'd passed. 'He has the hell of a leap in him,' I said, looking at Pepperpot as a groom took him and led him round.

As we spoke a shaft of sunlight broke through the cloud and fell on the knoll above us. Something reflected its light and caught my eye, and then I saw a black shape move along below the trees before disappearing round the hill. Realising that the reflection I'd seen was the sun catching a windscreen, idly I wondered what a car was doing up there at that hour of the morning. When the others had gone and were walking towards the Bentley, I mentioned it to Flinty.

Frowning, he said, 'I think we'll take a look-see. He may be still hanging around.'

About a quarter of a mile from where we left the field we found the way up the hill. We turned into a narrow, rutted lane and climbed upwards round two bends until we came to a short, straight stretch beneath the trees. There was a closed gate at the far end. Here Flinty pulled to a stop and we got out. The gate was locked with a rusty padlock which looked as if it had not been opened for some time. Flinty stared at the muddy ground. 'He's gone,' he said. 'And he wasn't just passing on his way.' He pointed to tracks in the muddy ground. 'Look. Here is where he turned.' He stared again across the landscape. 'He could see every yard of the gallop from here if that's what he wanted.'

'He was here for a bit,' I said. 'There are cigarette butts.'

Flinty picked them up and examined them. 'Parkinson of Haymarket,' he said. 'And they are more than just ends. I know of only one man who gets his cigarettes from Parkinson and throws them away half smoked.'

'Who's that?' I said.

'Never you mind for the moment. The point is he was here watching us. Who told him where we were?'

'One of the grooms?' I suggested.

'HRH's servants don't talk. Loyalty is their middle name.'

We were back in the car by this time. Flinty's fingers drummed on the string-bound steering wheel. 'How fit are you?' he asked. 'HRH wants you to ride Pepperpot in the Adjacent Hunts at Marleythorpe.'

I gasped. Never in my wildest dreams had I thought of this. 'Fairly fit,' I said. 'Is it because of his shoulder? Is it still playing up?'

'Mind your own business,' Flinty snapped. 'Don't ask any questions but be grateful for the ride.'

I had the feeling they were playing some game with me but I didn't care. Here was the chance of a lifetime, or two lifetimes if it came to that. As it happened, the problem of getting myself fully fit solved itself. Captain Pat was preparing Dainty to run in the Veterinary Corps race at Alton in Hampshire and Pirate had a horse which he wanted got ready and asked me to ride work on him.

Givenchy was the name Pirate had given his horse after the place in France where he had lost his leg. He was quite unlike the usual run of troopers, being a light-framed, thin-skinned sort and highly strung. But after we had worked them together for a few days it was clear that he could go more than a bit and could leave Dainty, whom we knew was no slouch, standing.

'He seems to suit you or you him,' Captain Pat said as we hacked home one morning. 'I'll have a word with Pirate. He might put you up. Then you'd have two strings to your bow, wouldn't you?' He smiled one of his knowing smiles, the news of my riding Pepperpot had got out. A paragraph appeared in one of the glossies:

> I hear that the Prince of Wales, who sustained a broken collar-bone recently when out with the Quorn, has given the ride on his good horse Pepperpot in next week's point-to-point at Marleythorpe to Daniel de Lacey, a young Irishman, who we have seen going so well to hounds in his first season.

I wondered what 'the watcher on the hill' thought of that, but my own thoughts were too full of the coming week to allow room for anything much else, though I did find time to ask Captain Pat if he had been able to ascertain the names of the Ascot stewards that day my father had been in before them. Yes, he said, he had, and the chairman on the day had been Major Sir Crispin Merevale, Bart.

Chapter Six

The days passed in a flash and before I knew it I found myself sitting on a bench in the barn that served as a changing room at Marleythorpe, about to pull on my jersey and go out to ride in the Adjacent Hunts race. I could scarcely believe it, there I was preparing to don the royal colours: red, blue sleeves, black cap. What a go! to use a phrase current at the time.

In the morning I had walked the course slowly, carefully and thoughtfully as my father had taught me. In those days point-to-points were still run over a semi-natural country under the jurisdiction not of the National Hunt committee but of the Masters of Foxhounds point-to-point committee, a very different body determined to preserve their links with fox-hunting and cross-country riding. To that end they laid down in their regulations that, 'the course shall be as natural a character as possible and typical of the country concerned'.

The organisers at Marleythorpe had taken these instructions to heart. The fences were cut and trimmed but not much more, and the water, for instance, was just that, an open ditch about eighteen feet wide. There was one place of which I took particular notice. You came down a fairly steep incline, at the bottom of which you rounded a flag, to be confronted by an in-and-out: a fence into a lane with another out of it. It was a place which needed thinking about, and I saw that others had anticipated action there: one or two picnic parties were taking their positions and a few press photographers were prowling about.

As I was pulling on my boots, a figure in a long greatcoat with the collar turned up darkened the doorway. It looked round and then crossed to where I was sitting. As the figure approached I saw between the wings of the collar the unmistakable features of the Prince of Wales. Immediately I began to scramble to my feet.

'Sit down, you bloody fool,' came from his lips, and then, with that boyish grin which had captivated so many men—and women—of his future subjects, 'I'm riding Flinty's and I hope you're not as frightened as I am!'

I remembered then seeing that Major R.J. Westcough's Bormont II was amongst the entries. I saw it all now. In view of Marston's reading of the riot act and the undesirable attentions of the press, they had directed the publicity towards me while HRH took the ride on Flinty's horse.

Just then Flinty came in. 'All well, David?' he said, and then, looking across the room: 'What's he doing here? He never rides in point-to-points. Not hot enough for him.'

It was Rupert Carleton sitting quietly in a corner and tying the bow of his cap in a businesslike manner. Flinty, frowning, stared at him for a few moments before turning back to us, 'Whenever you're ready, David, we'll get weighed out.'

Soon they left the barn together and after a bit I followed them, weighed out and went along to supervise the saddling of Pepperpot. That done I saw him led into the parade ring and walked in myself after him, feeling lonely amongst the groups of families and supporters surrounding the other riders. Up to now I had been buoyed up with the excitement of it all but, standing there alone among the crowd of crack riders and other swells, I wished my father was standing beside me to reassure me with his quiet confidence and presence as he had so often done before. It was borne in on me too that I knew nothing of the other runners. I had been left alone to ride my own race. I dreaded making a fool of myself and the colours I was carrying.

Suddenly I found Lady Val standing beside me. 'Nervous, Danny?'

'I think I'm going to throw up,' I said.

'Don't do that, it would spoil that nice rig you've got on.' Her presence beside me gave my spirits a lift. 'Pepperpot has done it all before, you know, and whatever happens the little man won't mind. He knows racing well enough for that. Anyway, nothing will happen. You've become our mascot, you know.'

It was then I noticed that she was wearing a habit and looking particularly striking in it. 'You're not going out too?' I said.

'Ladies' race,' she smiled. 'We're both in this together. So cheer up. You'll be getting up in a minute and then nothing matters. By the way, where is the little man?'

Flinty and the Prince had left it very late to enter the parade ring, but as we looked around I saw them coming in, HRH still with the collar of his greatcoat turned up round his ears. They chatted together for a moment and then Flinty came over. 'I wonder what that beggar is up to,' he said, looking to where Rupert was the centre of a little group. 'Whatever it is it's no good, I'll be bound. I see pressmen about too. They're not usually here. Something's up. Watch him, Danny. Are you OK?'

'More or less,' I said.

'That old fellow will jump anything. You'll be all right, you'll find.' With that he gave me one of his quick smiles and was gone.

Then we were mounting and going down to the start. There were eight other runners, making a field of nine in all. One or two didn't look particularly competitive and, I hoped, were there just for a good bump around. Mindful of Flinty's warning I kept an eye on Rupert Carleton. For his part he could never look anything other than what he was—a damn competent steeplechase rider. He sat there, shoulders hunched, leathers pulled up, staring out through his horse's ears, a man intent and ready for the business on hand if ever I saw one: his mount was lighter-framed than most of ours and looked more of a racehorse. I wondered where he had qualified, not having bothered to check on the racecard, and I felt very raw, young and inexperienced beside this hard-bitten tough. He came past me as we circled, walking slowly, grim and unsmiling. Whatever he had in mind he had a mind to do it. The Prince, on the other hand, was chatting in a friendly fashion to those by him. The horse of Flinty's he was riding was the one that had gone in the gallop with me a few days back.

We had not long to wait before the starter, a portly ex-major in the Brigade of Guards, lined us up and unfurled his flag. Rupert, I saw, had bagged the inside and kept it. 'Are you all right, sir?' the starter called to the Prince, and then, 'Well—ahem—go!' He dropped the flag and we were off.

The Prince went to the front straight away as I'd been told he was wont to do. The rest of us jumped the first two fences almost abreast, and after that the race began to sort itself out, the gents in top hats and double bridles, who weren't taking the whole thing too seriously, forming a little group at the back. To my surprise the pace was nothing like as strong as I had expected, scarcely more than a good hunting gallop with the Quorn. Pepperpot was well and truly into his stride by this time and it was all I could do to hold him. His jumping was quick and accurate and before I quite knew it he had jumped himself into the head of affairs behind the Prince.

So we came to the top of the slope leading to the awkward set of fences. Halfway down the descent Rupert passed me, his eyes on the Prince just in front, his face set and grim. Then I saw that there was a whole battery of press photographers lined up near the turning flag. I didn't know for sure what Rupert intended to do, but I believed that his plot was to bump the unsuspecting Prince off his line, drive him from the course before the sharp turn, into the arms—and lenses—of the photographers. This would make him look a proper Charley on a horse and give the press more fuel for their gibes at him, and I wasn't having it. I drove Pepperpot upsides of Rupert just as he was beginning to make his move towards the Prince. We came together and touched. Rupert's horse was thrown out of his stride and there was a stream of curses from his rider, who had to snatch him up. The Prince rounded the flag safely and sailed serenely on.

I had lost a couple of lengths in all this and what was left of the field began to close up. The bump seemed to have taken little out of Pepperpot. We rounded the flag, jumped the in-and-out without a pause and I set out after the Prince. I was intent on catching him and so were the others. HRH was never given any quarter in his races and we were really racing now. A rider in a red cap loomed up on my left and I heard the thud of another's hoofs behind me. We seemed to beat off the man behind, whoever he was, and together red cap and I raced for the next, a hedge. There was a ditch on the landing side of this, I remembered. I asked for a big one and got it. The other chap didn't. I saw red cap dive towards the ground and then I was alone behind the Prince—but would I get to him?

We were on good firm grass again now and Pepperpot revelled in it. He met two plain fences just right and I knew we were gaining lengths. I didn't look round but there was nothing near me so far as I could tell. It was between me and him. Ahead of me, at the top of a rise, I could see the finish, the roped-off straight and the crowds.

Pepperpot was full of running. Another fence fled behind us. The Prince was still ahead but the gap was narrowing with every stride. I knew it and I think Pepperpot knew it too. We came to the last at the foot of the rise. He threw a tremendous leap, gained lengths in the air and landed running. I sat down to ride and halfway up the straight I caught him.

But he wouldn't give in. The hill was getting to both of us now. Stride for stride we battled it out. The crowd was roaring on either side. Twenty yards from the post we were still locked level. I was blind to everything except riding that finish. Hands and heels I rode him out, not daring to go for my whip. And then Bormont's head appeared by my knee and dropped back. As the post came up we were a length to the good.

Pulling up, the realisation of what I had done came to me. I had beaten the most popular man in the land in a hard-fought finish. I wondered if the crowd would greet me by throwing bottles.

At least there was one who wouldn't. Turning to ride back I found HRH beside me. 'Well done, young fella,' he said. 'I'm always told the best jockeys pick the wrong horse of two!'

Considering he'd just been beaten by his own horse I didn't think that half bad, and, coming back through the lane of spectators, he clapped me on the back. 'Damn good race,' he said loudly so that all could hear. It was the sort of gesture which brought him instantly into the hearts of the country people, and as he spoke a ripple of clapping broke out. Here indeed was a man among us.

When I had weighed in I changed quickly and went down to watch Lady Val's race, getting there in time to see her win by what looked an easy four or five lengths. I had not seen Rupert since our race and intended to keep well out of his way, but when I went to fetch my colour bag from the barn I came face to face with him. There was fire in his eyes and a scowl on his face, and I resolved to get my say in first. 'I'm very sorry about that bump, sir,' I said. 'I couldn't keep my horse straight.'

'Why, you young cur,' he snarled at me. 'I've a good mind to report you to the stewards for foul riding but seeing whose horse you were on, this weak-kneed lot'd do nothing—'

'But, sir,' I said feebly, 'it was an accident—'

'Accident be damned. You're going to get a lesson in manners. Come round behind the barn and I'll give you something to remember me by.'

'I wouldn't do that if I were you, Rupert,' a quiet voice said. 'I'd pick on someone up to your weight or you may have to take on two of us.' It was Flinty who had come up behind us.

'You keep out of this, Flinty,' Rupert said.

'Oh, I don't think so,' came Flinty's quiet voice again. 'You see I keep wondering who was watching a gallop a while back and smoking cigarettes from Parkinson of Haymarket while he was doing it. I wonder, too, who alerted the press that HRH would be riding today and stationed them at that in-and-out. Who, I wonder?'

'Yes, lay off, Rupert,' said another voice, and I saw that Lady Val had joined us. She gave Rupert a cold stare from her cool grey eyes.

'You look out. I'll see you in hell before I'm finished,' he snarled at me. Then he turned and walked away into the crowd.

'Forget him,' Lady Val said. 'Congratulations, Danny, you rode the hell of a race.'

'So did you,' I said. 'How anyone ever takes on racing in a habit and sidesaddle beats me.'

'Makes it easier,' she said, laughing. 'You can't fall out of one even if you try. Anyway we deserve a celebration. There's a hunt ball tonight and you're coming, Danny. We can't do without our mascot.'

'HRH's quarters at eight for dinner,' Flinty said.

'He's gone off delighted with himself,' Lady Val went on. 'He loves old Pepperpot and he thinks the plan he made to keep the press away by switching rides worked a treat.'

'He doesn't know anything about Rupert's little game,' Flinty said slowly. 'And it's as well not to tell him for the moment anyway.'

'What was his game?' I asked.

'Adverse publicity,' Flinty said. 'It all mounts up. And it all gets home to Papa in Buck House.'

'Well it won't this time,' Lady Val said. 'Danny saw to that. There's champagne in the car. We can start the celebrations now.'

After I had fetched my colour bag we adjourned to the car where we polished off two bottles in no time at all. It was only when I was back in my rooms, changing, that I remembered to look for the name of Rupert's owner. Going to my overcoat I fished out the racecard. The name was there in black and white: A.R.J. Gretton.

HRH LIKED SMALL PARTIES and most of the guests had already assembled in his sitting room when I arrived. Truth to tell, I wasn't looking forward to the dinner or the hunt ball. I would know very few at either gathering, and the fact that I was the only one wearing black tails among the scarlet at dinner didn't help my self-confidence, either. The one consolation was that I should see Lady Val again.

She was there of course, and Flinty, but there was also a flashy blonde whose name I didn't catch and to whom HRH seemed to be paying plenty of attention. Rather to my surprise Roger Gretton and his wife were also in the party. To my even greater surprise, seeing me, he came over to speak to me.

'Terrible thing about your father's stroke,' he said. 'I'm truly sorry. Is there any hope?'

'None at all, sir, I'm afraid,' I said. 'At least, that's what the doctors say.'

He paused and then said, 'It was too bad what we had to do. But there was no option. It's mandatory. That's the rule.'

'Then the rule ought to be changed,' said a voice at my elbow. HRH had come up and had heard the last sentence.

'I'm inclined to agree with you, sir,' Gretton said. 'There have been discussions in that direction. But you know we move slowly—'

'Then you need shaking up,' was the reply, spoken quite sharply. When he had said this he moved off to pay more attention to the flashy blonde.

'HRH is right you know, Roger,' Flinty put in. 'Every trainer is at the mercy of his staff, and they're all at it, especially among the smaller stables, giving gee-up pills and patent remedies when they're not filling 'em up with slower downers. Why did you pick on poor Dick de Lacey, eh?'

'The evidence was there, what could we do?' Gretton was being backed into a corner and it was on the tip of my tongue to ask him if there had been a tip-off, but in that company I didn't dare. In any event I hadn't a chance. At that moment a footman appeared at the door, HRH made a gesture and we trooped into dinner.

The long hunting table in the dining room of the suite glistened and sparkled with silver and napery. Two footmen moved noiselessly about. The flashy blonde, glowing in the attention paid to her, was seated on HRH's right. I found myself at the foot of the table beside Lady Val. Though she kept the conversation going, her eyes were all for the Prince.

He was in tremendous form. Gay is a word one is not allowed to use in that context nowadays, but it is the only one I can think of to describe him at that moment. When he was in that mood it was as if a flame ran round the table and touched us all. He had that sort of mesmerism, an electric ability to make people more than they were. We seemed to come alight and move out of ourselves. It certainly wasn't due to drink, since I noticed that with the footman constantly filling our glasses with champagne, his remained virtually untouched.

'Will you run Pepperpot in the National Hunt Chase at Cheltenham, David?' Flinty asked him.

'By Jove that's not half a bad idea,' came the reply. 'Nothing I'd like better than a crack at the Cheltenham fences, except Aintree perhaps. Trouble is the press would get hold of it, confound 'em, and then certain people would come down on me like a ton of bricks and kybosh the whole thing.' The animation died for a moment and his eyes flickered in my direction. 'Better to be an ordinary sort of young chap,' he said. 'Beat me by a length on my own horse this afternoon, what do you make of that? I should have known better than to give him the ride, shouldn't I?'

I took a hasty gulp of champagne and didn't know where to look. The blonde seemed visibly put out to have lost her place, momentarily at least, as the centre of his attention. Lady Val flashed an appreciative look at me. 'You've won the race and now you've stolen the limelight,' she said softly.

We did not linger over the port and soon we were whisked off to the ball, which was held in the great hall of Patworth Castle some miles from Melton. Here the flashy blonde came back into her own for HRH, who loved dancing as much as he liked pretty women, monopolised her. I, on the other hand, was ignored among the crowd of socialites who all knew each other. Feeling rather like a wallflower at a débutante ball, I was on the point of wandering off to hide myself somewhere in a corner with a bottle of champagne when Lady Val came up to me. 'You're not dancing,' she said. 'We'll soon put that right. Come along.' She reached out a hand.

'I'm a hopeless dancer,' I said. 'I don't know any steps—'

'Nonsense. All jockeys can dance. It's a question of keeping time, that's all. Now then. That's an order.'

She more or less swept me onto the dance floor, where the beat of the band and her presence in my arms gave my feet a lightness to match hers. ' "The craze for pleasure steadily grows," ' she hummed in my ear, ' "Cocktails and laughter, but what comes after? Nobody knows." '

When the music stopped she laid a hand on my arm while her eyes roved around amongst the revellers. She was, I knew, searching for the Prince, and in vain. 'We need a drink,' she said abruptly, and led me through an arched doorway onto a terrace where there were chairs and tables set out. Leaving her for a moment I found a white-coated waiter and told him to bring a bottle of champagne to the table. As I was returning I found myself face to face with Pirate who was chatting to a tall, fair-haired younger man. 'Well done, lad,' he said. 'And your head is still off the block, I'm glad to see. By the way, this is Sir Crispin Merevale, your host, he owns the place. You may meet him some time in his other occupation, too.'

'I'm one of those dire people, a steward,' Merevale said, smiling. 'I'll add my congratulations too.'

So this was the steward who had conducted my father's initial enquiry. He was utterly unlike what I had imagined him to be—far younger, less pompous, and with an amused look in his eye. Altogether he appeared more approachable than I could have hoped if ever I got the chance to make that approach. The time was certainly not just then. I thanked him and passed on.

Back at the table, I found the champagne frosting in its ice bucket and filled the glasses.

'Now,' Lady Val said, 'you can say you're a man who danced with a girl who danced with the Prince of Wales.'

'And very nice too,' I said. 'I hope your feet are intact.'

We were laughing now. 'Cigarette me, will you?' she said.

I took out my case, opened it and held it out to her. 'Common fags,' I said. 'Nothing here from Parkinson of Haymarket.'

She drew a deep breath on the cigarette as I lighted it for her. 'Rupert,' she said, 'is a very nasty man. He goes too far always. And everything he's got he gives to the bookies.' Then her eyes fell on the slim gold case. 'What a lovely thing,' she said, picking it up from the table where I had placed it between us.

'It was my father's,' I said. 'One of his owners gave it to him when he won the Eclipse with Sang Froid.'

'I heard Roger Gretton asking about him. So there's no hope?'

'None at all,' I said.

Her eyes clouded for a moment. Suddenly, almost savagely, she stubbed out her cigarette and got to her feet. 'Let's dance,' she said.

The throb of the music came faintly to us on the terrace. It was one of those balmy nights that sometimes come to the countryside in early spring, and the formal gardens below were alive with fairy lights. Set on a high bluff as the castle was, the whole effect was magical. We seemed to be floating in some sort of ethereal space. Together we danced the night away and, at the very end, as we joined hands to the strains of John Peel and 'Auld Lang Syne', she said to me, 'You're coming to Huntercombe right now for the weekend, no ifs or buts.'

Together we made our way to the Riley. She had thrown a mink coat over her ball gown and I climbed in beside her. 'I'll have to pack,' I said.

When she pulled up outside my rooms dawn had come and gone. The strings of horses were already going out for exercise and the early morning had brought a chill to the air. 'I'm damned if I'm going to sit out here in the cold waiting,' she said. 'I'll come in with you.'

I had a sitting room, a bedroom and a bathroom down the passage. Turning on the gas fire in the sitting room for her, I went into the bedroom to pack. I changed rapidly out of my tails and then I threw what I guessed I would want for the weekend into a suitcase and hurried back.

When I entered the sitting room she was standing by the desk in a corner. In one hand was a cigarette and in the other my mother's letter. She was staring fixedly at the two photographs of Vincent Rossiter which I had left lying on the desk. Not a whit abashed, she smiled at me as I came in. 'I always read other people's correspondence if they're careless enough to leave it lying about,' she said. 'How is your mother?'

'Very well, I think,' I said. 'Hunting madly.'

It wasn't until much later that I began to wonder what had drawn her attention so fixedly to the photographs.

Chapter Seven

A puncture on the way and my changing of the wheel, which wasn't as simple an operation then as now, delayed our arrival at Huntercombe, and HRH's Rolls together with Flinty's Bentley were already parked in the forecourt when we drew up at the front door.

Huntercombe was a Tudor manor house, in size somewhere between a mansion and a country house. Lady Val led the way into an inner hall, square and compact, oak-beamed with a small minstrels' gallery. There a butler awaited us. 'His Royal Highness, the young lady and Major Westcough are on the golf course, M'lady,' he told us.

'I see. Get William to show Mr de Lacey his room, will you, Jenks,' she said. Then, turning to me, she said, 'I'm going to get out of these duds. You'll want to freshen up, too, I expect. Come down when you like. We usually meet here. Drinks over there—' She pointed to a drinks tray on a standing chest. 'Help yourself to whatever you want.'

I followed the butler upstairs and along passages until he threw open a door. It was a low-ceilinged room with a canopied bed and mullioned windows. 'You'd care for a bath, sir, I expect,' he said, opening a door in the panelling to reveal a modern, glistening bathroom. 'I'll run it for you.'

When he had gone I stepped gratefully into the steaming water and let it soak into my bones and muscles. I'd had a hectic twenty-four hours. I'd won a race against the heir to the throne, had a row with a leading gentleman rider, been to a royal dinner party, danced all night with one of the most sought-after girls in the Shires and was now a guest at her home.

In modernising Huntercombe, Lloyd George's earl had done well. The bath was long and deep, and there was every conceivable accoutrement including, unusually for that day and age, a bidet. The only touch of opulence was the yellow gleam of the taps which I assumed to be gold. Apart from that, the bedroom with its deep pile carpet, embossed writing paper on the desk and antique dressing table, seemed to typify the whole place, which reeked of taste, comfort and luxury. And it was, apparently, packed with servants. At Kilbarry we lived well, for Ireland, but nothing on this scale. I yawned and, in the midst of soaping myself, fell asleep.

It was the cooling water that woke me. My bag had been unpacked. Hurriedly I shaved and pulled on my clothes. Making my way to the hall I found my hostess, dressed in country tweeds, sitting in a big leather chair and reading the *Sporting Life*. Scarcely had I arrived when a side door opened and Flinty came in.

'A large pink gin, quickly,' he said, crossing to the drinks tray on the chest. 'I don't know how he does it. He never seems to tire. No sooner were we here than he had us out golfing. Eighteen holes! I'm whacked.' He gulped his gin.

'And the lovely Dinah?' Lady Val asked.

Dinah, I thought. So that was the flashy blonde's name.

Flinty chuckled. 'She rashly said last night, to get into further favour, I suppose, that she loved a game of golf. She little knew what was coming to her, poor creature. After nine holes she showed all the signs of wilting but the little man would have none of it. Eighteen holes or nothing. She's had time to regret those rash words.'

At that moment HRH and the flashy blonde, Dinah, came in. He was wearing the golfing knickerbockers we then called plus fours, a fair-isle jersey, co-respondent brown and white shoes, and looked as fresh as paint. She, on the other hand, was suffering. The blonde hair was bedraggled and she was wearing, I noticed, the sort of country clothes a town person thinks are right and which in the country look all wrong. As they entered I saw an all but imperceptible look pass from the Prince to Flinty, who immediately put down his glass and left the room. In a few moments he was back dispensing drinks after another slight signal had been exchanged between them. The flashy blonde asked with a sort of gasp for a cocktail called a sidecar. She probably needed it.

After we had made conversation for a few minutes, Jenks, the butler, came in. 'His Royal Highness is wanted urgently on the telephone,' he said.

'I'd better see to it if you'll forgive me,' the Prince said.

As soon as he had gone the flashy blonde put down her glass. 'I think I'd like to go upstairs for a bit,' she said. She then gave the ghost of a smile, and added, 'To try to repair the damage.'

'You do that, dear,' Lady Val said and, when the door had closed behind her, she looked at Flinty. 'You arranged that very nicely, didn't you?' she said.

A little later there was the rumble of the Rolls's wheels and, looking out, we saw it disappearing, with HRH inside, down the drive.

'That's the end of her,' Lady Val said with satisfaction. 'Time for lunch, I think. If she doesn't come down I suppose I'd better send her up something.'

Lunch was plain and unceremonious. As we sat down Lady Val said to the butler, 'Better send Miss, what the devil is her name, Flinty?'

'Carstairs,' Flinty said.

'Have Miss Carstairs brought up something on a tray.'

We had coffee in the hall. After the cups had been cleared away the housekeeper appeared with the news that Miss Carstairs had learned that the Prince of Wales had been urgently called away and felt that she should return to London.

'Very good. I'll take her anywhere within reason,' Flinty said.

'You could put her on a train at Melton,' Lady Val said. 'Good of you, Flinty. Always a shoulder to cry on. You'll be back, won't you? I'll show Danny the horses.'

The flashy blonde came down looking considerably more spruce but still not quite what she had been on the dance floor. There was a flurry of thanks and goodbyes, followed by the burble of the Bentley's exhaust as they drove away.

'Good riddance,' Lady Val said, drawing on her umpteenth cigarette of the day. 'Come on, Danny, let's look at the horses. They can do all sorts of things but they can't dance and they can't talk.'

The yards at Huntercombe were magnificent. Lady Val had twenty blood horses stabled at Melton but here were young stock coming on and replacements for the all-too-frequent injuries in the hunting field being schooled. Then there were her point-to-pointers, and in a lower yard her store steeplechasers and foals and yearlings for the few she ran on the flat. The whole place was spotless, the boxes were painted, polished and burnished, and all of it lay gleaming in the watery sun which had now come out from behind the low clouds.

We walked down the line of boxes. At one we halted. 'This is Prospero. I won on him yesterday, remember?' she said. 'It's my belief that he could go on to better things. They won't allow me to ride against you men, and I'm fed up taking on these fat cows in ladies' races—half my time is spent trying to keep out of their way. Will you ride him for me?'

I gasped. He looked the part. He was big and upstanding, and a pale chestnut. Here was another chance such as I had never dreamed of, and coming on top of yesterday too. She looked at me quizzically. 'You'll get lots of offers of rides after that win on HRH's horse,' she said. 'I thought I'd get in first. Well, what do you think?'

'You've taken my breath away,' I said. 'Of course I'll ride him for you. Are you sure?'

'I wouldn't have asked you if I wasn't, would I?' She tucked her arm into mine. 'Now let me show you the rest of the place.'

Arm in arm for the rest of that short, enchanted afternoon, we wandered through formal gardens, glasshouses carefully tended, and down through the woods to where a little river ran. Back at the house with the evening drawing in, the curtains closed and a log fire blazing in the big stone fireplace in the hall, we found tea and muffins waiting for us. Flinty had sent a message to say that he had been detained and would not be returning. Then the dressing bell sounded and we went upstairs to change.

Looking back I find it hard to believe the way we lived then. Was it I, as a youngster, who found a fire in the bedroom hearth, my bath run, my dinner clothes laid out, my shirt studded and linked? To me it is like a dream, as so many things from that time are now. Bathed and changed, I came down to the hall to see Lady Val standing by the fire, looking lovely in a short silken evening gown that set off her slim shapeliness.

As I joined her she indicated a jade cigarette box and then pressed a bell to summon the butler. 'Jenks creates the best champagne cocktails this side of paradise,' she said. 'It's the touch of the master hand that tells the tale, isn't it, Jenks?'

'Thank you, M'lady. I hope they're to your satisfaction, sir.' He handed me a brimming glass on a salver.

They were. So were those that followed. 'I've always been told that if you open a bottle of champagne you must empty it,' she said. And then, more sombrely, ' "Cocktails and laughter, but what comes after?" There's the rub, isn't it?' And she stared into her drink.

Later we dined together, in candlelight, at a small table set in front of the fire under the beamed ceiling. With Jenks and a footman hovering about, we spoke mostly of generalities, and it was not until we were back in the hall in deep chairs in front of the fire, our drinks beside us, port for me, brandy for her, that our talk became more intimate. We were both, I think, by that time slightly tight.

'And you, Danny,' she said. 'How is your quest going? Did you find out anything from the detectives?'

'Not much,' I said. 'They think one of the temporary lads did it, but we knew that before. They've narrowed it down to the lad who called himself Vincent Rossiter, but he's done a bunk. Gone to America and got lost.' Then, suddenly remembering, I said, 'That was his photograph on my desk you were looking at. He was a wanderer, apparently, and never in one place for long. You didn't have him here, by chance, at any time?'

'Good heavens, no. I wondered what on earth those photographs were doing there. Gone to America, has he?'

'So they say.'

'It's pretty hopeless, isn't it, Danny? Why don't you chuck it? Concentrate on your riding. You could go places, though I wouldn't count on more royal rides. That was a one-off. He likes to ride his own horses and does, whatever they say. Don't take any notice of what's said about his falls—everyone who hunts or rides races has falls, it's part of the game, but you know that as well as I do.'

'It's all that stuff in the papers,' I said.

'Damn the press, they're beginning to get him down and can you blame him? How would you like it if you were followed everywhere by a barrage of cameras and crowds congregating in the hope of seeing you take a jerk?' She lit another cigarette and sipped her brandy. ' "My falls have become a public topic," he said to me the other day. "Why can't they leave me alone, let me be a private person?" '

'If it was me I think I'd pack it in,' I said.

'He'll never do that, not willingly, he has too much guts, more than I ever thought he had. But that was one of the reasons he and Flinty rigged the deception yesterday, to keep the press away.'

'It didn't work,' I said. 'Someone split.'

'They'll make him give up riding,' she went on fiercely. 'And then what will happen to him? He'll take up golf, he says. Golf!' She put so much contempt into that word I could almost feel it. 'If he does he'll start to drink. He keeps himself fit for racing, that's why he's off the bottle now. He only drinks when he's bored.' Her words were almost falling over each other as she poured them out. 'And when he's bored he'll be easy prey for some floosie to get hold of him.'

I don't know what made me say what I said next. It must have been the cocktails and the wine and the closeness and companionship. 'Do you love him very much?' I asked.

'That's my business,' she said sharply. And then, so softly I barely heard it, 'More than anything.'

Silence fell between us until I broke it by saying, 'You mentioned there were those who would stop him racing and I've heard that there are people at court who don't want him there. What about Gretton? He's been friendly enough to me but he was one of the stewards who warned my father off.'

'Roger? You never know with Roger but basically he's one of that stiff-necked crew. Make no mistake, Danny, according to that lot Flinty, I and others, you too, to some extent, I expect, we're dross. In fact, it might be better if you didn't stay too long in this jungle of hard men and predatory women. Miss Carstairs was casting sheep's eyes at you. Oh, yes, she was, I saw it. Are you a virgin, Danny?'

I found myself blushing as I admitted, haltingly, that I was.

'What? A real virgin? Did you know that when one of those crosses Trafalgar Square the lions all roar and Nelson comes down from his pillar and takes off his hat? Has that happened to you?'

'Don't mock me,' I said sulkily. 'And I haven't been in Trafalgar Square recently.'

I was still sulking when I got into bed. Why, I asked myself, did she have to ruin a wonderful evening by reminding me of my inadequacy, for inadequate was what I felt in not having known a woman. A real virgin she had called me. I squirmed again at the description and all that it implied. Damn her, I thought, picking at the sheets.

At that moment I heard a movement near the bed and, looking up, saw her standing beside it. I had been so preoccupied with my misery and my thoughts that I had not heard her coming in. At first I thought that I must be asleep and dreaming.

It was no dream. She stood there looking down at me. 'My poor Danny,' she said. 'I've hurt you. I shouldn't have mocked you. It was foul of me. I've come to say I'm sorry.'

We looked at each other in silence and our glances held. Her hand went to the sash of her long silk dressing gown. It fell open and with a swift, lithe movement, she shrugged it off and stood there, the glow from the flickering firelight casting a sort of nimbus around her. 'I'll make it up to you,' she said. With that she lifted the covers and slid between the sheets beside me. Even now, after all these years, I can still recall the ecstasy of that first initiation, and at times the memory comes back to haunt me. She was careful, tender and kind, and when, at last, drowsiness was drifting me towards slumber, I heard, and can still hear, the words she whispered in my ear: 'Nelson is safe now.'

WHEN I ARRIVED at the depot next morning I was summoned to Captain Pat's office. 'You're late,' he told me. 'You were supposed to exercise the colonel's horse. That slipped your mind, I suppose.' He was right. It had done. I was still treading air after the most wonderful weekend of my life.

'I was away—' I began.

'I know. At Huntercombe. That's another problem. The colonel thinks you may be getting in with the wrong people.'

'I see,' I said. 'Is the Prince of Wales one of them?' This was impertinent and the moment I said it I regretted it. I waited for the wrath to come but Captain Pat wasn't one of those barking officers whose sparks fly off in all directions.

'He isn't, not yet anyway,' he said, mildly. 'But some of those around him are and you must remember that Colonel Probert is one of the old guard.'

'Who is it then?' I asked. 'Flinty? Why are they all so down on him? Is it because he doesn't try to stop HRH doing what he enjoys?'

He gave me one of his owlish glances. 'It's not for me to preach,' he said, 'but the heir to the throne can't always do what he likes, nor for that matter can you, as you will find out before you are much older.'

At that moment the telephone rang and he lifted the receiver. After listening for a minute he handed it to me. 'It's for you,' he said.

I took it from him, wondering who was making the call. It was Ginger Elton, the lad who had told me about Vincent Rossiter.

'I've seen 'im,' he said breathlessly. ''E's back, all toffed up in a trilby 'at an' all. Look, I can't talk more. I'm with Mr Barker now and 'e'd have the 'ide off me if 'e catches me usin' the telephone.'

'All right,' I said. 'Where can we meet?'

'Leicester races on Thursday maybe. I've a ride in the second.'

'I'll meet you outside the weighing room after the third,' I said.

'Crickey, 'e's comin'. I'd better bolt.' The line went dead.

I replaced the receiver, to find Captain Pat looking quizzically at me. Although I was boiling inwardly about having been brought down to earth with such a bump, I felt I had to explain the call. 'That was Elton,' I said. 'The temporary lad I tracked down at Plumpton. He said Rossiter is back in the country. He's seen him.'

'Has he, bedad? Did he say where?'

'No, but he told me he'd meet me at Leicester on Thursday and fill me in.'

'Leicester on Thursday. You'll be wanting transport. I could do with a day's racing. I'll take you.'

It was a gesture of forgiveness and, while mentally resolving that I must get myself a car, I thanked him.

'For nothing. I was told to keep an eye on you after all,' he said with one of his smiles. 'Now then, ever seen a bog spavin? No? Well it's part of your veterinary education and you'll see one now.'

Together, friends again, we walked towards the line of boxes.

ON THE TUESDAY and Wednesday I dutifully exercised Givenchy, the colonel's horse, and attended to my veterinary education at the hands of Captain Pat. The morning before we were due to go to Leicester I went into Captain Pat's office to see what he had in store for me that day. I found him frowning over a newspaper.

'Seen this?' he said, looking up as I came in. He chucked the paper across the desk to me. I picked it up. The print stared me in the face:

> THESE NAMES ARE NEWS. Son of disgraced trainer rides royal winner. Daniel de Lacey, whose father was warned off the Turf for doping, rode the Prince of Wales's Pepperpot to victory in a point-to-point race at Marleythorpe last weekend. His Royal Highness, recovering from a broken collarbone, when he was thrown from his horse in the hunting-field, was second.

I threw down the paper in disgust. 'They've managed to libel my father and insult the Prince in one paragraph,' I said. 'It's lucky for them my father is laid out and can't sue. They'd never have dared to print it, would they, unless someone had been feeding them information about my father?'

'It certainly looks like that,' Captain Pat said. 'But everyone in Melton knows about your father and, remember, the press were there in force at Marleythorpe.'

'I'm not likely to forget it,' I said grimly, wondering if this had scuppered my chances of seeing the Prince and Lady Val again. Mixing in that charmed circle had been heady wine and I wanted more of it: the charisma of the Prince had me in thrall. As for Lady Val, I suspected that she was one of that rare breed of women whose attitude to sex was much as a man's, in that she took what she wanted while at the same time remaining loyal to one, and that one was not and never could be me. During the night that we had spent together, twice I had heard her murmur in our fitful sleep the word 'David', and on the second occasion she had reached out and clasped me to her. It told me that the episode of the flashy blonde must have hurt more than she cared to reveal. All of this, if it did anything, only heightened my wish to see them both again. But no word had come by the time Captain Pat drove me to Leicester.

AT LEICESTER, Captain Pat went off almost immediately to seek out cronies and his trainer, leaving me on my own to watch Elton bring his mount home a hard-fought third in his race. He was good, I thought, and deserved more rides if he could get them; I had liked what little I had seen of him and mentally I wished him well.

Elton was waiting for me outside the weighing room and I took him off for a drink. 'That's a nice horse you rode in the last,' I said.

''E's all right; 'e ran a bit green. The guvnor said I done too much with 'im. 'E's terrible 'ard to please.'

Someone appeared in the doorway and said, 'They're going out,' and there was a general exodus to watch the next race.

'Well,' I said when we were alone, 'you saw him, you say?'

'Like I said. 'E was got up all posh. What's more 'e's dyed 'is 'air fair and grown a moustache.'

'How did you recognise him?'

''E 'ad a way of sort of twiddlin' 'is 'ands when lightin' a fag, and a kinda tee-hee laugh. I was sure it was 'im when I 'eard it.'

'Did you speak to him?'

'Nah. 'E was with the books, bettin' on the rails. None of your Tatts layers for 'im. But someone came up to 'im. 'E scarpered off pretty quick an' I lost 'im.'

'Would you know him again?'

'You bet.'

I took out a fiver. As he pocketed it he half rose to go, then he hesitated and sat down again. 'Anovver thing,' he said slowly. 'I've just remembered it. 'E talked a bit like a toff down on 'is luck, if you get me. We thought 'e was puttin' it on an' we ribbed 'im about it. Now, seein' 'im all dressed up, I'm beginnin' to think it was the other way round an' 'e was tryin' to 'ide 'is toff way of talkin'.' Then another thought struck him. 'Before 'e came to your father 'e was with Mr Connaughton. Someone there might remember 'im.'

Connaughton, I thought, Ormsby had mentioned him.

'Look, Guv, I've got to go,' he said. 'I'm to meet a fella who might get me a ride. What do you want me to do, Guv, if I see 'im again?'

'Don't let him know you've rumbled him,' I said. 'But keep an eye on him if you can. See who he's with, who he talks to and if you know them. And keep in touch.'

Another fiver changed hands and I watched him leave, whilst a roar of cheering, followed by an influx of people through the door of the bar, marked the end of another race.

Going back in the car, Captain Pat asked me how I had got on, and I told him of the conversation.

'I wonder,' he said doubtfully, 'if there's any chance he might be stringing you along. The odd fiver means a lot to these lads and I reckon he thinks there's more to come.'

'Perhaps,' I said. 'But I've a feeling he's genuine. Anyway, he's my only lead at the moment.'

We drove on without speaking for a few minutes, then Captain Pat said quietly, 'Are you determined to go on with this? There may be perils in your path. That wire in the fence—I don't know, it could be you'd be wiser to cut your losses and go home.'

'Are you trying to stop me?' I said almost angrily.

'No,' he said, mild as always. 'Merely pointing out the fences you may have to jump. And there's another thing. Colonel Probert tore up that direction from on high because he won't stand for interference, but neither does he like things happening in his bailiwick he knows nothing about. Pirate knows as well as we do that someone of influence pulled strings to get that instruction issued, but he doesn't know why, nor does he know why you're here or what you're up to.'

'What are you trying to tell me?'

'I'm saying that he is no fool. He is very strict and strait-laced in certain matters. He's one of the old brigade, as I've said before, and I don't think he's too fond of the Prince. If he thinks, what with your mixing in certain circles and those things happening, you're a disruptive influence then you're out and there's nothing I can do to stop it.'

'Then I'll go on on my own,' I said.

'You want to stay?'

'Of course.'

'It couldn't be mixed up with your getting too fond of those circles I was speaking of, male and female, could it?' he said, giving me a sly sidelong look.

'I can't think what you're talking about,' I said.

He chuckled in the way he had. 'Can't you? Bear in mind a wise man once said, "Put not your trust in princes." All right, if you must, you must. But you can't do it all yourself, you know. I think you'd better go back to Charles Ormsby.'

'That's good advice,' I said. 'I'll ring him when we get in.'

Chapter Eight

Having resolved to get myself a car, I acquired a secondhand Alvis 12/50 with a sports tourer body which was delivered in time for me to drive to Newmarket. The atmosphere from the sour-puss secretary was slightly less frigid this time when I entered the offices of Messrs Ormsby and Little, and I was swiftly shown into the inner sanctum. Major Charles, I saw, was sporting a different bow tie, crimson with white polka dots on this occasion.

'I gather from what you said on the telephone that you've made some progress,' he said as I sat down. 'Tell me about it.'

When I had finished he sat back and stared at the ceiling for a moment. 'The weakness of all Turf crimes, as you probably know, is that too many people have to be in on the secret. It's obvious if Rossiter has changed his appearance and come back and is in the money, he is blackmailing someone.'

'But who?' I said.

'That's what we've got to discover. First thing is to find Rossiter. Have you got those photographs I gave you?'

'Yes,' I said, and handed them over.

He studied them for a moment and then pressed a bell on his desk. When the secretary came in he pointed to Rossiter's image in the photographs. 'Have Crannitch blow that face up,' he said. 'And then get him to do a drawing of it.' When she had gone he turned to me again. 'If we could get Elton to indicate the alterations, the moustache and the hair, we'd have a sort of artist's impression, enough probably to pick him up and tail him. One way or another we'll find Mr Vincent Rossiter or whatever he's calling himself now.'

'Isn't he taking the hell of a risk going racing?'

'Not really, if you think it over. Only a few know suspicion centred on him, and he must believe the hue and cry has died down. I reckon he thinks he's safe.'

'We've no idea who he really is?'

'That's another question, though what you tell me of his talking like a toff is interesting. The first thing is find him, the second is watch him without his knowing it. I'll put a good man onto it. It would be best if you were to take the drawing to Elton. He might still shy off from one of us.'

'That reminds me of something,' I said. 'He told me since he came from Connaughton's there might be someone there who could tell us about him.'

'It's true it was from Jimmy Connaughton he came to your father. It's a gambling stable and up to all sorts of tricks. I wonder if we had a look at his list of owners would it tell us anything—' He crossed to a bookcase and took down the current *Horses in Training* from a shelf. Opening it he leafed through it and handed it to me.

N.J. CONNAUGHTON, Peterborough, I read with, underneath, a long list of horses and the names of his owners. Two names leaped out at me immediately: R.P. CARLETON and A.R.J. GRETTON.

'Good God,' I said, staring at them. 'Two of his owners are, well, I suppose you could say, interested in me.'

'Well I'm damned. Who are they?'

'Rupert Carleton and Roger Gretton. Do you know them?'

'I know everyone in racing. It's part of my business.'

'Captain Pat told me Rupert Carleton hasn't a bob. How did he get in there, how does he pay his training bills?'

'The answer to the first question is that he has all the right connections, to the second is that he doesn't. He gets commission on any new rich owners he introduces to the stable, he gives Jimmy something when he has a bet, either with the stable money or from information the stable feed him. It's a gambling stable, as I've said.'

'And Gretton?'

'Oh, nothing like that. Roger Gretton is a pillar of respectability. He's an influential member of the Jockey Club and carries weight in court circles, for that matter. I suspect he trains with Jimmy because he likes a bet. To me, I'm bound to say, Roger is a bit of an enigma. On the surface he's an affable, easy-going cove, though I've sometimes wondered—'

'Lady Val told me she thought Roger Gretton was devious.'

'Easy-going chaps sometimes get that reputation.'

'He was one of the Jockey Club stewards who warned my father off.'

'I know. I checked back in the *Calendar* before you came.'

'That notice,' I said, choosing my words as carefully as I could, 'leaves it very open to the suggestion that my father had a hand in the doping. That's what hurt him so much and that's what's been accepted by the public. That's why we have got to clear his name. Do you know who frames these notices or works out the wording?'

'They're drafted by a member of the secretariat who sits in on the hearing. Then the draft goes to the stewards for approval before they sign it and authorise its publication.'

'So any of them could alter it and change the wording as they wished?'

'I should imagine so. Are you suggesting that Roger may have had a hand in changing it so that it pointed directly at your father?'

'It crossed my mind. My father was convinced that he was framed. You know as well as I do that every winner isn't tested, not by a long chalk. Why pick on him? Elton told me the gossip in the weighing room was that there was a tip-off.'

'Weighing-room gossip often has a foundation in fact. If we could find out just where the gossip came from it would help. Who was the chairman on that day, do you know?'

'I do. Sir Crispin Merevale, Bart, of Patworth Castle.'

'He's far from being as pompous as he sounds. I know him quite well, he's one of the better stewards. We might get something from him. It all looks more and more as if there was some sort of conspiracy. I wish your father had told me more at the time. Have you any idea why he didn't?'

'My mother believes it was because of a plot against the Prince of Wales that he knew too much about. That's why he refused to take any action or go public in any way. He didn't want the Prince's name drawn into it.'

'And you think Roger may have been one of the plotters?'

'My father never named names, but since I've come here there do seem to be pointers towards him.'

'I'll keep an open mind. Any other names?'

'I've heard Lord Marston mentioned. He's been at Melton recently keeping an eye on the Prince, or so I'm told.'

'Lord Marston of Sevenoaks. He's the *éminence grise* at court. It's possible. Though unlikely.'

'He's a pal of Gretton's. They were snapped together at a smart wedding having a confidential chat.'

Ormsby got up and crossed to the window. With his hands in his trouser pockets turning over coins, he stood there for a few minutes in silence staring down at the street. In that silence I could hear a grandfather clock ticking. Somehow I had the feeling that a decision was being made which could affect my whole life.

Eventually he turned back into the room. 'If you are right,' he said, 'I think you should know what you are taking on. Accepting for a moment that there was some sort of conspiracy affecting the Prince, those who you may now be threatening stand to lose everything, as much as your father did. They're in positions of power and influence. They've shown how ruthless they can be and they can do it again.'

'I'm in now and I'm staying in,' I said stubbornly. 'I've got to find out the truth however tough it is. But how about you? You'll be in it, too.'

He gave one of his brief smiles and then in an involuntary gesture reached up and touched his bow tie as if it were a talisman. 'I've toughed it with tougher,' he said.

DRIVING BACK I had much to occupy my thoughts, but they kept turning to Lady Val. The artist's impression of Rossiter, which had been completed before I left, was in a manila envelope on the seat behind me. The Alvis was singing smoothly along, the wind whipped past and, as we neared the end of a long straight stretch on the Oakham side of Stamford, I caught sight of a figure standing by the roadside waving me down. Imagining that there must be cattle across the road or some such thing, I slowed. He went on waving and I pulled to a halt.

He came towards me and I saw that he had a cap pulled down over his eyes and a scarf muffling the lower part of his face. It was then that warning bells sounded, too late, in my brain. He didn't speak but leaned against the side of the car, his eyes studying me under the brim of the cap while his hand gave some sort of signal. With that a huge body heaved itself into the seat beside me. A masked face was pushed into mine and a massive hand appeared holding an ugly-looking knife which rested against my cheek. The first man stepped onto the running board and spoke. 'Drive in here,' he said, pointing, his tones muffled by the scarf.

There was a sort of recess in the roadway which gave onto an entrance where two rusted iron gates leaned askew between battered pillars. Beyond was a broken-down gate-lodge shielded from the road by a screen of ash, evergreen and sycamore.

'Get out,' the man on thc running board commanded.

I hesitated. Then the gorilla beside me spoke. 'You 'eard 'im. Wake up, sunshine.'

With that a fist like a pile-driver slammed into the side of my face. I was flung back against the seat and, as I tried to recover, he hit me again. This time my forehead banged against the boss of the steering wheel. Flashes flew across my eyes and I almost passed out.

Between them they dragged me from the car and into the gate-lodge. Inside, the wallpaper hung in strips, the windowpanes gaped, and there was no furniture save a table on three legs and a rusted iron bed. The big man threw me, like a sack of coals, into one corner. I hit the wall and it hurt.

'Don't kill him,' the muffled voice said. 'Just half kill him.'

The big man kicked me in the ribs.

'Now,' the voice said. 'How much did your father tell you? If you don't talk you'll get what he got.' Then the gorilla kicked me again, picked me up and slammed me against the wall. I wondered if my ribs were stove in.

'That'll do. For the moment anyway,' the first voice said. 'Now, once more. What did your father tell you?'

'I don't know what you're talking about,' I said.

'I think you do, else why are you hanging around Melton? You'll answer unless you want the same of what you're getting and worse.'

'He told me nothing,' I said. Despite the pain in my side, my brain was ticking over and I had learned something. Those mysterious marks on my father's body were now explained: they had beaten him up in an attempt to get information from him and failed. There must be, or have been, a plot of which he knew too much, or they wouldn't have gone to all that trouble to frame him and cover up. And now it had rubbed off on to me. It must, as my father had hinted, involve someone far bigger than any of us, and that could only mean one man—the Prince of Wales.

What they didn't know was that although those kicks hurt like hell I'd had falls before and could to some extent roll with the punch. The thick motoring coat I wore, too, took up some of the impact. I was hurt but not crippled and I could still think. I groaned and slumped. 'For God's sake leave me alone,' I pleaded. 'I don't know what you're on about. I'm in Melton to learn about horses.'

'Liar. Why did the Prince of Wales take you up?'

'It was an accident. I pulled him out of a ditch when he broke his collarbone, and he befriended me because of it. That's the sort he is.'

'You're lying,' the other said. 'And I'm going to hurt you more until you talk. How would you like to have your fingernails pulled out?'

'How can I talk when I don't know,' I said between groans.

'The right hand first, I think,' the voice said. 'Go ahead, Joe.'

But their mention of the Prince had given me an idea. 'You do that to me and I won't be able to ride a horse for the Prince tomorrow,' I said. 'He'll see my hands and he'll want to know why. He'll throw the whole works after you.'

'Hold it, Joe,' the one in charge said.

There was silence for a moment or two while I slumped back against the wall. The first man strode over and looked down at me. 'Somehow I don't think we're going to get any more out of him,' he said. 'Perhaps he's telling the truth. You've something to remember us by, anyway. Pick him up, Joe.'

Between them they brought me out to the car and got me into the driving seat. I hadn't, of course, been booked to ride for the Prince and I wasn't as bad as I'd convinced them. That, in its way, was a small victory. And there was something else running through my mind as I sat unsteadily behind the wheel.

The first man leaned over, switched on the ignition and pressed the starter button. 'I suppose you can drive,' he said. 'If you run out of road, too bad.' Then he sniggered.

He was beside me, very close. I knew now what had been bothering me about him all along. ''E talked like a toff,' Elton had said. So did this thug. And that snigger, ending in a sort of tee-hee, just as Elton had said, clinched it. With a quick motion, I reached up and pulled the muffler down from his face. The artist's impression stared back at me together with the additions Elton had described, the moustache and the fringes of blond hair beneath the edges of the cap. I had found Vincent Rossiter.

'I'll know you again,' I said.

He was so taken by surprise he jerked his head back and made a grab at the muffler. Off-balance he stumbled, giving me the breathing space I wanted. I slammed the gear lever home and let in the clutch. The wheels spun as we took off. Once on the road I rushed her through the gears. My foot was on the floorboards for most of the way back to Melton.

Back in my rooms I tried to examine the damage. I had a splitting headache but that, I reckoned, would pass. My ribs and round my back where the kicks had gone in, were a different matter. The weals were just beginning to show, but I knew from experience of hunting and racing falls that the real bruising would come up later. It all hurt like hell when I moved and I prayed devoutly that no ribs were broken. I supposed I should go to a doctor but that would have meant all sorts of enquiries and explanations which I didn't feel disposed to give. He might well stop me riding, too. I also found that my father's gold cigarette case and my wallet with forty pounds in it were missing. Then my eye fell on the buff envelope of a telegram lying on the table. Opening it I read: WILL YOU RIDE PROSPERO NOMINATION RACE HEYTHROP WEDNESDAY. VAL.

That settled it. No doctor.

Taking Rossiter's likeness from the manila envelope which the thugs had overlooked, I laid it on the table before me. His features were clearly etched in my mind even after that brief glimpse of them, and I did not think I need go back to Elton to complete the picture. Borrowing a box of crayons from Mrs Williams, my landlady, I began to shade in the blond moustache. That done I had a stab at the hair. The finished article wasn't very artistic but I reckoned Elton was unlikely to do better. Then I wrote to Charles Ormsby setting out what had happened in as much detail as I could, slid the letter and likeness into its envelope and walked to the post office. There I sent it off as well as the answer to Lady Val: YES DELIGHTED. DANNY.

As I once more climbed the stairs to my room, weariness overcame me. Though I wasn't much of a whisky drinker I poured myself a stiff measure and swallowed it with a grimace of distaste. Then I sat staring into the fire. Just what, I wondered, had I got myself into and where would it all end?

Chapter Nine

Forty-eight hours later I stood in the parade ring at the South Oxfordshire point-to-point wearing Lady Val's steeplechase jersey in her colours of black and gold and devoutly wishing I was somewhere else. I knew very well that I was in no condition to ride a race. My side was hurting damnably every time I moved and riding out hadn't helped. The bruises were well and truly up by now, and in colour ranged from dark black to deep blue shot with yellow. They extended from my rib cage round to my back. Luckily, and I thought I needed a bit of luck just then, they had missed my kidneys.

I should, of course, have cried off but there were several strong reasons preventing me. To be honest the one which weighed most with me was the longing to see Lady Val and be with them all again. But there were others. If I were to plead illness, that would entail explanations I was reluctant to give: there would be questions asked followed by possible police action. For the moment I had told Charles Ormsby and that was enough.

Walking the course had done little to reassure me. The South Ox point-to-point committee had included two post-and-rails and a double. I knew something about jumping timber out hunting, but that was a very different matter from taking it on at racing pace. I supposed and hoped that the horse, Prospero, knew more about it than I did. My general feelings of alarm and depression weren't helped by the very vague instructions Lady Val gave me. 'Be there or thereabouts at the second last,' she said. 'He has plenty of speed. Keep out of trouble and you've every chance.'

She had moved away to talk to someone else when I heard a voice at my side. It was the Prince of Wales. 'She thinks a lot of this horse,' he said. 'But I'm not sure his heart is in the right place. I don't like a horse with small ears. That's a lesson Flinty dinned into me. Don't be too disappointed if—'

'Riders up, *please*,' came the call.

A hand went round my uplifted leg and I was whisked into the saddle.

Down at the start I tried to collect my wits and look about me. The nomination race, with its crack riders from far and near, was an altogether more serious affair than the Adjacent Hunts I had ridden in before. There were no cheery top-hatted gentlemen having a jolly, here. Billy Burton-Brown and Mike Annerley, two of the elite of the point-to-pointing world who rode against each other regularly, were competing today. I didn't know whether it was nerves or pain that was making me feel weak and sick.

The first thing that happened was that they went off far faster than I expected, and I was left in the rear. Clods of earth flew past me and one nearly blinded me, so that we jumped the first fence all asprawl with me half out of the saddle. The bump as I came down wasn't much help to my ribs. Prospero didn't care for it either: he shook his head as if to say he wasn't accustomed to this and seemed reluctant to get on with things. Somehow I got him balanced again and then he caught hold of his bit and pounded along. We jumped the next fence cleanly but we had a good deal of ground to make up. After that came two more plain fences which he put behind him effortlessly, then we approached the first of the post-and-rails.

It was then that I started to make a mess of things. Prospero had speed and his gallop had taken him to the point where he was lying third, but I thought he was going too fast at that timber. I endeavoured to steady him, not realising quite how much of a passenger I already was. All I did was to make things worse. He missed his take-off and hit the top rail a right old belt.

Somehow he remained upright and I remained on top, I don't to this day know how. The second post-and-rails then confronted us, and this time I had enough sense to leave it to him. But the bang at the bar had taken something out of him, or else he had lost confidence in himself and his rider. He screwed over it somehow but on landing I saw we had dropped back again. I tried to take stock. We were three-quarters of the way round and the two cracks were duelling it out up ahead. If I was to put up any sort of a show I had to do something. Giving Prospero a kick, I went after them. The speed was there, he ate up the ground and, entering the field before the second last, we were upsides with them. They heard me coming and in a moment the three of us were racing for the fence, a weak-looking thing set on a small bank.

They had drawn fractionally ahead of me. I kicked as hard as my diminishing strength would let me. There was no response. Setting my teeth, I drove him with all that was left in me into the fence. But I was tired and in pain and wasn't sitting as tight as I should. There was a smash of birch beneath us as Prospero went through the fence's flimsy top. Down he came on his head, or so it seemed to me. He was near the ground but he didn't fall. Unsettled and unseated, I slid off his shoulder and hit the ground. It didn't do my ribs any good, but I was more hurt in vanity than in body as I saw the remains of the field gallop by me and watched Prospero's hindquarters disappearing after them.

At least I was spared the long trudge back. Prospero turned aside and ended up in a corner of the field. A countryman caught him and brought him to me saying, 'Here's your horse, mister.'

He seemed sound and there were no cuts anywhere that I could see. That was something. I got up and rode slowly back towards the tents and enclosures. Lady Val was waiting for me and one look at her face told me I was in trouble. 'You fell off,' she said. 'And I thought you told me you could ride.'

'Kindergarten stuff,' a voice behind her said. 'Go back to the children's meets. He needs a man on his back.' It was Rupert Carleton.

A groom took Prospero and I got down. 'Jog him up, Thomas,' Lady Val commanded.

'Well at least you haven't lamed him,' she commented when that had been done. Then she and Rupert went off together.

Miserably I made my way back to the barn where we changed, and sat on a bench contemplating my sins. Thinking it very unlikely I would ever ride in it again, I was in the act of pulling my jersey over my head when there was a little hush in the room. Looking up I saw the Prince of Wales making his way across to me.

'I've been commanded to tell you that there's a drink for you in the car,' he said.

It seemed odd that the heir to the throne of what was then the most powerful nation in the world should use the word 'commanded' to convey a message. It wasn't until years later that I, along with the rest of his subjects, learned to their cost that HRH was one of those rare men who like to be bossed about by their women. It's a sort of inborn masochism, I think. One of the reasons, I believe, that Val did not keep him was that she was in many ways too nice and did not exert her will enough.

'What about that horse?' he asked. 'Was he dogging it?'

'I'm not sure,' I said. 'I rode a lousy race. He made two bad mistakes which were mostly my fault. They may have knocked the stuffing out of him.'

'Hello, what's this?' His eyes were fixed on my side and the bruises in all their galaxy of variegated colours. 'That didn't happen today.'

Once more I had to think quickly. 'I had a fall schooling,' I said. 'I was kicked.'

'He did a damn good job on you then. Have you seen anyone?'

'No, sir.' I was desperate to change the subject. 'Will I lose the ride?'

He frowned, staring at the bruises again. 'We'll have to see about that,' he said. 'And forget about that fall. Happens to all of us. Think of the times I've done it—and you don't have to worry about the photographers!'

He left me to finish changing and then I went to the car park to look for Lady Val's chauffeur-driven Rolls. A small group surrounded the Prince and her, no doubt anxious to be seen in their company and hoping for the appearance of a *Tatler* photographer. But Flinty was there too, greeting me with his vulpine grin and pressing a silver beaker brimming with Krug into my hand. 'I've put in a word for you,' he said. 'Told her I didn't think that horse was all that genuine. She'll make her peace: it's started already by her sending the little man along to bid you to a drink.'

In fact she didn't speak to me then, contenting herself with a brief smile and a wave of her hand. She hardly had a chance, I told myself, so besieged was she by the group about her. Already, too, and before I was halfway through the champagne, I could see that HRH, who could spot a sycophant when he saw one, was showing signs of boredom. They piled into the Rolls, I gulped the rest of the Krug, surrendered the beaker to the chauffeur and they drove off.

The champagne had done me a bit of good but, going home, a long, painful and lonely evening stretched before me. I ran a bath and slid into the steaming water. Lying there, I felt my bruises and at each touch I winced. I'm not sure how long it was before I heard voices from below.

'Yes, he's in, M'lady. Come in from racin' he did and lookin' proper poorly. It's them horses—'

'I've got to see him.' It was Lady Val.

'But he's in his bath, M'lady. I heard him runnin' the taps.'

'I don't care where he is. The Prince of Wales asked me—'

'Oh, M'lady—the Prince of Wales!'

'Where is it, the bathroom, upstairs I suppose?'

'Along the passage, M'lady, but he's in the bath, oh!'

There were firm footsteps on the stairs and then the door was thrown open and Lady Val came in. 'Now then,' she said. 'Just what have you been up to? Let's have a look at you.'

I wasn't accustomed to entertaining ladies in my bath and made a vain attempt to cover up.

'Don't be a fool, Danny,' she said. 'I've seen it all before, remember. Good Lord, what have you been doing to yourself?'

'I had a fall schooling.'

'Tell that to your Aunt Fanny. I met Pat Terrier on the way in. He knew of no schooling fall.' She seated herself on the edge of the bath. 'I suppose that's why you fell off,' she went on. 'You are a damn fool, you know, Danny. The truth now.'

I gave in and recounted what had happened on the road—or most of it, for I didn't tell her everything. In particular I left out how I had identified Vincent Rossiter.

'They went to a lot of trouble to hijack you,' she said. 'Did they get anything?'

'My wallet,' I said. 'There was forty quid in it, and my father's gold cigarette case, the one you admired.'

'Damn swine,' she said. 'But those ribs of yours, they should be looked at. I'm going to take you to a doctor.'

She took one of the big towels from the clothes horse and I climbed out of the bath. Enveloping me in it she dried me. She was very close to me as she delicately touched the injured areas and her breath was sweet on my cheek. Her fingers were soft and deft and aphrodisiac. I felt an insane impulse to tear off her clothes and feel once more that splendid body vibrant against mine. She read it in my eyes. 'Not just now,' she said, giving me a gentle pat. 'There's a time and a place for everything. Clothes on, I think. Where are they?'

Dressed and in the sitting room I slumped into a chair. I really was feeling rotten and cursed myself for it.

'What you need,' she said, 'is a stiff drink and then the doctor. Is there any brandy?'

'There's whisky, Lady Val,' I said. 'But I hate the stuff.'

'I'll lush it up into a hot toddy and you'll find it goes down all right,' she told me. 'And stop calling me Lady Val. We're chums, aren't we?'

THE DOCTOR PROVED to be a fatherly old boy, well used to treating riding and hunting injuries as, in Melton, I suppose he had to be. After doing all the usual things with the blood-pressure machine, he ran his fingers lightly over my ribs and bruises. 'Any blood in the urine?' he asked as he came to the kidney area.

'No,' I said. 'It's clear.'

Next, I was sent to the local cottage hospital and X-rayed, before returning to the doctor's surgery. 'You're a very lucky young man,' the doctor told me. 'You have two cracked ribs and some slight bruising of the lung. Going out to ride in a race in that state could easily have damaged them further and even punctured the lung. There's extensive haematoma over the kidney area, but here again no real damage done.'

'Thanks, Doctor,' I said. 'But will I be able to ride?'

'I'm going to strap you up. You'll be off all work for a few days until the ribs begin to heal. And no riding whatever.'

'Damn,' I said.

'You're young and very fit, it shouldn't take too long. I'll write Captain Terrier a note to keep you right. Nice fellow, Captain Pat. We meet every now and then to compare notes over a drink.'

'Horses and humans, do you ever get them mixed up?' Val asked him with a mischievous look.

'Sometimes, dear lady,' he answered, smiling at her and responding to her in the way most men did. 'And one then wonders which can be the most difficult.'

WHEN VAL DREW THE RILEY up outside my rooms, she sat for a moment drumming her hands against the wheel. 'I've been thinking about what you told me of the beating up,' she said. 'The little man will want to know and I think I'll play it all down. He's not in the best of form at the moment. He's been summoned to the Palace. Papa wants to see him and that means trouble. He says he knows he's in for a ticking-off, probably about his racing and his friendship with Flinty, and he's afraid of his father, that's what's eating him. He's about the only thing or person he is afraid of. But he has all this on his mind.'

'Thanks for all your help this evening,' I said.

'Royal command,' she said, smiling. 'Besides, you're our mascot, aren't you? Can't let the mascot perish alone and in misery, can we?' She let in the clutch, the Riley gave a snarl, and she was gone.

HAVING SENT the doctor's letter round to Captain Pat, I was having breakfast next morning when there was a knock on the door and Mrs Williams came in. 'Gentleman to see you, sir,' she said, and a moment later Charles Ormsby entered. That morning he was wearing yet another bow tie, fashioned in regimental stripes.

He accepted a cup of coffee and said, 'I rang the remounts and heard you were on sick leave. Those thugs must have knocked you about more than a bit. How bad is it?'

'Not much to signify, really,' I said. 'Cracked ribs and bruising. More a damn nuisance than anything else.'

'How did the hijackers know that you'd be in Newmarket or how you'd be travelling?'

'I've thought about that myself. Anyone in the remounts would have known. A call to the office looking for me would have told them. I haven't checked but I'm sure that was it.'

'There's another thing. You were taken to a broken-down lodge, you said in your letter. Could you identify it on the map?'

'I expect so. I could have a try.'

Opening a briefcase he took out an ordnance map and spread it on the table. 'This is where I put it from your description,' he said, indicating a road on the map. 'And the lodge would be there, wouldn't it?'

With a quickening of interest I bent over the map. The drive passed the lodge and curved through marked trees to a large house. It was, apparently, quite an estate.

'Eston Court,' I read aloud. 'That's it. That's the place.'

'I thought as much. Would it interest you to know that that property belonged to Rupert Carleton's family?'

Rupert! I thought, Here we go again. 'But the lodge was falling down,' I said.

'Exactly. Rupert has gone through all his money and anyone else's he could get his hands on, including his father's. The old boy finally sold the place and went to live in Cannes. A local farmer bought the land. He had no use for the house and lodge and they fell into decay.'

'So Rupert could have known just the place, directed Rossiter—'

'It would seem so.'

'And Rupert, then, is mixed up in this plot or whatever it is?'

'Up to the neck, I'd say. And if Rupert is mixed up in it there's money for him coming from somewhere.' He finished his coffee. 'Are you fit enough to come for a drive?'

'Yes, of course. Anything to get me away from these four walls.'

'I've been on to Jimmy Connaughton to try to find out if he knew anything of where Rossiter came from. He wasn't very communicative on the phone but then I didn't expect him to be. But he'll see us. If you're ready we'll make a start.'

We drove through the countryside which was already showing signs of an early spring. Charles Ormsby clearly knew the way and threaded our passage along the narrow cross-country roads. A mile or so outside Peterborough we passed an entrance and then, almost immediately, came upon another where a sign pointed tersely: HORSES. A short drive flanked by elms, through which I had a glimpse of a square Georgian house on our left, led us to a stableyard. In one corner of this was a single-storeyed building with a portico, a miniature lodge of the sort built on some estates for their workers.

Ormsby parked the car before the portico, we went up to the open door and entered. Without hesitation he knocked on a door to the right and, in response to a gruff bellow beyond it, we went in.

Jimmy Connaughton, the trainer, was standing by the window as we entered. He was a man of just above medium height and built like a battleship. A round, bullet head was set deeply into massive shoulders. Thrusting this forward he stared bleakly at us. 'You're five minutes late,' he barked. 'Time's money and I haven't that much of either to spare. What d'ye want, Major?'

As I later learned, Jimmy Connaughton was a tough who had come up the hard way and didn't care who knew it. He had been for twenty years the head lad to one of the leading Newmarket trainers. An enormous bet on the Cambridgeshire had enabled him to set up on his own with a mixed string, flat and chasers, and some of the owners had followed him and supported him. His habit of speaking his mind had, oddly enough, not damaged his career. Those of the upper crust who patronised him dined out on his more outrageous pronouncements and verbal onslaughts. That, and the fact that he told his owners the blunt truth about their horses and produced winners when the money was down, won him patrons. But I could see from the start that the interview was not going to be an easy one.

'I know that, Jimmy,' Charles Ormsby said. 'And believe me I don't like taking up your time. But it's important to us as I'm sure you'll agree when you've heard me for a moment. This is Dick de Lacey's son. We're trying to find out who shopped him that day at Ascot.'

'And how the hell do I come into that? I didn't dope the bloody horse.' But as he said it he looked at me and I thought his voice softened a bit. 'I knew your father,' he said. 'A straight man.'

'Well, Jimmy, we don't think you had a hand in any of the business, believe me. But we've identified the lad who did it and who disappeared to America pretty quickly after it. Now you know as well as I that these lads never do those things off their own bat. There's always someone behind them, paying them off and paying them well.'

By this time the trainer was listening intently. 'That's true,' he said. 'Why do you think I keep 'em coming and going? Sell stable secrets for sixpence most of them would. It's them bloody bookies. And this doping is a nightmare. We're at the mercy of them. Why don't the Jockey Club alter the rule or bring in a proper system of testing? Why did they pick on de Lacey's horse, eh?'

'We're looking for a lad called Vincent Rossiter,' said Charles Ormsby. 'He was in your yard for a bit before he went to Danny's father. We'd like to know if you found out anything about him before he came, if he had any references through which we might trace him?'

The trainer sat glowering at us, then he said, 'If you could nail whoever was behind the doping then it might help us all. Rossiter, now, damned if I recall anything about him but my secretary might.' He got to his feet, went to the door and bellowed down the passage, 'Benson! I want you.'

There were footsteps in the corridor and a tall, thin, nervous-looking man entered. He might well be nervous-looking if he worked for Jimmy Connaughton, I thought.

'Vincent Rossiter,' Connaughton shot at him. 'He was here about a year or so ago. That mean anything to you?'

The secretary frowned in thought.

'Come on, man, it does or it doesn't.'

'This may help to refresh your memory,' Charles Ormsby said quietly. Unfastening the briefcase he took out the two photographs and laid them on the desk before him.

The secretary took them up and studied them.

'That is him all right,' he said after a pause. 'He stuck in my mind.

Odd sort of chap, not like the ordinary run of lads.'

'Any idea where he came from? Did he have any recommendation with him?' Ormsby asked.

'There might be something on the personnel file. I'll go and look.'

In a few minutes he was back, a bulky folder under his arm. 'It's hard to keep track of these lads,' he said. 'But after looking at those photographs it all came back to me. He interested me when I interviewed him. He seemed a cut above the usual run somehow, and I asked him what experience he had and if he had any references. He said he'd always lived with horses and he produced a letter. He left in a bit of a hurry as I recall and never asked for it back. Here it is.'

Ormsby took it and I leaned over his shoulder. In scrawled handwriting this is what we read: *I know the bearer, Vincent Rossiter. He has experience in handling horses, strapping and feeding*. The signature made me catch my breath. It was: *Rupert Carleton*.

'Well, who was it from?' Connaughton barked at us.

'Rupert Carleton,' Ormsby said.

'That beggar,' was Connaughton's comment. 'Why the hell did you take him on?' He glared at Benson.

'We were shorthanded at the time,' Benson said. 'He looked as if he was down on his luck and I know what that's like. I asked in the yard how he was getting on and they told me he was good at his job.'

'Too bloody good by the sound of things,' the trainer growled. 'It's as well he didn't stay here long. Anything else you gents want? I've work to do.'

'No thanks, Jimmy,' Ormsby said. 'We seem to have got what we came for. We're obliged for your time.'

'I hope you nail that bastard, Carleton,' Connaughton bellowed at us as we were leaving.

'I thought you trained for him,' Ormsby said.

'Not any more. He shopped me once. No one does that to me twice.'

As we left, we could hear Jimmy Connaughton's voice bellowing at Benson.

We lunched off bread and cheese and beer in a pub. As we finished Ormsby said to me, 'This afternoon we have another call to make.'

'Oh?' I said. 'Where?'

'Patworth Castle.' He caught my surprised look and smiled. 'I've made it my business to see Crispin Merevale,' he said. 'I ran into him by accident on purpose at Sandown. I sounded him very obliquely about the tip-off in your father's case, and he said to let him think it over.'

'Does that mean he'll go back to his other stewards? They'll shut him up, won't they?'

Ormsby gave a short laugh. 'Nobody shuts Crispin up,' he said. 'He's independent and he'll make up his own mind. The only reason he's stewarding is that he smashed himself up so badly in the National they told him he'd never ride races again. He'd been elected to the Jockey Club a year or so before. He was young and energetic and he was a godsend to the old stiffs, so he got accelerated promotion. But he takes his own line and sticks to it. He's agreed to see us. By my reading that means he's prepared to talk.'

Patworth Castle, which I had only seen hazily that night of the hunt ball, looked enormous as we drove up. It was set on a cliff and with its battlements and turrets it towered over the vale below where the best of the hunting country stretched into the misty distance.

We climbed the curving drive and passed under an arched entrance into an outer courtyard. Here another archway led us to a smaller courtyard where Ormsby drew the car up near a vast gothic doorway. 'Half of this is bogus,' he said. 'Victorian Tudor stuff. No wonder Crispin wants to get out of it and go racing. It'd drive me mad.'

We were led through a maze of corridors and finally into a gloomy library, all dark panelling, heavy tracery on the ceiling and ornate, cumbersomely carved bookcases set into its walls. Crispin Merevale was standing by a massive stone fireplace embellished in its centre with a coat of arms, where blazing logs roared their heat up the great chimney. Another man rose from his chair as we entered and Crispin introduced us. It was Lord Marston.

'Afternoon, Ormsby,' he said, giving the detective a far from friendly nod and directing his hard stare at the bow tie. Then he transferred that stare to me.

Lord Marston had the face of a mournful bloodhound accentuated by two purple-veined dewlaps on either side. His eyes were hooded and wary and I could feel them boring into me. He said nothing by way of greeting or otherwise but turned abruptly to the baronet. 'Well, Crispin, I'll be off,' he said. 'Thank you for seeing me at such short notice. No, don't bother about that,' as his host reached for the bell. 'I'll find my own way out. Knew it well enough in your father's time.' He bustled off.

'Sorry about that,' Merevale said as the door closed behind him. 'Had to see me about the monarch's health—but we won't go into that. Now then, Charles, it's about that rotten affair of Dick de Lacey's doping, isn't it?'

'That's it, Crispin, we're trying to discover who was behind it.

We've heard that the buzz in the weighing room was that there was a tip-off. That might give us a lead. Hinted about it when we spoke at Sandown. Can you help?'

'I've turned it over very carefully in my mind. It would benefit all of us if whoever was responsible was found. It might even bring about the changing of that rule which I've never liked, but that's another matter. Yes, there was a tip-off.'

'Can you elaborate a bit?' Ormsby said. 'Who, for instance, took the tip-off? Was it you?'

'It was a phone call to the weighing room asking for me by name and saying that it was urgent. I went to the phone and took it. I can't remember the exact words, of course, but it was brief and to the point, that de Lacey's horse in the third was doped.'

'I don't suppose the caller gave his name?'

'Hardly. When I asked who was calling he put down the phone. I debated whether it might be a hoax and whether I should tell my fellow stewards. Then I decided that I must, and I also felt I had to say that we should act on it and if the test proved negative no harm would be done. In the event, of course, it didn't, more's the pity.'

'Can you tell us anything else about the call—the caller's voice for instance?'

'It was disguised, no doubt about that. I did get the impression that what he was disguising was an educated voice.'

'What was the dope? Can you remember?'

'Cocaine, smeared on the tongue it was thought.'

'Cocaine,' I said. 'But surely it's illegal to have it?'

They both looked at me, almost pityingly. 'There's plenty of it around if you've got the money,' Merevale said, 'and arsenic too. A goodly percentage of trainers use it, some of them those at the top. They say it brightens their coats and it's harmless used in small doses. That's what they say. I tremble to think what will happen if random testing is brought in. Goodness knows what heads might roll.'

'HOW ARE THE RIBS and bruises?' Ormsby asked me as we drove back from Patworth Castle.

'Hurting as of this moment.'

'Six o'clock. Opening time. We'll pull in here. I expect you could do with a drink. I know I could.'

It was a country pub with a creaking sign over the door. Ormsby bought the drinks and we made our way to a dark inner parlour. It was early; few drinkers were about in the public bar and where we were was empty and private.

'Bit of a coincidence, isn't it, Marston being there?' I said. 'Is he a member of the Jockey Club too?'

'He is. He never goes to meetings, I believe.'

'Still, he might be anxious to find out from Merevale just what we were coming for and what we wanted from him.'

'If he did, and tried to influence Crispin Merevale, he picked the wrong man.' All the same, I thought, I wouldn't strike Lord Marston off my list of suspects just yet. But Ormsby was going on. 'He doesn't like me much,' he said. 'I crossed him once and he never forgets.'

'Do you think Marston may be in it?' I said.

'Possibly, though if he is, he's at the top and we've got to start at the bottom—with Rossiter. We've got to find him and make him talk.'

'That may not be easy,' I said, remembering my encounter with him.

His mouth set in a firm line. 'First find him,' he said. 'The rest will follow. I'll see to that.' Reaching down to the briefcase he had brought with him, he opened it and took out the photographs and the artist's impression. These he placed on the table before him and studied them for a long minute. 'It's my belief,' he said, 'that many of the people I mix with don't know their own fathers.' With that cryptic utterance he shuffled the photos and the drawing together, replaced them in the briefcase and we left the inn.

HARDLY HAD HE DROPPED me at my rooms than I had another visitor. It was Captain Pat. 'So,' he said. 'Off work, are we? I came round earlier to enquire but Mrs Williams said you'd gone off with a gentleman in a bow tie. Charles Ormsby, I presumed.'

'That's right. We had some enquiries to make.'

'I see.' He took the doctor's letter from his pocket and glanced at it. 'Haematoma and cracked ribs, the doctor says. Would it be too much to ask how you sustained these injuries? I heard some cock-and-bull story about a fall out schooling which I didn't for a moment believe.'

'You might as well know since everyone else seems to. I got beaten up.' I told him what had happened, ending up by asking, 'Did anyone phone for me during the day and ask where I was, do you know?'

'As it happens I do. The call was put through to my office. It seemed a very ordinary enquiry. I told whoever it was that you had gone to Newmarket. I assumed it must be one of your smart friends: you mix in such high society nowadays. By the way, tell me about that horse, Prospero. Lady Val stopped me yesterday on her way to see you and we discussed him. She has high hopes and great plans for him, but is he any good?'

'I don't know,' I said. 'I thought I got nothing when I asked him, but then I rode such a rotten race—'

'I was there. I asked Billy Burton-Brown about the race when I saw him afterwards. He told me you were going much too well for his liking when you joined them before the second last and he was seldom as glad to see anyone go.'

'HRH did warn me he wondered if Prospero was all that genuine.'

'Did he? He's no fool about a horse. Maybe the horse is a dog, or maybe he's moody like some humans. On their going days they can be the best, on others they can't live with the worst. I shouldn't be surprised if he's one of them.'

'I'd love to find out. Do you think I'll keep the ride?'

'That's up to Lady Val. She seems to have taken a fancy to you. It's between you and the horse, isn't it?' He gave one of his chuckles and then became serious again. 'But I'm afraid I've a bit of bad news for you. You've lost the ride on the colonel's horse. He says if you're off work you can't ride and he wants to run him Saturday.'

'Oh, hell. Who has he got?'

'You won't like this—Rupert Carleton.'

'Rupert! For God's sake, why him? I thought he didn't bother about point-to-points.'

'He doesn't usually, but he's been making the racecourse proper a bit too hot to be wholesome for him recently. Then he met Pirate somewhere at a dinner party and asked him for a ride. Pirate said Carleton could tell him more about the horse than you could and he's to have him for the rest of the season—if he wants him. That's it, I'm afraid.'

'Rupert,' I said. 'Everything seems to come back to him.'

'Cheer up. Rides come and rides go, you'll have to get used to it. I'll drive you to the point-to-point Saturday if you're still under the weather. We'll see how Givenchy goes for Rupert.'

Chapter Ten

Almost the first person I saw when I arrived at the point-to-point meeting that Saturday was Flinty. He came up to me smiling and after asking about my injuries he said, 'I have news for you. You've kept the ride on Prospero.'

My heart leaped. 'That's marvellous,' I said. 'And I'm sure I have you to thank for it.'

'It's true I put in a good word for you, but it was the little man who pulled it off. He's ridden enough races to know what it's like to miss out. He told her it was damned unfair to think of ditching you after one bad ride, that you were only starting and that it would do you untold harm. His word is law in that quarter as I expect you know. But you only got there by a short head. Someone else was after it.'

'Don't tell me who it was, I can guess: Rupert Carleton.'

'You've hit the spot. He's been dripping vitriol in her ear ever since that race last week.'

'He doesn't usually condescend to point-to-points you told me.'

'He's short of the spondulicks, I believe. Anyway, there it is. She's in love with that horse. Got a fixation on him the way women have. And she has great plans for him. You're to come to the little man's lodgings this eve to discuss them. But it won't be a long session. We're off night-clubbing.'

The colonel had entered Givenchy in the second race on the card and to watch it I took up a position on the hill where we had parked the cars. There I was joined by Charles Ormsby. 'I hardly expected to see you here,' I said.

'I get about,' he said. 'I heard Rupert was riding and I thought I'd come along. What about this horse Givenchy? You've exercised him. Has he shown you anything?'

'He can go a bit,' I said. 'I don't know about the other runners.'

'Billy Burton-Brown has one in it,' Captain Pat, who had just joined us, said. 'But they're backing the colonel's horse for pounds, shillings and pence. I can't understand it.'

'By God,' Charles Ormsby said. 'I wonder . . .' And he hurried off.

He was back in a few minutes with a look on his face of one who has just made a pleasant discovery. 'Come to the car after this,' he said to me. 'I have something to tell you.'

'They're off,' I said, raising my glasses.

Naturally I wanted to see how Givenchy went under Rupert's strong handling, so I watched with more than usual interest the colonel's colours of amber and white. Rupert had him in the middle of the field most of the way, then when they began really to race he moved him smoothly up. Most of those that were left began to drop back, but two came over the last together: Rupert Carleton and Billy Burton-Brown. There followed a desperate set-to up the straight in which Givenchy was subjected to Rupert's full treatment in a finish. He knew how to handle a whip as good as a pro in a tight finish, and he got up by a neck. But when a horse was subjected to one of Rupert's roustings in a finish he didn't forget it in a hurry, and this was Givenchy's first time out. Captain Pat hurried off to have a good look at the winner and to see how many stripes of the whip were decorating his coat.

'The money was down,' Charles Ormsby said quietly as we made our way to his car. 'I haven't been idle,' he went on as we settled ourselves in its seats. 'Something about those pictures of Rossiter has bothered me ever since you came in and reopened the case. Take a look at this.' He reached over and took from his briefcase another copy of the drawing from which my embellishments had been removed. 'Remind you of anyone?' he asked as I studied it.

'Gosh,' I said. 'Yes, now you mention it—Rupert!'

'Exactly. He's Rupert's younger brother, or half-brother would be more accurate. I'd acted once for one of Rupert's ex-wives and remained friendly with her. We had dinner together recently and she told me the whole story. It seems Rupert's father didn't sire this fellow though he had to give him his name. Gervase Carleton, that's who he is. But the old man knew very well he'd been cheated and hated him from the start.'

'Who was the father?' I asked.

'No one knows except, I suppose, the mother, and she died without telling. Whether the old man's hatred had anything to do with the way he turned out I don't know, but Gervase proved to be a wrong 'un fairly early. He was expelled from two public schools and did a term in clink for forging someone's signature on a cheque, leaving a stack of unpaid bills behind him in the West End. Thereupon fond papa kicked him out bag, baggage, the lot. He drifted into the wrong end of racing having changed his name about three times, and he survived somehow in the way these characters do. He was always good with horses and that helped.'

'But where does Rupert come in?' I asked.

'That's the quirk in the story. The two of them got on well, it seems. The ex-wife told me Rupert did his best to look after him, rescuing him from the worst of the scrapes he got into and giving him money. It was about the only decent thing Rupert ever did in his life, according to the ex-wife, which is the sort of remark you expect from an ex-wife, as I hope you'll never have occasion to find out.' He paused to light a cigarette.

'What then?' I asked.

'It's obvious, isn't it? Rupert recruited him for the job of doping your father's horse and he's now either blackmailing Rupert or Rupert has him under his thumb and is keeping an eye on him. One way or another they're in it together. It was Rossiter doing the betting for Rupert today. I thought it likely when I heard they were betting on a cert. I went down and spotted him.'

'Did he see you?'

'I took good care he didn't.'

'But we've got them now, haven't we?'

'Not so fast, my young friend. We've still nothing really on Rupert yet. It's no offence to get someone to do the betting for you. And we both knew there's more in this than meets the eye. I've put a tag on Mr Rossiter—I brought one of my chaps with me just in case. I had a feeling something like this might turn up. Keep in touch, I think things may now begin to happen.'

WHEN I LEFT HIM I watched HRH win one of the regimental races that were a feature of point-to-points then. By the time I reached his rooms at Braden Lodge, corks were popping.

'I gather Flinty has told you,' Val greeted me. 'I want you to ride Prospero for the rest of the season.'

'He has and I don't know how to say thanks,' I said.

'Well, don't then.' But she smiled as she said it. 'How soon will you be fit enough to ride out?'

'In a few days, I hope. I mend quickly.'

'I'm entering him in two or three nomination races and then the Liverpool Foxhunters',' Val said. 'You'd better be fit.'

'Gosh,' I said. It was all I could say. The Liverpool Foxhunters' was then run over the full National distance. It was every GR's ambition to ride over those fearsome Aintree fences and I was being offered it. This was beyond anything I could have hoped for and it left me speechless. Seeing me, the Prince gave one of those quick smiles of his. 'You deserve all the luck your father didn't have,' he said. 'I hope it goes well for you.'

On that note I left them to their night out in the bright lights and went to look for Captain Pat. I found him, as I thought I might, at Givenchy's box. The horse was a sorry sight, listless and drooping with a series of raw, red weals across his quarters. 'He hasn't eaten up,' Captain Pat said. 'And I'm not surprised. It'll be some time before he sees a racecourse again. What the hell did Rupert think he was playing at?'

'He backed him,' I said.

'I thought as much.'

'What did Rupert say when he came in?'

'He told Pirate he was going so well he had to take Billy on and then there was nothing for it but to battle it out or they'd have been in trouble. He always has an answer.'

'How did he know he was good enough to back him?'

'That's my fault. He asked me about him and I told him we thought he might be something special. But I warned the swine he was highly strung. I have an idea too he had someone watch him work. I'll take damn good care he doesn't ride him again. You might be lucky and come in for the ride, whenever it is.'

'I'm lucky twice over then. I've just come from Val Spenlove. I've kept the ride on Prospero.'

'Have you, by Gad. That's a bit of a turn up, isn't it?'

'Flinty and HRH fixed it. She's going to run him in the Liverpool Foxhunters'.'

'I hope he's as good as he looks. Here's the colonel now. I think it might be wiser if you were to fade gently away.'

Walking back, although I knew that sterner things than riding races should be occupying my thoughts, I could not bring myself to do other than dream of Prospero and Aintree. But the following afternoon I was brought back to reality with a bump. There was a telegram waiting for me in my rooms. It read: MEET ME BUCK'S CLUB TOMORROW 11AM OR NEAREST. ORMSBY.

WHILE I WAS BREAKFASTING next morning, before catching the early London train from Melton, Mrs Williams bustled in with the post. It consisted of a letter from my mother, which I put into my pocket to read on the train, and a small registered package. Breaking the seals on this I tore open the wrapping and my father's gold cigarette case slid out onto the tablecloth before me. There was no note or letter with it that I could see and after staring at it in astonishment for a moment I picked up the wrapping to examine the address label. But this told me nothing, either. It was printed in blue ink and had a London postmark. I was still frowning over it when I heard Mrs Williams's voice from below. 'Mr de Lacey, you'll miss your train.'

Hurriedly pushing the case and wrapping into a drawer, I grabbed my hat and coat and made the station with a few minutes to spare. The train was in on time and in my first-class carriage I took out my mother's letter. It contained little beyond some scraps of hunting gossip and news of her horses until I reached the end. *You seem to be seeing a lot of Val Spenlove*, she wrote. *Beware! Did your father ever read Mr Kipling to you? 'A rag and a bone and a hank of hair', and if you don't know the rest then find out!* I need scarcely say I didn't know the rest and I put the letter in my pocket while I tried to figure out where the cigarette case had come from.

BUCK'S CLUB WAS the first London club to install a bar, and it was there that Charles Ormsby was waiting for me.

'You're giving up an awful lot of time to our affairs,' I said. 'I only hope it's not wasted.'

'I'll tell you why I'm doing it,' he said. 'First, I'm interested in righting an injustice if I can; second, it may concern the heir to the throne and is therefore my duty; third, and many people would say most important, your mother has paid me a handsome deposit.'

Mention of my mother reminded me of her letter. 'You know a lot,' I said. 'Do you know a quotation from Kipling—"a rag and a bone and a hank of hair"?'

'Kipling, the soldier's laureate,' he said. 'I do know that thing, or some of it. It goes on, "we called her the woman who did not care but the fool he called her his lady fair." ' He paused and looked at me, 'Why do you ask?'

'I heard it somewhere,' I said, mentally trying to digest it.

'Hm,' he said, giving me another hard stare and reminding me that here was someone whose probing mind worked all the time. 'Well, we have work to do. We've located Mr Vincent Rossiter, or Vernon Radley as he calls himself now.'

ROSSITER—OR RADLEY, which I'd better call him from now on—had taken up residence in a block of flats near Marble Arch known, so Ormsby informed me in the taxi, as Co-respondent Court. There was a commissionaire at the door and a receptionist behind a desk in the foyer, but neither of them questioned our credentials as we marched in.

Ormsby led the way to the bank of lifts and we went up to the third floor. There, about halfway along a dark corridor, he paused before a door with a card on it inscribed: MAJOR VERNON RADLEY. 'Major, indeed,' he said. 'He's come up in the world. He usually goes to the pub round the corner about this time, I'm told.' As he spoke he took a bunch of what looked like keys from his pocket and bent over the lock. In a few moments there was a click and the door swung open to his touch. 'Kid's stuff,' he said.

We stepped into a short hallway. There were two doors on either side, both of which stood open. One gave onto a bedroom, the other to a sitting room and kitchenette. Ormsby checked the rooms quickly.

'I say,' I said, when he came back to me in the hall. 'Isn't this frightfully illegal?'

'Of course it is,' he said rather crossly. 'That's why I'm doing it.'

On the floor of the hallway was an envelope addressed to Major

Vernon Radley. Ormsby picked this up and studied it for a moment. Then, taking a penknife from his pocket, he slit it open and began to study its contents. 'We've come to the right place,' he said, handing me the letter. There was a cheque pinned to it and it was written on Braden Lodge writing paper. On it was scrawled: *Thanks for your help. We worked it well*, followed by the initials *R.C.* The cheque was for fifty pounds. It was made out to Vernon Radley and signed Rupert Carleton.

While I was looking at these, Ormsby was prowling about the living room, finally coming to a stop before a desk in the window. On it stood a half-empty bottle of whisky and a used glass. It was littered with circulars and unpaid bills, among which was a leather-bound book. Picking this up he examined it. 'It's a diary,' he said. 'This might be interesting.'

He took it to a chair and began to leaf through the pages. 'It's a five-year diary,' he said. 'It was a year ago your father was warned off, wasn't it? It all began at Ascot, as I remember. Listen to this: *June 3rd.* That was a week before Ascot. *Got the stuff from R.C. Hope it works.* That's Rupert Carleton, I'll be bound. I think we may just have struck gold. Give me that letter from the hall, will you?'

I brought it to him and he looked at it again. 'He signed the letter with his initials,' he said. 'And the cheque, of course, with his full name. That ties him in with the diary entries for R.C. I'll hang on to these.' He replaced the letter and cheque in their envelope and put them in his pocket. 'The cheque would probably bounce anyway,' he said. 'But there's more in the diary.' He turned over the pages. '*June 11th*,' he read out, '*It worked! Bf won by three lengths. Enquiry. de L sent on. He must go. Now for the pay-off from R.C.* Even if the rest of it doesn't live up to what we've seen and heard I think Mr R. Carleton is in some trouble. Up a certain creek without a certain paddle, you might say.'

'Why on earth did he write it all down?' I asked.

'So as to have a record and a hold over Rupert, I imagine.'

'And leave it lying about?'

'It wouldn't convey anything to anyone unless they knew what we do. When did your father have his stroke?'

'Last August.'

He turned back to the diary. 'Good God,' he said and read out: '*They seem to have fixed de L*!'

'That must have been when he was in America.'

'It was. Let's see what he says about coming back. Here it is. He's got a bit more expansive: *Fed up with this bloody country. Champagne like Epsom salts. Returning whatever R. says and he can pay up.*'

At that moment there was the sound of a key in the lock and then steps in the hall.

'Oh, Lord!' I said.

'Panic not,' Ormsby said coolly, almost as if he had been waiting for it. 'If it's the gallant major, he's in for something of a surprise.'

The door opened and a man came in. It was Rossiter alias Radley and I recognised him at once. I could now see the striking resemblance to Rupert, but there were also differences. It was a far weaker face. Where Rupert looked what he was, a roaring tough and hard nut to crack, this chap's mouth had a curl of indecision under the fair moustache and the eyes were pale and watery.

'What the hell—' he exclaimed as he saw us. 'Burglars, are you? I'll call the police—'

'You do just that if you wish,' Ormsby said. 'The phone is over there. But take a look at Mr de Lacey there. There's a small matter of grievous bodily harm outstanding between you, apart from several other things I could mention. Go ahead, what's stopping you?'

He looked at me and recognition together with fear suddenly flared in his eyes. Then he caught sight of the diary in Ormsby's hands. 'What are you doing with that?' he shouted, pointing at it. As he pointed he picked up an ebony ruler from the desk and made a lunge towards Ormsby.

It was the quickest thing I ever saw. At one moment Ormsby was sitting there, the diary in his hands. The next the diary was laid aside and he was on his feet, clasping the wrist that held the ruler. It went up behind Radley's back and spun him round as you'd spin a top. A single push sent him reeling off balance towards the far wall. He hit it hard and collapsed with a crash onto a spindly sofa, where he lay gasping with shock and surprise.

'You try that again and I'll break your arm and probably your neck as well,' Ormsby said equably. The bow tie, I noticed, remained impeccably in place.

'What do you want? If it's money I haven't any,' Radley said.

'I know that,' Ormsby said. 'It's a little information which I rather think you can give us. How is your brother Rupert, by the way?'

He lay there, looking at us, his eyes darting from one of us to the other, finally coming to rest on Ormsby. 'Who are you?' he said. 'You're not CID.' Then, recognition dawning, 'I know you. You're Ormsby, the private rozzer, paid for digging up dirt.'

'I wouldn't have far to go to find it here,' Ormsby said.

At that, all at once, having realised we had no official status, he began to bluster. 'What the hell do you think you're doing?' he said. 'You've nothing on me.'

'Is that so,' Ormsby said. 'Try this then.' He began to read the passages from the diary. 'R.C. That's your brother Rupert Carleton, I don't doubt,' he concluded.

'That'll never stand up,' Radley said. 'You stole the diary, you tampered with my letter. You can go to hell.'

'Try pulling his fingernails out,' I said. 'That was what he suggested doing to me. I owe him something, and for what they did to my father.' Involuntarily I took a step towards him.

'Hold it,' Ormsby commanded as the other threw up a hand as if to ward me off.

'I had no part in that—your father,' Radley said. 'I was in America. It was Rupert and you'll never touch him. He knows too much. He's connected, with half the court and three-quarters of the Jockey Club.'

'Rot,' Ormsby said succinctly. 'We've got you where we want you. You'll find out how quick your precious connections can drop you.'

Suddenly Radley began to whine. 'You don't know what it's like, being the black sheep,' he said. 'I didn't ask to be born, did I? Why take it out on me? It was Rupert who was given everything. All I got were kicks, cold shoulders—and hatred.'

'I didn't come here to listen to confessions,' Ormsby said coldly. 'Save that for the dock. Where is Rupert now?'

'Where you can't touch him, in Monte Carlo playing the tables with his winnings. Damn him, he said he'd take me with him. What's in that cheque?'

'Fifty pounds.'

'Fifty quid? He took twenty times that out of the ring!' Cupidity, fear and venom were all beginning to work on him. 'That bloody Rupert,' he said. 'He got me into this.'

'And paid you well for it?'

'Like hell he did. Shipped me off pretty quick to the States when he thought you were closing in on me. A few ponies when I did the job, that's all I got.'

'The job? That's the doping? Why do it then?'

'Rupert said there was money in it, big money.'

'Where was this money coming from?'

'I don't know. You don't pester Rupert for information when he has hold of the bit. I think he had the arm on someone.'

'And you came home to put the arm on him?'

He sulked at that. Then he said, 'He told me the source was drying up. That's why he had to work that bet. Listen, what's in this for me?

I'm flat broke. At least give me that cheque.'

'The diary and cheque are staying with me. They'll do as evidence. Would it interest you to know that Rupert has got you mixed up in something that may well concern the Prince of Wales? That's treason. Do you know what the penalty for treason is? It's hanging by the neck until you're dead.'

Radley sank back onto the sofa. I've often heard of people turning deadly white but I'd never seen it before. His cheeks really did take on an ashen tinge and he stared helplessly at us.

Suddenly Ormsby stood up. 'That'll do for now,' he said. 'Just remember we've got you by the short hairs. We can hand on this information at any time to those who can act on it. Come on,' he nodded at me.

It was then I remembered something. 'You've got the forty quid you pinched off me on the road,' I said. 'That should keep you going for a bit. But why did you send me back the cigarette case? You could have pawned it for a bob or two.'

'Cigarette case?' he said, looking at me open-mouthed. 'Oh, that gold one. I never had that. Rupert took it.'

As we reached the door, with a final flash of defiance, he shouted, 'You'll never get Rupert, you know. He *likes* living dangerously.'

ONCE OUTSIDE, Ormsby turned to me. 'What's all this about a cigarette case?' he said.

'I forgot to tell you before,' I said. 'It came in the post this morning. It was pinched off me when they beat me up.'

'Did you keep the package?'

'It's in a drawer in my rooms.'

'I'd like to take a look at it. I'll come back to Melton with you.'

But the package told him as little as it did me. He stared at the address and postmark and finally put it down. 'Beats me,' he said.

'What will Radley do now? Will he run to Rupert?' I asked him.

'He won't. He's scared of Rupert. He'll lie low for a bit. I'll pay him another visit tomorrow while he's still in shock. I may have to do a deal with him. Your first aim is to clear your father's name, right?'

'Yes, but I want to nail that bastard Rupert for what he did.'

'Step by step. He can't do much in Monte and I rather think their little plot about the Prince may be falling apart.'

At that moment there was the sound of a car drawing up outside. Going to my window I looked out. 'It's a Rolls,' I said. Then I saw a door open and a figure step out. 'It's Sir Crispin,' I said. 'What can he want?'

'We'll soon see.'

In a few minutes he was ushered in. 'Afternoon, de Lacey,' he said to me, stripping off his gloves. 'And to you, too, Charles. I thought I might find one or both of you here. I rang your place of business, Charles, and found you were meeting de Lacey in London but didn't expect to be away all day. Riding any more winners, young fella?'

'He has a ride in the Foxhunters' at Aintree,' Ormsby said. 'So what brings you here, Crispin?'

'Since you came to see me I've been considering the whole matter of Dick de Lacey's warning-off. I've always hated that rule as you know. Your object, both of you, I take it, is to clear his name?'

'We were discussing just that when you came in,' Ormsby said.

'Whatever way you look at it,' I said, 'the public think he did dope that horse and the press have more or less said so.'

'Very well. That being so we must try to get the warning-off notice lifted. I've been taking soundings and there is very considerable sympathy. There was a Jockey Club meeting last week and I felt I had enough to mention it in general terms under any other business.'

'How did that go?' Ormsby asked.

'There was opposition, not much, but some. It was said it might be establishing a precedent. Luckily I was able to cite the case of Bob Sievier who was let back after two years, over a different matter, it's true. They mumbled and bumbled a bit, but I think on the whole I carried the day far enough anyway for you to make an application on your father's behalf.'

'Who were in opposition?' Ormsby asked.

'Now, Charles, you don't expect me to quote names from a private meeting,' Merevale said. And then, to me: 'I'll draft your letter of application for you and I'll write in in support of it. If they do grant the lifting of the warning-off notice we should try to get them to say that no blame attached to your father in the matter. That will need delicate handling. By the way, have you got any further with finding the real culprit?'

I was about to blurt out a reply when Ormsby quickly forestalled me. 'We're making progress,' he said. 'I'd prefer not to say any more just at the moment.'

'Hm, well, tell me when you do get anything. In the meantime I'll take a few more soundings and let you know, de Lacey, when the time is ripe. Good luck with your riding.' At the door he paused. 'By the way,' he said, 'that Jockey Club meeting, Roger Gretton was there, and Marston, who seldom comes.' The door closed behind him, leaving Ormsby and myself looking at each other.

Chapter Eleven

Then began what was the most exciting and at the same time most exacting period of my short life so far. My next outing was the Garth at Arborfield. Prospero behaved impeccably, the famous Arborfield brook held no terrors for him, though it floored several of his competitors. I had him in front most of the trip and he came away to win comfortably. After winning the nomination race at the Garth my fall was forgotten and offers of rides came pouring in.

There is no denying of course that my association with the Prince of Wales helped my racing career. Those with a horse to sell realised that it did them no harm to say, 'that chap, friend of the Prince's you know, rode him and liked him,' and many were not above slyly suggesting I slid a horse into the Prince's stable. One such even brazenly suggested that, 'there's ten per cent in it for you if you pull it off.' Fortunately I had enough sense to refuse that ride. Just the same I found that I was being offered rides here, there and everywhere.

There's no denying I was spoilt. I was young enough to believe that you made your own luck and that I was making it. But I had enough sense to keep my feet on the ground and my head out of the clouds. I kept a still tongue in the weighing room and above all did not try to make capital out of my patronage by the Prince. Nor did I ever try anything on in a race but, knowing my inexperience, I was learning all the time. As a result both Billy Burton-Brown and Mike Annerley accepted me. Once they had done this they did all they could to help, except of course in the actual race when no quarter was asked or given. ' "Look after yourself, no one else will": that's what my guvnor said to me when I started,' Billy told me once. However, it wasn't all plain sailing. There were clouds in the sky, and the first of these concerned Prospero. I won the next two nomination races on him, but despite those I was still not entirely happy about him. Nor were Flinty or HRH. The only person who believed utterly in him was Val.

'Get him off well, keep him up in the van, let him run his own race and with luck his speed and his jumping will see him through,' had been Flinty's advice to me. This I had done and the luck had lasted. There was no question of his ability to jump, but in the last of those three races I thought I detected signs of his sulking, and he hadn't really yet been asked to battle. Had he the heart for the struggle that would be required at Aintree? That was the question which the four of us discussed endlessly.

'Carry on the way you're going,' Flinty said. 'After all it's worked so far. What do you think, David?'

'I'm not one to give an opinion on the tactics of race-riding,' the Prince observed with his ready smile. 'I'm far too busy trying to stay in the race to think of anything else.'

'You're not fair to yourself, as usual,' Val said hotly. 'Anyway, I don't know what the three of you are bothering yourselves about. He has won three on the trot, hasn't he? What is in the Foxhunters' to beat him?'

'There's that thing of Billy Burton-Brown's, The Clinker,' Flinty said. 'If he comes out of the United Hunts at Cheltenham all right, he'll go to Liverpool.'

'What about us?' I said. 'Where do we go next?'

'A school at Jimmy Connaughton's on Monday,' Flinty said. 'He lets us do that when the hunter chases start. Then the Hunters' race at Colwall the next week to give him a taste of the racecourse proper. Both of those should sharpen him up after the point-to-points.'

'There you are then, Danny,' Val said smiling. 'And see that you don't smash yourself up in the meantime.'

The second cloud concerned my quest for the clearing of my father's name. Whenever I tried to get in touch with Ormsby to find out how he was getting on it proved surprisingly difficult. The sour-puss secretary kept putting me off with one excuse or another and when at last I got through to him all he would say was: 'It's going reasonably well but just at the moment the less you know the better.' I wondered just what he was up to and if by chance he had been in touch with Crispin Merevale. With some trepidation as to how I would be received I rang Patworth Castle to find out.

The baronet, however, was his usual friendly and approachable self. No, he said, he had heard nothing from Charles Ormsby. 'But,' he added, 'I have news for you.'

'Good or bad, sir?' I asked.

'A bit of both perhaps. I've had a word in private with Lord Benby who is the senior steward this year. They're going to meet to consider the application. But he stressed its unusual features. As the application is being made by you on your father's behalf, they want to have a look at you. That means you'll have to appear before them in person.'

'Oh, Lord!'

'It's not unreasonable, you know. It could be that you might want to take up where your father left off. If you were to apply for a licence to train they'd know about you and have you on record. And they knew your father and felt for him, so you will at least be in with a chance. I'll brief you about the hearing and go with you to lend support. You'll get official notice of the date and time.'

'I really don't know how to thank you, sir, and I know how grateful my mother will be.'

'Forget it. Go and ride a few more winners and we'll pull this one off, you'll see.'

TWO DAYS LATER we brought Prospero to Jimmy Connaughton's for a school. He was to go over the chasing fences with two older steeplechasers and Jimmy himself came down to watch it. Somewhere in that cold heart of his Jimmy had a soft spot for amateur riders, possibly because he had once been one himself; he always interested himself in their doings and allowed the use of his schooling fences on designated days to point-to-pointers and their riders.

There were others besides Jimmy there too, which may have been explained by the presence in the school of the Prince of Wales. It must have been one of his last-minute, spur-of-the-moment decisions, as Flinty had not mentioned it to me, nor did I think he entirely approved of it, for he stood there frowning as he watched the horses being brought out. The Prince joined me as we walked towards them.

'I'm coming with you,' he explained as he swung himself up. 'Recognise him?' He nodded to his mount. 'It's your old friend Pepperpot.'

The third member of our party was, I was equally surprised to see, Ginger Elton, riding a big, rakish chaser of Jimmy's. 'Wotcher, Guv,' he greeted me. 'I'm back with Mr Connaughton for a bit. Bin ridin' a few winners yourself I see.'

There I was between the Prince of Wales, the highest in the land, and a stableboy, or stablerat as they were sometimes called, and a spirit of pure mischief possessed me. 'Your Royal Highness,' I said. 'May I present Ginger Elton, one of Jimmy's work riders.'

The boy goggled and almost immediately I was aghast at my own temerity. In fact there was no cause for alarm, for once HRH was among horses and horsemen he was one of ourselves. 'Jolly good,' he said. 'I hope you won't knock me down.'

Jimmy had spared nothing in constructing his schooling ground. It was a huge field set amongst the flat acres and bordered by a screen of trees. There were hurdles for the hurdlers, smaller fences for the education of the young, and bigger ones to smarten up the older and more experienced. These latter were in two lots of three and four respectively. The first contained an open ditch and the second, placed a little way from the others on a curve, contained a replica of a water jump simulated by a chalked-out sheet. Although the horses could be pulled out at the end of the first set of fences, we were to face the lot.

I was placed between the two experienced horses and, with a shout from Jimmy, we were off. The plan was, so Flinty had told me, to take them steady so as to give Prospero a feel of the thing. 'Let him have a look at the ditch, don't worry about the water, he'll jump it as it comes. Bustle on over the last two if you like.'

That may have been the plan; it wasn't carried out. Straight away the Prince on Pepperpot jumped into what I can only describe as a headlong gallop. There was nothing for it but to hurtle after him, Elton's old chaser devouring the ground and Prospero matching strides with him. I had never been so fast over first fences in my life. Beside me I heard Elton mutter 'Cripes' as we flew them. For whatever reason the Prince was making this a trial not a school. We had a look at the ditch but not the way Flinty intended. The others stood back and made nothing of it. Prospero put in a short one but he got away with it and we went on.

In a way the Prince had cooked his own goose. Pepperpot was really only a hunter, though a very good one, and these were racehorses, even if Prospero was as yet an embryo. At the bend Pepperpot began to drop back. Elton by now had entered into the spirit of the thing—the wrong spirit to my mind—and was setting the other horse alight. It was the next best thing to a race.

The distance between the last two fences was longer than the others. Here Elton came off the bit and forged past me. Immediately I thought I felt Prospero falter. But the fence loomed up. Whatever else there was about him he loved jumping. He flung it behind him, out-jumped the other and landed running. Then we pulled up and I slid to the ground near the Prince, Jimmy and Val. 'He's a smasher, isn't he, Jimmy?' I heard Val say to the trainer.

The Prince drew me a little apart and then, with that truly regal ability to make a fact out of an opinion, he said, 'That was all right. Nothing wrong there.'

To my mind there was everything wrong and for the first and only time in our association I could cheerfully have throttled him. Fortunately he did not wait for an answer and his next words disarmed me. 'She's set her heart on getting a good one to follow up her father's triumphs, and she thinks this may be it,' he said. 'I wanted to find out. I don't want her hurt, especially now, any more than may be.'

With that he turned back towards the others and I made my way to the cars. Here Flinty, looking glum, joined me. 'I'll come back with you,' he said. 'I came with the horses.'

He spoke very little on our way but when I pulled the Alvis up outside Braden Lodge he said brusquely, 'Come in, we'll have breakfast.'

Breakfast proved to be a bottle of Krug, devilled kidneys, kedgeree, scrambled eggs laced with smoked salmon, and coffee.

'What did you make of your fellow?' Flinty asked as we ate.

I thought I'd better tell him the truth as I saw it. 'One thing is sure,' I said. 'He has the hell of a leap in him. As for the rest, I just don't know. I still think he may not battle. He's unpredictable.'

'About as unpredictable as my royal master. He only decided to put himself into the school at the last minute and I had to tell Jimmy to pull his other horse out. What was he playing at?'

'He said he wanted to find out about Prospero for himself.'

'Damn queer time to think of doing it. Something is eating him and I wish I knew what it is.'

'He said he didn't want her hurt, especially just now.'

'It's to do with those bastards at court is my guess. They'll want him to drop her.'

He went off then to change for a day's hunting and I drove back to my rooms to bath and dress before resuming my veterinary education with Captain Pat.

In my rooms I saw a typewritten envelope lying on my table. Opening it I found a summons from the Jockey Club stewards to appear before them on the coming Friday.

CRISPIN MEREVALE was as good as his word, letting me know that he would be with me that morning in time to give me what he called my 'riding instructions' for the hearing. Before he arrived I received a postcard on which was scrawled *Best of Luck—VAL*. And hardly had I glanced at it than I was handed by special delivery a long, brown, official-looking envelope. Inside was a legal document with a solicitor's letter attached. It was headed: HARDING, HENSLEY AND BARTON with an address in Lincoln's Inn and it was brief: 'Dear Sir,' it said, 'We have been instructed to forward you the enclosed affidavit sworn by Gervase Carleton, otherwise known as Vincent Rossiter. Kindly acknowledge safe receipt.'

Eagerly I read it, racing down the numbered paragraphs, and then going back to scan them again with care. 'Gervase Carleton, otherwise known as Vincent Rossiter, gentleman, presently residing at Braxton Towers, Marble Arch, London, made oath and said—'

The gist of it was that under the name of Vincent Rossiter he had been temporarily employed by Colonel Richard de Lacey at

Madagascar House, Newmarket. As such he had been 'solely and only' responsible for doping the colt Bloemfontein when under the care and supervision of the said Colonel de Lacey and, further, that Colonel de Lacey had no knowledge of, or association with, the doping carried out by him, which required the utmost secrecy, skill and diligence owing to the strict security maintained by Colonel de Lacey in all matters concerning the horses in his care. He went on to swear that no other persons in the stable had been concerned in the matter and if he received payment it had come from outside sources. After the incident, fearing exposure, he had emigrated to America, but had since returned. He made this affidavit voluntarily from sincere regret for his actions, with the object of clearing Colonel de Lacey's name.

When Crispin Merevale arrived I showed him the affidavit and he read it carefully. When he had finished he said, 'I should have guessed Gervase Carleton would be mixed up in something of this sort. He's a thorough-going bad hat. It's typical, too, his pointing the finger at someone else with his talk of payment. Where'd you get this?'

'It came by special delivery a few minutes ago.'

'I think I see Charles Ormsby's fine hand in it somewhere, but you and I mustn't know that. And we'll have to be careful how we use it. The stewards aren't over fond of lawyers or legal documents.'

'Who are the stewards I'll be appearing before?'

'Lord Benby will be in the chair. He's a fair man, he doesn't like that rule and I'm sure he'll be sympathetic.'

'That's something. What about the others?'

'There's Lord Giles Tevern. He has the habit of listening and asking just one or two questions plumb to the point—and there's Roger Gretton.'

'Roger! Good Lord, how?'

'He was elected this year to fill the annual vacancy. Your guess is as good as mine how Roger will go. Now, when you go in make sure you're respectful. Don't put their backs up or you're lost.'

'Will you be able to come in and give me moral support?'

'Not at first, I think. They'll want to see you alone. But I'll take care they know I'm on the premises. If they don't ask for me I'll wangle my way in one way or another.'

With that we went downstairs to the street. I hadn't slept much the night before, tossing and turning, wondering what questions they would fire at me and how I would answer them. At any rate, I reflected, as I climbed into Merevale's Rolls, the tumbril taking me to the place of execution was doing it in style.

It was then long before the Jockey Club moved to Portland Place and their headquarters were still at Newmarket. My heart sank lower and lower as we approached the town, and the fact that we were kept waiting in an anteroom didn't do much for my nerves. At length I was told I could go up.

'You're off. Good luck,' Crispin said, giving me his friendly smile.

A steep narrow staircase led to the door of the stewards' room. As I climbed it I could almost hear my knees knocking together. At the top across a small landing were the ornate double doors to the stewards' room. As I approached them, wondering whether I was supposed to knock or await a summons, they were thrown open and I was ushered into the 'star chamber'. The whole scene is indelibly implanted in my memory.

Immediately in front of me was a polished mahogany table. I was positioned to stand facing the three stewards. In the centre was the senior steward, Lord Benby, who had a pair of immense bushy eyebrows and a bald dome; on his left, Roger Gretton and on his right, Lord Giles Tevern, slim and erect with a thin pencilled moustache. There was also a flunky in attendance, who acted as a sort of secretary. I hadn't long to take in these details for almost immediately the senior steward addressed me.

'We're here today, Mr de Lacey,' he said, 'to consider the application for the lifting of the warning-off notice imposed on Colonel de Lacey as a result of the drug administered to the colt Bloemfontein when in his care and under his supervision. You make this application on his behalf?'

'Yes, sir,' I said. Oddly, rather like riding a race when the gate goes up, I suddenly felt my nerves go away from me and I could concentrate on the job in hand.

The chairman continued. 'Your father, we are informed and accept, is seriously ill and cannot make the application himself. Your mother, I believe, has given her authority for you to act.'

'There's a letter on the file, my lord,' the flunky said.

'Very well, now I just want to ask you a question before we proceed. What is your present position?'

'I am at Melton Mowbray, as a learner with the veterinary staff.'

'Then I am correct in saying you have no personal interest in that you have no ambition, for the present at all events, of applying for a trainer's licence yourself?'

'No, sir. Not at all. In my spare time I'm trying to become a reasonably competent rider.'

I thought I saw a sympathetic smile flicker across Giles Tevern's

rather saturnine features when I said that, but it was Roger who spoke next.

'Then surely this application is misconceived,' he said. 'Your father is, to put it plainly, permanently incapacitated. He will never train again. It gives me no pleasure to say this, but the application appears to me to be quite pointless. The rule is there.'

So, I thought, Roger has for once come firmly off the fence. But Lord Benby was speaking again. 'Mr Gretton has a valid point,' he said. 'In the tragic circumstances surrounding your father it cannot benefit him. Briefly then, why is this application made?'

This was the very question I had been dreading. I had racked my brains how to answer it without appearing to criticise stewards. But suddenly I knew what I had to do. I'd take the plunge and risk it. 'It's to clear his name,' I said.

'Are you suggesting that the notice in the *Calendar* was misleading?' Roger said menacingly.

I was into it now and had to go on with it. 'I can only say, my Lords and Mr Gretton,' I said, 'that press and public have placed the blame on my father and he himself, in the position he is, can do nothing to convince them otherwise.'

'We're not here to cater for press and public,' Roger Gretton said contemptuously.

It was Tevern who intervened. 'Wait a bit,' he said. 'I seem to remember that at the original hearing Crispin Merevale, who was chairman of the stewards at Ascot, gave evidence. He very strongly stressed that when de Lacey was before the local stewards he had quizzed him thoroughly as to his stable security and was satisfied that no blame could attach to him. In fact as I now recall he said that he wanted that recorded. And now I understand that he has written in supporting the application.'

Lord Benby rustled through the papers in front of him and found Crispin's letter. Peering into his half-glasses he took a moment to read it. 'That is true,' he said. 'He repeats it here. I wasn't at that hearing. You stood in for me, Roger. Do you remember it?'

'Vaguely,' Roger said.

'There should be a record of that original decision which was conveyed to Dick de Lacey at the hearing,' Lord Benby said, and then, turning to the flunky, 'Have you got it, Masters?'

The flunky produced a massive leatherbound book. Opening it he leafed through the pages, found the appropriate entry and placed it before the chairman. 'It's here all right,' he said when he had read it, 'with the recommendation Crispin suggested. Let me have another look at that warning-off notice.' Again he rustled through his papers.

Having read it, Lord Benby frowned. 'It does differ from the record,' he said. 'What de Lacey was told at the hearing makes clear that he was absolved from blame and that it was the rule and the rule only which convicted him. The warning-off notice omits that and it could be interpreted that he was guilty of the offence. There's something in what this young man says. Do you know anything about the omission, Roger?'

'No, I don't and I cannot see it makes any difference. As I said before, the rule is there.'

'Yes, but what about justice being done, and also being seen to be done? Do you know, I think we should see Crispin. Is he here?' He looked at me.

'Yes, sir,' I said. 'He drove me down.'

'Did he?' He addressed the flunky. 'Ask Sir Crispin if he'd be good enough to come in to us.'

In a few moments Crispin entered. He was immediately asked to sit down and a seat was pulled out for him along one arm of the horseshoe. I was left standing, but never was I so glad to see the arrival of anyone.

'Good of you to come, Crispin,' Lord Benby said. 'Now, about this application. You have written a very strong letter in support of it.'

'That is so. I was firmly of the opinion and belief that Colonel de Lacey could in no way be implicated in the doping and indeed I asked that the warning-off notice, when published, would indicate that it came about solely by reason of the mandatory provisions of the rule.'

'Well, it didn't. Can either of you throw any further light on this?'

It was Roger again who answered. 'How could we?' he said. 'We don't draft the notices. But I'd like to say that the real culprit, if there is one, has never been identified.'

'Oh, but he has,' Crispin put in. 'I think Mr de Lacey has a document which I believe you should see.'

Now I took out the affidavit and unfolded it. The flunky came round and, taking the document, brought it to Lord Benby.

'What is this?' he said as he took it. 'A solicitor's letter. Harding, Hensley and Barton, I see. "Gervase Carleton, otherwise known as Vincent Rossiter",' he read aloud. 'Gervase Carleton, God bless my soul, what next?' And then, as he read on, 'Good God!' He finished reading in silence and then sat back. 'You'd both better read this,' he said, handing it first to Tevern.

When it came to Roger he looked at the solicitor's letter. 'Who are these people?' he said. 'They may be any East End fly-by-nights—'

'They've been my family's men of business for generations,' Lord Benby said. 'I think you may take it that it's quite genuine.'

'Gervase Carleton, that's Rupert Carleton's younger brother,' Tevern said.

'Yes, I'm afraid it is,' was Lord Benby's comment. He said then, looking at me: 'You've no information as to who instructed the solicitors? It was not yourself, I take it.'

'No, sir,' I said. 'I only got it by special delivery this morning.'

'The solicitors won't tell, that's one thing certain,' Tevern said. 'They're hedged about by all sorts of privilege. But there's one other matter. I've heard a rumour that the Prince of Wales is interested in this case.' He looked at Crispin. 'Has he mentioned it to you or have you discussed it with him?'

'I have, informally,' was Crispin's reply.

'What did he say?' asked Lord Benby.

'Surely this must be pure hearsay,' Roger interjected.

'Are you suggesting I'm lying?' Crispin said dangerously.

'No, no, not at all, I assure you,' Roger protested. 'I only meant—'

'Hearsay be damned,' Benby growled. 'This isn't a court of law. What did he say, Crispin?'

'I asked him if he would give it his support and I give you his exact words: "I should think I jolly well will," was what he said.'

'He put nothing in writing,' Roger muttered.

'I believe that is not his practice,' Crispin said, coldly. 'But since you ask I should perhaps add one other thing.' He looked hard at Roger. 'He said he wondered could there be anyone else behind it as it was all a bit fishy to his mind.'

I thought I saw Roger shrink into himself at that.

'That struck me, too,' Tevern said. 'Especially in view of the tip-off to you which you mentioned. And there is in that affidavit a reference to Carleton being rewarded.'

'It's suspicious certainly,' Lord Benby said. 'Perhaps we'll take it into account. Well, then, if there are no more questions—no? Then, gentlemen, if you would be good enough to wait in the committee room we should be able to let you have a decision shortly.'

Once more we sat and waited. The minutes passed interminably. 'They're taking a time,' I said. 'What do you think they'll do?'

'They won't throw us out flat, I'll bet on that. They're arguing about something.'

'With Roger for the prosecution.'

'It looks very like it, and what's more it's not his form. I had a good look at him when I was telling them about the Prince of Wales and I thought he looked frightened. I don't understand it.'

I thought I was beginning to do just that, but I held my peace. And then the door opened and we were summoned once more to the stewards' room. This time I was told I could sit. The flunky actually pulled out a chair for me. I hoped it was a good omen.

Lord Benby peered at us over his half-glasses, and addressed us. 'We have discussed this application, and come to a certain conclusion. Because, however, of the unusual nature of the matter and the apparent confusion between what was recorded at the stewards' hearing and the subsequent notice in the *Calendar* we have decided to obtain legal advice as to the published wording of our decision. This is solely to avoid any further confusion concerning what we intend to convey. As soon as we receive such advice, and we shall seek expedition, the notice will appear in the *Calendar*.'

'But—' Crispin said.

Lord Benby held up an admonitory hand. 'I'm sorry, Crispin,' he said. 'That's all I can say at the moment.'

'SO WE STILL HAVE to wait,' Crispin said to me as we drove back. 'But news of your application has already filtered out in the way these things do. They'll want to clear the air and put the matter at rest once and for all. If Benby says he wants a quick answer he'll get it.'

And with that, I had, for the moment, to be content.

Crispin dropped me at my rooms. On my table was a typically belated telegram from my mother wishing me luck. I ought to write to her, I thought, telling her the events of the day. That telegram reminded me of Val's card, which I had stuffed into my pocket when the affidavit came. Now I took it out along with my father's gold cigarette case, and lighting a cigarette I looked at Val's card and read its brief message. How thoughtful it was of her to send it, I said to myself, and perhaps it had brought me luck. Then, turning it over, I glanced at the address. As I did so my eyes fell on the cigarette case lying beside it and then went back to the card. Something clicked in my mind as I read it, and a cold hand closed round my heart.

Chapter Twelve

It was a strange week of waiting. I had little time to spare for thinking about anything except myself: the growing certainty hovering in my mind that I had found the key to all that had happened; the anxiety about the ride on Prospero ('You won't sleep for a week,' Billy

Burton-Brown had cheerfully assured me when discussing Aintree after one point-to-point); and hanging over me the result, whatever it might be, of the enquiry. On Wednesday I had rides in a point-to-point and the following day, Thursday, saw the opening of the National Meeting at Aintree.

I didn't expect to be asked into the royal party, nor was I, but Captain Pat, kindly and loyal as ever, took me under his wing. There was much to do at the remounts so we decided to give the first day a miss and reserve ourselves for Grand National day, then a Friday, and, of course, the Saturday, when the Foxhunters' was run and I would put Prospero—and myself—to the ultimate test.

On the Thursday morning I went early to Captain Pat's office to find out if there was anything in the *Calendar* about our enquiry since Thursday was publication day.

'Here's something to gladden your heart,' Captain Pat greeted me. He had an opened copy of the *Calendar* in front of him. Passing it across to me he indicated an entry with his finger. Lord Benby's request for expedition had been effective. I read:

> The Stewards of the Jockey Club, in view of further evidence now made available to them and for the purpose of clarification only, desire to state that no personal involvement was ascribed to Lieutenant-Colonel D.R. de Lacey in the warning-off notice required by Rule 176 regarding the administration of a drug to the horse Bloemfontein when under his care. The said warning-off notice is withdrawn.

I read it twice. When I put it down I felt that one of the weights had been lifted from my mind.

'That's what you came for, isn't it?' Captain Pat said. 'Now go and win your race and Bob's your uncle.'

'I must send a telegram to my mother,' I said.

He pushed a pad of telegram forms towards me. 'When you've done that,' he said, 'we'll start our rounds.'

I suppose few now remember the supremacy of the Grand National Meeting in those far-off days, the glamour and excitement of it all. Before the Second World War it was the acme of the steeplechasing scene and, indeed, of the winter social scene, too. There were then none of the 'semi-classic' chases in the fixture list, run on park courses throughout the season, and the Cheltenham Gold Cup was in its infancy. The National was the be-all and the end-all, the culmination of ambition and achievement, the crown every owner, rider and trainer strove to gain.

All the best and indeed some of the worst horses were aimed at it. Endless were the discussions as to what was 'a National type' and deep were the pockets out of which money was poured in trying to find one. No other race came near it in either prestige or prize money. Its winner, wherever he came from in the handicap, was the hero not only of the day but of the year. The Friday night celebrations in the Adelphi Hotel were legendary.

And the Foxhunters' Chase, then run over the full National distance of four miles three hundred and eighty-six yards, was its amateur equivalent. The fences then were great green straight-up barriers with none of your present-day sloped-off aprons and softened tops. Horses had to be built like battleships to survive the shock of impact with those unforgiving obstacles, and they had to gallop and jump if they were to win or be placed at Aintree.

CAPTAIN PAT HAD ENGAGED a room for me near the course. 'You're not going to join those celebrations in the Adelphi, my lad,' he said. 'Not if I have to chain you to the bed. You may not sleep a whole lot but you'll be fit and well the morning of the race.'

I don't think I had ever felt so lonely in my life as I dined alone in those rooms. There were battles yet to come, and a confrontation I dreaded above all things. I had no one to confide in, and anyway I could not share what I knew until I had made certain. I had to solve this one alone, even as I had to ride Prospero alone.

To distract my mind I turned once more to the form book and the entries for the Foxhunters'. There were eighteen probables, Billy's The Clinker and Mike Annerley's Raison d'Etre amongst them. When I checked on a runner called Kindly Note I found that he had run in an amateurs' steeplechase back in February, ridden by Mr R. Carleton. I began to wonder. When, next morning, I opened the *Sporting Life* and saw the confirmation of Mr R. Carleton as the rider of Kindly Note in the Foxhunters', it didn't do anything for me at all.

But Prospero moved smoothly and well in the early morning warm-up, showing no signs of temperament, and that helped to build my confidence. It was while I was walking back from this that I heard a voice hailing me. 'Goin' ter win today, Guv?' it asked.

Turning, I found myself face to face with the cheerful countenance of Ginger Elton. 'I'll tell you that in a few hours' time,' I said. 'What are you doing here? Mr Connaughton hasn't a runner, has he?'

'Mr Connaughton, nah. I'm not there any more. A new batch of lads was comin' over from Ireland an' 'e chucked me out. I've gone freelance.'

'Good Lord, that's taking a bit of a chance, isn't it?'

'Things are tough, but there's allus room at the top, isn't there?'

I felt in my pockets and dug out a fiver.

'Thanks, Guv,' he said. 'Best o' luck this afternoon.' He moved away and then stopped. 'That school we 'ad,' he said. 'I was talkin' to one of Mr Burton-Brown's lads that came with the 'orses. That one of theirs, The Clinker, 'e said 'e's the 'ell of an 'orse. But 'e needs to be 'eld up. 'E's only got one run and it's 'ard to get it right. 'E'll be comin' after you if yer in front. Thought that might 'elp.'

I was digesting this piece of information when I was joined by Crispin Merevale.

'Who was that you were talking to?' he asked curiously.

'A lad called Ginger Elton. He was with my father when the crash came,' I said. 'It was he who put us on to Rossiter. He's gone free-lance now to try to make his way. He's had a few rides and I've seen him. He looks good. Perhaps you'd give him a chance some time?' I added, remembering that he had the reputation of being encouraging to the young.

'I'll bear it in mind,' he said. (He did, too, and a few seasons later when Elton was amongst the top ten in the jockeys' list we would sometimes laugh together about how he had made his way.) 'I've been away in Scotland or I would have been in touch before,' he added. 'You've seen the *Calendar*?'

'Yes,' I said. 'It's a marvellous result—thanks to you.'

'We were lucky. Benby has always disliked that rule and he is trying to bring about a change. And that mysterious affidavit didn't do us any harm. Ah, here's someone who can throw some light on that.'

Charles Ormsby was strolling towards us, a copy of the *Calendar* under his arm. 'You've seen this,' he said to me holding it up. 'Satisfied, I hope?'

'More than that,' I said. 'And it's all due to you both.'

'That was a very interesting document which arrived in de Lacey's rooms the morning of the hearing,' Crispin said. 'You wouldn't know anything about how it was obtained, would you, Charles?'

Ormsby's smile was childlike and bland. 'I can't imagine what you're referring to,' he said.

'I rather thought you wouldn't,' Crispin said. 'But perhaps you can help us on another matter. Gervase Carleton—just where is he now and what has happened to him?'

'As a matter of fact, I can tell you. Unregrettably, I suppose you might say, and unregretted certainly, he has left the country—and he won't be coming back.' The grim look I had first observed in

Gervase's flat had returned to Ormsby's features. 'Do you know, I don't think I would pursue the matter any further if I were you—either of you.' He gave a brief nod and then wandered off.

Crispin's eyes followed him as he went. 'That's the way it goes,' he said. 'Some go up, some go down, and some just go away. But for you it's over, isn't it, and it couldn't have turned out better.'

But of course he was wrong. For me it was far from over. There was the unfinished business in which I had become entangled to be cleared up; and there was Prospero's race to come.

Somehow I got through the intervening hours before I entered the weighing room to change and weigh out. The tension in the jockeys' room was almost palpable: people spoke to each other hurriedly or fell glumly silent. There were frequent visits to the loo and someone in one corner was being quietly sick into his handkerchief.

Nothing, however, could quell Billy Burton-Brown's ebullience. He had been up all night or most of it, he confided in me, at the Adelphi celebrations. 'I've a head like an over-ripe melon and a mouth like the bottom of a parrot's cage,' he said. 'Oh hell, why do I do these things?'

It was then that Rupert Carleton came in. His eyes fell on me and he strode over to where I was trying with shaking fingers to secure my scarf round my neck. 'What have you done with Gervase, you little rat?' he said.

I stared at him in amazement.

'Don't play the idiot boy with me,' he snarled. 'He's disappeared and you're behind it somehow. I'll get you for this, if not today, later. You wait, you little swine.'

He moved off but not before I had time to notice that he had put on weight during his absence from racing. His face was fleshier and didn't have that tight, hard look which comes from constant riding. A few minutes later we were called out.

They were in the ring, waiting, Val, Flinty and HRH. I walked up to them, touched the brim of my cap with my whip and gave the 'half-nod, half-bow' described by Pirate, and which protocol demanded, to the Prince. I was rewarded by a brief smile but I was struck immediately by how quiet they were; even Flinty's cheery grin was absent. 'What can I tell you?' he said to me after a moment. 'You know Prospero better than any of us. Keep him there or thereabouts. Let him run his own race. That's how you've won on him before.'

'You will win this race for me, won't you, Danny,' Val said.

The saddling bell rang then. HRH walked with me to the horse. He could have remained aloof and on his dignity, but that was not his way. 'Good luck,' he said when Flinty put me up. There was a wistful air about him as he added quietly, looking up at me, 'I only wish I was coming with you.'

A Mersey mist was hanging over the course as I rode out onto it past the packed stands, and it occurred to me that those on them would see little of the race that day. For myself I was in a tangle of emotions. Nerves had gone as they mostly did once I was on the back of a horse, but something must have happened to cast a cloud over my friends and there was Rupert and his threats to be borne in mind. I had better watch out for him. I had memorised his colours, green with a white sash, and to my dismay when we lined up I found them beside me. The starter mounted his rostrum, his hand on the lever. Out of the corner of my eye I saw Rupert edging forward.

'C'mon, jockeys.' The starter's hand went down, the gate flew up—and Rupert pulled straight across me with a hoarse laugh. His horse was perfectly balanced and he was off and away. As for me it was enough to make me snatch Prospero up and to throw him out of his stride. By the time we got going most of the field was streaming along ahead. There was no hope now of lying well up from the start, and I knew that my worst fears had been realised: out of the firing line where he wanted to be, Prospero was sulking. Plodding away he showed none of his freedom and fire, and as we approached the first I wondered if he would bury me. My fears were unjustified; jumping was what he liked and enjoyed; he stood back and threw it behind him as fluently as ever.

So it went on. At Becher's he never touched a twig and the drop meant nothing to him. But we were toiling. 'Let him run his own race,' were my instructions. I knew they were right and knew instinctively too that were I to get at him in any way it would only make him sulk the more. He was having one of his moods. Rupert's manoeuvre had worked better than he could have thought. There was nothing for it but to sit and suffer—and hope.

We floated effortlessly over the Chair which I have always thought the most difficult fence on the course whatever they say about Becher's. And then suddenly, nearing the stands, Prospero appeared to wake up. Whether it was the noise from the enclosures or the sight of the crowds I don't know, but all at once it was as if he changed gear. His stride lengthened and he landed yards over the water before going out into the country again. There was a feeling of unleashed power and I knew that once more I had a racehorse under me.

Gradually we began to pick up our field. His jumping, as always, helped, since we gained lengths in the air. Unwittingly I had done what the experts said should be done at Aintree over the full course—ride it like a hunt first time and then go after your race. Prospero, too, had conserved his energy, and some of the others were tiring. He made nothing of the second Becher's and at the Canal Turn, to my astonishment, I found myself amongst the select few. The leaders, though, including Mike Annerley, were well ahead. Where Rupert and Billy were I had no idea.

Coming to the third from home I was clear of the pack but with little hope of catching the two in front who, if anything, had increased their lead. It was a formidable obstacle, five feet high and with a five-foot-six-inch ditch on the landing side. Prospero, however, had all his running still in him and I went into it full of confidence. As I did so I heard a shout behind me and on my left. 'Pull out, you little bastard!' It was Rupert.

He was coming on my inside. That he meant having me in some way, foot beneath the stirrup, perhaps, as he bowled me over, I had no doubt. Thoughts of my father lying there like a vegetable, and what he had done to make him so, flashed through my mind as I heard that hated voice. He thought he could do what he liked with me. It was either him or me, and I had learned to look after myself. I slammed the door in his face.

There was another shout and an almighty crash as he went out through the wing. I hadn't any remorse for what I'd done. He had taken his chance and paid for it.

Prospero's strength and his jumping kept us both upright. We survived the far-side ditch with only a nod. But the two in front appeared even further away. Races, however, can change in the instant. At the second last both of them came down and I was left in front. There was the pack, what was left of them, behind me, and Billy, too, to be reckoned with, if he was still standing. Remembering Ginger Elton's warning of that one devastating run of his and Prospero's doubtful courage, I kicked for home to put as much daylight between us as possible. With Prospero still full of running we landed over the last and then that long, interminable straight stretched in front of me.

At the elbow I was still in front, apparently unchallenged. But Prospero's stride was beginning to shorten. Where was Billy? Then I felt rather than heard that there was someone behind me. I sneaked a look under my arm (which I shouldn't have) and there he was bearing down on me, unleashing his run.

He was gaining with every stride. Would Prospero hold on or fall apart? He heard those hoofs, too. Oh, God, where was the post?

I prayed Billy might be feeling the effects of the night before. He was driving for all he was worth, but perhaps he'd timed it wrong, perhaps he'd tire before the horse. Would Prospero pack it in?

I have a theory that some horses who are not genuine battlers won't really try until they are collared. The threat behind them keeps them going, cowardice rather than courage urging them on. Prospero rallied, gave a last desperate surge. Billy could get no further. In the little that was left, Prospero held on. We passed the post a diminished length to the good.

The first thing I remember was Billy reaching across to take my hand. He was puce in the face and blowing more than his horse. 'I thought I had you caught,' he got out between gasps. 'Why the hell didn't you stay at home?'

Minutes later I was getting down in the hallowed winners' enclosure under the canopy and Val was throwing her arms round me and kissing me. Then, as I sat on a bench in the changing room and someone was opening champagne, Flinty came in to tell me that I was wanted in the royal box.

There weren't many people about when I got there. HRH, who I think was in many ways a shy man, did not like large gatherings. But Flinty was there as ever, dispensing drinks and hospitality, and Val and also Roger Gretton. He came up to me immediately, smiling his ingratiating smile. 'You'll have seen the *Calendar*,' he said. 'I was very glad we were able to do that for your father. You may have been surprised at some of the questions I asked but, you know, someone has to play the devil's advocate at these enquiries.'

I felt like kicking his teeth in; fortunately I was spared having to reply by Flinty coming up to me. 'He wants to see you,' he said. 'He's outside.' He nodded to the front of the box.

I found him there, alone, staring out at the course. 'Well done, Danny,' he said, and I think it was the first time he had addressed me directly by my Christian name. 'You've pulled it off. Lucky chap. Everything is in front of you now. Make the most of it while you can.'

There was about him an air of indefinable sadness, as if something was coming to an end. He stared out over the abandoned, empty racecourse, its huge fences, great green bulwarks in the gathering dusk. Moments passed and I was wondering if I was dismissed when he spoke, still looking out over the course, his hands on the rail in front of him. 'They're going to make me give it all up,' he said.

I hesitated and then, greatly daring, I said, 'Is it your father, sir?'

'No,' he said. 'It is my mother. I can refuse my mother nothing.'

Even then I think I saw dimly that deep in him he longed for a woman's dominance. It was his tragedy and, I think, the nation's, and certainly that of all who loved him, that he found it in someone who never really cared for him. She added to the domination he longed for the spice of sex and so captured him and held him in thrall all the rest of his days.

We stood together in silence for a moment. Then there was a stir in the box behind us and he turned to go. As I stood back to allow him to pass he paused to give me that brief, intimate smile of his which once received was never forgotten. 'There's nothing like it, is there,' he said. 'Don't let anyone ever tell you otherwise.' Then he was gone.

Following him I came face to face with Val. 'Thanks, Danny,' she said quietly. 'You've been avoiding me. Why?'

Our eyes met, and I knew then that she knew what I had guessed and that my guess was right and I knew she was going to be hurt and that there was nothing I could do about it. 'I want to see you urgently and alone,' I said.

'Very well,' she said. 'Come to Huntercombe tomorrow morning.'

Then she, too, was gone.

CAPTAIN PAT AND I dined together that night at the Bell in Melton. Champagne flowed and we discussed the race endlessly.

'What about Prospero, now?' he said.

'I wouldn't be surprised if he never won another race,' I said. 'Except, perhaps, on his own terms. Billy should have won it. He might if he hadn't been up all the night before.'

Captain Pat smiled. 'Bacchus, or so I've heard it said, always renders his bill.' Then he looked hard at me. 'Rupert Carleton is badly smashed up. Did you know that?'

'No,' I said. 'I didn't.' In all the flush of victory I had not thought to ask and no one had told me. 'How bad is he?'

'Pretty bad. He's unconscious and will be for some time. There is a fractured skull and multiple injuries to his back. You didn't give him much room.'

'My father didn't get any room at all,' I said. 'Anyway, how did you know what I did?'

'I was down at the last fence and could see it. You were lucky there was that mist and no view from the stewards' box.'

'He was going where he had no business to be,' I said.

'And you are growing up,' he said.

The waiter placed a bottle of brandy on the table beside our coffee. 'With the compliments of the management,' he said. I poured myself a stiff measure while Captain Pat surveyed me closely.

'You've won all along the line,' he said. 'You've cleared your family's name; you've won the race of your life; they're calling you the find of the season amongst GRs; you're something of a royal favourite and yet you don't seem very happy. Is it Rupert?'

'No,' I said. 'It's not Rupert. He got what was coming to him.'

All he said was true. Everything had gone my way these past weeks. I'd won the enquiry and the race, and the whole business was dust and ashes in my mouth.

NEXT MORNING I drove to Huntercombe. Jenks told me Her Ladyship was in the library. He showed me in and closed the door.

The library was a compact room panelled in warm oak between its bookcases with their gilded wire fronts. There was a blazing fire in the hearth, two deep sofas flanked it, between them was a low table on which were the daily papers freshly ironed. She stood by the fire, one hand on the chimneypiece, the other holding the inevitable cigarette.

She was wearing, I remember, one of those tweed costumes of mannish cut, fashionable at the time and made by a male tailor. On her feet were handmade brown brogues.

Above the chimneypiece was a portrait of her father, a handsome man with a snowy moustache. He gazed into the room with the same level glance from his grey eyes as his daughter was directing at me, and I knew that she knew why I had come.

I took the cigarette case from my pocket and laid it on the table. 'Thank you for returning this,' I said, and then placed beside it the wrapping in which it had come and the card she had sent me wishing me luck. 'The writing matches very neatly,' I said. 'You're not a very good forger, are you, and you didn't even think to change your ink. You were behind it all. You betrayed him. Why did you do it?'

'I wanted him for myself,' she said simply. 'I was in love with him. You ought to understand that. You're half in love with him yourself.'

'There are two of us then,' I said. 'I fell for it and for you. My mother warned me. "A rag and a bone and a hank of hair", she said. "But the fool he called her his lady fair." '

'She never liked me nor I her.'

'You used me,' I said. 'You kept me on a string, under surveillance. That was why you took me up, gave me the rides, why you put me on Prospero. Why didn't you put up your pal, Rupert? I wondered at the time but I was blinded. It seemed such a marvellous opportunity. I know better now.'

'It wasn't quite like that,' she said. 'It's all been torturing me. But how did you find out?'

'I first began to wonder,' I said, 'when I saw you and Rupert together in Newmarket, just after the business of the wire in the fence. Then there was the leaking of that private gallop to Rupert. No one but you could have done it though I tried to persuade myself otherwise.'

She made a small gesture as if to interrupt me, but I had rehearsed what I wanted to say through a sleepless night. 'Let me go on,' I said. 'Then, later, when you came to see me after I had been beaten up: you came because you wanted to find out just what had happened and perhaps to discover if I'd told them something they didn't know. I remembered how you had seen Gervase Carleton's photo on my desk after the hunt ball. I guessed then that you had recognised him from the likeness of Rupert and realised I was onto something. And you wanted to keep the beating up from the Prince, didn't you?'

'You have a right to be bitter,' she said. 'But you don't know it all. Since you have guessed so much I'll tell it to you.'

We were sitting now, facing each other across the low table. 'It all began with Marston,' she said. 'My association with HRH was common knowledge, let's face it, and the court didn't like it. They felt it was getting too deep. Marston sent a message he was coming to see me. He came and it was to warn me off. "If you think he'll marry you, you are out of your mind," he said. "Apart from the fact that he is an inconstant man, fickle in his devotions, it is out of the question that he should marry a commoner of no family at all." '

'He was playing it pretty tough,' I said.

'They are tough, these people. "So you want me to give him up," I said. "That," he said, "is our present intention." We were silent for a while, as he pondered something and I thought about asking Jenks to throw him out of the house. Then, finally, he said, "Of course, there is another alternative." I asked him what he meant and I remember his exact words. "There is," he said, "a strong feeling at court and among certain of those close to him that he does not want to be King. It is felt, too, that he may not be temperamentally suited to kingship. If he were to be prevailed upon to renounce, it would solve many problems. Perhaps you could be the means of doing this, and I may say you would be doing crown, state and yourself a signal service were you to succeed. Think it over, my dear." Then he took his leave.'

'What did you do?' I asked.

'I thought on it. And the more I thought, the more it seemed to give me hope. He'd often said to me how he wished he'd been born without the trappings of royalty. I wanted him so desperately, you see.' She drew on her cigarette and continued to stare into the fire. 'I knew him so well I was certain such a suggestion could not come directly from me. Because he's been badgered by the court and that old father of his all his life he is deeply suspicious of anyone close to him giving him advice or trying to influence him. But I was sure if I didn't do something Marston and his lackeys would get him away from me. Rupert was riding for me then, and we were fairly close. I didn't know what I know now, that if there are two ways of winning a race, the straight and the crooked, Rupert will always choose the crooked. Anyway, I had no one to turn to. I couldn't mention it to Flinty. I talked to Rupert.'

'So it was Rupert's plan, whatever it was.'

'He said if we could orchestrate the press to step up their campaign about his reckless riding and how it was endangering the throne, it would help to persuade him he wanted his sport more than the throne and he'd chuck the succession away. It's all been artificial, you know, that press campaign. Rupert was behind a lot of it.'

'What happened next?'

'He said he wanted money to set it all up and like a fool I gave it to him. I persuaded myself it was harmless but what I didn't realise was that with Rupert he can never stop. He wanted more and more and then he had to bring Roger Gretton into it. They're cousins, you know.'

'Good heavens, is everyone in this set related?'

'Pretty well, save for me and a few others. Roger, anyway, was easy prey. There's a vindictive streak in Roger. He's never forgotten some row HRH had with him a year or so back on tour. Besides, he loves intrigue, and I think he sees himself as Marston's successor as the *éminence grise*.'

'I shouldn't wonder. He's tricky enough for anything.'

'Rupert got him to step up the whispering campaign at court against David, so that it would be borne to him on the grapevine that none of the present crowd wanted him and would be happy to see him go.'

'And all the time Rupert was bleeding you of money.'

'Yes, and worse. David would enter his horses in point-to-points all over the place to try to put the press hounds off the scent. Several times Rupert tricked me into telling him where he was running. Then, as I discovered too late, he alerted the press to the correct meeting. David was furious and couldn't understand how the press were always there when he was riding. It gave Rupert another hold over me. He threatened to tell David it was I who had spilled the beans.'

'He blackmailed you?'

'That's it, damn him. Oh, Danny, I'm coming out of it awfully badly, aren't I? The things we do. Let's have a drink. Maybe that'll help—' She went to the bell and rang it.

When Jenks came in she told him to bring a bottle of champagne and open it. When he had gone and the glasses were filled, I said, 'I can understand this, or I think I can. But I have to know—how did my father come into it?'

'That's where it all began to go hideously wrong. The plan Rupert came up with was for Roger to persuade HRH that it would be better for crown and state if he were to renounce, and that he would be far happier himself. He'd often said that he'd be better off as a "plain lousy aristocrat". They thought they could play on that.'

'It would never have worked, though, would it?'

'It might well have done. At that time he was disgusted with everything except his life here. He might have fallen for it if the right approach had been made.'

'And it wasn't, I gather.'

'No. Roger, being Roger, reneged at the last moment. He said it wasn't his place to go to the Prince, using as his excuse that there was some personal feeling between them. They'd have to get someone else. But they picked the wrong man.'

'My father—'

'He was close to HRH at the time. Roger suggested him and they went to him. They dressed it up, of course, Roger at his smoothest; but your father saw through it all. He exploded. Said he'd see them damned first, and then he threatened to go to HRH and tell him the whole thing and expose them. They were terrified.'

'So they framed him.'

'Rupert did. Rupert was behind it all. Your father was in the royal party that Ascot, which made the disgrace all the more spectacular.'

'I begin to see it clearly now,' I said, putting the bits and pieces together in my mind. 'When they thought they had him disgraced and muzzled they heard he might be taking a libel action where everything could well come out. So they lured him to Brighton.'

'Rupert again. I verily believe he meant to kill your father and dump him and the car over Beachy Head. I once heard him say he wouldn't hesitate to commit murder if he thought he could get away with it. They had an encounter. When Rupert tried to beat him up he had the stroke and Rupert left him there. He boasted of it to me, thinking if I knew of it it would increase his hold over me.'

'Don't forget Roger,' I said. 'He managed to get onto the stewards' panel who sat in judgment on my father. How did he do that?'

'It would be easy enough. They're all chaps together. He could say to one of the sitting stewards, "You won't want to take this, old boy. Very embarrassing. I'll do it for you." '

'And that would give him access to the draft notice for the *Calendar* and he could fiddle it.'

'They thought it had worked a charm. But Rupert could never lay off and he wanted to go on bleeding me. He continued to gee-up the press and stir opinion against HRH. Then you came along and they started to panic again. Rupert put that wire in the fence. That's what you saw me arguing about with him in Newmarket. He just told me I'd started something I couldn't stop.'

She paused and sipped her drink. 'But I tried,' she said. 'Telling Rupert about that gallop was the last thing I did. By that time I knew I was about to wreck your life as well as my own. I told Rupert he could do what he liked, he'd get no more blood money from me.'

'He told Gervase, I remember, that the money was drying up. It must have been about then that you got the cigarette case back and sent it to me. Why?'

'The swine, I thought, when you told me of it. They wouldn't even leave you with that memory of your father. I went to him and demanded it. He laughed at me. "Take it to your fancy boy," he said when he threw it to me. "That's what you're down to now." '

She looked at me while I fiddled with the stem of my glass. 'I know what you're thinking,' she said. 'But it wasn't the way you're seeing it—my taking you up, giving you the ride on Prospero. I wanted to help and I hated him for what he had done to your father and was trying to do to you. And, Danny, I was, I am, fond of you: do believe that.'

I hoped I could believe her. But I was not finished yet. 'Rupert is out of it now,' I said. 'But what about Marston and Roger?'

'Marston knew nothing of the plot against your father. All he was concerned with was pulling strings.'

'But Roger was in it up to the neck.'

'Not quite as deep as that. He'd never have condoned what Rupert did to your father. I believe he was horrified when he learned of it. He was frightened then and he is terrified now.'

'I still don't think he should be allowed to get away with it,' I said.

She looked at me steadily. 'Do you know your Bible, Danny?' she said. 'The good book says there is a time to love and a time to hate. You've had your share of hating, Danny. Don't go on, it'll eat your guts out. Roger was only a catspaw, a go-between. Let him be. He's got to live with himself.'

We stared at each other for a long minute. Suddenly I saw that she was right. 'Very well,' I said slowly. 'I was thinking of going to

Crispin Merevale and asking him to bring what Roger has done to the attention of the Jockey Club, but I won't now.' As I spoke it was as if a poisonous cloud had been blown away.

'Well done,' she said quietly. 'And it all may have been for nothing in the end,' she went on. 'It looks as if pressures the other way have won. Did he say anything to you?'

'HRH? He told me his mother has asked him to give all this up.'

'None of them understands him. He's not really one of them. He's some sort of throwback, Danny.'

At that moment Jenks came in. 'His Royal Highness is on the telephone, M'lady,' he said.

SHE WAS AWAY some time while I sat on sipping the champagne and looking at the portrait of her father. I could have liked him, I thought, a no-nonsense ironmaster who had fought his way up through the thickets of influence, social prejudice and snobbery. There were also portraits of Spenlove's two Grand National winners on the walls. In his quiet way he had shown them that a plain man could conquer their world even if he could not be one of them.

At last she returned. She wore that same sad look that had haunted them all during the past week, only now it was stronger. She sat down, twisting a handkerchief between her fingers. Then, 'It's all over,' she said. 'He's going back.'

'What did he say?' I asked.

'They've won,' she said. 'We've known something like this was coming. It's his family this time. If it was only the court, I think he'd go against them just for the hell of it. But this—' She drew a deep breath and fought back tears. 'He's giving up Braden Lodge. That's the start. He says he'll come up regularly for the hunting, but I know they'll play on him and fiddle his engagements to keep him away. It will be out of sight out of mind for us here.'

'But his racing?' I said. 'That's surely where his heart is?'

'It's in abeyance until next year. He says he may persuade them to give him one more season, but I know and I think he knows that it's all over.'

'And Flinty?' I said.

'He'll be dispatched pretty smartly back to his regiment in India. The War Office will fix that, you'll see. It's finished, Danny, finished.'

She was right, I knew. It was like a light going out of our lives. If I could feel that, how much more must she be shattered?

'Do you still hate me, Danny?' she said then, breaking the silence.

'You know I don't,' I said. 'Not in a thousand years.'

'What will you do now that what you came for is over?'

I too, was alone, rudderless, lost, after all that had happened. I would never go back to university, nor did I feel ready to return to Kilbarry and my mother. 'I don't know,' I said. 'I haven't had time to think—'

She stood up and came towards me. I rose to meet her. 'You'd better stay here, Danny,' she said.

'Why?'

'Someone has to look after the horses—'

'Is that the only reason?' I asked.

'No,' she said, and now she was very close to me. 'It's not. There must be something left. And you were once our mascot, weren't you?'

Epilogue

I had not finished reading the typescript when it was time to leave Dermot de Lacey. With his permission I took it with me, and it was late at night before I turned the last page. Next morning at breakfast Max Melville was silent and abstracted, and I guessed he was anxious to take up his pen again. Certainly when I told him that I wanted to see de Lacey before driving to the airport, he readily agreed and disappeared into his study.

'I shall have to see my partner,' I told de Lacey, who I found once more in his father's living room. 'But I think I can assure you now we shall take the book on if you agree.'

'Of course,' he said. 'It was a strange beginning to a long life, wasn't it? I don't think anything was ever the same to him again.'

'Then he stayed?'

'He did.'

'And her? I feel I must ask you that. It's obvious—'

'That I'm not her son?' He smiled. 'You are quite right. She was killed in a point-to-point the following year. She was never really in love with Father, you know; but she was fond of him and he filled a gap in her life. All her love was squandered on the Prince, and he knew that, I think. When the Prince went out of her life she was filled with a sort of death wish.'

'What happened to him then?'

'It nearly broke him up. But she left him all the horses and a stack of money to go with them. He threw himself into his racing, taking rides on anything, and I've been told it was as if he, too, wanted to break his neck. But he didn't, though he broke nearly every other bone in his body, some of them twice. He was successful; he rode all those winners I told you about.'

'Did he ever see the Prince again?'

'Sometimes. He always said HRH was never a fair-weather friend. On the rare occasions he came up to Melton after that season, he sought Father out; and when in the end they made him sell his string he gave him Pepperpot, saying he wanted him to have a good home. Father never lost his admiration for him.'

'The abdication didn't change his opinion?'

'Never. HRH used to say that there was one throne he could not abdicate, and that was in the hearts and minds of Leicestershire folk who had known him. Father blamed all that followed on "that creature" as he called her. He said she meant to have him from the first. And he wanted to tell something of the other side of the story. So much of denigration had been written about him and he had nothing but contempt for those who abandoned him.'

'He lived to a great age,' I said. 'What happened afterwards?'

'He tried to get into the RAF in the last war but he was too old to fly. They made him an intelligence officer and he was badly smashed up in a bombing raid on an airfield. My mother was his nurse and he married her. It wasn't a great success, I'm afraid. They had little in common and they drifted apart. After the war he took a pack of hounds in Ireland while my mother stayed in England and brought us up. Memories of Melton were always with him.'

He picked up one of the folders, glanced at it and put it down. 'You know,' he said, 'I think he was right. She ruined him. She played on his worst instincts and she bled him white financially. And she was determined to alienate his old friends. But Father loved him till the day he died, and what he has written is a sort of testament to it.'

I took the typescript and caught my plane. As we soared out across the lush green fields of Cork and over the Irish Sea, I knew that my visit, which had started out so unpromisingly, had not been in vain. Max Melville was writing again, I had been afforded a glimpse into a society as remote to my generation as the sands of Ozymandias, and into the character of a man who might have been.

JOHN WELCOME

John Welcome has recently celebrated his eightieth birthday and to mark this special day and his contributions to racing, his local racecourse in Wexford, Ireland, honoured him by naming one of their races after him. John Welcome has had a lifelong involvement with racing, riding in point-to-points and hunting, and in 1961 was elected to the National Hunt Committee, the governing body of steeplechasing in Ireland, where he served two terms as its Senior Steward. He has also owned a number of racehorses and has had, as he puts it, 'a few winners, but it was such a long time ago now I don't suppose anyone will remember their names.' His other passion has always been writing, and from jotting down short stories as a schoolboy he has become a distinguished racing novelist and biographer. He has contributed to newspapers and magazines, including *Horse and Hound*, *Country Life* and the *Spectator*, and reviews crime novels for the *Irish Independent*.

In *Royal Stakes* the author focuses on the pressure surrounding the Prince of Wales before his abdication. Throughout the halcyon years before the Second World War, John Welcome and the Prince of Wales mixed in the same racing circles but they never met even though they had acquaintances in common. 'Several of my friends were racing cronies of the Prince of Wales and they told me many, many wonderful stories about him. He loved his hunting and racing and was completely fascinated by it. It was the one thing he really wanted to do and go on doing and the Court stopped him. He then became a man without an anchor, torn in two by his love of racing and his sense of duty.'

Even at the age of eighty, John Welcome is still busy with his writing. He is finishing the last book in a trilogy and has been commissioned to write the life story of one of racing's greatest artists, Gilbert Holiday. As he writes he looks out onto green meadows full of young racehorses that he is preparing for their trainers. It is natural inspiration for yet more novels.

PICTURE CREDITS: page 191: © John Earle; pages 318/19: © Wz-Bilddienst, Wilhelmshaven; page 363 (centre): ©Wz-Bilddienst, Wilhelmshaven; pages 380/81 (bottom left and right): © Martin Bronkhurst; page 401: © Gotfryd; all other photos between page 318 and page 400, author's own; page 527: Mark Gerson. The publishers would like to thank the following people and organisations for their help in providing art reference: page 427: John Frost; page 473: Neill Bruce, Motoring Photolibrary.

179X